Book One: Lost Hope
By Mark P. Bromley

Artwork on the book cover by Mark P. Bromley

First Edition was published in 2022. First Edition written January 2022
Yoranthium: Book One: Lost Hope. Written By Mark P. Bromley

Distributed in the United States and Around the World
Began as a crowd funding project in December 2021

Published By Mark P. Bromley Enterprises Publishing

Library of Congress Control Number: 2023924454
ISBN: 979-8-9909482-3-5 June 2024

First Edition
First Hardback Print on Demand June 2024
Uploaded as Ebook June 2022

Book One: Lost Hope

Dedication

By Mark P. Bromley

I only love you.

Whom else would I dedicate my books too?

No character is you in the book I just love your name.

I'll likely do that in every book just so I know you are here with me.

With love always anywhere in this world and forever.

Yoranthium

Book One: Lost Hope

By Mark P. Bromley

Contents

Yoranthium

Book One: Lost Hope

Chapter One: Upon Awakening

By Mark P. Bromley

Dreams of fantasy take flight in the waking hours. Our thoughts are not our own but that of the sweet blessings we have been given by those who care most about us in life as we age to maturity. The world belongs to many and not all are of fortune or fame. Your hopes can be lost especially when one has become too complacent living in a dream.

A gentle breeze was felt on the cheek of Kumithra. She was stirring from her slumber as she felt the morning sunlight warming her skin exposed from the pure white Yoranthium silk blankets of her bed in the chambers of the princess. She heard the sweet melody of the birds tweeting the greeting of the new day as she tried to remember the most pleasant of dreams, she had just had that night.

Her dream was that of the captain of her palace guard Rarailmuir. He was strikingly handsome and muscular and has always been the icon of lust and inspiration to Kumithra. She dreamed of a life where they had settled in as King and Queen of Yoranthium. They had wonderful and beautiful children. All the people of the land and the world of Ishormot hailed them as their saviors and liege lords and the Potentate of all the elf kingdoms in the world.

It was such a fantastic dream. All the people she had ever known were in that dream. All was good and great with many blessings. It was the life she as a little girl had always aspired too. For why not. Yoranthium was a great kingdom and has lasted for over five hundredths revolutions of the seasons after it's founding on this remote, to the warm side, island far from the main founding kingdoms of the known elf world. Which was to the cold side of Yoranthium where the forever winters covered the ground. Most of all she had been aspiring to be wedded to her long admired and highly respected captain of the guard Rarailmuir.

Rarailmuir became a legend to her kingdom and was appointed as the captain of the guard at a rather young age for a sea elf. His deeds became heroic; he cared and preserved the lives of so many. Kumithra was smitten with Rarailmuir when she was one of many whom he saved. Twenty-thousandths Yoranthian's of the Grand City had been saved from certain catastrophe. They all owed their lives to her hero and desired husband Rarailmuir.

Reflecting back four revolutions ago to that burned half city. She remembered how he busted through splintered beams and burning fire finding her in the wreckage of her classroom. That had caught fire from an attacking dragon. The dragon that Rarailmuir had called upon the unborn God's blessing had slain. Bringing and end to a nightmare rampage that cost so many lives of the old guard and a third of the people of the city.

Kumithra recollected as a child of fifteen revolutions how afraid she was. The fire of that burning building terrified her. She was unable to save herself and was trapped. Rarailmuir broke through all the debris and fire. Like a Juggernaut hearing her cries for help. He grabbed Kumithra in his very strong and powerful arms protecting her. That is when she felt the first pangs of love and the strength of her hero, savior and love Rarailmuir. Holding her tight. A sensation fell over her in his embrace against the warmth of his chest and the sound of his beating heart. She knew that day she loved him.

It was since that day. Whenever she was given the chance to meet with or see Rarailmuir. She would greet him with gifts and swooning. She knew in her mind that Rarailmuir was aware of her. However, she wasn't sure if his feelings for her were the same. Well, she was only a silly child back then. Not a fully blossomed and blooming female[1] she had become over the last three seasons. She had been only an enamored child completely pathetically undeveloped, not fit, not suitable and uninteresting to him. She was swooning for an older adult male of great respect and renown in her city.

Thankfully, Rarailmuir hadn't taken a wife, had no children. Was only a mere eight full revolution's older than she. As Kumithra remembered the dream, she realized this beautiful morning was more than just a dream to remember. She was now the age of marriage among her people. She had now become nineteen revolutions of seasons old. She was now considered a fully developed female by her very age and by her form as she had grown from her childish flatness to a figure of a pear-shaped hourglass that adult males pined for. She had quite the dream and today of all days she was sure her parents would not object to her expressing her feelings for Rarailmuir. Today as by tradition of Yoranthium is her wedding. Where she is to take a mate as chosen by her father King Sinderthion. As this tradition was custom of

---

[1] While promoting Yoranthium in 2022, I was accosted for the use of Female and Male by the cults of political oppressors. I have to explain we are talking about Elves in this story and they are not Humans and this means they can't be represented as Woman or Man. These terms with Man would identify them as Humans and are omitted for the purpose of narrative and world building this difference is appropriate.

royalty and her place as a princess among all known kingdoms of the world of Ishormot.

She was so excited and giddy with delight. She smirked with an expression of amazement, wonder, and a plan of action and a day of days for her to be in love. Often are the whims of the youth upon becoming of age. A wedding was a day princess's had dreamed of and readied for across Ishormot. Since the first day their mothers and protectors had to explain why they had a cycle and their duty. It was in keeping with the design of their God of birth and creation. Princesses and all matter of females had the responsibility to bare the children of Ishormot. For her it was to foster a King and a successor to the throne of Yoranthium. Being her responsibility and duty for kingdom.

Kumithra shot up in bed. The covers falling off revealing her near see through nighttime apparel. Barely remaining on her delicate petite form. Nearly revealing more bare skin than it should reveal and barely enough to cover her. As if by magic the clothing shimmered and always stayed in the right place to cover her body. The cloth was of the softest most royal shear cut of the harvest of Yoranthium silk. Sought out for it's seductive nature by all other kingdoms. Yoranthium silk weave was magically imbued and would shimmer with the sun in warm tones of reds, oranges to gold.

She had gone to the window after getting out of bed. To listen to the birds, breathe in the fresh tropical air and feel the sunlight touch her skin. Skin of integrated and interlaced light blue patterns of shade to pinkish patterns of highlights. As a sea elf, having a pattern of subtle soft almost seamless scales. These scales would shimmer in a subtle energetic slightly noticeable prism of warm light reds, oranges to golds as the sun shined on her. Her hair was alabaster that would also shimmer in the sunlight just like the silks and her skin. It was a magical property to all living things on Yoranthium and the sea elves. Her ears were different than main land elves, as they had been meant for swimming in the open ocean. Pointed at top and two tapered and diminishing points on the back of the ears that could seal themself from ocean water and hear underwater sounds with a second membrane. Right behind the ears was three concealed and small gills. That allowed sea elves to breathe for four parts of a twenty four-part day underwater.

Kumithra's eyes were small and narrow. Perfectly positioned forward facing and a soft lovely color of purple iris, black pupils. When she smiled, her eyes would seem to close. She had a petite nose that was very cute. Her cute lips were small and ample and a shade of pink. With her eyebrows being thin and attractive as if they had been treated by the local beauty shops in the finest part of the city. Her cheeks tapered to a tiny chin atop an eloquent thin neck of fine specimen.

Kumithra hadn't noticed she wasn't thinking about palace guards and gardeners and all the people who made living in the Palace possible outside the window. The females were going about their work in getting the palace ready for this wedding day to her Rarailmuir. Yet she had forgot there were many males looking up at her as she was hanging halfway out of the open window in her nightgown. As guests had been arriving and soldiers being stationed on the grounds for this day of the wedding.

With her eye's closed taking in the wonderful smells of a new morning and the flowing trees of pink flowing petaled leaves and tropical plants in the garden below. Then she opened her eyes. Quite a few of the males had their mouths open and couldn't help but drool ever so lightly. She was a very attractive sea elf after all and their princess. Becoming a practiced siren that learned to manipulate the males in Yoranthium on her many outing with the seductive Huspecia her protector of chastity.

Slightly embarrassed she darted back into her room. Blushing ever so slightly knowing she had given quite the show in her nightwear in broad daylight. Satisfied she could turn heads and garner the admiration and desire of so many males. She had worked on her feminine magics since the age of sixteen revolutions of the four seasons old. She would deliberately wear loose garments over her chest as her breast developed to becoming a lady. Developed to a pleasant pleasing size over the past three revolutions.

She would let the collar fall loosely just enough to see when she bent down in front of boys and adult males. Catching if they would try to sneak a peak at her breasts. Hoping to see or even catch a glimpse of more of her that she never revealed. She knew how to tease the males and she liked doing it often. Practicing

discretion and never around anyone of the guard or the court. Only doing so with her partner in crime and armed protector Huspecia.

She and her crown protector learned early how to get males to see her as a seductress without revealing anything. Something her father secretly knew she did and had secret guards always watching her without her knowledge. Concealing secret agents of the guard unknown to her. Rarailmuir had assigned undercover guards to protect her. As with many females after knowing the will of creation, she so much wanted to be considered a Siren from the books and tales of fancy. Romance, she had read in school of sailors being drawn to their doom. Legends of mermaids of the deep ocean were known to do, by the ways and wiles of seductive sorcery. Huspecia was so kind to aid her with such mischief as she reached to obtain the blossoming maturity of this day. The two were brought up together with similar flights of fancy.

Her father a King Sinderthion, discouraged and never approved of her dressing provocatively. Often, she had to cover up before going out on her own with her guards and protector. She always found ways to get around that over the years. Especially with dearest Huspecia her faithful appointed protector. On multiple occasions the two girls played out their imagination on the males around Yoranthium. Never knowing that the fear of many of the males wasn't nervousness but that of knowing who she was, the daughter of the King. Many males knew she was engaged to Rarailmuir the captain of the guard. No weaker male would challenge the Grand City savior and defender that defeated a dragon.

Eventually swimming at the forbidden beach was all the real fun she and her protector could have. When Yoranthium Navy ships and sailors would be present to watch and admire them frolicking on the rocks attempting to lure the Yoranthium navy to their doom with their playful taunts of youthful sexual innuendos in very attractive and recent stylish swimwear.

Her mother the Queen Zantkara approved of her behavior as being desirable but not too desirable to avoid trouble. Kumithra had blossomed into quite a female very capable of using her attractiveness to command respect and many admirers.

She went to the mirror as the head maid; Godmother and her mother's protector entered the room. Thernya was an older

female who was the chaperon of her assigned by her mother the Queen. Thernya arrived in Yoranthium for Zantkara to marry her father the King Sinderthion. Thernya was Queen Zantkara's protector. Arranged marriages of royals were commonplace to keep the peace with the small kingdoms such as Forumth.

Thernya was a heavyset female but with strength that could best some of the palace guards. A female even Rarailmuir was afraid of. Thernya was notably handsome in the face that was not a sea elf but from another kingdom Illustrom. Her skin was bronze and wrinkled and blessed with rather sizable breasts and strong defined cleavage. Thernya was taller than most sea elves at six and seven of a king's foot high very much as tall as Rarailmuir. Yet she was old the revolutions of time sadly robbed most of her beauty.

Thernya was the head of royal household affairs and closest friend of her mothers much like Huspecia was to her. Well trained in defense and always had two deadly chain daggers hidden on her person. Thernya was invaluable she had raised Kumithra along side her mother as her own daughter. Thernya lost her love and child long ago in her youth. When Kumithra was born Thernya was there and blessed the birth as her divine protector. Believing she was Kumithra's mother and gave birth too her instead of her true mother Queen Zantkara.

Thernya had informed the princess "Your bath was ready, and you should be very attentive to your body and image this day. A suitor has arrived for your hand in marriage this very day. Do not forget to eat your breakfast on the table I placed by your bed." Speaking in one of the most gentle and musical voices of the highest quality.

"Oh, Thernya do you think Rarailmuir will be there?" Kumithra had said with wide-eyed and enthusiastic gleeful hope.

"I don't think so." Thernya replied. "Rarailmuir was called away this morning for training with the Yoranthium guard at your fathers command."

"You mean Rarailmuir will not be here?" Kumithra exclaimed in panic. "It's my day... I don't want... I..." She stopped herself, as she never told anyone that she wanted to be with Rarailmuir since the day he rescued her. Just assumed everyone knew.

"Kumithra, you know you are the princess of Yoranthium. Your mother wouldn't want you to waste your life or make a bad decision. It's for the people of Yoranthium. You do understand?" Thernya who cared just as much for Kumithra as her own mother did since she was born.

Tears were welling in Kumithra's eyes that she fought to keep down. The disheartening news was like being slapped on the cheek or bopped in the nose. She had known and feared she would not be allowed her dreams and was prepared to suit the good of the people of Yoranthium's future. This custom was believed the prosperity of the unborn God. This might mean giving her hand to strengthen ties to other kingdoms. Just like the appeasement of her mother's hand to that of her fathers for the Kingdom of Forumth.

Reluctantly Kumithra returned to common sense royalty. A mannerism and poise she was trained with since her birth. The tears welling in her eyes went away and her prim and proper lady of the land came to bear. "My purpose is for Yoranthium and our people." She said devoid of any feeling and with a regal tone of voice.

"That's good to hear my fine young female of royalty and a princess of Yoranthium." Said Thernya in a parental voice similar to her mothers. "Your mother made this sacrifice for her people many years ago. Look how much love, caring, and beauty is in your life. Not all arranged marriages are bad things. Your father was up all night making a choice for you. I'm sure Princess Kumithra you will be fine and find love eventually for Yoranthium with the suitor your father has decided for you."

"Yes, I know my mother Queen Zantkara of the fiefdom of Forumth did say how much she loved my Father King Sinderthion. I remember them both holding me in their arms from the day I was born. I remember that throughout all the years the love they gave me. How could he deny and turn Rarailmuir away? Never mind that. I'm sure my loving parents made the right choice for Yoranthium I guess." Kumithra said nearly choking on her words and faking a trusting pose that what she said was right when it felt so wrong.

Thernya's smiled and then became an expression of duty. "Well, I'm sorry my lady for the news. However, I have a bath to flavor with the proper lovely perfume salts, and I need to get your

make up ready and we'll do your hair up very nice and make you the finest princess of all the land we can. Yes, I'm sure all will be fine trust our unborn God is watching us and blessing us this day. You get ready and I'll take care of all the details, and you'll be right as this morning sun on this very fine and beautiful day." With a smile and some rose colored hue returning to her cheeks.

Thernya turned and went back into the bathing chamber to prepare the bath and arrange the beautification ceremony for this auspicious day of coming of age and the selection process for the good of Yoranthium's future. Leaving Kumithra alone in her room. Where she was stifling a scream of agony and suffering.

Kumithra's head sunk a little low. As she grabbed a brush to stroke at her long flowing hair down to her waist as she muttered to herself. "No Rarailmuir. The dream wasn't going to be real. I felt it was so real just moments ago and I was so hoping. Yet, Rarailmuir wouldn't even be here today. I was so hoping for him to be waiting outside my room this morning as he was for all those years after father knew I had feelings for him." Was it because she never said she had those feelings? It was so obvious she shouldn't have had to say anything. Could it be no one knew because they hadn't been observant?

A sigh was heard coming from her. "Oh well. Let's make the best of this day. I really haven't met many males wanting to court me. If my mother could find happiness, I should be ready to do the same." She thought. Brightening up a little knowing her father never makes mistakes. But not to pick Rarailmuir and send him away for the day, kind of feels like a mistake.

She walked to the mirror next to the bathing chamber. "I know Rarailmuir would demand combat for my hand. I suppose that's why he was sent away."

Kumithra flicked of the right strap holding on her nightwear revealing she was wearing no undergarments as the right side slipped off parts of her body that slowly became viewable in the mirror. Then she flicked off the left strap and the entire frail and light nightgown fell to the floor. She was standing naked before the wardrobe mirror and stopped to admire her body. As today she would have to offer herself to her husband, as is tradition for such events and wanted to make sure she would be perfection.

Kumithra was petite with silk like skin, very soft to the touch and shimmering as the sun light from the window danced on her skin and soft unnoticeable scales. Her breasts could be seen and were subtle, pert and quite ample and shapely. Just the right size with soft protruding tips of singing seduction and transgression that would sharpen a male's eyes as if arrows had been sent his way, of a darker roasted hue and perfectly symmetrical. A tiny waist and a well-established tiny belly button, Soft and strong looking abdomen with a flat stomach and a perfectly curved back and widened hips just enough where the hip bones protruded and defined just enough to be attractive and unquestionable that any male would find her nudity mind boggling and an enigma to solve for a lifetime of love and happiness. A perfect sacrifice to whatever beast her father found for her.

Having a body that would last for countless of revolutions as the highest level of physical limits of any mortal females lifespan. Sea elves for the most part did not have body hair except for a little in the lower region near the lustful lobes. This was very apparent on Kumithra's small and petite form with very nice smooth silken legs. That didn't need any leggings to accentuate the beauty and shapeliness. Attached to even matching feet of an attractive women and nice small toes well groomed and very soft.

She grabbed a container on the table by the mirror a canister to apply a softening tallow used prior to bathing and worked it into her skin and entire body as the bath would improve her skin even more. As if such perfection was even possible for her suitor would have the finest bride to himself by this very evening, as he must to satisfy his curiosity. Hoping that groom was Rarailmuir.

"To bad for Rarailmuir. I've been hoping this body would be his. I had imagined having his strong and wide hands softly with care, touch and caress me this very night. Such a waste." With an tsk, and taking a deep breath entered into the bathing chamber.

In the bathing chamber Kumithra's maid Thernya was waiting for her. "You are such a beauty my princess. Your suitor this evening is going to be very delighted with your bodice as his bride. You do the royalty of Yoranthium an honor with how well you have taken care of yourself. I just wish I was still young and

could give you a challenge in beauty." So said Thernya attempting to elevate Kumithra's spirits.

"You were young once? I never knew that." Said Kumithra with a joking smile concealing the anger she held over the news that she was not wedding who she would have liked. "I'm okay with today I was just hoping for more."

"Yes, I was young once and quite the looker." Thernya said with a smile. "I think I could have given your mother a challenge for your father. Now please let's get your bath done and get you ready we are running out of time."

Kumithra went to the side of the sunken bath in the floor and stepped down some ivory marble steps trimmed in gold overlay with swirls and symbols of youth and frolicking in play about bath time. Much of the bath's art works on the floor, on the walls was all done in ivory marble laced with gold of childish images. Images of toddler tales she was fond of as a child. Now she had outgrown much of those fabled childish tales.

On the other side were a table and a stool that was nicely made with padding and embellished with decorative arts of beauty and lovely shapes of hearts and other designs. Hand crafted from some of the finest craftsmen in the Yoranthium capitol city. There too was an oval mirror in the middle with facial perfumes and makeup and care items with additional handheld mirrors and tissues and other side mirrors magically lit by spell magics on the frames to give the best appearance to finish out ones beautification routine.

Kumithra stepped into the tub and slowly sat down in the warm bath water as Thernya began sponging her back after having moved Kumithra's hair over her left shoulder.

"I don't know what your father had seen in the male he decided should be your husband. Too young for me and too brash." Thernya said.

"You don't like the suitor my father picked? Is he a horrible male?" Kumithra asked unsure of what Thernya was telling her.

"No not at all I think he's very kind, maybe a hero to his people. So, your father and Huspecia think." Thernya said with some auspicious connotations.

"What does he look like?" Kumithra wanted to know out of curiosity.

"I don't know how to explain. He looks like anyone, I guess. He's strong and healthy. Something of a common sort of person you might casually see around the grounds of this palace. Fit I would say like some of the guards. So, I think normal looking would be good enough to say." Thernya said with a shrug and facial expression that was not exactly the truth as she lifted Kumithra's right arm and began washing it. "You know I've been bathing you since you were a child and I'm so proud of how you turned out."

"Thank you, Thernya for your dedication you are like a second mother to me and a very good friend. But don't change the subject. I'm terrified of meeting some suitor I know nothing of." So said Kumithra as she bathed her chest with a soft lofti cloth only found on Yoranthium typically used for cleansing and purification with her left arm.

"I'm not playing with you. Your father picked the best suitor for your hand. Or so he thinks. But I'm sure the suitor is a lord but not royalty. I think he might just be less than your father would want for you. But don't worry he's a leader and has a good enough reputation. A good reputation that's well received and respected by his people who are here on Yoranthium." Thernya said with little disappointment.

"There's only the one suitor, Thernya?"

"Yes. Now switch arms." Kumithra had stopped washing her chest moved her hair over her right shoulder and lifted her left arm for Thernya to clean as Kumithra moved to her lovely left leg out of the water to start cleaning it slightly turning to her side.

As Thernya finished cleaning her left arm she let Kumithra finish her bath and clean her right leg and body to her liking. Along with her hair and face. Kumithra rose to get out of the sunken bath. Thernya then told her some startling news. "You need to get dried and get ready. In about half this time glass your suitor will be waiting for you outside your chamber to escort you through the garden and to the banquette hall."

"What?" Kumithra exhaled in panic "He's going to be out my door? I've never met him. Why must he be outside my door? He should be down in the hall not outside my door. Only Rarailmuir should be outside my door. I barely know this suitor fellow."

"Yes, your father thought it best you two walk through the garden. So, everyone can see you both together." Thernya said with a frown on her face.

"This is not my dream, Thernya." Said Kumithra loudly and in disappointment.

"Dreams seldom come true for most people Kumithra I should know. I'm thankful to be your maid, your friend, and as a second mother and divine protector to you. This was not my dream and my love and champion, and child died before we could wed. You are much more fortunate than I. Please remember that and do your best to make this the best day you can. Tonight you will be wed. Soon you'll bare an heir to the kingdom in short order. It is the way of things before the unborn God of creation and true cycle of life." Thernya said imploring Kumithra to reason and stay rational about this day.

Her sanity was pressed thin. "You are right, Thernya. I will have to make do even if it's not my dream. So many on this isle of Yoranthium only have what we do and make on this isle. We might be a rich sea kingdom yet there are many lesser and worse off fiefdoms and kingdoms not as fortunate as ours. I will be the princess Yoranthium needs. I will marry as my father and mother sees fit and bare the heir of this kingdom. As is expected of me as the future Queen of Yoranthium." Kumithra said with conviction and certainty like a real princess would proclaim for her people.

With that she rose out of the sunken bath and grabbed a towel imbued with drying magics and stepped up the steps carefully drying her breasts, chest, arms, neck, head, hair and back. Then raised her left leg up the steps to the top and dried her leg and then followed suit with the right being pulled from the water as she bent over to dry her right leg and finally handing the towel to Thernya to dispose of for cleaning.

"Thank you, my princess you are an example to all, the people of Yoranthium. It has been my honor to serve you all these years." Said Thernya with tears welling in her eyes. "Now let's do your hair." With that the naked Kumithra sat on the padded stool before the make up table in front of a large mirror where she could see her face all the way down to her bare breasts.

Thernya disposed of the towel and quickly returned to fix Kumithra's hair in sea elf Yoranthium royal wedding fashion.

Creating two long braids of six strands on either side of her head. Leaving the split of the hair only in the back of her head while shifting the front and top lose and somewhat over the top of the forehead and combed to the left side. The ponytails on either side were then lifted on the sides of the head making a cross in the back and covering the part in the back of the head. Then were lifted above and behind the ears, curving over on the top and then trailing down the back evenly spaced. With some remaining hair on the sides slightly curled down the sideburns line.

Finally the headpiece was installed between the two ponytails down the back. It was a rigid starched cloth board of a thicker silk made on Yoranthium. It went from down the middle of the back rising fastened between the ponytail ends. The headdress went straight up in back, above the top of the head where it sat eloquently on the top of the head. Curved to the front ending in a point and creating a halo above the head. On the Halo a transparent shear cloth of silk of white for purity would be installed to surround the back of the head and slightly swept over the ears leaving just enough of Kumithra's face open. The final front facial veil resting and for now placed on top of the halo. So Kumithra could apply her make up.

"Ah, that should do it and so in fashion these days. Now if you will excuse me while you do your make up and perfumes. I'll be out in the vestment preparing your gown and getting dressed myself with the other retainers for today and prepare your undergarments. I know you had your breakfast don't forget to do your teeth for you will be kissing today." Said Thernya, with a smile and satisfaction of the hairstyle and veil preparations for this glorious day.

Kumithra looked at herself in the mirror satisfied with the hair and head dressing. It was time to administer the facial make up to impress everyone at the pairing. Yes, to care for her dental hygiene as well. Caring for one's teeth is very important to impressing persons around you in the court. Then she began her facial beautification.

First came the foundation and the smoothing out any blemishes of her skin to be nicely colored to match her youthful complexion. Then she put some highlights into her cheeks and continued on to shadowing her eyelids with a pale color of muted

purple and blended it in with a subtle lighter blue that sparkled. After that she worked with her alabaster eyebrows and smoothed them beyond the perfection they already were. Then came the eyeliner in black with the edges trailing to a point at the outside edges of the eyes.

With a quick change of tool she ordered her eyelashes to look all so eloquent. Finishing off with the same purple and light blue melded lip color. She had to admit she had never been so beautiful and striking with her make up. What was wrong with her, she wasn't getting married to Rarailmuir, but she dressed as if she was. Still dreaming and not wanting to let go of a relationship she thought was established with Rarailmuir. Kumithra stood up from the dressing table and walked out naked into the vestment area of her chambers. Thernya was changed and so were some retainers.

Thernya was awed and exclaimed. "Wow, you are so beyond beautiful today! Come here and let's get you dressed." Thernya said as she passed Kumithra her lacy under pants. That was like body tight shorts up to her belly button and tied in the back. That Thernya had to help tie. While still behind Kumithra. Thernya placed a strapless lace white bra securing the fasteners in back. Followed by a similar corset on Kumithra. Her bodice was a frame that didn't need a corset. Then one leg after the other was the furled upper leggings undergarment. Then stockings of white silk knitted in back and tied off with a ribbon bow just above the knees. Sinching the corset although completely not needed was tied sharply in the back. Next came the Yukata wedding robes.

The first Yukata robe was a soft silk robe used to protect the body from discomfort. Next came the inner trim that would be the less formal wear layer and lace edging, arm cuffing of white. That would cover the legs hemming her gait in to force her to make smaller feminine steps; running would be out of the question. No escaping her fated marriage now. This second layer silk would provide an illusion giving a subtle hint of walking while floating as if not touching the ground. Then came the second inner layer robe that would accentuate the make up of a blended light purple and blue into a lavender. This evened out the headdress and make up to tie in the wedding dress.

The final robe was more like a heavy coat. A Kimono made of starched silk that would signify the occasion in this case it would be white for purity of virginity with a long flowing tail that would require a retinue of courtesans of eight to carry past the garden and into the main hall. It will be detached as the bride was asked to turn to face the audience and would become part of the carpet on the isle.

The final kimono folded left over right. Had trim strands of lavender and purple and a stiff collar worn to majestically reveal the nape of the neck in back. Then finished off with a wide belt that extended just under the breasts and ended at the top of the waist tied in the back in a very pretty bow of considerable size similar to butterfly wings. Measured at two kings foot tall and wide with trailing tails that would rest on the carried long skirt from behind. Accentuated with an inner light blue and purple lining. Then finished of with a two kings thumb tip ornamental lavender bluish rope that sparkled of mithreal, a valued metal of Yoranthium. And would be tied in an intricate rope tying fashion of infinite wedded loyalty that would require some skill to remove. Every husband should be tested for patience and kindness for the gift of their bride.

As this process of the wedding dressing was taking place. Thernya had several other maids enter the room to help dress Kumithra. Helping each other to get dressed quickly as well in similar fashion yet much simpler. Being a basic dress to Kumithra's style of wedding dress. The long flowing tail of the dress was folded and pinned in place behind Kumithra just right below the bow in the back. This would unfold when they get to the exit from the Royal Housing just before going out to the garden.

Kumithra looked in the Mirror and realized this dress was exactly what she had dreamed of on so many nights. "Oh my, Thernya how did you know? This is exactly what I dreamed of on my wedding day. It's so fantastic and beautiful. Even my shoes with the Four thumb high platforms and the lacing along my calf's feel great and look so lovely. You out did yourself."

"Thank you my lady my chamber of maids are in attendance now and we can go and meet your suitor in the hall." Said Thernya holding her arm out towards the door.

“I think I'm ready, oh don't forget my long gloves. Got to have those and my earrings, I almost forgot.” said Kumithra more excited more now than ever. “It's amazing what a nice set of clothes does.”

Long gloves of white shimmering silk were put on her outstretched hands and pushed up her arms to her elbows under the open large hanging sleeves that stopped about the width of the side of a hand’s length before the hand. Then came the earrings of golden loops with a picture in the bottom that would magically change of various sparkling stars and the rising of dawn giving way to subtle ocean spray and calm seas to tropical flowing plants and repeating the imagery over and over in various areas on the Wedding silk that was random. Making Kumithra one of the loveliest people in the room.

The wedding Kimono had magics of illusion designed in it by a fabric’s mage. All controlled by the images in the earring, the same images that would be reflected in the entire retinue’s white fabric kimonos. Images pale in color attractively displayed slowly over time. Giving a peace and tranquility of soothing reflection of beauty. All the displayed images on the dress would be wedding themed and designed to impress.

Kumithra was so obsessed with her own dressing she didn't notice that her entire retinue now filling the vestment chamber had all been dressed and changed in a simpler robe of two layers and a simpler tied belts that were tied in the back with a cloth down the back that was square and flat, all depicting the same imagery in her earrings.

Thernya then attached the veil on the front of Kumithra's headpiece concealing her face. The maids had the similar yet shorter headdresses and no veils. Thernya and the eight other maids positioned themselves behind Kumithra.

Yoranthium

Book One: Lost Hope

Chapter Two:

What of our dreams

By Mark P. Bromley

Dreams are often not the goals of our lives. We share this world with others, and our goals will change if we allow them. Careful of what you dream for many will tread on them. Unless you take the time to earn and nurture the dreams you had wished and relied upon.

The bride was prepared. Thernya and the eight retainers were already dressed. Similar yet simpler with the elderly belt tied to the back. A flat cloth folded over at the top and tucked under the bottom of the large waist belt instead of a butterfly bow. They are not to marry they are simply the retainers that will fall away once the marriage is announced, and the tail piece of the wedding gown is detached and lowered to the ground as the groom and bride turn to face the crowd at the end of the ceremony.

Thernya had once hoped for this day. Yet the world of Ishormot was not as kind as Yoranthium. Wars were fought and champions and children died. Wealth was random and uneven and not fair. Life for many not of a Royal hold never got such weddings. Kumithra was never aware of the inequality and inequity and disadvantage of people. Even for being so wise and learned. Seldom are elites educated to the true world.

Kumithra never realized how few real weddings she had ever attended. This expensive wedding never happened for her father or her mother. Forumth was a poor kingdom not as fortunate as Yoranthium. The rules of conquest and submission of fiefs to larger kingdoms had to be cemented quickly over twenty revolutions ago. Kumithra was much more fortunate than many ladies coming of age. Most royals wed the way her father and mother had been. Never resulted in love of true hearts. Kumithra was very lucky that her kingdom was special to recover so quickly after the dragon attack in four revolutions.

It was great to have found a kinder kingdom and fantastically magically laden Kingdom of the heart the unborn God shined brightly upon them and blessed this land of Yoranthium. As King Sinderthion a kind and benevolent male took the peace offering from the fiefdom of Forumth to be his bride. Queen Zantkara enchanted King Sinderthion when he met her. Thernya was there as the Queens protector to witness the magics, the entire love affair unfold. Which was remarkable considering the circumstances.

Peace was made and not a drop of blood was shed. Thernya was there when Kumithra was born. She was the one to first pull Kumithra from the womb of Zantkara as she pushed. Time flies and the child once in her arms and loved by her parents in their arms is now a grown female. Tears welled up in Thernya's eyes.

She was blessed to raise Kumithra as nearly her own. That was ever so much Thernya's child even if not by birth as she has become quite a female on this very fine and dreamy wedding day. Her voice raised and slightly choked with pride and sentiment, which steadied and sounded so regal and official.

"We are ready, please open the door. Maiden of Honor Huspecia, second to Kumithra her devoted friend and court appointed overseer of this wedding by King Sinderthion and Queen Zantkara of Yoranthium." Huspecia was Thernya's second child she raised from being orphaned as a baby. Ishormot was a cruel world that took the lives of many parents. It was the nature of the deep dark that festered in this world to break elves hearts by denying children the warmth of a family and stability. Denying many the knowledge of parental love.[2]

Thernya cleared her throat. "Suitor to be readies thyself to receive the hand of Princess Kumithra who has come of age and is ready to be wed. To make the long walk to the bridal hall where the Kings and Queens of Yoranthium are made. Thus, proclamation is by the Head Maid, Nay, the second mother of Kumithra. Being I, Thernya in her most official role as Godmother and protector. Proclaim that Kumithra is a female of nineteen revolutions. Unto the unborn God is blessed and be wed this very day. You will from now until all the days forth to bring into this world a gift of a blessed heir and child of the realm. To be proclaiming Kumithra the one to be wed this day."

Trumpets sounded a challenge and then the drums began to beat from outside the Royal Housing. As a retainer at the window waved the signal that they would be proceeding and descending the stairs to the courtyard.

The door opened in pace with drums that was beating outside in tempo. Beginning slowly as horns began to play ever so softly a melody of a wedding preparation. The first person seen in the spacious corridor was Huspecia and protector of Kumithra's chastity. Huspecia was dressed the same as the bride with the belt being tied in the back with a similar butterfly bow. Matching Kumithra as per tradition of bridesmaids.

---

[2] Even in the USA bad elected politicians savagely destroy families and their stability taking all they worked for away. Homelessness never ending begins, inequality and injustice flows from the failings of Globalist Socialists.

Huspecia was very much the same in petite figure as Kumithra. Yet had larger set of eyes of opal, hair that was a shifting yellow, red orange to gold, and one of a kind bluish green interwoven color skin with green as the highlight and a pale azure transition in shade. Along with the same shimmering scales of sea elves.

Huspecia had thicker lips and a more rounded nose and jaw line. Her webbed hands were bigger than Kumithra's and was her feet. She was just five and six king feet high slightly smaller than Kumithra. Although in the wedding procession dress you couldn't tell. Huspecia's breasts were considerably larger than Kumithra's. Yet her buttocks were less round, and her hips were wider along with her chest measurement. Nearly a perfected hourglass shape and fit from her rigorous combat training as a royal protector.

Huspecia said loudly and formally with much exaggeration on key words. Each word metered, paused, clearly pronounced exquisitely theatrical intonation. "I'm here to examine the bride. All appears to be in order, and I accept this bride to be. I, Huspecia approve and ensure she is fit and ready to be given to the captain of the guard Lord Bronanes of the Mundrunche. We are here to solidify a wedding and a matching that is in the best interest of Yoranthium. Please accept this arranged marriage by command of King Sinderthion and Queen Zantkara and this suitor Lord Bronanes the captain of the guard of the Mundrunche as decreed by your father King Sinderthion and Queen Zantkara?" The long lasting exaggerations of all titles and names dragged out the proclamation. Was only a question answerable by Lord Bronanes?

Huspecia moved to the side. There was Lord Bronanes. Dressed in a suitor's vestment by tradition. A long sleeved Yukata folded left over right. Covering a strong muscular chest with various golden tattoos similar to the males of the warrior cast of Yoranthium. Specifically tied to the Yoranthium Navy. Which was common for suitors of the Yoranthium throne to adapt to local royal body art embellishments. The sleeves were similar to the wedding gown in design. The color was on one-side squares of red and gold and on his right side stylized ocean waves of light blue and dark blue in a repeating pattern. This was the traditional wedding outfit of Yoranthium.

The leggings were a continuation of the open Yukata. Loosely formed around the legs following the same color scheme. Most male clothing was designed for mobility and action. The belt was a dark green tied simply crossed over in the front with tassels larger than a male's hand width. The boots were highly polished black and open toed as it was familiar that the webbed toes of sea elves be free for swimming in the water followed by easily removed geta sandals that fitted to the boots. His gloves were black and ran up his sleeves. Sea elf gloves are designed for quick removal as the webbed hands of the sea elves were often needed for swimming should the need arise as water enhances and activates the webbed fingers and toes. The headdress for the males in a wedding was a band of golden laurels from behind the head to the open front.

Lord Bronanes was shorter than her true love only about five and eleven king's foot high slightly taller than Kumithra who was only five and seven king's foot high. With her heels on Kumithra was about six and one kings foot tall. Lord Bronanes was a tad short, not only that he had a nasty scar on is right cheek and his skin mostly interlacing dark blue shadow and light hazel illuminated. Having sea elf shimmering scales. Except pale where you could see his veins under his skin across his right face. Suffering burns in his youth. These burns went from the top of his head down to his lower legs. Heavily scarring the right side of his body.

His eyes were weird as one squinted on the right likely do to the laceration on his face. His eye color was a pale brown color and lacked luster. Seemed like he was glaring like an accusation was being made. His hair was combed on the left side, long shoulder length and black as night as for the right side his hair was missing again due to the wound and burns on his face. When Lord Bronanes tried to smile it was more like an awkward sneering.

"My lady for whom I just met." he said in a slow difficult to pronounce his words and slurred speech. Caused from the injuries on his right jaw down to his throat. "I Lord Bronanes of the Mundrunche, Captain of the Guard of my homeland. With permission of our lady's protector of chastity the ever so kind, generous and sweet and lovely Huspecia. Do accept from King Sinderthion and Queen Zantkara of Yoranthium the hand of Princess Kumithra to be escorted on this day of twenty-seventh day

of the suns harvest five hundredths revolutions of the sun shining on Yoranthium to be the one chosen for this great honor of our kingdoms."

With this and a great smile from her closest friend Huspecia. Kumithra's heart sank and although she hid her disbelief of her suitor. She said, "I upon my father and mother, King Sinderthion and Queen Zantkara and with the blessing of my protectors." Taking a quick hateful glance toward her friend in disbelief with little enthusiasm. Finding it difficult to look at the ugly wounds of Bronanes. Wondering why her father even approved this marriage suitor. He was so difficult to accept let alone look at.

Knowing that her veil hid her faces expression, as she couldn't see Huspecia's smile. "I, do accept in the traditions of Yoranthium and the expectations of our two peoples the hand of Captain of the Guard Lord Bronanes of the Mundrunche to be my escort and the one selected for my marriage before the faith of our God the one yet to be born that will save our world and bring salvation to our lives." If only someone could save her from this fate. "Fortune the day is bright, our lands are well, our sea is plentiful, we prosper, and the birds sing of the blessings we have received. May our good fortune always continue united this day together."

With that Kumithra took small hesitant steps towards her husband to be Lord Bronanes, as her robes were so tight limiting her steps. It was easy to conceal her reluctant acceptance of Lord Bronanes as her suiter. Upon nearing Lord Bronanes, he waited for Kumithra's hand to be extended towards him. Her hand raised and there was an awkward hesitation by Lord Bronanes as he took her hand. Admitting he was terrified. "I'm so nervous about this, I do hope you are okay. I know I'm not exactly what you are hoping for." Said Lord Bronanes with such sympathy that it took Kumithra off guard. Even with his roguish and harsh looks while slurring his rough voice he seemed quite kind and gentle. He was more her age perhaps only a revolution or two older.

As she watched Huspecia take up a position next to Lord Bronanes and placed her hand on his back for encouragement. Then quickly removing her hand with a quick glance to the hidden face of Kumithra. As Huspecia's face was also hidden by a difficult

to see past veil, then said. "Right let's get on with this wedding. Let's go you two love birds." Again, she elbowed Bronanes.

Traditionally the bride's protector wore the same outfit as the bride including a veil and did also require eight maid retainers to carry her long flowing dress in the back as well. The entire host had some difficulty descending the stairs, as they had to break into two formations to get to the lower landing and assembly hall. Descending from the upper floor royal chambers down two curved descending staircases to either side. Made of marble covered with red carpet lining in the center of the steps and curved banisters. Trimmed in gold embellishments and decorative Yoranthium historically illustrated leafed columns. Created by the stone shaping mages.

The main vestibule was of the same white marble on the walls. Supported by large Columns in larger scope to the banister columns. The upper windows allowing more than enough sunlight to fully illuminate the hosting chamber that opened down a short hall from a study and coat room to the side.

Fortunately, the hall was wide enough for fourteen large males to stand side by side. So, it was no problem for all the retainers to line up and prepare the procession towards the main door. The doors were arched to three kings height and just short of that wide, with two doors opened wide and guards at the ready lined along the wedding path. Outside came in the light of a view of a splendid garden.

The guards came from both the Army and the Navy. The Army represented the colors of the golden fields at harvest and the blood of the people symbolized as yellow and red squares. The Navy was represented with dark and light blue altering waves for fair and stormy seas. This was seen under the bottom head of the tips of the tall spears the guards held in one arm on top by the pointed, triangular, long and thin tapered banners.

Their shields were small round bracers with the same colors representing them and their tabards also reflected the same color that covered their armor of light weight scale dragon plated mithreal mined from the main mountain on the coast of the island towards the Cold lands and to the Sundown of the island. Their helmets were simple pointy helmets with curved brims that shined of polished mithreal and their leggings and open toed boots were

blackened leather of high quality. The soldiers stood at rest along the path to the king's hall from the royal housing.

The garden was beautiful this morning. It glistened with dew from the humidity cooling in the morning. The ivory whitened marble gleamed, shined, and sparkled and even glittered as if the stars themselves fell to Ishormot for just this day. Many different kinds of flowers blossomed in this tropical paradise with the bees coming out early and the birds chirping their songs of love to lure their mates. It was a breath taking moment and the entire wedding host felt awe and exhilaration for this day was wonderful like a blessing and a gift from their unborn God the heir maker of champions, heroes, love and hope.

The wedding host stopped just short of the door. Thernya raised her arm and the retinue pulled out the pins holding the two flowing dresses laced white cloths from behind them and stretched out to approximately eight kings length behind Kumithra and Huspecia with the trailing skirt fully stretched out. That the retainers quickly took hold of fanning out to the full length of the long lacy and grandiose tail was unfurled. With the maids being evenly spaced. Thernya would be orchestrating behind the entourage.

Another motion from Thernya and the beating drums and the horns drifted into silence as the guard stiffened and stood at attention pulling their pole arms tighter and more strait. Then with a twist of the wrist by Thernya's raised arm a new song began, and it was a real wedding march not a wedding theme that played before. This was the signal for the wedding procession to move forward. The soldiers with their spears and shields at attention awed the assembled guests to murmurs and then silence.

People on the far sides of the garden behind the soldiers behind the trees and gardens gathered to witness. Had scrambled for the best location to watch the affair unfolds in reverence and hope. These guests outside had to pay tribute for the honor of their loitering arrangements of attendance as royal weddings had not been cheap.

Out of loyalty to Yoranthium the loyal guests spent their meager earnings for a very expensive one of a kind wedding. Those of lesser means attending behind the royal band began to cheer as they seen their Princess and Huspecia and Lord Bronanes along

with eighteen retainers followed by a procession of other well to do and noble families marching right behind them.

With several children up and down the outside flanks from the start of the procession to the end of the procession all tossing Yamazakura pink flower petals out of a magically refilling baskets. Each flower girl dressed in a light child's Yukata similar to the retainers with the same changing scenes on their gowns as was displayed by Kumithra's earrings. The girls toss pink petals of flowers that fluttered to the ground as the lightly falling petals the same pink flowering trees in the garden. A little boy dressed very similar to Lord Bronanes had also escorted each of these little girls.

Following the measured footsteps of Kumithra the entire retinue did their best at keeping in step walking with one small step with the right followed with one left step to match the right stepped out of the Royal Housing. With a slight curtsy first to the right and then another step and curtsy to the left which was repeated for every step to honor the crowd that had been assembled for this once in a lifetime moment for the future of Yoranthium. With Bronanes and the boys doing a slight bow.

Lord Bronanes stuttered a moment and softly spoke. "I'm sorry you might not recognize me. We have met before. I know there is nothing I can say to explain how honored I am to be with you on this special day." Just then he stopped talking as Huspecia accidentally bumped into him.

"Huspecia are you okay?" Asked Kumithra. There was an audible gasp of surprise and few murmurs from the assembled spectators. "We are being watched you know."

"Yes, it's these shoes I'm not use to them. I'll be more careful."

"I know these shoes are a bit tall. We did practice in them for a few days preparing and I never seen you falter before." replied Kumithra "But never mind that. Lord Bronanes. What kind of groom are you?"

"My lady I'm a naval commander who recently got promoted by my father Admiral of the Mundrunche who is in charge of the fleet of my kingdom." Said Lord Bronanes with pride as his slurred voice filled with confidence. "I'm surprised Huspecia hadn't told you as she is the one that arranged all of this for just this day. I'm so proud of her assistance. We did notice you two

swimming off the coast by the shoals as my assigned training skiff prepared to pull into port. Most beautiful and enchantingly intoxicating Siren I had ever seen. I was nearly tempted to crash that training skiff into the shoals. If it wasn't for me being a sea elf too I would have gladly drowned for my Love."

Kumithra was shocked and blushing noting the air seemed to get a little too warm yet didn't want to show her slight change of expression and demeanor toward Lord Bronanes instead she decided to be angry and politely said. "Couldn't you have said something yesterday Huspecia when we were in the marketplace, the gallery or at the beach? I did notice the ship of sailors you decided we should tease yesterday."

Huspecia said, "I didn't want to ruin the fun we were having, and it was a very great day especially when we got to the beach and swam for a few sun wanes until we returned home tired. I did know Lord Bronanes was on that ship and wanted to amuse you Kumithra with one last moment of us working our wiles on some lonely sailors. Especially your unknown suitor Lord Bronanes Knowing it was our last day with you being single and not betrothed. I just wanted to play like we did as kids."

"Oh, I see and I understand Huspecia." Kumithra said in disbelief. "Just forget about some important details. We practically made fools of ourselves sing to them hoping to be like the mermaids and sirens of the sea." Kumithra's ire was picking up in the disappointed tragedy this wedding was becoming.

Lord Bronanes interrupted. "I hope I'm acceptable to you Kumithra. I know I'm not royalty, but should that really matter? I know my image isn't the best. But I am a very loving and caring and kind person who was awarded greatly for heroism as a young male during that disaster by a dragon that caught many buildings on fire revolutions ago. It's where my injuries came from. It was also where I had met the former captain of the guard Rarailmuir. On a few occasions I had visited the palace over the years at his side. I'm so hoping to meet him today. Perhaps he can give away the bride."

Kumithra was finding it difficult to conceal her disgust and anger with the misappropriate comment from Lord Bronanes. Rarailmuir was the captain of the royal guard her father wouldn't replace him ever. Something awful must have happened and her

father was upset. Often Kumithra was scolded for swooning too much around Rarailmuir and playing like girls do with the males that they admired the most over the revolutions. Kumithra was worried now more than ever.

She out right just a few days ago expressed her love of Rarailmuir in front of her mother, her father and the entire court. She quite literally couldn't control herself. Her lustful passions and female desires got the better of her as her libido had blossomed. She thought she was daydreaming. Rarailmuir was her goal and lustful interest since the day the dragon attacked, and she was rescued.

Just days ago, Rarailmuir surprised her in the court of the King. She hadn't seen him enter behind her throne and she was fantasizing out of boredom and day dreaming of her and Rarailmuir. That she failed to maintain her princess demeanor and let the mistake that upset her mother and father and her feelings fly free as she was of age and her hormones got the better of her.

She shot out of her throne and grabbed Rarailmuir and hugged him with a kiss on the cheek. This sent a big shock through the entire court. At first Kumithra thought it was just a daydream she often did that during boring days at the court. But it wasn't a daydream. The entire court noticed. Her father and mother noticed and had scolded her. Raising their voice to Rarailmuir to leave the courtroom immediately after delivering the status reports that all was in order and no dangers to the Kingdom of Yoranthium was on the horizon.

The entire court was shocked, and her mother and father appeared disappointed and angry at the uncontrolled outburst. Kumithra did notice that Rarailmuir kept his poise and politely and even with affection of want, smiled and winked at her on his way out.

Hopefully that wasn't why he was sent away. Hopefully he's still the captain of the guard. If Lord Bronanes is right though and Rarailmuir was demoted? Kumithra could feel her heart sink, anxiety rising, panic began to well in her. Her rushing heart beat faster, and she started to breathe more irregularly. As hot flashes of anger mixed with regret and disbelief filled her mind. Could all this be because of her? Her eyes began to narrow, and she was no

longer aware of the world around her as water was welling in her eyes.

The sounds around her were fading. She was walking mostly on automatic just as she had been trained without a care or a thought just completely void of any reason or conscious thought. At least she spent revolutions training for this day as Kumithra in her automated mode kept to her training. Oblivious of her surroundings and could no longer hear a thing not the trumpets, the drums, the clash of the metered symbols or the cheers of the crowd. Even though she could feel Lord Bronanes strong soft and small hand holding hers and helping to escort her. She was simply no longer aware of her surroundings.

Anxiety and panic and fear took over and her heart and mind raced faster than she could process. Did her actions a few days ago doom her love to a miserable end? Her father the king was known to be brash and deliberate in dealing with what he perceived to be threats to the kingdom and especially very protective of his daughter that on a few occasions her father had swung a sword and used fire ball magics to dispel evil men and monstrous persons from harming or getting near his daughter.

'Oh, no!' Kumithra wildly thought did something awful become of her Rarailmuir was he sent to the mines or the dungeons or to harvest pearls and that's why he's not here?

She couldn't breathe. The tightening of her throat was hard difficult silent breaths. She could feel a throbbing in her head. A flat no color no shapes a nothingness filling her vision. She was finding it difficult to manage herself.

She made it to the palace not noticing the pillared long columns encircling and supporting the large three-tiered palace. She went up the stairs and hardly remembered stepping up any of the nine stairs. Each column went from the base of the dais of stairs of the oval building rising into the sky and supporting the ceiling of the palace at about fifteen king's length high.

Upon entering the building there was an oval of offices on three floors stretching down a short hall of six wide and then of six king lengths long. With doors in the middle of either side or with half pillars exposed in the walls. The building was made of white sparkling marble that shined much like Kumithra's hair and sparkled like the stars at night rested on the floor during the day.

Once the procession moved past the hall. The chamber of the throne room opened up into a wide oval space with columns and pillars supporting another flat roof for a few kings lengths until becoming a dome around the entire center of the building. Five-Hundredths revolutions of Yoranthium Kings, Queens and notable persons statues stood between the pillars around the entire hall.

On the outside the dome was covered in gold leaf and the lighting rod in the middle was a symbol of Yoranthium with a hero of it's founding holding a trident to the sky. Inside it was a magically painted fresco that moved to detail the history of the founding of Yoranthium. The voyage from the mainland and the heroic discovery and the peace with the local sea elves and the rise of the Kings of Yoranthium for five-hundredths revolutions made what Yoranthium is today.

Kumithra made it to the steps of the throne not noticing how the hall had been arranged for the banquet in honor of this marriage arranged by her father. After approximately eighteen lengths of her father, she had made it to the steps of the dais of the throne. Where she unconsciously ascended the nine steps up to the dais.

Once on top about two kings length she, Lord Bronanes, Lady Huspecia and the entire retinue had stopped as the court of lords and ladies and the children of the procession veered off to take their seats or stand at the sides of the red carpet that was encrusted with golden historical references of courtly duties performed. Trimmed in a gold egg and dart lining the outer edges of the carpet they had just walked on, and the same carpet covered the dais of the throne.

Where there behind her father, mother and a clergy priest of the deity of the unborn God they worshiped was three thrones. The largest was three kings length high and on either side on the kings right a thinner two kings length high throne for her mother and a single king length high narrow throne where Kumithra had sat when attending court.

Of course, Kumithra noticed not where she was. She was no longer really at the wedding and was filled with dread, anxiety, panic and finding it hard to breathe as her heart raced and her head pounded a dull thud that choked off the world too her.

No one else could see it. Kumithra was beginning to lose her strength and conviction. She was becoming stiff and locked her legs standing before her father. She was aware of smiles from her father and mother the clergy and saw their mouths moved but heard nothing. She looked over momentarily to see Lord Bronanes soundlessly speak and noticed the puffs of air of Huspecia speaking from behind her veil. But heard nothing and looked away. The world was beginning to become hazy and blurred.

Then she felt Lord Bronanes strong, soft and thin hand drop from hers on the left and a stronger hand that was thicker and more familiar. A hand she dreamed so many times that would touch her body ever so softly. Taking hold of her right hand. She looked to her right and the world focused ever so slightly.

To her right stood a taller than her father sea elf of chiseled square jaw with a dimple in the chin, thick strong lips that Kumithra dreamed of kissing. A sea elf shimmering scaled interlocking pattern of dark blue shade and dark bronze highlighted skin with thick male lips. Having a strong strait nose broad in nostrils that has never been broken. Eyes of gold sun fire irises around black glistening pupils. Followed with modestly thick eyebrows with a dark golden mane of long flowing hair that was well kept with two braids on either side meeting in a braided ponytail in the back. To the front of his face a dangling thin Therica hanging to the side. Thericas being a fashionable braid that Kumithra put there herself over three revolutions ago dangling down the right side of his chiseled face.

He was strong and dashing wearing a similar to Lord Bronanes wedding wear quite handsomely and Kumithra saw his muscular chest heave up and down she had wanted to touch on many occasions. It was Rarailmuir he was holding her right hand.

It was too much and like a candle being blown out by the wind she had seen the world going dark around her. Her head shifted upward, as her eyes rolled behind her eyelids and her ankles and knees felt weak and bent awkwardly in the tight Yukata she wore around her legs and her waist began to bend as she felt herself falling towards the floor.

Rarailmuir was quick and while clenching Kumithra's right hand he spun round to catch her in mid fall. His hand landing to the side of her left breast with the edge of his palm touching her

nipple concealed under the wedding Yukata and the rest of his hand under the arm pit of Kumithra's left arm.

".... Kumithra, Kumithra... Can you hear me?" Ever so faintly she began coming back to consciousness and seen Rarailmuir's face mere inches from her veil staring with large, concerned eyes. Deeply, concerned and lovingly at her.

She could feel the warmth of his hand under her arm on the side of her bodice and slightly on top of her breast and nipple. Oh, how long she had wanted to feel his touch and it was so assuring to her. As he caught her and kept her from falling to the floor so she could regain her poise in front of all the people she loved so much in life. This wasn't a dream this was real. The nightmare wedding was a ruse and a trick. Rarailmuir was indeed her true suitor after all. Dreams do come true.

But what of Lord Bronanes, where did he go? She had to know, and she looked to her left. He was still there. It all started to make more sense. As Lord Bronanes was now holding the hand of Huspecia and just the day before at the beach Huspecia waved at the ship and sure enough there was only one sea elf waving back. It must have been Bronanes.

Huspecia deliberately went to that secret beach location for years and it was to see Lord Bronanes departing and returning to Yoranthium. But still Kumithra had questions as now she realized Huspecia didn't accidentally stumble and bump into Bronanes. They had carefully plotted a trick and played a game on Kumithra. Rarailmuir, Thernya, Huspecia, Bronanes, her mother and father and the entire court was in on it.

Remembering the story of Lord Bronanes was just as remarkable as her rescue. Yes Kumithra began to remember. She remembered a story from long ago. It was hard to remember for her own story of her own rescuer took precedence and she was so enamored with Rarailmuir that she never paid much attention to the second of the captain of the guard. How selfish for her not to remember. Bronanes was Rarailmuir's lieutenant. Huspecia's love story is what she forgot, for Huspecia's love was Lord Bronanes.

On the same day the dragon had set the city on fire. Rarailmuir inspired another young male student who became his squire. That young male was Lord Bronanes who looked up to

Rarailmuir as someone he had always aspired to become. Bronanes was two revolutions older and a senior schoolmate.

When Rarailmuir crashed through the burning debris and into the crumbling classroom to save Kumithra. Lord Bronanes was like wise motivated and was the second to enter the burning classroom where Huspecia was also trapped and in danger. Yet Lord Bronanes was not as lucky or fortunate as Rarailmuir. Bronanes suffered burns, a severe laceration and injuries in his rescue of Huspecia.

That must be how Huspecia fell in Love with Bronanes. Months after the incident Huspecia spent a lot of time with the healing clerics and it must have been to care and swoon over Bronanes. Her injured savior was being treated for his injuries. Huspecia. '...Had a patient to care for.' Is often what she said and learned some healing arts from the clerics going there for Bronanes.

Kumithra deserved this little joke. Four revolutions she had forgotten these events and was singly focused on her love interest with Rarailmuir that she never really paid attention to another story of love and romance that was with her everyday. Huspecia's hero Lord Bronanes, heartthrob and her savior a husband to be.

Just now, Kumithra remembered and to think she was so forgetful all these years. At the hidden beach every time it was Huspecia that insisted when they would swim there and why they both would try to seduce the sailors of the ship Bronanes was on. The ship would change constantly and one of them was the Mundrunche. Which was undergoing refit in the hidden secret docks.

The Mundrunche wasn't a fiefdom or a kingdom it was the pride of the Yoranthium navy and currently being upgraded with knew secret upgrades. Was the Admirals ship that was being refitted with some new magics by the Mages College at the hidden harbor. If her legs could move in this wedding dress she could kick herself for not realizing all this. Mundrunche in sea elven language meant the 'victories of heart, love, duty, honor, and kingdom.'

She was fooled by all those closest to her and even Thernya set the stage for this ruse this very morning. Kumithra was known to be a bit naive and often acted rash and a little reckless. There is no doubt she had this coming for being so insensitive.

"Are you okay my love?" She gazed up to realize she had regained her footing. With the height of the platforms on the shoes making her almost as tall as Rarailmuir himself. Kumithra could look him strait in his loving and longing passionate and caring eyes.

"Did you forget to eat your breakfast this morning? You know you have to keep up your strength. But don't worry my love we will be wed this day soon enough and on to the luncheon banquet where we can get you back to full health in no time. Sorry for the joke we didn't know you would take it so badly my love. Hopefully we can continue." Rarailmuir smiled upon her wishing to keep her well.

She listened to his words like they were a spell on her. Raising her left hand and placed it on top of Rarailmuir's right hand pushing his hand deeper onto her breast for she so much wanted to feel his warm touch upon her. Then changed her mind as she was in a room full of those who cared much for her, and she placed her hand in Rarailmuir's large strong soft and tender hand and lowered it off her body.

"Yes we can continue, you are right I had been told to have breakfast before my bath by Thernya and simply forgot knowing what day it is. I was dreaming of you." Kumithra had said with some subtle confidence to Rarailmuir, and she looked upon his darker bronzed blue skin that was chiseled and strong and yet so soft and so attractive to her all these years. She was so enamored that her stare even from beneath the veil dug into Rarailmuir's very soul knowing and yearning to be with one another more intimately.

Rarailmuir was slightly blushing feeling the impact of Kumithra's soul touch his even through the gloves and through the eyes staring tentatively into one another's obscured by a veil. It was difficult through the veil to feel each other's souls. Something that Kumithra had believed in since the stories of romance and love her mother and Thernya use to read to her. How does this soul touching work? Maybe she had to wait to be unveiled or something that she didn't understand. But she read everything about wedded true love souls. This simply didn't make any sense. Her soul failed to touch Rarailmuir's.

Rarailmuir must feel the same way. He had too. No wife no children and no one in his life. Bronanes was the only second one

close to Rarailmuir and he's in love with Huspecia. Kumithra had tried so often to be around Rarailmuir every day surely they were soul compatible. Even when he was so busy with his duties she would find him.

Why is it so difficult for their souls to combine like in the stories? Perhaps it's a wedding thing and couples must wed to soul synchronize. Maybe and hopefully it's when Rarailmuir touches Kumithra in the wedding chamber. That's when they bare their souls to one another. Not all couples have their souls locked. Some do it out of convenience, others for the sake of children, yet all learn to love and even her Father didn't soul sink with her mother. It wasn't until they met at the peace parley with the kingdom of Forumth.

Look at them now they truly love one another, and they loved her too. She was more loved than the King loved his sword. The sword was the treasure of Yoranthium. Why couldn't Rarailmuir sync with her soul? As the princess of Yoranthium she should be able to sync her soul with Rarailmuir. Perhaps she was trying to hard, because she could feel Rarailmuir's soul was near but would not sync with her for some reason. Perhaps the books she read on the subject are wrong. After all those books had been fairytales of love and the soul. Taught to her in religious studies.

Perhaps it was best not to dwell on such trivial matters. Soul binding meant everything to Kumithra and her idea of a perfect dream of a marriage. Making for a perfect marriage of the heavens and cosmos. Or perhaps she was being selfish again and expecting too much. It might be better to relax and not be so uptight. Kumithra thought and perhaps this would fix the soul dilemma she was creating for herself on this fine wedding day to her one an only Rarailmuir.

Yoranthium

Book One: Lost Hope

Chapter Three:

Dreams become Manifest

By Mark P. Bromley

Sometimes if our dreams are shared with those around us miracles of life, love and happiness inspire us to make these dreams of ours to manifest becoming truths. But not all dreams last and sometimes even the dream can turn to a nightmare.

"Uhm, Uhmppf!!!" Raised the voice of her father, King Sinderthion. A rather strong voice well heard in the echoing hall that amplified his voice so all could hear. Sinderthion was a tall sea elf by two kings thumb heights taller than Rarailmuir. He was tall and lanky yet very physically fit for an elderly sea elf of one hundred and three revolutions. Sea elves lived long lives similar to their kin from the mainland of the Potentate. He was younger than Thernya by far.

Having black hair that was ragged and short cropped with a top knot of hair that was long and flowing over the back of his crown tied off with a brilliant displayed top band of silk treated leather lacquered with gold inlay. The crown was a simple thin band that displayed the royal line and symbology of the sea elves land of Yoranthium through out its established history depicting the strength of the land and the heart and soul of the people. The crown on his head was quite simple with laurels on its side and only about one kings thumb thick.

His black beard was swirled and well groomed short cut to his face along with a thin wispish mustache that accentuated his parse and strong lips. Above the mustache was his well-defined and highly dignified nose that was slightly crooked with a scar he sustained in battle years ago fighting to take the fiefdom of his Queen Zantkara and her brother. Winning that battle adding Forumth as a vassal fiefdom of Yoranthium.

The scar was slight and on the middle of the nose, yet it was a deep cut. His eyes were thin like Kumithra's and purple his eyebrows similar to Kumithra's as well. Which it was hard to say if she got her eyes from her father or her mother for they were both very similar. There was no denying that Kumithra did not get her fathers smile but that of her mother Queen Zantkara.

Queen Zantkara was standing next to the King with her arms folded in front of her hips. The Queen was unquestionably ravishing and in stature similar to Kumithra. The Queen had her hair done to similar fashion, as her daughters the hair color of her mothers was very similar to her daughters. With a facial line very much the same. This is whom Kumithra got her lovely, good looks and lips from along with the same physical features of her mother's apparent shapeliness.

Both her father and Mother wore matching dark naval blue robes accented with red underlying robes of a high royal nature that suited the wedding very nicely. The queen's crown was lighter and thinner than the kings and accentuated her earrings that matched the ones Kumithra was wearing on this fine day. That also reflected images in their clothing. Her mother had a belt on that matched the retainers and was tied in the back with a top sash square and flat just like Thernya. That was matching royal color to her royal queens dress.

"So, with all the drama this wedding, I do hope that we can proceed with my daughters, Princess Kumithra's union to General Rarailmuir of the Yoranthium guard. Also continue with this ceremony to set in place forever the marriage of the princess's protector Lady Huspecia and her husband to be Captain of the Yoranthium's Guard Lord Bronanes? Does anyone object? Do we have a challenge? Can my daughter please stay attentive and on her feet?" With that a loud but short bit of laughter and merriment filled the chamber from all the attending guests. No challengers stepped forward for there was no guard or other male in the room except Kumithra's father even remotely capable of defeating Rarailmuir.

Kumithra had a strange thought about a foreign visitor she met half a third season ago at a local popular pub in the gallery. In the back of her mind, she had wanted for him to suddenly appear and demand a challenge. After all what princess's wedding wouldn't be complete without males fighting for her heart and love and hand in marriage. Yes, Kumithra thought so haughtily of herself and was somewhat spoiled in this aristocracy. She felt a little sad that that foreign male wasn't here to spill his blood for her.

Several moments passed and Rarailmuir looked deeply into Kumithra's eyes. Speaking softly. "Are you ready my beautiful lady? I had loved you and waited and watched you mature and blossom all these years?" Kumithra was speechless and liked and yearned for this blessing of mating her flesh with that of Rarailmuir's. Along with being bashfully ashamed of the right out comment of copulation that surely her parents had heard. Rarailmuir did covet her in secret all these years and only now

confessed his love, lust and desire for her in such a definitive physical method. It was as if a dream came true.

She knew Rarailmuir to be much older and he had never taken a wife and so many had tried to land him for he was very much a popular heartthrob all over Yoranthium. Many females swooned for Rarailmuir. Often giving Kumithra quite a challenge for his attention. She was often aware of the rumors and stories and the swooning of other young and old Yoranthium girls in this kingdom. Even heard the rumors of impropriety and scandal that was all proven false over the past revolutions. Lies of red district scandal that would send Kumithra to tears and rage and forgiveness of thoughts found to be baseless against her love Rarailmuir.

It was quite the wild ride of untamed griffon riding and nail biting. All for naught for Rarailmuir was always found to be true of heart. Yeah, She was partially choking and whispered trying to regain her voice. While blinking her eyes as her imagination and dreams was becoming a reality. She was near screaming and jumping up and down with anxiety and excitement she had won the prize of the land the hand and heart of her physically attractive male Rarailmuir. True of heart true of physical form the best Yoranthium had to offer. She was the princess and always deserved the best. Being aware of other ladies of the court that must have envied her. They could challenge her, yet ladies of the court would unlikely stoop to brutal combat, as it would tarnish their female image and grace before their love of a male.

Rarailmuir let go of Kumithra's left hand and swung around facing her father. Loudly stating echoing in the grandiose hall. "Yes, my king and my queen for the sake of Yoranthium and the future of our kingdom we are ready to join my hand and heart to your daughter Princess Kumithra. We are also prepared to tie the hands and hearts of my second and most loyal Captain of the guard Lord Bronanes and my wife's faithful protector the Lady Huspecia in a dual wedding. The ages of Yoranthium's history will speak kindly and reverberate our dual union. We are gathered under this very Royal and regal dome before the King and Queen of Yoranthium in sight of our lord God who is yet to be born. Of course, by all means bring forth the Clergy and let the holy matrimony of two unions this day commence that are founded in

devoted love, kindness, and caring." With that he raised his left arm holding Kumithra's hand horizontally. That signified they are ready to be united in love, heart and soul forever and at the same moment Lord Bronanes did the same with Lady Huspecia's hand in his.

King Sinderthion and Queen Zantkara had been diligently collecting taxes for this wedding of their daughters for some time. It would be revolutions before another wedding of this scope and interest by the lords and ladies would ever be again. The costs to make this the first of it's kind and the most widely anticipated and historical event would only be a once in a lifetime affair. The King and Queen had known of their daughter's interest in Rarailmuir since the day he rescued their daughter. They had also recognized the long-standing love of Rarailmuir's squire and closest friend Captain of the Guard Lord Bronanes and his Lady Huspecia.

The princess was so blind to that love story that was at her side all these revolutions. That creating the Royal double wedding would justify to the citizens of Yoranthium for all the taxes being spent and all the taxes being collected. Especially a massive sum that came from a foreign lord of some Tovorian House that Rarailmuir defended in the local streets.

The Foreign Lord donated Potentate coin to be spent in this wedding budget. This wedding was well financed and boosted the Yoranthium economy.[3] Why not over do the festivities and double the marriage rights for both the Princess and her Protector were of equal merit and value as they were both equal daughters of the King and the Queen. The princess was their true daughter and Huspecia was their adopted daughter.

"Then let the wedding commence!!! Bring forth the Archpriest of our faith and let him bless this most sacred of days by uniting these two couples before me King Sinderthion and Queen Zantkara. On this day the twenty-seventh of five hundredths and twenty-three years of our flourishing Kingdom of Yoranthium!!!" He exclaimed with considerable pomp in his most notable royal voice so all could hear. The king and queen smiles

---

[3] A common failing of nations is the reliance on other nations coin in the false boosting of their economys. Vassal nations are created when other economies are servant to a benefactor economy.

widened and the Archpriest of the temple of the God to be born took his position in front of the two couples to be wedded.

The Archpriest was known as. 'The whispers of the womb' or he who would be the voice of that which needed to be heard and was waiting to be born. Who would be called keeper of the words of God that would become our protector and savior. So was their faith and belief in life above all was the most valuable asset of the people of Yoranthium. The beating heart of the people and the kingdom of Yoranthium was based upon in the spiritual philosophy and theology of the kingdom of Yoranthium.

Their belief's and politics are why many female sea elves would be married so early in life to males that could bare them many children. Why the education of the island was so good and great and the envy of many kingdoms. Love and caring was at the heart of this kingdom and this was good and considered the most holy of purposes before their God.

The priest wore a tall spearhead shaped oval mitre on his head about half a kings arm length high. That was edged in white with a red soft silk insert in the front trimmed in gold symbolizing the faith and disciplines of their belief. That contained in the lower part of the front the symbol of Yoranthium and combined coat of arms. The symbology of alternating red and yellow squares and then the alternating light and dark blue waves of the ocean that surrounded the island of Yoranthium. In the middle was a symbolic golden heart of the beating sea elf heart of their unborn God representing the philosophy of life and love of the people of Yoranthium.

Atop and emblazoned on the mitre was the light blue sky of clarity above the land and waves on the left and right of the purple mountains that surrounded Yoranthium. Of four alternating dark and light purple images mirrored and repeated to each side rising up into the sky. Representing the mountain that was the wealth of Yoranthium that supplied the metals, like mithreal steel and other raw resources that built the very cities and defenses for the kingdom. The rest of the vestments of the priest were a simplified heavy starched and thick white priests kimono. With a neck wrap that dangled over the shoulders and down the front with runes of blessings, protections, and saintly wisdom trimmed in gold and shimmering like the silks do in Yoranthium.

The priest was an old male. He had lived a very full life and was the third generation of the head archpriests on the island. It was said early in life the clergy from the same family had always heard the voice of the unborn God. That one day the Kingdoms heir would bring into this world the child that would be the embodiment of the Holy Scriptures and the legend of the God who would bring love and compassion to all the lands of Ishormot. Who would be the savior of all Ishormot in a time of need.

No child has yet been born and many possible saints had risen to great accomplishments and heroic deeds. All had perished in their efforts and were only worthy of being saints and champions and angel messengers of the unborn God. A warning to the darkness growing that it will fall before the light of their God to be born. This was the belief in the life of the unborn to be the heir to inherit the light of their most holy God and blessed savior.

The priest had a small, tiny face in the flamboyant attire. Almost to the point of comedy and was all wrinkled and his eyes whereas if they were closed but just enough to reveal his eyes were silver and one of his pupils had developed blindness.

"Let us all who assembled here today please rise as we wed these two couples before the unborn God and witness a blessing this day of hopes that our God will find his means to be born unto our lands." All the people rose as instructed. Quieted and silenced for reverence to why they attended the wedding. This was the moment they had been waiting for the entire morning as the zenith of midday was nearing and they all felt the pangs of hunger for the wedding feast to begin.

The priest then had attendants at his side. It was a young boy and girl. Both part of the retinue that entered the hall earlier. Both of the children had golden inlaid with silver shimmering strands of unbreakable mithreal laced silk ropes in their hands. These long ribbon lashes were the instruments of binding the wedding couples lives and souls and hearts to one another.

The priest then turned to the girl standing before Lady Huspecia and Lord Bronanes. The Archpriest bent over ever so slightly as the girl had raised the bonds of marriage and handed them to the Priest. The children were picked at random. The belief of the marriage ceremony was that the child giving the wedded couple their band of bonding was the gender of the first child the

wife would bear to her husband. Such was the faith and hope of ceremony and belief. In this case Huspecia would be blessed with a girl so the tradition symbolized. The little boy with the wedding band for Kumithra meant she would bare Rarailmuir a boy.

The priest then took the wedding bindings and walked over to Lord Bronanes and Lady Huspecia. "It is before our God yet to be born. That we witness a couple that is to be wed before the light of our God to be born. That they bring full a circle of life and foster a loving care for the future of those to be united as husband and wife. Who shall be known before our God in marriage." The priest paused for a moment and then asked. "Lord Bronanes do you have your oath and vows for Lady Huspecia?"

Lord Bronanes slurring his voice responded. "Aye, I have the words I would like to say this very day. I offer to my lovely and caring wife to be Lady Huspecia. The finest and most tender feminine that has been with me for many years." It was a sea poem Lord Bronanes had prepared for just this occasion. That he sung to a typical navy shanty. Not only that many of his shipmates from the Mundrunche were in attendance at the wedding. They added their voice and few musical instruments of their own making to the musical poem they had been practicing. Even Rarailmuir knew this song with a deep male voice he too also sang in the chorus.

Titled: Cast anchor yet love we wed is on the shore.
(Chorus)
"Oh, way, o' way, with anchor cast off we sail.
Oh, way, o' way, with sail unfurled we sail.
Oh, way, o' way, be long the leagues we travel.
Yet way, yet way, our hearts had never left shore.
(End Chorus)
(Solo Lord Bronanes own writing a gift to us all.)
For our hearts have love they have true love of the one we leave on the shore.
Our hearts that yearn for the tender touch, embracing of our love on the shore.
We put our hearts to the hazard that just like a siren she has called to us with her love.
To return, return. Return as promised from the sea to wed our love.

(End Solo)
(Chorus)
Oh, way o' way, with anchor cast off we sail.
Oh, way o' way, with sail unfurled we sail.
Oh, way o' way. be long the leagues we travel.
Yet way, yet way, our hearts had never left shore.
(End Chorus)
(Begin Solo)
We find our hearts are tied we find our hearts are bound to a soul calling us to return.
To a lovely lady lovelier than the sea, who will shipwreck us on her shores.
Our hearts are full of love and song, and we are glad she holds us in her caring arms.
For her soul is the port we now call home for now our souls are one.
(End Solo)
(Chorus)
Oh way, oh way, with anchor cast off we sail.
Oh, way, o' way, with sail unfurled we sail.
Oh, way o' way, be long the leagues we travel.
Yet way, yet way, our hearts had never left shore.
(End Chorus)
(Begin Solo)
May my sweet Huspecia be my love.
For lovely, sweet Huspecia is to me like a dove.
I did find solace in her heart the day of trial.
By she tendeth to me so tenderly every day on the dial.
I healed with the love and the kindness of her heart.
That she would always find my heart like a dart.
Like a Siren I would willingly give too my life.
So should she become my loving wife.
I will care to my last day unto Lady Huspecia.
For my heart and love and life belongs to my dear Lady Huspecia.
(Singularly only Lord Bronanes sings this chorus.)
Oh way, o' way, with anchor cast off we sail.
Oh way, o' way, with sail unfurled we sail.
Oh way, o' way, be long the leagues we travel.

**Yet way, yet way, our hearts had never left shore.
For my heart will wed my lovely Huspecia this day my refuge and love from the waves."
(Fini. What a lovely sea shanty.)**

Lady Huspecia elbowed Lord Bronanes. "What was that? Poetry? A song? All your guard on the ship too just had to sing it as well didn't they?" She started to giggle while embarrassed even while blushing under her veil.

"It's a sea shanty me and my crew was singing yesterday I made for you. The last bit I made it up yesterday whiles you where on the shoals in that two-piece revealing swimwear. Could you not hear the song?" Inquired with a smile, Bronanes knowing Huspecia loved the piece because of the way she would giggle when he made her blush or happy.

"Often I hear some kind of song from your ship, but you are often too far away for it to make any sense to me." Said Lady Huspecia.

"Really then there's more you'll need to hear. I wrote them all down." Bronanes said with some glee in his heart.

"Well, my dearest we'll have a lifetime together for you to sing to me. Huspecia said with such tenderness and hopefulness that the songs only get better with age.

Kumithra noticed that Rarailmuir had also sung the terrible and awful wedding shanty of Lord Bronanes. She was quite amused and smitten by the terrible shanty. Yet Rarailmuir had a fantastic singing voice she was never aware of. It would be his turn soon enough to enchant her heart with what he had prepared for her.

"Very well Lord Bronanes!" Exclaimed the priest trying to get Huspecia's attention to focus back on the wedding.

"Yes indeed Lord Bronanes." Said King Sinderthion with a huge smile and somewhat a very loud and room filling laughter. "I had no idea you were so talented with love shanties from the sea. Your men and General Rarailmuir knew, had practiced the song as well. I shall have you teach me the fine arts of how to woo a female with sea shanties so I can impress Queen Zantkara."

Queen Zantkara although amused and enjoying the moment. Looked at her Husband in disbelief. "Don't you go and

start turning our kingdom into a series of sea shanties by Lord Bronanes. You don't need to sing to me to have my heart my husband Sinderthion." Queen Zantkara said and moved right next to her King and placed her left arm behind his back and rested her right arm on his heart while leaning over to kiss him on the cheek. Reaching with her feet pressing off the floor up to her husband's lips as he knelt over to meet her lips. That lasted for quite a few moments as astonishment came from the guests with tumultuous approval and cheers.

The kiss slowly ended and the king lovingly saying to the court. "Queen Zantkara this is not your wedding it is our daughters and her finest suitors, the General Rarailmuir's and the Captain of the Guard Bronanes. We are wedding both our daughters this day. Yet if you insist we'll have three weddings this day and reestablish our love for one another as well." King Sinderthion said lifting his left arm and tenderly touching the cheek of Queen Zantkara who slightly blushed and smiled.

"My King, with your permission to continue." Said the Archpriest. Wanting to keep the double wedding on track. He was prepared for only the two weddings and there wasn't a third wedding band.

"Quite right, let the weddings continue as planned for we still have the matter of getting my daughters hands married this blessed day." Said the King.

After turning back to Lady Huspecia, the Archpriest then inquired. "Is there anything you have to say as your wedding vows to your Lord Bronanes Captain of Yoranthium's Naval Guard?"

"Of course, I Lady Huspecia do have and express my vows. I'm prepared to bare my soul and my heart and love of my desire. Of my life commitment to be the one to give Lord Bronanes the children we have so much spoken about."

Lady Huspecia took a deep breath and paused a moment, adjusted herself and reached over with her left hand and brushed so caring at Lord Bronanes facial scars and burns and then took another deep breath returning to a more rigid stature. Under her veil her lips began to move and taking a deep breath through her delicate nose. With her breasts greatly becoming larger and lungs filling with air and slowly closing her eyes the part began opening of her lovely mouth. Ever so slight began a very smooth and

growing sound so beautiful you would imagine it to be the song of a true siren of the waves of the queen of the mermaids. Her voice was far beyond the vocal octaves of many of the best sea elves professional orators.

The song was not words it was sounds. Beginning in an octave that only sea elf ears alone could hear. Quite soft and smooth and long tones playing a magically enchanting and enthralling tune. Sounding like all the angels of the cosmos was singing through her singular voice. That for moments lasted as the crowd of people slowly became very silent and all that could be heard was Huspecia's song. Echoing off the convex domed ceiling and dancing off the walls amplified by the construction of the building and exceeding the sound quality of the most famous opera halls found in the lands of the potentate. A real song of a siren if there ever was a mermaid that could sing around Yoranthium. Huspecia would be that mermaid.

Her voice was never heard like this before. Kumithra was taken by surprise. There had been many lessons Kumithra learned about singing. She learned from Huspecia. Kumithra never knew this lovingly beautiful seductive voice of Huspecia it was beyond beauty. Kumithra was doubtful she could ever match the voice of Huspecia's song of the Siren. The tones and melody's were beyond the range of any sea elf maiden. The only other creatures of the sea prized for such a voice was only the mermaids that surrounded her mother's home island of Forumth.

Huspecia continued to sing the tones becoming longer more deliberate more soothing, gentle and enchanting. Yes this was an enchanting spell. This song, her voice echoed off the dome and you could see a perceptible glow around everyone inside the Hall of the king. Bronanes was enthralled and looked lovingly beyond the veil of Huspecia into her closed eyes. Huspecia's eyes opened met Bronanes eyes and their souls bonded and caressed each other's. All so gently and deliberately synchronized and in tune soul dancing and binding.

The couple's souls were an amalgamation of true love and romance that was indistinguishable. Explaining in the song a lifetime of feelings, hopes, ambitions, and love. Love, emotional, physical, real that was figurative and imagined. This is how Huspecia's song felt in the very soul of any couple or anyone in the

world who ever had true love for another. It was two hearts becoming one, two souls merging in ecstasy. Becoming the joyous elation of life, hope, ambitions and aspirations that were the yearning of the heart. The circle of life and love and children and futures and the greatness that... Well, there is only one real word for the feeling. LOVE.

More than that it seemed only Kumithra and Rarailmuir was immune to the very powerful enchantment that seemed to extend far beyond the Palace Throne and out into the garden. The song could be heard in the birds and the wind and seemed like the entire island was enchanted. In fact the island of Yoranthium had rare minerals that made the island special. Throughout the entire island was brought to life and to love and not only shimmered but began to glow.

The entire island was enthralled in Huspecia's song. Huspecia was aware of her voice the most beautiful she had ever managed and as if the unborn God had blessed her this day. She was unaware of how the entire court felt the song in their hearts and very depths of their souls. The entire island had been exceptionally gifted and blessed with her sirens song.

All, except Kumithra and Rarailmuir were impacted deeply to their very souls with Huspecia's enchanting and ensorcelled song of the deepest of life affirming true loving hearts. That radiated towards the heavens and the cosmos of the universe. Just at this time and moment there was among the stars an alignment of the cosmos. That if having access to scientific equipment on a spaceship and had observed the timing of this song. You would have found baffling energies and affects that were beyond science and could only be explained as magic.

The entire court and everyone on Yoranthium who could ever share their souls with another had been soul binding. Had embraced, held hands, reached out to touch one another with tender and caring love as the song continued in such sweet melody and tempo so deliberate and enchanting. Even little boys and little girls who were fated in their futures would be bound by their souls. Had stopped being children just to look at one another's eyes. A soul binding of couples that were never known of in the world of Ishormot was taking place on Yoranthium over Huspecia's siren song.

This song of the heart of the soul of love being bound to those we had been connected to from our births in one life to the next. Was by the heavenly conjunction triggered around the world of Ishormot and all that lived had been impacted to some extent even at great distances as far and beyond as the Potentates kingdom and other lands to the deep dark abyss of the Hell fires. Souls were alive and imbued with sensing and knowing.

Kumithra was looking at her Rarailmuir under her veil yet had diverted her gaze to a distant part of the sea where eye's like Rarailmuir's yet of a blue sun fire instead of gold. Shared this moment. She could see a caravel and a male looking back at Yoranthium. Which wasn't right for her true love was Rarailmuir.

Even the Archpriest with a tear in his eye over the beauty of the song had looked over to his love. She was a nun of the unborn God and head of the Healing Clergy. That secretly in the past they had broken their vows just to be with one another for even among the clergy love does happen.

The crowd had many ladies and lords and all in attendance holding hands binding their souls. Some were moved to kissing and other signs of their affection for one another. Even those who pretended or spurned their love and soul binding to another could not resist Huspecia's sweet voice and powerful vocals and the depth of love of the heart and the very soul that every living thing across the known planes of creation could ever know. Loves truth could never be deceived. Imagine adrift upon the beauty of the cosmos beyond the stars and looking into the depths of creation. The glory for love at its heart, spiritual, real, metaphysical, in fairy tales and all worldly knowledge this was the song Huspecia was now singing.

This song was so lovely that Kumithra and Rarailmuir who seemed unaffected witnessed the King and Queen lock eyes and kiss and meld their bound souls in love real love. The King and Queen's kiss was unworldly it transcended everything Kumithra thought a kiss could or would ever be with a telling of truth of love and the passion of the heart.

Rarailmuir looked at Kumithra and whispered looking into her eyes past her veil. "I have no idea how to top this. How about you?"

Kumithra turned her eyes back to Rarailmuir's and could only see the eye's of another far off to sea. It took some time for her

to break the spell and let the sun fire blue fade into Rarailmuir's sun fire golden eyes. Before she could respond.

"I have a song very similar to Huspecia, but I'm not gifted with that voice she's been blessed with. I doubt I'll be any better, but I will try for you my love." Kumithra wanted to feel what everyone was feeling but seemed denied. She was confused about the eyes she had seen half a third of a season at that pub in the shopping gallery of the Grand City. She clenched her hand on Rarailmuir's to express her warmth and love for him. Which broke the effects of something strange and weird to her.

Huspecia's Siren Song continued for some time and was impressive, full of love, and the mysteries of all the known realms of the cosmos the finest concert of all there was had been given. That eventually came to an end with astonished silence for long moments after. No one said anything, as they were all still sharing their very souls that were locked and seemed unbreakable to those they were bound to.

As the enchantment faded the glowing of the island of Yoranthium began to fade to normal, as the conjunction of stars in the system of Ishormot had ended. The court applauded and approved of the intense enchanting and enthralling song shared by Huspecia. Without ever knowing the world of Ishormot was awaking from a very beautiful dream this very day.

Queen Zantkara then realized where the voice of Huspecia might have came from. No one on the island knew of Huspecia's lineage. But now she suspected. Zantkara kept quiet for some secrets not even her own people were open about. Not in public. Yet now the King would need to know. There is a prophesy about this in Zantkara's homeland. But that would have to wait.

This was a wedding and Lady Huspecia and Lord Bronanes had to commit to their pairing and their souls were truly bound to one another for such a song to be sung by a true Sorceress of enchanting siren songs of the deep ocean.

The Archpriest was in danger of giving away his past transgression of love. He was still locked in his gaze across the room to the Arch Nun. Fortunately, his eyes were small and unnoticed by anyone else. He shook his head and pulled out the Book of the Unborn God for the groom and the bride to place their

hands upon. Reciting the oath of faithfulness in their holy marriage.

"Is there, are would there ever be a challenger to contest this matching and Soul paring this day?" After several seconds surveying the room the Archpriest then said. "Being there is none to contest this pairing of these souls. Then we take it to be a true paring and the souls are mated before our Lord and this pairing is now blessed to be."

"Lady Huspecia do you take Lord Bronanes to be your soul partner for the honor of Yoranthium and before the sight of your God who is yet to be born?"

"Yes, I do take Lord Bronanes to be my Soul Partner from now and forever before our God to be born." This said Lady Huspecia with a large smile and was so happy that she finally said those words.

"Lord Bronanes, do you take Lady Huspecia to be your soul partner for the honor of Yoranthium and before the sight of your God who is yet to be born?"

Lord Bronanes was still looking into Huspecia's soul as if her veil wasn't obscuring her face. He nodded his head as if hearing something distant and gladly replied, "With all my heart and all my Soul I am one and will forever be the one that will be forever yours my sweet, sweet Huspecia."

The Archpriest had cracked a smile and realized this was in fact true love and something of an enriching odyssey and curiosity. He so much loved happy marriages that would stand the test of time no matter what challenge they may face. They would face it together. Considering the wounds Lord Bronanes had suffered all these years. The fact Huspecia was always in heart and spirit and soul always bound to Lord Bronanes. This was truly a gift worthy of his priesthood and commitment to the spirituality of his people. "Then let this blessed union before our God to be born be solidified as a testament to the values of Love in the kingdom of Yoranthium before King Sinderthion and Queen Zantkara."

With a pause Lord Bronanes was about to lift Lady Huspecia's veil so he could kiss her to finish the marriage ceremony. His hand was stayed by the Archpriest as he gently tied and bonds both Huspecia's and Bronanes to one another with the

wedding binding he held in his hands. Firmly placing their bound hands on the book of the God to be born.

"Wait Lord Bronanes we have one more set of vows to deliver this fine morning. Witnessing the vows of the Princess Kumithra and General of Yoranthium Lord Rarailmuir. Let us have two unveiling at the same time for this blessed union of two soul bound couples before our God, King and Queen of Yoranthium." Said a very happy and gleeful Archpriest. He so liked being in charge of Blessed wedding ceremonies.

"Very well, we shall wait the approval of my lord and liege to bless our wedding with that of their own. That all of Yoranthium shall bare witness as their princess and lord the honor and duty that is rightfully theirs this fine day. As me and my lady Huspecia are still so anxious to hear and witness their vows that they must be so patiently waiting to top my lovely lady Huspecia's song of love."

"Thank you Lord Bronanes and Lady Huspecia. Patience is a virtue, and you will have a lifetime to cherish the ceremony and memories of this day. I pronounce you husband and wife. Just hold a moment for the unveiling." Said the Archpriest as he lowered the holy book from their hands. The Archpriest scanned the room looking for the little boy to retrieve the second band of holy union.

"My King Sinderthion and my Queen Zantkara. We come to the grand event of this wedding day. We have only to BIND, with a wedding BINDING…" The Archpriest stressed hoping the boy who was here a moment ago would quickly return with the wedding binding. "…to complete this morning marriage so that we can have your daughter Princess Kumithra soul bonded to her rather dashing and handsome soul partner General of Yoranthium Rarailmuir..."

The priest was running out of things to say to procrastinate and delay the wedding long enough for the boy with the wedding binds to return. Where could that child have run off too? That boy was nowhere to be seen.

Yoranthium

Book One: Lost Hope

Chapter Four:

Dreams Fade into Nightmares

By Mark P. Bromley

Fairy tales are the stories we like to believe in the most. That is the reflection of the perfection of a dream. Yet dreams fade and die and sometimes get tragically cut short.

Rarailmuir saw the boy during Huspecia's song towards the end. The boy was glowing like sunlight was under his skin. Then time seemed to slow down, and the boy walked to Rarailmuir. Time had stopped. Apparently no one noticed. Yet only Rarailmuir did. The boy had light golden hair a light golden skin like the main land elves yet had shimmering scales very much like that of the sea elves with eyes of gold and sun fire purple and looked very healthy and strong.

The boy spoke to Rarailmuir matter of factually. The Childs voice was a father speaking to a child. He spoke. "I will come to you twice and empower you to defeat your enemy and save that which is important. The first will be soon and the other you will have to wait for. You will be filled with knowing and of light. I will spare your memory until the second coming. You will not wish to remember the pain, suffering, and loss that is to come. As at those times you will remember like a purpose of old and known to you.

You will only live to be someone else until the time is right. You will know what you will have to do for love, forgiveness of your sins. To make everything right and be the hero for just those moments Yoranthium needs. You are blessed to be my champion saint and protector for all your people a name to be remembered and renewed unto the praises of your God. A birth of a hero to a hero as is the way of your God to be born." The boy said and then handed Rarailmuir the wedding bindings and stepped back.

A halo of sunlight formed around the boy's head. What looked like wings of sunlight formed behind the boy. The boy faded into pure light like a ray of sunlight reflecting off the dust in the air. Then the boy was gone.

Rarailmuir thought he was dreaming and must have been mistaken. The little boy must have had to run off. He never seen anything like this and refused to believe in myths of angels. Yet that weird conversation with a boy made no sense to him. Now, he realized he had the wedding binding in his hand. He quickly wrapped the wedding band around his right wrist tightly so he would not lose it for some strange reason. Then grabbed Kumithra's hand as time resumed.

Suddenly there was a loud commotion coming from outside and then dramatically bursting into the wedding hall. "Sire, Sire, the navy is no more. There's darkness on the horizon moving fast

to fast. We are doomed, sound the cloisters Yoranthium is under attack!!!" So yelled the injured warrior fainting in his last breaths and then fell to the ground near death.

There was no time to examine the messenger. What was a nice sunny morning becoming dark. Candles had to be lit and light magics were being tended to as a crashing of thunder and streaks of lighting flashed in the open doors and the windows just below the dome. A harrowing wind picked up and light debris started flying around the room. While clothing and other light items began to wave harshly in the tempest that was now transpiring.

The celestial controllers had their magics in place. Had said this day would not be ruined by storm at sea or a drop of rain for this was the calm months and the astral celestial magistrate had promised in their never wrong weather forecasts. The weather was to be clear blue and calm cloudless skies for this day.

Screams and panic and anxiety started filling the room. People were alarmed for many surmised dark magics were the cause of this terrifying weather. Yet no one had time to debate or decide what to do next. Loud explosions could be heard in the distance. Then followed by massive impacts on the dome of the throne hall causing cracks to form in the roof and then suddenly the dome ruptured, and parts of the dome fell to the ground killing a few of the guests instantly.

Panic and screaming could be heard. While a dark orb some six kings lengths high in size had sailed across the room and impacted just before the wedding host. Landing just a mere kings length in front of Kumithra and Rarailmuir. The meteor impacting and landing on top of the Archpriest and...

No, no, it couldn't have happened. Yet it did. The meteor had landed and impacted where the king and the queen were standing just minutes before crushing them and rolling away revealing nothing but crushed blood bathed streaks of squashed remains of whom it had savagely just been killed. King Sinderthion, Queen Zantkara and the Archpriest were now and forever dead and crushed too a mulch of elven remains.

Kumithra and much of the wedding host and assembled guests witnessed the most gruesome sight they had ever seen in their lives. There was crushed bone, muscle, skin, innards and so much blood, too much blood. Very loudly many guests feminine,

male and an entire host of witnesses screamed in fear and panic and in shock. Kumithra felt it the worse for she had just lost her parents. She didn't know what to do except to scream in terror at the loss in complete disbelief falling to her knees with outstretched arms reaching for where her father and mother had once stood.

Huspecia had lost her adopted parents and could only plow into Bronanes, Tears in her eyes. Both were locked tightly and Bronanes understood and in shock of what had just happened as the sky quickly darkened the room into a gothic nightmare and horror no sane person could or would be able to believe.

Rarailmuir grabbed hold of Kumithra with both his arms to protect her and comfort her. Looking around the room to determine what to do next. He noticed the thrones were destroyed by the meteor impact. The Kings sword of Yoranthium was on the floor not far from them. A whirling noise could be heard coming from the large orb that impacted inside the throne room. Cracks were forming on the outside of the round and rough object that was smoking and smoldering. Then the cracks worsened as parts started falling off the orb revealing a Mechanation.

Mechanation's were decided by known kingdoms to be illegal weapons of warfare. The known kingdoms signed treaties of war. Someone, some army or kingdom had violated those accords. Mechanation's were excessively brutal weapons of war and who knows what their purpose was or their intended design for the Mechanation had so many capabilities.

Mechanation's are by far the most formidable and threatening object that was near impossible to harm. It was a metal steam driven device of deadly magics of death and destruction on a battlefield any warriors would be hard pressed to defeat in open combat. Not with the current weapons at hands of ordinary sword, spears, and daggers. Magics would be needed, weapons much more dangerous to use.

Regardless there was a Mechanation freeing itself from the round meteor like object that just killed the Archpriest, the King and the Queen of Yoranthium. With blades and arms and red-lit eyes becoming more apparent. The Mechanation came to life and worked on freeing itself from its container. It was huge over six kings in height. It was a killing Mechanation designed to murder and kill all that was in its way.

"Bronanes to me!" Commanded Rarailmuir. "Have Huspecia protect Kumithra and remove their bows, veils and heavy outer coats and use your blade to break free their dress so they can run. Like so." Rarailmuir pulled a knife out of his boot and cut Kumithra's butterfly bow off, removed her veil and stripped her of her outer coat. Then Rarailmuir adjusted Kumithra's inner garments exposing her bra and corset underwear furled leggings and over the knee stockings. Using his knife to savagely cut the Yukata into a short dress and quickly tied it around Kumithra's waist. "You the remaining wedding host do the same to your dresses. As it should give you better combat ability and capability to run fast. Thernya you take charge your king and queen is dead and now the princess is our queen. Protect Queen Kumithra!!!"

Bronanes and Huspecia sobered up and broke from the consolation of one another. Rarailmuir's booming commanding and decisive orders was echoing in the chamber and overpowered the fear building in the collected wedding host. Rarailmuir's commands were comforting and forcibly obeyed and perceived of great strength and regnant voice. Snapping the minds of the fearful to crystal clarity of purpose and most urgent response.

Kumithra was confused she didn't know what was happening tears had destroyed her make up. She was sobbing in fear like a frightened child barely able to see. She felt Rarailmuir grab her and undo her wedding dress as if it was tissue. Savagely undress her and then redress her. Right there on the floor of the throne room. She was confused was Rarailmuir making love to her? Right here, right now? Was the wedding over? Did they have a great wedding? No that can't be right her mother and father... No, they can't be dead she must have fainted this is a nightmare and she's unconscious. No, that wasn't right either. This was real. All she had to do is look upon the bloody crushed pulp that was her parents. "Rarailmuir!" She cried. Frantically reaching towards him to hold him tightly like a frightened child.

Rarailmuir had to assure her with a confident hug and a sense of well being and warmth. "Kumithra you will be okay. I had just adjusted your wardrobe to suit the situation. We need to get you to safety my Queen, for you are now the Queen. You are the hope of Yoranthium now. The time for tears is over you need to be

a Queen for now." Rarailmuir had said with a commanding look into her eyes.

Kumithra began to become a little more relaxed and was comforted by her champion, her love, and her... Husband? They hadn't wed. What does that mean? She felt confidence and courage in his embrace. All of this relaxed Kumithra. She was becoming much more in control of herself for every brief moment that she held Rarailmuir in her arms and her in his embrace.

Speaking with a calming voice. "You are my queen now. I'm at your command. I'm your general. Yoranthium is under attack. Your wedding gown is going to be in the way, so I simplified your clothing making it combat ready. You have to escape with the wedding host with Bronanes, Huspecia and Thernya as your protectors. They are better trained and were trained to be your protector by decree of your father the former king Sinderthion of Yoranthium. I slit your dress so you can run and it's nice you have those magical shoes on your lovely feet. Even with those heals they will let you run fast enough to escape. But first I have to retrieve the sword of Yoranthium it's my rightful place as your King and I must stop the Mechanation from harming more Yoranthian's."

Kumithra understood and as her veil was discarded on the floor she had seen her outer robe and butterfly belt had been quickly removed by Rarailmuir and her legging were now exposed as Rarailmuir had tore her Yukata down with his knife. It was now a short somewhat provocative dress that was quickly tied at the waist revealing her chest and bra and corset. If there were more time to think, one would think that Rarailmuir was a renowned dressmaker for seductive women's apparel, being quite in fashion around the singles corridors of the city. The Red District was commonly visited by many of the Yoranthium workers, guards, lords, ladies, sailors, and fishermen were known to visit. Rarailmuir is a soldier, maybe when there is time Kumithra will have to inquire.

Rarailmuir helped her to her feet and Huspecia now dressed similar to Kumithra along with Thernya and their retinue was near her. She could see the maids and Huspecia were all armed with chain daggers they had carefully armed themselves with and hidden in their dresses. Kumithra was unarmed, as she was not trained in the art of combat but more in the arts of the royal court

and peaceful diplomacy, receiving only a slight bit of training from Thernya and Huspecia with the safer rope dart variant made for novices.

The whirring in the background was turning in to clangs as the crumbling outer meteor rock like material was rendered to ashes and dust. The cling of blades the gnashing of metal claws and slashes in the air could be heard. The puffs and whistles and hideous sickening screeching of released steam began to fill the room among the horrified screams of women and children and some of the males not fit for combat.

The Mechanation was preening and preparing itself as the outer meteor fell away. The Mechanation was there to make war and murder Yoranthian's. Many Yoranthian's were confused and some were already in flight. The Mechanation was with a more hateful and destructive purpose than the sea elves preparing themselves for fight or flight.

The dragon attack years ago left the Yoranthium army weakened, for many of its older veterans were slain in the attack. Many of the new guard wasn't much older than Rarailmuir and inexperienced as Yoranthium only had a minor conflict on Forumth in recent history. Much of the guards were terrified upon seeing their foe. They had never been trained to fight a Mechanation.

Rarailmuir looked longingly and regretting he would not wed this day and have Kumithra as his reward for so many years of service to King Sinderthion. He was sad he would not get to swoop her off her feet. Saddened he didn't get the time to be romantic to her for he so wanted to be intertwined with her this night. Hoping to finally conceive his heir. That would now never be as he had hoped just moments ago. There would be no time to make an heir. With a loving look at Kumithra and a sudden overpowering respect for his handiwork on her loosely defined combat garment. Not to mention the sight of the entire retinue of seventeen maids and Huspecia now all dressed similar to Kumithra.

Becoming a total of nineteen sexy maidens of war. Rarailmuir was indeed pleased with his styling for converting wedding gowns and wedding apparel into combat succubus of seduction. Even other males and palace guards were longing and

staring at the now less than formally clad and no longer veiled women in the striking combat alterations.

He snapped back to reality and with a true general commanding tone of voice. "Thernya and Huspecia take the retinue and guard the Queen keep her safe as I retrieve the sword of Yoranthium! Bronanes to my side! Order the guard of the land to assemble with us to fight the Mechanation. Order your lieutenant Dabensir to take command of the guard of the sea and save as many women and children and evacuate them to the hidden submerged caves on the warm sundown side of the shores."

"Thernya. You and the wedding retinue take those long sleeves and discarded cloths and make bags and satchels and use them to carry off as many foods mostly bread and fruits and vegetable and preserved meats that you can as supplies. You'll need that on your escape out of the city, as I'm sure you all need some kind of meal for the hard journey ahead of you. Have Dabensir and sea guards then defend the women and children escorting them to the hidden caves and the secret flotilla where the Mundrunche is stationed. The Mundrunche is fully refitted by now."

"Tell the men you find along the way to find a weapon and wage war, having them assemble at the front lines. Dispatch runners and riders and get the guard of the cities of Sea Shore and Farmer Town assemble and reinforce Yoranthium's capital. Turn them to the city and send them to the fighting and tell them. 'They must defend those you love with your lives for Yoranthium is at WAR!' If we fail, we lose all we love this very night."

"Aye sir, it had already been done. I'm your second for a reason sire. I know my duty to you my General and to my Queen Kumithra. Lady Huspecia is already in motion my lord and Lord Dabensir has began the throne room evacuation." Bronanes pointed out as his Sea Guard the Shore Guard had been well drilled for emergencies and conditions of war. Rarailmuir was a very effective and planning leader that had worked tirelessly to improve the guard.

Lord Dabensir was young about twenty revolutions old. He was a squire from a young age with an unusual martial ability rarely found in the youth of Yoranthium. He was quite commanding and tall. Very ruggedly built and looked like an older

male of twenty-five. With a long crop of dark brownish bronze hair, modest sized ears, large sapphire blue eyes and a large bulbous nose. A very strong jaw line with no facial hair and a very strong bulk of sinew and mussel. His skin being of an interchanging blue and dark blue to purple skin, Wearing the wedding guard outfit along with armor, spear and shield.

Dabensir was the male for the job; he was off to the side standing with the guard of the waves when he heard the call to duty. He was already on top of the situation and Lord Bronanes didn't have to say very much to him. Dabensir already knew what to expect that is why he was a Lieutenant at such an early age. "We are now in rescue and defense operations Lord Bronanes and General Rarailmuir. It is my honor to take your wife Huspecia and the Queen and escort them to safety. I will do this without fail." At that, Dabensir shouted orders to his men and began moving the wedding guests to safer locations in the Throne Hall towards the open main doors.

Rarailmuir had released the Queen from his hold. Discarding her like she was not important. Throwing away her hand as if it was a piece of refuse that he had no need of. He saw something more important and special to his people of Yoranthium. A sword he coveted and loved more than his Queen. It was the sword of kings the sword of Yoranthium that made one king. If he could prove he was able to use the weapon he would be King of Yoranthium even without being bound by marriage.

Deliberately he rose and with much power in his strides he strode across the throne room carefully avoiding and walking around the blood and remains of the dead. Looking toward the broken and pulverized thrones. His goal was the Sword of Yoranthium that was on the floor shining, glowing, pulsating and calling to his hands. This was a defining moment for Rarailmuir he would gain his objective defined by courage and a test of combat by using the unique magical weapon to defeat the Mechanation.

The King sword of Yoranthium was an ancient long sword single or dual handed weapon about a kings length long minus a kings foot, imbued in this weapon was incredible and indescribable ancient magic. Found on Yoranthium by its first king. Which was at the center of the island in a stone statue of a defeated hideous monster a long time ago. The remains of which turned to powder

and faded away in the wind once the sword was removed. So, the story goes.

The sword hummed with magic and knew when it was needed and had a soul of it's own to protect the kingdom of Yoranthium. It was made of the island metal in some ancient ritual no sea elf living on Yoranthium understood or knew about. It was encrusted with runes no one understood in an ancient language that was forgotten and words that could never be spoken by any scholar that had studied the weapon.

The Sword was simply called the Hero's Blade, the Kings blade, or the blade of Yoranthium. With many scholars renaming the sword as the famed legendary blade known as the King's Blade of Yoranthium. Famed by many scholars and desired by many kingdoms and many lands for it was a work of art that was beyond the blacksmiths of the Frozen and Volcanic kingdoms of the under dwellers to the far cold.

If there were any sword of any real magics on all of Ishormot this would truly be such a weapon. Hailed to is a gift from their Unborn God to the people of Yoranthium as granted by the Archangel Eriderion, first champion saint of all Ishormot and the known elven kingdoms a story that felt familiar played in the mind of Rarailmuir. Fabled as one of the most powerful if not the most powerful blade. Wielded in mythic tales of unbelievable legends by the Archangel Eriderion slayer of the Leviathan.

Only the strong and the right person of great love for their people of great character, courage, love and heart could wield this weapon. The magics contained in this sword were spectacular and no one knew its truth of worth.

Rarailmuir remembered the advice of King Sinderthion when he was only a lieutenant of the guard. "Rarailmuir. When you wed Kumithra and bare me an heir to the throne. I will teach you a secret of the sword and what is the truth behind the legend of the sword of Yoranthium Kings. This sword will be yours and you will become the King of Yoranthium." Sadly, it would seem with Sinderthion's untimely death that secret will never be known to Rarailmuir.

"Learn these days well Rarailmuir that it's not you or your position or who you are that can use this weapon. It is the strength of your heart and the life love in your arms in this world that gives

you the ability to wield this mere focus of strength. It is only a symbol and never to be thought of as a weapon. It is only an extension of you and your heart and your love. Remember that Rarailmuir and build your heart and build your love for Yoranthium, your Queen and your heir and you will wield this sword. It knows its wielder; it knows our heart it knows your love."

The king was always a kind of swashbuckling romantic and was prone to over exaggerating the concepts of love and heart and that of truth to his people. He wrote books, poems and even made songs but it was his wife Zantkara who really had the gifted voice in the kingdom. Rarailmuir remembered Queen Zantkara's songs they were things of love and beauty so much like the sounds of song by Huspecia just moments ago. Pity Rarailmuir never got to see if Kumithra's young voice could ever match those songs.

Rarailmuir had reached the Kings Sword. Reaching down and quickly picked it up. Casting off its sheath to the side on the polished marble floor almost in the bloody remains but just shy. The Sword just like his love welcomed his embrace coming home from a long journey. It was warm in his hand and felt as he had used this weapon all his life, yet this was the first time he ever held such a great weapon. It was as if he was holding his love in his arms. It was like the legends of old; Rarailmuir could feel its legendary powers fill his very soul digging into him and finding his source of strength.

The sword then possessed his body and for a quick moment without a thought the sword swung up to protect Rarailmuir as the Mechanation's large ax came smashing down on the sword. Which might have just been paper as the Kings Sword sliced right through the Mechanation's axe. Rarailmuir's arm ached from the quick movement and was a bit sore. He felt the blade pulling and drawing forth of him physical and emotionally.

No one has seen the Kings Sword in use. Yet Rarailmuir had felt weakened by the sword in that block the sword did for him of it's own accord. It glowed with a light that enveloped Rarailmuir. Could this be the light the boy spoke of? Was this the first light that was mentioned by that boy? He saw himself in light and it issued forth breaking up the darkened Throne room.

This was a time of great peace in the kingdom and only for the battle of Queen Zantkara's hand did this weapon of the King

ever see the battlefield. A battle King Sinderthion won by diplomacy more than by conquest without needing to wield the sword in battle. Kumithra's uncle the Lord of Forumth offered the hand of his sister Zantkara to bind their kingdoms and her uncle becoming a vassal fiefdom of Yoranthium.

Any King of Yoranthium never drew the sword in battle since the first king. The first king only pulled the sword from the dead beast that faded to nothingness. Someone else used the sword to kill the unknown great beast. That someone was claimed to have been the Archangel Eriderion.

The Mechanation simply didn't care it had lost an ax. It had many weapons to bare on Rarailmuir and it simply engaged a gear, moved a mechanism, and spun another weapon into place and took a swipe at Rarailmuir this time with a scythe to no avail. Rarailmuir dodged the swing. Then a claw came out and tried to grab and crush Rarailmuir. While a round cylinder was rotating into place and a red flame could be seen growing in the barrels chamber.

The sword swung down, and an explosion projected away from Rarailmuir impacted the mighty Mechanation destroying its claw and removing multiple limbs and a pointy arachnids like legs from the Mechanation. As fire then flamed on the sword and a flame quickly began engulfing the Mechanation. Although this Mechanation was sizable there were two canisters on it's underside somewhat protected. The flame from the king's sword ignited those canisters.

A second explosion ripped the Mechanation asunder, and it crumbled to the ground and its red eyes had gone dark. Oddly any flying shrapnel harmed not a single person in the area. As random people that would have been impacted by the debris of the destroyed Mechanation had magical shields block the debris from hitting them. This was truly a powerful sword of considerable magics.

The crowd cheered as they seen this awesome and amazing bit of combat prowess by Rarailmuir. He defeated that which was thought too dangerous and deadly a Mechanation so easily with the Kings Sword. The swords magic did all the work. Rarailmuir could feel his strength draining and the sword becoming heavier. King Sinderthion told Rarailmuir. "The sword demands a heavy price to

those it protects. Do be careful how you use it for it drains you of your strength. Fight wisely and not recklessly, to command the sword. If the sword commands you it will not be yours for very long."

"By the unborn God, king Sinderthion was right." This sword did all the work and taken from Rarailmuir his strength. Rarailmuir staggered weak back from the Mechanation he had just destroyed. He thought it would be best to sheath this sword for now and use it sparingly as his strength returns. This sword was truly a double-edged sword not only in blade but also in how it's magics worked.

Quickly he looked behind him and sure enough there was the scabbard for the sword. Quickly he snatched the scabbard off the ground and sheathed the blade.

The draining effect on his strength had ended by the scabbard that protects the user from the swords magics and he only held the sword by the scabbard now. It was too risky to unsheathe the weapon, so Rarailmuir simply held it up before all to see.

By keeping this Sword and having used it in battle that makes him king by Yoranthium tradition with no other king to dispute his claim. "I Rarailmuir now have used and am master of the Kings sword of Yoranthium. I proclaim my right to succession as your king." Even though he was not officially wed to Queen Kumithra. "I King Rarailmuir of Yoranthium takes his rightful place to rule for the sake of our people!" Even with the broken dome. Rarailmuir's voice echoed in the chamber.

Cheers echoed in the chamber from those witnessing the use of the sword. Proclaiming Rarailmuir as King. No one contested the proclamation by Rarailmuir he was the fiancé of the Queen he was the General and by trial of combat with the sword all had witnessed Rarailmuir protect the Lords and Lady's and the Queen of Yoranthium from harm of a deadly Mechanation.

The assembled host of Yoranthian's felt safer now that Rarailmuir has taken his post as the new King with the sudden demise of the former King and Queen. Rarailmuir awkwardly got back to Kumithra. She reached out to him for an embrace. He simply moved the sword to his side away from her and grabbed her wrist. "Kumithra, this sword proclaims me as your King." He was awkwardly gloating and boasting as if competing for the title of

who leads the kingdom. Was an argument that Kumithra couldn't win.

"I need you to join Huspecia and Bronanes and the rest of the wedding host of children and women and weak elves. You must stay alive for you are the last of King Sinderthion's line and I swore to protect you before your father." He said with eyes of duty to defend his kingdom, calling his bride weak. "Bronanes and Huspecia take the Queen to safety." Handing Kumithra off by a pull before a forceful push.

Rarailmuir had roughly released her, just casting her aside rather savagely for Bronanes and Huspecia to tend too. Like his would be bride was just some oddity and a thing of unimportance. "Do not let any evil befall her and take her with all those needing refuge to the sunken caves. Where the emergency fleet was located. That the Mundrunche and assigned to be refitted. If things get worse and the enemy overruns the shores we need to evacuate to Forumth Queen Zantkara's brother will have to give refuge."

"Aye my lo… King Rarailmuir." Became Bronanes slurred response as he remembered part way through that his mentor is now the king. "Lieutenant Dabensir, take your men send out the scouts and find us a safe corridor through the city to the outskirts. We must protect the defenseless wedding host and civilians we pick up along the route. Avoid all enemy contact if possible."

Dabensir was eager and had the sea guard assembled and ready with their spears with banners removed to do combat if necessary for a fight. "Scouts to be at the ready." Eight scouts lightly armored and armed with short swords and bows and arrows assembled before Dabensir.

"Scouts assembled sir." With a salute the Sergeant reported standing at attention in front of the eight scouts.

"Proceed down the hall at haste and let nothing bar you from your duty. Scout out two hundredths kings lengths and then report conditions to me as I move the wedding host forward." Dabensir said with duty. The scouts did a ceremonial about face and then broke formation to head towards the main doors.

Bronanes was satisfied with Dabensir's ability to command. Yet was bothered and he turned to Huspecia who was helping Kumithra adjust and prepare to evacuate the throne hall. "I don't like this Huspecia."

"Why?" Huspecia inquired.

"Rarailmuir seems strange to me after he got that blasted sword. Didn't it seem a little off to you?" Bronanes looked over to Rarailmuir and was annoyed and a little jilted. He knew Rarailmuir as a squire of his. Never was Rarailmuir this rash with persons closest to him.

"You worry too much Bronanes. I know you worry a lot and well Rarailmuir is under stress. I'm sure it's nothing but we need to leave the defense of Yoranthium to Rarailmuir. We have our orders and Queen Kumithra is now our responsibility and so is the evacuation of the citizens of Yoranthium that can not fight." Huspecia replied making sure that Bronanes remembered his duty.

"Huspecia, do you think we'll have a better day once the clouds are gone, and the winds die down? The lightning is very scary." Kumithra was acting odd, she seemed to be unaware of the current situation. Then she ran over to a flowering large tropical plant in a wedding planter. The flowering plant had a multitude assortment of five ovate petal flowers that had a dark blue center. With a light blue faded white to a medium hue. Surrounded with a purple outline and then followed by white fading into a dark blue on the edges of the petals. The flower had in the center a long pink pistil with yellow stigma on the ends.

Kumithra picked two of them and ran back to Huspecia. She placed one in her hair right side over her ear and into the bun behind the ear. Then she did the same thing to Huspecia's hair and grabbed both their hands locked together and outstretched arms. "You remember my mother use to put these flowers in our hair." Kumithra was beginning to smile in merriment. Was just about to start spinning in circles with Huspecia as if they were children again. Remembering a day with her mother and father when she was introduced to these flowers with Huspecia for the first time.

Thernya fortunately intervened in the nick of time. Before the spinning began. "We don't have time for this my ladies." Thernya looked at Huspecia and whispered. "You need to be gentle and firm. Don't let Kumithra out of your sight Huspecia and don't let her get out of hand. She's in shock." Huspecia seemed to understand. "Queen Kumithra you look nice with your hair. But we have things to do right now for your People. Follow Huspecia

and do as she says. If you have any questions come and find me quickly."

"Yes, yes, of course my mother gave me you Thernya." With that she let go of Huspecia's hands and gave Thernya a big hug.

Bronanes looked at Huspecia. "What is wrong with the Queen?"

"She's in crisis, she lost, we lost our, her parents and is going to be acting weird because of the loss for some time. This is going to be difficult getting her out of here." Huspecia was worried about Kumithra as she continued to remember good memories of her father and mother and forgot there was trouble and they're in danger.

Tears filled Huspecia's eyes as she witnessed her charge and her queen failing to keep her poise. She didn't remember it was long ago when her true parents abandoned her. Huspecia didn't recall or even know why and developed a strong resistance to loss. She was a tiny baby back then. Saved by the Yoranthium Navy and vaguely remembered the small face of a kind little boy whom she married this day.

It was hard on Huspecia as well for the King and Queen adopted her and raised her very similar to Kumithra. Yet maybe Huspecia thought she was spared these feelings being just an orphan and not tied by soul and blood. Maybe that's why she was more reasonable and acted better than Kumithra. She knew loss and experienced it shortly after she was born. She wanted to believe she was steadfast and unbreakable and longed for nothing. She just didn't realize she was deceiving herself. Huspecia was fighting her heart and feelings preventing her from realizing her new loss and breaking down.

Bronanes realized Huspecia was being strong for her loss. Knowing Kumithra needed her and insisted. "Get her something to drink and eat immediately. I've seen this condition before." Which he did on the deck of the Mundrunche when his father found Huspecia and brought her on board. "We need to simply keep her as calm as we can and being she missed breakfast give her something now." Bronanes seeing the conflict in Huspecia actions spoke to comfort her. "You have me my love. I'll be at your side."

Thernya reached over and found a fruit and gave it to Kumithra after pealing her off her. "Your mother wants you to eat my princess queen. You need to keep your strength up. We have a long journey." Princess, Queen it was so much for Thernya to rationalize for Zantkara was so close to her, just as close as Huspecia was to Kumithra, and she was missing her Queen for a second time.

"Yes my mother and father it's time for lunch. Thank you Thernya. Where are we going on this trip?" Kumithra said remembering the days she would go on field trips with her father, mother, Thernya and Huspecia.

Bronanes quietly put his arm around Huspecia while Kumithra couldn't see. "You look fantastic with your new dress and flower in your hair." With a smile and a wink.

"Oh, just stop it!" Huspecia lovingly brushed into Bronanes.

"Can't be helped, I love you and we'll survive this together you and I Huspecia and we'll protect and save the Queen with Thernya's help. We have a guard and scouts. We will make it together my love." Turning to the crowd of frightened ladies, children, and some of the males that might have been part of the court.

Some males of the court might be an overstatement as they cowered behind the ladies. "Keep the group tight. Many of you have never been under a guard. Do not get in the way with or interfere with the guard. Follow their instructions, for it will be your only way to live through this. Eat when we say, drink when we say, move as we say. Above all stay behind the guard at a distance and keep safe out of harms way."

Bronanes said accommodatingly as the court civilians understood and paid attention. "Always stay behind the guards outer perimeter we can not guarantee your safety if you get past us. If you do as we tell you we will be victorious together and make it to the sanctuary and the evacuation port."

With this the guard ordered their charges and they followed and gathered the recommended supplies and adjusted their fancy attire to be more mobile. Bronanes was pleased with his command and his disciplined guard.

Rarailmuir from the side of his vision could see Bronanes had his group all assembled and worried about the state of mind of

Kumithra. Perhaps he should have been more caring and sensitive. He did hand her off to Bronanes command rather cold and harsh. He reveled in having his new title as King and the sword like a new gifted toy at the longest nights festivities of the plentiful harvest. That he was disappointed that his gallant behavior and manners had failed him. The plan was working, and he accomplished his goal to become King. A King at war and it was now a falling kingdom.

Yoranthium

Book One: Lost Hope

Chapter Five:

Flight and Fight

By Mark P. Bromley

War is ugly, messy, terrible and a horror best to avoid unless you have no choice. The war in Yoranthium is about to begin. Flight is what you do when you have something valuable and preciously special in this world to protect. Fight is what you do when you want to prevent all that you love from being taken away forever. Dreams are worth fighting for especially when they are of love and the matter of the heart.[4]

[4] The Importance of love the heart and the most precious of life that of our children whom are products of our love, hopes, and dreams.

A dragon years ago killed so many older veterans leaving behind a legacy of youth and the young to take their place. Rarailmuir was far too young at twenty-seven to be a general and so was much of the guard he commanded this day after four revolutions of rebuilding the Grand cities shore guard. The sea guard didn't fight the dragon and was at sea.

The land of Yoranthium was vast and the Grand city housed over twenty thousandths in population. Farmer Town housed an estimated fifteen thousandths. Sea Shore housed thirty thousandths sea elves and other cultural refugees fleeing oppressive tyranny that many kingdoms including the Potentates home of all the elf kingdoms had descended into. [5]

To the cold sundown before the small land bridge to the main mountain was an overlooked town of Under the Rock that housed around seven thousandths of miners, metal smiths and artisans. The small artisan village of Worm housed two thousandths of skilled silk farmers and manufactures for Yoranthium.

The Yoranthium prison was on the water break island of the sundown side of the water break just sunup of Sea Shore. The prison housed one thousandths and two hundredths of convicted criminals who labored on pearls and assisted with the exportation and importation industry of Yoranthium.

The entire guard after the dragon was peaceful and under populated in the Grand city. Mostly ceremonial and operated as roughly formed police was not ready for war. It was in the process of rebuilding. Each city of Yoranthium ran their own affairs and independently maintained their own guard. This is why the older guard from other towns did not replace the Grand cities old guard after the dragon attack.

Sea Shore was swamped with a high influx of refugees. Alarming news of the worldly kingdoms began outlawing the belief of the God to be born faith. Many kingdoms reverted to the cruel worship of the eight deities of old and the one. In Yoranthium freedom was second nature to sea elves and so was love.[6]

---

[5] Populations create scope and depth of world and will become a factor in the series of Yoranthium.

[6] 21st century politics was trying to control religion to promote the false religion of government so elected tyrants could see themselves as false gods to the people they would oppress. (Global Socialism)

The last safe haven for many who followed the unborn God had become pilgrims flocking to Yoranthium. Sea Shore was the hardest pressed and its guard was delegated to administration and enforcement of refugee codes of immigration. Farmer Town had a small guard managing farmers; Under the Rock and Worm had no real guard just a peace patrol.

Rarailmuir reflected on an encounter of some petty lord Jintru, or something like that. He protected that drunken Jintru from the Sea Ghouls that jumped Jintru in an alley. Jintru's donation to the guard aided the Kings tax collection supporting this wedding a major contribution that was collected half a third season ago. Sadly, he wasn't here to challenge him. Rarailmuir would have liked getting in a good word with him.

That foreigner from the potentate's kingdom did sign in and was denied audience with the King. He wanted a monastery for combat monks for the God to be born. Just more refugees fleeing oppressive lands that Yoranthium could not sustain. To bad Jintru didn't bribe the magistrate with the wealth provided from him for this wedding. That Jintru surely would have got his monastery of monks established in Yoranthium.

Perhaps Rarailmuir was also not of sound mind reflecting back on the cost of this shattered wedding. Trying to remember he was now a King, and his Kingdom would fall thinking like this. There was a war he needed to focus on winning.

Dabensir and his scouts had reached the main entrance to the throne hall. Reaching the entrance upon stepping outside into a world that was moments ago a paradise and now a version of hell. The city and courtyard were in shambles. Trees and foliage and buildings were burning. Lightning was crackling across the sky and impacting buildings all throughout the city. Many of the buildings were not upgraded with lightning protectors such as the palace. Causing combustible burnable materials to ignite in flame and causing parts of stone buildings to crumble and fall to the ground. Much of the courtyard was in chaos as guests, the musicians and the guard on the outside of the throne hall were leaderless and confused in panic.

It was looking like a nightmare and smoke and debris was flying everywhere. More Mechanation Meteors could be seen streaking through the sky and randomly impacting in parts of the

city much further toward the outskirts of the cold side direction. Screams could be heard, fear, and terror was it's sound and shouts and commands and pleadings of the random persons of Yoranthium could be heard calling out for help.

There was no doubt that the stench of death and wounded was in the air. The very terror of terrorized plagued sea elves was upon the air. Weeping and crying, screams in all directions could be heard and so many needed help, distracting the hero's to come to their aid and rescue. There simply wasn't enough guard to go around and chaos was quickly ensuing and the darkness of the clouds and lighting with the tempest of the winds outside was something strait from horrors hidden in the back of their minds. Becoming real and manifest with terrible dread.

"Guards to your posts, I lieutenant Dabensir are your commanding officer!!!" The few close to the door had heard their new leader and turned and looked at Dabensir. "Scouts gather our forces and bring them here. Tell the shore guard to form up here at the Throne chamber and tell the sea guard to render aid and assistance to the people and help as many as they can escape the city and to the sunken caves. Do not let the enemy follow those whom you escort. Thus being the order of king Rarailmuir. We will place the emergency station here in the Throne side chambers we just passed. Start sorting out the injured. Find every healthy male and tell them to report to the nearest Sergeant of the guard for further instructions to defend Yoranthium and all for whom they love." Dabensir noted there was enough good troops among the guard and continued. "Pass the word and hold your ground. Get the siege weapons out and all the magics out. We have Mechanation's and who knows whatever is invading our shores this night."

A scout was dispatched back into the throne room and reported to the King and Bronanes. "Sire the exit is currently blocked by people. Lieutenant Dabensir had taken charge and is clearing the path as we speak. It gets a little worse the lightning from the sky is hitting the buildings and catching the city on fire. It's going to be hard for us to find a clear path. As more meteors have been impacting through out the city and there is no telling how many Mechanation's are about." Said the scout grimly and wild eyed.

"Captain of the Guard!!! You must do what you can to get your immediate group outside the city and be the first to the secluded caves. We must establish a refugee zone there and defend it adequately as it has siege and magics available to defend much more adequately than we can here in the city. Go now Captain of the Guard and take the Queen with you immediately!" Rarailmuir commanded insisting this is the correct course of action.

Rarailmuir as the General and now King knew the entire status of the arsenal and garrisons of Yoranthium's defenses. Yoranthium had great difficulty rebuilding after the Dragon. He disobeyed orders specifically to rescue Kumithra and in so doing the dragon had destroyed much of the siege and magics Yoranthium would need in this war this very night. Rarailmuir was going on instinct for he really had no plan.

Plans of war usually happened when kingdoms diplomatically proclaimed war on one another. Battlefields were debated and usually avoided the cities and major towns of commerce. There was a set of rules for warfare. This enemy simply ignored those laws of warfare, and they will have to be held accountable to the civilized kingdoms of Ishormot for breaching decorum. Declaring war had rules and traditions to follow after all. This kind of attack was cowardly, and the cowards are going to pay. This Rarailmuir had declared unto himself. Part of Rarailmuir didn't mind the chaos on the other hand. He was sure such a cowardly dark magics induced conflict would have a short ending.

Bronanes knew his new King was right. If they were going to evacuate the island or have any safe staging area for such an activity they needed to control the secluded caves to the warm sun drop side of Yoranthium. This battle here at the throne is not his assignment or his task. Bronanes heard his father's force was destroyed. That meant the Navy was in bad shape. Leaving the Mundrunche fleet the last of the Navy. His father the Admiral was likely dead. The best Navy on all Ishormot was no more.

Good thing that Lieutenant Dabensir gathered the troops and began an emergency staging area. At least the main door was now a bit safer. With sturdy confidence Bronanes commanded. "You heard your king it's time to move out. Thernya and Huspecia tend to the Queen all the other house maids and sea guard protect

the rest of the people that join us in this endeavor if you see we are being followed or under attack raise the alarm. Look out for any useful magics or devices along our way if we meet resistance from Mechanation's. Follow my lead."

With that Bronanes gave a motion with his arm by holding it high and then dropping it to point forward. With his spear in his hands, he headed straight to where Dabensir was standing guard and organizing the outer throne room defenses. "May the unborn God be your protector my King. May we meet again victorious."

"Very the well Captain of the Guard Bronanes may we meet again victorious and may the unborn God watch over you. Protect the weak defend the helpless." Rarailmuir said and then took a rear guard position behind the sea guard and host of women and children leaving the palace for the secluded caves.

The shore guard then became the final host behind the king protecting his flank as he strode behind the sea guard headed out of the throne room. Dabensir's orders were showing some results as Clergy of Healing had begun to enter the room setting up treatment areas and bringing wounded into the reinforced center of the administrative offices on the outer edge of the Throne room. Avoiding the Guard as they left the throne room. Good enough location as it was better protected and less likely to collapse and was designed for war if... When it did arrive to Yoranthium.

"Dabensir, there you are now delegate your responsibility to another fit commander. I have need of you and the scouts to continue your mission and find us a safe way out of here. By order of the King." Bronanes had looked sternly at Dabensir instilling in him a sense of duty for the new King and Queen of Yoranthium.

"You there, how long have you been with the shore guard?" Inquired Dabensir to a young male that seemed capable as he had heard Dabensir and got the treatment center up and running and got Healing Clergy doing their tasks and organized the chaos outside the Throne complex.

He looked young and somewhat new to this work. As they all did. He was frightened yet managed to lead where there were no leaders. His complexion was rough, and he had a pit marked face indication that he suffered from facial blemishes and like many soldiers from the lower cast hoping for fame and fortune as a soldier in the guard. He was about twenty revolutions old and had

yellow green hair that he must have died with a magics hair tonic under his helmet. His eyes were orange with a hint of gold and his skin a medium hue of blue and teal. He had a round face and a strait nose with narrow eyes. "My name is Metiur, red district watch commander. I accept my assignment as commander of the throne post."

"Then with the power of the king invested in me you are now the Commander of this post and will command this post until relieved." Dabensir stressed the command ensuring that Metiur understood.

"I the Captain of the Guard Lord Bronanes orders the sea guard to join my escort and to rescue every able body as we go that is maiden or child to follow us out of the city. Lieutenant Dabensir begin your scouting mission and report back every fifty kings feet while sending patrols to scout every five hundredth's kings feet for a safe path. Commander Metiur defends our retreat."

Yes sir could be heard in stereo, as both the Lieutenant and the Commander understood their instructions. Dabensir gave additional instructions to his scouts, and they began their mission. While the entire sea guard joined the flight retinue, and the shore guard became the fight retinue and stood at attention as king Rarailmuir began to stroll out into the garden.

"Commander Metiur! I your king request your attention." Rarailmuir watched as Thernya and Huspecia had supported his Queen. Recognizing that Kumithra was eating some food and drinking some water and began regaling stories of her father and mother with a flower in hers and Huspecia's hair. Rarailmuir was truly worried that his Queen was having difficulties understanding how to deal with the conditions she had found herself in. Perhaps not even aware of the amount of danger she was now in.

Hopefully he made a good choice and the right choice. Bronanes is a good soldier and sailor and knows much of survival. But with so many defenseless women and children in his ranks it's hard to say if they will even make it out of the city alive before night fall. If night does come they would be tired and exposed in the open for yarns (a hundred kings length). They'll cross open farmlands with sparse walls and houses and barns. Perhaps a few keeps along the way would be the only refuge possible but that was

ten yarns outside the city. A hard-pressed forced march on foot indeed for protection from whoever their real enemy might be.

So many random meteors are still impacting the city mostly to the cold side and Rarailmuir was truly worried that his bride would not make it out of the city if they ran into a Mechanation. The sword used him to stop the behemoth in the throne room and now it was simply in his hand in a scabbard and would likely not be of use against more than one or two without great cost to himself. "Bronanes if you manage to find magics arm yourself immediately there is an armory down the street you are on! Do what you must to keep the queen safe and avoid the Mechanation's if at all possible!!!" He shouted not certain if Bronanes heard him.

Bronanes turned and waved he understood. Still looked behind him and seeing Rarailmuir concerned and looking at Kumithra. Uncertain if the choices he was making as King was right. Bronanes thought that makes for a decent king at least he questions his instructions and Bronanes will have to safely navigate the city as they head out of the sun drop side of the garden exit into the tenement district where they are going to pick up more females and children as they leave the city. They would have to do it quickly and they would not search any building for the distance was long and they needed to get to the keep before nightfall.

Metiur had run over to his king. Stood at attention pulling his spear to his side. "Commander of the guard Metiur at your service my king."

"Enough with the titles just call me your King and I'll call you Metiur. Understood."

"Yes, my king." Metiur saluted.

"How many in number are the troops on the ground?" Rarailmuir was trying to understand how large of a force he had.

"We number at about fifteen hundredths my King. That's without the sea guard of seven and a half hundredths that went with the Captain and Lieutenant." Metiur was good at math that was for sure.

"Have we searched to secure siege weapons of ballista, trebuchet's, and mortar's?" Rarailmuir was getting a bit ambitious.

"Currently in progress the nearest armory was destroyed by lightning, exploded and destroyed a city block. With lots of dead

and injured that had been coming in from that direction. We had to go to the further Armory on the outer walls. My dispatch should be returning shortly. The good news is the Clergy of Healing accessed some magics and we have been issuing two or three magics to each forward of the line soldier." Metiur was proud of his initiatives.

It was a good thing the guard began arming the Clergy of Healing and creating small caches of magics in their storage holds just in case the healers had to be warriors. Rarailmuir could have used some combat monks. The magics storage solution was a good suggestion of former King Sinderthion, as that is now proven invaluable. Rarailmuir looked to the Royal housing that had been struck many times from lightning.

Fortunately, no one was inside, and all the guard stationed there were assigned outside the morning on wedding detail. He looked at where Kumithra use to reside, and it was no more. Now just a bunch of flames. Rarailmuir was relieved he knew Kumithra would have thrown a tantrum if she knew all the things she valued were now destroyed. Such as her diary she uses to tease Rarailmuir and even tempted him to read on occasion. Only catching him when he tried to pick... Break the lock on it. Maybe he was more upset now that he could never read it.

"You there soldier." Rarailmuir scanned the area for the most competent appearing soldier. After getting a yes my king. "Go round up some civilian men and put them on fire detail. Do what you must to douse these flames and use as many able bodies as you can muster. You are my new fire brigade." The soldier gave him a "Yes my King," and began rounding up civilians ordering them into service as the fire brigade.

The king was happy the soldiers accepted his new title he was truly a king in his war torn kingdom. He could see the soldiers standing braver and taller around him. Their confidence in their King gave them confidence in themselves. He knew their names he trained them all and he knew who could perform their duties he was their general for a day and now their King.

Suddenly to the right a mechanical noise could be heard as the Sunup wall was impacted and impacted again. By loud hammering of what sounded like a ball and chain in rapid motion was being used on the wall. Fact is it was a reciprocating steam and

magics driven hammer that was pulverizing the outer wall. Dust came flying off the wall and cracks were forming. Towering a quarter above the wall was another Mechanation that was sieging the wall to the palace. There was a significant amount of loud hissing coming from behind the wall.

"Magic's to the ready we have company!!!" Rarailmuir warned Metiur.

"We are on it my King, magics to the Sunup wall. Move the wounded towards the Sun drop wall. Protect the king and the injured!!!" Metiur had said. "Tighten the perimeter and lookouts, stand your ground and report any difficulties! Steady your hands do not waste any magics wait until the wall falls and then use your magics." Metiur had some real charisma and command ability. The soldiers did as they were instructed running to the side of Metiur. The King couldn't be any prouder of Metiur's command abilities as thirty or so guard responded.

Rarailmuir was indeed proud of Metiur for looking a little jittery and young he was definitely on top of his duties as a commander. Metiur was a watch commander of the worst district in the Grand city. Fantastic examples of Rarailmuir's ability to instruct his troops and defend Yoranthium. Maybe he didn't need to find cover. With soldiers like Metiur he could win this war his guard would be victorious, and he would truly be the King of Yoranthium and his Queen would no longer be required for his title as King. Rarailmuir said softly. "We can win this war. We have the tools we just have to deliver a killing blow to the enemy."

After several more impacts the long wait of anxiety and dread ended. The wall crumbled and fell. The Mechanation was fully exposed but the guard with the magics hesitated and arrows pierced them, and small explosions impacted the front line of the guard as the magics hit the ground before those shot by arrows did. The arrows didn't come from the Mechanation but a host of catfish looking monsters known as the depth dwellers. The depth dwellers were massive they stood on average two kings height tall. Their heads were curved somewhat like a shark but with catfish whiskers about their nose. Their mouth was rows of rows of sharp teeth. With a top fin on the head that would collapse and expand as it breathed. No ears just small, protected holes and dark black tiny

eyes on either side of the head where they looked left and right often to get their bearings.

Their skin was gray covered in dull scales covered in glistening slime. They had two massive sinewy arms and two massive and muscular legs ending in webbed hands and feet with black half a kings foot black claws. They also had shark tails half a body length that made them powerful swimmers and something to avoid in the deep as they ate everything even themselves. They wore primitive armor and loincloths mostly strapped on of metals and fish shells. Their weapons were bone made and shaped by magics they only knew. But the weapons were massive much larger than any weapon his guards had and longer than their spears.

The bows the Depth dwellers used were crossbow like weapons that fired three arrowhead tipped bone bolts. The head movement of their eyes made them bad shots. As apparently they shot their own with the bolts they fired. But it didn't matter to them as their skin was thick and they had a lot of blubber under their skin to keep them warm in the very deep parts of the ocean. From where they came, this muscular blubber of theirs made their skin like the first layers of a heavy leather shield. Many said the depth dwellers had a city to themselves under the waves located at the deep valley abyss and the flames down below. The Valley of the dark deity of the depths so was the legend. A dark deity of nightmare proportions that legends told of elves that went mad looking at such a being.

It was just bad luck for the guard who fell before these monsters. Yet the magics did more damage to the front ranks and Metiur tried to restore his command and tried to get the magics unit to reassemble. But it was no use they saw too many of their friends die to quickly terrible and awful burning deaths from the magics. The bolts would have been easy for the guard to fight past but the fire and the explosion was too much. Some of the soldiers dropped their helmets to the ground because of ringing in their ears and were now useless and vulnerable.

Metiur was soon the only one up front with his spear ready to attack and it seemed he would charge thinking it would inspire courage in his command. Inspiring indeed and Metiur was a credit to himself, but he had no one behind him. He was on his own and didn't know it. Foolish.

Rarailmuir didn't want to pull the sword, still felt drained from the first time. He couldn't let Metiur fight this on his own. He couldn't let the Mechanation along with the host of the depth dwellers slaughter Metiur. He had no choice so he put his hand back on the sword hilt and could feel it draining him ever so slightly like a curse was upon him. He had heart he had a love he should be able to use the sword but why not? Why was the sword cursed with draining him? He was pulling the sword out of his sheath and another soldier that was running away had stopped.

The soldier, Fedarious realized the King was going into battle and wasn't retreating. The soldier wouldn't follow Metiur because he thought Metiur was going to get them all killed after the magics went horribly wrong. However, the King was going to save Metiur and if the King would defend the guy the soldiers teased. Then Metiur was indeed a worthy commander and Fedarious felt bad for betraying Metiur. "Protect the King." is the shout the guard gave. All the soldiers looked over and saw the King pulling out the king's sword and rallied to their king's initiative. Taking up the posts to the side of Metiur. Where Fedarious showed up next to Metiur with a hand on his shoulder to let him know he was no longer alone.

The remaining soldiers with the magics began throwing their orbs at the general direction of the Mechanation. They didn't' have to be accurate as the host of depth dwellers swarmed closely around the Mechanation trying to get through the wall. Like wild beasts rampaging and blood thirsty. The guard just had to aim in the general direction of depth dwellers. Explosions rained down on the attacking force. The Mechanation was being damaged and parts, limbs, over sized weapons and the wrecking ball and reciprocating hammer had been removed.

The Mechanation fell to its side as it lost a couple of its pincer like legs. The depth dwellers were worse off. As the magics burned and it was then learned they were weak to flame and unable to defend as many only had spear like weapons and their massive cross bows. The hissing became louder, and they felt pain and some died by the fire and the explosions. Yet it seemed pointless as more depth dwellers simply took their place.

It was no doubt this unit had orders and the throne room was it's goal. They must be after the king and the lords and ladies

of Yoranthium. It was good Rarailmuir had sent them past the sundown gate as they were out of sight at this moment.

Suddenly a flame erupted from the Mechanation's barrel. The flame shot out strait toward where Metiur and Fedarious were standing. Metiur was on fire and so were several soldiers over thirty in all. That had returned to his side including Fedarious that noticed the King pulling his sword getting ready to attack that put his hand on Metiur's shoulder to let him know he was now a brave friend worthy of the respect of his men. It was horrible, over thirty soldiers were on fire and screaming being burned and dissolved horribly by fire. The garden was on fire the pink petal trees of sakura were on fire the flowers were burning. The marble stone itself seemed to melt as the yellow flame turned blue and blasted like a furnace everything in it's path as the white marble blackened into an oozing bubbling slag.

Rarailmuir pulled the sword out as the depth dwellers cautiously advanced. Depth Dwellers were truly mindless beasts of just one purpose. That's all the depth dwellers did was follow a purpose blindly with no real care. Who was ordering them? None seemed in command and followed some kind of mysterious unknown command.

Soldiers on fire everywhere they were running tripping and catching other soldiers on fire. Rarailmuir had simply pointed the sword in the direction of his burning soldiers and the Mechanation and the depth dwellers. The sword of the king lit up again and fed on Rarailmuir's heart on his love on his strength it was eating a hole in his very soul draining his being as his eyes became white-hot crackling with lightning and possessed by the sword.

Then a big flash of light erupted, and the sword made an arc with his arm. Horizontal in line with the landscape, the light wave crescent shot forth towards the burning soldiers. Extinguishing the flames on the soldiers and reducing in intensity to a thin crescent. Impacting the swarming depth dwellers only cutting down the front row pouring through the wall by cutting them in half. Then just as before it got to the Mechanation, and the crescent funneled down the flame barrel tool on the Mechanation and the canisters behind the Mechanation once again ignited and the depth dwellers for eight kings length the opening in the wall and all around were incinerated. Rarailmuir dropped the sword

and fell backwards onto the ground unconscious. The sword drained Rarailmuir entirely of his energy and strength.

A soldier saw the sword of Yoranthium clang and clatter to the ground. He saw the sword and it called to his eye and gave him his purpose. Xern a disreputable soldier that always did wrong and was known as a cheat and gambler and chased after the worst of the red district had to offer. Xern a criminal and corrupt guard had been reprimanded for many misdeeds and was destined to be expelled from the guard with no recognition. His corruption investigation and trial were complete only waiting sentencing. Xern drank too much, entire bottles of farm sake the size of a king's forearm. Xern was often cruel, abusive, and unfit for duty. Saw the Kings sword and knew that the male holding it would be king.

Xern decided that if Rarailmuir fell then he was unfit to be king. Xern could be king and thus defeat the investigation his so-called King was responsible for. He grabbed the sword and felt nothing. It was just a sword. He swung the sword and nothing. No light, nothing just a swoosh. He aimed it at another soldier. Tried to cut down the guard with the swords magics. Having failed, nothing happened, Xern told him, "Back away, I have the sword I'm your king now!!! You obey me!!!"

A short laughter broke out and then the soldiers remembered they had wounded this is war. The king had fallen. The closest to Xern was Metiur he rose to his feet with his armor falling off of him and his skin was new. He was naked and had new skin his pocked marked face was smooth. He could remember the intense pain as he was roasted alive he remembered his eye's boiling and popping. He couldn't see he was terrified dying alone his brain was telling him it was hot, it was hot, hot, he felt his legs burn away as he fell his hands burned away he felt the armor on him cook his chest like a fish shaped pancake he would get from the street vendors. He was about to die as he smelled his own flesh and his brain cooking it was a terrible way to die. Yet because of the king he was brought back to life from the brink of death. He was whole again and healed. He owed the king and seen Xern with the kings sword and the king on the ground. "Xern you know you can't fight! You have been a problem soldier from day one! You are no male, and you are no King! You have no heart Xern, and no one will follow you! EVER!"

Xern took the sword and ran off. He had a confrontation with Metiur once before and was afraid of Metiur. He ran for his cowardly life into the deserted throne room down the hall up the dais, slipped and fell on the remains of the priest, and former king and queen, and picking himself up covered in gore mopping up most of the blood. As he comically slipped for some time trying to get on his feet, then after crawling to his feet, he ran past the first fallen Mechanation with the sword clutched in his hands. No one pursued him. He wasn't worth the trouble there was more important matters to attend to but now Xern was a deserter and betrayed his king. The penalty for that are capitol punishment and his death.

"Tend to the King!!! Clergy of healing your priority is the king. He seems to be breathing and just unconscious. My naked brothers in arms today you witnessed a miracle of the heart of the king. He gave himself to defend us all and now we owe him our very lives he pulled us to life back from the grave." Metiur received the respect of his men and they bowed before Metiur and named him their new commander and knelled to honor and cheer.

"Metiur, Metiur, Metiur lord commander we pledge our loyalty and service!" Proclaimed Fedarious who admired Metiur in more ways than one for his bravery. "What shale we do now Metiur? We the 'brethren of burning death,' are now yours to command."

"What is your name soldier?"

"Fedarious my commander."

"Fedarious we need clothes pick me out some clothes as I organize a uniformed patrol to check the perimeter for hostiles." Metiur was duty bound and his nakedness would not get in the way.

"Where will we get clothes my lord?" Fedarious was oddly staring at Metiur. Not making eye contact.

"From the dead take just what you need, find some weapons and find out if the warm side gate armory has weapons. Of course, if you see a weapon no one no longer uses acquire that as needed." Metiur witnessed a miracle on the battlefield it gave him hope.

Next time he will not be fortunate as the king no longer has his sword. 'The brethren of the burning death.' Metiur liked the name it made his new loyal squad sound like something to be

feared. He could hear other guards that were far from the fighting as they admired him and his new unit. Perhaps it was the nudity of his new unit, they were all strapping young men that were all physically fit. They too began calling them 'the brethren of burning death.' as they began chanting the name believing in what they witnessed was a true miracle this very day for the King had saved them all.

"Men on rotation the first squad take scout and return after five kings length and report your findings and then you will be relieved for chow. Second and so on squads rotate out to the throne room there is still food in there. Eat your fill and then do a reconnaissance of the fallen enemy's kill any of them still alive and scout the perimeter for any more threats. We are at war, and we will rotate squads until the food is gone." Not a single male giggled at Metiur, as he may have been naked but by far better endowed then many of the other soldiers and seemed very confident even in the nude. Metiur and his loyal men earned respect for what they had gone through and today was a glorious day for Metiur as he proved himself in battle.

Rotation of the guard and scouting went well, and some time passed.

"Commander here you go. We have royal Yukata's and some minor gear we found at staging areas." Fedarious on his return gave unto Metiur a royal Yukata the same design as Rarailmuir was wearing and a chest plate and a spear. Fedarious quickly got dressed and went over to tend to the king. "Good Job Fedarious take command as I check on the king." Metiur was surprised that Fedarious managed to pick out a perfect fitting uniform.

Metiur checked on the king and he was still unconscious being tended too by three female healing clerics of experience. Their lead spoke with Metiur, "He should be coming around soon, he's okay just weak right now." She had seen Metiur in the nude before he had put on his clothes and was blushing looking at him with desire.

Metiur was at the king's side and looked upon the king's face. He thanked the cute healing cleric clearly not interested in her.

Rarailmuir stirred back to the dismal world and noticed Metiur looking at him and was surprised he was alive. "Metiur so it wasn't a dream, the sword saved you." He said with a smile. "Nice new uniform I see."

"Yes my king. I did burn and nearly died along with the brethren of the burning death. It's now what we are called as your personal guard." Metiur stated with relief for the king and pride in his new command.

"Burning Death?" Rarailmuir remembered inside and down the hall of the first door in the throne room there was a cache of armor taken from some hostiles deep-sea elf raiders that tried to terrorize Sea Shore a few years back. That him along with king Sinderthion foiled and kept their armor and knowledges. "Go through that door down two rooms and you'll find armor fitting of your units new status. It's magical and should protect you all and it's a fit for you the 'Death Guard.' You'll be my personal protectors." Rarailmuir was sitting up and being tended to by the trinity of healing clerics.

Metiur was excited! He found new magics armor and weapons. He rushed down the hall and found the door and opened the room. There was enough armor for his unit and they would look uniform. Wearing the royal wedding male Yukata's and guard chest piece, with a large black belt with a demon skull for a belt buckle. There were boots that had knee padded armor of death skulls, tapering down by five skulls down the boot and provided excellent knee protection. There was a demons skull buckler and a long sword of quite eloquent and brutal design curved just right, heavy and different than any sword on Yoranthium and can be used single or double handed. The shoulder was a single demon skull to be worn on the buckler arm that also had a demon skull gloves like the boots defending the elbows. There was a helmet of a demon skull. Looking like they just stepped out of the flames of hell. It was good and frightening and made his unit look intimidating and nothing to trifle with.

Metiur issued the gear to the soldiers and uniformly passed out to his thirty men as they took their turns dining in the hall. Metiur and his men now belonged to the Kings personal Guard. The Death Guard was simple and neat not as complex as the burning guard. There was just one more thing that Metiur had to

do. He had to find the best pieces for his King Rarailmuir. Which he did. Then he grabbed some water and cloth and went to the dais.

There it was the crown of the former king Sinderthion. It wasn't damaged for it was mithreal made of the mountain. Metiur picked it up as it still had the former king's hair and skin and gore with blood dripping off of it and cleaned it. Wincing at the gruesome sight. As it became clean he polished it and then presented the King his new combat gear similar to the Death Guard with no helmet but the kings crown.

"Fine work Metiur, I your king am honored." Rarailmuir took the armor and adorned himself with the weapon a Sukenobu as called by the invading raiders at Sea Shore that he personally interrogated.

The Sukenobu was a long curved blade of considerable balanced weight and felt light in the hand or two hands depending how you fought with it. The length of a long sword just slightly larger than Yoranthium long swords, With a very exceptionally sharp blade on one side that had an artistic and purposeful unevenness to how the blade was sharpened like a mountain landscape in the distance. It was a delicate and powerful weapon and much stronger than many swords made in the elf kingdoms. That went on Rarailmuir's right side just nicely and matched the Yukata style he was wearing. Then he placed the kings crown on his head and found it a good enough fit but just a little larger that it sunk down closer to his eyebrows. He could feel the weight of the crown he wore, as it felt heavier by the moment as his head began pounding with what to do next. The fight had just begun, and he already lost the kings sword.

Yoranthium

Book One: Lost Hope

Chapter Six: All Hail King Xern

By Mark P. Bromley

Even in war in our best of the rank and file exist those of despicable and reprehensible behaviors. They see themselves as rulers and leaders of the people but in reality they are not more than criminals that only spread deception, fear and terror.

Xern was covered in the blood of the Archpriest, the former King and Queen of Yoranthium. He slipped in the throne room not knowing what had happened. He didn't see no bodies in front of him and hit the puddle of blood and gore. He had difficulty getting up that he ended up mopping up that floor and soaking all that blood into his clothing and hair and on his exposed skin. Fact is it got into every crevasse under his clothes, and he could feel all that blood he slipped and sled around in soaked all the way though onto his covered body. Managing to get up and continued to run he found the back entrance to the Throne Room and departed through the direction of the deserted cold gate.

He was running down many streets getting lost down the winding darkened streets not knowing where to go. He ran into a frightened soldier of the lower ranks that was running from a Mechanation as his comrades in arms were dismembered in quick fashion. The lonely soldier recognized the sword and never met Rarailmuir or Sinderthion. He was younger than Xern about twenty. Xern was an older guard recruited because of his expensive reckless depravity that limited him and indebted him to the red district of the Grand city. The guard was in need and offered a wage and Xern survived the dragon attack drunken in a brothel that fortunately wasn't the dragon's goal.

The dragon never touched the red district. It made no sense as many other buildings and streets were a light and a blaze with dragon fire. Xern remembered the horrors he had witnessed that day, the panic and the confusion and the burning smell of the dead and dying. The dragon did swoop down the red district street but never attacked. The dragon had looked as if it would. But the red district was oddly spared the dragons fury. Which was fortunate for Xern in the calamity the gang that had power over him died a terrible burning death. His gang was no more, and the dragon cleaned his debt. The dragon did Xern a favor and he got a tattoo of the dragon on his arm. Below that tattoo an inscription in forgotten tongue. That said. 'Dragon kills as the king of demons bathes in their blood.'

Xern was old, lonely, resentful and spiteful because of his age. Xern was able to convince the young soldier he was indeed the king himself by holding aloft the sword of the king. "My king, what's happening? You are covered in blood. It must be bad

everywhere if you are here without a guard. We got to run my king that Mechanation fell out of the sky, and we tried to fight it, but my entire unit is gone. I'm all that's left and I'm too young to die. We got to get out of here and report and regroup. How do we fight such things? My weapon is useless against such a monstrosity." The frightened guard showed Xern a damaged, bent and dented blade. It was true he did try to fight the Mechanation to no avail.

Xern looked at the soldier and lied. "Your job is to protect my retreat you need to stop that thing by attacking its legs. They are soft at the hinge, and you will prevail. Protect your King! Would I ever let you down if I thought you couldn't do it?" As he pushed the terrified young guard back in the direction of the Mechanation.

"Yes my King, I'll do my best but I'm only one soldier." He began to turn towards the Mechanation taking a couple of steps backwards toward Xern.

"You have Yoranthium's blessing by the will of the unborn God and I as your witness. Defend the king. You will prevail. Charge!!!" Xern pushed the young male just a little to send him in the wrong direction.

The soldier yelled at the top of his lungs and plunged straight towards the Mechanation that just killed his entire unit, with unparalleled conviction of purpose. He would protect Yoranthium and be its savior and hero and champion of the king. He didn't even get close he was hacked into four parts by bladed whips that sliced through the darkness so fast it was hard to tell where they came from. Just shining silver slivers could be seen and then crimson. As the young males body parts fell to the ground in gruesome slushy sounds of raw meat being fed to a grinder.

Xern winced at the sight. But at least the soldier died and could tell nothing about meeting him here. As he got closer to his home the red district of the Grand City. He ran hearing the Mechanation's all around him. Feeling safer only when the Mechanation's noises were getting quieter and sounded distant. He could hear others in the city screaming, running, yes as long as that noise got more distant, he was safe. Xern stuck to the shadows and stayed as quiet as possible to avoid all the Mechanation's. Fortunately, all the meteors had stopped bombarding the city only the lightning was still striking buildings and catching the city on

fire. The impacts of lightning sending heavy stone and debris randomly around him.

Xern rounded the top of a hill and could see the city around him. It was bad. Fires braking out everywhere the lightning was everywhere, choking smoke everywhere. Worse than the dragon attack. Suddenly a huge explosion took place and a fantastic number of screams could be heard and silenced as it would seem the Cold side main armory had been hit by huge lightning strikes that destroyed an entire city block. Leveling everything including two Mechanation's. That armory housed a major supply of magics and siege weapons. Whoever attacked this island didn't care who lived or who died using such a weapon as this magics storm cloud of destruction. Oh well, thought Xern not his problem. Just kept running to his safe place, that he now calls home in the red district.

Xern was always like this. He was born in the bad streets. Where enforcing the laws of Yoranthium was difficult more than most districts in a city this size. The bad streets began with the kids when they had been young making those abandoned resentful of the community, hatefully cruel and abusive toward others. Children were forced into gangs and the adult leaders of the community would beat children into gangs. Doing deeds of crime out of threats, intimidation and body extractions of lesser-used body parts by older criminals in the gangs. With death and execution or forced suicide often being used to enforce group cooperation. Establishing loyalty to the gang out of fear. Many of the gangs top leaders were rejects from the guard who learned military tactics of the most cruel and brutal methods. Many of the gang leaders that were as old as Xern had served in the guard to learn skills of the military to strengthen their criminally brutal methods.

Criminals trapped into a life of crime and cruelty by abuse and neglect from childhood. Xern was recruited early but was found out to be kind of weak. The tougher criminals took advantage of him in more ways than one. Sometimes forced into submissive acts by cruel perverts and miscreants. Xern wasn't liked by the gangs and was left with making his earnings from scams and petty theft. Like the sword he now carried. Without city guards it was easy not to get caught committing crimes in his youth.

By Xern's teen years, this was long before the dragon attack. Dealing with crime changed for a time in his niche of the city. As King Sinderthion had a well established guard, the old guard, which improved the conditions in the city. He got caught and was unable to pay a bribe. Yes although there were guards they were an improvement but not too much better than the crime gangs. This inability to pay a bribe sent him to the Break Water Prison farming pearls. By adulthood he was freed and given compensation for his work diving deep in the ocean of the pearl fields. Fortunately, a kind and caring sea elf councilor gave him useful advice. The first kindness he ever knew to settle a farm.

That payment tided him over for some time as he tried his hand at farming and was doing well. He hid his past, changed his name tried at honest living and even swooned a lovely country farming gal to be his bride. No one knew him in the local one street hamlet on the outskirts of Farmer Town.

His gang never forgot about what he owed them for they were greedy and often cruelly and brutally selfish. Debts were never forgotten by organized crime. Debts could never be repaid. Debt was a tool that organized crime festering in the guise of government officials used to traffic persons and enslaves the masses. The debts just kept growing faster than you could ever repay. The criminals never meant a debt to ever be repaid, it was a scam for steady income and indentured slavery to the organized crime lords.[7] Crime feasted on abuse of debt and the kingdom simply looked the other way. To many lords and ladies of the court were the crime bosses and the Grand City was ripe with scandal and corruption that the King and all his males could not subside.

His old gang found him and burned his fields and home for not paying his dues and fees. Leaving him with no way to make a living or pay anything. Then when he didn't pay they came again and murdered his wife to be, as they made him watch and witness her get assaulted. Ultimately murdered her horribly while he was forced to watch by his gang.

He was told that is how traitors are dealt with in the gang and to make amends he had to come back to the gang in the Grand

[7] Much like our modern world of forced debt and credit where much can never be repaid forcing an indentured slave life style of our modern 21st century no better than confederate slavery of old.

City. They took more than enough of his money to pay his past dues then indebted him even more. Back in the city he had found some honest work for a time and became a laundry and cleaner for his gang. But getting up there after eighty revolutions his remorse, loneliness, sadness, drunkenness, and wanting to forget and thoughts of suicide and desire to get out of the gang life got the better of him.

He found 'Dresdie's Love of the Depths and Darkest Desires.' a house of ill repute and lovely women in scantily clad dresses outside and inside. To him it was paradise and a safe haven. A bar on the first floor and you could buy the women drinks, for them to talk to you. Or for the right price you could get an upper room with one of the lovelies for the night. He became a regular after his day job.

Apparently Dresdie the owner of the brothel took a liking to him. Protected him from the gangs. He would spend his wages there until the day he no longer had a job. But he was addicted and found work cleaning and caring for Dresdie's brothel. Tended the bar, cleaned the rooms, and managed the females and their clients. Learned how to manipulate customers just to be rolled for their immediate wealth and dumped in the sewer canal behind the brothel.

Especially the land and sea guard when they were in town. He would set them up and rob them. Confuse them with all sorts of feminine desires and fantasy and on many occasions selling a few off for sexual favors as distractions to rip them off. The only thing protecting the drunken land and sea guard patrons was their own patrols that kept them from too much trouble in the red district.

Dresdie's shop became infamous and ill reputable, and the guard warned their own to steer clear of the place. But it never stopped the guard; many forgot the warnings and went there anyway. The guard were young and of that mindset that they are tough, unstoppable, and invincible. Only to get rolled and taken down a notch or two, the guard protected and saved their own from worse fates in the red districts dark and poorly lit back rooms. Some of the guard got so drunk they often mistook males for females over a matter of dress and length of hair and make up.

It was a guard that took care of other guards and got them back to the barracks that made Xern think about another life as a

guard. He remembered a rather scrawny young guard of dark blue and bronze skin and golden hair and golden sun fire eyes enter Dresdie's place long ago. He was only there for a short time and met Dresdie herself. Apparently he was of low rank and wanted to be an officer of the guard. Dresdie offered him power via magics and he accepted meeting with Dresdie in the back rooms. He was a drunk and seduced by the matron of the place and that went on for seasons.

Xern never seen Dresdie take an interest in any male except that one guard. She often disapproved of Xern and how he treated the other ladies working there. Then that guard who was really well behaved for a drunk stopped showing up to the place and Xern thought he must have been rolled or killed or locked up by his own mistakes. As often happens when a guard not knowing the rules of the red district becoming drunks in this part of the town.

Dresdie had disappeared at the same time that guard stopped showing up. While a new matron the attractive Gethia took over her duties. Gethia kept Xern in line promising to make him no longer a male, for some reason Xern having feared Gethia, was enchanted by her. Knew not to try anything for two other attractive women watched him from the shadows. He so much wanted all three but was terrified by them.

Then a quarter a third season later a dragon swooped in and destroyed much of the old guard and burned half the city and the King increased the pay to be a guard. Xern pulled his drunken self out of Dresdie's brothel and signed up. It was that drunken guard that Dresdie liked so much that talked him into joining the guard. That fool told Xern he could be an officer in the guard and told Xern of the lucrative opportunity as a guard. Boasting and bragging of the achievements and laurels of the Guard and its great-defined history of five hundredths revolutions and "...here's to many more!"

He wasn't that strong and looked like a puny and wimpy version of the recent king Rarailmuir. He had no real physical strength just a strength of will and charisma. A desire to rise to power in the Yoranthium guard, Dresdie liked that dark skinned sea elf and offered him enticements of power and even promises of marriage and an heir. Oh, Dresdie insisted he should marry her.

Perhaps that's where Dresdie disappeared to for over a year. Perhaps she did marry that foolish guard and they had a child. It was long enough for things like that too happen. As Gethia and her two attractive guards terrified Xern into searching for another job. Sometimes the rooms of the brothel were covered in blood since Gethia took over. The janitor of the bar was getting tiring and not to his liking.

Xern joined the guard. It wasn't to his liking either. He found it hard to do the training and was not a favorite of any other guard. He never moved up in rank and he just took his guard money and went to Dresdie's as a customer, and it was great. He knew the system and knew how to work it. Gethia was now just a bar girl of the highest quality. Dresdie had returned more handsome than before with a new zest of life and rosiness in her cheeks. Often telling Gethia they will soon have their plans in motion. Whatever that meant Xern never understood the relationship of Dresdie and Gethia.

Fact is he made mad coin being in the guard and as customer and former employee. He knew how to pull scams and how the corruption worked at Dresdie's. He brought the gambling of cards to Dresdie's and made good money. Learned to manipulate the lower ranks of the guard and get their money too. Enough to buy the big bottles and drink himself silly and rent out the top room for his hangovers to wear off.

The guard was over for him. He screwed up one to many times. A pending investigation was launched on him. He went absent without permission; he fought with other guards, even stabbed with a knife out of fear one patrolling the red district one night.

That guard was trying to help him back to the guard barracks, he was drunk and obnoxious, delusional and Xern picked a fight instead. In the scuffle with the patrol that guard almost lost an eye and had to be sent to the healing clerics to be healed. That guard never knew Xern was one of them, he kept away from that guard as much as possible in the red district. Because that guard was a good fighter and didn't need a knife, but Xern needed a knife he was a frightened coward by nature not guard material.

Metiur was that unfortunate guard on patrol that night, stopped out of pity to help Xern off the ground in his own vomit to

get him back to the barracks. Metiur got attacked instead. Xern remembered Metiur he had the pocked marked face. Remembering all this right now Xern rubbed his right cheek remembering his jaw got dislocated from Metiur's impact from his fist on Xern's skull. That was long ago yet it still hurt to this day. It's why he ran away with the sword when confronted by Metiur.

Metiur was a powerhouse, strong, resolute and followed a code of conduct. Even for having his low rank Metiur had the honor and distinction of duty as if he was an officer. Only one punch from Metiur nearly knocked Xern out and as he staggered to the ground that's when he got the upper hand and slashed at Metiur. With a knife from his boot. Even with his right eye nearly being removed and unable to clearly see. Metiur rose up and clenched his fists and threatened to beat Xern to a bloody pulp.

Metiur wasn't even worried about the knife that did so much harm to him in Xern's hand. Xern was frightened of Metiur and ran away. Metiur chased Xern for several blocks until other guards found Metiur and talked him down and to see the healing clerics. Just a bit ago, Xern ran away again when confronted by Metiur, Xern was weak and was a coward and Metiur just keeps laughing at him for a second time. This time Metiur terrified Xern in the buff. Even naked Xern couldn't challenge Metiur.

'Metiur will meet his God soon enough,' Xern thought. Remembering how terrified his drunken self was when facing off with Metiur. Yet the Healing Clerics and this blasted sword fixed the scars of that drunken heated night. Metiur was more handsome and stronger for their encounter. Xern is a coward and that's why his life is what it is and why he is headed right back to it. But he has the king's sword and now even for having blood all over him. He's worth something now he's worth the ransom of Yoranthium. He could start over a new life maybe in Forumth. Far from this hellhole of the gangs in the Grand City. Some criminals just will never learn.

Xern rounded a corner and there was the red district. It was only a street with about ten buildings in all with the sewer canal behind the buildings. It smelt badly outside from the raw sewage flow. It was that sewage canal that created this street. No respectable person would live here or open shop unless you had been a wanted criminal or the worthless. Once inside the shops

incense burned and you couldn't smell anything terrible, just sweet perfumes of incense. The street was dark only one building was lit with red lanterns. All the other brothels and bars were dark and empty and not lit up, with two of the buildings on fire and burning. The dark clouds, lightning and Mechanation's had closed the street down.

Only one brothel 'Dresdie's Love of the Depths and Darkest Desires.' was fully lit up with a new magical flashing sign stating 'Girls, Girls, Girls.' As if that sign was meant for him. "Well, I hope they have booze too because I'm thirsty and a bath would be nice." He said with some excitement. Noticing a scantly clad prostitute of rather large breasts and nice cleavage in a long shear see through Yukata and wearing only a bra and under panties beneath it. She smiled at Xern and raised her arm and motioned with a kiss from her lips and then mimed with both arms as if she was pulling at his heart and pulling him to her heart with a wink. "Nice," Thought Xern. "This sword does have magical powers." Xern was so confused that it was difficult to discern which sword he had thoughts of.

Xern was floating on air. He only smelled the sweet perfume of the seductress before him. He was gliding on air towards her and as he neared her soft voice enchanted him. "Xern my king my love, you need a bath before you touch us. Enter my king I have other maidens for you. This night we will give you a fine sensual bath. There is drink just three floors above in the kings room waiting for you my sweet. You are the king right?"

He nodded his head like he was a young male. Nervous and afraid and letting her lead him around. "Yes, a bath and then let's play, drink and have more." So smitten with desire and the attractiveness before him and upon entering two more even less clothed trollops were there past the bar by the stairs behind a beaded curtain with walls of red and pink velvet decorative paper covered walls. Past the velvet red booths and pink tables of gold trim with lighted love candles that romantically lit up the room. There was a billboard by the bar. It had the painted portraits of the floozy's available and lit by magic flame from behind showing their expensive kingly price. The other ladies were not lit and cheap. The three Xern saw where lit up, meaning available, and

their price was of the highest according to the billboard. Xern indeed was a king he deserved the best.

Xern turned to kiss the moll who brought him into the building feeling an ecstasy of love he never knew or felt before. The harlot held up her hand to stop Xern. Placing two fingers on his lips. "Oh, my King you are far to bloody for me to kiss you just yet. Let us give you a sponge bath and soak up all that crimson fluid of former life. Then I and my friends will truly give you a night you never knew." Said Gethia who had disguised herself. She seductively blinked her eyes and looked down at her large breasts. Causing Xern to do the same with his eyes and he realized she had bared her chest down to her bra and could see her medium bluish nipples peaking over the top of the small bit of cloth passing for a bra.

Xern obeyed and the two dolls at the stairs slowly turned and went up the stairs while turning occasionally to blow kisses to Xern or wink seductively and caressed the railings of the stairs and around a corner banister so alluringly. Rubbing themselves on the wall in up and down motions and exposing their legs and buttocks from the very transparent Yukata's of pink with flowers that reminded Xern of what he was hoping for most providing he could deliver. Xern was never with three babes at once this was a fantasy of dreams. Xern bit his tongue as his open mouth issued forth his wandering provocative tongue licking his lips and drooling more than a little.

"Now, now my strapping young king Xern. Don't go wasting that blood on your lips. Let us clean you first before you get too much enamored and enthralled by our lady wiles." Gethia had sounded musical, and her voice reverberated in his ears and mind as if he began making love to the three ladies in his minds imaginings.

Dreaming and upon entering the romantically lit room on the third floor of the brothel. Xern saw several bath buckets some empty some full of water that shined just a little differently. Some of the bowls had glass containers attached to them that were of a light purplish hue. There were many sponges stacked to either side of a nice pink colored tiled area. Each tile had roses on them and writings in strange runes. This area was large enough for all four of them to fit comfortably in and was meant for bathing and a

chair that Xern was taken too and laid in. To Xern's left he noticed an eloquent and massive king sized double bedding of quite a royal nature made of solid dark brown wood and laced with gold and silver etchings of love and the depths of intercourse of the deepest darkest desire. That moved and flowed around the woodwork calling to his pleasures. The sheets were silk and died red and pink and the mattress was heart shaped with a mirror above it. "That'll come in handy."

The two other maidens knelt to his sides as Gethia stood in front of Xern. He felt his clothing being removed all so gently and seductively. He saw his clothing come apart piece by piece and didn't mind he was excited and noticed the lady's had discarded their clothing too. He could see their bare frames all of which looked like triplets of the same image as the disguised Gethia. Just what he wanted in his queen to be triplets. Hopefully they all had the same name it would be easy for him to remember them all. Perhaps when tonight is over King Xern would proclaim Gethia and her twins Queens of Yoranthium. Why not it would seem they would deserve it this night.

He could feel himself becoming stiff and relaxed all at the same time. He watched as the courtesans placed his clothing into one of the bowls and as by magic the blood was removed and filled the light purple jar under the cleansing bowl and his clothing looked as if new as all the blood was removed.

Then the maiden's used the sponges on his hair and chest and face. Worked on his legs and arms and all over his body and every crevasse got a good cleaning. It was true he was a bloody dirty boy and needed a bath that was exactly what he needed. He was overcome with excitement. Not caring to notice how the fluid cleaned the sponges and drained the blood into more light purple jars. What did it matter anyway if these ladies wanted the blood they weren't monsters? Just sexy elven females for the city are a safe place from monsters. So enthralled by pleasure he forgot the world as it was now. Xern seen these call girls working here before many times catering to the lords and some ladies of Yoranthium that got robbed in this place. Making Dresdie wealthy.

Xern knew these hoochie mama's do not disappoint they had quite a taste for their clients and providing for the lords and ladies exceptional happy endings. The bath was ended and Gethia

so seductively said. "My, my, Xern you have grown into a big male." As she reached down he could feel the other two touching him as well down there. It felt good he stiffened and tingled.

"Yes, yes, I as your king desire you three to be my Queens." without a thought.

"We will be your Queens my King." Gethia began kissing Xern on the lips and his mouth opened and it was a very long kiss, and he was breathing through her kiss as his breathing became more difficult he had to pull away from Gethia. Gasping for air and wanting to kiss as deeply as they had just done.

Gethia had moved Xern past the open window with screams, explosions, and the sounds of fighting and crying and dying. But to Xern it sounded like the most romantic magical music he could imagine, as he was willing to be intertwined with these three lovelies tonight. His queens were very professional and well attentive to their kings needs. He felt the two maidens' on his sides drift away and opened his eyes. They were at the double over sized heart shaped bed that seemed to get bigger and more comfortable the nearer he got to it. He could feel Gethia pushing into him. He could feel her warmth touching and moving rhythmically on him.

Then she pushed him down onto the bed. Where the other two women pulled him all the way up and rested his head on the pillows that obstructed his view and was so soft. The other two maidens didn't leave his side. They crawled into bed with him. One on his right the other on his left. They each locked one of his legs in theirs and pressed their breasts on the side of his body. And they began kissing him and licking his ears with what seemed like unusually long tongues. He was in so much ecstasy it was hard for him to see. He was paralyzed and could not move.

Gethia was the last thing he saw. As she smoothly pressed her body up from his feet to his legs and up his chest like a snake. That was warm, soft, and made Xern stiffer. Gethia then sat up on his chest he could see her, and the flower was blooming. She looked at Xern with a sinister smile, looking into his eyes. She sat so heavily and provocatively on his chest that it was hard for him to breathe. It seemed she was breathing in his breaths. Then she turned round and Xern could see her back and long flowing hair. She bent down and down she went finding his stiffening point and applying her soft velvet like breath and then Xern closed his eyes

tightly and began groaning and moaning. Love of the depths of the deepest darkest desires was true indeed.

Xern didn't notice a fourth lady entering the room. She had long chromatic changing hair that was simply strait and very long down to her ankles. Her frame was very thin and taught. You could see her muscles well defined and wore a dress of brilliant red trimmed in pink that was nontransparent that hung around her neck and was tied at the top of her long slender legs to a long flowing cloth between her legs. She was over one and two kings foot high. A very tall female, the chest of the dress was open and layered loose cloth exposing down to her belly button. Held together with four strands of gold bindings. Her eyes of sapphire blue, of medium size, clear complexion with makeup of black and black lips with a crimson red line in the middle and outer edges. A long slender nose and well defined cheeks with five black dots horizontally following the lines of each cheekbone and a rune on the forehead. Her skin was whitish gray foreigner. Along her arms and legs were more runes of an ancient forgotten language not known of on Yoranthium.

It was Dresdie herself the matron of the brothel. She had entered the room and upon doing so the two maidens at either side had touched Xern's eyes and he was now asleep, mostly. His sleep was in reality a trance still living his fantasy.

The two playful ladies then slowly walked over to Dresdie. The one on her right kissed her neck and raised her right leg on Dresdie's uncovered right leg. Placed her right hand on Dresdie's abdomen and left arm over the shoulder to playfully touch her matron's ears ever so playfully.

The other lady followed suit walking over to Dresdie. This lass too raised her left leg just like the other and placed her right hand on the matrons backside while placing her left hand on Dresdie's small breasts and began playing.

Gethia had noticed Dresdie enter the room and was finishing off Xern happily like a meal of scrap of meat to a hungry wolf was tossed her way by her mistress. Raising her head and Xern was no longer stiff he was now asleep. "There that was nice. Don't worry Xern will never yearn or need another maiden in his life. I finished him off; he has more in common with a eunuch than a male now. He just appears to be a male, but I fed deeply into him

and took it all away. I wish you fed me like this more often Dresdie. I have no care for these mortals the way you do. Just a meal to my kind."

Gethia then began to transform. She was no real female she became only three kings feet high and was now squatting on Xern's chest. He was having difficulty to breathe as her large pig like snout sniffed the air sucking at Xern's breaths. She had large wings to either side of a bulky misshapen hideous figure for her size, no breasts no nipples just a squat misshapen beast that had some sparse hair all over and a tail that ended in an arrowhead point. Two rounded goat horns over the backward pointed ears that were smaller than the elves. Her head was bald and monstrous red eyes above the pig like nose and a smile of razor sharp teeth in points. She was a succubus and could shape shift into the wooing form of an elven female with ease, as they are masters of illusion. Gethia was now in her true form.

Dresdie then blushing and wanting no more of the attention she was getting from the two maidens flicked her hands towards them to shoo them off like fleas. "Enough you two you've done your job for tonight and I'll keep my promise to our kind for Yoranthium will soon fall with the gifts you provide this very night."

The two trollops transformed into shades, which had no true shape, and left down the stairs. You could hear them laugh as they opened the door to the outside and left with the ring of the bell on the door. While entwining with one another walking down the street like phantoms. As shades often do.

Gethia looked at Dresdie in an awful and terrible whispering loud voice. "You know this is going to cost you one day Dresdie." With and increasing sinister smile. "Our Deity patron of the Dark Deep and Hell fires of the sea abyss is expecting no complications."

"There will be no complications as long as you offer me the sword." Dresdie was scanning the room not able to see what she wanted. "I also require the blood for my rituals to destroy the cursed blade. What have you done with it all Gethia?"

"So, my powers of illusion do work on you too, Dresdie. Remember that." Gethia flicked her wrist and the sword wrapped in thick cloths was revealed along with the three jars of elven

blood. "You know Xern forgot all about that sword apparently not enough heart to use it. It burned us touching it and we had to work quickly to wrap it for you Dresdie. The pain we suffered for you was too much." Gethia showed the burns on her hands.

"Awe you poor thing, got burned for touching a sword." Faking sympathy.

"Not just any sword this is the sword of saints of the unborn God that created this island long ago from our masters pet. As long as that sword exists our master can not return for his pet will never return." Licking her hands as they healed with what she took from Xern. "You must hurry and destroy it Dresdie as quickly as you can before some other fool tries and finds it. We do not want a chosen champion wielding it for the damage it can cause to our plans."

"I will destroy the sword Gethia, you provided me nicely with the blood Xern so thoughtfully gathered for our plan. I have more than should be required for the spells needed to end this cursed sword of damnation. I have more than enough to call the possessor of the heart that must die to destroy the sword" Dresdie walked over to the three blood jars and then marked each one by etching on the glass. "Let's see." sampling each one with a long pointed tongue that came out of her mouth. Making sounds of delight as she sampled the blood. "This is King Sinderthion's blood, this is one here is Queen Zantkara, and oh I wasn't aware of a third person. It tastes of my old lover who looked into my soul at the wedding. It's the Archpriest my little internal spy to the royal family. How nice this will come in handy." Then dark black portals opened under the sword and blood containers and turned white in the middle with bubbles of black dots tapering to the edge swirling outwards and the sword dropped and blood containers fell into the portals and disappeared.

"Fortunately, I accept the compensation for this evening it will extend my life for sometime. I do hope your place remains open in the future Dresdie, as I've enjoyed the convenience of this red district of yours. It's a wonderful buffet of elven half-lives and perfect for my nest to sire more succubae and incubi from the hellish lands of the deep abyss. Many of my kind enjoy the feast you provide. Pity it should end as it kept us demonic kind from being observed in this city of theirs by their defenders. Sad to see it

all come to and end but joyous that our dark God of the deep has a way to fully return for there are eight other demons of his council in wait for their real master to arise." With that Gethia's wings stretched out as she flew out of the window to catch up with the shades that were her protectors.

"Sleep well Xern, Fool of Yoranthium. You did your job better than the one I assigned this task too. The other one decided to play hero. Don't worry Xern you'll be given a chance of revenge in the future. As this day ends sleep well in your old dusty and dirty bed. It's been some time since you been home. Enjoy your drink you earned it. As I'm sure you'll wake up never suspecting a thing but a last weird and strange lusty wet dream."

With that the room changed it was just four wooden walls, broken door, and a window. With Xern's old rotting dusty bed in the corner. Dresdie turned to leave and flicked her wrist and a portal her size opened in an oval of black and then whitened in the middle as bubbles of black expanded in the whitening area and when the portal was large enough Dresdie entered and then disappeared.

As Dresdie left her brothel the lights went out the magic of the night was gone and the sign outside had disappeared, which was a nice touch by the magics of the two shades. Now the entire street was as it should have been dark with lightning striking all around and no one except the screaming in the distance and the sounds of the Mechanation's. Sounds of some weeping and moaning and just the right amount of suffering.

Xern's was dreaming pleasantly. Believing he was still making love as a king should with his new queens. He was asleep and no longer was covered in blood and no longer had the sword and he was drained and would never desire the touch of a female form again in his lifetime. That is the power a Succubus with no restrictions will do to any gender if they are given enough time.

All Hail, Xern the Fool.

Yoranthium

Book One: Lost Hope

Chapter Seven: Flight out of the Grand City of Yoranthium

By Mark P. Bromley

Love is worth protecting, the weak are worth protecting, the youth and those to be born are worth protecting.[8] Defending what we love and care about most is why you run away from battle so that what you love and builds your heart survives the atrocity of war and destruction. Flee with that which is precious to us so we can rebuild in the light of Love and the Heart and God at our side.

---

[8] Rage against the dying of the child of the womb a weaponized legislation condoning the harm of the innocent, the defenseless, the weak and unsuspecting a cruelty of hate by partisan politics of ignorance in the early 21st century.

Fleeing the city was much more difficult than it would appear especially on foot with so many civilians to protect. This group will not stop and fight it must flee and guard it's rear. Many were lords and ladies and nobles and policy makers with children all dressed for a wedding wearing geta or high platform shoes of highly polished formal attire. Dress geta of clopping and clickity clacking on the cobble stone streets, some stumbling to try and keep up with the guard.

The sounds of battle could be heard all around them echoing off the buildings and choaking alleyways of the city. Sounding like phantom voices and sending shivers up and down the spines of all. The guard was tense and ill at ease. It took time for scouts to report conditions and some scouts never returned. A non-returning scout was a good suggestion that direction would be too hazardous of a risk. Providing the scout didn't desert and betray the sea guard. Sadly, there simply was no one to spare to find out what had become of the lost patrols.

It was not hard to think negatively given the situation. This is the sea guard; they don't like land they were meant for the sea so it would be unlikely any of them would desert here on shore. Sea guard knew the sea like sea elves taking to water, as was their nature. They went out the sundown gate far away from that nasty and filthy red district. None of the guard would be foolish to go Cold side anyhow. With the majority of the Mechanation meteors that had flown overhead had impacted far to the cold side of the Grand City.

The past midday darkness and terrifying lightning impacting the buildings around them was terrifying. Some buildings exploded and heavy stone had fallen on some civilians that tried to join the Flight. Other's were trapped behind fires and could not escape. Most of the buildings were thatched and wood framed with shingles made from the bark of trees from the logging industry. It was sad that Bronanes force could not stop to render aid. That activity of rescue would have slowed their chances of a safe retreat.

Bronanes knew he had to find a way to move faster. This is taking to long and they could still hear the fighting they just fled behind them. Then they heard a big explosion. Must have been Rarailmuir using that cursed sword again on another Mechanation

and more death and destruction. Those noises eventually got more distant and silent after running until many were tired. Insisting on taking a break and moaning of how much suffering the forced quick march to flee was causing them.

It's been quiet for a few moments for now. Perhaps and hopefully Rarailmuir is now a true king and getting the situation under control. Anyone capable of slaying a dragon like Rarailmuir did revolutions ago. Saving the lives of all that is in Yoranthium now must be able to achieve victory here too. Or at least rise to the challenge. Bronanes imagined how heroic Rarailmuir must be right now. Incentivizing his action and determination.

Rarailmuir was the inspiration for Bronanes to rise to the captain of the guard, he gave him the courage to ask Huspecia to be his love. Bronanes was smitten with Huspecia since before the day he rescued her from the fire. Having no memory of when he was several seasons old that he was there when Huspecia was found. He remembered admiring her and keeping his distance out of nervous ineptitude. He was shy and kept his distance as she had many bigger and gallant males swooning for her attention. If he tried speaking with Huspecia they would cut him off. Threaten him and intimidate him.

Even when rescuing Huspecia. Bronanes was nervous and afraid. It was the closest he ever got to her. Never saying what he meant to say. Although it seemed Huspecia always wanted to speak with him before the day of the dragon attack. He just looked away or found a reason to run away he wasn't even allowed to enter the palace grounds. Then the dragon showed up and relentlessly attacked the school as if looking for a specific target. The fire was terrifying. Bronanes had a real fear of fire. He was running down the hall and heard Kumithra screaming and Huspecia would be near she always was. He knew Huspecia was in danger, and he was nervous, afraid for his own life and might have just become a coward and saved his own worthless life. He was torn. Didn't know if he should even try with his fear of fire.

Then Rarailmuir showed up busting down doors, grabbing kids and explaining to them how to save themselves. "What are you waiting for? Some teachers to teach you to value life?" He said to many groups of children in the school. "Seize your future, take

control of your lives and when you can save yourself you can save those around you!"

Bronanes heard those words and courage grew in his heart, bravery grew in him that day.

Many of the students heard Rarailmuir. Heard what he was saying. Even the ones screaming in fear heard him focused on survival. The student's listened and followed the orders of Rarailmuir. Out of the fire and towards safety. Bronanes found his inspiration in Rarailmuir. Seeing him move with purpose and his bronze, blue mussels. Bronanes saw the face of bravery and strength to overcome your own weaknesses and be bold, to become brave and not to fear or hesitate.

Bronanes was one of the last students and was about to make an exit and save himself. But heard the cries of Huspecia and that of Kumithra the princess trapped behind doors and fallen burning beams in their classroom. Rarailmuir didn't seem to want to go in, but he said, "Damn, why does this have to be so hard." Then Rarailmuir burst through all the wreckage and strait towards Kumithra. He couldn't save both or the other four in the classroom. Rarailmuir needed help.

Bronanes had to seize his future and decided it was all or nothing and chased in after Rarailmuir. Huspecia was behind lots of burning debris. She only screamed out because she saw Bronanes in the hall thinking it over.

She was there along with the rest of the class a total of four other terrified and frightened students, two boys and two girls of royalty. One of the boys was cowering in the arms of another girl Huspecia didn't like much. That boy in her arms was trying to court her before the fire. Now he didn't care just wanted that other girl to hold him.

Huspecia knew out of the entire student's Bronanes was afraid of fire the most. Then he saw Huspecia and began trying to overcome his fear. Thankfully following Rarailmuir and hearing Huspecia's calling for help made him brave and willing to face his own worse fears. Rarailmuir was powerful and just plowed through the debris for Kumithra.

Bronanes kicked at the debris and punched at it knowing he was getting burned in the process as the debris was hot on fire and was difficult to move. Yet he managed to break through all that

debris. He saw the others weren't hurt or injured and shouted at them to save themselves and follow Rarailmuir's lead. They did so and followed Rarailmuir as he left the room with Kumithra. The boys use to bully Bronanes over his love of a girl out of his league. This day as Huspecia smiled upon her savior Bronanes he seen her smile before in his early childhood. He didn't mind the burns he had suffered soothed by her smile that staved off any pain he suffered.

After that day Dabensir, Leorth, Ardrian, and Teirdith were in admiration of Bronanes for he had saved them. What was better is that Huspecia saw him and grabbed his hand, to help push off a beam that wasn't really holding her down, jumped up and looked into his eye's with great bravado she then said. "Save me so we can get out of here and spend our lives together." Bronanes was smitten with her charms as she wasn't afraid, and she was pretending to be trapped. Just to see if he would save her. She liked him by her very words and very actions. Then again she liked him on the day his father pulled her from the sea abandoned.

She could move and pulling her forward he grabbed her back and pushed her to a safe area next to the door they had entered just as Rarailmuir was leaving the room. "Follow Rarailmuir he'll save you!" He winked at Huspecia and then the ceiling came crashing down on him this is where he got his scars and burns. He was buried under debris and his face lacerated by a sharp hot nail protruding from one of the burning beams falling on him. As he heard a terrified scream from Huspecia the first he would ever hear from her, Huspecia is seldom terrified of anything.

In great pain, bleeding and on fire he pushed up and lessened enough material he crawled out from under it. Huspecia looking at him on fire and had screamed a second and last time he would hear from her and grabbed his hand that wasn't on fire and dragged him to the hall. Her strength failed her, and he fell into the hall. Bronanes rolled until the fire was out. He was screaming in agony and pain and then looked at frightened Huspecia's eyes. He was badly burned and bleeding from the deep wound on his face. "You'll be okay, you'll be okay. Don't die, don't die my Bronanes, I love you." Frantically sincerely caring as she knelt to pull him up on her arms.

He stopped feeling the pain and stood up grabbed Huspecia's shoulder and her arm around his back under his arm and they made it outside some kings lengths and a Healing Cleric was there and that's when he lost consciousness.

Bronanes never knew that Huspecia only had eyes for him. Since that day she was at his side in the Healing Clerics halls tending to his wounds, having meals with him, reading stories of fairy tales and courage and how to over come being different and knowing what love was. Yes, even stories of love the mushy stuff was what Huspecia had read to him. A lot of kissing books made Bronanes ill, but he loved hearing her voice and never complained. She would listen to the healing clerics and apply salve and bandages even help him move about.

Remembering that day at the old school gave Bronanes courage for what he was doing. He had many people now to save and a sea guard at his command. It was getting difficult for him to focus and Huspecia and Thernya had their hands full with Kumithra. She was in battle fatigue and feeling the pangs of loss and regret and disbelief all at once.

Kumithra was unable to process her loss. How could she? She lost her mother and father at her wedding along with his Huspecia. Of all things to go horribly wrong in her life you would think the dragon was bad for all the harm it caused in the Grand City. Yet this was worse. This was the pain many students felt when they lost their parents years ago. Some of them were in this very crowd here and now.

Something needed to be done.

Kumithra was sad her eyes were in tears she had snot running from her nose and the ash and dirt was getting all over her white dress and leggings and in her hair. The braids were getting dirty with ash and soot in the air. Her hair was keeping its shape, as it was braids that could hold up to anything. The new Queen was a disappointment.

"Huspecia, do you or Thernya have any ideas how to conceal the Queen. We can't let these people see her like this. Some of them lost their parents years ago due to the dragon attack. They mourn their parents too. They can't go through it again themselves." Bronanes said with sympathy and concern for the worsening condition of the fleeing host.

The lightning from the sky set buildings on fire. A city that recently with the material shaper magics was rebuilt about one in a half revolution ago. Now they had to live the nightmare again. Yoranthium simply couldn't get a break with the amount of conflict now impacting the kingdom. That was a conflict free Kingdom that lasted over five hundredth's revolutions.

"I have an idea. We need to go down that street there." Thernya pointed down a street that was often used to house Carriages and carts for various assignments around the city for mobility. That warehouse was a central hub for transportation and would house over seven hundredths horses and two hundredths carts, buggies, and carriages.

"Are you suggesting we use carts and carriages? Thernya that's a great idea they were supposed to be ready this afternoon for the wedding parade." Bronanes recalled the plans to take them to a scenic hotel for their evening's bridal banquet.

"Not only that there's clothes down that street too. Sensible ones. The royal dress shop attached to the Royal Guard's outfitter." Huspecia piped in.

Kumithra agreed. "Yes my father and mother shopped there, you remembered Huspecia they use to..." back to sobbing and crying.

Bronanes was concerned if Huspecia would soon be losing her mind too? Wanting to shop for clothes at a time like this? "I don't think shopping is something we should be doing Huspecia, snap out of it! We can't let you become a liability."

"Liability! Now listen here my sweet!" Huspecia with some ire in her voice exclaimed. "Rarailmuir might have made it possible for us to flee in these wedding Yukata. However, this wear is not appropriate for us to think we have a chance to escape the city in. It's too bright and too provocative. Offers no protection. We need sensible attire and it's at that store next to the carriage store house." Placing her hand on her hips causing her brassiere to expose the tops of her cleavage.

"You look ravishing and quite attractive; just thought you should know." Bronanes eyebrows shifted up and down with an expression of lust. "Yet you are right there are too many of you all dressed like that. We won't make it like this." Bronanes came to reason and agreed to 'operation shopping for clothes and operation

carriages and horses.' A bold dual plan just what those fleeing the city needed. This would mean no more stops until they were out of the city and at the outer keep. Any other civilians would have to fend for themselves. Yet the Queen of Yoranthium must be protected for the sake of her people above all. It was Bronanes duty.

"Thernya!" Turning his lovingly gazes at her bodice and realizing how right Huspecia was to the inappropriate attire. He almost got too excited looking at all nineteen of the wedding retinue similar in provocation. Then he rubbed his eyes and shook his head.

"Bronanes turn your eyes to your wife. I'm much too old for you." Busted! For his ogling. "What do you want?"

"I want to know if you think there are horses in that carriage house? Do you think we can get good apparel at that shop down there?" Bronanes said keeping his eyes on Huspecia's... Rarailmuir's dress making skills was a secret blessing for any of the males and several sea guards agreed.

As Huspecia looked at Bronanes with a little anger and amusement Thernya explained. "The carriage house street seems to have taken little damage from the lightning as the buildings are better protected from storms with lightning rods. No fires to report. Just looks deserted. Horses are in the carriage house it's a main carriage house for the palace and commerce of the city. They should have been preparing all the carriages this morning for after the wedding. We need to move quickly before that changes. Huspecia and I will take the ladies and get suitable clothes. While your men and those men get the carriages and horses ready." Thernya was good with logistics, and she should be she was the head of household affairs, assigned queens protector, and trained Huspecia in her duties to protect Kumithra.

"Right my ladies. The men and me will ready the coach and you ladies will shop for clothes. Now, I just want to stress. No cosmetics. Just grab your change of clothes and assemble at the carriage house. Dabensir you and your scouts need to scout a clear road out of the city on horseback. You guards take ten squads and protect the shoppers. Rest of the men aid in readying the carts, buggies and carriages. It looks like we will be a mounted unit." Bronanes said with confidence and strict command. "Once moving

down the road. Scouts will ride ahead and report on single horseback. We stop for nothing and no one, we are to simply protect the Queen and what we have on hand."

Huspecia was holding Kumithra and came up along side Bronanes. "Don't think I didn't notice you eyeing Thernya like candy you migrating Narwhal."

"What. I didn't. I wasn't being a Narwhal. You all dressed yourselves this morning. It's your fault, no it's Rarailmuir's fault for dressing you all that way." Said Bronanes in his own defense. His arms were out and palms held toward the sky and he shrugged. As Huspecia pinched his cheek and took off with the rest of the shopping patrol with glee and a hop in her step excited to go shopping. Along with the soldiers and the two hundredth or so civilians that were badly dressed. Fortunate for them it was a clothing warehouse.

Kumithra was excited. "I hope you pick out something my father would approve of, Huspecia and Thernya. I remember shopping with my father...." Then she became sad again and started sobbing.

Huspecia whispered. "He was my father too, Kumithra. I know, I remember, I can never forget."

This is how it went down.

'Operation Shopping for suitable attire.'

The civilian's, the wedding retinue and the ladies over two hundredths needed to change their clothing fast. As their guard of ten squads and some guards moved with civilian's under guard in all directions as they quickly moved down the street. The shopping patrol upon reaching the clothing warehouse knew immediately what it was and took up positions around the building with light patrols scouting the corners. It was the military supply warehouse where many recruits to the guard get their first set of gear. This was going to work nicely as the entire group of civilians was guaranteed a decent set of apparel. The quickly deteriorating war torn streets indicated a need for haste. It would work quickly and efficiently. No more clickity clacking on the cobblestone streets.

Thernya had been in charge of issuing when this building was rebuilt in the city. The builders used shaping magics to quickly rebuild the magical Grand City and the plan for the city was

hundredths of revolutions old. Rebuilding was easy with the office of architectural magistrate as elven magics shaping was supreme in crafts of all kinds.

Thernya had no problem assigning experienced guard members to each isle inside the massive clothing warehouse. One soldier for each isle as the apparel was issued by quick measurements. The host was ordered behind changing blinds as they got issued their gear and above all they would be getting rid of any flashing colors or any clothing that shined too brightly and replace it with a duller military silk kimono, hakama, boots and gloves designed for sea elves that accentuated their form and ability to swim in water.

Interesting thing about sea elves is that they could jump in the water and not worry of wet clothing or dampened silks when getting out. As their skins adsorbed water and utilized water as nature had intended. Their clothes would dry fast before the sun had to do its work as their sea elf skin absorbed and quickly dissipated excessive water.

To keep from giving themselves away Thernya had ordered all outfits to be the same in colors. Only the badges on shoulder and over the heart would display Yoranthium colors of the land and the sea. The uniform was composed of long boots that were tight, open toed, black and would rise just over the knee and could be left folded down depending on how you laced the boots along the outer sides. Followed by a loose yet tightly defined dark brown set of fashionable leggings, corsets and strapless bra's for the women.

The Kimono top was of a dark maroon color and folded over on top with big sleeves stopping at above the elbows. Then tied off at the waist with a large black belt that if they were preparing for war this heavy starched thick silk belt cloth would also support waist armor and swords. However, the host is civilians and do not fight and it's easier to move without the armor. The belt was two kings hand width thick and could be folded to any thinner thickness as desired. Tied into a square knot in the front and either left that way or spun to the back for better comfort and support.

On the ladies the Kimono almost looked like Rarailmuir's fancy design for the retinue. However, this one covered their breasts up to their necks folding left over right and short to just above their upper thighs. Tight pants and long laced open toe boots

along with foot fitting sandals. The sandals would attach to the bottom of the boots and cover the toes. Designed to be kicked off when entering the ocean for the sea guard.

All of this was meant to fight in and there were a variety of pouches and additions for weapon holders and other gear available. Those with interest simply equipped what they felt they needed. Such as arm holding loops that would keep the long sleeves of the kimonos out of the way for aggressive sword fighting stances. The holding loops interested Huspecia and Thernya and they collected a good number of oils and ointments and stored some of them with Kumithra. The oils were used as special compounds to counter different types of dangers like fighting demons and such. Hakama were also offered, and these were used for more official dress style options that some felt better in and less revealing leaving it at the tight pants and long boots.

To think Rarailmuir was the designer of the guard. He was the General and had the final say. It would also explain the male Yukata's for the wedding. He signed off on those too. Exposed chests, none of the females complained why would they? What was it with Rarailmuir and wanting to show skin in formal attire? Questions we'll never know the answer too. The ladies fortunately had to be thankful for him not designing the original wedding dresses.

There were also gloves that didn't' impede their hands and were thick and offered some arm protection of black heavy silk that had metal protection up to and over the elbows with a solid armor piece that protected the top of their hands and allowed their webbed hands to expand freely should they have to swim. As this outfit was perfect for the sea guard. Some equipped backpacks, satchels, blankets, and extra sets of clothing and under garments. Some even managed to find cosmetics for they might not use them now. None the less some wanted to impress their partners down the road. If a pleasant time would ever surface from this dark day for one could only hope.

Kumithra saw a helmet of ancient purpose and after dropping her flower to the floor she put it on. It was round on top with sea elf top embellishment and symbology of sea dear antlers that went off to the sides symmetrically. Then at the bottom of the bowl was a band and under that a round cone of three segmented

sections expanded to protect the back of the neck too the shoulders and was bent in the front to reveal the face as it was tied onto the chin. Kumithra had looked at Huspecia when wearing the oversize helmet telling it reminded her of her father getting ready for battle. And then she began sobbing again.

The helmet was a special order for General Rarailmuir the artisan delivered it in the morning it was the only one of it's kind. The guards themselves didn't have to change. Although their dress uniform was flashy it was functional and satisfactory military ready for a fight. Only over two hundredths civilians needed gear and it was easily procured. A few of them objected complaining they are not soldiers. They were ladies and lords of the court. However once in the care of the military, "One size fits all." Was Thernya's reply. As for the children they had emergency dark colored Yukata's for the children and simple open toed slippers that bound around the ankles.

Now the host was well dressed and nothing much to note except the shelves got emptier in the warehouse and now it was difficult to tell the difference from anyone of the civilian hosts except for the color of uniforms. The sea guards liked their fancier uniforms as opposed to the standard issue. Along with armor and helmets and had weapons. They also stocked up on a range of belt pockets and items and oils to combat different kinds of hostile enemies including demon breads and other creatures common to Ishormot. Several sea guards were trained in some healing magics and equipped them with what they could get on the shelves of this fully stocked station.

'That's right.' Thernya thought perhaps I should verify my retinue is armed. Looking at Kumithra in the helmet, Thernya thought about arming her. The Queen was emotionally compromised, and it was too much of a risk to give her a sharp dagger of temptation with her weakening values of self worth. Thernya seen this before and wasn't new to such emotions. Thernya years ago, lost her champion and her child and it cut her deeply. So deeply she had thoughts of finding her loves in the world after, if it wasn't for Zantkara entering her room baring her pregnant stomach.

"You got to feel this it's amazing!" Zantkara was excited.

The Queen placed Thernya's hand on her large and round stomach. The hand with the wrist Thernya had planned to slice open, just moments before the Queen interrupted her. Thernya hid her intentions, and the Queen was unaware of her attempt as she hid the knife behind her. Zantkara simply came in and placed Thernya's hand on her belly. Zantkara didn't pay attention to Thernya's chain dagger being slightly hid from her view for she was used to Thernya training with the weapon often and nothing to suspect.

With Thernya's open hand on the Queens stomach. Kumithra kicked Thernya for the first time. "That's right my Thernya you are going to be a mother along with me, I can't do this without you." Zantkara had kissed her cheek as Thernya felt another kick from Kumithra and then ran out of the room down the hall. "Oh, Sinderthion, Sinderthion I have something for you." Zantkara's friendship at the last moments of truth... Her daughter is in turmoil, both of them and they had saved her life with their respective love.

Thernya brushed a tear from her eye and sniffled. No she's not going to fall into this trap she has two daughters to care for. Thernya heard Huspecia's whisper about her 'father too.' King Sinderthion raised them both. Thernya would have to watch them both. Kumithra was the biological child and would hurt now but likely recover easier than Huspecia. Huspecia knows she's an orphan and as such lost the parents she only knew, and they weren't her real ones. Huspecia might be brave now but down the road losing a second set of parents would be hard on her. Fortunately, Huspecia has Bronanes now and Thernya. They would both need their Godmother Thernya soon enough.

Thernya's strength was needed. She was the head of household affairs and now leader to over two hundredths civilians, lords and ladies and many children. She had obligations and keeping Huspecia and Kumithra her daughters alive was her duty, that duty was her motherly love for her children, for they are her children she raised them just as much as Zantkara did. They would survive they would make it to the caves. They had too, for her children and their future of Yoranthium.

'Operation hitch the carts and buggies.'

Bronanes and Dabensir separated from the shoppers. Their group had over six hundredths of the remaining sea guard in it. Their object was next door to the Yoranthium uniform issuance facility that also had a boutique that sold to the civilians fancy dresses, suits, fancy Yukata's, kimono's and styles from all over the known world of Ishormot as a means to raise revenues and taxes for the kingdom. Much of the white formal dresses and lords and ladies dresses paid for part of the royal double wedding.

Dabensir and his scouts ran past the main doors to the carriage house and down to the end of the street. Signaled to set up a sunup side and the cold side watches. While other scouts were sent to scout the road, they had planned on using for their next operation, 'Ride like hell and hope nothing blocks the way.'

Dabensir gave Bronanes the signal with his spear that the area was clear from down the road. Bronanes looked at the carriage house door. It was slightly a jar for a heavy set massive door. Peaking from behind the crack between the two doors was a girl child. She ran away the moment Bronanes eyes caught her. "Prepare yourselves there are people inside. You four, two on each side help open these doors for our entrance."

Several guards got their spears to the ready and stood in formation of a half circle as the doors were swung open by the two guards on either side of the door. Inside was a bunch of frightened carriage house workers. They arranged themselves preparing for a fight as smells and sounds of livestock wafted from out the door. Horses would nay in the background.

The carriage house workers would be no contest for the Kings guards of the sea. The citizens were armed with only a few pitchforks, scythes, hay bail pincers, hoofing knives, and various low-grade knives and cutlery along with a few staves and shovels. Just a mere hundredths or so with the children including the little girl clinging to their legs. They were not fighters and if they tried they would die, and their children would be harmed in the conflict.

"There's that sweet little darling I saw just a moment ago. You must be her father. I'm Lord Bronanes captain of the kings guard." Starting at the top of his head he rolled his hand down in a form of theatrical bowing to his new host. "We are here to rescue you." He stood at attention and smiled. "I do hope you have a name too sir."

With uncertainty and hesitation. "I'm Leorth and this is my daughter Rubius. We don't want any trouble we just want to be left in peace. Don't you have enemies to fight on this dark day of hell?" Leorth was frightened and was worried that Bronanes and his men would murder them. Leorth hadn't seen the enemy and didn't know what was happening.

"My good Leorth and your charming child Rubius. I'm not here to harm any of you. I'm actually here to take you to the secluded caves and safety. We could always use more able body fighters and well look at you. You make Yoranthium proud." With some pride and quick salute and open hand gesture he began stepping forward towards Leorth. He lowered his own spear to the ground keeping his other hand from his weapons.

Leorth wasn't sure but Bronanes although a scared snarling looking, and intimidating man rang of truth. Leorth could hear his daughters heart beating as she buried her face in Leorth's carriage drivers green Yukata covering his legs. Leorth knew the hundredths of them were no match for the guard outside. This was the sea guard they are no slouches when it came to fighting. Many revolutions since Yoranthium's founding they had fought off other kingdoms and pirates. Yoranthium sea elves, in the Potentates kingdom were known as one of the deadliest encounters on the open sea. Books discovered by the Yoranthian's found out the mainland elves feared the sea elf's at sea. Just as much as sea elves feared the deep dark abyss and hell fires deep in the ocean far from the resorts of the lollygag islands.

"Captain of the Guard, I submit." Leorth fell to his knees before his lord and dropped his weapon along with the rest of the frightened civilians that were unsure that was the right action, yet they did it reluctantly anyway. Following Leorth's lead they all had children nearby and knew they were no match.

Bronanes reached into his chest pocket and pulled out a large cookie and a bag of them. He gave it to the girl Rubius, "Go give these cookies to your friends I'm sure you are hungry." The girl looked at her father and he nodded for her to do as told. Then Bronanes reached down with his hand and grabbed Leorth. Pulled him up off the ground and hugged him. "Leorth, I'm sure you forgot me but here we are again."

Leorth pulled back and was thinking then he remembered the male who saved him his wife Teirdith and his friend Dabensir who joined the sea guard for his family. "Bronanes that is you the hero who saved my family from the dragons fire. Dabensir's wife Ardrian is here along with my child and his children Dueith, Vatalorn, and the infant Indirid."

"I need you to go relieve Dabensir." Bronanes pointed at the nearest sergeant and he ran to relieve Dabensir. "Well, I didn't know you all got married, why didn't you all tell me?"

"You weren't around after the dragon and honestly we just lived our lives. Likely just like you. Whatever happened to Huspecia. She wasn't around the school after the fire I heard she was at the Healing chapel. Something about burns unit and helping others. It's a pity she was quite the looker." Leorth was one of the boys that frightened Bronanes away from Huspecia and use to bully him.

Bronanes simply said. "It turns out she only had eyes for me. She took care of me I was the one with the burns and now today we were wedded. You should know you were here getting the carriages ready I see."

"You lucky male, you got the best of the deal. Living in the palace and all. Glad you got to live your dream." Leorth said humbly. "Yes we are almost done getting the carriages all ready."

Dabensir came into the room and saw him and grabbed him by the head and messed up his hair. "Leorth haven't seen you since yesterday. You narwhal. Are you still pining for Huspecia before your wife? Speaking of wives where's Ardrian?"

Tapped on the shoulder by Ardrian. Dabensir turned around and saw her holding Indirid. Then Dabensir's other two children grabbed his legs. "Daddy's back!" They said lovingly in union as Dabensir looked into his wife's eyes.

"Found our hero Dabensir it's our old friend Bronanes." Leorth said while Dabensir then realized who Bronanes really was. These five old acquaintances hadn't seen Bronanes since they were rescued. Didn't see his injuries and stopped pursuing Huspecia. She spent all her days caring for Bronanes when not with Kumithra. The school was burned to ashes and most of their education was home schooled for the past four revolutions and as

they came of age they all managed to pair themselves with those ladies nearest to them all.

"Okay guys enough, we have business here. We need to get these carts, wagons and buggies up and working and hitched to all the horses. We needed it yesterday. We got the malepower. Start getting this process over and done with we got more females and males joining us soon. Including the lady Huspecia and Queen Kumithra." Bronanes ended the reunion and then began issuing orders.

Leorth interjected. "The Queen is going to be here? That's why we are here. We had the marriage carriages ready this morning. Then the darkness fell and lightning all around. Many people ran down this street and hid in the buildings across from us."

Just then lightning struck the building to the warm side across the street and it burst into flames instantly and women, men, and children could be heard burning alive as the entire turpentine shop went up in flames. "How many more are in these buildings?" Bronanes was terrified there was a magics factory on this street too.

Leorth looking frightened again and worried. "There are about thirty to fifty people in each building. We got to save them as many as we can. We have enough carriages for everyone and horses too."

"Good to hear Leorth." Bronanes gave Leorth a firm grab on the shoulder a congratulations for becoming a hero himself. "Dabensir your family will be safe here, go and take some guard and evacuate the buildings to this location. If you find the magics grab those too we might need them."

"Quite the day for several side missions Captain. I your faithful, Lieutenant of the Yoranthium Guard, will not fail you." Dabensir wanted to impress his wife with his new title Lieutenant of the Guard and Ardrian smiled and yearned for her hero's return. Giving him a quick kiss on the cheek and as he left she waved at him with Indirid's tiny hand.

Dabensir had his men scour all the buildings asking the inhabitants of scared and frightened males, females and children to come out. At first none dared for it was dark, lightning everywhere and wind gusts. The fire of the turpentine and paints building got

warmer as more fuel was burned and the nearest buildings began to catch fire. The buildings shared common walls not divided by narrow alleys.

This prompted those two buildings to unload it's people quickly first. Then seeing that those people were being helped and assisted and assessed for health. Sure enough the others in hiding came out to be rescued.

The number of civilians that needed transportation increased dramatically. It was getting questionable if there would be enough transportation and getting these people to safety was a priority. There was only a couple of sunwanes of daytime left. The darkened clouds might have darkened the day but by nightfall it would be much worse, and it would be terrifying to remain in the city past dark with no streetlights to guide their way.

Horses were matched to carts, bindings and lashings and mounting gear attached to the carts. Guards that had skill were assigned to each cart as lookouts, defenders and drivers. Cart after cart quickly got pushed out to the streets and Leorth and his wife assigned people to load up as many as possible into each cart, wagon and carriage.

Bronanes heard a unique trilling nay of a very special horse. It was a shape shifter and belonged to King Sinderthion it was Wertomeer the sea stallion, appearing like a horse but a thin and longer snout larger eyes and smarter than most horses. With a spiny and webbed mane and similar ears on the side with no nostrils just air holes four of them with two on either side on the back of the head they were more like whale blow holes and had sealing membranes. The sea stallion had a larger ribbed chest that looked very much like a smaller sea horse but on a normal horse body with toed hooves that had webbing between them. This horse was special. On land it was like a horse and has four legs with a fish like tail. But in the water it transformed and was more like a dolphin mixed with a silkoe as it adapted and adjusted to the water. Sinderthion found Wertomeer on Forumth when he was saving Queen Zantkara.

"I'll be honored to ride you out of here friend of King Sinderthion. You must accept me for this place will likely burn and you along with it if you stay." Wertomeer simply looked at Bronanes and understood. The sea stallion was said to understand

by telepathy. Ability Bronanes didn't have. Bronanes had no problem placing the saddle on Wertomeer and the tack. Bronanes brushed Wertomeer's soft shimmering scale like skin as he walked the sea horse toward the entrance.

There coming around the corner was the shoppers detachment. They were all uniformed now and looked very much alike. Brought with them extra clothing they distributed to persons in need. Thernya and Huspecia were still holding Kumithra tightly. Huspecia still had her flower in her hair while Kumithra was wearing a helmet too big for her head.

Bronanes looked over to a gypsy carriage they had impounded recently. It was rustic but it was fully enclosed with small windows that you could see out but not into. It's exactly what the Queen needed to not draw attention. It wasn't hard to instruct the wedding host to get in their carriages, carts, buggy's, chariots and this gypsy monstrosity. Time was running short and Huspecia didn't want to bother Bronanes because he was masterful in organizing this exodus.

Huspecia just handed Bronanes some of the same clothing with the Captain of the Guard rank on it, hakama, leggings and boots. That he wore in folded down pirate fashion. A common officers helmet similar like Kumithra's except it fit his head and was made for him. Along with body armor and pauldrons and mounted knights waist skirt. Bronanes rushed off and changed with Huspecia's help and then returned after several minutes. Truly looking like a knight of renown and a true officer in command. Complete with a face piece of a commanding smile.

Dabensir returned with crates of magics as ordered. "Sire the men are assembled the guards and scouts have all reported. We are ready to move forward, and we should distribute these crates to our defenders should trouble arise. We have several carts, and we will lash them to the backs of the more robust carts as we move this caravan out of here.

Bronanes went to Wertomeer and got on the sea stallion. Huspecia noticed from atop the Gypsy cart admiring how handsome Bronanes was and how inspirational to all the refugees and his sea guard. "What a leader." She said out loud and the guards around her agreed while you could hear nothing from Kumithra for she had fallen asleep on Thernya's lap like a child

within the gypsy cart. The unfortunate Queen had cried herself to sleep in Rarailmuir's helmet still on her head and to its side.

"Today is a terrible day." Bronanes was giving a speech to raise the hopes of the refugees and the guard. To give them confidence and directions, "Hold to your love hold to your heart, for this day will end. It will soon be night and we are going to race against time and hell to the outer farms keep and we will succeed. The road is long and rough and do expect some bumps and bruises. Do not fear for fear is failure. Believe in your guard for they will serve you well and you will live, and we all will be stronger helping each other as we flee with those hearts that are so precious to us all. Be brave, have courage, and believe and trust in our hearts and our love as your strength. The unborn God watches over us and with all these blessings we will prevail!!!" Bronanes still needed to work on his command skills as the speech was well received more out of kindness than enthusiasm.

Their spirits were raised, and it wasn't long as the wagons and carriages began moving, it was exciting at first. Like being in the royal parade. Until all the carts were on the main road as the scouts galloped ahead with great rapid speed. The wagons began to get faster as the whips of the reigns could be heard as clicks and "Yah's," increased the speed. The wagons and the horses all of it got faster and faster on the main road they were for sure trying to outrun hell. Bronanes commanded from the rear and would use Wertomeer to go up and down the ranks. Wertomeer was the fastest of all the horses in the stables of the Grand City.

They moved incredibly fast, and nothing bared their egress from the city at the speeds they had taken that was somewhat reckless and dangerous. Persons in the carts bounced and got tossed about except Kumithra who simply was too exhausted to be bothered by the constant bouncing about in Thernya's cushion of a body. The sea guards were good pilots and masters of their coaches. Light was fading they made it to the country and farms passed for all those that had a window.

It wasn't long but they did reach the Keep of an old fort that was on it's way to the sea caves the outer defenses of the Grand City where they would hold up for the night. The day light ending and the Dark clouds made the coming of the night darker behind them as the setting of the sun was nearing and about to touch the

rim of the far off peaks. The setting sun was striking as the Darkness didn't cover the entire island of Yoranthium after all. It was nice to see the setting of the sun and the pink tropical Yamazakura foliage in the distance and that of other trees and open farmlands.

Yoranthium

Book One: Lost Hope

Chapter Eight: Fight Part One: Situational Awareness

By Mark P. Bromley

Can't fight what we do not know or understand when we cannot see. It is true that knowing your enemy goes a long way in understanding how to defeat your enemy. We cannot protect the ones we love if we do not understand who your enemy really is. Or how they are destroying your unalienable way of life, liberty and pursuit of Happiness.

A group of six that passed the outer guard with purpose and a mission was approaching King Rarailmuir. The Royal Magistrate of Map Makers a key unit of advisors and strategists that can recon vast land areas and display by magic illusions of the real time conditions of any battlefield. By use of magics known as mechanoids they can deploy to conduct surveillance operations and spy on enemy positions. These mechanoids were of a wide range of magics design. This means Rarailmuir's guards will have knowledge on their side and a possible means to victory.

These six mapmakers were all dressed like one another in black thick kimono's of a priesthood nature that were shimmering with silver belts of island silk. With a long dangling sash one kings foot from the bottom of the kimono tied in an interlocking square holding the belt and kimono in place. They were all pale blue skin, bald and had eyes that were somewhat translucent. Eyes were larger than a common male and composed of multiple angled lenses something like ommatidia that flashed in chromatic hues.

Each mapmaker wore glasses over their eyes of a telescoping nature and had additional lenses to the side of the main lenses covering each eye. Lenses would reflect informational pictures and various information as the lenses would switch pending what information the mapmaker was examining. The glasses were firmly fitted to each eye with a black material that kept all six of them looking directly forward and you could not see between the lenses and the eye sockets on the side. You would think they could not see around them, if it wasn't for the effectiveness of their psychic and telemetry abilities that feed them the required information to navigate the world around them. These mapmakers seen the world on levels beyond normal sight.

They had devices in their ears of bronze same metal as the glasses and a wire that ran down by thin under the skin wires connected to an implanted device on their throats. Around their sea elf ears they had a thin metal of bronze that circled the front of the ear. Running up the forehead, on top of their heads and behind their head on either side disappearing under their skin. This metal that then went under their skin and into their brains. With an array of tiny antennae sticking off to the sides of the metal ear loops looking like spikes following the line of bronze on their heads. The kimono had large collars of white shining metal like silk that

curved up around their heads and occasionally a small electrical shock could be seen sparking quickly between the collar and the neck apparel crackling through the spikes and rows of miniature antennae.

The six mapmakers approached Rarailmuir outside of the throne room. "My King we are the royal battle command and have maps and surveillance that would be useful on the battlefield. Let us enter the main throne room and set up on the dais." They did this in unison and in a mechanical tonal quality. Sounding more machine than elf.

Metiur was at Rarailmuir's side as several wounded were being treated in the administrative halls of the throne hall. "Should we use the conference chamber to determine our next strategy with the map makers?"

"Yes. Mapmakers use the conference chamber just down the hall to the left. There is a table much like the dais and we'll have to work on a smaller scale than intended. Do set up there." Giving a hand gesture the mapmakers disembarked from the King.

With a royal bow, "By your leave our King we will be ready as soon as you arrive." The mapmakers said in unison as one was louder than the rest. They hurried for they knew time was important.

Fedarious had returned with news from a returning scout. "My King this sea guard scout has returned with men that are able to join our fight. They came from the carriage street where Dabensir had taken all the horses, Wertomeer, wagons, carriages and buggies along with many citizens unable to fight successfully out of the city. They met no resistance and are now at the out lining keep on the edge of the farmlands. All assembled females and children along with unfit males for combat are with their unit. Queen Kumithra is reported safe and in no immediate danger." With a relieved sigh he stood at attention.

"This is good news. Thank you sea scout Tombulin." Rarailmuir knew all his guard for it was his duty and honor to serve with them as their General and now their King. "Take food and drink and then check back in with the Sergeant. I will need you and the use of your horse soon enough to send messages to Lieutenant Bronanes."

Rarailmuir then turned to Metiur. "Let's check out the situation with the map makers."

Rarailmuir and Metiur with some haste went to the makeshift command room that was down the hall. This room was initially used for parliament of legislative drafting efforts with foreign dignitaries that would barter various agreements with Yoranthium.

The room was rather big about eight and a quarter king's length and fifteen kings foot wide. There were smaller columns half submerged in the walls of white alabaster marble and wall carvings of intricate design depicting peace treaties and achievements of many treaties signed in this very room that would animate to display the culmination of many of the kingdoms finest moments. Many of the palace walls had historical moving frescos of marble placed there by sculpture magics. In the middle of the room was a massive sakura oak table that was dark in the center and edged with gold lace around the edge of a leafy pattern that repeated and ran on top of a lighter layer of sakura maple.

Yoranthium had various kinds of sakura trees most having pink flowering leaves year around. The wood types had been varied and the same and comparable to Oak, Maple, Ash, and many other types not to be confused with the tropical large, leafed variety trees that were blues and greens.

The sakura trees were common along with bamboo that usually were treated with new resins and wood shaping magics of specialized artisans. That was called lacquering and specialized pressing techniques infused with mithreal mined on Yoranthium. Making many wood made items very exceptionally strong and nearing metal fabrication. Especially if applied to specialized cloth and coated with additional gel resins and magics compounds.

The chairs had curved legs and rounded delicate looking yet comfortable backs that you could sink into made of the finest leathers and there were about sixteen chairs with one chair being the largest designed for the King at the head of the table. The chairs looked like bergere with only the kings having longer back than the rest. All having a lacy leaf motif of sakura cherry wood that was gold leafed and padded with a diamond nailed backing. The main cress at the head of the chairs was that of the Yoranthium crest and coat of arms.

The magic lights of hovering orbs that were at ceiling height in the chamber were dimmed. The six map makers had been in the room and already had their magics at work on top of the table that was a semi-opaque and translucent view of the island of Yoranthium with the current storm at sea disrupting the waters. "My king we are ready to serve you and the storm conditions are ready for your review." Said all six-map makers as their eyes light up in a trance and they were connected to one another as they surrounded the table.

The Map Makers were gifted with the magics of telepathic connections to a large array of magics called mechanoids that were used to monitor and watch key elements of the island for the kingdoms security. Only the Royal Magistrate of the Map Makers who had been selected at birth had access to this level of Yoranthium security. Much of the magics mechanoids being only to their level of understanding and were a top secret to the people of Yoranthium. This information was restricted to those as high as the Lieutenant and above to the King and Queen of Yoranthium. Now Metiur learned of this and was quite astonished. Many people would be shocked to know how far these kinds of magics could intrude into their lives.

Many larger kingdoms of great wealth had fewer of these resources. Yoranthium was envied by the Potentate of the elves founding lands for excelling beyond their level of sophistication. Yoranthium had at its disposal the best services. Some of the most fantastic magics that were acquired by various means knowledge that caused envy and fear from the main land elves.

Much of what Yoranthium excelled at in magics and knowledge came from many raiders and other encounters with the island and sunken deeper kingdoms. These kingdoms were further side of the warm equator and towards the sparsely explored depth dweller kingdoms of the deep dark fiery abyss of hell. Where the directional compass would flip as to which direction was the cold side in the windless zone of Ishormot seas.

Yoranthium's navy never really had to go far. The raiders came to Yoranthium with their new magics and knowledge. Rarailmuir made a successful career at retrieving these magics and knowledge and passing it on to the mages college. The mages

college was Yoranthium's secret magics and knowledge research and development services.

The mechanoids were miniature devices that belonged to the ancient culture ruins that were discovered five-hundredths revolutions ago. These kind of magics made Yoranthium's security services and special units the best on all of Ishormot. The magics of which could only be controlled by the sea elf's that demonstrated the highest telepathic abilities and capabilities of linking themselves to the mechanoids and each other to project the map seen on the table from their very eyes in a dark enough room.

These map makers began their lives as gifted highly psychically gifted children. Sadly many came from parents often of a less wealthy class. When learning of these special individuals cruel parents would sell their own children into slavery, captivity and a black market. Fortunately, the Mages College often found them first. Yoranthium mages had been feared upon discovery of gifted children and often cruelly treated.

The mages often would use forget spells and simply remove the mage attuned child from parents who could not understand their child's true value. The Mages College would take such unique sea elves and augment them with mage magics and training. A sea elf mage was a secret of Yoranthium and often thought of as a demon to those who did not have the ability to understand their unique qualities.

There were many different classes and subcategories of mages and would have a wide range of designations. Such as celestial observers, mapmakers, shapers, crafters, magistrates, healing cleric, clergy, magics viziers and many other titles and rolls. To have the title mage denoted a high ranking magics user who obtained a fantastic level of knowledge of forgotten techniques that could only be found and mastered in the mysterious ancient and hidden keeps and ruins covering the underground of the isle of Yoranthium. With all the acquired knowledge being stored in the mages college compendium.

One mapmaker began to talk with the other echoing in lower voices. The map scrolled and zoomed out to see a larger area around Yoranthium. "As you can see the epicenter of the storm is from a raised tower in the ocean close to the lollygag islands chain; to the sunup warmer side about a hundredths leagues from Sea

Shore. The tower is of dark obsidian and next to the lands of the deep dwellers and runs extremely deep to the bottom. It was difficult to get a mechanoid out that far as the storm has disrupted many magics in the region. The guard posts had been destroyed on the volcanic peaks of the Lollygag islands. Including all Yoranthium vacationing pleasure resorts. As of now no sea elves are known to be alive on the Lollygag island chain."

The voice changed to another mapmaker as the other subsided to a softer echo. "The storm cloud that darkens our sky's only extends past the outer defenses of Farmer Town and the Grand City. While totally enveloping Sea Shore where the Navy off the coast was doing drills and exploring suspicious activities, only a small scout craft escaped delivering the warning of eminent attack. The destruction of the Navy is still a mystery. We do know that sun light does exist past the outer keep defenses on the Sundown side of Yoranthium."

With a change to another mapmaker, "Sea Shore is under heavy siege by unknown forces that have been moving quickly through the city and defenses. Having captured the Break Water detention facility as a forward operating post. A small force was detached and used portals to reach the palace that was defeated by you our King. As only two Mechanation meteors impacted near the Palace grounds. Those were fired from heavy powder magics cannons from a massive structure that emerged from behind the water break. It was believed to be some demonic island sized sea monstrosity that is unknown."

With another switch to another mapmaker, "We believe from evidence that over two-thousandths plus large Mechanation's have impacted on the Cold side of the Grand city and up to Farmer Town. These Mechanation's are currently invested in activities pushing further cold side away from the Grand City. Armed units are engaged until defeated by the Mechanation's while the Mechanation's is herding the unarmed towards containment area's. Purpose of captive taking is still unclear at this time."

A new voice from the mapmakers, "Lightning strikes although uncontrolled it would seem are more likely to strike key area's and armories that our unknown enemy has intelligence about. Our enemy likely is the depth dwellers from the deep world. Lighting rods of sufficient quality such as the one still protecting

the Palace grounds easily mitigate lightning strikes. Many of our armories and other stores do not have these lightning rods in place. As just moments ago lighting destroyed the carriage house and many fires are now out of control in all districts of the city, with exception of the red district. It was good the sea guard decided to utilize the carriages and saved the horses from certain doom."

Switching again. "Sea Shore is losing and their fight is a grim one. Their command structure completely collapsed along with many units in the cold side districts of the Grand City. Farmer Town's governor Colusious did not attend the wedding as it was first harvest season and Farmer Town was out and about doing their diligence this morning. The land guard of Farmer Town has been delegated to withdraw from the city as ordered by their Governor. They are retreating to the shoal keeps on the cold side of Yoranthium. Most of Farmer Town including all males, females, and children and a caravan of supplies including heavy weapons are being taken to the keeps. It would appear that Governor Colusious plans to resist and defend at the keeps. That should supply ample defense and protection from the Mechanation's that are being slowed by search operations as they reach Farmer Town looking for citizens to capture."

The last mapmaker began to take over. "The situation is dire in the Grand City. Without direction many Grand City guard and citizens have began a move towards Sea Shore. With no leadership they have fallen to confusion and do not know of the dangers they are running into. More over the lightning strikes have intensified here in the Grand City and many blocks are burning out of control: Grand City will be lost simply by the intense lightning strikes and the many warehouses of magics and other combustible materials stored too closely. It is advised to vacate Grand City toward only three possible locations at this time. Farmer Town and face the Mechanation's. Flee to the outer Keeps for safety along with the Flight group. Or we can push towards Sea Shore and try to hold the last bastion defenses on the outskirts of Sea Shore. The Sea Shore command has completely collapsed, and the Depth Dwellers forces are rapidly advancing along with unknown horrors. It will be difficult to aid Sea Shore at the Last Bastion defenses unless we move to contain the aggressors, now!"

Rarailmuir was sorry to hear the bad news as it would seem this enemy had planned this invasion for some time and had a considerable stronger force. Unless there was the Mages guild and the Mages College of Yoranthium that could turn this tide, "What of the many mages we have on Yoranthium? Can we get portals to improve coordinating our efforts and improve our non-existing communications? Use the Mages to move our troops about through portals?"

One mapmaker began the report. "Mages College to the cold side of the grand city was destroyed. They were in the process of testing and the majority of all mages were in attendance at the college. Sadly over hundredth's of Mechanation's attacked the facility before the mages could fend for themselves as they have done in the past. The Mages College was simply overwhelmed and taken by surprise. They did put up a good fight and only destroyed about two hundredth's Mechanation's until all mages were killed. All other mages have gone missing and are presumed dead. Intelligence reports that there was dark magics and demons witnessed in some local mage killings." A very grim report and troubling as demons have been sighted in this war actively disabling Yoranthium's defenses.

"We have only one option at this point. We must fight for Yoranthium the best we can." Rarailmuir was determined to defend his new role as King. He just achieved his goal. Yoranthium was finally his. Even with Metiur looking surprised. "We must resist the invasion and push back. We will take our Grand City forces to the Last Bastion and we will protect, as many civilian's as possible. Even if Sea Shore falls we will hold them at the Last Bastion our last defense of Yoranthium."

Metiur was troubled. "My king we are out flanked. We have Mechanation's to our backs if we go to Sea Shores Last Bastion defenses. Not to mention reports of demons and other creatures unknown on Yoranthium porting into locations behind us."

"No, we don't Metiur. The Governor Colusious forces will occupy the Mechanation's. He will buy us time as those shoal keeps are many and have a labyrinth of defenses that could hold out against the Mechanation's and the invaders for hundredth's of years if need be. The problems of demons porting in require certain specific blood magics and I hold this charm I purchased

from a merchant with the local clerics. May the unborn God protect us and my parents rest in peace." Rarailmuir showed an artifact from old of Yoranthium just as fabled as the Yoranthium Kings sword.

The amulet was an old ancient simple metal necklace of bronze. Known as the,'Heaven's of Heart.' That depicted the sun with rays in a large rectangle and two hands unfolded on top a cross with a newly born child in the hands and the heart of Yoranthium on the child's body. There were demons to either side in the lower corners cowering in the symbology. "This necklace protects the wearer, and the wearers influences from demons preventing all under my protection from being harmed or even impacted by demonic portals. The demons are rendered inert and can only witness but are forbid to do anything to my charges or that which I have influence over. Such as my command and my host. This means wherever I go is protected from demon attacks. Yet doesn't mean they can't spy on us." Rarailmuir was certain he was right for some scholar of low merit told him so.

After the dragon attack Rarailmuir searched Yoranthium feverishly for a means to defend from demonic forces finding a medallion he believed was unique and powerful. He heard about a visiting sales person of mystic items in the marketplace and was amazed by the story and protective powers of the amulet. Purchased it out of belief and was certain of the amulets protective properties.

Metiur was amazed at this news for the demons really frightened Metiur from when he was a child. He had witnessed demons before and it was a reason he lost his parents long ago prior to the dragon attack. It was a terrifying incident and even some priests had been killed in the event. Metiur studied some of the metaphysical and mysterious concepts and could identify quite a few demons and terrifying monsters of the deep dark. He stopped his studies when he felt certain books pulling his mind apart of terrifying creatures that no elf should know of. Some of which was rumored to be part of the deep dark kingdoms.

"I've heard of this artifact and I'm glad you have it in your possession my King. There is a problem we need to address." Metiur said with some urgency.

"What would that be?" Inquired Rarailmuir.

"It's the Arch Nun. I think she's a shape shifting demon?" Metiur was a little shaky on his accusation.

"You aren't experienced in demonology are you now, Metiur?" Rarailmuir was curious.

"Yes I am. Demons took my parents and many priests of the unborn god in my youth. I studied trying to understand them. I believe this very night that the Arch Nun is a demon by her aura and shift in her eyes. I wasn't sure until I saw her tend the wounded and saw her lick some blood off her hand. She enjoyed it." Explaining what he saw.

"I believe you." Rarailmuir surprised Metiur once again. "I do not wear this because it's a fancy piece of religious jewelry. I wear this because I do not want my demons harming those I love and care for anymore. It is my penance and my attempt at forgiveness." There was a time Rarailmuir sought power as a younger male over eight years ago when he was twenty revolutions old. Back then he was less than he is now. Often when evil befalls the sea elves they turn to self-introspection to understand what they may have done wrong to bring such evil as demons among them. "Where is this Arch Nun right now?" Rarailmuir questions very concerned for those in immediate harm.

"I was watching her and then she went around a corner. I tried to follow however she disappeared. After searching I believe she may have gotten suspicious of me as I made a clumsy mistake on following her. She might have used a portal" With a shrug a little doubtful and unsure.

"Very well the demon must have left to report our conditions. We'll have to move out and leave this behind. This palace is safe from the lightning strikes. We can't take the injured they would likely slow us down and would be in considerable danger and a great liability. We'll keep the fire brigade, a handful of healing clerics, and a small detachment of a hundredth guards to protect this location." With some considerable thought Rarailmuir believed this plan would work.

"I recommend my king that we keep the citizen brigade with fifty guard. I doubt the citizens are in any shape to mount a decent defense at the Last Bastion." Metiur had a perfect solution for an imperfect problem of tactical logistics.

After some consideration the King agreed. "Yes that sounds good enough. Making tough decisions in war is not easy. Time is essential and we cannot be overwhelmed with the on coming depth dweller army and leave Sea Shore defenseless. Besides the last remains of the Grand City in a day or two will only be this Palace location after the city burns." He felt awful for leaving the small force behind and realized there was no other choice. Their only hope was holding the last bastion and haste was required.

In unison, "What of us the map makers my king. Surely we can not stay here as we are of high value to the enemy should they know of us." Said all six in unison.

"Metiur, have Fedarious lead the death guard to defend these six until we have a secure location at the Last Bastion." Rarailmuir had a contingency for everything.

"Yes, my king." Metiur was again impressed with his king for being so prepared.

"Keep them safe and out of combat. Once a location of safety is secured at the Last Bastion. Have yourself and the death guard report back to me. Fedarious is to lead the mapmaker's protection. You Metiur will stay at my side coordinating and commanding the other ranks." Rarailmuir seen Metiur nodding in agreement and turned to the Map Makers, "How many troops will we have for this?"

The six map makers quickly calculated. "With all the recent incoming guard and citizen's. The palace will have a hundredth fire brigade, two hundredth citizen conscripts, five to ten hundredth's injured, hundredth healing clerics, fifty guard."

Pausing and recalculating, "The king's force will be ten and five hundredth's, with over two hundredth's healing clerics, six map makers, twenty-nine death guard, one King and one support staff. We will be out numbered greatly but do expect to pick up two tens of hundredth's of Sea Shore guard. Plus the defenses of a fully stocked Last Bastion defense chain of keeps. Along with five hundredths guard already located with in the Last Bastion defenses."

"We got to make this stand. We will not let Yoranthium fall. Follow your king and we will be victorious." Rarailmuir was assuring confidence in his command. That was well received by Metiur.

Then from outside there was a commotion in the courtyard a conflict not from the making of the enemy but that of the Guard in a heated argument with a darker seedier side of the Yoranthium kingdom.

"Fedarious take charge of protecting the map makers, Metiur with me to the Courtyard Garden. We must see what the trouble is." Rarailmuir raced to the courtyard and there standing with a few hundredths of thugs and known criminal gang members was their crime boss Orichen.

Orichen was a rather heavyset dark skinned sea elf of larger stature by one king's hand taller than Rarailmuir remembered. He had beady eyes and a terrible scowl often smoking a glass pipe of some sort of drug. He had a scar on his chin and tattoo's of black ink up and down his bare arms and on his open chest covered with a black leather vest that had the symbol of his gang on the back. A terrifying undead demon skull with six inch incisors and claws, they were known as the Sea Ghouls. There were metal spikes on his shoulders of the vest. His hair consisted of three strait vertical standing Mohawks from back to front rigid red fins. He wore a large red sash that blew in the wind and two rather large pieces of heavy and over sized daggers. With black trousers tucked into black boots that folded over about half the boot length down his calf.

"I'm here to dispute the King for the throne of Yoranthium as is my right of heritage being the great, great, great God child of the brother of the founding King. You Rarailmuir are an impostor!" Orichen was hatefully looking at Rarailmuir and pulled out his two heavy daggers and spun them around effortlessly. Then pointing directly at Rarailmuir. "You will now die!"

"Any scribes. Write this down for the history of Yoranthium although we do not have time for this filth. Let it be known Rarailmuir the King of Yoranthium accepts the challenger and will teach him the errors of his way. It is time Orichen that you face true Justice with your death and become nothing to Yoranthium's future." Rarailmuir had many personal issues with Orichen. It couldn't be better having this opportunity to pay Orichen back for the early days of abuse and neglect Rarailmuir had at the hands of Orichen's crime syndicate as an orphan.

This was before he ran into King Sinderthion who intervened in his trial and transmuted the sentence from the prison to the royal guard. "Guard stand at the ready if any of the thugs interfere cut them down! This will be a more than fair fight in your favor Orichen. You are no King and you are no General and you are no Captain and you are not a well trained warrior as myself." Boasting Rarailmuir approached Orichen with his arms to his sides and palms of his hands out front. "Come get some." Rarailmuir motioned with his open palmed fingertips. No weapon in his hands. "I've been hoping for this for some time. Once you are defeated your men will fight for my cause. To the front lines and the Last Bastion defenses."

Orichen began his attack and with spinning blades he ran at Rarailmuir. Taking a quick downward slash. Rarailmuir just stepped to the side and grabbed Orichen's arm and let him continue on in his direction down and onto the ground continuing past Rarailmuir and tripping in his own momentum. Rolling head over heals and his three stiff standing fins fell to the side and one of Orichen's daggers spun out of his hand clattering for about two kings lengths until coming to a complete stop next to a guard standing at the ready with his spear.

"I'm telling you now Orichen you are not a match for me. You never were and never will be." Rarailmuir was looking at his fingernails grooming and not really caring too much as Orichen pulled himself off the ground. "King Sinderthion saved me years ago from your diseased gangs. While you learned how to lie, cheat and deceive. I learned to lead with love, truth and heart." Rarailmuir said getting back into his form ready for Orichen to make another mistake and attack him again. "Let's try that again."

Orichen was angry. He would not let Rarailmuir make a fool of him again. He was about to go and retrieve his dagger. The guard standing over the knife shook his head in disapproval and denial. "Using parlor tricks won't save you Rarailmuir. I've been killing people long before you came along."

"Only when they are tied down and immobilized and can't fight back. You are in truth a coward Orichen." Rarailmuir was taunting him.

Orichen charged at Rarailmuir again as was expected. This time Rarailmuir caught his wrist and twisted it awkwardly upside

down with Orichen's elbow facing up and now twisted behind his back. It wasn't a problem to remove his dagger as Rarailmuir had full control over Orichen's movements now. Rarailmuir pulled his sword with his left hand and flipped the sword effortlessly in his palm and moved it right to Orichen's throat.

"I'll give you a simple choice. Follow me as your King or die here right now Orichen. It would be a waste to end your life here when there is a battle waiting for us. The future of Yoranthium is at the Last Bastion. Make your choice Orichen, I need the conscripts and I need a forward patrol so I don't waste any of my valued guards as scouts." Rarailmuir kingly commanded Orichen to surrender and he obey.

"In the gang we are not generous. You should kill me as that is how we work." Orichen was still being defiant.

"Is that what you really want?" With a chuckle, he mockingly spoke to Orichen. "Or for once in your wasted life would you want to take that life and make a difference that matters?" Rarailmuir demanded a better answer with reasoned confidence.

Orichen looked down and saw his life glinting as lightning flashed on Rarailmuir's sword. He could see he was frightened and was about to die. He had made a mistake trying to think he was a King. Rarailmuir was by far a better King and Yoranthium would need him. "Very well my life is yours to command along with my gang." He sneered in a unassuring hesitant voice. "King of Yoranthium."

Knowing the difference of countrymen, friend, foe, enemies and those you can unite and tie to your side is an important quality of true leadership. "Then go collect your daggers and your gang and head past that breach in the wall and down the first street in the sunup direction. We the guard will follow you and expect a guard to command you from time to time as we head for the Last Bastion keeps. Call out or run back if you encounter trouble. You are not on your own, you have the Kings guard to back your men up." Hoping for some understanding and looking for any deception from Orichen. "I do not trust you and if anything seems off. My guard will terminate all of your gang. So be what I expect and we will get along famously. Who knows maybe you can become a hero instead of a zero."

"Yes, I understand and we are at your command my King." Orichen was sincere and then was released by Rarailmuir and he gathered his weapons and put them away. Turned to his host of thugs. "You heard your King we are on recon patrol and we will do as asked for Yoranthium." The thugs were shocked. Just like that they were conscripted into military service for Yoranthium under a different King that by the gangs own means was now their boss. Orichen lead the recon conscripts with his pride gone and his head low. They headed out the breach in the wall. Down the street as his king ordered.

Orders were given by Rarailmuir to Metiur, and Fedarious The units were established to protect the wounded to be left at the palace and Rarailmuir's and Metiur's main force was on the move past the breach and on the main road about sixteen kings lengths behind Orichen's gang.

The entire force under the King moved at the rate of the mapmakers to keep them well defended and protected. The mapmakers would become an essential asset for planning. That was the only way in this communication black out that the King would know how the defense of Yoranthium was going.

Lightning still rained down from the sky. Impacting buildings with large chunks of masonry landing haphazardly all round. Occasionally impacting into a thug or a guard and causing moments of chaos with quick emergency orders being barked to regain control; Assistance being rendered to fallen and injured thugs and guards alike. Sometimes the debris was so massive from the lightning strike that one or two would be entirely crushed and beyond saving. It was even more difficult as the lightning would strike flammable buildings and catch them on fire. Where females and children and frightened citizens could be heard perishing in the flames.

There were no side missions of heroics trying to save anyone in a damaged building there was no time. They simply lost their lives in the cause to defend Yoranthium. If the Last Bastion fell, Invasion of the entire island kingdom was certain, and all survivors would be captured and facing a worse fate by the brutal nature of the depth dwellers. The depth dwellers are ravenous creatures of appetite and there were more deadly and horrifying at sea experiences of innocent swimming sea elf's being eaten by depth

dwellers more than any other sea monstrosity attack on a sea elf that had ever been reported.

Rarailmuir didn't like losing so many citizens and guards, although he didn't mind losing the conscripted thugs. The thugs were monsters themselves in sea elf form as he was nearly one of them once long ago. In fact, it was Orichen that tried to force him to murder an innocent family and children. Orichen called it toughening. But it was becoming a monster. That is what it was a monster like a demon despised by every kind and loving person. This is not what Rarailmuir was.

Orichen thought Rarailmuir was weak for not doing what his loyal band of thugs did for their place at Orichen's side. They were all child murderers. They did terrible things to loving families. Forcing the tied and bound parents watch as their children died. Rarailmuir thought of this as he was forced to ignore pleas and cries for help down the streets to the Last Bastion. He wanted to save them but simply had to hold the advancing enemy as a priority. This was different than the gangs. As King he had to march his army to the real enemy and by doing so save more lives than those dying around him on this street. Their loss was for the security of Yoranthium. He had to convince himself.

Rarailmuir had plans for Orichen's gang of murderer's. Oh yes, simply killing Orichen would have been to kind. By the time they get to the first line of defense the conscripted thugs and Orichen would stand their ground and defend Yoranthium with their very lives before Rarailmuir would risk his own guard. Rarailmuir would watch as these cruel children of Orichen died before his eyes.

Over half those thugs pursued Rarailmuir in his early youth. When he was seventeen. Rarailmuir wasn't interested in a gang life. He had joined the guard and in need of a wife and child at the time. He did find the only other person that could help him become strong and the future King of Yoranthium. Even if she was somewhat cruel herself at least she did know how to love and had, well a dark heart but a heart, nonetheless. Those dark magics of hers and rituals made Rarailmuir strong. He felt tainted by sin back then a curse that the Unborn God's clerics could not remove. He turned to dark magics, blood magics that made him feel as if his soul was released from a prison of weakness.

Rarailmuir had ordered the weapons helmets and shields removed from any fallen guards. Having collected six helmets, he went back to Fedarious. Fedarious had been doing a fine job protecting the mapmakers. "I know these helmets do not aid the Map makers abilities however they must keep their heads safe. Have them put on these helmets and these gloves. Here are some additional water supplies. I cannot stress how invaluable their abilities are to Yoranthium. You're doing a splendid job Fedarious."

"Why thank you my King the death guard is always at your service and defense." Fedarious was grateful for the consideration of his Kings attentiveness.

"Metiur, when we get to the Last Bastion." Whispering just to communicate with Metiur. "I want you to ensure the conscripted criminals stand the front lines and the front guard. I do not want to sacrifice any of our guard. The Sea Ghoul conscripts are all baby killers and family murderers. Its time for them to do their duty for Yoranthium's defense and it should be them fighting or dying first."

"I agree my King I will put any of them running from battle to the tip of our spears. Yes, they will fight for the lives of our people or die over the next few days. I will see to it." Metiur knew these awful criminals and their ways of gang membership and was intolerant of their evils. This is why Metiur often went on patrol in the red district for he did seek out justice for those harmed by such evil.

Yoranthium

Book One: Lost Hope

Chapter Nine: Flight Part Two: Flight and Fright of the Impundalu

By Mark P. Bromley

Lightning strikes and birds take flight. Demons become manifestation of seduction into flights of fantasy often infect the youth with lustful wants and desires beyond their control. Lightning breaks the sky, and the flicker of lights plays tricks in the darkness on those who take shelter thinking that thick walls will be their defenses. Often failing to realize they should have looked up to the lighting in the sky.

Kumithra awoke on a soft bed that was more of a bench, inside the Gypsy cart. She wondered if what she experienced was just a nightmare. It seemed so real and she remembered not being as queenly in dealing with the nightmare of her mother and father dying. She could feel that she ran out of tears and was dehydrated. Noticing a decanter of water nearby she quickly drank from it greedily while water spilled from her mouth.

Remembered being completely confused, sad and weirdly odd in her actions. Wiping the water off her chin with the cloth of the gloves she was wearing. She remembered breaking Huspecia's heart and that of Thernya. She really hurt Huspecia, forgetting that even as an orphan she is really her truer than a biological sister. Huspecia was as much the former king and queens child as was she.

Kumithra was worried she had strained their relationship over being so selfish and uncaring. She looked around and realized she was inside a Gypsy cart where she fell asleep so exhausted from her confused tantrum of losing her parents. Her eye's ached from the tears that had dried on her face. Using some of the water from the decanter to quickly clean her face incompletely not aware of the dust and ruin of her makeup hidden by the oversized helmet she was wearing.

Coming to the realization that she and Huspecia are now the same. Orphaned. Fortunately, Huspecia has Bronanes, Kumithra has no one at her side to fill that gaping and painful hole of loss in her heart. Rarailmuir was not at her side and they were not wedded this day. She was alone in a dark wooden box of the Gypsy cart that felt she was locked away in a coffin. Like some nightmare she couldn't wake from.

It was real her mother and father are dead and she was such a frightened child. She was sad and could no longer cry. Her tears were for the moment gone for she selfishly thought of only her needs and wants. When her kingdom was under attack, and many were suffering. Many suffered just like her four revolutions ago from the deadly dragon attack. She sat in the darkened gypsy cart feeling very low as the helmet she found that was to be Rarailmuir's flopped forward on her head covering her eyes. That helmet was too big for her head with her dirt encrusted ponytail

buns that held it for the most part in place the last most comforting worldly belonging of her would be husband and love.

Pushing the helmet up so she could see. She pondered on what she should do next. They had stopped and an orderly sound of voices could be heard. She heard something of the outer keep. Perhaps that's where they are at the outer keep. The cart was motionless and this means they had stopped likely for the on coming night.

Getting up from where she was sleeping moments ago. She looked around and couldn't find Thernya or Huspecia. Where could they have gone? How long was she asleep? Then she heard Thernya outside of the sealed cart. Kumithra felt she was intentionally locked inside purposefully hidden from sight for the way she acted. It was right of her protectors to do so. The dragon caused her people so much of the same suffering she was going through today.

"The Queen is asleep. What she has been through took a heavy toll on her mind. She could be a sleep way past dark into the morning. You sea guards must protect the Queen and guard this gypsy cart let no one but I, Huspecia and Lord Bronanes enter this cart upon penalty of death." Thernya said with implied expression of authority. The Guard did their duty and obeyed. "I have to find the keeps resources and fetch water and cleaning cloths, food and drink." Wanting to know if the guard understood their duties. "For the Queen."

"For the Queen!" Repeated the sea guard.

Then she heard Bronanes. "Huspecia. The keeps custodian guard had informed me that the defenses have been upgraded since last I was here. The citizens are all being treated and cared for and have been moved to the inner defensive hall under the keep. They are being provided and cared for. Our guard is now augmenting Keep defenses. However my lady, my dear sweet Huspecia, I have something to show to you and I need to show you the upgrades. Please follow me my love."

"You do, is it something wonderfully beautiful? I know you my husband you are up to something." She giggled. The cart shook and that meant Huspecia had gotten off the Gypsy cart. You could hear their feet clacking on the cobble stone floor as they both hurried and walked away.

'Where could they be going? I got to follow and find out. They are up to something and I want to know what it is. Sounds romantic and they haven't been blessed by their Queen.' Kumithra was thinking. She saw a dark brown blanket and wrapped herself in it like a hooded robe. Then she spied on the floor of the gypsy wagon a door on the floor. She saw an indented latch and tugged at it. It would not open so she pulled harder and still nothing.

She was thinking and saw some curved scratches along the side and a lock ahead of the latch. She didn't have a key and she was running out of time. Then she remembered reading a book about thieves. She was a princess. A noble, and none the less was entertained about the high adventures of a thief's life. Her mother would scold her for looking at such books. Yet her mother had so many in her room on the lower shelves. She read them in secret not even Huspecia knew. She remembered something about hairpins and locks. Hairpins made for good tools for picking simple locks such as the one on this hatch beneath her feet.

Oh, she had many hairpins in her hair. Reaching up and under her ridiculous helmet she found a hairpin sure enough. She did a little bending of the hairpin into a tension pick and went over to the lock. She stuck the pin in the hole and worked it around quickly just as the forbidden book informed her. It worked with a click of success her smile widened her eyes became large and her heart jumped with excitement.

She had picked her first lock and it was ecstasy. She never had so much joy she wanted to pick more locks and realized that would waste time only needing this one. Time is essential so she grabbed the latch and turned it in the direction of the scratches and sure enough there was another click. Success again. Then she opened the hatch with dirt encrusted on its bottom from outside. Lifted till the hatch leaned back on its hinges.

Kumithra carefully dropped down from the hatch of the Gypsy cart. Oh, was she good only a little bit of the dirt on the bottom of the wagons door hit the ground and got on her blanket. She was low to the ground with her hands to the side on the floor and back legs carefully bent. All those years in the exercise of stretching her limbs in the training of yoga paid off quite nicely. She was almost one with the shadow of the carriage and almost flat enough to be the floor. She would tell herself in her mind. 'Be one

with the shadows.' As it echoed in her head she swore she heard her mothers voice comforting her and proud of her.

She was looking around and noticed seven guards around the cart and there were carts and buggies and horses scattered very close to one another. Lot's of guards and lots of people still being instructed and arranged passage through the keep and the reception hall under the keep. Guards at the doors to the stairs and somewhere tending to light magics to improve the light conditions as the dark clouds above the keep were getting darker as the sun was dropping.

The guards were sure to notice her if she came out from under the gypsy cart. She needed a distraction. Looking around she saw one. There were several metal amphoras of liquid, maybe water, maybe milk, which knew? Hopefully they are empty she thought. Looking around she saw a large rock embedded in some mud on the wheel well. She dug it out and it was of good weight. So she threw it. Missed, she hit a passing female in the leg as it bounced off a far wall. The female cried out in pain and it distracted a guard who tended too her. Almost and nearly making eye contact where Kumithra had been hiding. It was close as the guard blamed it on some silly child that must of thrown the rock.

So she looked for another rock from under her carriage and spotted it right on the bottom of the hatch. She reached up and pried it off the hatch. The hatch came slamming down and nearly caught her fingers. Dust poured off the bottom of the door onto her and the ground. Upon impacting the ground the dust rose and hit her in the face and nearly caused her to sneeze. She couldn't help it the dust made her stifle her sneeze as she made a really high pitch terribly funny type of sneeze like a high pitched mouse whimper. The hatch had made a loud thud and the guard turned to look at the gypsy cart.

"Queen must of have woke up." The guard remarked jokingly.

"Yeah, she might of fell out of bed, as it's not a queens bed. Me thinks." Other guards started to laugh and made other jokes.

Which irked Kumithra. She was tempted to chastise the guards for making fun of her and restrained herself. She had to get to that door and up the stairs and she was lagging far behind Huspecia. Carefully she took the second rock and threw it at the

stacked amphoras. An audible ping could be heard as the amphora was empty and it shook violently yet nothing happened.

The rock just bounced off and hit the guard in the head who was assisting the lady. That guard was looking around looking for the child who threw it. "All right kid, come on out that's enough with the rocks!" The guard went in the wrong direction and was terrible at deductive reasoning as to where the rock came from.

This was getting time consuming and there was a need for another rock. She found one more rock apparently not hard to find. Prying it off the underbelly of the cart and this was the biggest and heaviest she had yet found. After carefully aiming she hit the same amphora and it teetered as the rock fell next to it and after several moments the amphora fell to the ground. Creating a cascading effect of destruction. The entire stack could be heard creaking and moaning audibly as many people near that area started to look at the stack. Suddenly the amphoras began tumbling and falling to the floor. Not all of them were empty. Some were water.

A huge spill was in progress as amphora after metal amphora emptied it's content and hit the ground making a huge mess with all the guard looking over at the disaster along with the other people and spooking the horses. That distracted even the guard around her wagon that made a perfect opening. Where Kumithra could stick to the shadows and make for the door. Noticing the door guard had moved away from the door making the perfect opening for her to go unnoticed.

Kumithra in her dark brown robe stayed close to the ground, stayed in the shadows and made her way to the door from under cart after cart. Like a shade of night embracing the floor and shadow. What she learned paid off from her forbidden books on thieving. No one took notice as she scrambled up the steps and into the door stopping just inside to the left leading up the spiral steps. No one seen her and she was awesome. "Yeahay me." She whispered, as her flexibility physical training was very useful.

Kumithra was not as stealthy as she had hoped. There was a kid named Dueith that noticed the Queens antics, he's been enamored with the queen since he saw her. Making his own plans to capture the heart of his love as he watched her wagon. Dreaming that they would be inseparable friends. What did he know, but just

tales he heard spun for he was was the age of seven revolutions old. Confusing infatuation with what he barely understood was love.[9] He watched her cart hoping to see her again. This is how he witnessed the entire stealthy events of the greatest girl he ever known unfold.

She didn't get in the door fast enough because a guard the one looking for the kid with the rocks. Did notice the Queen slip into the door. He was going in that direction thinking he found the kid. Yes he found the one throwing the rocks but didn't know it was the Queen.

Dueith saw his desired heartthrob was in danger. He picked up a rock throwing it with as much force as he could muster. Struck the guard in the back of his helmet to the left. The guard forgot about the door he found the kid throwing rocks. Turned with an angry scowl towards the child. All the child said next was, "For the Queen!!!" As Dueith took off in a direction away from the door and made the guard chase him. The guard caught him easily for his legs were longer and stronger than Dueith's and grabbed him by the ear for justice to be served. Dueith was hoping that perhaps tomorrow him and the Queen could be friends and play outside.

The Queen realized she wasn't as stealthy as she thought. She'll make it up to Dueith. She thought as she saw his apprehension sneaking a peak back out the door. Perhaps when there is time she will have to pardon him in a royal fashion. That would be later for now Kumithra had a mission. She had to catch up to Lord Bronanes and Huspecia as they were ahead of her.

There were many steps to climb. On the way up Kumithra looked out an open door to the outside wall and thought she saw a flash of bluish lightning and a nude male. He was pink in color and had the oddest eyes. Kind of looked like Rarailmuir in her mind. She stopped for a moment and was wanted to go to him and then like a flash of lighting he disappeared. Some guards appeared at the far end on patrol. She shook her head and went up the landing thinking she was seeing things. Then again another open door and

[9] An illustration of bad perverted child assessments in the 2020's that falsely claimed children and minors should be gender altered by a greedy selfish medical tyranny trying to profit by harming minors. Children take time to understand concepts of gender, love and affection and are immature and innocent in their early years.

flash, just like lighting a yearning nude pink skinned Rarailmuir, she wanted so desperately to reach out and feel his embrace. Just like that another flash and the naked male disappeared and she heard the guards.

"Did you see some strange lighting flashes followed by something like a elf sized pink bird?" A guard was saying and Kumithra could hear him as his voice echoed up the stairs.

The other guard replied. "Birds? I don't care much for those fowl things. Get it, Fowl. Never mind. I think you are seeing things and the lightning is playing tricks on you." Making light of the absurd question from the first guard. "This lightning hasn't stopped since this cloud hovered over the land. At least the sun set is nice."

Kumithra believed she was still feeling the effects of this morning on her very soul and mind. Nonetheless. Up the stairs she went to her goal the secret rendezvous of Bronanes and Huspecia. Upon reaching the upper battlement she noticed the heavy stone cover to the stair well was open and she could hear Bronanes speaking to Huspecia.

"...lovely is this not? I thought you should see this wonderful sight." The storm clouds stopped short of the Rim Shoals Mountains that surrounded the island caldera and didn't cover all the farmer's fields. "I saw the sun going down and as the sun touches the Shoals Mountains. You can see this rather strikingly beautiful sunset."

Bronanes and Huspecia were watching the sun drop and touch the Rim Mountains of Yoranthium. It was a sight to behold and one of unmatched tropical landscape, like an oil painting mixing into the darkening sky and clouds while the stars began to peak. The vermilion and purple and pinks of the sky were something not to be missed a once in a lifetime scenic experience of fantastic wonder and amazement. The sun touched the tropical trees of Green, blues, gold's, and various sakura trees pink leaves in the distance after making striking high-resolution silhouettes of the mountain rim.

Turning the mass expanse of the farmlands into a paradise of vibrant picturesque golden glowing fields of sunset the most picturesque romantic time of the day. With the typical shimmer of the island and the dark clouds creating high contrast and well

blended subtlety. It would take a master painter to paint this scene. This beyond words sunset landscape would not last long. The other worldly twilight sunset was a blessing to the mind and heart of anyone who seen it. There where only two times in a day that the sun touched the world creating the warm glows of the most artistic visions created by nature the art of the dawn and the dusk the golden times of the day.

Bronanes and Huspecia were now silent and caught up in the moment of the most beautiful sunset they had seen compared to the horrors they had witness after a fantastic wedding. Bronanes right hand was holding Huspecia's left hand with their wedding binding loosely tying them together and only shared in their palms. Just above the waist their other hands were holding one another's backs. Pressing them close and in contact while watching the sunset they were getting ready for a kiss. The kiss to seal they're love and seal their marriage hesitating and waiting for the word to commence.

Yet it would not be official. Kumithra was just in time. As Queen it was her duty to preside over such moments and the scenery would make this one of the best if not the best in the entire world of Ishormot moments. It was an honor that fell to her and it was an honor and a gift she had to see for her mother and father in spirit would have to know. Know that at least one out of two daughters on this very costly wedding day had the Royal blessing that the vows were sealed, and they were now fully bound to one another.

As Bronanes was looking into Huspecia's eyes their very souls were already intertwined in a commitment deeper than physical love or expression could explain. Suddenly they felt two hands clasp the bottom and top of their bound hands and pull them looking away from the sunset. It was Kumithra, smiling in her over sized helmet that almost fell in front of her eyes hiding and concealing the dust on her face.

"I your Queen can not let you commit with out my authority. I Queen Kumithra of Yoranthium officiate this blessed union of the Captain of the Yoranthium Guard Lord Bronanes, to the Queens Protector Huspecia who is a sister too me to be wed this day. The vows have been stated, no challengers have protested for Huspecia's hand. I pronounce you both Husband and Wife before

our God who is yet to be born. You may now kiss the bride as decreed by the blessing of those who came before and will come after by the order of Queen Kumithra of Yoranthium. You may now kiss the Bride." Kumithra gave a gentle smile as what began softly and ended in a crescendo.

With that Kumithra let go of their hands and both Bronanes and Huspecia looked at their Queen and accepted her statement with a blush and a smile. Glad that the Queen of Yoranthium arrived in time to bless their matrimony. Stating at the same time. "We are honored to have your blessing before our God to be born, Queen Kumithra of Yoranthium." Then they turned smiling to one another and a little giddy before the setting sunset. As Kumithra's words meant everything to Bronanes and Huspecia was happy for she was recognized finally as the Queen's sister.

It was the most exceptional moment Kumithra had been dreaming and hoping for her sister and herself even if she would be denied. One out of two weddings at least ended well and that isn't bad. Huspecia and Bronanes should have their marriage blessed by the Queen for they had earned it with a long dedication of love and commitment to one another. This is only a minor repayment for all of Kumithra's blind selfishness to acknowledge the marriage this day.

Bronanes and Huspecia's smiles faded to a serious look. A look only one of love, of the heart and of desire as they locked their eyes upon each other, and their souls combined in bliss. Desire to commit their souls to one another grew ever so stronger. Their heart rates were racing. Even with all the days they spent together. They never frolicked or truly kissed and were inseparable best friends forever. But now they are lovers. Blood pumped to their faces each passing millisecond was a lifetime of love in the making. Their very souls had bared all and there was caution. Terrified of a defining moment. Could they even kiss one another, and would it be to their liking? The terror of this moment for our fated lovers was the most horrifying moment of great anxiety.

The anticipation was swelling in Kumithra. Maybe she was standing too close. She simply walked backward away from the lovebirds. Time agonizingly slowly pressed on and was it ever going to happen? Maybe something was wrong it was taking too long. Kumithra wanted it to take time and be memorable romantic first

kiss, but this was too long of a wait she would have preferred the collision of two celestial fast moving objects to this long overly exaggerated wait.

It didn't matter for Bronanes and Huspecia the world had disappeared they lived in the sunset becoming the very nature of life of love and of the heart. As their heartbeats synchronized the deeper and the deeper they explored one another's eyes and the depth of their souls. They remembered all the love they shared and every moment from the beginning of their life together up to this moment. Smiling as the day they did when seeing each other from their infancy on the deck of the Admirals ship the Mundrunche.

They yearned for each other's touch and lusting to know the sensation of touching each other's lips. They could hear one another taking deep breaths and could from their hands holding one another feel the anxiety and the trembling of their nervousness. A nervousness and fear and dread they had panic growing in their very souls for this was a first for them both a defining moment and testament of their lifetime.

Then Bronanes let go of Huspecia's hands. His right hand reached behind her back. Her left dropped lifelessly to the side. His left went behind her head, supporting her head and neck. Her right arm grabbed behind his back as her left leg lifted and wrapped around his right leg and flexed tightly. Bronanes was moving his mouth closer to hers while turning his nose to the right and she turned her nose slightly to the right. They could smell each other breathing somewhat heavy with desire and a little hint of lust and ecstasy of the moment. Their lips began to pucker as their tongues moistened their lips preparing for what was to become.

Their eyes closing in prayer that this one kiss would be divine and blessed by the celestial heavens. A long pause again just the width of a seed between their lips. Their hearts were touching, the warmth of their body's aching for one another. The pain they had suffered waiting for this moment a moment of truth was overwhelming as Kumithra held her hands to her heart. Right over left she could feel their heart beat in hers for this kiss was better than any romance she had ever read. Each and every romance books all claim to be the best kiss, do they not? Yet in the end are just words this moment words would fail in translation. Only the

feeling and the emotion and the art of life could ever exist for just this precious amount of time.

This kiss was beyond words it was beyond experience. It was the first it was the last it was the beginning of the end the Alpha and the Omega. This kiss would define eternity and infinity of time space. It would be the building block of husband and wife and would establish the very definition of the children they would bring and raise in this world. They paused because there would only be this one kiss. After that, their love would have to compare to this one kiss unto their dying days.

The long hundredths of revolutions of the seasons had come to an end and motion resumed and that too took another eternity the lips that were partially open moistened by their tongues. In a hunger and pain of yearning, wanting, and jousting for the proper posture. Relaxed, flexed and rived with a supple trembling as they were feeling each other's gentle breath on each other's lips, and they felt the outer tips touch and pressed into the soft succulent meaty flesh with the taste of their own salt of their nervousness and panic. It was nice as their lips touched.

Eyes tightened being closed. They could feel air from their nose take the place of air from their mouths touching their skin and their lips. The last of the day's sun dropped behind the Shoal Mountains. Creating a burst of transcending light across Yoranthium and their world. Everything becomes radiant with gold light energy of the cosmos filling their souls with serendipity.

What seemed like eternity were just a few moments. For Bronanes and Huspecia it was eternity and a lifetime living together. The dusk began to turn to night. They both began pulling with vacuum gentle on each other's lips. They loved the taste of each other's flesh and breath and saliva as a gentle ply of tongues touched each other's lips. Suggesting they were both ready for a more intimate encounter and that would consummate their marriage and truly bind them for a life of happiness.

It was the most exquisite kiss and this telling and witnessing can only be a tribute to such a feat.

As all great moments in life do have their time and just as they began the same time dilation of pulling away from a kiss takes place. As their eyes opened and they look into each others eyes with knowing of the feeling of real love and compassion and the heated

moment they had been counting on. At first they didn't want to betray the kiss for they are concerned of the other's feelings and their face is of no expression.

A simple blink of the eye that flutters like a stationary butterfly wink at one another. Then the cheeks grow rosy and begin to blend as a subtle corner of their mouths transform in unison into a smile of acceptance, happiness, glee, and mutual commitment. Knowing they are blessed and dreaming of the future they would wonderfully share. Wishing to be by one another's side forever even when apart. By this time their hearts have slowed their beats are timed and synchronized. Carefully and tenderly Bronanes lifts Huspecia and straitens her back up. Her leg reluctantly let's go of his for her flower had moistened and thickened as did his pistil.

The final moments of the sun set left a glowing golden glow on the surrounding of the end of the kiss. It was like two angels have wed and their halos are now visible. Kumithra's work as the Queen was done and now she simply wanted to leave the lovebirds alone. And went back down the steps to not intervene or spy on her friends no more. Bronanes and Huspecia will have to figure out on their own what to do next.

Kumithra soon looked out a defensive opening and noticed multiple flashing of lightning moving about in the sky. It was lightning but moved like birds. It was odd lightning she never seen before. She simply continued down the stairs. She was feeling love, holding her heart with both hands on top of her chest. She yearned for her hero, her champion, and her love Rarailmuir. She was a female and didn't know the comfort of a male. She had just witnessed one of the best kisses she would have wanted.

Reaching the landing she noticed the door was open and a flash of lightning got her attention. She looked out the door catching the red round eyes of a bird. Not a bird, it was a nude male of pinkish skin, with blood red crimson hungry golden sunfire Rarailmuir mesmerizing eyes looking at her. Calling to her. She was ensorcelled and realized he was there for her. She couldn't resist and like in a trance she opened her arms and walked toward the nude pink Rarailmuir just waiting for her hug and her touch.

As she got closer it wasn't Rarailmuir. It was a male sized bird a demon bird known as Impundalu. Sometimes called a

Lightning bird of myth not native to Yoranthium. They could shape shift as a nude male and enchant females on the Lollygag islands at night in a storm. So were the myths of the resort of the Lollygag islands to keep women from staying out late at night and prevent unsavory nocturnal criminal ventures. Ventures ruining a paradise resort from falling into a den of demons such as the red district.

Lightning was a special talent and the Impundalu followed the harrowing of a storm. It was said to prey on unwed women and was a vampire feeding on their blood. Before Kumithra could come to her senses. Just like lightning, her arms were in its powerful claws and she was being lifted off the balcony. Without a scream for she believed she was in her loves arms being swept off her feet.

A guard had noticed the abduction by the lightning bird demon. He rang the bell. "The Queen is under attack by flying demons, the sky is full of these flying monsters. Archers the ready!!! To arms, to arms!!!" Alarm bells began clanging in the distance.

Just like that. Before Bronanes and Huspecia got the chance to further their love they were brought to duty once again. Readjusting themselves and grabbing for their weapons and armor they had discarded. The clamor of the guards rose in ferocity. The birds descended from the heavens and arcs of lightning and blinding flashes took so many guards by startled and frightened surprise.

The moment Huspecia got to her chain knives she let one lose towards one of the birds. Slicing it through the belly as it fell to the ground in front of her screeching in its death throws. Knocking her off her feet with a last discharge of lightning before dying. As Huspecia got to her feet with Bronanes help. She saw the dead over sized demon bird crackle with lightning on the inside turning it's outer body into a blackened husk that crumbled as the lightning in the body itself shot towards the sky leaving a crumbling black pile of dust. The chain blades from Thernya were a blessed holy weapon and highly effective on demons.

The guards below were struggling to spear the birds as the birds darted by lightning from one random position to another. Not even the archers could get a clear and clean shot and were now pointing their bows randomly and firing blindly. It didn't matter

much, for these birds could not be harmed with normal weapons. Any successful shots simply caused an Impundalu to scream and disorientate the guards while continuing their attacks on guards at lightning speeds. Several guards on the pulpits and tops of the keep got pushed over the sides and caught in mid air and torn apart as the lightning birds flocked and used their claws to shred and long beaks to feed on their blood. Shredding them in their claws fighting over the bodies in mid flight.

Oddly Kumithra was noticed to be limp as her captor was carrying her further and further away. The birds were not interested in tearing her apart. Kumithra was being abducted and it was obvious a dark power was responsible as the bird headed to the cold sunup side of the city in a deliberate direction for some unknown purpose. With a sense of urgency several Impundalu followed.

At the bottom of the keep a female on Wertomeer rode out from the keep. It was Thernya. When Thernya found out Kumithra was abducted. Her stubby swollen legs moved faster than any guard. It was like Thernya was young and she spun around to avoid several elves in the way and it was like an acrobat and went strait to the seas stallion. Wertomeer was fast and gave pursuit of the birds that have by now flew so far away Kumithra was on her own. Thernya rode with desperation and intention her eyes full of purpose, duty and blood lust. She knew what was going on and what must be happening. She was planning her attack for she had an idea who was behind this night of demons and Impundalu of all unholy things and doings.

Bronanes could hear the sound of Wertomeer and grabbed Huspecia as she spun her chain daggers over her head keeping the Impundalu from getting close for the silver laced daggers were blessed and deadly to the vampire birds of lightning.

They both took a look and noted the direction Thernya took off in.

"We got to have the guards deal with these demonic creatures and we got to get out of here and follow Thernya for our Queen is in danger." Bronanes exclaimed to Huspecia as she nodded in agreement while she cut down two more Impundalu. They didn't wish to fail their standing order to protect the Queen.

More guards and archers came to the top of the keep shooting arrows and swinging their spears at the quick moving lightning birds. One of the guards got too close to the edge and three Impundalu slammed into him and pulled him from the roof top screaming as other Impundalu fed off him to a bloody and grisly end.

They were making no impact in the Impundalu numbers. The same couldn't be said of the Impundalu as they took one and another guard out with impunity. The Impundalu accomplished what they came for and one by one. Those that got their fill of elven blood with a bolt of lightning took off in the direction Kumithra was abducted.

The remaining dwindling numbers of Impundalu were a menace. The battlements of the keep were becoming a disgusting sight of blood and entrails and feasting vampire birds. Dabensir along with a squad of sea guard then charged out on the battlements with glowing and magics imbued spears, long swords and arrows flying from enchanted bows. The magics blessed weapon oils were effective and designed to deal with demonic hosts with oil's of blessing, incantations to ward off evil and runes of demon slaying.

Then some other guards under the command of Leorth arrived out another door. Swinging demon oiled blessed weapons and shooting more demon oil blessed arrows. The remaining birds had their fill of blood for the night and they ascended like lightning into the dark skies above following the rest of their flock.

Bronanes was thankful for the quick thinking of Dabensir and Leorth. Acknowledging their efforts for saving the terrible evening and preventing the loss of more lives. The battlements were now caked in entrails and blood and torn and shredded guards. "Dabensir and Leorth." Bronanes rushed to them in a hurried activity. "I'll need you two to take charge of the keep as I and Huspecia have to follow in the direction of Thernya and find out what has become of the Queen."

Leorth was a little uncertain, "I don't know much or how to run the sea guard, and I'm just the operator of the carriage house."

"You'll be fine Leorth, like we use to play as children. You have all the experience you need and we will be triumphant this night." Dabensir was proud of his friend Leorth.

"What shall we do once daylight comes Captain Bronanes?" Leorth was worried if Bronanes never returned.

"If we do not return by the morning. Head for the caves immediately. It is more defensible than this location. Get everyone to the ships. Wait a couple of days and then Dabensir will take command of the Mundrunche and the fleet and take our refugees to Forumth." These would become the standing orders of the captain of the guard.

"There are some nearby storages of farms at the caves. You will use to discard the carriages once we reach the caves to hide our migration. I do believe we have enough ships for all our citizens and even livestock ships capable of holding the horses as transports. We should be capable of accomplishing our goal, captain Bronanes." Said Dabensir.

Not much needed to be said, as Bronanes had picked a fine elf to be his right hand. Dabensir had likewise found another who he could count on. In this the chain of command was not broken. Bronanes felt confident in his decision to leave the keep and have him and Huspecia track down Thernya and thus their Queen.

Bronanes and Huspecia descended the stairs of the Keep to the first floor and found a couple of horses that were the best rested. Gathered some needed supplies and spoke with healing clerics to acquire a small parcel. Should they have need of medical aid.

This consumed quite a bit of time. Bronanes and Huspecia together had saved considerable time working closely together. That they were soon mounted and out the main gate and down the path that Thernya had taken. The trail left by Wertomeer's haste was obvious and clear to follow even in the darkened darkest night. Above far out of sight was the moon that would be in eclipse soon on this very darkest of the dark and utterly darkest of nights.

Thernya rode Wertomeer rather roughly and you could hear the sea stallion's breath become raspier and heavy and difficult. This was King Sinderthion's pride and was rode into a few minor conflicts the one on Forumth. Wertomeer is an intelligent steed and known of it's purpose. Not only did it understand Thernya it's goal was to serve the queen the daughter of his former master.

Wertomeer could sense Thernya's attention and could smell the birds in the air and the scent of Kumithra. Following that Wertomeer knew better than Thernya where the queen was being taken. It was going to be a long ride at night and there are so many dangers that they would have to proceed with throwing caution to the wind. Speed and haste of the utmost importance and in the dark for there was no telling how many other kinds of demons Dresdie had placed in their path. Wertomeer was a deep-sea stallion and the dark was more illuminated in his changing opal eyes.

Thernya knew long ago it was a mistake to let Dresdie live on Yoranthium yet King Sinderthion was compassionate, too understanding and much too forgiving. The former king wanted to believe people of sinister intentions could through the process of mercy find a way to better salvation. Some souls are beyond salvation. Thernya knew Dresdie, she had grown up with Dresdie. She once believed Dresdie had a kind heart. But that was when they were young. When they use to live across the sea on the main lands of the country of Illustrom and studied minor magics from one another. When they were similar to Kumithra and Huspecia.

Thernya hoped she was not noticed leaving the keep for this is her mission and her mission alone. The last thing she wanted was for her pupils Kumithra or even Huspecia to die at the hands of a wicked and twisted demon witch Dresdie. That could be the likely fate of Thernya. Tonight was a ritual night of the darkest darkness desires.

Yoranthium

Book One: Lost Hope

Chapter Ten: Fight Part Two: Attack of the Impundalu

By Mark P. Bromley

War is ugly. When caught unprepared choices must be made and those choices all lead to many dying. This part becomes quite messy and for those to squeamish you might want to skip this chapter. The horrors of war are most fowl.

She was one of the greatest healing clerics in Yoranthium. Spent years learning her craft at the Mages College and with the Healing Clerics. It was her duty and heroic destiny that she decided to remain behind to care for the injured in the Palace of the King. She had worked tirelessly and then needed a break from all the blood, wails and cries of injury. She walked toward the dais and the broken thrones. Was surprised to see multiple lightning flashes from overhead. Not as intense as the big blasts of lightning destroying the city just small flickering flashes. In a way it was beautiful to see the lightning and no rain just occasional gusts of wind that would subside. Then abruptly pick back up terrifying everyone. Inside the palace the doors protected them from the harrowing unpredictable tempests. Fortunately the winds magically seemed to die down and didn't return for a long time.

Then another flash in front of her and this was the most handsome nude male of her dreams. Her lover wasn't far away. He was still tending to the wounded. Or was he? As she become ensorcelled in the magic of the moment. She looked at the nude male before her and saw his face and brilliant longing blood red hazel eyes, loving his pink skin. Working her way down to see the feather that tickled her fancy and what she really wanted to see.

With no disappointment, she was with her lover and he was motioning her to come closer. She took one step after another. Trying to excite her lover she had wanting to be intimate with for the past season. She was getting closer and closer and then more lightning flashed next to her as she felt heat. She loosened her Yukata and exposed more of her breasts. Perhaps she was dreaming because she was with three well endowed males all of which was her lover and wildest desire. She began to loosen her clothing even more generously and share her love with her identical triplet set of lovers.

Letting her right hand touch the abdomen of her lover to the right and reached out to embrace her lover on the left. While baring her nude breasts to her lover in front and licking her lips and biting the lower lip ever so seductively. The lover in front of her leaned in to give her a kiss on the neck. Feeling a little discomfort for he was a bad kisser, with the trickle of wetness down her body. Was he drooling? She still wanted more not

noticing the blood trickling down her body from her neck while she began feeling the same terrible kissing from her other two lovers.

Her real lover another healing cleric of youth and lower rank, who had been looking for her as it was time for them to have nourishment. Stumbled upon the grisly sight. She was half naked and being fed on by three elf-sized birds. Pink birds with red eyes and long beaks stuck into the neck and chest of his love.

With blood trickling down her nude body onto the clothing barely hanging to her arms and lower body. He let out a scream calling his loves name. Instantly there were more bolts of lightning around him and he felt lifted into the air as his love was like wise and they both met a terrible end as lightning flashed birds showed up with their talons ripping and tearing at them severing their limbs. Exposing the entrails and innards. The Impundalu fed on them like a feeding frenzy just like the sharks in the ocean were known to feed.

Then many more flashes of lightning entered into the palace from the Mechanation's hole in the dome. Even more started entering through the open hall arched doors. More of the Impundalu were also flashing like lightning outside around the civilian conscripts and the remaining guard. The commanding sergeant ordered his men to go back to back defend and stand their ground for they were under attack on all sides.

It was no use, the guards were encased in metal mithreal armor on the chest, on their arms and shoulders and a helmet. The lightning birds simply struck instantly in the center. Causing a chain reaction that would break the guards from their back to back formations in an explosion of electrical shock. A few would fly about half a king's length to their death while others would be knocked down receiving lightning burns and trying to recover from electrical shock and disorientation.

That is all the birds needed as the Impundalu used their sharp beaks to pierce their armor. Body armor, helmet, pauldrons, any armor even mithreal laced would not stop their beaks and these birds were ravenous. The Impundalu didn't care as they savagely gathered more than one to each meal that was quickly torn apart. Leaving elven body parts scattered all over the ground.

It was much worse inside the Palace as the Throne hall was over ran with Impundalu. Most the guards and defenders were

outside trying to defend the inside. None thought about the gaping hole in the palace ceiling. The guard was too busy to close the door. The injured females, males, and children were a buffet for these Impundalu.

The females had it the worse. None of them saw the birds they only saw an orgy of ecstasy of masculine elven males embracing them. Seeing whom they loved that was returning. What they believed affection with nothing more than evisceration and shedding their blood. So much gore that males and children would be horrified and then panic running right into a lightning bird that would claw them, drive their beaks into them, pluck out eyeballs from their sockets and pull out their insides lungs, hearts, intestines, muscles and all. The Impundalu only wanted the blood it's all they cared about. They would use their claws and beaks to squeeze all the blood they could from the torn flesh and even crack the bones for the marrow.

The guard was trained to deal with demons. They had demon oil in their belt pouches. None of the guard thought these vampire birds were demons. None of them ever fought an Impundalu. Let alone a massive flock of Impundalu. The demons didn't give them time to think. They were as fast as lightning and could enchant the females with lustful desires by eye contact.

The only ladies immune to the effects of the illusion of the Impundalu were those who had soul matched. Love wasn't enough nor marriage, to be immune was to bind your soul to another. Yet for these wedded by the soul, it was little a haven from the ravenous birds. Now it was simply all out slaughter of any elf in or around the palace grounds. It mattered not to the lightning birds what gender or even if they had ensorcelled or beguiled the feminine. They Impundalu just feasted on torn and bloody flesh while devouring every drop of blood greedily.

The guards and conscripted weapons could only use brute strength to bash at the birds only driving one off as another replaced it. Not a single weapon they had could penetrate or even harm the Impundalu. None of them thought about using their oils or even the few magics they had on them. The most experienced of their command had died horrible gruesome deaths. Their ranks crumbled and were leaderless and had no directions it was everyone for themselves and the chaos worsened.

The conscripted civilian's were next to useless. None of them had any real combat training and were facing demon Impundalu. Only stories of these creatures came from the lollygag Isles. As some resort visitors were said to never return. Many thought it was to keep people from visiting the fox isle in the chain. Where Lollygag islander natives had their private community and wanted all visitors to stick to the resorts and pristine beaches. Why not tell them about vampire birds to keep visitors away.

The stories of the Impundalu were always just small tales of one bird that would have demands and a moral or lesson to teach to youngsters. Most of the morals of the tales were to avoid promiscuity or disloyalty avoiding the sins of the flesh. None of the stories ever mentioned the pure terror and horror happening this night.

No one knew the Impundalu lightning was a force of destruction for most of the young adult books of their time only said that it was a metaphor for speed. In reality it was a terrible uncontrolled mussel spasm of death. The lightning was real and shocking and enough to cook an elf internally. The Impundalu restrained them for the flowing blood is really what vampires feed upon. Yes these birds could have been much more brutal if it wasn't for their lust of feeding on blood.

Now here they are late in the night after the high eclipsing moon returned on the darkest dark night. How could there be so many. The island was free of these birds. No reports ever. This storm cloud of darkness was odd the night of darkness and the moonless dark night. Wind howling as it blew around them and lightning all around. It brought destructive lightning and no rain. Not a drop of rain, the night would have been more terrifying than it now is if there was a dismal downpour of rain. It wasn't like any tempest ever seen moving in on Yoranthium. This storm was terrifyingly strange. Then it brings this nightmare of blood thirsty Impundalu a plague of death and evil and gore.

The conscripts quickly broke ranks and ran in all directions looking for shelter and safety from the vicious birds. Many would get struck by the lightning, drilled and killed in the back by the birds. Even picked up in their claws and pulled up in the air and dismembered by several birds all at once.

Some of the civilians ran past the gates and into the city along with the conscripts. It was pure chaos even with orders being called out by the Sergeant. It would seem no one listened and then the Sergeant's voice was a high pitched scream and he too was ripped apart and silenced. A new leader sometime would rise up to take control. That voice too would fall silent after exclaiming in pain and great suffering their failure to defeat these birds.

There was a lot of confusion and outside the gates of the breach in the wall. In all directions they went there was Impundalu attacking and slaughtering them. A small group of three was being chased and if they had been paying attention as they ran into a raging inferno of a burning building. They would have known the Impundalu stopped following them. The Impundalu was weak to fire. Fire could ignite the glands under their skin that made the lightning possible for the birds. But panic and fear and the need to run got the better of them. They never looked back as looking back was always met with death. So the fleeing elves ran into the burning building as the top floors collapsed on to them.

The weakness of the Impundalu went unnoticed as much of the lightning was by magical demonic and glandular means. Even magics used for heating are not of flame but a glowing orb. This thing about fire was unknown to those that sought refuge at the palace. Even if the fleeing elves knew of the effectiveness of fire on Impundalu, it would of likely made matters worse, for one should always be careful how you play with fire. Least you get burned.

The Impundalu wasn't the worse of what was coming. The torn and dead body parts scattered all over the place from the Impundalu attack. Began to twitch. The dead body parts were infested from a demonic possession disease carried by the Impundalu a disease that would reanimate dead tissue. The broken, torn, bloody mess of entrails, bones, skin, guts and gore began twitching. The twitching looked like uncontrolled spasms. Of course, only the bones that had mussels and sinew attached actually began to move. In an unnatural and frightening contorted way that seemed incredibly painful. The limbs quickly contorted and convulsed blindly searching around. Then success one limb found another and found another skeletal bloody body part and joined.

This unholy abomination wasn't trying to be elven in the slightest just a mound of flesh with oddly created and contorted limbs. Not just one. Many were forming from the torn, discarded remains. Misshapen horrifying and unfathomable bodies were being created. An arm and leg would form a body and that body would form a mouth of jagged teeth of random shattered bone and a tongue and nose. For some reason eyes even when absorbed into the fleshy lump was impossible for the things to use.

Some of these shambling oddities of demonic terror had ears and could hear the Impundalu having difficulties with the doors down the halls. Bird wings have no opposing thumbs, difficult to turn a door handle without a thumb and just feathers or a long proboscis for a beak.

Some of the survivors had run down the halls, and stairs and had run into various rooms of the administrative sections of the palace. Small groups of surviving elves would find themselves in the rooms, slamming the doors shut just as the Impundalu pursued them down the narrow corridors. Once the door shut behind the survivors they would brace the door as the Impundalu battered the door with great force.

Thankfully these palace doors were sturdy and strong. The doors held against the super strength of the vicious vampire birds. They only had wings and over sized claws unable to turn a doorknob. Which would have simplified the battering process to break into the room for the sake of turning a doorknob. Even the escaping ladies and females became immune to the seductive nature of the ensnaring process of the Impundalu eyes. The solid doors kept them from making eye contact with the maidens who were defenseless against the Impundalu's charms by avoiding the mesmerization of the Impundalu.

This plan had worked, but for how long. Eventually they would need food and they would have to leave these side rooms to foray. Some groups hadn't given a thought to their new prisons and how to escape. This was only for a few moments the Shamblers heard their Impundalu masters crying for assistance to get at the blood behind the doors.

Slowly the Shamblers came down the hall. There were many Shamblers and some went up the stairs to the higher floors. The Shamblers would reach a door and then with a deformed hand or

foot with fingers and a thumb. Yes the Shamblers had thumbs. The Shamblers hands would reach up to the doorknobs and begin to turn them with great unholy strength. The panic inside the room could be heard as praying and desire of blessings could be heard on the other side to spare the elves in the rooms. Some of the elves would try to stop the doorknobs from turning. The Shamblers were too strong the doorknobs turned until the latch released the door and the Impundalu pushed down the doors quickly out numbering the inhabitants of each room.

High pitched screams came from all over the city all night long. The feast of the Impundalu could be heard in the distance. Rarailmuir and his group were ordered to continue forward keep moving to the defensive keeps. A defense line was important for the nightmare kept getting worse and worse and only a fortified post would suffice Impundalu could be seen by the guards coming their way.

"Demon Oils at the ready, saturate your weapons and pour some of it in your sheaths should you need more oil. These are demons." Rarailmuir called out the orders.

Metiur and Fedarious did know about the Impundalu and heard of the demon birds. They both had when growing up with a fascination of such unholy studies. They heard the stories read a book or two but never thought these creatures could be real, just terrible stories to tell children visiting the Lollygag Islands and keep the resort clean of transgressions of lust. No reason to question Rarailmuir's instructions. He had issued the demon oils to all guards along with other useful items tucked into their service belts.

Metiur asked. "Should we go back to back my King?"

"No!!! Stay loose. Archers prepare your arrows with oil. When the birds get close shoot them. If you see small lightning shoot it. These birds will seem like lesser flashes of lightning. These are Demon birds do not look them in the eyes and if you see a female looking at the bird. Kill the damn bird." Rarailmuir was angry he didn't think he'd be attacked by demon birds, he thought he would be spared such things. What is wrong with his medallion he boasted of? Where did this blood magics come from? He realized it didn't matter. There was enough blood everywhere now

this very night. "Death Guard protect the map makers. Ensure we lose none of them."

Rarailmuir seen one of the Impundalu coming in for the attack and ran towards it and sliced strait through it's gut with his sword. "Anyone not doing anything get out torches. The filthy birds go up like kindling." Just playing a hunch considering the depth dwellers and most demons don't like fire.

The Sea Ghouls saw what was coming and they armed themselves with torches as instructed and came up from behind Rarailmuir's rear and engaged the Impundalu. The Impundalu were terrified of fire and retreated some distance still stalking the group.

"Thank you, Orichen. It seems you finally realized your real purpose in life to defend the King." Rarailmuir said with some sarcasm.

"I'm not defending you I'm defending me and my Sea Ghouls. I'm of the founding blood this Yoranthium is more mine than yours. No damn demon bird is going to make a meal of us. However we can't keep these torches up forever they only last a small hourglass." Orichen was hoping that Rarailmuir had answers.

Which Rarailmuir did. "Archers we need fire arrows to the ready. Fire when ready and clear out the birds when they near."

Fedarious was given leave to take up arrows from Metiur. "Archers to the ready. Stand by the Sea Ghouls and let them protect you if any birds get close."

The Sea Ghouls would lower their torches to make it appear less threatening to the Impundalu and then the birds surged forward. They filled the sky waiting for a chance. "Oiled blades to the ready." Rarailmuir shouted as the birds began their attack.

The archers waited and then the birds were in close range and they opened fire. It was a splendid show of fire works as the Impundalu exploded as the fire arrows impacted them. Even better for any bird to close to another also exploded and a huge number of burnt and dead ruptured birds fell to the ground a king's length away from Rarailmuir's forces. The strategy worked better than planned as the remaining Impundalu realized they could not defeat these elves as they did with so many. This unit of elves was prepared.

It would seem the Impundalu demons were not the monsters they had been, to so many unaware. A person with knowledge such as Rarailmuir their King was definitely a godsend to his men as he knew exactly how to fend off these foul assailants.

A few Impundalu had used the air to their favor and came at the group like lightning. Appearing in the middle of their ranks. Several Guards got killed instantly and a few were being lifted into the air. As fire arrows flew through the sky causing the Lightning birds to explode. A good number of Impundalu exploded and so did many guards get consumed by the very fireball of an explosion in the middle of the group.

"Stop firing the flame arrows inside the ranks. Change to oil arrows!" Rarailmuir was angry. Several of his guard and others had been killed or injured by a few archers that let loose with fire arrows while the Impundalu were inside their ranks. Nearly causing panic and putting more guards at risk of fleeing in the chaos.

It took a moment for some of the archers to change their arrows to oiled arrows. More of the guard got killed as they failed to use their oil weapons effectively. This was getting out of hand. The ranks were being broken the Impundalu had successfully infiltrated behind their lines and began attacking chaotically. It was coming down to each elf for himself.

"Rally and press to the warm side buildings. Use them for cover. Get closer to the buildings on fire. Do not enter any damaged building." Just as lightning struck one of the buildings catching it on fire. "Sea Ghouls, spread out and cover the guard with your torches."

A Sea Ghoul ran over to some guard and got to close to an Impundalu and hit it with his torch. An explosion erupted not only killing the bird but also setting alight ten other guards who began running in all directions. The Impundalu are clever and got out of the way. Yet the other guards had no where to go and one burning guard ran into another that had several magics on his person causing an even larger explosion. This killed a considerable number of archers and guards all at once.

The Impundalu were learning how to use fire to their benefit. Several Impundalu started to organize themselves making a net to trap Rarailmuir's forces. The Guard was being pushed

back along with the Sea Ghouls. As the bodies of guards became undefended the birds would swoop in and feast on the dead scavenging for blood.

"Twenty Archers stagger yourself with a Sea Ghoul and use fire arrows for distance only. Sea Ghoul's arm with demon oil swords and douse the torches. No more hand to hand torches. We are going oils only at point blank range the rest of the archers to oil arrows. Cover one another and do not allow any more of these demons to destroy our ranks." Rarailmuir was looking around and saw some familiar streets in this part of the Grand City that offered more protection from over head attacks and would funnel the birds. Leaving the birds one direction to attack them.

"Okay everyone we are going to take the tight alley's and back streets." Rarailmuir began backing the rest of his unit towards the narrow alley.

The Impundalu appeared to understand what the plan was and saw the narrow alley the elves were moving towards. With a loud call and terrifying screeching, a group of Impundalu broke off and quickly filled the side streets before the alley to block Rarailmuir's strategic retreat. Then a small group of birds flew straight into a burning building and exploded killing a good number of guards trying to use the tenement as cover.

Fedarious saw what was happening and realized more guards are going to die if he didn't act. "You Sea Ghouls with me, we need to engage and take as many of these birds out as we can." The Sea Ghouls followed Fedarious at reckless and headlong charge at the heart of the gathering Impundalu to their retreat. Directly into the gaggle of the flock blockading what appeared to be the Impundalu's leadership. The raider's sword Fedarious held was saturated with demon oil and sliced through the enemy ranks with ease causing the birds to panic and rush towards their leadership. The Sea Ghouls acted in the same manner and hacked with their axes, swords and daggers with demon oils in a similar fashion as Fedarious.

The birds were in retreat as they lost their wings and ability to fly and the distance between Fedarious and the Sea Ghouls increased. Fedarious sheathed his weapon and grabbed a bow and flame arrow from one of the archers. Having strung it back with the notched arrow. He almost let the arrow draw him in as he sited

what he knew to be the leading bird. He let the burning arrow fly. The flaming arrow arched high and curved downwards on its target. The shot was flawless as it burned into the bird trying to protect the groups leader and erupted in a fantastic fire ball of an explosion that leveled two buildings in the process and the high pitched squawking of a hundredth or so Impundalu perishing in the fiery aftermath.

Fedarious and the Sea Ghouls along with the other Archers had been hit with the shockwave from the blast sailed through the air for three king's lengths. Knocked to the ground motionless. Metiur upon seeing this broke ranks without hesitation. He ran over to Fedarious fallen body on the ground. Leaned next to him and raised his head to look into Fedarious's eyes. They were closed. "Oh, God, come back Fedarious. You fool, why get yourself killed for these stupid birds?"

"Metiur, your my champion," Somewhat silently and in a silly voice. Fedarious's eye's rolled open with a sinister smile. "I didn't know you cared?"

Metiur let Fedarious's head drop and hit the ground with a thud. "Seeing you are okay enough to fool around. How about rejoining the ranks. We still got birds to fight." Metiur looked around and realized there was a lot of smoke, dust and soot covering everyone. "Sea Ghoul's back to your posts. Use any spare cloth and use it as a face mask so you can breathe. All this smoke, dust from collapsed buildings, and soot is going to choke us before long." The cloth masks worked well on the dust, dirt, and smoke but couldn't conceal the smell of the death and decay all around them. The cloth masks wouldn't stop airborne pathogens only heavy dust particles.[10]

Already enough choking and difficulties breathing could be heard among the remaining force. Rarailmuir was already giving commands. "Cover your mouths and noses before we choke in this dust and smoke." Rarailmuir tore at his Yukata and ripped the lower portion using his blade to help cut some off to cover his face. "Metiur! Where is Metiur?"

---

[10] A valid lesson in 2020 over the false issuance of phony mask mandates that festered foolishly into the year of 2021. Mostly a political message to silence the common people and deny them first amendment rights.

Looking around Metiur wasn't at his post another death guard showed up in his stead. "Metiur went to assist some fallen guards, my King."

"Take these cloths here and give them to the Map Makers to cover their mouths and noses." Rarailmuir trusted Metiur and knew he'd likely get back to his command soon enough. He saw what Fedarious had heroically done. It was the collapse of two robust tenements from the massive explosion that now filled the air with choking dust along with the smoke and the soot.

Rarailmuir watched the death guard return to his post. Then turned to the alleyway egress. "Magics, throw your orbs far from us and hit those birds. Their command is broken and we can now press into the alley."

Several guards with Magics on their hips staggered an open line and started throwing their magics at the birds. It was true the Impundalu were leaderless and couldn't commit to any formations as before. The birds began to break ranks as their numbers began dwindling.

It took the guard some effort to tie cloth around their mouths and noses to lessen the effect of all the dust and smoke in the air. The entire guard, conscripts, and Sea Ghoul's were becoming hard to identify. They were all getting caked in thick dusty soot that heavily encrusted them and filled the air.

There were some odd new sounds all over the street a sloshing and cracking of bones sounds. Looking around the dust was moving on the ground. One of the Sea Ghouls went over to a small half a kings foot high mound of dust that was convulsing on the ground. He poked at it with his short sword. A hand erupted from the ground with great force and a small bit of arm came with it.

The hand landed on his shoulder and the wrist section swung around with a rough mouth filled with wood splinters, sharp rocks and sharp bones. Bit into the Sea Ghouls throat. The Sea Ghoul fell to the ground and more odd discarded and torn body parts of fallen guards started attaching and biting into the Sea Ghoul as his gargled terrified screams got heard by other Sea Ghouls. One acted quick and thrust his torch into the transforming Sea Ghoul and lit him on fire. The contorted concoction of living sea elf and dead broken and deformed body parts twisted

contorted in pain and ungodly screams and then silenced as it was completely engulfed in flame.

More movement under the dust and the mounds of dust kept getting bigger as more and more body parts reassembled themselves in weird and odd distorted manifestations of fleshy mouth type creatures based on the features of elven body parts. A new danger was approaching and it was slow moving something easy to avoid but dangerous nonetheless.

The twitching looked painful to watch and yet mesmerizing it melded and created some kind of hideous monstrosity. Forming odd ears, and nasal passages and it's own internal organs that varied from one Shamblers to another. The mouths were gnashing hungry and kept chomping menacingly towards what it deemed as food or something to stalk and kill. The teeth were bones, rocks, wood, sharp debris of all sorts of sharp objects and it drooled foam and congealed blood.

These Shamblers were more like some kind of pet. It's masters of course were the Impundalu who obviously had mastery of dead body parts of their victims. The Impundalu had lost the battle and were leaving the area and the Shamblers began backing away following the Impundalu. The Impundalu were feathered birds of elven size and the dust and soot covering this block was not good for them. As bird's even vampire lightning birds they still had to breathe air. The birds had no means to craft dust masks to survive in these conditions of their own making.

The Sea Ghouls backed away from the larger Shamblers and simply burned the smaller ones that were in the way and around the group of sea guard and conscripts. The staggered group of exhausted fighters simply fell in and followed directions from Rarailmuir that was hard to hear behind the masks.

Rarailmuir could feel himself getting weaker from the continued sustained conflict with the Impundalu. He only had one objective now, to keep moving. Get down that narrow alley way and head for the secret passage there was an underground sewage passage. That was long and a considerable distance, a secret route from the Grand City to the Last Bastion defenses. Meant as a secret means to reinforce and supply the keep via the Grand Cities initial island defense plans. The Last Bastion would be reached in less than a day. Quicker than having to traverse over land and

through the difficult marsh forest. They wouldn't get there until after the morning. They would be tired and exhausted it had accommodations and they could set up and recover at rest. It was getting difficult to know if this was night or day so much destruction on one block with dust flooding all the blocks for who knows how many streets? It was dark and cold and miserable.

A Shambler rose out of the soot in front of Rarailmuir. He simply pulled his demon oil covered sword and sliced the Shambler in two. It twitched as if it was in even more pain and began to blacken and solidify and then stopped moving and crumbled to dust. One thing for sure the demon oils were much more effective on these Shamblers than fire was. Just a nick would be enough to poison it and end it.

At least that was worthy of note and many of the guard followed suit as they encountered more body remains of their force and dispatched them. A few guards would kneel and make a prayer to the unborn God to bless their fallen brothers and guide them in their next life to be born unto.

The Map Makers had been silent this entire time. The Death Guard proved invaluable at keeping them protected. They insisted to move closer to speak to the King. Which Metiur facilitated along with Fedarious at his side.

"What do you need?" Rarailmuir inquired.

"Sire the alley path you plan to take dead ends." One of the Map Makers said.

"The birds will not have easy access and we can easily defend." Another said.

"If we use the sewer at the end of the alley we should have a strait shot to the lower catacombs of the Last Bastion." A third one said.

"Yes that is where we are headed." Rarailmuir pointed out.

"We simply wanted to let you know of the conditions down the tunnel." The fourth had replied.

"We need to get out of this dust and soot for our magics can't be maintained." from the fifth.

Rarailmuir was curious about the tunnels. "Is there a problem in using the tunnels?"

"No, we have our magics there too. It's clear." Said the sixth. "Most direct route to the Last Bastion. Of all the ways underground is currently recommended."

"Very well then we will make it down the alley to the sewers and to the keep. Knowing there is nothing in our way." Rarailmuir could see the exhaustion on his unit's faces. His force was haggard and couldn't take much more of this forced march until they got too exhausted. "Fedarious, Front and center!"

Fedarious was frightened, the King wanted him personally. He was likely in trouble for braking ranks. He ran over to the Kings side saluted and stood at attention. "My King."

"Fedarious next time be more careful. Do not get yourself killed in duty." Rarailmuir reached for an item in one of his belt pockets.

"My King, I know..." with a tremor in his voice fearing discipline.

"Don't interrupt the king when I'm speaking." Rarailmuir found what he was looking for. "For bravery above and beyond the call of duty, proving leadership and initiative to do what needed to be done. I King Rarailmuir bequeath to you the award. Protector of the People of Yoranthium." Rarailmuir reached over to Fedarious's chest and pinned a metal on him above his heart on his breastplate. The medal was what King Sinderthion gave to Rarailmuir for saving the kingdom from the dragon attack many revolutions ago. Fedarious's quick action saved the King and his fellow Guards for disrupting the Impundalu's command structure. "You are dismissed Fedarious, let your courage inspire those whom you lead in the future." Rarailmuir could see this inspired his guard and was uplifting to their spirits giving them an added boost in strength to push forward.

Fedarious with a sigh of relief and accomplishment, "Yes, my King, by your leave." He nodded and ran back to the death guard. Fedarious knew about the medal he was now wearing. He was in the crowd years ago when Rarailmuir was recognized for his achievement and given the award from King Sinderthion. He inherited a legacy of the guard this day an award that meant a lot to many of the guard. Rarailmuir's victory over the dragon was legend to the people of Yoranthium and to wear that very same medal was the heart of Yoranthium.

Upon getting back Metiur eyed Fedarious. "Well aren't you special? You were just lucky, you do know that right."

"Don't be jealous Metiur, one day maybe if you are lucky you can be as good as me." Fedarious then found himself in a headlock.

"Just let me know next time you do something that almost gets you killed. I'm here to make sure that doesn't happen." Releasing Fedarious after messing with him a bit. Metiur was proud of Fedarious and they both smiled.

The unit moved out in a protective and defensive posture down the alleyway only encountering a few Impundalu. They were disorganized and couldn't mount a decent assault on the wary guard. It was easy enough to use demon oils on arrows and swords to cut them down. No Shamblers followed them. The air began clearing and they had managed to clear the heavy dust and soot from themselves as breathing became easier towards the end of the alley.

They would only get a small reprieve of fresh air to breathe by the time they got to the sewers and opened the cover. It reeked of bowel movement material and stank something fierce. Their masks were put on their faces again as one by one they descended into a sewer system that was cramped and they had to move three abreast. Surprisingly the cloth masks didn't do much to cover the stench proving ineffective against biomass.

The sewer went on for some distance until past morning. With smaller pipes leading to other cisterns and sewer pipes under the streets. Eventually they reached the end of the tunnel and it branched out to smaller drains with water emptying out into the main line from this section of the Last Bastion. There was a ladder up to the top cover. Having climbed it Rarailmuir pushed it open and realized he was now in the lower catacombs under the Last Bastion.

The funeral rights of the Last Bastion Catacombs belonged to both Sea Shore and Grand City out skirts of their territories. There's a chapel to the unborn God above and to the side the halls went to steps leading to the lower lavatories and the showers as well as the barracks, stores, dining and assembly halls.

His guard was slowly emerging from the sewers and Rarailmuir was bothered by the lack of guards on the lower levels

there should have been at least two. No one was around no guards found or on duty. Other than the noise his own guard was making, he heard nothing.

Rarailmuir split his command and sent half his unit to scout the cold side while his half scouted the warm side of the Last Bastion. He gave them orders to station guards and use the showers as needed. The boilers were still stoked and working. If they met any Last Bastion patrols to make contact and let them know they are here with the King and have their commander find him. As long as there were no dangers noted or threats of eminent danger the guards are to get some rest and rotate patrols.

Rarailmuir knew the Last Bastion he was stationed here for a time before the dragon attack. He knew the commanders chambers was to the warm side and it housed it's own personal bathing chamber with pumped in cold and hot water. Quite a new development using boiler magics, water storage towers provided the water pressure for the pipes. An offshoot of creating aqueducts to farm the land and send fresh drinking water to the cities on Yoranthium.

Once Rarailmuir inspected the area he found no Last Bastion defenders. The total missing guard and no signs of conflict baffled Rarailmuir. He stationed his guard using Metiur and Fedarious to manage the affairs of the command. He wanted to go check the logs to see if there was any mention where the guard went.

Rarailmuir found the commanders quarters and saw the journals but he was still caked in grime, dust and soot. He decided the first thing was a bath and that's exactly what he did. The water was hot, and he soon filled the bath water and stripped off his armor. He brushed off the grime on his armor and found all the needed polishing tools he even found a replacement commanders Yukata for when he finished bathing. The Yukata was of the Shore Guards colors. Along with replacement trousers and boots that fit.

The bath was exceptional, and he worked on his body from head to toe making sure to wash away all the dirt from the day. One of the most sensual baths he has had in what felt like forever. He even almost forgot how lovely his own bronzed dark blue skin was like and missed his long flowing dark golden hair. He could feel his mussels were in good shape and his pecks were rock hard

along with his abdomen. The only thing missing was a specific feminine touch for his bath the day after the wedding. He thought of Kumithra and how nice it would have been to bathe with her. It would be nice if the wedding went as planned to be in a bath with his very young wife and Queen? Remembering how when he caught her from falling he felt her very firm breast. Which excited him and he yearned for.

He hurried his bathing because he was on duty and there was a war and he had to defend his kingdom. He got dressed and found the commanders bed and decided he was too tired and fell asleep. His dream was filled with two females squabbling over him and even in the phantom shapes of his mind. He knew who they were. They were trying to kill one another over him Rarailmuir the King of Yoranthium. This lucid dream satisfied his longing and missing companionship in the lonely bed. In known Yoranthium history he was the only King to have slept alone after his wedding day.

Yoranthium

Book One: Lost Hope

Chapter Eleven: To Govern the People

By Mark P. Bromley

Farmer Town has been separated by a deadly enemy knowing they are on their own with so many precious lives in the Governors hands. Governor of a city sounds like a dream job and a temptation to abuse that power granted. Power is for the weak minded. Compassion is the real strength of leadership. Bad leaders run ahead of their people and leave them behind. Good leaders run behind their people. Ready to respond to all problems with good solutions to save lives. Placing the slowest and most vulnerable at the head of the pack while protecting them with the best and most competent that can quickly respond to any situation.

Governor Colusious had to evacuate the city to the cold side Shoal Mountains where ancient keeps had been located. That could save his people from being slaughtered. There was a massive hoard of Mechanation's approaching Farmer Town.

Colusious was short only five kings foot tall and two kings thumbs and fit for having a bit of center. He wore his status of office lightly believing in his people rather than believing he was in control. He was bald and eyes were green with large black eyebrows and of a medium hue of blue and brown, yellow interlacing pattern skin. He had a black beard that was thin and strait about a king's hand in length to a point and no mustache. His nose was crooked, and his jaw was wide with thick lips for a mouth.

On his chest was a medallion of heroism given to him by King Sinderthion for protecting and fighting for the rights of his farmers by bringing sensible concerns to his Kings attention to help the farmlands of Yoranthium prosper. Along side a tiny seashell necklace made by his daughter. His idea's in agriculture improved their yield and made Yoranthium a key exportation hub of many sea kingdoms and especially that of Forumth that was part of the parley that won the hand of Queen Zantkara. In these days of strife Yoranthium's crops provided for many nations of Ishormot.[11]

The medallion had the heart of Yoranthium's God of the unborn in the center and the common symbol of the people of Yoranthium. This medallion was only gifted to those who provided great achievement and guided their city to excellence. Awarded to those picked by the King and Queen to run and manage the larger municipalities as a badge of office along with a laurel of silver leaves that identified his station upon his head with an open front. Silver was considered more valuable than gold in seafaring nations.

He wore the medallion on the outside of a stiff and thickened Yukata of lime green with pink set of five petal flowers running around the collar and down the lining. With a darker green belt and more darker pink sakura flowers running around the belt. He wore leggings under the long Yukata and simple geta that were a kings thumb off the ground. He always kept a journal

[11] Early 21st century Globalist Socialism's attack on farming and agriculture in the guise of climate crisis.

with him. A very well organized and exceptionally disciplined elder that was older than King Sinderthion.

Farmer Town was unique and had a rather routine lifestyle for so many citizens that called it home. There was real peace of mind and freedom as most of the time the people spent their days caring for their crops, livestock and living wholesome family lives. Where there was some corruption and decay in the Grand City and Sea Shore. Farmer Town was spared those distractions and they simply lived a good heart warming and love of the land lifestyle. Farmer Town had its troubles. Those troubles were often quickly dealt with fairly and by the magistrate that the governor presided over.

This day started out well. As it was a big day for Farmer Town hauling in essential crops in the first planting season out of three on Ishormot. It would be the shipment for Forumth as detailed in the articles of mutual agreements. The day of preparing a major export was a busy day in Farmer Town. Requiring the governor to magistrate legal responsibilities along with traditional and celebratory functions. This is why he did not attend the best dual wedding that Yoranthium ever had.

Then again he wasn't invited, for he objected to the wasted tax collections for a dual wedding of the ages. It would only last the day and linger for a quarter a third season. None of the farmers or common sea elves would benefit from such wasteful spending. Except just those corrupted, entitled and privileged as the elites of the Grand City. Single selfish wasteful weddings all over Ishormot was a rarity and only a handful benefited at cost of so many that should be allowed to spend their coin of the realm the way they individually saw fit. Instead of having their money spent for the selfish wishes of a handful of monarchs.[12]

Governor Colusious had felt something bad would befall Yoranthium for a long time. Although King Sinderthion was kind and had great heart and love, he was ultimately blind to worsening

[12] The collapse of Democracy by a Monarchy of oppressive reform by Globalist Socialism the new NAZI of early 21 century thinking. Caused by the tyranny of dysfunction 20th century fake sciences of Sociology, Psychology, and Political Science. The fringe extremist philosophies opposed by Aristotle and Socrates leading to wealth hoarding by excessive taxation and predatory real estate creating 21st century slavery and human trafficking.

conditions of the Grand City and Sea Shore. That dragon's unholy attack four revolutions ago created the disparity that not all of what remained to the King of the Grand City was able to fix or correct or properly magistrate. The very means the guard used to collect taxes was somewhat harsh and unrealistic. Crime had risen in the land and only Farmer Town was spared these gangs. Although the unfortunate farmstead, occasionally being burned by inner city gangs was becoming more common. Those Farmers came from the prison and could not escape their pasts. Once in the gangs, a sea elf was considered property and was never free of the gangs.

There were many oversights and mistakes of King Sinderthion's young and inexperienced magistrate and guard. The young upstart appointed magistrates of the Grand City was unable to maintain authority and the city was falling to waste and abuse. Farmer Town had offered aid many times. Yet the Governor of Sea Shore opposed Colusious's plans for development and strengthening the Grand City with the old guard of Farmer Town. The corrupt Sea Shore Governor had an old nun that often controlled the policies and enforcement of Sea Shore. Some how the same corruption was witnessed in the Grand City. It was rumored that the Sea Shore Governor would wed that demon witch of an Arch Nun. Only to be proven false and just a rumor as a new scandal took place.

A scandal of the Archpriest and the Arch Nun being romantically involved and that halted the unholy union of the Sea Shore Governor. It was already unholy for a Nun never married and was supposed to remain chaste. It just wasn't done and wasn't in keeping with the unborn God's belief. Ultimately the scandal was never resolved, and the investigations ended without any reason given. Books of speculation of drama and intrigue could have been written on this scandal of Sea Shore but only as fiction. As all the investigations disappeared along with a good number of investigators abandoning the cases.

Even with the growing corruption and bad management of the Grand City by the lower level magistrate. Sea Shore's problems of rampant uncontested migration of refugees, rising crime rates, condoning of street criminal behavior, and internal issues of negligence all the way up to the Governor of Sea Shore.

Made Sea Shore the worst of all the cities on Yoranthium. Allowing the King and Queen to live peacefully thinking that the Grand City was prospering. Creating costly and expensive distractions and entertainment and too many lower level charities that were nothing more than profiteering fronts that never repaired or serviced the issues. Concealed by slight of hand, trickery, and deceptions. That was leading Yoranthium to financial ruin and projected collapse.[13]

Colusious was thankful; Farmer town was spared all these bad magistrates appointed by the very leaders that were corrupt and cruel. Unfortunately, that same barbarism of monarchy also prevented his hopes to unite the Farmer Town authority of older guard to that of the younger guard in the Grand City. Rarailmuir oversaw the guard in the Grand City. He was too young and brash and harsh and imposing poor tax collection method's that were excessive. Colusious could not deny that Rarailmuir was the best of the magistrate the Grand City could hope for. In it's ranks of growing mass corruption. Rarailmuir inherited the corruption having been born into a tainted background rising above it and showed a promising kind and noble heart. Even with the hope of Rarailmuir it was obvious to Colusious that darkness was falling on Yoranthium and today was the real truth of the arriving darkness. That promised and brought destruction to Yoranthium.

Colusious did send delegates of Farmer Town with recording magics and presents. Romanticizing he so loved, like all sea elves do, the age of a girl becoming a lady and taking a mate. This was a dual wedding for both of King Sinderthion's and Queen Zantkara's children the greatest representative of the Yoranthium sea elf culture. It was their way of life and time of greatness in Yoranthium and a blessing of life and the heart of their God.

Colusious met Princess Kumithra, who was naive but young and a good top magistrate. She was kind and fair in her lower level responsibilities and Huspecia her protector was a gentle and compassionate person as well. Colusious saw his possible

---

[13] In the 2020's many cities in the USA worsened similar to life in North Korea the USA version of it. Elected corruption was rampant and oppression and Global Socialism on the rise especially in the authors home town. Global Socialism the worsening of National Socialism in the guise of the democrat party Nazi's Emerge group politicians.

reconciliation's of Farmer Town and the Grand City in the princess. He even liked the fact the princess would argue on behalf of the citizens and ideas of elected council over just monarchy. Unfortunately, he had feared she would likely not change the way things are. She would simply grow with her Rarailmuir and continue the aristocracy of Yoranthium. She was a promising aspect to the throne even if her Rarailmuir embraced the values of the old throne. It would have been interesting in time to see if Kumithra would tame Rarailmuir and both could have adverted this doom that was upon their shore.

Colusious objected to the dual wedding. For expressing his reason of corruption and excessive taxation he wasn't invited. He got out of line just a bit trying to force the issue. Barely managing to keep his Governor title in the process. He was almost considered an insurrectionist and threatened with imprisonment for treasonous thoughts.[14] King Sinderthion was hot headed upon the allegations by Colusious. Then calmed down and forgave Colusious for he valued the council of Colusious above all in the court.

Colusious was hoping for a different kind of wedding for the King's daughters in Farmer Town. For a quarter a third season starting right after the first harvest was a festival in Farmer town. The Mate Matching Festival that went for two-thirds of a season. A festival intended for soul binding females of age to males of age, soul finding and forging binding loves and hearts. The festival was a boon to all those too poor to afford expensive royal weddings. Colusious was hoping the King and Queen would match their daughters at the Farmer Town festival to bring their two cities closer together. Where Colusious would be able to change and correct the corruption of the Grand City and improve King's Sinderthion's reign.

By introducing his magistrate to replace those unfit in the King's magistrate.

It was quite a dream and if he could get all of the Grand City to partake in the Farmer Town festival he could get Sea Shore, Worm, and Under the Rock to become part of it the year after. The plan was for the combined Yoranthium Fair Grounds it would

---

[14] This is a report of worsening corruption caused by the foreign Global Socialism buying corrupt politicians in the USA. As they gained their ill gotten power they falsely accused opposing politicians of insurrection in 2020-2021.

have been a glorious dream of uniting all of the people of Yoranthium and moving towards a new form of governing the people.

Colusious loved his King and Queen and was torn over the issue of upsetting them by objecting to the dual wedding of his daughters. Some corrupt magistrates bent the King's ear and lied about Colusious's plan that would have improved Yoranthium nearly destroying his Governorship and placing his life at risk. Those corrupt magistrates in the Grand City was behind the rise of an Orichen and his Sea Ghouls. He remembered in front of his family in their carriage having to fight a desperate battle leaving the Grand City at the end of that evenings political disaster a little over half a third season ago. That forced the magistrate to close down all visitors to the Throne for a bit. Orichen was a descendant of the first king of Yoranthium. Being blood of the kings had a significant influence in the growing corruption of the Grand City.

This day dark clouds and lightning in the distance around the Grand City was the on coming storm as a result of his failure to change Yoranthium for the better. Colusious had witnessed this terrible darkness roll across the land in the distance. While many wave after wave of orbs landed on the Cold side of the Grand city.

After a small amount of time, off in the distance the mages college had magics going off, large explosions, bright flashing lights, Lightning flashes and things both of light and dark flying in the air. Who or what attacked the Mages College during their exam time was unknown. The mages were in testing and likely taken unaware when the first wave of monstrosities assailed them. It was not a very long amount of time. Parts of the mages college towers and battlements and other fortifications had been seen collapsing. It was hard to tell if it was from outside or inside. One thing for certain it was anarchy and chaos. One could only imagine the horrifying moments until the complete destruction of the college. Colusious could only watch as the last tower fell.

A portal opened in the central magistrates office behind the open balcony doors. A powerful gust of wind could be felt and sounds of explosions. Just one massive explosion echoing as the final tower of the Archmages was rent asunder and some debris came through that portal. A badly injured and burned and bruised mage named Satoria flew through the portal as it closed and flew

all the way toward the open balcony door and impacted the governor in his back almost sending him over the railing.

Turning to see what happened. He was looking at a young lady who must have been in her later teens revolutions old. Dressed as a mage with soft pink eyes crushed in the expression of intense pain and anger and sadness all at once. Pink eyes that filled the entire eye socket, her hair was short and red metallic as much of it was singed and burned, she had a small nose and mouth and back sloping ears and was of a dark vermilion and yellow brownish interlacing skin tone. She was robed like a novice that started the training as a mage. The glowing eyes was an indication she was a prodigy and perhaps so important that some older mage must have cast her through the portal to save her, but why just her? There had to be other gifted students.

Satoria's mages garments had been torn, they were thick and not revealing of a dark purple heavy kimono, under it a lighter lavender Yukata. Tied off with a thick band that was black and housed many hidden items that only mages knew of. She was a skinny young female of some elegance as seen by her hands and sandaled feet.

Then from the warm direction towards the Grand City came a loud explosion not far in Farmer Town. Governor Colusious had to look. It's where his wife and child were. It was his farmhouse that had exploded burning on fire, and he could see it in the distance. He collapsed to his knees. Saying "No, No, No." He could not believe his family had died. He felt the impact deep in his heart as his soul of three became a soul of one. The soul binding that many sea elves went through connected them not in just life and love but to their very feelings that they could sense at great distances.

The child mage prodigy known as Satoria saw his hand on the banister and reached out with hers she didn't know why it was as if someone else was doing it. Her head twitched quickly to the right. She used this contact to feel his pain and to search for the truth of his family. It was true they were dead she could sense with her magics. Then she not knowing the Governor Colusious searched his mind. She understood he would save his people. His loss and sadness would prevent him from being the hero his people needed.

Satoria said, "Forget!" Wiping out his memory of what just happened. She wiped out his memories and gave him new ones. That his wife left on a sea journey for the land of the potentate and would return at seasons end. Which was standard to make arrangement of exports and imports. Then Satoria made the Governor think she was his child replacing the fact his child was much younger replacing his memories with that of the Archmages of Satoria life at the Mage College.

Satoria's real father was a drunk and terrible thug in the gangs. Her mother was nothing to her father just a night of lustfulness and was raped. The mages found her by their magics taking her to the Mages College long ago. The Arch Vizer made arrangements with the mother whom did not want a child of a monster. Satoria's real mother was about to set sail for the dark temples of the hollow womb in the land of the potentate. Abortion was not allowed and not condoned by the belief of the Unborn God of Yoranthium. Satoria was saved from becoming a ghost in the womb. The Archmage sent the Vizer mage as the sword of Yoranthium in a vision had revealed the importance of Satoria to them.[15]

It was impossible for the mother to understand her child was not exactly of her's or of the father's being. The child was unique and different and at conception made of a new special soul that deserved life as equal as any other child. Her mother agreed to give birth to the child and let the Mages College take her. Before her abusive father would ever know and exposed her to the darker not meant for children side of the crime festering in the Grand City under Orichen's gang. The Archmage made her thug father forget about her. Even made Satoria forget about her terrible thug of a father that was cruel and would have abused her.

Satoria didn't know this forget spell it was odd that she just remembered how to use it, as her head twitched awkwardly. Governor Colusious was a compassionate male a father she could admire. Reminded her of the Archmage and the Vizier mage and how kind they were to her. By making him forget the death of his real family. She could keep him reasonable and able to save the

---

[15] Early 21st century conflict of the value of the unborn child and the cruelty of abortion themes in politics.

people of Farmer town from the Mechanation's and their fire magics that killed so many mages at the college.

Satoria was gifted by the Arch and Vizier mage the compendium of Yoranthium. That had been rushed in their final moments fighting for the Mages College. She was an oddity and quick study in line to ascend to the Archmage one day. She was tasked with a barrier protective field while the Arch and Vizier mage worked behind her. This compendium wasn't meant for her she didn't know what the Arch and Vizier was doing. All this knowledge much of it forbidden and ancient knowledge was forced into her mind. Best stored in the compendium than in her head. Even the Archmage and Vizier couldn't store such knowledge. Satoria didn't know all of the compiled and completed compendium had been forced into her memories. All of it, Magics of madness, was burning in her mind and she could see much. It was too much for her to hold in her mind. As she had a sudden shift in her thoughts over the effects of the forget spell she didn't know how to cast.

Satoria could feel the knowledge hidden inside her mind, wanting to expand and drive her mad. The Archmage wanted to save the knowledge of Yoranthium as his priority and the old male didn't want to risk it himself so he tested it out on her when she was in the middle of holding up a barrier thinking the Archmage would likely save himself.

Satoria after doing the forget spell screamed in agony and pain. It was worse the compendium was in her head and it was a twitch of extreme pain that subsided magically. She looked around for persons she knew where here. She couldn't see the Arch or Vizier mages. Why weren't they here? She thought they would save themselves and not just her. She wasn't as important as they were she wanted to sacrifice herself for them. For she…

The voice of the Archmage could be heard. She looked to her right. He wasn't there, "Satoria we've escaped with you and the compendium. It worked. I'm the one who did the forget spell. Looks like I can possess your body."

Then Satoria jerked her head left. "Yeah don't get any idea's this is our protégés body." Came the Vizier feminine voice. "Sorry we got to be here to keep the compendium stable, Satoria."

Colusious witnessed Satoria talking to herself and could not hear the other mages in her head. "How did you two get in here with the compendium?" Satoria was talking outloud to herself. Forcing Colusious to be worried and concerned for Satoria his child.

Satoria pulled her hand off of Colusious's and felt a confusion of her thoughts as images began impacting her and she screamed a little the psychic impact of more than one mind and the magics of the compendium overpowered her for a moment. It was terrifying she could feel their egos in conflict with her own. Multiple suggestions. At seventeen revolutions she was too young for all this and now her two older mentors were speaking in her head. The Archmage took over her body and cast the forget spell.

"I hope you are okay, daughter. Are you in pain? What happened to the mages? I'm glad they sent you home, I couldn't stand losing you." Hugging Satoria like he lost his family, for which in truth he did. He couldn't tell which was destroyed his home or the Mages College. Now his daughter was alive and escaped destruction that he witnessed. Yes he fell for the forget spell. She hugged him back as the pain subsided pretending to be Colusious daughter that she shed tears for.

"I'm fine just a little singed. I'll be okay." She deceived Colusious and was sad for doing so. Satoria killed and destroyed Colusious's memories of his infant child daughter and replaced it with memories of her away at the Mages College. She felt terrible for wiping out his memories of raising a child that was good. Better than her memory of childhood. These were the tears she shed for Colusious. In those erased memories was his wife and him and the bundle of joy.

He read books to the child, danced and played and slept with the child on his chest. Picnic's and friends and play dates with other children and the zoo, and the sea coral reef off the coast and the land of play, in Sea Shore and a trip to the lollygag islands. So many good memories that any child such as Satoria's past would have been pleased to have had. Colusious was a great father a caring loving father. She shed tears for the loss that she caused of his memories of his devoted family. That she found more room for in her cramped mind. Should a day come that she can give them back and let Colusious remember.

"Satoria, you need to stay close to me and the guard. Use your magics they taught you to help as you can. I must get as many people out of Farmer Town as possible. We'll head to the shoal keeps up cold side." He looked into Satoria's eyes.

She wasn't sure if her spell worked because she looked into his eyes, and he didn't see her exactly it was a mix of her and his recently lost child. She wasn't sure if Colusious understood how old she was? She was now a changeling and will have to apply the forget spell often until she could make a focus for him to wear. It must have been all the magics knowledge crammed into her brain. She didn't know anything about spell focus until just now. There right before her was a seashell necklace that was gathered and made by his real daughter. When her adopted father looked away she bit her thumb until it bled a little and she imbued the blood to create a rune on the shell of permanence and forever the ancient rune 'Satoria' was inscribed by magics she didn't know.

Again, she shrugged her eye's sporadically to the left. "There, that should do it, now all you got to do is place it on the cats neck." Clearly hearing the voice of the Vizier.

As Colusious turned to look at her again his eyes changed and did really see her as his child and no longer focused on the distance where his home once was for she erased that from his mind too. He now accepted this new gift of a necklace from his daughter Satoria. Placing on his neck as Satoria had asked.

He walked out of the office with her elbow locked in his and hand and hand swinging it with a parents pride and directly to the city guard commander. "Commander we need to evacuate the city to the Shoal keeps. Deadly Mechanation's are heading this way and the people will be in extreme danger as the explosions are getting nearer." Satoria had plenty of time to funnel information about the attack on the Mages College into Colusious mind. "Grab enough necklaces as you can so my daughter can imbue them with communications magics and we can network our strategy more effectively."

"Who's this?" The Commander knew Colusious and thought it strange to have some young female sea elf hanging off his arm.

Satoria was close enough that she managed to reach out and touch the Commander. While her head sporadically jerked to the

right. Performing the same forget magics and adjusted his memory of Colusious daughter. With another tear streaming down her eye as she realized that little child was so much loved. She realized she would be doing this to everyone in Farmer Town with what she had planned to do. It was too horrifying and seemed evil. To conceal this child as she took over it's place in life. She didn't even want to say the child's name for it would destroy her inside. Reflecting on demonology studies and how names had powerful meaning to defeat demonic possession. Yes just like that this child's name was just as powerful and did this make her a demon and a real changeling?

Her head jerked to the right. "Get a grip Satoria. Not all magics are easy on any of us." The Arch was explaining to her. "It's not perfect for I or the Vizier to be here."

Then her head jerked left to the Vizier. "We wanted to live too Satoria but this compendium needed us to keep your mind from melting. We are now the guardians of the knowledge of Yoranthium. You need to simply accept you are now the protector of this knowledge."

Jerking to the right. "With us and the compendium. You Satoria are the Archmage of Yoranthium and a secret that must not get out."

Jerking to the left. "That's right you must not be discovered everything that is a secret of Yoranthium is with us right here in the compendium. If you are discovered and found the deep dark one of the hell fires of the abyss will relentlessly and ruthlessly rule Ishormot. Exterminating all Fae and Elven kind."

"Understood." Satoria's eye's dried as she found understanding, as a mage should. Satoria saw the odd looks she was getting from the Governor and Commander knowing she must seem awkwardly weird having these internal conversations with her Arch and Vizier mages. She tapped the locket of the commander with the same open wound on her finger and devoured more memories of the child the ruling body of Farmer Town loved so much. Erasing the little darling of Farmer Town. As she tried to not know and store the memories she was absorbing and replacing. That only crushed her heart little by little and saddened her true feelings.

“Ah, it's your daughter returned from the college. Right away Governor I'll have those necklaces as you ordered. I'll just go to the jewelry store across the street there and get some.” The commander rushed off with a couple of close guards and then after a few moments as Satoria cast a few more spells jerking her head to the right each time and imbuing the necklaces by inscribing blood from her finger on a massive number of them. Jerking her head left. While some time passed as Colusious, and the Commander and the Farmer Town guard was organizing a retreat.

Then came a wonderful thought. The Vizier told the Arch of the teleport magics in the Compendium and launched the necklaces that landed on the necks of everyone who met the governors daughter. Which worked like a charm.

Satoria's head jerked left. “Teleportation what a nice magics.”

Her head jerked right. “Just what we needed, and it works so well, no more confusion and now all are accepting Satoria.”

“I'm still getting weird looks the more you two speak in my head. Looks like I'm talking to myself and creeps people out.” Satoria said looking at many odd and weird looks of subtle fear she was getting.

Jerking her head right. “Don't worry Satoria, we mages always are doing weird and strange things. They'll get use to it and accept you just fine, as a mage they will never trust.”

Jerking to the left. “Mages are outcast Satoria, you had the convenience of living at the college. It's a refuge for us weird mages. It was decided long ago by the King and Queen to protect our kind.”

“Protect, what do you mean?” Satoria was curious.

Jerking her head to the left. “Mages had been misunderstood in most kingdoms. We are considered like demon witches and monsters. Persecuted and irrationally hated.”

Jerking to her right. “There was a mage purges a hundredth's of revolutions ago. They hunted us and burned us on crosses. Crosses we worshiped to our God to be born on. It's in the compendium. Many mages died.” The Arch grew a little remorsefully quiet. Satoria could feel his pain. He lived a long life and was an object of these purges of mages. Satoria could feel his

mental images flood her mind of savage and brutal beatings and mages burned on the cross of the unborn God.

Jerking her head left. The Vizier too was in these purges and it was difficult for both of them as magics suppression was a real magics of those with no magics. The Vizier ran alongside the Arch and she fell and he rescued her and if he fell she did the same. Fights broke out and only one kingdom of founding elves gave them safe haven. It was some kind of hold and the information wasn't being shared. Sharing the faces of the mages that had been lost to the mage purges of the mainland's. Then the awful truth that the younger mages use to make jokes of why the Arch wore a gold emotionless mask and why the Visor wore a silver emotionless mask and never showed anyone their faces. They had been captured and tortured by a branding of iron to their faces by magics that would never let them heal. Revealing them as mages to all who seen their faces.

Satoria was being flooded with images and it would take time for her to understand. Then she felt that the Arch and the Vizier were much closer than she imagined that there was a deeper story and she simply realized they were losing time. Knowing this the Arch and Vizier ended the story of images short with how they traveled here with the first refugees of the Mainland Elves and that the founding of Yoranthium was different than the stories suggested and much older too.

Satoria put her hand in front of her. "Enough!!! I can't learn everything that fast. We got to help Colusious and his people and whomever we can now." Satoria tried thinking on the Compendium for an answer and she accessed it and found it.

Jerking to the right. "I knew it you do have great meditation skills."

Jerking head to the left. "Great idea. But dangerous, it'll take your power to do this you know that Satoria."

Jerking head to the right. "You'll have to meditate frozen in time for this is very demanding and draining."

"Yes all three of us can do this, together." Satoria found the mass portal spell. She could save all of Farmer Town, many others and attuned mages. If there were some left?

Head jerked to her right. "Yes this would do well if you teleport to the shoal keeps and port everyone there. You can petrify

and focus an illusion to hide the keeps and make an inner world fooling all that they are still in Farmer Town and safe."

Her head jerked to the left. "Very dangerous and powerful magics of a forbidden kind. It could cost you your soul for trying to save so many. Don't know if this is the right choice for you Satoria. You risk incursion magics that could nullify you. If you were an ordinary mage."

Her head jerked right. "That's right incursion is not to be taken lightly. You don't know where you'll end up petrified and awakening. Very risky."

Satoria looked forward. Not noticing all the assembled people wondering why Colusious's daughter was so scary and talking to herself. "We must try, it'll hide the magic and only our God to be born could detect such a thing. So said the Compendium."

Jerking head to the right. "Where did you read that?"

Satoria pointed it out to them. The Arch and Vizier were good but not good enough at reading the ancient texts of what kingdom use to be on Yoranthium so long ago.

Jerking head to left. "I don't know, you sure you can read that, Satoria?'

Head strait not looking at the gawking crowd collecting around her with growing fear in their eyes as the sounds of the Mechanation's could be heard in the distance getting closer her father was with her slowly pulling her along in this conversation of hers. Wondering if he could get them to put her in a wagon. "Yes I can read it just fine. I have a wonderful idea."

Satoria faded and disappeared in front of her father and frightened peoples of Farmer Town most of them wearing her necklaces if not all of them. She appeared in a massive hall deep inside the ancient ruin keeps along the cold bound side of the Shoal Mountains. Raised her hands and light magics spun off her fingertips that in turn caused ancient light magics to illuminate and began warming the chamber she was in and down various halls to other similar chambers a series of illuminations brightened.

Head turning right. "My, Satoria you are incredible for your age and lack of talent. You seem to read the forbidden magics with ease and understanding. Quite a unique protégé."

Head turning left. "These rooms you see in your mind are massive and easy to conceal. Look over there isn't that an attunement pedestal? Seen them in their other incursion site locality but not in their original place. This looks new."

Her head strait, "Incursion is a likely high probability. This attunement pedestal is new I just formed as we teleported." Satoria could hear shock and amazement from the Arch and Vizier. She also felt that they were excited and thrilled at the new aspects and possibilities. All four sides of the dark stone black podium attunement pedestal were covered in designs of a cross with open hands of a baby with a heart with the God to be born symbology. Across the bottom and along the sides having symbols of angels and cupids and the carving of the illuminated sun shining from above. This magic was as Satoria explained and was attuned to the nature of the one and only true God.

Satoria went to the pedestal and got up on top crossing her legs and folding her hands under her robes. As her form began to solidify and become more solid made of the same material and petrified. Across the world and in time another corresponding pedestal emerged made of marble and on top a marble version of Satoria emerged as a living statue. The suns energy danced on her sculptured form of the white marble in some garden pedestal. The energy of nature and the sun and cosmos feeding both pedestals and Satoria could feel its energy. Radiating through her, yes incursion was a fact and a reality but not for now. Day or night the energy of nature and the cosmos filled her.

More than that the eyes of an ancient hero the origins of the sword of Yoranthium had opened and was looking at the face of the creator. A smile of knowing and a final resolution and act occured instantly performed by the Archangel Eriderion. The Vizer, Arch, and Satoria were speechless for that moment of understanding. They were witness to the tale was not a fable it was true and Eriderion was a true Archangel in the graces of the creator. Then it faded and the three mages returned to their world knowing where the source of great energy came from.

Satoria focused with the now meditative silent Arch and Vizier. They were concentrating and recreating a larger version of Farmer Town and lands within the very chambers of the Shoal keeps on the cold side of Yoranthium. This illusion also extends

outward concealing the passages and entrances of the keeps to simply feel and be the same as the rim mountain range and you could not see or find any of these keeps if your heart was corrupted by deep darkness.

Having created a perfect environment that would provide food and water and all that they would normally need to live in Farmer town a barrier was created. Created to fool those now living in Farmer Town that this was real, and their home protected from a calamity that lay outside. That danger outside the keeps was true. These magics were undetectable by demons; witches or even dark mages for the true God is a belief of the heart, soul and love. Without that belief one does not know this magics.

The illusion was made true enough. Satoria opened portals to gather people from all the lands not infected with demonic powers or had mage abilities and attunements. Portals opened in Farmer Town to all people heading to the shoal keeps. Satoria telling them to enter to be saved as the Mechanation's were closing in on them and the keeps were too far away. Even though Colusious had been the hero of his people. He simply couldn't move them faster than the advancing Mechanation's. He saved his people by buying them time as Satoria prepared the required magics to help Colusious save his people. She was in Colusious's head and knew his heart and he would be the greatest of hero's on Yoranthium this day. He had saved many and the good people of Yoranthium.

Colusious was surprised he didn't know what to think. His daughter was calling him and everyone to enter the portals. "Everyone it's my daughter we are going to be safe!!! I Governor Colusious promise you!!!" His voice echoed from every portal that opened and each white radiant bubble-forming portal of sunny gold bubbles accepted the people entering them. They walked out into the safe streets of Farmer Town and found their homes as they left them that they thought had burned or were destroyed by Mechanation's. The illusion let the people entering this farmer town to believe they were simply returning to their lives. Safe from the impending doom, safe from demons and Mechanation's as an augmented forget spell took the places of charms and necklaces and simply gave them a piece of mind.

The Mechanation's had almost been in range of the fleeing people and the real Farmer Town was burning as Colusious looked behind him. He walked backwards into the portal finding himself in a safe Farmer Town. He stood before the Statue of a meditating Satoria his daughter. Realizing her sacrifice to save the people of Yoranthium. Came at a great cost and she was now made of stone. Thus he wept falling to his knees reaching out.

In the darkness, a difficult to maintain portal opened a few days later. The combined meditation of six Map Makers was heard by Satoria calling to her knowing were they where was not safe. She opened the portal of light and the mapmakers loyal not to the King but the Mages entered. She realized there were more in the Last Bastion and couldn't get the rest of Rarailmuir's guard but instead the gate slipped in time to a several days before Rarailmuir arrived, before the darkness blocked her powers as incursion took hold. Satoria managed to get that Commander and Guard of the Last Bastion before Rarailmuir and the Map Makers arrived.

With no more mages she lost contact with the Last Bastion and could not reach Sea Shore or anyone in the Grand City or outer defenses as dark psychic energies canceled her abilities. The secluded cave was invisible to her abilities and she never thought of checking the oceans or thought too much about under the rock but she did manage to save some fleeing from the Grand City and Worm days later. Worm and the Grand City housed minor mages of shaping and crafting magics.

Her powers were not as great for the invading Demons and Mechanation's had made if difficult. One demon witch of unusual powers was blocking her own abilities she gleaned from the Compendium. That Demon Witch was looking for the Compendium of Yoranthium in the rubble of the Mages College. Fortunately, Satoria, Arch, and Vizier made it impossible for her to ever find the compendium. Then the Yagrallmagrund's came on shore and a new danger to Satoria's abilities became apparent.

Satoria had began fighting along with the Arch and Visor the darkness kept getting stronger on Yoranthium and her Incursion point felt a shift and there would be another. Incursion wasn't a danger but a distraction that could impact many as an anomaly of what is or could and shouldn't be. As her Incursion point impacted another demonic Incursion point that shifted the

very history of the lands of Ishormot. Satoria was in a battle of paradoxes of incursions ripping at the seams of the natural and supernatural. Twenty revolutions ago an agent of the Deep Dark One had unleashed a dark incursion.

For now, many Yoranthian's were saved and hidden in the very ancient rim shoal keeps of the rim shoal mountains of ancient unknown architecture. Architecture found only in the compendium. Thanks to a little unknown mage of Satoria and the Arch and the Vizier for sequestering away the compendium from the forgotten civilization on Yoranthium.

The people owed their very lives to Governor Colusious for leading his people to safety. Hailing him as a great Governor that spared them a nightmare. All forgetting Satoria and after a nights rest none the wiser of what actually transpired as they went about their lives. The Governor Colusious would look at the statue of Satoria and Forget his loss and he even forgot who the statue was in time. As time passed and never noticing that occasionally the statue wept.

Yoranthium

Book One: Lost Hope

Chapter Twelve: Kumithra's Abduction

By Mark P. Bromley

Time to bring to an end this fairytale of a princess. A plan was made before the dawn of the elf kingdoms long ago. Yoranthium before it's imprisonment by the ancients was a purpose to serve the demons and the deep dark lord of the hellish depths of the fiery abyss. Bring an end the cursed sword and the legacy of the light. Abort the unborn God. Bring about a demonic world. Casting the kingdom of fae and elves into darkness and enslavement. Upon breaking and destroying a heart of virgin purity.[16]

[16] Oddly enough this thinking manifested in the partisan politics of the early 2020's as there was real plans to defame the good religions of morals and ethical values. To replace them with globalist socialism a new false religion of dependence of oppressive and tyrannical governance becoming the cults of woke the cults of extremists philosophies, legislation of lies to replace truth began in the 20th century of fake sciences known as Sociology, Psychology and Political Science and into the 21st century.

The Impundalu that attacked the outer keep on the sundown side of Yoranthium. Had flown fast and long leaving anything on the ground far behind. There was a dark broken old and forsaken five level windmill of multiple broken rows of blades. That had rusted solid and creaked trying to move and it could not the strong winds gusting and trying to topple the old creaking and moaning building. This dilapidated windmill was an old stone design and resembled a large battlement tower. It would have been torn down long ago if it was not purchased and renovated by a wealthy Grand City tavern owner named Dresdie.

Who had taken residence here for longer than ten revolutions ago. Many parts of the old windmill stonework had been recently renovated. It was a large industrial mixed use windmill with milling processes on many floors. Broken mill elevators that use to supply harvested grains and mined materials. Broken and ruined storage silos and harvesting containers surrounded the rebuilt windmill in much worse shape.

It wasn't known who repaired the building. It was for sure this was rebuilt in the recent decade revolutions. This is where the returning Impundalu were headed too. Some of the birds even having eaten their fill and following their lead bird kept eyeing their prize with strict instructions to bring her safely to the top of the windmill. They were creatures of vampire habit. They could smell her flesh and her blood and the pounding of her heart calling to them. Even the bird that was holding her in its talons was squeezing her arms so tight. That the bird's claws were digging in to her skin and tiny trickles of blood began streaming through the darkest night air. Only the other vampire demon birds could see the succulent blood flowing from her arms. They so much were gluttons for blood.

Occasionally the head Impundalu had to express its dominance and keep the other Impundalu at bay with a snapping of its beak or a sound of voice or lightning from its mouth that had ended the corporal existence of some of its kin in a fiery explosion. Show of dominance by force kept the vampire birds at bay for the Impundalu always had a master. A demon witch was always their master no matter what.

They only existed when summoned and called forth by the power of darkness and a demon witch needing a familiar. These

Impundalu were to obey Dresdie for she owned them and if they betrayed her they would instantly die. Familiars have brains and for these birds they were not so clever. If they killed their prize and failed their mission it would be the end for all of them. Still these fine feathered birds couldn't get that in their brains. They would still be tempted to sample that snack of queenly blood before them.

By this time Kumithra was so ensnared in the diabolical illusions of the Impundalu that she had fallen to a deep state of trance, dreaming while in the air. Or it could have been unconsciousness and a trance like state as she had been bleeding out for several leagues across the land. Her blood simply fell back to Ishormot and dotted the landscape of Yoranthium.

She was beguiled and locked in a fantasy love and infatuation. With a blood red turning sunfire gold eyed pink naked skin of her Rarailmuir was exciting and new. She would try speaking with him. Not a word would come back to her. He would quickly blink and quickly twitch his feathered hair around with and occasional squawking. That was enough for Kumithra to understand her magnanimous husband as she snuggled in large soft lined nest of fluffy fir. Fir she knew that he gathered just for the bed lining of their nest. She snuggled next to their clutch of their children of eggs, while his warm feathery wing would hug her giving her the softest and most warm hug she ever had in her life.

Resting her head on his chest was like a down pillow. She would imagine herself strolling down the street with her hand in the wing-feathered tips of her big strapping handsome cock down the Grand City gallery street with a large size latest fashion baby carriage. Inside the carriage would be their offspring a clutch of three or five eggs. At each egg count Kumithra would forget how many eggs she had in her nest. She was blossoming with pride at the envy of every other strutting cock that also was her Rarailmuir. That would try and get into a pecking fight with her tiercel of a husband.

Kumithra's husband was faithful and so was most of the world in that askew illusion of hers. It was a nightmare dream she could not simply just awake from for the Impundalu's were master of feminine hallucinations. Their world would take over and replace the ambitions of any maiden especially if they had someone

they loved. That it would seem only the imaginings of ones love is all it takes to be deceived.

As the birds closed into the tower, the roof was flat and a person of chromatic hair and tall lanky form in a red seductive dress that barely covered her skin was waiting impatiently. Her name was Dresdie. She was tapping a very tall thin spiked stiletto with heels the length of a king's hand that lifted her feet to simply disappear into her long legs. She was getting impatient the time of the lunar eclipse on this the darkest of darkest nights of Yoranthium was nearing. She began smiling.

Once she seen her Impundalu's she captured on the Lollygag Islands were with their target Princess Kumithra. Dresdie was satisfied with her choice of familiar. Her plans had worked and worked too well. Impundalu's were a good choice for a familiar for she liked their pink feathers. Not bright but they served well and were easy to command.

The birds began landing on the roof along with the head bird flying close to Dresdie and dropping Kumithra to the ground. Kumithra was still unconscious and still dreaming. Falling to the ground with pink, rosy cheeks indicating she must be enjoying her imaginings of her life with Rarailmuir the Impundalu. Then the lead lightning bird flashed and abruptly landed, and eyeing Dresdie insisting on a promise being delivered. Familiars do not simply provide for free they demand a promise of a prize and payment for service rendered of the Impundalu.

"Ah, yes my dearest Impundalu you have done well. You had brought me this diabolical and sinister evil child. Yes you should all be rewarded." The leader Impundalu had a blood marked rune for 'fetch,' on its forehead. Dresdie placed it there before the flock was sent to the keep. The rune reminded the bird of it's objective that proliferated on all the Impundalu clones. An objective to retrieve by blood Kumithra. By the ancient power of blood magic using the blood of Queen Zantkara stored in a jar she obtained at her brothel from Gethia and the shades. That is how the bird knew who to grab and abduct unharmed to Dresdie. Using the blood magics of her mother to find the daughter.

Unharmed except for the talon marks that dug into Kumithra's arms.

Dresdie grabbed the throat of the Impundalu before her. She had

the jar of blood in her hand labeled Zantkara. She shoved the blood vial into the open beak of the bird. The bird panic was frightening as it tried to pull away. Dresdie wouldn't let go and it was obvious from her very thin form and apparent lack of muscles. That Dresdie was demonically strong and could easily overpower the Impundalu, the Impundalu's skills at illusion also failed against Dresdie for she was no ordinary female.

Squawking and squeaking trying to break free, Dresdie's thin weak looking hand and frail thin muscled arm was like a steal trap with the strength of a giant. Lightning would hit Dresdie to no effect as she dumped Zantkara's blood down the beasts throat. The Impundalu was choking on the blood. Trying to cough it up and vomit the blood. It was no use Dresdie has magics that would make it impossible for the Impundalu to do nothing more than accept the gift of blood. The bird flopped around and began staggering on its feet. It was in great pain. As it was having problems staying on it's ever fattening feet and fattening body.

Walking over to Kumithra. Dresdie marked Kumithra with Zantkara's blood in the small amount that was left in the jar. Magically the blood spread itself down from Kumithra's forehead and all over her body under her clothes. The blood was writing the runes on Kumithra's body just as Dresdie recited the ancient words to be inscribed on the sacrifice. As the runes wrote on Kumithra's skin burning red and smoking. Dresdie levitated the unconscious Kumithra and went inside and down the steps to the top floor under the roof of the windmill as the door closed by magics.

The bird had fallen on its side. It grew larger and larger until it's pink feathers fell off revealing a pink skin getting more and more transparent as the blood swelled in the bird. The rest of the Impundalu realizing Dresdie wasn't around. Pounced on the blood sack that was their leader and feasted. They feasted well and as each had their fill and moved away. They would multiply to even more Impundalu and more Impundalu by lightning. There was an endless hoard of Impundalu more hungry and thirstier for blood than ever before. The supply of magics tainted blood gone. The Impundalu had to find a new source for their growing unsatiable hunger.

The wind blowing from the Grand City toward the windmill was full of life and blood. Bringing the faint hard to hear screams

and succulent suffering of the Grand City sea elves the Impundalu couldn't resist. The Impundalu could taste the blood and the fear on the wind. They had taken flight in great numbers headed towards the palace in the Grand City. Not interested in a lone rider. For one meal is not as good as many.

Dresdie walked down the stairs as it opened into a large room that appeared well lived in. Modestly lit with light orbs in the ceiling corners around the chamber that was circular. This room was full of tables, cauldrons, magical instruments for alchemy, enchanting and many volumes of books. Books in the forbidden and dark magical arts or that of demonology and runes of ancient and magical purposes. There were many vials and jars of various compounds but only one bottled jar of blood with the name of Zantkara on it. Zantkara's was nearly gone with only a little congealing on the bottom of the jar.

In the middle of the room was a two kings foot high dais that was lit with a cylindrical glowing shield of transparent barrier of muted light to the ceiling. That housed and encased the Sword of Yoranthium as it was levitated with dark lightning impacting its surface. It was like a battle was being fought inside the cylinder of light holding the sword. Each dark lightning impacting the sword, the sword would flicker with an equal amount of bright brilliant white and blue lightning impacting the shield barrier. The blade would flash and throb with a pounding noise on the barrier as the sword appeared to wish to free itself. The sword began to pulse even more and began shining the closer Kumithra came to it, the throbbing on the barrier getting louder and louder. Where cracks could be seen in the barrier. It was humming partly as if it was relieved but also the sword was in pain and alone.

Across the room was a door that was braced open looking out to a dark hallway that must have gone to another set of steps to the lower level. Across from the door was a space that had a set of chains and was attached to a dark image of eyes. The eyes were of an alien nature not normal eyes, but hour shaped and dividing eyes of red and black like floating oil was contained in the eyes. Oddly shaped mouths with sharp teeth in a random display with tentacles and claws and pincers and stingers of scorpion tails, with demons of many kinds moving in the fresco. It was truly hideous and evil a symbol of the deep dark one and a host of deformed and mutated

minions flowed in the mosaic a mosaic that looked alive and would burst into this room at any moment.

The deep dark flaming hell of the abyss was the source of great pain and suffering on Ishormot. Monstrous sea creatures would rise from its depths and terrorize shorelines. Chaos was attributed to the oceans of Ishormot. Life was said in ancient knowledges that all life came from the deep dark abyss. Thus, oneday eight devils of the highest power set foot on the mainlands and created a division of the Fae.

The very natural being of the Faefolken were divided and the birth of the Elven species began as the tear of the heavens fell upon Ishormot. Known as the tear of the founders. A tear of the pain of a God to be born shed in the nightmarish turmoil of the Faefolken wars. The Faefolken many were corrupted and served the eight demon devils of the one deep dark chaos. Becoming the Altered Fae capable of great sins and evils and plagues on the world of Ishormot.

The Fae of the Dawn, were the Fae of the natural world of Ishormot they tended to the world and grew the nature of all that is good. They served the Founder Elves and the first of the fallen tear of a God to be born. The Fae of the Dawn taught the fallen tear. That became the original founders of the Elves the values of the unborn God and that they had a purpose that was kin to the Fae of the Dawn. The Elves were adaptable in body and form and could alter and change along with help of the Fae to be more to rise and bring the real power of the Fae to correct a deep dark corruption from killing their world.

The eight devils learned of the plot of the Fae against their dark master the one. Launching a plot to adapt the tear of the founder elves to the purpose of the deep dark ones. The tear must be wiped clean and the God to be born aborted. The founders were in the way and twisted demonically possessed elves would change their species to service the eight and bring this world back to the deep dark and kill the fae of the dawn. Only the Altered Fae deserved a place on a world of the one deity of the deep dark truth of fiery hell of the abyss. There was no room for a sad tear of a crying unborn God to exist on Ishormot for it fell from the heavens and not of this world.

Kumithra could smell a strong pungent odor that had her

awaken. She never had seen the pale chromatic haired maiden before. Standing before her using a small tissue of waking magics in her hand to wake Kumithra. Dresdie's face looked upon Kumithra with disgust and much anger and hatred. Kumithra couldn't move and did not know why and then she found out with great difficulty looking down and to her left.

Kumithra was chained to the fresco of the deep dark void of the deity of the abyss. She was intended to be the virgin of purity sacrifice. She was far more than that. Perhaps overkill in this unholy ritual. Her arms were pulled to the sides and her legs were crossed right over left and shackled at the feet. Then her head was held in place by a shackle on her neck. "Let me go, you don't have to do this." The gravity of the situation dawned on Kumithra. The moment she realized she was tied to a sacrificial alter of the worst and most demonic kind. "I'm Queen of Yoranthium I have wealth and whatever you want." Tear's welled in her eyes as she heard such rituals do not end well.

Laughter was Dresdie's response to the pleas she was hearing. "Queen, all I know is that you are a spoiled princess groveling for your worthless life. I doubt your mother would have cried like you." Then Dresdie pulled out some torture devices on the table near by. "I could have used these to crush your mother's toes or fingers." Then she grabbed a sharp knife and held it to Kumithra's fingers on her hand. "I could also take each of your knuckles." Then quickly moved it to her nose. "I could give you a pigs snout and remove that tiny nose of yours. You know what? This ritual demands this."

Dresdie pulled out a hammer and a large spike pounding and driving the spike in Kumithra's feet. Kumithra could do nothing but scream as cracks formed in the Sword. Kumithra was in intense pain yelling, "stop, stop it, please...." Until Dresdie did stop faining surprise at what she had done. Stopped only long enough to change to a new spike and lick some of Kumithra's blood from her upper lip. Then another spike was hammered into Kumithra's left hand as Dresdie laughed and smiled at the cries and wails coming from Kumithra.

When that was done she waved another spike in front of Kumithra's eyes. "Would you like to trade your nose my dear, perhaps not that interesting. Oh, well." Dresdie pounded the spike

into her right and enjoyed the wailing until it turned to fear, blubbering, tears and snot. As Dresdie's long forked tongue licked the blood off her right hand. Filling a wine cup with Kumithra's blood to drink it. "I so enjoy a young virgin vintage. Your heart will be strong in my chest. As it's almost time for us to begin the ritual." As the blood of Kumithra began to prepare Dresdie's body for the heart transplant she would perform with this very ritual.

Faintly and weakly Kumithra wanted to know. "Why would you do this to me? I've done nothing to you. I have never met you." With much distress sobbing and sniffling pathetically pleading for her life.

"Done Nothing!!!" Dresdie knew she didn't know; she never knew for she was a naive child living a lie of fairytales and never understood the plan. "Seems I will have to tell you a story. It all started with this pathetic sea elf. So sad and pathetic he didn't even have a name. Not a good name from the terrible people who raised him. I gave him his name a good one. A name of a champion long ago, that fought in a war of the three kingdoms. I was quite fond of in my more innocent days as a mage."

"Who was a mage of legend and a warrior that was a champion of the battlefield and feared by the other two armies? It was said in legend that famed warrior mage walked the planes of the dead and would return to life. Death after death he would revive to life, for he had no soul to lose. I thought it was a fitting name for who entered my brothel and wanted to mate with me." Dresdie enjoyed the fact Kumithra still didn't know whom she was speaking of.

"That male I named after a great hero of the spirit bird elves. An ancient tribe who fought a three crown war wishing to be king and never was. That fool who was named by me entered my brothel, he wanted to join the guard and have a meaning in life. He was young at that time only about twenty something revolutions old, gangling tall push over, pathetic and weak. He didn't have the strength, toughness, or will power only drive, motivation and ambition willing to do whatever it would take. He said to me he wanted to be powerful. In his own words, 'No matter the cost.' Even if it would be a lie." Dresdie was talking about some stranger Kumithra never met.

"I don't know who you are talking about? I don't know why, why you are doing this?" Kumithra didn't understand what Dresdie was saying. "I don't even know you. I'm sorry, I'm SORRY!!!" Training she was given by Thernya just apologize hoping they will accept it and release her out of pity or by mistake. As often in the kingdoms, identity of one person often got confused with another of similar appearances.

"Sorry? You don't even know anything. Foolish. You are part of a plan dear; I made this plan. Now before you die you do deserve to know why. Another pathetic young ignorant petulant child deserves to know. Know their place and know their roll. You are the virgin I picked for this ritual. You do deserve to know." Dresdie grabbed her chin to look her in her tear filled eyes and then turned her head at the sword that had a few cracks in it. "You are here to do one of two things. Destroy that sword or transfer it's power to me. That is what this ritual is for. I could let you die with knowing nothing. But, then I'd be having so little fun. I like tormenting you just as I like playing with my food and pulling parts off bugs. Dissecting rodents because I can."

Kumithra before now thought she was royalty and above bugs and rodents. She was terrified to know her killer cared nothing for her and belittled her to lesser creatures. "I don't need the sword. It's yours. Please, please, please let me go. Nothing bad will happen to you." Kumithra was being naively sincere and honest while pathetically pleading for her life.

Dresdie just cackled even more. "You would like it to be easy wouldn't you? What or whom do you think is going to save you? My birds have by now killed your entire run away cowardly army. No one's coming for you." With more fiendish laughter, "This is a ritual that requires your death, in a painfully terrible manner. You'll be bleeding more than you have ever in your life. You're over a third of season cycle will pale in comparison." With that Kumithra was going to cry out again and in went the gag into her mouth by Dresdie's hands. "You need to listen to my story! We'll start your murder ritual soon enough."

"Where was I." Dresdie thought a moment. "He was skinny and weak. I sweet talked him and he couldn't take his eye's off my body. He couldn't help groping for me. I hope you approve of my body; I think it's very nice." Dresdie did a little seductive dance

before Kumithra. "That nameless imbecile couldn't keep his hands off me. He wanted to do many things to me and I was so willing to teach him, he was exactly the answer to my problem and ultimately a disappointment. I began experimenting on him as I brought him here to this place. I enchanted him and he saw what I wanted him to see."

"He thought this was a palace for the longest time. He was a fool it only took a quarter a third season to wean him off the fantasy and to the truth. He wanted the royal life. Agreed to get the sword for me and I would help him rise in the guard's ranks." Dresdie was thinking because she didn't want to give too much away not too soon.

Hopefully this princess was stupid and didn't see it yet. The ritual wasn't ready yet the darkest of darkest nights wasn't synchronized yet. "I did rituals and he sold parts of his soul to the deep dark. He had spirit. I never saw anything like it. He got stronger and well defined by my rituals. I admit I wanted him for myself. He was fit in more ways than one before I began the rituals. After the rituals he could bat around ten or more males like flies. He became drunk on his new strengths and powers." Dresdie looked up for she could see the ritual time had begun and she was in a hurry to complete this task. "He failed to bring me the sword and now we can begin the ritual for I had another willing to do the job."

Dresdie then grabbing Kumithra's Yukata top, where the two halves covered her. Tore it apart and out of her belt to expose her bra and girdle. "My, my sweet have you blossomed. Pity you would have made a great addition to my brothel. Some of the lords and ladies would have paid any price to violate you. You don't even need a girdle to keep your figure. I could have sold you for a high price. After that you would have been in a cage waiting for all those boys you use to tease." Admitting she had followed her and was never seen by Kumithra.

"You would have been starving and dehydrated waiting for some sadistic male to pity you and love you for I would have lured them with you. They would give you minor thanks and that's about it as they abused and neglected your body. You would be even shallower and broken in more ways than you could know. Fading away and I'd likely have to keep you chained just so you wouldn't

try to end your life." She tore off Kumithra's girdle and cast it to the floor. Then traced with her sharp fingernail under the left breast a line of blood just under Kumithra's left rib cage.

"Yes this will do nicely." Dresdie went to the table with Healing cleric knives on it. "Pity to think how much more of your fathers court I would have owned if I could have sold you to the highest bidders. I could have owned your father with lies that you were safe. Allowing you being raped for realm coin. Day and night sequestered in the basement of my brothel. Along side the soiled linens and smelling garbage." For Dresdie was the head of an elven trafficking ring and many abandoned and forgotten and missing sea elves found themselves sold into slavery in far lands like the potentates Kingdom. Many of the trafficked elves were male and female much younger than Kumithra. Stolen, kidnapped or even out right bought from their awful parents.

Some of Dresdie's trafficked elves. Had been provided by corrupt magistrates that taught the youth magistrates to admire trafficking as a way of life. Just more examples of how corrupt Yoranthium was becoming. Having twisting and distorting education of those too young in Yoranthium with false and misleading narratives such as sexual choice. The subject of sexual choice would only lead to abuse, cruelty, neglect, and degradation of the souls of the youth[17].

Some of these corrupt magistrates had been the principals of Kumithra's school. Kumithra was too young to understand why some of the students never returned and disappeared. Choosing to believe they moved away or some other deception. Never wanting to know the truth and didn't care. The poor and disadvantaged was never seen or recognized by monarchy. It was the corrupt magistrate and school authority that kidnapped children into the elven trafficking of Yoranthium.

Kumithra stirred and screamed in panic. She couldn't move and she was partly naked and could see runes and some horrible fresco below her waist coming to life and tiny demon hands reach out to her trying to pull at her loose Yukata. She was chained,

[17] 21st century the fake sciences via the perverted children of the globalist socialist movement, found it lucrative to buy corrupt politicians in the USA and the world to push false gender legislation's. Targeting minors to stripping parents of their rights to protect their children from abusers of sexuality exploiters of minors to savage lies.

shackled, crucified and couldn't move. She saw Dresdie looking for a knife on the table before her. "Stop, stop, stop!!! As Queen of Yoranthium I command you to stop!!!" She is beginning to sob uncontrollably. Trying to command by force of office. Kumithra had a commanding voice she was taught well by her father and mother.

Dresdie lived for pain and suffering she relished the chance to torture her captives. "You a Queen? You got to be kidding me. I'm the one with the King's Sword." Dresdie showed Kumithra the sword was becoming white hot. "Once I change my heart with yours. I'll have the king's sword and I'll be your queen. You will bow to me. Oh, no. You'll be dead." Laughing mere inches from her face as her face distorted showing demonic eye's and sharp demonic teeth as her tongue rolled out licking the cheek to Kumithra's left ear trying to enter it as she closed her outer membrane of her ear.

"My Rarailmuir will save me!!! You can't defeat my love Rarailmuir!!!" Crying out in a fantasy of her hero and husband breaking through the door just about now. Yet nothing no Rarailmuir and she was feeling weak and still believing in fantasies.

Dresdie just about to lick Kumithra's gills behind her ear to violate her body just laughed as the over sized helmet on Kumithra's head hit the floor. "Rarailmuir, Rarailmuir is your hero?" More laughter. "Silly child, poor, poor silly child. Rarailmuir is the name of the hero of the three army's war. Living as a spirit without a soul. Forgotten to time and apparently to Yoranthium history." Mocking Kumithra with callous and uncaring sinister sympathy. Shaking her head from left to right and some tsk's. Dresdie just laughed at Kumithra like a terrible person playing with candy they had no intentions of giving to a wanting child.

"I met Rarailmuir long ago. Before he even met you child. Were you not listening to the story? Let me explain. The wasted no name loser sea elf is (stressed) Rarailmuir; he was to give me this (stressed) sword. He was in the (stressed) guard. He wanted to move up in the (stressed) ranks. He wanted to be (stressed) King."

Dresdie cackled and hesitated during the ritual. "You should be told the entire story it would destroy you. We were wed

to my master of the deep dark. He never knew he thought it was the unborn God. Not very bright about theology and rituals Rarailmuir is a fool. Unlike the war master mage where his name originates from." Widening a sinister smile towards Kumithra.

"You're a liar. He would never wed a monster like you. He's kind and generous and he has no wife or child.." Kumithra exclaimed and was silenced by two fingers from Dresdie on her lips.

"Wrong again naive princess. He collects taxes and intimidates to collect more than he should. You don't know what he does on guard duty. You don't even know what he did with me after we wed. He did have a child. He gave me his seed. I had seduced him, and he was mine and did anything I told him too at that time. He had too. He was nothing when he met me just a fool avoiding the life as a street thug. He was nothing." A portal opened on top of an empty place on the table. A jar with a deformed sea elf infant that looked only partially formed sat on the table floating in a liquid with a bite taken from it where it's heart would have been.

"This is mine and Rarailmuir's child. He has no knowledge of. I had removed this child before his knowing and replaced my heart with its heart. For it's my body I should be able to do with this unborn life as I please.[18] Now shouldn't I? For I needed its heart to prolong my life." Dresdie looked with great evil at Kumithra moved her hand to her left breast and patted the top of her chest in rhythmic beats of the heart.

Kumithra eyes were welling with tears. She could hear the heart beat of Dresdie louder and louder in sync with the pounding on her chest. As she looked at the nightmare baby, lifeless, cold in preservative magics on a shelf. The unborn baby's tiny, deformed body and misshapen head along with putrid darkened skin was sad and terrible to look upon. She felt sad for the child that never got to know life and live among the sea elves with hope, caring, kindness, and love. Only a demonic monster could have been so cruel. Was an old life worth more than a new life?

Dresdie was watching as the tears built in Kumithra's eyes. Not realizing the tears was for the unborn child more than

---

[18] A war cry of the cults of extremist views that detested life of the unborn that a third of the population was abusive towards in the 21st century a plea of ignorance to create false misleading legislation and elect wicked politicians.

Rarailmuir and no longer for her condition. Dresdie didn't know or understand the new tears from Kumithra, was for the aborted soul on the table. "Rarailmuir was my tool. I heard about you. I watched you from within your own throne room for years. I followed you in the city. Rarailmuir was always too old for you. You never cared for him. You needed a hero, and I sent that dragon to burn down your school. That's when you finally noticed your hero. I told Rarailmuir to save you. I told him it's how he'll become king one day. He only wanted to be King, and I simply provided a plan."

"Kumithra you never mattered to Rarailmuir he only saved you, so he had a way to the throne by your hand. Yet he spurned your hand for that." Dresdie pointed to the sword. "He just wanted the symbol of the king the sword of Yoranthium." knowingly from experience. "I was there in the throne room yesterday. I watched as he picked up the sword. The fool protected everyone with a charm he was wearing from me. I could only witness. Pity he doesn't understand the truth of the sword or the medallion. Rarailmuir doesn't love you child. He loves me!!! I'm his real wife. That is his real child."

Then the tears started to flow down Kumithra's face. This is when Dresdie started to collect her tears on the tip of her inner fingernails and placing what she was collecting in a vial. "That's okay cry. I know how hard it must be for you. No male to marry you no heir for Yoranthium. This night begins the end of this Kingdom and the return of the Greater darkness and the new Queen the one before the eight." like a mother just to coax more tears from Kumithra.

Filling a vial with Kumithra's tears. She just let Kumithra cry and sob on the ritual stone. Of contorting and twisting ever changing demons and monstrosities. "The nameless heathen known now by me as Rarailmuir came to my red district looking for love a life and a crown. His ambition was to become king. I told how there would be a way for he had to love me." Smiling knowing these details hurt her more and more.

"Love me he did. Our nameless hero was like most males weak and guided by his lower region and lust. Lust I provided and cast. It wasn't until I gave him the name Rarailmuir then he really became a believer in himself. I should never have told him about

that hero of the three armies war. Should have given him a more common name. He was weaker than your father who almost betrayed your mother for me!" Flashing her body in a sexy kind of way in that single piece of red cloth she called clothing.

"Of course, I cheated I tried to slip into his bath one night trying to confuse him in disguise as Zantkara. But that sword was near by and gave me away. It almost didn't matter to him. I'm a looker and have been for a long time." Dresdie lied for she was spurned. King Sinderthion was loyal only to Queen Zantkara her mother. The soul mated couple could not be fooled or misled. The eyes would always know whom they were with. There are more powerful magics and the King and Queen knew of one of the greatest magics. Kumithra since she was born became the bond of those magics.

Kumithra realized when Dresdie was lying about her father. Even though her life was weakening, and her heart was failing. Lightly all so quietly that Dresdie didn't hear. "Liar."

"Now Rarailmuir however he was young and young men your age are easy to beguile for they are weak in the knees. They pine for any sexy female who comes their way." Said Dresdie collecting more tears.

"I, Dresdie, gave him the plan of how to become king. He only needed you. All he needed is a silly child to admire him, a silly princess that was given forbidden books. You read my books on thieving, on forbidden love and romance. Those were cursed books of the darkness the cause of the division of the fae. You read my poison of your mind by ignoring Zantkara your mother. That lower shelf was I putting those books there for you to read of the shadows. Then the day the dragon I unleashed on the Grand City was perfect."

"Rarailmuir did as I directed, and he followed me out of love of his wife. We mated just before he left to save you. I promised to bare him a child, and there you go. It's right over there." Pointing to the dead fetus Dresdie ripped from her own womb. "That heart is the heart inside me and now. I'll replace it with yours." Having satisfied her collection of tears.

She reached over to the scalpel on the table. She poured some of Kumithra's tears on the blade. Stripped off her left shoulder strap of her red dress. Revealing her pale and paler

breast and nipple down to her waist. Then plunged the blade into her chest. Making a deep incision under her left breast, under the rib cage pulling the scalpel to the right making a large incision to her sternum.

Upon pulling the scalpel from her chest no blood flowed from Dresdie. Just some black thick oil like sludge percolated to the surface. Switching the scalpel to her left and trembling and wincing in great pain. She carefully reached into the gaping wound and pushed her hand further and further in and up behind her breast and ribs. Dresdie was reaching and searching for her heart pushing her diaphragm, lungs, and veins out of the way. Dresdie was in the most intense pain she had ever felt with difficulty at breathing as if having asthma. Scrounging around for something small and hard to find.

Then she found it. Quickly she removed her hand painfully from her chest. Her skin began to turn black, gray. She appeared to stop breathing. Which didn't matter to Dresdie for this is what the ritual demanded. Dark powers of demon magics were preserving her life. Driven by rage and anger and hatred of the child who sequestered her husband's heart.

Upon opening her hand Dresdie smiled with a little laugh. She had extracted a tiny black oozing beating heart. Then she looked at Kumithra her eyes turning red and serpent like. It was the look of a demon and a witch. Ancient magics was keeping Dresdie alive.

She was a demon witch after all. Raising her right hand and turned the palm toward Kumithra. "It is only fitting Rarailmuir's first born heart desecrates the vessel of my new life with the power of the deep dark one." With that she smashed the tiny black heart on Kumithra's face. Starting at the forehead and working her way down over the eye, the side of the nose and right cheek and down to the mouth where she tried to rub the heart in to Kumithra's mouth, but she would not open her mouth.

"You don't want to taste Rarailmuir's first born. Why not? He betrayed you and married a female he wasn't faithful too. I am by far a better lady than a Hussy like you." Dresdie slapped Kumithra on the left cheek and squeezed her jaw in disgust. As her left hand rose with the scalpel she shoved Kumithra's head back

into the frieze with great and painful force. As the demonic animations grabbed at her braids and kept her head stuck in place.

Dresdie reached for the vial of tears and administered enough to clean the blade. Then with her left hand she made a deep incision into Kumithra from under her bra and under her rib cage starting to the left of the sternum and slicing as far to the right in a quick and brutally painful manner just to hear Kumithra's screams of suffering. Blood was pouring down Kumithra's abdomen down her belted waist and trousers. Some of the blood poured down her long boots while some found it's way inside her boot on her left leg and dripped onto the cold stone floor as steam rose from the warm blood freely flowing from Kumithra's chest.

The pain wasn't over as Dresdie smiled viciously licking her lips at the sight of the blood. "Virgin blood, blood never spoiled by a male. Having a virgin heart beating in my chest. I do hope it makes me one again for it has been hundredths of revolutions since I was so young. This is delightful, I feel giddy again." She reached toward Kumithra with her palm up, facing toward her and her fingertips penetrated the gaping bloody wound forcing her way in slowly, desperately and to inflict as much pain and suffering as possible. More screams came from Kumithra as her chest burned and it was hard for her to breathe. Turning Kumithra's screams into a fight for air.

Dresdie could feel her to be new powerful heart beating faster and faster inside Kumithra's chest. The suffering was so pleasurable that Dresdie was indeed receiving the best orgasm of her life. Dresdie was screaming like the first night she was with Rarailmuir. Her eyes rolled behind her head and she screamed in excitement for the thrill she was having been very similar to a bedded cosmic experience.

Then she found Kumithra's heart. Dresdie could feel her hand grasp her heart and she stroked at it before clenching it tightly. Kumithra couldn't breathe. She was in great pain her heart was being pulled and she could feel her heart disconnecting effortlessly from her body as the trauma confused her brain.

At the same moment the encased Sword of Yoranthium was changing. It was cracking and reforming and becoming transparent fading as one sword and then blackening into a more sinister version. Dresdie could feel the heart of Kumithra moving

closer to the cut in her chest. Then she notices the flicker of life fading in Kumithra's eyes. "Kumithra, don't die on me you have to see your beating heart as I place it in my chest. Don't you go and die on me too soon Kumithra. You have things to witness and see. You'll have plenty of things to tell your mother and your father in the hell fires of the dark deep abyss. DON'T YOU DIE!!!"

The pain and suffering were simply too great and with out love or knowing love she could not exist in this world. She would rather be dead than alive as tears rolled down her cheeks like a flood. The world was blurring, and she was losing any interest in her own wellbeing. All that she had ever known was taken from her this day. Rarailmuir wasn't Rarailmuir, he was a stranger she never knew. Never knew his real name.

From the story she was an object to the throne and nothing more. It made sense why she wasn't with Rarailmuir now. He did push her away like she was a plaything. She was just a means to and end. When her father died. There was no reason for Rarailmuir to marry her. She wasn't the Queen. He was a soulless disciple of the deep dark. He worked for Dresdie. He gave her the sword. He killed Yoranthian's with the dragon attack. He faked her rescue. Rarailmuir was the one who set the fire in the first place. Just to fool a foolish girl into believing in hero's and true love. Rarailmuir tricked her heart into a prison cell and held her captive. That true love was gone and at the wedding their souls did not find one another. Rarailmuir faked that too. He had a wife and she seen his dead child. In a jar and a sad hateful story of how it was ripped from the womb to prolong an old hags demonic life.

Her love never loved her she was just a pawn. Kumithra was just a silly stupid girl. She lived in fairytales and fancied a wonderful kingdom of magics and kindness. Painted in rainbows and unicorns. She believed in a beautiful world and the wonderful life she would have had with Rarailmuir, but it was all a lie and her parents were dead and the world she knew was no more. Kumithra's life slipped from her she closed her eyes feeling her life force and soul depart her body.

The sword of Yoranthium faded and was in a transitional state. As Kumithra's heart began easing out of its chest cavity held in Dresdie's hand and slipping towards the incision. The heart was still beating, gleefully and gladly Dresdie realized that...

Kumithra had died.

Yoranthium

Book One: Lost Hope

Chapter Thirteen: The Broken Heart

By Mark P. Bromley

Love is sometimes fleeting and elusive and is not what our dreams manifest in fairytales. Reality can be brutal and evil can be cruel and abusive to harm that what you thought was true. To the point your heart is ripped from your person, and you would rather be dead than to live in a nightmare.

"Awe, she is dead! Weak little princess tried to pine for my husband Rarailmuir. You deserve this death." Dresdie looked toward the sword as she was pulling the dying heart from Kumithra trying to keep it pumping for she needed her living heart to complete the ritual.

The sword was transparent, and it started to break apart. The cracks on the sword separated into many parts. The sacrifice was working the sword of Yoranthium was going to change allegiance to the dark deep. It would be a sword of doom for anything on Ishormot in Dresdie's way. Maybe becoming even more powerful than her master the dark one. She turned her gaze back at the dead Kumithra. Keeping the heart beating and pulling it slowly out of her chest cavity.

Suddenly a silver glinting blade followed by a silvery chain flew through the open door of the dark hallway. Thernya tossed her chain dagger at Dresdie and slashed her right arm. Forcing Dresdie to release Kumithra's heart and withdraw her hand from her lifeless chest. With a rather abrupt release of the heart and a hand full of blood that went flying in an arc as Dresdie turned to Thernya.

Dresdie turned in pain and screamed in anger so loudly that the very vibration impacted Thernya and sent her out of the room crashing onto the wall just past the door. "THERNYA!!! You will die this day sister. You betrayed us, failed to kill Zantkara and steal the child. You refused to murder this child in the womb and bring the fetus. You rejected our power over these mortals. Look at yourself. You are OLD Thernya. You could have had everlasting life. Now you have grown old. You are no match for me even your demon slaying daggers will fail you this day."

"Leave my daughter alone!!! She is my child, and you will not..." Thernya had seen Kumithra with a gaping wound in her chest and blood flowing down her body and pooling on the floor. Runes of blood glowing red hot all over her exposed skin and that her head had fallen forward as she was chained to the deep dark montage behind her. The ritual of betrayal had begun and Dresdie's plan to usurp the deep dark ones throne was in progress on this moonless and darkest night. The ritual Thernya had once in your younger days trained for was in progress.

Tears came to Thernya's eyes. She was too late to save her child again from Dresdie. "My Daughter! What did you do Dresdie? Not again. No!!! This is evil this is wrong. I can't believe you would continue with this madness knowing this is not the right path!" Thernya was enraged and threw her chain dagger at Dresdie as her eyes watered and blurred throwing her aim off. She missed.

Dresdie laughed fiendishly. "You can't even hit me. Thernya former sister you could have had this power; I would have shared with you the glory that is to come. You refused this gift. You failed to bring it forward on a night like this on Forumth. Also, the night that Zantkara was to give birth. You failed thrice. You are going to die tonight sister. You should have taken my offer." With that Dresdie used telekinesis magics to pull Thernya towards her. By will of force just dragging Thernya by her toes on the ground towards the outstretched hand of Dresdie. Grabbing her by the neck. Thernya was in shock and fear for she never new Dresdie had such powers. Dresdie could tell Thernya had gone too soft and flabby. "You put on some weight. You really think you can fight me?"

Then Dresdie threw Thernya at the bloody feet of Kumithra. "Look at your new child she is dead too, Thernya. That's thrice. Two times you failed or is that three if we count your champion too. All your failures are in three. Why is that? You should have wedded him for he was vulnerable to my charms. He really betrayed you Thernya. As I took his love from you."

Thernya reached up to Kumithra. "Wake up my child, my daughter don't die on me. Comeback, return to me, don't let her take your soul. You are stronger than you know." She was attempting to cast a blood spell in Kumithra's own blood to reverse the cursed runes on her body. Yet the ritual was too strong the moon was dark the clouds artificially made this night the darkest night in defiance of the natural order of the cosmos. The counter spell failed and Thernya could feel her strength drained from the meaningless effort to cast a spell of protection.

"That's enough my unmother. You failed to protect her and now I will not let you try to save her." Dresdie flung Thernya using telekinetic magics across the room back towards the wall by the open door and smashed into a table breaking it and fell to the

ground in a heap. Then Dresdie snapped her fingers and Thernya's body contorted, and you could hear several cracks of various bones in Thernya's body painfully snap like twigs. Thernya was old and the pain put her in shock. She felt death closing in and this would become her fated final end.

Dresdie appeared to weaken a little as it took quite a bit of magics to snap so many bones and toss Thernya like a rag doll around the room. Especially when Dresdie had already rid herself of the former lovers fetus's heart. "Thernya now watch as your adopted daughters heart becomes mine." Dresdie walked towards Kumithra and was about to put her bloody hand back into her chest. All Thernya could do was watch and realize she was failing to protect her own daughter for that is who Kumithra was to her.

Then suddenly another chain dagger flew from the open door and impacted Dresdie in the leg. She screamed in pain and the dagger was burning her as flashes indicated Dresdie might catch on fire any moment. Dresdie then cast another spell and moved her leg like a ghost from the dagger as it dropped to the floor and was quickly recovered by Huspecia. Dresdie's leg was healed yet again it came at great cost to Dresdie as she was a little weaker for the effort of great magics that would be nothing if she had a heart.

"Your apprentice, Thernya? I get both of you tonight and both of you will die. That chain dagger of yours is so out of date." Dresdie then broke the jar with the fetus of hers and Rarailmuir's child. She quickly took a bite out of the dead fetus and opened a portal to remove the dead fetus of a boy from the room.

She was having difficulty without a heart, and she used a lot of magics in the current fight. She needed a heart now and by biting into the dead fetus she could use that flesh to make a new heart to deal with this fight. She had lied the Chain daggers are deadly to her and there was no way she could complete the ritual in time before the dark moon rotated on it's axis and becoming a lit moon again on a darkest, dark of night. It would be impossible to destroy the sword now unless she had more power, and the fetus flesh would do the trick. The dead half fetus of a sea elf and demon witch was blood magic that gave her Rarailmuir's strength as long as he lived. Her blood magics became Rarailmuir's beating heart to be her strength and reinforce her magics. Rarailmuir's heart was a good investment for it made her very powerful feeding on the flesh

of that dead fetus that was their child. The dark twisted stem cell magics, of a symbiotic parasite is what Dresdie had become or so she thought but there was more she didn't fully understand.[19]

Bronanes finished preparing his sword, dagger and spear with the demon oil. He came into the room and told Huspecia to care for Thernya. Bronanes then turned his spear towards Dresdie. Yelling a battle cry as he charged in like a gallant hero with true aim to strike Dresdie down. With a war cry Bronanes charged right at the gaping hole under Dresdie's bare left breast.

It was for naught and an inane action. Dresdie simply motioned with a finger she flicked from a clinched partial fist and brushing it across her thumb of her left hand. Having lost power and reachieved her strength so quickly, Dresdie knew something strange was empowered within the fetus. Bronanes flew to the far wall crashing into some shelving with an impact that shattered the sturdy shelving and crumpled him to the ground. His spear fell from his hand and hit the barrier holding the cracked Sword of Yoranthium and the spear burned and disintegrated.

Bronanes noted the destruction of his spear realizing that barrier is something to avoid. He reached to his right side and pulled his sword with his left along with a dagger in his right. Jumped back to his feet and prepared for another assault on Dresdie.

Huspecia saw Thernya on the ground in great pain. She ran over to her but was like wise just like Bronanes picked up off the ground and thrown to the other side of the room, headfirst into the wall where a sharp piece of stone cut her forehead and she crumpled to the floor for several moments motionless. Suffering a mild concussion.

Dresdie then opened two portals with no effort and a couple of dark shadowy figures began to enter the room. Something in the fetus was more than she realized for her powers should not be so great having to regenerate her heart. Bronanes threw his dagger at

---

[19] A twisted medical development in the 21st century where many believed in the murder of unborn children to be come cannibals of the healing property of dead human fetus stem cell research. Many facing death embraced this grim resolve of stem cell research thinking they would prolong their sinister natures. From Discussions with a dying man who wished to live even at the cost of their own soul in early 1990's.

one of the portal demons emerging. It was a direct shot and the demon screamed in a loud deafening high pitched shrieks as the portal imploded and a phantom body got cut in half and then disappeared into vapor.

Dresdie then once again pulled Bronanes too her as Huspecia was starting to revive and push herself up. Bronanes then felt Dresdie's hand on his throat, crushing his larynx. He tried to swing his sword down. Dresdie with her free hand displaced Bronanes sword. Having the intention to push Bronanes skull against the barrier of the sword to his death.

Huspecia then managed to spin around and seen her husband turning bluer than his skin had ever been. She was horrified and frantically moved her hands on her bodice looking for her chain dagger. Yet it was too far away across the room and Thernya was in too much pain to be of any use. Bronanes was about to die a horrible death.

The moon became a sliver of light above the dark clouds covering Yoranthium. The time of the deep dark, dark night had come to an end. The ritual failed the distraction paid off. The sword of Yoranthium pulsed like a faint heart beat and reassembled itself turning white hot as the barrier began to break. Kumithra's chest took a deep breath and her heart that wasn't removed in time began beating again. The manacles holding her to the hideous Mandala behind her were turning white hot along with Kumithra's neck, wrist and ankles. As the crucifixion spikes in her feet and hands dissolved. The wounds of the spiked limbs closed, mended and healed.

The activity in the room stopped in place and time became relative to the moment. As the shackles melted the blood from Kumithra, the blood runes and the black smeared dark fetus heart began to peal. The pealing became like petals, pink petals of the yesterday's morning trees in the garden of the palace commonly known as Yamazakura. Floating upwards with a glow emanating from Kumithra.

Kumithra lifted her head and she saw Bronanes in a death grip from Dresdie as Dresdie smiled fiendishly at all the destruction she was causing. There was the portal and the shade emerging. She saw Huspecia on the floor looking at Bronanes knowing she was about to lose her husband. Then she saw Thernya

was on the ground in terrific pain and suffering. Kumithra knew if she didn't act her mother and sister and brother would be dead. The last of her remaining family would die this very dark past midnight and dreadful terrifying evening she couldn't allow not one more of her closest family to perish this night.

The shackles melted Kumithra floated across the room towards Dresdie and then she balled up a white hot fist and let it loose on Dresdie knocking her into the shade that just emerged out of the portal and sending the shade back to where it came.

Dresdie upon the impact felt incredible pain and screamed as Kumithra's fist had burned her jaw. Creating a gaping hole that you could see the inside of her mouth and flinching tongue. Bronanes fell to the ground after being released and gasping for air.

Huspecia's wound on her forehead healed and Thernya's broken bones and injuries healed as she got back to her feet. Kumithra's blood on Thernya did like before, peeled off like Yamazakura petals. That then upon rising to their zenith fell to the floor. Kumithra was angry and her eyes had become pure white blinding lights that shot a hateful stare at Dresdie. Eye's of such intensity that lightning could be seen crackling in her eyes. Kumithra's voice was that of a powerful angel. "You will not harm my mother, my sister or my brother!!!! You will die!!!!"

Dresdie looked at the sword. It was whole again and burning bright white and had shattered her barrier spell as arcs of lightning could be seen coming off it. Then Dresdie saw the wicked look from Kumithra as her braids came undone. Her alabaster hair was being blown like the wind in all directions. Her wound was healed, and the runes were gone and the white hot ends of her arms and feet and those eyes with small amounts of lightning coming out of them. Faint angelic wings could also be seen.

Kumithra viciously smiling with an intention to destroy the demon witch Dresdie. Kumithra was something more than just a mortal. She was being fueled by the anger of souls that demanded vengeance for the sins of Dresdie. These souls were that of infants and children trafficked by Dresdie. They were abused, neglected, torn, enslaved, beaten and many other terrible actions leading to their deaths. Kumithra was becoming not just angry but filled with a spirits demanding absolute vengeance. Elven trafficked souls

drawn here for justice and to the only magistrate that had reason to care. Dresdie convened this court of lost souls demanding Kumithra to dispense justice.

Dresdie underestimated the Sword of Yoranthium. It was more powerful than she understood. These souls tied to her crimes and sins fueling Kumithra's vengeance frightening her. Dresdie did not know Kumithra thought of Thernya like a mother or Huspecia like a sister and that Bronanes was now her brother. The heart of a family is powerful magics,[20] the heart of a saint was even more powerful as it communed with the souls of vengeance and justice.

This sacrificial chamber of horrors was never enough to destroy the sword. This ritual was doomed to failure for Dresdie underestimated what Kumithra really was in spirit. She woke a sleeping giant of latent energies. Dresdie realized she was next to being destroyed. Dresdie could feel the power flowing from Kumithra already searing her flesh and burning her to her rotten core. In haste fleeing to her portal and she simply pushed with her legs towards the Portal and disappeared before Kumithra had a chance to land another terrible blow to her, that perhaps would have killed Dresdie.

Huspecia and Bronanes looked at Kumithra and couldn't believe she had saved her rescuers from certain doom. Then they remembered Thernya as it seemed Kumithra didn't need their help after all. Bronanes and Huspecia ran over to Thernya and helped her to her feet and hugged her. Kumithra returned to normal as she gently drifted to the ground and became her normal self again. She tightened her Kimono over her chest and used the tiny side strings to tie it back together with out her belt, which was over by the helmet on the floor by the cracked and broken ritual stone that once held her shackled. All the demons gone, and the mosaic were blank and empty.

Kumithra never looked at the sword of Yoranthium and it simply turned back to it's shining glory and fell hitting the dais it was on and then falling off to the back making a clang on the floor

---

[20] Sinister and evil politics of the 21st century Globalist Socialists elected politicians attacking the foundations of family and spiritual faith in the USA and worldwide by a vicious and dishonest Cult of the Woke. Families of faith are strong and this they the evildoing politicians of the cults of left would learn to respect life and heart of family before the Century was out.

and spun under a table into the shadows. No one cared to look or find the sword and simply left it out of their thoughts.

Kumithra ran over to her mother, sister and brother and gave them a hug. Thernya, Huspecia and Bronanes heard what Kumithra said. They were never certain how Kumithra thought of them only had it in the back of their minds. But they are the only family she really had left, and they rode like mad to save her this very night. Not just because she was their Queen. Kumithra was their sister and child and became the center of the hug. Thernya pulled her to her bosom's giving her the biggest hug ever and kissing her on the forehead.

This was the first time Thernya realized that she was truly Kumithra's mother and Kumithra was her child along with Huspecia and Bronanes who was now her son in law. It was a moment she had always wanted since she lost her family long ago. This family of hers was a moment she wasn't sure of but now she knew. Thanks to a swift kick from a child that was not yet born that kicked some sense into her nineteen revolutions ago. They were all orphaned and they are all now family. Yes that would be the word to describe it. For if there was any family or love or heart to save in this terrible attack on Yoranthium let it be Thernya and her new loved ones.

"You are all here. When did you get here? I'm so glad you are all alive and I was afraid I'd be alone." Kumithra said while ending the long hug.

"Kumithra are you okay?" Inquired Thernya with tears of joy in her eyes. "You were dead just moments ago and now you look refreshed and healthy again. I saw Dresdie killing you." She said grabbing Kumithra to her bosom again. "I'll never let go of my child again, my daughter, I love you too much." A hug of motherhood so long in time that was more than twenty revolutions in the making.

Kumithra had to struggle a bit fighting for air. "If you don't let me go, I think your hug might kill me." As she failed to push herself away from the power bear like hugging with Thernya.

"Yeah, you better let her go Thernya, you are suffocating her." Huspecia said as she was in Bronanes arms and receiving affection on her cheeks from her Hero.

Thernya released Kumithra and realized this place was not that safe. Dresdie could attack them again. "We can stop this family reunion we need to get out of here. This is a death trap if Dresdie returns." Thought Thernya knowing about the dangers they are in.

"It's getting really late at night. We can't go very far from here. I'm very tired." Kumithra was looking very haggard from her ordeal. "After what happened I don't think Dresdie will challenge us again, I think I really hurt her." Then with a thoughtful resolve decided on a plan of action. "We are too tired to travel and vulnerable in the open. Maybe we should move to a lower floor and rest next to a fire and head out in the morning. It's way too dark with this sightless sky above and those demon birds still about."

Thernya thought it out. "Yes you are right. Just grab your weapons and head down to the lower levels as a group. We'll stay on the bottom floor for the night."

Bronanes, Huspecia and Thernya quickly gathered their weapons and surrounded Kumithra who was exhausted at the door to this chamber of horrors. Bronanes held up Huspecia and Thernya held up Kumithra as they descended the stairs to the lower landing. Bronanes gathered some blankets from the horses and Wertomeer outside and then came back in as Thernya gathered some wood for the fireplace on the lower landing. Bronanes also had some rations of hardened and salted meat and some fruit and passed out a healthy portion for all and some water. Huspecia lit the fire with some strike stone and metal she had on her as they huddled together for warmth. And soon after some idle talk fell asleep.

As all that was transpiring another person had entered the windmill unnoticed concealed in the shadows. From outside the interloper had been watching as the birds had left. There was a person moving under cover in the shadows. He had a mission. He couldn't believe he was fooled and tricked. He knew where Dresdie was going he's been there before. He woke as night fell and he came to the windmill. There were two horses and the king's steed outside, eating the grass. He heard some noises from inside the tower and figured Dresdie must be getting hers. Xern snuck inside the windmill quietly and with much stealth at concealment.

Xern was a highly practiced thief and knew much of how to hide in the shadows. Been doing it since he joined the gang's and he was good at it. Perhaps the only thing he was good at in his criminal life. Hiding in the shadows and likely the best as he had used it often hiding from Gethia and her two guards. Never knowing how good he was at stealth. Back then he never knew that Gethia and her Guards were born of darkness.

Xern had snuck all the way to the top and the corridor extended far past the door and there was lot's of deep shadows for him to hide in. There was a makeshift screen and behind it had a stool and a deep bowl along with a corked flask of some kind of healing liquid. He watched from the shadows behind the curtain of a makeshift evacuation chamber as it was a long set of stairs to find relief outside. Dresdie was a powerful enemy to be reckoned with. Noticed how she managed the captain of the guard, Huspecia, Thernya and Kumithra who was dead on the far end of the room.

Dresdie was about to kill everyone that was left alive of the old kingdom. Then Xern saw his objective the Sword its power was beyond belief. He was going to have it once more. The sword glowed and was giving off power and broke the barrier like glass as it crackled with lightning and released a wind in the room. He witnessed the Queen coming back to life and how her bare skin renewed itself and all the blood and gore turn into pink petals that floated around the queen until falling to the floor. Witnessed her great strike on Dresdie and watched as some sharp teeth in Dresdie's misshapen mouth went flying across the room.

He saw it all. The power of the sword reviving the Queen was incredible along with healing the rest of the old crown. Then the long mushy bit unfolded and it sickened Xern. But he could only watch from the shadows as he saw the shiny mirror like sword fall to the ground and behind and under a table. Falling into the shadows. The group had gathered their weapons yet forgot about the sword and left the room not even looking Xern's way. They all looked like they been through a lot, even for being refreshed by the sword. He heard their plans for sleeping on the lower level.

None of them came back up to get the sword. Apparently it wasn't important for them. The King's sword was important to Xern, however. He never admitted to being a fool. 'Here's to King Xern.' He thought as he went over to retrieve the sword. He

reached under the table in the dark and felt the sword. Slowly he pulled it out from under the table as to not make a sound. There it was in his hand once again. Yet no mirror like reflection dull and lifeless and unimpressive looking. It was common metal again. He shook it thinking he could activate its beauty once again. Raising it above his head to see if it unlocked power. Failing to do so with no avail. It's just a sword again.

Xern saw all the pink petals and the broken stone by the wall where Kumithra had been shackled. There on the ground was a green belt and a wellmade helmet. That looked like it belonged to a King. Xern grabbed the helmet and put it on, and it was just a tad bit loose but with a headband of some cloth it would fit nicely. A helmet fit for a king.

"King Xern that is." He said getting worried someone four floors down might hear. He needed to get out of here before anyone noticed so he wrapped the sword in the cloth he found on another table and strapped it to his back. He was quite a good sneak thief and he melded in again with the dark shadows of the windmills stair well. He was almost to the lower landing when Bronanes had opened the door returning with blankets and if it wasn't for the blankets blocking his view. He would have seen Xern standing next to him. Xern got lucky and undetected. He fell back into the shadows.

"Thernya you really rode Wertomeer my father's sea stallion and it's just outside? Just to rescue me?" Kumithra surprised by Thernya's gallant ride to rescue her. She was wrapped in a blanket snuggled right into Thernya.

"Yes, I had to save my daughter and my Queen. I know the most about Dresdie and some day I'll tell you the story. You deserve to know, for you saved me more than once Kumithra." Thernya had tears of joy and relief in her eye's as she pulled Kumithra's left shoulder and entire body towards her as Kumithra's eye's had closed before the warm fire. Falling asleep comfortably snuggled against Thernya under the blanket.

"Hey look, there they are asleep Huspecia." Bronanes gave a kiss to the forehead of Huspecia as she was kissing his neck to repair the damage of the chokehold.

"Why my husband what are you saying." She moved her right hand down low and slapped at him. "Not tonight my dear."

Bronanes was moving his right hand up and down her back under the blanket they shared. "This isn't my idea of a wedding night anyway." With a giggle as Huspecia told him no. "I'll wait, there's something I got to show you when we get to the Mundrunche." Holding her right hand to keep her from whacking him again.

"Like the captain's cabin?" Huspecia's eye's lit up lustfully.

"No." Bronanes was flattered. "It's better and much more fun." The fated couple continued with more jousting of lovely small talk.

Xern was shaking his head, waiting for them to sleep. He didn't want to open the door with it creaking the way it did when Bronanes entered with the blankets and the rations. Those two lovebirds were annoying and spoke lovingly for a while until they finally fell asleep before a nice warm fire on the first floor fireplace. Xern use to like watching love birds it use to excite him he was a pervert. Yet for some reason this no longer interested him, and he was somewhat sickened by it.

Xern then had his chance to leave, and he slowly and carefully opened the door by lifting its weight to keep any stress off the hinges from squeaking and it worked well. He was silently out the door and had closed it.

There was Wertomeer the famous kings sea stallion. 'A fitting ride for King Xern,' so he thought. As he neared Wertomeer the sea stallion reared it's legs and kicked him directly in the stomach. Oh, did it hurt. Xern went flying a king's length and had difficulty getting back to his feet. He was in pain and hunkered over. He was certain to avoid Wertomeer because it looked like the sea stallion was debating if it should kill him. Fortunately, his ribs were only bruised. The bruised ribs were painful but not broken.

He eyed another horse an ordinary black mare that looked healthy enough. The horse didn't fuss too much and he gave it a name. "Stone, come with me. Charcoal black stone." The horse responded to his clicking and he simply got on top of the saddle and rode away. Heading back towards the Grand City. King Xern rides again.

The morning had come, and the dark clouds had remained. Yet the day was noticed as there was more sunlight and it was easier to see the world around them. The fire was running low and

the small group in the blankets was well rested, warm and happy. They drank some water and ate the meat.

Bronanes, Huspecia and Thernya got the horses ready. Kumithra stood inside by the outer door and was troubled by the tale she was told about her love Rarailmuir. She was wondering how he was doing and if he was even thinking of her. Did he just want the crown and not her? She remembered how he dropped her hand upon seeing the sword. It was like she didn't even matter or exist.

Then Kumithra remembered the sword upstairs. She ran up the stairs and stopped before the room where all the evil took place. She was terrified of entering the room again. She had died in that room. It was only because of the distraction of her saviors did she come back to life as the time of the ritual ended with a sliver of moonlight. Yet she needed to retrieve the sword. So she quickly entered the room and frantically searched and seen nothing. But in some dust on the floor she saw footprints, and a hand drag the sword out from under the table. Someone had stolen the sword last night. This place wasn't even remotely safe if someone could sneak around them last night.

Then she remembered Rarailmuir's helmet that fell off her head. She went over to claim it among the Yamazakura petals. The Helmet was gone and only her green belt remained. Upon claiming her belt and securing it to her waist she hurried to leave the room.

She ran down the stairs and almost tripped as she got to the final landing and used the door to pull herself back up. Upon opening the door she saw the other three. "The sword is gone and so is my helmet! We had a sneak thief visit us last night!" Revealing the startling news.

"We know already." Thernya was feeding an apple to Wertomeer. "Apparently he took one of our horses last night too." There was only Wertomeer and a golden brown horse outside.

Bronanes broke in. "Wertomeer got a good swipe at our thief last night. Here's where Wertomeer was standing and here's where the thief with the sword impacted the ground from being kicked by Wertomeer. Way to go Wertomeer!!! You should have killed him. Damn horse thief." Bronanes was looking better this morning. His scar was smaller and his burns were receding and he had more hair. He walked over to Huspecia.

Huspecia was feeding some straw to the other horse and preparing the horse for two. "We'll have to go easy on our mounts. Although they are rested we had to ride pretty hard to get here in time." Then she looked at Bronanes for the first time in the morning. She realized he was looking different and his scars were mending faster than she ever could imagine. "What's with you Bronanes?"

"What, What, why are you looking at me that way?" He had always been self conscious of his looks.

"Your burns and injuries Bronanes they are healing magically." She blinked her eyes and it gave Bronanes selfconscious introspection. Huspecia could see Bronanes becoming nervous. After all these years knowing Huspecia never really cared about his deformity. He was still ashamed of his scars. "Your scars are a reminder to me Bronanes the day you rescued me. I love you and your scars. Now they are fading." She hugged and kissed him just so he knew not to be bothered over his wounds that were healing.

Kumithra chimed in. "My father said the magics of the sword could heal people. I know you all had it rough last night but look we all healed and I came back to life."

"There you go Huspecia, there's your answer. Magics at work here. Do you like what you are seeing?" Bronanes asked with a smile brighter than he ever had in years. Pretending to be a model and puckering his lips at her and winking weird like.

"Yes, our unborn God, yes. I love your new look." Huspecia seductively with much desire was eyeing Bronanes. Realizing that Bronanes accepted her new appraisal of him.

Oddly Bronanes skin was continuing to mend. He could feel the tingle under his skin. Yet the sword of Yoranthium was nowhere to be seen. "We'll walk for a few leagues towards the sea caves. Then we'll double up for a few sunwanes and take the mounts to a soft trotting speed until a few leagues from the caves. Where we'll rest up the mounts and walk our way in. Hopefully with any luck Dabensir and Leorth will have everyone from the outer keep there. Then we'll start stage five and prepare the caves and check on the Mundrunche fleet for readiness to set sail in the next few days." Bronanes realized his helmet was left on the horse. He forgot to put it on before entering. Which would have made him

late to stop Dresdie's ritual. Now he didn't want to wear it as his face was now mending.

Kumithra heard the plan. However, was thinking of Rarailmuir and what she had been told. She was looking at the Grand City that was burning as lightning never stopped hitting just the city. Kumithra couldn't see any Impundalu in the sky. Perhaps they only hunt at night.

She was distraught and saddened. Thinking about all the betrayal of love Dresdie told her about her would be husband. How he had a wife and a child that Rarailmuir's witch of a demon wife tore out from her own womb ending its life. Just so Dresdie could feed off Rarailmuir's strength. Feeding and biting into that aborted fetus like some kind of demonic vampire. This was heart breaking and Kumithra didn't want it to be true. But she saw the evidence. Dresdie was evil. Why would she be honest with Kumithra? 'Dresdie would lie she wanted to kill me.' She thought. Dresdie did lie about seducing her father.

Her answers could only be known by seeking the truth from Rarailmuir. What would he say or do upon her asking him to explain? Rarailmuir loved her he heroically saved her. He let her put that Therica on the side of his face out of fanatic love for him. He knew he loved her; he was a hero a general he knew... he had to know... Yes, he had to love her for him to want to marry her. Dresdie must have lied.

Thernya saw Kumithra deep in thought and looking troubled and a little sad. "Kumithra we are ready to go."

Kumithra was troubled and was in deep thought walking along side Thernya. Behind the horse of Bronanes and Huspecia who seemed to be enjoying a romantic stroll. At least they looked happy. But each time they would snuggle and said sweet things to one another. Just reminded Kumithra how much she was missing and she hated it. She found her family and still felt alone for her fairytale wedding was just fantasy.

"Thernya, do you think Rarailmuir loves me?" Looking a little sad and very uncertain.

"Why yes! I asked him with my dagger by his throat two days ago." with a smile.

"No, you didn't ask him with your dagger at his throat?" Kumithra was surprised and in shock that Thernya would be so ruthless.

"Right after he left the throne room after your romantic outburst. I had to know if he cared it's what a mother would do for her daughter. A daughter that saved my life more than once." She gave Kumithra a quick hug.

"More than once?"

"Never mind that. Rarailmuir has always been honest with your Father and Mother to my knowledge. I would think he loves you very much. He went out of his way to save you in that school fire. If not for him that dragon would have burned everything and then Rarailmuir rescued you and chased down the dragon out of the city saving twenty-thousandths of lives. All of what he is doing was just for you. He killed that dragon for you Kumithra. That's what he told your Father and Mother. I'm sure he loves you Kumithra." Thernya said with confirmed certainty.

"You don't think he ever had another wife or another child. He is older than me by quite a bit." Her mind was full of doubt and lots of Concern. Doubting Thernya because the dragon was the set up for Rarailmuir to save her. Thernya might not be the one to speak with on this issue after all.

"Dresdie messed with you didn't she. She got into your head and lied to you. Dresdie is a monster I met long ago. She is never to be trusted and she will say only what she needs to get what she wants. That ritual last night." Speaking with some difficulty in finding how to explain it. "It was meant for you to die. Dresdie could only kill you faster by trying to destroy your belief in life and love and matters of the heart. She would say anything to mislead you even using that fetus on the table." Remembering the deformed horror on the table. "What was that anyway Kumithra she ever tell you?"

Kumithra lied. "I don't know what it was. It was terrifying and sad. She claimed she took it from a female's womb by force. You are right Dresdie is a monster. Let's forget about it and enjoy this day together." Then Kumithra fell silent and Thernya was worried for a bit.

As the group got closer to the end of the dark clouds the beauty of the daylight started to shine. The warmth on their skin

and their shimmering began to return on their sea elf scales and Wertomeer. They took in a glad and welcoming breath of the sunny air and warmth on their skins.

They spent the rest of this day basking in the sun until night came and they could see the stars for the first time since this nightmare began. The land was safe and no one was around and they set up camp creating a covered fire. To prevent alerting anything that could be flying in the sky. Nothing bothered them all night. They got their rest and continued in the morning.

They rode at that point and the sun and the wind were nice. Getting closer and closer to the sanctuary caves and could smell both fresh and sea water as there was a waterfall covering the entrance of the sanctuary caves feeding high peak impassable mountain water to it's basin.

Kumithra didn't want to go inside. She wanted to return to the Grand City. Her family wouldn't understand if she tried to escape and head to find Rarailmuir on her own. They would never let her go. They were ordered to protect their Queen. She would have to think of a plan to escape.

Yes she would have to find a way that they would not suspect that she was gone. Yet they would know once Wertomeer went missing. She realized her father Sinderthion taught her a lesson about Wertomeer. He could hear the inner voice of her father and would act upon it. Her father used that ability on Wertomeer to win a battle on Forumth when he said he had to save her mother.

Kumithra wondered if it would work for her. Being the child of Sinderthion. The group got closer and was preparing to walk the rest of the way to the secret caves. That Kumithra talked Thernya into letting her hold the reins of Wertomeer. This went well without a hitch. Then Kumithra looked at Wertomeer in his eyes. Wertomeer then let her know with his mind that he knew her and accepted her as his master. Kumithra asked if Wertomeer could run and hide until she comes out of the cave in a day or so. Wertomeer said he understood.

Wertomeer reared on its back legs and started getting crazy. It looked like Wertomeer would hurt Kumithra and started prancing around until Kumithra had to release his reins. The entire group was surprised and in shock. No one could touch

Wertomeer and the sea stallion was out of control and looked angry and dangerous and simply ran away towards a small forest a league away from where the group stood.

"What happened to Wertomeer Kumithra?" Bronanes asked.

"I don't know he went crazy maybe it's the waterfall or the cave. I don't know but I'm scared of Wertomeer. Let's just get to the cave. What is one crazy sea stallion when we have more important matters?" Kumithra asked the group.

Thernya agreed with Kumithra. "Let's follow our queen. Consider Wertomeer a loss it was a hard ride and I admit we might have misused Wertomeer for him to run away like that. Let's get to the caves and settle in and decide what next to do."

Kumithra's plan had worked. Wertomeer understood her and acted well. She even thought she was in danger in the crazy prancing of Wertomeer. The psychic connection to Wertomeer revealed he would not harm her and just wanted it to look real enough to fool the others. That had been the plan.

It was a sneaky plan. A plan that would require more planning and hiding in shadows. Very not like a royal Queen but more like a sneak thief. Kumithra was distraught at treating those closest to her this way.

Yoranthium

Book One: Lost Hope

Chapter Fourteen: Hidden Caves

By Mark P. Bromley

All that which is precious and of value to us is those we love and protect in life. Seeking a place to hide and recover and hoping that one day we can recover what we lost. Caves are a risk but sometime our sanctuary in times of darkness and just a staging area for what to come next as a place to unwind and recharge and prepare. Soon an exodus will be required.

Kumithra was still considering her options to escape her protectors and set out on her own quest to find Rarailmuir. She had to know the truth. What Dresdie told her hurt her. Hurt her badly to the point she gave up on life altogether. Luckily the ritual ran out of time and her heart brought her back from the dead. There is no doubt she would have perished and the sword of Yoranthium would have served an evil cause of Dresdie. What the plot may have been is completely unknown.

She could not simply just leave her protectors. Huspecia, Bronanes, and Thernya wouldn't just let her go. They would follow her and protect her at their own peril. Dresdie almost killed all four of them. Even as they're Queen she couldn't just command them. Wait a moment, Could she just do that? Could she just give them an order by their Queen not to follow her? This idea of royal decree didn't occur to her until just now. She felt she had grown and learned a lesson.

As she walked along looking at the lovely waterfall and how bright this part of Yoranthium was compared to the lingering dark cloud behind them. She noticed lots of footprints poorly covered and disguised in haste. Horse hooves everywhere and other minor debris and rubbish only a large group of sea elves would leave behind. There were no signs of the carriages. Those must have been abandoned at the keep. Fortunately it was only a few sunwanes at a brisk walk to get to these caves. The tracks left by the refugees leading to the waterfall and around to the sides that entered the hidden caves.

The entire band of refugees from the Grand City must have came this way along with the remaining sea guard. Bronanes had his orders to protect these people. The people of Yoranthium are the real power behind the title of the Queen and Kings of Yoranthium. Without her peoples safety and their lives. There is no kingdom.

Kumithra was only a princess a few days ago. Now it felt like revolutions had passed. She was still acting like a Princess and thinking like a thief. A Queen would not think like this. Trying to sneak out was a plan. She had some slight success a few nights back. Yet that was more cowardly and not noble. What of the boy that saw her? What did she teach that child with her methods? The thought she was guilty of acts that were not noble gave her much

concern. Her plan to escape the caves by the shadows felt dark. Then she told Wertomeer a valiant and gallant steed to hide and wait in the shadows. What kind of Queen was she becoming? She didn't want to appear dishonest and one that could not be trusted.

Rarailmuir claimed to be a King. Discarded her the moment he saw the sword. He dismissed her and pushed her away. He did have an excuse there was that Mechanation. Kumithra could respect it but surely there was a kinder way if Rarailmuir in truth cared for her? She was yesterday's princess and a failure as a Queen. She was so wrong in her deceptive methods around those she cared the most for. Dresdie was wrong and lied and then? Then what?

Kumithra knew that Dresdie wanted to make her lose hope and feel worthless. That would only work if much of what she said were truth. To say at least her twisted version of the truth. Twisted but the truth nonetheless she felt her will to live fail from Dresdie's words. Kumithra knew that some of what Dresdie said had to be true. The story of an aborted child that belonged to him a male she knows little of. Rarailmuir would have to explain. If Rarailmuir couldn't explain then he shouldn't be King and Kumithra should be fighting for her kingdom. It's what the Queen would do.

"Thernya, Bronanes and Huspecia." The Queen was building her courage and clearing her throat. "I am your Queen and am giving you a command."

Thernya looked at her. "A Command, my Queen?" Kumithra's eyes were on fire like her father the king and her mother use to do when seriously giving instructions. They expected to be followed without question.

"What is this?" Huspecia inquired as Kumithra shot a stern punishing glance for speaking out of turn.

"My Queen?" Bronanes with a Yoranthium salute at attention with his hand to his forehead with the back of his hand turned to the sky. Performing a proper Yoranthium guard salute. Bronanes believed in values higher than his own.

"Yes, I'm your Queen and there is no King on Yoranthium." Kumithra was dignified and commanding as she eyed her remaining family. "Rarailmuir is not the king, you only have a Queen and that is me. Do not think less of Rarailmuir as a general he has served Yoranthium well and protected his Queen

when I was weak." She strode to the left and turned to the right like her mother use to do when addressing the guard.

Thernya recognized the pacing. She had seen it many times when guards or even her got out of line. She was never prouder of Kumithra as right now.

Huspecia was shocked. Kumithra frightened her and made her stand still at attention like her mother from time to time did when finding out about bad ideas she introduced Kumithra too while playing around as kids.

Lord Bronanes smiled realizing the Queen was truly speaking and he's seen Queen Zantkara do this on occasion.

"You three are very dear to me. I have a mission that only I alone can complete. I'm the Queen of Yoranthium and must remain here and find General Rarailmuir." Expressing her intentions and feelings. Along with years of trained discipline the three protectors wanted to speak but were silenced not knowing what to expect.

"I have orders for you three of the utmost importance. A Queen is not a Queen without her people's lives being first and foremost in her mind. You have in that hidden cave many Yoranthian's and my subjects that need your help, experience and protection, more than I your Queen. I will not abandon my kingdom. I will do what must be done to give my people no matter how little a chance to live beyond today." She stopped pacing and looked back towards the Grand City. The Grand City was in darkness, crackling with large bombardments of lighting, burning and smoking and concealing tiny flickers of lightning in the distance a city that was lost.

The Queen continued. "Yoranthium is at war. Your Queen isn't meant to run from her kingdom. She is meant to face the enemy and fight to defend her people. Yesterday I was a silly princess and today I had saved you my family and it is time I defend my Kingdom. Your orders by your Queen are to save the people in these hidden caves. Take them to my Uncles land of Forumth. That is your orders. Do not follow me and do not worry. I will find Rarailmuir and inquire into his actions. This is something only I the Queen can do." Turned to her three family members she had left and with a tear in her eye. She was afraid she

may never see them again and she was hoping them the best of luck with their duty to save her people.

"We are sworn to obey my queen." All three said at once worried about Kumithra's safety and wellbeing. What are the people of Yoranthium without the last of their monarchy and the unbroken linage of their queen?

"These are my Orders to my Guard, the Yoranthium Guard and defenders. You are to save my people and by doing so you serve the Queen and you're Kingdom. Do not make this difficult or hard. I will not accept your disloyalty. I expect you to follow my orders. If I perish in my mission then you Lord Bronanes and Lady Huspecia are the King and Queen of Yoranthium. Both of you this moment forward Heir to the throne of Yoranthium and the next in line. Lest contested by Governor Colusious then you are to determine that based on the loyalty of the people of Yoranthium." Completing her immediate commands and thinking if she had covered everything they would need to know and perform their duties.

Oh, No. Kumithra thought as the three quickly came after her. She failed and was going to be forced into the hidden caves. They broke ranks and came at her with their arms outstretched. They reached for her and instead of pushing her to the ground or trying to tie her up. Or even throw her over their shoulders or carry her against her will into the hidden cave. Bronanes, Huspecia and Thernya were far stronger than she and could overpower her. Kumithra's protectors simply hugged her with tears in their eyes and backed away one after the other. Understanding with great humility of reverence and great respect towards their Queen. Completely understanding her intentions.

Thernya was the first. "Take care my Queen we'll be here preparing for the next two days. You do what you think is right. It's what Queen Zan..." Then she broke into tears. Unable to complete what she wanted to say. Her daughter was all grown up with her own purpose and she knew it was personal between Kumithra and Rarailmuir.

Huspecia was the second to hug her. Huspecia kissed Kumithra on the cheek and said. "Don't forget these." Presenting her with her set of chain daggers. "It's not safe out there and even though you still have much to learn with chain daggers. Just

remember keep the sharp pointy blades aimed at those you intend to kill. I obey you my Queen and we will meet again." She backed away and consoled Thernya her mentor. "I taught her well Thernya don't worry the Queen will be okay."

Bronanes was last and he bowed on one knee before the Queen. "Queen Kumithra you are like your mother. A strong and fine Queen who will lead as she see's fit." Bronanes reached to his side and grabbed his belt and unfastened it so he could present his faithful side companion a short sword and scabbard still covered in demon oil. Offering it to the Queen. "This sword is just a sword it isn't much but you can use it to defend yourself. Please accept my gift and with the weapons we offer. You will be defended as we three had promised to do."

Bronanes was finding it hard not to tear up and cry. But like most strong willed males of his linage he would not cry. He just sniffled. "Take good care my Queen. Your final orders will be obeyed and I the captain of your Royal Guard. Commanding our Queens Yoranthium Navy along with the Mundrunche fleet. The oldest and finest ship of the Navy of Yoranthium will save your people. Thus I swear unto death. For the Queen of Yoranthium." Before rising. His right hand grabbed the Queens left hand and he kissed her hand. Letting go. He stood and saluted and did an about face military style turn. With his right leg behind is left and pivoted on the toe of his boot and then turned away at attention and walked to Thernya and Huspecia.

Kumithra stood there for a moment and just blinked. Her plan has simply worked she didn't have to try to sneak around again. She just did the Queenly thing and her family obeyed as she had hoped. She was sad and took a few steps back and then turned and walked away. She was heading to meet Wertomeer in the woods. As Thernya, Bronanes and Huspecia said nothing more and just watch her walk far enough away.

"I knew she would eventually act more like her mother Queen Zantkara. I'm so proud of our Queen. Thank you both for understanding and aiding Kumithra. You both do her much respect and service. Look she's going to where Wertomeer is, I knew she planned this and we should be proud she took the right course." Thernya was smiling with her tears and was being supportive of Bronanes and Huspecia.

"When did you know?" Asked Huspecia.

"I didn't know until last night. I knew about that ritual. I was a student, more like a slave of Dresdie a long time ago. That was in another time a lifetime ago. I was on the wrong path and living in the dark shadows. Dresdie was on borrowed time last night. If she didn't complete the ritual the Sword of Yoranthium would not change its master. All we had to do was delay and interfere until the moon's light returned. You all did a wonderful job." Thernya gave both of them a hug.

"Last I saw you and Huspecia were on the floor when I came charging in. Exactly how were you going to stop her Thernya?" Bronanes wanted to know.

"I had two sets of chain daggers. Here Huspecia I have a spare set for you. Seeing you gave yours to Queen Kumithra. I had enough strength to continue the fight" Pointing down to a pouch that contained a magics vial. "I was going to use this potion to heal myself while Dresdie turned her back and then strike true with another attack. Then Kumithra would revive at the end of the ritual as the moon returned for the sword wasn't destroyed and she still had her heart."

Huspecia scoffed. "I don't think your plan was working Thernya. It was my dagger that made her turn away and deal with me. That idea didn't last long. Let's face it. We're a very good distraction at best and we would have died last night. If Bronanes hadn't arrived finally buying enough time for Kumithra to save us we would have died two nights ago. It took all three of us. What is she anyways?" Huspecia had to know.

"Dresdie's a high priestess of the Deep Dark One the lord of the evil gods of the eight. She is a demon witch and conspires with the unholy to bring the elven kingdoms to ruin. Then she became something worse perhaps one of the demons of eight. Her real plans are to usurp the Deep Dark One and assume the hollow throne of the damned. Think she could undo time and events by incursion magics. Last night we fought true evil and we only delayed it and nearly paid with our lives in the process. Queen Zantkara and Kumithra is my only reason for living and they saved me after Dresdie murdered my champion and my child."

Huspecia never knew this about Thernya and it was a lot of information. Both Huspecia and Bronanes spent years in the halls

of the Healing Clerics and learning the faith of their unborn God and legends of a savior. Evil wasn't a word they knew and now because of last night and nearly dying in their first encounter. Huspecia felt that a new deadly threat was truly stalking them in the darkness of the shadowy fringes of their perceived world that came with the dark clouds and wind covering most of Yoranthium.

Bronanes didn't like the story either. He never heard such nonsense about actual evil as a being. He always thought evil was a deed by the criminal or the sick. Thernya's words were true. He felt that solid unevenly powerful grip on his throat and felt that Dresdie's hand claws of fingernails digging into his skin and crushing his larynx and none of his training from Rarailmuir or his father the admiral was enough to save him. "So that was a real face of evil? Thernya you'll have to prepare us if demons are going to plague us these last few days on Yoranthium before we head to the open seas and Forumth."

Thernya was forth coming with more information. "You are only sea elves and I'm a mainland elf from Illunstrom, kingdom of the Third Elves founding. As sea elves you might know the surface of the water down to over two hundredths depths. In the belief and service of the Deep Dark One we learn there are worse creatures and evils deeper than you know coming from the fiery abyss. Deep, deep, deep in the darkest abyss of the ocean lives true evil and destruction that has always plagued our world."

Thernya was trying to be careful not to create too much fear. Fear she was taught from forbidden books of unmentionable evils and demons and monstrosities the world is better never knowing about. It could only breed madness to dwell on such things. "Like the gigantic monsters used to fire the Mechanation meteors. It's likely the very creature that did away with the best Navy in this world that is known as Ishormot. The masters of the surface ocean have been the Yoranthium Navy. There are other creatures too just as dangerous and only few and far between stories of horror exist that even speak of such demon monstrosities of the Deep. Even the kingdom of the Deep Dwellers is known and they live on the precipice of the Hell of the Deep Dark One."

"Oh stop!!! Thernya now you are just playing." Huspecia was agitated because of the size and scope of evil in this world was

getting way out of hand and leading to despair. "You make it sound like we should give up for all is lost. Just lose hope?"

Bronanes walked over to Huspecia's side. "We have love and heart my lovely." Putting his arm over her arm and giving an uplifting sermon. "We have each other and we believe in a saintly God of the light and that of renewal of life with the birth of life. It is our teachings our God is mighty and the all-powerful. I'm sure we are meant to be stronger than any evil we will face. Have courage my love. For if Thernya once followed them. Then found them to be a lie embracing our unborn God. Teaching us how to defend against them. Not to mention the powers of the Sword of Yoranthium. Kumithra our Queen returning from the dead to save us. I'm positive we have the will to overcome evil."

"You speak truth my Lord Bronanes. I, Thernya did see the faults of a fake evil one. Yes it is our lot to suffer and overcome our condition and rise above our problems and push for a better future always working for the light. Seeking the truth of our understanding. We of the unborn God are not without our saints and angels and those matters of the divine. I was lost when Queen Zantkara and Queen Kumithra found me and saved me. We together must do as our savior Queen has ordered us and save her people." Thernya now understood the Queen's command even more and it made more sense letting her go. Beginning her mission to find Rarailmuir. Hopefully they can reconcile.

"Oh, look a cave, wonder what's in there? Let's not get to in over our heads. I don't think any of us count as clergy. So let's get inside and speak with Dabensir and Leorth. Let them know everythings going to be okay." A smile returned to Huspecia's face glad not to be speaking anymore about evil things. Changing the subject away from a meandering of theology that they themselves are not prepared to lecture.

Upon entering the cave they were met at spear point and some sea guard carrying torches and light orbs. "Who goes there, friend or foe!!!"

"It is I, Captain Bronanes your commander and royal protectors at my side." Bronanes eyed his sea guard. "It is good you have taken defensive positions. Take us to Dabensir so we can understand more of the condition of our egress over the next couple of days."

The guard stood down putting their weapons to their sides and saluting the three. Having an escort was assigned to guide them to Lieutenant Dabensir. They had some minor chattering with the guard and each other on what seemed like a long narrow passage. Wide and high enough to move large items and two horse widths into the caves as large sized stone doors were slid to the open to allow access into a longer corridor that was well braced and supported by carved magics of stone shaper crafters and miners. Every few king's lengths there were light orbs with a torch lit every other three light orbs. Stacking spare stacks of torches by each door for emergencies and defense. It must have been an idea of Dabensir to stagger the torches least those Impundalu demons attack. Bronanes asked their escort, and it was exactly as expected.

The Hidden caves were created long ago as a refuge and retreat. More than that the Yoranthium Navy as a secret facility housing the Yoranthium's secret shipyards also utilized these caves. Where the Mundrunche was recently upgraded to a new class of sea elf ship. The sea elves do breathe under water and had the magics and technology that only the sea elves could create over five hundredth's revolutions of never having been involved in any serious destructive war. War was never known on Yoranthium until yesterday.

Upon reaching the final sealed door about fifteen in all with tunnels that ran about ten kings length each. The caverns expanded into an enormous underground courtyard. Just before an inner defensive wall behind a moat of spikes and lowered draw bridge before an open portcullis. Many sea guard, citizens, children and horses could be seen as they were getting organized and moved into the underground keep.

Dabensir had heard of Bronanes arrival and was waiting along side Leorth who had now been given a uniform of the sea guard under the rank of Dabensir. "Lieutenant Dabensir reporting to the captain of the sea guards Lord Bronanes, Sir." With an official attention and salute.

"Very good Lieutenant Dabensir, report." Commanded Bronanes as he returned the proper salute.

"After you had left sir the sea guard set watch and the broken and torn body parts became a threat at the abandoned keep. We simply torched the remains and cleared the fortification.

The lightning birds never returned. Upon sunrise we gathered the citizens and abandoned the carts and just took the horses with us to the caves to lessen the burden considering it was in a day and a few sunwanes marching distance from the Keep."

Dabensir took a deep breath. "We camped in the open and no dangers befell anyone and we had a relative peaceful night."

"With acting commander Leorth we managed to get the citizens and sea guard along with the horses to move all the supplies and magics we could muster to this location. We saw to the defenses and prepared to wait out a siege for your return my lord. Good news is that we have more than enough ships to handle all citizens and sea guard. With six ships fully prepared and ready for war should they be needed. Including the fully refitted Mundrunche as your command ship." Dabensir was proud of his recent command and activities and it shown on his face. He had performed his duties beyond expectations.

"Lieutenant Dabensir and Commander Leorth, you are both a credit to this command and I'm proud you are able to lead effectively and well in my leave." Bronanes gave them a smile of admiration. "Let's get these people hunkered down in here for a few days and send out five scouting groups to the surrounding farms and acquire any additional resources and save more citizens over the next couple of days. Have all scouts report back the morning of the third day for I plan on taking the citizens and our sea guard and remaining navy to Forumth as instructed by the Queen who has joined the Land Guard along side General Rarailmuir." Bronanes wanted to lay at rest any questions of the Queen's whereabouts by informing Dabensir of the intended purpose of the Queens absence.

"I thought the General is now the King?" Leorth wondered in surprise at Rarailmuir being just the General and not the King he was told about.

"The Queen did not wed. Queen Kumithra proclaimed Rarailmuir is not officially the King, and we are under the command of the Queen. Furthermore I Lord Bronanes and Huspecia have been decreed the new Regents upon the Queens return. This is witnessed by Lady Thernya the Royal protector and surrogate mother to the Queen, so you know this to be true."

"We have no doubt's sir." Dabensir was exceptionally loyal to Bronanes. "I'll give you the tour and explain conditions of the caves fortress and the conditions of the ships."

"Ladies, Huspecia and Thernya. Please forgive me for leaving you unattended as I see to our defenses and means of transport to Forumth." Bronanes looked Huspecia in the eyes.

Huspecia didn't want him to leave her but she understood his responsibilities. "Very well my Lord. I and Thernya will tend to the conditions of the citizens and get organized here for what we need and should distribute among the manifests of your navy."

Thernya agreed with Huspecia's decision. "As head of the royal household affairs. I do believe I'm a perfect fit to head up this initiative with so many civilians to plan for and a half a third season journey by sail to Forumth. You should also send a scout to the mines and Worm to have them evacuate to the land bridge shores to be evacuated."

Dabensir motioned to a nearby guard to aid Thernya as directed. Then turned back to Bronanes and Leorth and began walking away towards the cave keep.

The Keep was old, existed here long before the sea elves inhabited Yoranthium. It was different than the shaped stone found in the earlier part of the cave passage. It was massive single shaped stone with shaped ports for arrows and anti-siege weapons leveled around five floors to the roof of the cave. The portcullis was wide and only two floors high. The massive overhead Portcullis was about a king's length in width. With three more portcullis and sliding black obsidian stone doors between each Portcullis behind the ones starting in the front.

Between the stone main entrance was oil pour holes that would slow any enemy trying to breach the doors. The outer wall was a single defense wall that went from one side of the caverns wall to the other. Entrances to the Keep wall interior could be found once they were on the other side of the wall. The stairs were shaped stone steps and the doors were thick lacquered reinforced mithreal wood.

Once on the inside of the keep you could see a similar wall to the outer coves about a hundredth's king lengths on the other side that was longer and higher than the first. At eight floors high, with the same door set up but in reverse. The inside area had many

tents set up kind of like a bazaar open market. Much of this was meant to support the auxiliary Yoranthium fleet of Naval ships and for specialist facilities of new magics and development. With the citizens setting up some resting and food areas as the open inner court became their current refuge.

Bronanes, Dabensir and Leorth had a significant conversation as to the limits of defenses of the keep for only two days. How they would supply the Navy on the other side in the hidden sea cove shipyard facilities of the cove side keep wall. The conversation covered all the problems and the logistics needed to sail the refugee fleet to Forumth. Covering this rather lengthy and tedious proceedings and overview. The group then left the staging area inside the keep and made their way to the sea cove.

Once at the sea cove there were many ships capable of transporting the large retinue of refugees. The ships were being fitted with sails and tack and balanced for the resources at hand. If not combat capable they were given one central main mast a jib and a spanker for sails. Ships with more masts were reduced and the spare masts given to those with less. This way all the transports could maintain similar speeds.

While shipyard designers and shipping artisans paid attention to the demands of their elven contents and supplies for the half a third season slow sail to Forumth. Providing the weather could be relied upon and no bad winds or dark clouds would follow them.

Most of the citizen ships were not ready for high seas and would become liabilities in such an event. This is where Bronanes had hoped the Celestial mages would prove to be correct and this magical dark storm would not impact their plans and all would be smooth sailing. The trip could take half up to a third of quarter and if double that time the supplies would become difficult if not for the fact they are sea elves and able to fish as needed. Survival on the sea was not going to be too much of a logistical nightmare hopefully.

There wasn't enough sea guard to support all these ships and there weren't enough citizens trained to sail. The real difficulty was training up crews, instead of just hoping for calm seas and smooth sailing. The most difficult of tasks was to get citizens informed and trained up in two days to manage a sail craft

competently. A long detailed instruction had to be given by Bronanes. Dabensir and Leorth being the ones he relied on in creating and combing the civilian's to take on the assignments of sail captains and breaking them into groups of five to ten to pilot each watercraft as the sailing crew. Weapons would be issued to the conscripted boat crews of a few bows and arrows. The rest of the citizens would be required to make and use.

Fortunately, they are sea elves. That falling in the water or even flooding a craft wouldn't be a problem for them. As they could swim up to about two hundredth's depths underwater for about a two-thirds of the day. Mostly the foods and other supplies simply needed to remain dry unless they tried to fish. Raw fish was often a menu item of delicacy to the sea elves. As there were preferred methods of preparation even under the water for all kinds of catch.

The most difficult aspect that Bronanes had to deal with was how to crew six naval ships of the line. The Mundrunche needed a crew of two and fifty hundredths, while the five light frigates required a crew of two hundredths each. The sea guard lost some good sailors last night and the auxiliary fleet only had a skeleton crew to guard the port facility. Sadly none of the navy has reported from his fathers command or Sea Shore. Making for a crew of four hundredth's short and another hundredth's needed to fill the transports. Leaving Bronanes only a hundredth's each combat ship. He could conscript. Finding skilled conscripts always proves difficult. The conscripted would fill the lower ranks on the watercraft but that would only increase each crew by about fifty more each. The dangers of any naval battle would be great.

The conscripted would have a low rate of surviving any real combat actions and it would be assigning raw recruits to their doom. Bronanes was the son of his father the Admiral. When he was old enough his father placed him on the Mundrunche as the new refitted command ship was being built. Bronanes was expected to be his father and thus an officer and never attended boot camp for the Navy. His first day at his father's side was dangerous. His father had to grab his arm or clothing or his ear to keep him out of getting killed frequently. It was like being chained to his father like a convict. Bronanes learned to excel at command but being a deck hand not so much.

It wasn't until he healed enough after the dragon attack that he then became an instructor at the Naval school. He actually learned more from the senior ranking in the school than being a teacher. He could only drill commands into the students. Bronanes learned a lot about rigging and sailing. Where he finally became a competent deck hand.

He also learned of the new naval magics and this is why he became the captain of the Mundrunche. The Mundrunche was that new refitted ship and why it needed a larger trained crew. Fortunately for him the essential crew was among the remaining sea guard and he took those one and fifty hundredth's and fifty conscripted to fill the ranks of his command ship. It was the fastest ship and could respond better than the other five frigates.

Thankfully the Mundrunche and the five combat frigates were fully rigged with three double sail masts, two jibs and a spanker each. The Mundrunche about fifty revolutions ago was the pride of the Yoranthium navy it was a full sized combat command ship back then. Time replaces these ships and today it was nothing more than an over sized frigate.

The ships of the line were better off than the transports. The transports were a standard hull of coated wood simply designed to float and hold cargo for import and exportation. The combat ships constructed of a special process using the tree sap on the island and various varnish, sealants and high grade mithreal lacquering. The naval lacquering involved a high quality sap from the Yamazakura trees unique to Yoranthium. Mixing that lacquer with mithreal dust and recoating the wood and following up with a fourteen-layer process made the wood of the combat craft very strong. Nearly and almost to the same quality as the mithreal armor used by the land guard in heavy plate mail of the older kingdom some three-hundredths revolutions ago. The Fiber lacquering method was with much greater benefit and made for a very light ship construction technique that made Yoranthium ships faster and stronger than other ships from other kingdoms.

Bronanes could see some of the special magics being loaded into the Mundrunche. Black stone slurry was being funneled into the housing below the deck in the center. The black stone slurry was a high-energy fuel for the new systems installed. Untested and claimed would replace sail one day. New magics to facilitate the

firepower of the ship were being loaded. Along with the magics acquired from the supply storage back at the carriage houses. There was ballast being loaded into gunnery storage. Bronanes was satisfied the shipmasters in the yard knew their duties and had been on top of all the preparations for the fleet.

He could see several tugboats had been preparing to pull the ships through the narrow passage to the open ocean in a couple of days. They had also been rigged to be towed themselves by some of the refugee transports as extra seating for passengers. All the ships were being prepared no matter how small for the exodus that would be taking place.

Bronanes had been quite busy with Dabensir and Leorth all day. They had a few laughs while planning the navigation and exodus and Leorth was a carriage master not vested in understanding naval terms. Leorth was a quick learner and would become one of the first of ten in his class to train other sea captains for the refugee transports. Good thing Leorth could tie knots of rope in his carriage knowledge with understanding nautical terms. He was at the head of his class understanding navigation. Leorth was allowed to join the other guard commanders that would be assigned to guiding the refugee fleet.

Plans were made on the first day as to what to expect and it became apparent the two half third of a season journey had a learning curve to all the transport captains that didn't know how to navigate their ships. Bronanes would tell them, "There's nothing like getting on the water to learn how to swim. Fortunately, you are all sea elves and swimming is what we all do best. So, trust in your instincts as sea elves and pay close attention to the sea guard assigned to help you. Learning to command a small transport isn't that difficult if you work together and communicate well enough."

Leorth was becoming more confident as the training went on. He was a fine student and aided the rest of the class and showed to be a good choice by Dabensir for command. Leorth was already helping those in class that needed assistance. Even in a quick test. Leorth stopped filling in his answers and reached over to one of his classmates having problems and got them back on track. Leorth thought he failed, as he didn't finish his test.

Bronanes pulled him over to the side and congratulated Leorth in front of all the students for putting his own ambition to

the side to assist others. As Bronanes stressed the only way a ship and fleet works is by helping one another to succeed. The rest of the trainees understood this lesson well and by the end of the day they looked ready to lead a flotilla. Bronanes was proud with great confidence they will be ship shape.

The Caves were well lit by the time nightfall outside the cave came. The only way they knew in the hidden cove that it was night was from the crack of light at the mouth of the cove to the open sea becoming dark. Or from the scouts returning from their duties to gather more citizens. The order was given to close all entry points and only a night watch would be posted in the cove to monitor the ships as the rest moved back into the keep. The guard would be rotated, and the mealtime would be issued for all those to attend. Other than that, there had been no threats this night and no alarms had been raised.

Bronanes finished his duties. He found Thernya preparing meals with the cooks and Huspecia was with her. "So how was your day?" Smiling Bronanes hugged Huspecia from behind kissing her on the cheek.

"Good, the people are in good cheer." She was helping some of the sea elf children with their meals. As several of the refugees had began playing music in the background singing about their voyage from Yoranthium and glad for their protection of Lord Bronanes, Dabensir, Huspecia and Thernya. They hailed the Queen for fighting to protect them this night with her own sacrifice.

"I'm glad but I have something to show you, Huspecia." Bronanes grabbed Huspecia's hand pulling her to the door. Quickly escaping as no one was looking and as not to attract attention.

"Don't stray too far you have responsibilities you two." Thernya said as they left the room. Nothing escapes Thernya.

Bronanes ran with Huspecia down a few small crevices that she was unaware of. It was a series of secret passages. Then Bronanes doused the light orb. He began kissing her and started to undress her. She did the same to Bronanes. Their eyes adjusted and opened.

Huspecia was amazed she could see there was living strands of a plant hanging from the ceiling and other plants around them

all of them growing in this dark cave. They could glow and glow brightly these plants did. There was a pool of water in the middle of the room and steam rising from it. Noticing the glow of soft magically illuminated moss on the bottom of the hot pool. "Oh, my. How romantic Bronanes you could be at times. I never knew this place existed."

"Come along Huspecia, join me this water is wonderful, and I so wanted to show you this wonder. Look at you my love, your body is so nice." Bronanes moved into the water and Huspecia couldn't help but notice and admire Bronanes body he was fully healed, as well being so excited as he got into the pool. Yes she would follow him into the pool she would follow him anywhere as she got more excited.

The water was very warm, and she pushed her body close to Bronanes. They had kissed for sometime. Sweat pouring down their exposed skin above the warm water. They had been touching each other's body for a long few moments. The warmth of the tub was relaxing and restful being soothed by the warm water in the pool.

Bronanes then relaxed too much and fell asleep. His head fell back and began snoring. Huspecia could feel he was out cold and snoring loudly. Expended from the very busy day. No longer up for what he was planning. Huspecia was a little disappointed but was in this warm pool feeling very tired herself and simply cuddled next to Bronanes. The two had a long day and overexerted themselves.

At least Bronanes was a romantic and had thought about Huspecia. Their life together just began. There will be more chances for them to make love to one another.

Yoranthium

Book One: Lost Hope

Chapter Fifteen: The Mission

By Mark P. Bromley

Time to find out what is true and what is not? Is often one of the real questions in any relationship even those that have not been fully committed to or realized. Why would she have rushed into a marriage when she never knew the past? Swooning and dreaming never really talking or being romantically involved was the price for being an infatuated child to shy to even take the time to be romantically committed?

Kumithra had left her protectors behind at the hidden secluded cave that accessed the hidden keep and the cove for their refitted and newly designed Naval ships. Experimental class naval craft and storage for older transports removed from service or deserted by their crews. It was a shipyard cove used for many purposes and that of storage. Kumithra knew they would be okay and Bronanes, Huspecia and Thernya was the best chance that the people of Yoranthium that could escape had.

She had to know what was becoming of her kingdom. A kingdom her father King Sinderthion and her mother Queen Zantkara had been building ever since she was born. Rebuilt anew since the dragon attack that resulted in great loss of life. Rarailmuir became Yoranthium's greatest defender after he managed to slay the dragon.

The dragon attack had set back many of the plans of the Grand City and utterly decimated the shore guard upper ranks. Farmer Town and Sea Shore along with the mining town was never touched and much of the economy of Yoranthium remained in place. There was only a minor drop in Yoranthium's exports and an increase in imports. It wasn't enough to suggest any real problems of Yoranthium to defend itself or to remain the economic trade giant it had become in the known Kingdoms. Not significant enough to encourage a military coup from any kingdom Kumithra was aware of.

Perhaps what Kumithra understood about Dresdie was right. There was a greater evil that Yoranthium never knew much about. There are other kingdoms and from time to time raiders and pirates and invaders from unknown shores would try to ravage the sparse shore localities. Namely Sea Shore. She remembered one set of raiders. They attacked Sea Shore wearing some fearsome garments. Primitive looking yet frightening, and she was quite young at the time.

They had skulls for armor and some of the finer weapons that taught Yoranthium a new means to fold their metal and forge new fearsome single sided curved blades. More powerful than the long swords and short swords Yoranthium use to covet. They even had new composite lacquered bows and a special wood that was used in the new remodel of the Mundrunche. Providing a new and untested method of sea travel. Better than wind and better than

oars. The first of it's kind promising a revolution in industry and was the future.

Those raider's who provided the new knowledge and magics, were a pale skinned kind of deep-sea elf. They claimed to live deeper in the sea. Deeper than a dual hue skinned sea elf could go. The sea elves of Yoranthium only could go about two hundredth's depths deep before their lungs would not function. These deeper cousin pale gray sea elves traded with the Depth Dwellers. Rarailmuir was the one that broke them in interrogation and brought them before her father and mother.

That pirate captain made contemptible comments about her. That's when Rarailmuir looked at her, she nodded, and he backhanded the pirate captain, blood and teeth came out of his mouth. Kumithra remembered smiling to Rarailmuir for protecting her honor, virtue and chastity and then the pirate captain fully complied with questioning.[21] Even when she asked him how he liked the taste of his own blood and he better hope she forgives him or worse was going to happen. What exactly she wasn't sure but Rarailmuir whispered in his ear and he got more frightened from what Rarailmuir said was worse. Yoranthium benefited much from the interrogation of the deepsea elves and learned their technologies.

Kumithra was changing inside from her encounter with Dresdie. Now Kumithra was searching for Wertomeer in the woods, Clicking and calling and thinking of Wertomeer. She was going to ride into the Grand City, find Rarailmuir at the palace, and question a male that was a skilled interrogator. Who by now was more than that, a King that didn't have any need of his wife and queen. He successfully lied to her all these years and had a wife and even a child. She must be mad thinking she could match wits with such a scoundrel, one that fooled her father and mother for years after the dragon attack. Fooled them enough for her to want him as her husband.

Kumithra was smitten and infatuated with Rarailmuir when he rescued her. She felt his powerful arms covering her in safety and protection all so comforting. Even felt the warmth and strength of his hand on her bodice that moistened her feelings.

[21] Seems out of character but is part of an extrospection larger concept explained later in other books of the series.

That she wanted and yearned for and never forgetting how it felt to be in his arms. Listening to his heart that was strong and sound and dreamy as he ran with her out of the building.

He had saved her and looked down upon her with kind sun fire golden eyes. The most magnificent eyes she ever knew. Having saved her that day and looking upon her for a moment, he looked up and placed her on the ground outside and then ran off. Like a hero running back to help, she wasn't even sure if he did go help others. That was something she imagined and wanted to believe.

Rarailmuir was charismatic he had always been a fine leader in the guard. He trained most of the royal guard after it had been decimated. She doubted the shore guard would ever listen to her or even follow her? If she asked the shore guard to arrest Rarailmuir would they? Or would they simply laugh at her and lock her up instead? Becoming the Queen pretender and traitor of Yoranthium. Likely becoming a traitor to be executed for opposing Rarailmuir and betraying her love over revenge for being spurned.

This wasn't going to be easy. She knew she couldn't demand combat with Rarailmuir. He's tall, strong, and a master combat trained tactician able to defeat dragons. Not just any dragon but a mythical dragon of legend, one that use to be hailed as the guardian of Yoranthium. Rarailmuir is one of the best if not the best on all of Yoranthium or all of Ishormot. What is she going to do? Swing her chain daggers around. Try to poke him. Use her short sword. Try to kill him, she shuttered at the thought. From what she heard from Dresdie murder was on her mind. Act of vengeance for betraying her love.

By now Rarailmuir is sure to have one of those death skull swords in his hands. He no longer had the King Sword. Some other thief came in the night and stole it or Dresdie returned and claimed the sword again. Rarailmuir no longer held the sword of Yoranthium. No, she will not be able to fight Rarailmuir for her throne. She would only have to hope the shore guard respects her as their Queen. That is unlikely. Rarailmuir sent her away. More than that he pushed her out of the way. He did that in front of all the Guard they would know she was nothing and only lived by the word of Rarailmuir. She was fortunate to have Huspecia and Thernya and discover that Bronanes was a kind male that followed her protectors and swore allegiance to her.

She should have brought them for this adventure. It would of made this easier but at a great cost to the safety and lives of her people. She made the right choice sending her protectors to save her people. Hopefully they can save as many as possible. Which from her last count was sadly very few.

As she was walking in deep thought about what to do, she suddenly heard a twig on the ground next to her snap. She looked to her left and there was Wertomeer. Silent and she didn't even know how long he was there? Could Wertomeer vanish? She looked over to her left and realized the sea stallion's scales of soft skin were somewhat translucent and solidifying. She turned to Wertomeer and bound her thoughts and learned Wertomeer was expecting her later at night. Then she explained how she got here early. Wertomeer was relieved and happy she chose a strong bold path, as a Queen should. Flooding her mind with thoughts of her father as his way of comforting her.

Wertomeer was aware of her choice to find Rarailmuir. Wertomeer was fond of Rarailmuir too but a little disconcerted as to the Queen's reaction. Wertomeer needed to know the truth too and was more than willing to take Kumithra towards danger to find out the fate of her Kingdom. She got on Wertomeer and headed towards the Grand City the way they came with the Carriages. Upon reaching the outer keep night was falling and she had to rest feeling her energy draining and being depleted from all the stress from the events at the terrible windmill tower still impacted her.

Kumithra slept closely with Wertomeer to stay warm. Wertomeer was a great partner for her bed and Wertomeer dreamed of dreams of his past with Sinderthion and his conflict for the hand of her mother Zantkara. Most of it was faded memory and tales with no words just actions and the life of Wertomeer's life in the sea until the first day he met and let Sinderthion tame him under the waves, a purely fantasy and magical tale of Sea Stallion meeting boy. Boy becoming a warrior and riding his closest friend a war stallion into battle for the hand of his Queen. Kumithra was well rested in the morning. Heading past the outer keep to the bridge and the main road of the Grand City.

The journey back was saddening as an exodus of refugees took place. Kumithra ran into groups of refugees fleeing the city

hundreds of them at a time. They knew Wertomeer from stories of her father and other legends told in Yoranthium. They knew from Wertomeer she had to be their Queen and obeyed her to head to the hidden cave she explained to them how to get there. That they only had two days before the ships would leave. Each group had things they brought with them, some of it useful and some of it worthless. Hopefully the ten of hundredth's she sent to the caves would make it and escape to Forumth. Worried if they had enough ships for so many.

This gave Kumithra great satisfaction to be held in high esteem by her people. They didn't accost her or vent their anger or frustration. As many of the people she met had been there when the dragon attacked, and the horrors of death and destruction isn't new to the people of the Grand City. Mostly they were confused and didn't know where to go. Many had no choice but fled as the buildings burned or collapsed and heard terrible cries and fighting in the streets.

The refugees from the Grand city had families with them and children staring wild eyed and terrified. Not knowing where to go or what to do. Upon seeing their Queen and the famous Wertomeer. They would tear up as hope crept into their eyes. Some even fell to their knee's thanking their unborn God for a sign. A sign they had a chance and opportunity, for their Queen had appeared to them, alone and riding a symbol of bravery and their saint. Kumithra helped them on their journey to the hidden cave for salvation, hearing stories of her bravery being told of her by her people as they departed. Her spirit was uplifted and her mission was validated as she saved lives and rode into legend.

Kumithra did not disappoint the refugees. She knew their plight. She had just lived a much worse fate two nights ago. With the power of the sword and the love and heart of her remaining family she had managed to overcome complete despair that let her very life force fade into the darkness where she had witnessed a light at an end of a passage. Then a voice that told her, "It is not yet near your time, your journey has just begun. Return to your body for Yoranthium needs..." Needs what? She couldn't remember the rest from an ancient and old voice that was soothing and kind and benevolent. Needs what? She wasn't sure. Remembering this just now as refugees flocked to her.

The refugees would ask for her blessing. Would make the religious sign of a cross from the top of their heads to their abdomen from the left shoulder to their right shoulder. Then double tapping a heartbeat above their hearts. Like she was a champion saint. They would from time to time hope for her gentle hand on their foreheads and some would kiss her hand. Causing her eye's to fill with water from the attention and her modesty made her blush at first. Then she got use to it wondering if her father or mother ever experienced this. Which she recalled some of Wertomeer's thoughts on her father and there was a time this happened to her father.

It was imperative she reached the city and the palace and meets up with Rarailmuir and confronts him for his accused sins. She just kept moving forward with Wertomeer. She needed to know if he loved her. Still wondering how to handle this affair of her Kingdom. Did he ever love her or was she just a weak foolish child being abused and neglected for the throne by Rarailmuir? This saddened her but not as much as the dreadful eerie sight of the Grand City.

A tear ran down her cheek. It was clear the city was even worse for wear. Fires raged out of control. Entire blocks had been leveled by the bombardment of massive lightning strikes. It was only a few days since this took place. Kumithra had to stop for she ate nothing and needed some of the food she was given back at the windmill. She was looking at the city in disbelief. She never has seen such devastation and destruction.

She knew of no known weapon capable of such malevolence and it wasn't getting better it was getting worse. Only lightning in the sky, large huge lightning that was more intense now as it made longer contact with parts of the city exposing bare ground and fusing it like black glass. This could be seen from a distance, and it was terrifying under the darkened sky. As if where the Grand City was located had some significance. Had a terrible purpose and the city was in its way. Who or what's way was uncertain? Kumithra had no idea, only speculation that the Grand City was important to a purpose of some dark evil cause of this war.

Winds would ebb and serge with strong gusts to lessening winds. Small wind devils could be seen circulating through the city, some becoming powerful enough to pick up some small debris and

scatter it about. At one point Kumithra thought she seen a person get picked up off the ground and impaled at a distance. If these gusts of winds gained in strength then the city would certainly be leveled in no time.

The lighting rods of the larger buildings wouldn't be able to deflect destructive tempests. Birds of pink could be seen in the sky and they would dance like lightning. Kumithra was really horrified about riding into the Grand City. Something in the back of her mind about last night told her of nightmares that was more of a reality. As she began to recall how she ended up at the sinister events of three nights ago. The birds were swooping down and she could see sometimes, the birds had something in their beak she couldn't make out. Then she saw it. A group of five birds had picked up some person. The poor person was torn apart and this was happening all over the city from time to time.

She had to risk entering the city. She had to find Rarailmuir. She had to brave the horrors of the sky, for she was fast on Wertomeer. Her steed would be quick and smart and get her to her destination. After finishing her lunch. Adjusting her clothing and mounting Wertomeer. She pulled out her chain dagger to a point she could swing it overhead at the birds if they gave her a problem. These Impundalu would be no match for her weapon that could kill demons. Hopefully the road would be easy. The main road she remembered using after the bridge appeared vacant.

Wertomeer was aware of the dangers. His skin began to shimmer and shift in light. Kumithra was amazed at what was transpiring for her own soft smooth and hard to notice scales began to dance in light's similar to Wertomeer's. She and Wertomeer were becoming translucent and she could see the outline of her and Wertomeer, as they began to blend in with the surrounding cityscape upon entering. Her clothing wasn't changing until her skin reached a zenith of light that cascaded over her outer garments, the saddle and the bridle and tack. Her and Wertomeer had become invisible upon entering the city. Perfectly concealed from the sight of demons flying about the city.

There were many horrors and gruesome acts of barbarity unleashed by the tempest of lightning, wind, fire, and destroyed buildings. The vile acts of the pink lighting bird that floated, glided,

and flew in the skies and sometimes used their lighting to be in one part of the sky and appear in another. Was worse than those burned to death or crushed. The birds tore them from limb to limb.

She even realized unfortunate women would be enchanted upon eye contact with the birds, as she had once been. That is when she remembered the nude male she wanted with lustful intentions. Including what she knew now was a hallucination of her Pink Rarailmuir's like a nightmare dream she could not break free from. These birds were sinister and pure evil. The ability to target women in a seductive way and conceal their true bloodthirsty intentions was awful. She couldn't dare intervene for doing so would place her at great risk. She would lose her invisibility and knew as a female she would be ensnared the first time she made eye contact.

These Impundalu needn't to entrance the minds of their meals. These birds just liked doing it for a sadistic and unholy abusively cruel means to play with their food. That is all the elves represented to them. Food. It was much worse than just that. There was a shadowy figure of a mound of something slowly following the flight paths of the Impundalu, like a mindless servant or slave. Then even under the darkened sky. Light eventually fell on it. It was a mound of limbs, remains of torn elves. It was a massive shambling blob of collected elven parts. Twitching and distorting and convulsing with weird, shaped mouths full of broken bone, stone, wood, debris for teeth, sniffing and listening. At first the Shambler appeared to sense Wertomeer's clomping, and it was slowly moving towards them.

Suddenly a group of Impundalu cawed and sounded out. The Shambler obeyed their masters and slowly shambled over to the birds. There was a small tenement. Kumithra could hear screams of panic and worry coming from behind the door. The birds battered at the door with their claws and ramming it with their elven sized bodies and strong foreheads. A latch on the door was the only thing keeping the elves safe from behind it. The Shambler approached and with a twisted, twerking spasming hand and arm, or was it a leg with a hand. Reached out to the door latch and activated the latch.

Kumithra's eyes widened, she heard frightened children. A panic cry, "I can't hold the door it's to strong!"

Kumithra turned Wertomeer toward the house under assault she couldn't let children die a horrible and awful death of dismemberment to become a Shambler. Wertomeer knew what to do as his powerful flanks surged with energy and power Kumithra had never felt between her thighs sitting on the saddle. Her excitement flushed to her face turning her cheeks red in delight. She gave out an ecstatic war cry. Raised the chain dagger over her head and charged down the street just as the lead Impundalu was busting down the door. Catching the Impundalu and the massive Shambler off guard.

Kumithra's blade swooshed through the air. Slicing upon brutal impact right through the birds. Two of them lost their heads immediately like hacking vegetables in preparation for a meal. The blade kept spinning and sliced the Shambler that groaned in pain and began blackening and exploding in blackish dust as the blade finally struck home impacting across the hasty lead bird that knocked down the door. Striking the back of it's head with the chain that stopped the motion only to cause the dagger to swing across the birds right side of it's head and flying point first into the birds eye and ending up in it's brain. There wasn't much commotion coming from the birds or the Shambler. No screams or real outcry's they simply died, blackened into clumps of stone dissolving into dust.

Kumithra had to retrieve her dagger from the Impundalu's collapsed mess of pinkish feathers. So she got off of Wertomeer's back and he shot her a look of approval of her courage but to be more careful. Pick her fights sparingly there is too many Impundalu and Shamblers for her to try and fight every fight she runs into. Not to mention she had to be rescued in her first encounter with the Impundalu's. She's vulnerable to their demonic charms. She was bending over the fallen Impundalu and pulling out the dagger when the elves she saved ran up and approached her.

"It's the princess, we were saved by the princess!" A maiden cried out who had a child's hand in her embrace. The little girl was ecstatic and surprised. The princess of Yoranthium was one of her favorite tales in the city. Pushed herself out of her mothers hold and ran over to Kumithra and gave her a hug so tight it felt the child would never let go of her leg.

"You saved us!" The girl had huge purple eyes and pale hair just like Kumithra's at her age and darker blue bronze skin like Rarailmuir's. She was surprised and amazed and infatuated with her idol. "I knew my princess would be a hero, even when all the boy's said girls could never be such things."

Her brother ran over there and looked at Kumithra. "It was Rarailmuir he must have taught her everything she knows." For it was obvious the little boy admired Rarailmuir just as much as the little girl admired Kumithra. "It is the princes she… I take it back girls can be good too." He hugged his princess too.

Kumithra was released by the children hugging her legs and seen there were more infatuated children. No doubt told fairytale after fairytale of fables Kumithra could not begin to fathom. Truth is it was made up stories told of the bravery of the Royal family of Yoranthium. Yet she had some idea as she did read some of the fiction of thieves and forbidden romance along with many other teachings when she was their age. Including some that were about her that fan's would write about. She ran into her fans and she lived up to their expectations, for this moment. As she risked her own safety to save the children she heard crying out.

Looking upon the adults of the group she noticed they too were like most refugees. Tired and exhausted. Wearing clothes they had on for the past days as the afternoon was approaching this third day. They would be hard pressed to reach the cave but they would have to try. Don't let her efforts to save these children be invane for the love of their God. Isn't her God not the protector of children?

"I know you all had been through quite a lot. I do know of the hidden caves under the waterfall at the warm, sundown side of the island. If you can read tracks there should be plenty beyond the outer keep. Follow those many tracks of refugees. You have about a day and a half and you must hurry. Take the main road and across the bridge. Take this oil and put it on the weapons of your bravest. They had been armed with simple cutlery and blunt weapons." She handed them the last of her demon killing oils she was given in the sword belt Lord Bronanes gave to her.

The little girl was a little sad. "You won't be coming with me my princess?"

Kumithra gave a hug to the girl. "You join your parents and your brother. Your Princess is now your Queen and I have Kingdom business to attend too." Looking at the rest of the group of refugees. "Yoranthium is now a war zone. Your only safety is the hidden caves. Be quick if you value your lives and for any of you with skills. Seek out Lord Bronanes, Ladies Huspecia and Thernya they will have assignments for you to save Yoranthium." Eying the child with some thought. "You'll have to be your mother and fathers princess and protector in my place."

The little girl understood and decided. "Yes, I'm princess Kumithra the protector of my people. For Yoranthium!"

The parents, children and all the refugees in the group heard their Queen. Realizing she told them to meet the other legends of their lore at the hidden caves. The children's eye's sparkled because they were being saved by their fairytales, and they had to hurry. Just like the adventures they had been told before bedtime. They were excited and couldn't wait to meet their hero's of fantasy.

Kumithra didn't have time to wait and simply ran to Wertomeer and swung herself on to his back and turned him back towards the main road. She reared up on the hind legs of Wertomeer amazing the group of onlookers. There was no doubt in their minds they had great admiration for their Queen. She alone on top her heroic mount accomplished a feat none of the cowering adults had the strength to do themselves, for they knew not of the demon fighting oils. Now thinks to their Queen they had courage, hope, a direction to go and a reason to believe in their new Queen, along with a new tale to tell their children at night. Kumithra moved at a quickening speed down the alley to the road and then like magics her and Wertomeer was no longer to be seen.

Her and her mount had once again vanished from sight just as they entered the city. Kumithra looked behind her and saw the group she had saved. Carefully navigate the main road staying to cover and hoped them well and as they disappeared out of sight. It was some distance before Kumithra got to the junction that led to the carriage house. She turned right back down the carriage street and noticed most of the street had been destroyed by fire and was still spreading to the other buildings. The Carriage house was partially collapsed at this point and still burning. It was a massive

structure and reinforced. The trail of carriage tracks still fresh from the past few days.

Then Kumithra remembered there was clothing supply right next to the carriage house. Fortunately, the building for Yoranthium guard uniform issue was still standing. She could smell an awful smell coming from her clothing and noticed how ragged it was getting. She shouldn't waste time with her own attire. She had a mission and she decided to ride past the entrance they used and looked to the left and saw the storefront entrance.

Through the door she saw it. A Yukata similar to the black and red trimmed Yukata her mother was wearing. Yet this one had short sleeves over the long flowing sleeves and was a dark purple with cranes all over it. The Yukata was short and simple enough to adjust. She could simply remove the underlying Yukata and wear the other Yukata with the current boots and leggings she had on. She felt violated wearing this Yukata that Dresdie had torn open and removed her corset so she could cut into her and grab her heart.

Yes, Kumithra would feel better changing this Yukata and belt. There was a nicer golden belt of velvet that had a top and bottom silver lining. Kumithra moved to the side in front of the door and got off Wertomeer. Entered the shop making sure not to be spotted by any Shamblers or Impundalu that had not been in the sky around this part of town. As there were no elves on these streets they had already been evacuated.

Kumithra entered the shop and found new under garments and disrobed as Wertomeer stood invisible and on guard. She found a new bra that matched of a soft black and red metallic trim along with under pants of the same. Then put on the leggings of purple and her boots with finally the dark purple cranes Yukata and golden silver trimmed belt. Then she saw it, over in a corner. A chest plate meant for her mother the Queen. It had gathered some dust and was segmented in black lacquered mithreal plating. Trimmed in metallic dark red rope. Snug to the hips and rounded just right for the breasts to fit inside. This breastplate fit her like a glove for her body was very similar to her mothers. It was armor fit for a Queen and Kumithra wore it well. Tied with leather straps on the side and on top of the shoulders with light feather like lacquered pauldrons. Along with loose fluted waste guards that

folded over one another. Kings foot length leather straps with black lacquered trim mithreal on top and studded into the leather, runes of inscription of holy texts from the God to be born. Right below the groove separating the breasts was a cross with hands outstretched and the baby with the heart of Yoranthium protection from demonic forces.

Then she found a helmet met for her mother. Of the same design and it was a small top hat piece that sculpted to a point in the back. With a mask in the front and a dangling chain mail of black mithreal that covered around the back of the helmet going down the entire length of her hair with an inner red silk cloth and padded inside for comfort. She put the helmet on and it was light and silent imbued with magics of protection, comfort and stealth.

Having quickly completed her new outfit she quickly returned to Wertomeer that was pleased with her new attire. She even found some long leather gloves matching the Yukata to complete the look. She found the mithreal to be very light as if not wearing armor. The magic of this armor was worthy of the master crafters of Yoranthium and fit their new Queen nicely. While reminding Kumithra that she is filling the role of her mother exemplary. In the small of the back was an inscription, "Made by Society Monks of the Grove." A symbol and guild Kumithra had no knowledge of on Yoranthium.

She did have some doubts to the armor intention. The design appeared to match that of the forbidden thief books her mother didn't want her to read. That was a secret book that belonged to her mother and not Dresdie. That book was simply called, 'The Society, for members only.' She mounted Wertomeer and got her chain daggers to the ready and pulled on the tack. Becoming invisible and on their way back down the street that turned from the gate to the palace and into the open doors of the outer palace gate. Passing the now collapsed buildings to either side and into the palace yard.

She first thought of a bath and looked at the Royal housing. It was demolished and no more. The gardens she had passed days ago were burned and destroyed. Blood was everywhere and discarded remains of clothing and armor littered the grounds. Weapons scattered on the grounds everywhere. Those who sought refuge at the palace had met a grim end. She looked to the palace

and could see the Impundalu resting, searching taking flight. She even saw the terrible Shamblers slowly lumbering around inside the palace.

Kumithra was certain Rarailmuir wasn't here. She saw the broken wall on the sunup wall where it was breached. Burn marks and bodies of torn and eviscerated remains of Depth Dwellers. There was enough evidence of boot marks and efforts to clear a path in the remains of a second Mechanation and Depth Dwellers to indicate a large Yoranthium force of Guards had left the palace days ago.

Kumithra knew there wasn't no elves alive here just the Shamblers and the Impundalu taking up nests left around the palace. Inside the palace there were oddities and other instruments of value to aid in this war on Yoranthium. She was alone and no match for the demonic forces inside the palace. It would be suicide to enter the palace and Wertomeer agreed. The Impundalu seemed well fed and uninterested as many of them began sleeping.

The sun was getting ready to set on this day. Kumithra had little time and simply kept moving through the breach wall hopefully taking the same path as Rarailmuir. She made her way past all the bodies of the dead Depth Dweller and noticed some of them had been infested with parasites of the deep ocean. Realizing a bite from a Depth Dweller or touch from one could be a death sentence with the shear number of parasites of the deep these creatures lived with. The stench was enough to almost make Kumithra fall off Wertomeer and her mount found it very offensive and difficult to navigate.

Soon enough they had passed that zone of death and decay and moved forward and it didn't get any better. Burnt pink feathers were everywhere. Broken parts and more slowly moving Shamblers covered and caked in dust, soot, and debris. As a major battlefield opened at one street with boot prints, armor, weapons and collapsed buildings where explosions must have taken them down. She knew from this sight she must be on the right path. The amount of death and destruction was that consistent of a large band of soldiers in conflict. It must have been horrible and a terrifying battle. Only Rarailmuir and his shore guard could have survived this and kept moving on.

Pink feathers, burnt bodies, Guard armor and even Sea Ghoul jackets. Littered the battlefield. Why was the Sea Ghoul here? Did Rarailmuir and the guard have to fight them too? This battle confused her, and she worried about the condition of the guard.

She simply kept following a swath of footprints that lead to an alley and eventually to a sewer cover that was moved and replaced. There was no way Wertomeer could follow her anymore. She tried to move the sewer cover. She wasn't strong enough to move it. It was too heavy. She had an idea to use the short sword on her and create a fulcrum to move the cover; the sewer cover defeated her. Until Wertomeer's foot came down on the short sword and opened and moved the cover aside. Moving the cover just enough for her to get into the sewer entrance.

At this point Kumithra realized she needed to say goodbye to Wertomeer. Before dropping down into the sewer tunnel. Kumithra would reach up and grab Wertomeer's head and gave him a hug. Looked him in the eyes and told him this is as far as they could go together. Wertomeer understood as Kumithra undid the bindings for the saddle, bridle and tack and harness. She kissed Wertomeer on the cheek and told him to head to the ocean and safety. Wertomeer backed away regretting he could not accompany her and realized he would not get to know about Rarailmuir. He turned from her and looked back a last time and then ran off as Kumithra dropped into the sewer tunnel.

The smell was even worse than the rotting Depth Dwellers yet there was no parasites or worms so at least not so nasty. Her height was good for this tunnel, and she could easily navigate it. Yes there was enough evidence an entire force led by Rarailmuir came this way. She silently moved down this passage for some time, as it got darker and darker. The visor of her helmet had some magics to it for it let her see in the dark well enough. She could make out the tunnel and see the ladder at the far end. It was a long tunnel and it opened to many pipes feeding bath water and wastewater to the tunnel. Which was running and smelled horribly new. Letting her know sea elves must be securing the Last Bastion.

Well at least they have baths she thought. How nice it would be for her to take one after all these days. Her hair was getting matted and difficult to manage and dirty. She felt grimy even with

the new clothes and armor. War is filthy business and not much fun. She couldn't imagine why Rarailmuir picked this life. It was the same life her father picked, and her mother was part of. This armor of her mother's was different and not truly made for war very not like her fathers. Silent, Dark, melded with the shadows and an eye mask shaped to her eyes that let her see in the dark. Who was her mother and why did she try to keep Kumithra from reading about thieves?

She had found the ladder and began ascending the ladder thinking it must be dark by now. It was a long journey. Thankfully Wertomeer now free of the city had been fast enough to escape. But where exactly was she now. She's never been here. She spent most of her time at the palace, school, shopping and the hidden beach entertaining the crew of different ships Lord Bronanes was on. His training cruises on various training ships. No time for this place. As she ascended the ladder she heard a voice. Shore guard voices. They were here.

"Did you see that? Orichen and the Sea Ghouls met their demise and defended us just as the King wanted." Said a guard.

"Yeah didn't think those low lives would amount to nothing. Yet the day is ours and we have held the last bastion for another day." Relieved from a long day.

"It would appear we can hold the keep for a long time. Stores are full." Pride was brimming from the first guard.

"Do you think the bodies of the Sea Ghouls are going to keep in the back over there?" worried but more of concern.

"Yeah I'm sure they'll be fine. If it keeps going like this we'll be marching on Sea Shore soon enough. I think this war is about to turn for the better." Proud and hopeful like a Yoranthium guard would be, "Rarailmuir had put Metiur in charge while he sleeps in the commanders chamber. I wish I knew where this keeps Guard was. Why they vacated their post?"

Kumithra reached the top of the ladder. She now knew where she was at the Last Bastion. She could see this cover wasn't sealed and open halfway just enough for her petite form to easily get past. She even knew where the commander's chambers were. She visited here with her father revolutions ago as a child. Her father and the commander of the Last Bastion were great friends of many Yoranthium conquests. He had a daughter and they

played in the Last Keep a few times. Never remembered that child's name and tried to learn it many times. Kumithra's memory failed her.

All Kumithra had to do is find a safe way to sneak over to the commanders chambers. Which wasn't hard the guards were lazy and not minding the open sewer grate. Mostly interested in talking and looking at some bodies of citizens in leather jackets that were dead and had a marking on their jackets of the Sea Ghouls. A local criminal gang Kumithra was told to avoid and never interact with. Their bodies piled in a corner with elven blood pooling at the bottom. Not the way a guard would be treated. More like the Sea Ghouls didn't deserve honors in death. Why should they? The Sea Ghouls murdered sea elves often that were children and families. So Kumithra was told. She still felt sad for them they are sea elf's of Yoranthium too. Hastily out of fear of being caught she said a quick prayer for them.

The lower basement of the Last Bastion was under ground and lightly guarded it was easy for Kumithra to sneak around in the shadows. She finally found the Commanders chambers and entered it simple enough. There was Rarailmuir he was asleep. Fresh from a bath and Kumithra could smell it. She so much wanted to bathe but that would be a mistake. She pulled her chain dagger. Getting closer and closer to Rarailmuir. He slept in the nude with a robe that failed to cover his strong physical form. Kumithra watched as his muscular chest heaved up and down and tantalized her imagination and she traveled with her eyes down his body and seen the small mound of hair down lower and was not disappointed by the sight of his less excited valued member. Her eyes lit up on it and she moistened her lips and felt a wave of heat cascade over her.

She wasn't here for his body, but she did desire every curve and strong muscular muscle she saw of his body. Then she came to reason. For her to debate the problems of his infidelity and dishonesty would be too complicated. It would be easier if she just used her dagger and ended Rarailmuir here and now. Not fussing over whom the rest of his guard should follow. He'd be dead and they would have only their Queen. It would be the only time she would have. Yet she hesitated. Was it his body calling to her? Indeed, it was just that she was infatuated with Rarailmuir. She

was fixated on his breathing chest and masculine features. That she didn't see his eye's open.

Even in his half sleep Rarailmuir knew Kumithra even with her face hidden under the black lacquered helmet. Rarailmuir did not know he had her chain dagger at his throat. And simply said longingly, "Kumithra?"

She was caught and couldn't complete the deed she was thinking about. She couldn't murder her Rarailmuir. Yet the dagger was proof of her intentions, and she was sure he had seen the dagger at his throat. Gazing upon and taking a last look at his golden sun fire eyes looking at hers. She knew he fully knew it was she.

She turned nearly tripping over her own feet. Having difficulty scrambling back to her feet. Crashing into the wall and into the door. She was frantically panicking and rushing not thinking, not breathing. Then she was out of the door and slammed it behind her. Just long enough to come to her senses. Then as silently as she entered the chambers she moved at great speed down the hall, silently into the shadows. As she checked to make sure she still held her dagger and didn't leave it behind.

Sure enough her dagger was still in her hand. She was racked with dread for he must have seen the dagger at his throat. He'll be having the guard come after her and she would have to escape. Yet she was so tired. It was a long day. She spent most of her energy getting here. She found a closet that was full of equipment, many blankets and it was easy enough to hide in. Kumithra covered herself up. Knowing she would likely never be found and she instantly fell asleep.

Yoranthium

Book One: Lost Hope

Chapter Sixteen:

Fleet of The Mundrunche

By Mark P. Bromley

The last Naval fleet of Yoranthium is to set sail for Forumth. The last defense of the defenseless, with only six Yoranthium Navy combat ships, to protect the light and repel the darkness spreading across the land. Evils of war wanting to end the lives of those we have found precious to our hearts. What chances do they have when an entire navy of cutting edge ships could not defend the shores of Yoranthium from this terrible war of demons?[22]

[22] Written before the wars of Ukraine and Israel brought on by the ills and woes of Globalist Socialism formerly of National Socialism origins creating strife and ignorance in the early 21st century.

Thernya knew many things. She had been the head of household affairs since Queen Zantkara took King Sinderthion to be her husband. With this secret cove of Yoranthium being in the direction of Forumth it was one of the first locations Thernya became knowledgeable of.

She knew exactly where Bronanes and Huspecia ran off to last night. Not a big secret that Bronanes and Huspecia wanted to consummate their wedding vows. They had been in love a long time. They went to the hot springs hidden down the small side tunnel. Leading to an under ground paradise of glowing in the dark plants that thrived in caves like this from the very uniquely enriched soils of Yoranthium.

Thernya had put on weight for being an older female and no one to care for except her two adopted daughters. They worked her to the bone, yet it was fun for Thernya to attend to them. She had difficulty navigating the tight tunnel that a young sea elf in the prime of their youth would have no problem navigating. She eventually made her way to where the hot spring pool was located and took a shockingly quick look and then hid herself around the corner. Slightly embarrassed for both Bronanes and Huspecia were naked sleeping in the hot spring.

She smiled thinking it was a great way for them to consummate their marriage. She was happy for them to finally get a chance to physically know one another. However, Dabensir and Leorth were lost without Bronanes and many of the females and the children and the other citizens need Huspecia's guidance. They're the living embodiment of the Regent to the Queen of Yoranthium now.

Thernya at the top of her lungs echoed in the hot spring chamber. "My Lord and Lady it's time to wake up!"

Huspecia was the first to wake and got her bearings. "Thernya how do you know we are sleeping. Did you sneak in here to spy on Bronanes my husband?"

"No, my lady. I just came here to let you both know you are needed and need to get dressed and guide these people. It's your duty as Regents. I do hope you and Bronanes satisfied yourselves." She shouldn't have said that and bit her own lip scolding herself in reflection. Thernya had been wanting to learn all the details from Huspecia.

Huspecia knew this and looked at Bronanes who was still asleep and not in the mood. “Nothing happened Thernya, we were too tired last night.”

Bronanes woke up at the time hearing the disappointment from Huspecia. He reached over to her and felt her body. “Sorry my love. I am pleased to see your body for the first time. It's everything I imagined and more.” He was becoming aroused and wanted to take Huspecia right then and there.

Huspecia grabbed his hand and gave him a light slap quickly whispering not to be discovered. “Thernya's here around the corner, time for us to get back to work. I'm sure we'll get another chance.” Huspecia pushed herself away from Bronanes and got out to dry herself. Which for sea elves doesn't take long as their skin alters itself naturally and quickly to wet and dry conditions.

Bronanes could only watch as he too stood up and admired Huspecia's nude form as she was dressing. “Your body is excellent Huspecia well have to try this again, soon, real soon.”

Huspecia looked behind her to see Bronanes and he was fully erect and standing up in the hot springs. She had a smile from ear to ear and was about to run back towards Bronanes but had to stop herself for Thernya was right they needed to get back to the group and help. “Stop Bronanes! I want you too. I want you so awfully bad and I want... You know full well what I want. But we have work to do and Thernya is just around the corner.” With her blushing and whispering.

“Thernya you can leave. We'll be there soon enough. Give us a few moments.” Bronanes had said with his intentions of taking Huspecia right there and then.

“A few moments? What? Who do you think I am Bronanes? Not going to happen. You better get dressed a few moments might be okay with you but I'm more demanding than that.” Huspecia scolded Bronanes for being hasty and brash.

“That's right Lord Bronanes women can't be rushed, and you need to understand patients.” Thernya's voice came around the corner and she bit her tongue knowing full well her advice wasn't wanted.

“Shut up Thernya, I love you, but you got to go. Leave us alone we'll be there momentarily.” Huspecia said laughing a bit as

Bronanes felt silly and embarrassed losing his enthusiasm while watching Huspecia getting dressed. All that was left was getting dressed and ready for the day.

Thernya was laughing as she realized she had dampened their spirits while making her way out of the tight fitting tunnel. It wouldn't be long before Bronanes and Huspecia were themselves again and assisting the people of Yoranthium. She went out and got some food ready and set up a small table for Bronanes and Huspecia to have breakfast. Sure enough they made their way out of the cave still frolicking and touching each other lovingly in play and provocative jest. Thernya smiled and waved them over to the table as they had breakfast.

Bronanes and Huspecia went over their itinerary and realized their schedules were full and difficult for them to find the time for each other. As their duties just like Thernya was significant. Wondering if this is how mornings went for King Sinderthion and Queen Zantkara that had difficulty keeping their hands off one another.

Eventually Dabensir and Leorth had found the lovebirds and met them at the same table for breakfast. Along with their wives and four children. Apparently it looked as if Bronanes and Huspecia that Dabensir and Leorth found time with their wives. As the paired couples were much refreshed, tired, but refreshed and grinning pointed ear to pointed ear.

“Looks like you two need to learn some time management before you have children.” Leorth with only one child sat there looking at Bronanes and Huspecia knowing they had failed last night as Teirdith shot Huspecia a look that she should be telling her a secret of relationship success.

“I think you are right Leorth. Seems someone is a little hurt from last night.” As Dabensir played with a sausage on a fork and turned it to it's side. “Blue jam for your toast?” He was trying to give it to Bronanes. While his wife Ardrian took a seat next to Huspecia and whispered in her ear. Letting her know the secret to three children.

“We got to get to work this morning, Dabensir and Leorth. Leorth, you still got a way to go today to even get close to being a real ship captain. Don't worry about me or, or, or... Never mind.” Bronanes was caught of guard from all the kidding around.

"I'll need to go over the supply list and need your help Ardrian and Teirdith along with Thernya and your children. Yes they can help too." Said Huspecia pinching Rubius's cheek. Making Indirid giggle and smile nestled to Ardrian's chest.

"My first duty is to check the outer defenses and check on new refugees and set a watch to bring them into the cave keep. Dabensir I need you to assemble the men this morning and get Leorth and his first class to start training the other inexperienced transport captains for sail lessons. Sail lessons are a high priority and I want to know Leorth if you feel up to the challenge? Tell the truth always I know I'm expecting too much for just one day of training." Bronanes looked at Leorth and could see competence in his eyes and fear of command knowing he had a long way to go. Fortunately, Leorth's abilities as a carriage master of the royal stables made him good choice to lead the sail crews.

A day or two of training must be enough. Bronanes had been learning and was still learning for over a decade. When he began at age five to learn under his father the Admiral. It was the only reason he was so gifted and capable now. Ability could be taught in a couple of seasons. It wasn't hard for anyone to learn. Experience is what taught skill. Experience takes a long time, and it must be on the deck of real ships that teach the true magics behind sail craft and ships.

The Navy was in the classroom built on Knowledge about one tenth. Experience was nine tenths and that is where you found skill. Without experience no amount of education would make a true sailor. Experience made skill, was an art form making you more able. Only getting good as long as you had access to the work and rewards to make experience worthwhile and motivational. Yes, reward was the key to get a new sailor to becoming the best they will ever be. No reward nothing good ever comes of anything. Bronanes worked tirelessly to make sure his Sea Guard was rewarded with providing a meaning for life and being realistic in their assignments.

"I know the importance of my role. As long as Dabensir is near by, I know we'll do fine my Lord Bronanes. I'm confident not to fail you as you have so far proven to be a great protector of my love and life and family." Leorth was really sincere and serious.

"Well don't go getting too serious, lighten up have fun and stay on course. I think you might even impress yourself Leorth and do give Dabensir the support he needs too. It's good to be with you guys again. Remember we got lots of family and people of Yoranthium to care for. Do me proud." Bronanes had eyed them both and got up to get ready for his mission and kissed Huspecia on the lips.

"I'll see you later this evening before we push off to sea. Two mornings from now." All they needed was hands on training in an emergency was always good for experience. Bronanes just didn't want any to feel stressed or that expectations were too high. Having so much to do in so little time made it difficult to balance with such massive risks. There would be half a third seasons to get good on their way to Forumth and hopefully by their God to be born, the seas would stay calm.

Two mornings was a short amount of time in all reality. Several new refugees groups said they had met the Queen and she sent them. Bronanes was happy to hear the news and informed them to check in with one of four ladies. Who coordinated all the new arrivals and created manifests to log where and how they were preparing the transports. Skilled artisans had been busy at the cooking facilities drying and preserving food for the half a third season journey. Food was tight but plentiful enough that the magics used in the processes sped up and minimized the time it took to fully provision the fleet. Tooling and supplies for fishing nets and trawling fishing lines being issued to all the transports that were slow moving and fitted with essential stations and training, supporting and understanding of duties and responsibilities.

Bronanes knew that the faster frigates of his naval military command would take half a third seasons to Forumth. Then realizing the slower qualities of the transports it would take longer. Maybe up to a third a third seasons. Bronanes worried for time at sea the longer it took with so many refugees could be dangerous. It would put many at risk of sickness, disease, and well there was a lack of amenities. He had to be positive and hope for the best. With so many how many options were there? The demons and Mechanation's would slaughter them if they were discovered here.

The work and preparations was hard and the day flew by. More Yoranthian's were trained and educated in their new duties rather quickly. The refugees were all in good spirits even if getting a little haggard over the adaptation of the new training and preparations they would be making. They felt close to one another and every late evening there was merriment and song that uplifted the group of refugees. Keeping their spirits was good and the experienced sailors were told by Bronanes to be kind and understanding. Have fun with the people in the evenings and sturdy educators in the day. Keep their hopes up and lessen the fear by contributing to the evening's merriment. His Sea Guard had family and kin among the refugees and understood.

The guards at the door kept vigil and noted no immediate threats approaching the cave. Bronanes would meet up with Huspecia and this day and the next day was so busy that it would always end up some what the same with them being to tired to get involved. With the third day only difference being that Bronanes and Huspecia kept their skivvies on as Dabensir and Leorth's wives and family found out what they were up to with the secluded hot spring. Thanks to a slip of the tongue from Thernya.

It was a very active night at the hot springs with the kids floating face down in the water by the morning of the fourth day. They are sea elves they don't drown in warm water. That only happens if they exceed two hundredth's depths, where their lungs can no longer expand due to water pressure at those depths.

The morning of the fourth day the last group of refugees arrived, the ones that were saved by Queen Kumithra. They made it just as Bronanes had ordered the doors sealed and that all the Sea Guard was needed to prepare and crew the ships.

Among the group of twenty were ten retired sea captains and it was mostly their kin. Many had some skill in fishing off the coast of Yoranthium. It was a stroke of luck as Dabensir and Leorth had a shortage of captains and were designating a few transports with questionable captains. Bronanes was also happy to hear from the child that hugged Kumithra for saving her. He was really amazed at the story of Kumithra charging down three Impundalu and a Shambler and defeating all three with a chain dagger. It amazed Thernya and Huspecia the most when they heard about it. Their Queen was alive last they knew and fighting

for her people in the literal sense. It was a miracle this group got here in time and it was a miracle they brought much needed help. As many groups came.

The docks became a busy hub of activity as the refugees gathered to be issued their directions to join the fleet and which transports they would be on. Thanks to Queen Kumithra more refugee's and some with sailing talent arrived to fill the sparse ranks needed to sail the craft out of the hidden cove and into open waters past the shoals beyond the mouth of the cave.

Bronanes had ordered Dabensir and Leorth to their ships that would be the guide to all the other ships heading up and leading the flotilla of refugees towards Forumth. Dabensir took his frigate along with a guide boat that was rowed out the narrow passage and into open waters along with two other frigates fully fitted and rigged for sail to be the protectors of the head of the fleet.

The frigates all five of them had been fitted with two bow mounted jibs, three masts of a forward, amidships and aft triple sail and a final spanker on the fantail of the frigates. Their hulls were partially of the special refitted magics lacquered treated wood and stronger than modern shipping of this time along with Yoranthium mithreal studded side plating for added defense. They were about five decks in height with the main deck open to the air, followed by the gun deck just above the water line and three more decks that were submerged and underwater.

The third deck was for the crew and the fourth deck was storage. The Keel deck was designed differently on sea elf frigates and was known as the wet deck. As the Keel deck was filled with water and designed for various additional duties to access the undersides of the ship. As the sea elves lived in water and could make use of a flooded deck. The keel deck also allowed for ease of egress for divers and marine operations as well as mounted two torpedo magics tubes forward, port, starboard, and aft. Sea elves learned long ago to attack mainland enemy ships via under water and this secret of the Yoranthium Navy spelled disaster for enemies that did not understand that sea elves can live underwater and use this means to launch submersible attacks and defenses.

The frigates had an array of magics powered cannon number about twenty-two cannons on the port and starboard for a

total of forty-four guns. Two guns mounted to the bow and two guns to the aft. With sixteen magics held in reserve for depth charges that would be released to port and starboard aft slides. These magics depth charges could be rigged and weighted for specific depths and timed.

In deck top lockers the sea elves had repeating harpoon guns that could be fastened to the deck railing and smaller magics gunning cannons. Most of the deck edge mounting was spaced between the rigging as space onboard allowed. This would allow up to twenty small arms mountings per port and starboard.

The crew in all would require a few hundredths including marines and service members. As the rigging of the ship and all the quarters of stations was very labor intensive for these fast frigates. Mostly steered by an aft wheelhouse and below deck piloting gang that had a call tube installed along side the helm to call down orders along with a repeat calling station that would ring to set course and double ring to acknowledge course changes.

Most of the actual piloting depended greatly on the wind for the frigates and the setting of the masts the main, jibs, and spanker. You could say the steering was mostly for fine-tuning the actual directional course adjustments.

In truth the frigates originally were supposed to undergo modification like the Mundrunche yet didn't get the chance making them old no longer of the line. They had only begun minor conversion with their hulls. Only the Mundrunche was modified for a new roll in the Yoranthium navy. As Dabensir and Leorth had began crewing the first three frigates and transports that were filled with refugees out of the cove harbor and into the deep ocean by row boats and preparing their sails. Bronanes had decided it was time for him to show off the Mundrunche new propulsion system that needed comprehensive sea trials and testing. No time like the present. So, he thought.

Bronanes was worried his hopes of this new untried test of the Mundrunche would fail. He looked across the harbor where he saw Thernya working to load up the transports with the refugees. She was being very stern and commanding to the refugees. Telling them what to bring and that they couldn't bring bobbles and trophies of their former lives. She made them understand only essential items, as space was limited on the transports.

There were many that needed equal room as storage for provisioning and support for half a third season was more important than their treasures that should be safe to keep here at the harbors for their return. Bronanes wasn't sure they would return any time soon. The darkening clouds, demons and Mechanation's made all that questionable at best with no standing army or navy.

Then he eyed her. Or to say Huspecia had eyed him. She was waving to him as she was helping load more refugees who were worried about the moving of their ships. Many of the refugees hadn't really been on a boat. Many for being sea elves never spent any long time at a beach for being shore bound and the ocean moved differently. It was a unique experience for many of these land loving sea elves.

Although they had been born sea elves doesn't mean many of those fixed to run of the mill shore bound lives ever stepped foot on a boat or swam in deep water. There would be a lot of fear at first for those not familiar with the ocean. They are sea elves they all adapt to the comforts of the waves soon enough. Especially when they find out they can breathe underwater for some time before needing to come up for air.

Huspecia was waving as Bronanes caught her in his eyes and she in hers. It's like he could hear what she was thinking. 'Oh he sees me. Over here, over here.' It was her voice in his head.

'Huspecia can you hear me?' He thought and then waited for a reply. Just a silly thought.

Huspecia stopped for a moment not really too worried about it. Suddenly realizing she could hear Bronanes thoughts to her from across the harbor. 'Yes, yes, I can hear you. How is this even possible? This day is a weird one isn't it.'

Bronanes thought with a smile on his face. 'You know I think I've heard your voice in my head all my life. I never told you my dear. Didn't want to seem crazy. I didn't think it was real just my imagination.' Confessing a secret, he had thought about for a few years now. Just now coming to the realization of another truth of paired sea elves.

'You knew this? You could hear me? How long?' She was curious because there was so many times Bronanes knew things she only thought about and never really told him.

'Since you came to the healing clerics and felt love for me.' Bronanes replied.

Huspecia was somewhat embarrassed as some of her thoughts had been of a sensual nature of Bronanes and she thought it out loud enough for him to hear it in his mind. 'How could you not ever tell me? I thought things wishing you could hear me and it...'

'Beautiful.' Was Bronanes thought in exchange, 'I had those thoughts of you too. I never tried to think them too you. Sorry you didn't know. Now we do my dear.'

'Yes we do my Narwhal.' Huspecia said with much lust and impatience as it had been days since they had their wedding and haven't been intimate.

'I've undressed you many times my Huspecia and soon enough we'll get our chance hopefully. I do want you so badly.' Bronanes couldn't help but think of her that way.

All she could do was shake her head with a seductive smile and biting her lip and she flooded Bronanes mind what she wanted to do to him. Her thoughts of him were and had been very inappropriate, carnal yet agreeable.

'Huspecia I'm busy here don't excite me that much. I just wanted you to know I'm getting ready to test out my new ship. Well old refitted new ship the Mundrunche. It's classified as a protector class fast frigate.' Huspecia looked a little ejected as Bronanes love of his ship and the sea seemed to be more important than her. 'You'll love it Huspecia, the Mundrunche is just like you now so lovely and beautiful...' Bronanes had to hesitate as Huspecia thought another seductive thought to him. 'Okay, I got it Huspecia! Stop!!!' Bronanes was grinning ear to ear from that thought. Knowing Huspecia understood him. Not to compare the Mundrunche to what she had to offer.

Bronanes almost fell into the bay, as he got closer to the Mundrunche thinking about the thoughts Huspecia gave him. "Lower the masts and make ready the magics black slurry." His well-trained crew knew what Bronanes meant. The sail was rolled extremely tightly and folded to fit the mast booms. After the sails were stored the rigging was fully disconnected from their lower deck locations and tightly wound round each main mast boom and main telescoping pole.

The bow jib booms were also telescoped under the deck along with all three main sail booms. Dropped to the deck and lowered into a special housing that ran under the center of the fantail. The ship configuration didn't have a fantail command deck like the other frigates. Instead, it had a central command cabin and a strange kind of transparent view port slits only about the size of a kings hand wide and a row of narrow kings foot wide gaps of lacquered walling between the circular windows.

Bronanes had walked across the gangplank, as the Mundrunche was being prepared and transformed into a ship with no masts. Many of the spectators had been expecting the oars to come out of the side of the ship but seen no holes for oars. Just that the cannons on the lower deck that was fewer than the other frigates by six, from twenty-two down to sixteen cannons per side with the gun ports being sealed. The hull of the Mundrunche was completely transformed and was of the lacquered wood and mithreal metal sided making it look silver and metal more than wooden.

"Prepare for steam and increase the heat of the boiler!" Bronanes called to the crew in the conning. That's what was called the centralized command room that had a sliding hatch that was open of the same mithreal lacquered wood silver material. "Store all top side gear and make ready to steam forth." There were tubes on the side of the back of the Mundrunche transom that gave off steam as it pressed open flaps that were designed to keep sea water from entering. Opening only when the steam was greater than the pressure outside and quickly resealing.

There was a noticeable multiple stroke pumping and banging coming from the Mundrunche that was faint but could be heard like a heart beat. "Take in the mooring lines and pull in the gangplank." The dock crew removed the moorings and tossed them to the deck where the deck crew pulled in the ropes and stored them in their watertight cabinets. The docking crew ran across the gangplank and then joined the deck crew to pull in the ropes. Freeing the Mundrunche from the pier and pushing off with rods to keep the ship from the pier and creating distance from the boat to the pier and the bumpers. That protected the pier and the ship from damaging one another should they impact.

After the Mundrunche was more than two kings height away from the pier. "Partial Quarter forward." With that the Mundrunche began to move slowly as the steam engine located on the storage deck in the aft center began turning the impeller of a sea jet propulsion system. Water was being siphoned through a water intake fitting aft of the ship that was protected by mithreal grating that allowed water to be sucked up by the impeller and then transferred to a stator blades system. The first of it's kind. Bronanes didn't know if it would work. He's only seen it in test bays before today.

The steam engine with the magics of the black slurry feeding the boilers was working as seen in the test bay and water was being ejected back aft pushing the Mundrunche. The on looking refugees were amazed and never seen a ship move without oars or sails and simply could not believe three jets of water was propelling the frigate forward. "Engineer how are the gauges and boiler doing?"

The Engineer Boson was a new posting on the Mundrunche. It took twenty sea elves to elven the required stations. All of them had to monitor valves and measuring instruments of a nature Bronanes found difficulty in understanding. Much of it was simply magics especially how the black rock magics ensorcelled slurry was able to provide the fire needed to boil the water and create no waste product of black smoke.

Those crafty mages of Yoranthium had their secrets and this black slurry was one of them. There was enough filling the fuel cavities of the Mundrunche to power this ship for two days. Then it would have to revert to sail. This was a good test of it's system not to mention impress the refugees with the might of the Yoranthium Navy. Which was being very well received, by the onlooking spectators, while lifting the spirits of the refugees with jaw dropping cheers of amazement. "All systems are running at top efficiency Captain." Said the engineer with beaming pride.

The Mundrunche was moving forward and nearing the end where it needed to turn. "Drop the bucket pilot and turn to starboard."

The pilot at the helm was a youngster not more than seventeen and new to his job. Performed like a season professional for he was chosen for this specific duty at age fifteen. Another new

system was that of a fluid based tubing magics, hydraulics it was called, again crafted by the mages at the college. That operated part of the bucket diflectors system and turning of the water jets. Operated by two levers next to a steering wheel where the boy sat.

There was a compass that showed the degrees of a full circle of three and sixty hundredths. Starting at the Cold to ninety degrees each for sunup, warm and sundown sides before going back up to cold. The Mundrunche bow was sitting at two-thirty three hundredth's as it's directional bow orientation increased to a new heading of three-twenty hundredth's aiming for the narrow opening of the entrance to the open sea. This maneuver involved no forward motion the jets simply turned the boat and then Bronanes gave the command to resume forward heading. Commanding to haul and store the bumpers.

The Mundrunche's was a sight to behold and gave the people hope they hadn't had in days they seen the amazing magics at work here and the first of it's kind. Yoranthium's pride, Yoranthium's magics, Yoranthium's strength. There wasn't much room for storage on the third or fourth decks. The Mundrunche after it was converted much of the compartments need new protections in place to house the extremely hot boiler and the steam engine.

The dangers of steam leaks were deadly and could if not aware of them could cut an elf's limbs clean off. If there was a loss of pressure in a gauge the crew would have to use a cleaning mops or broom sticks to check ahead for any leaks. Advancement wasn't without risks. Some of the magics in use the mages warned to monitor it closely and shut down the boilers and engine when situation got critical. Only the steam engineers knew what that entailed with these magics in use.

Although Bronanes was well instructed what to monitor along with some command officers, known as Boson's of various titles, on the conning station. Where there was a gauge wall to aft and being watched and logged. Logging was the books the mages wanted so they could improve and understand these magics better.

Oddly except for the light pounding heart beat of the steam engine the Mundrunche was quite silent moving through the water. A few more course adjustments at the right time easily got to the entrance of the Harbor just as the sail frigates had began picking

up the wind in their sails with a wind coming from three and ten hundredth's toward cold. The Mundrunche then turned to port and set up a defensive watch a few leagues off the coast.

Watching as the rear frigates took up a watchful post just behind them as transports began following the lead frigate to a safe distance and the other first frigates taking up a port and starboard shepherd post to protect the refugee transports. A steady stream of transports could be seen leaving the hidden port and the number was significant and sufficient to house all the refugees with still some room to spare. Even the Mundrunche with its cramped decks had quite a few refugees onboard along with a decent number of the best sea guard and marines.

Bronanes had missed his father. He hadn't heard word of any survivors and none of the refugee's had known anything about the actual fate of the Yoranthium navy. Sailors die even officers and Bronanes knew this all too well. He had experienced loss and seen ships go to battle stations. Raiders from time to time attacked the rich merchant ships off the coast of Yoranthium and Bronanes was there to interdict the pirates. Usually Yoranthium ships out matched the pirate and it was easy work. But now this was war and the entire Yoranthium navy was destroyed quickly. The enemy had to have something terrible and Bronanes had to be ready for it.

A signalelf on watch had reported the entire count of transports had been filled all personnel have boarded and no one was left behind according to flags and signalelf aboard the transports. Then confirmed as Huspecia could still telepathically communicate with Bronanes with some difficulty because of the lacquered mithreal hull of the Mundrunche. Reassured Bronanes that the count of transports and refugees was complete and accurate. Dabensir's family and Leorth's family was with her, and they were all doing well, As Thernya was ahead of them somewhere in the middle of all the transports.

Bronanes was relieved as he saw the ships colored flags of the frigates indicate the condition of the fleet and the signalelf's were on top of their duties. It was going quite well as they began slowly moving the ships to a heading of Three and forty hundredth's. They had finally left the coast of Yoranthium by thousandths of leagues. The sea on this side of Yoranthium was a bright sunny day. The dark cloud could be seen but wasn't moving.

It was stationary over most of Yoranthium. The sea was rippling like a calm ocean with no other indications of a storm and sailing was smooth. Seagulls could be seen in the distance and water birds would skip out of the water and dive back down. Hopefully smooth sailing for the next two or third a third season as the Celestial observers noted.

Then a new signal came from the frigate Resolve on the port aft of the transports. "Captain of the Resolve reporting two unknown ships heading one and twenty-five hundredths gaining on us. Unknown class, unknown purpose, appears to have guns at the ready."

Bronanes knew at this distance it would be hard to know the purpose of those incoming ships. Can't put the transports at risk. The Resolve and Spirit and the Mundrunche will have to drop back and prepare to fight the incoming unknown crafts. "Signal the Resolve and Spirit to head One and twenty-five hundredths ahead of the Mundrunche by one half league. Mundrunche will observe and intervene when needed. Do not let the unknown ships pass until we know if they are friendly. Disable them and kill their crew if they are foe. Prepare the guns and load the tubes. Make sure deck crews and the marines are ready in the hold for under water warfare and have the Keel lookouts crew their periscopes. Watch for boarders, or under water activities. Prepare the deck guard to discard boots and prepare armor and weapons for further instructions."

This is the part Bronanes hated the most. Defining if there was a threat incoming or if it was friendly ships. With pirates they would often simply wait until the time was right to raise their colors and attack. Tricking any thing less than the Yoranthium navy. Yet it could be more Yoranthium ships. It kind of was a problem for Bronanes didn't know the status of the main fleet. Except from a scout that collapsed all the way from Sea Shore at the wedding. That was days ago half of a quarter of a third of a season had passed. That scout could be wrong and there could still be other navy ships. Yet the report these ships are unknown configuration would rule out the Yoranthium navy.

It took many commands to get the sail frigates into position and in front of the Mundrunche. Bronanes simply disengaged the

impellers and stopped the ship while the steam engine kept on beating away.

The sharp-eyed signalelf were keeping a close eye on the approaching black colored unknown ships and the tarnished black sails. It looked like pirates and no signals from those ships could bee seen. The signalelf on the Yoranthium ship reported the strange ships had their gun ports open and might also have tubes. Bronanes had ordered deck guard to arm themselves with bows and arrows as well as harpoons and even the deck hands had been armed. All of the tension was getting greater and mounting. Many of the sea guard only had faced battle just days ago at the outside keep. Not many were involved in that skirmish. It was obvious as Bronanes looked out the conning ports that many of the sea guard were nervous and worried filled with anxiety. It would be their first naval battle in a long time.

Hopefully it was pirates. Not sea elves or those raiders of the deep sea elves. Hopefully just some shore elves failing to put their guns away. Bronanes would be happy with that. He could use more ships by the time they got to the land bridge for the farmers and miners to join them. Got to protect the Refugees.

Then Huspecia contacted Bronanes. She was worried. 'Is everything okay?' She thought to him.

'Huspecia you shouldn't be here it could get dangerous drop back to the other transports don't get lost.' Bronanes thought to her but only parts of the message got through.

'Shouldn't, dangerous, get back, other transports, get lost?' Huspecia didn't understand Bronanes message and replied. 'Transports.... not on...fleet slow...wha....'

Abruptly Huspecia couldn't be heard and Bronanes asked for a fleet report. The signalelf reported, he couldn't make out any signals. The range to fleet was too great. "There is only a single transport trying to close in to the aft but no signals." Looks like the fleet had halted by dropping sail that the signalelf couldn't confirm.

Suddenly there was a volley of two cannons and then another two cannons. The black ships in the distance declared themselves as enemies the moment they fired shots.

"Report bow observer." Bronanes jumped to action stations.

"Resolve and Spirit report shots fired from hostile ships they are out of range and the shots fell short." Reported the bow signalelf.

"Signal the Resolve and the Spirit to engage the enemy ships. Concentrate fire on the one to port first and then finish the other one off. Apparently they have split targets, and this should be easier to target one on port first. Disable that then disable the other. Prepare for underwater activities and use your marines and deck forces to port first and hold starboard should these be water born pirates." Bronanes ordered the signalelf, and he did as he was told.

The Spirit and Resolve signaled their compliance and reported they seen something below from the aft keel observer. A sea monster was under them of considerable size and was headed towards the refugee fleet at high speed. A cruising speed that the frigates could exceed if they turned back now. With the bulk of the refugee fleet out of range the other three frigates would be caught unaware.

It would be unlikely the other three frigates were even in range to interdict the underwater sea monster. No way to effectively signal or relay a message at the current distance the Mundrunche was from the nearest transport that of Huspecia.

Yoranthium

Book One: Lost Hope

Chapter Seventeen:

Sea Monstrosity Tredinak

By Mark P. Bromley

The deep dark ocean has never been fully explored many things and stories of the deep abound on Yoranthium. From time to time terrible Monstrosities surface and are known from folk tales. Legends and myth of sea monstrosities to be terrible and frighten even to the sturdiest of sailors. Those who make their living on the oceans in their tropical paradise know on the surface all is calm but what lies below is something to be wary of.[23]

[23] Our world is large and we know little of our own oceans a critical environment key to the life of Earths Biome. Worry more for how we treat our oceans for the waters is crucial to all life on our world and Ishormot.

The defense Bronanes had planned on was now lost. He had to make a new command decision, one that would test the three ships to their limits. It was obvious the gunshots from the unknown enemy were meant to distract them from the real threat. A sea monstrosity that was heading straight past their defense and towards the helpless refugees that staggered for quite a distance and likely out of sight of the lead three frigates. Half of the refugees could die and so could Huspecia, Ardrian her children and Teirdith and her child. Bronanes couldn't let that happen as it would destroy his command and Dabensir and Leorth would lose hope in Bronanes as a leader.

Bronanes knew the Resolve captain Terrance and the Spirit captain Zultier. They are fine captains, and they had some combat experience with his father the admiral. They had fought some hard fights in the past and had lost sea elves under their commands. Experienced sea captains capable of fighting two hostile ships that split their attack and had been pushing against the wind. While the two Yoranthium ships with the wind in their sails can move faster and are well stocked with the new hull refitted reinforced hulls. Along with new magics, new cannons, and many newer weapons and folded metal blades to repeal boarders.

Bronanes had requested. "Keel spotters have you seen anything beneath the water?" Bronanes was certain that the Resolve and the Spirit had the upper hand and if they ran interference and targeted one enemy at a time they should make good time in crippling those ships. They don't need to sink them. Just disable and catch them on fire, destroy their sails and ability to repair. It would take a long time to sink a wooden ship. Wood floats and if these are other sea elves or water pirates. They would need to kill as many bastards as they could. Stop their ability to fight on. Buying time for the refugee fleet to make good time to Forumth and safety.

"Sir."' the keel speaker in the conning responded. "Sea monster spotted it was described as a myth sir. It's a Tredinak or so that's what both the observers said. Moving at mid speed below us." The keel speaker was in complete disbelief. The Tredinak was a terrible myth told to every child who admired the sea. It was a large creature the same size as the Mundrunche. To a fishing boat

it was a real terror even for a frigate it's power was said to crush the hulls of ships over a hundredth years ago.

The Tredinak had a crustacean shaped body. That could devour a transport and all aboard. Four huge crab like pincer claws in front. Round domed shaped black glistening smaller eyes from the front of its head and down it's back. If it surfaced vertically exposing its underbelly from the sea it would look like elven eyes on its underbelly above a shark's mouth full of row after row of teeth. Believed to have two arms middle of its body along with massive, elongated sea elves arms with three joints and hands ending in smaller tentacles instead of fingers. Fingers of multiple uncountable lengths of various sizes from one king length to fifteen or more in length, small wispish tentacle on its hands. With as many as six large octopus tentacles that helped it's shark like tail move quickly in the water just under the arms. Moved at cruising speed for the Mundrunche underwater. A deadly sea monster never seen around Yoranthium just tales further off the coast of the Lollygag Islands and more myths that come out of the deep dark hell of the abyss.

Bronanes could not let the sea monster go unchallenged. Fortunately for Bronanes the Mundrunche was more than a match for the Tredinak. "Signal men tell the Resolve and the Spirit they must deal with the black ships themselves. The Mundrunche must defend the refugees and stop the sea monster."

Bronanes waited for a reply from the two ships, and they replied. "Happy hunting and the unborn God protect you." Respectively: as reported by the signal Boson.

"All deck crew store the deck weapons, close the gun ports, get below deck and rig for underwater running. Prepare all torpedo tubes for firing solution. Turn this ship about and maximize speed to target, active sound bounce." Sound bouncing was using sound to bounce off targets to see things that was difficult to see underwater. This new sonar magics very effective method that the Yoranthium fishermen used to find and locate large groups of fish. In this case Bronanes was hunting the Tredinak using reflective sound.

The Mundrunche turned around in very little time as the pilot engaged the drive and the bucket on the water jets to quickly pivot the Mundrunche with no listing to either side. The waterjet

was a flat and smooth turn not even a shudder of the ship. The steam engine and the gauges were in the right range, and all looked good with the boilers. The Mundrunche was surpassing cruising speed and moving towards top or flank speed. Just below emergency speed. The deck crews had finished stowing all gear and final checks were made by the bosons on deck then gave the all clear that all went below and secured all hatches. The Mundrunche was ready to take on the Tredinak.

"Fill ballasts and dive to match the Tredinak's position. Boson of the deck, close all conning hatches." Bronanes heard the conning boson give him an aye and all was ready. The sound bouncer worked as intended and gave the range to the Sounder engineer on duty.

The Pilot gave a command. "Down bubble, Mundrunche submerging." The Mundrunche was the first of it's kind the magics came from a deep sea elf raiding party that lived below two hundredth's fathoms. Much of the magics the mages had used came from understanding the deep sea elves own ship that was retrograded and studied for its magics. Mundrunche may have not been the first submarine or under water vessel. As for Yoranthium today marked their kingdoms first day of submerged vessel usage. Hopefully the magics of the Mages College would prove useful and not fail. Bronanes had an entire fleet of refugees to defend and the Tredinak was aiming straight for Huspecia's transport. That simply would not do and his Huspecia would not be food for a crustacean.

The down bubble hit a five down direction of a ten down maximum the bow plane group along with three boson's was located on the fourth deck. They had moved by hand, fins that looked like whale flippers into position for the ship to sink beneath the sea. The conning tower could see out the windows as the water washed over the bow and flooded the deck. It was the first time sea elves had seen such a thing and it reminded them of home. They loved the water and felt as home to them. The fifth deck and the ballast tanks had crew living in them and it didn't bother the sea elves as these chambers became full of water. They simply dogged down the hatches to these chambers and stood watch. Ensuring the systems of these new magics worked as they had been intended.

“Range and depth of the Tredinak?” Bronanes needed to know.

“Depth forty fathoms and rising nearing the first closest transport. Range zero point two-fiver of one third leagues, one point eight zero leagues to first transport.” The sounder reported.

“Ready to fire forward torpedo's at point one zero of a third leagues to target, adjust course to maintain depth with the beast. Set timers to self destruct torpedo's if they overshoot by twenty sub-moments.” Bronanes could see from the sounding and plotting magics table displayed by the ships cartography boson. The cartography boson was a lesser vassal of the celestial mapmakers used on Yoranthium ships to a lesser extent than the bound six previously discussed. The cartography boson could display real time information of the immediate ship combat information providing detailed moment-to-moment navigational assistance to the captain.

The Mundrunche headed straight for the Tredinak and closed range faster than the sea monster anticipated. The range between the two competitively sized combatants fell within the Mundrunche's firing solution. “Fire.” Came Bronanes order and two magics laced torpedo propelled by magics accelerator launched from the forward tubes.

The torpedos were fast and the Tredinak seen from it's dorsal black bulbous eyes the incoming threats. Didn’t expect such a threat and was surprised to see an underwater attacker hunting it. The Tredinak turned effortlessly to face the incoming torpedo's as the speed took the Tredinak off guard.

The first Torpedo sailed by harmlessly but close enough that the Tredinak took a futile swing at the torpedo. The second torpedo impacted the Tredinak's right hand and exploded. Ripping apart the hand and sending the multiple twisted and deformed tentacle fingers in all directions. With impact bursts rippling and nearing the Tredinak doing even more damage until the energy dissipated. While the first segment of the wrist and arm was shredded causing the Tredinak to let loose a terrifying telepathic scream that impacted the crew of the Mundrunche making them wince in pain for a few moments. Out the view ports dark oozing blood could be seen coming from the Tredinak's stump of a right

elven like arm. Thus explosion set off the first torpedo doing even more damage.

Bronanes wasn't ready for such a psychic scream. It took him a few moments to get his bearings. The Mundrunche needed to change course. Bronanes intended to put the Mundrunche in harms way and between the Tredinak and Huspecia's transport. "Level bubble, veer two degrees to starboard, ready starboard tubes. Seal and prepare forward tubes for another shot." Bronanes shouted the same command three times before the rest of the crew had fully recovered from the Tredinak psychic scream of agony. The beast received significant damage to its right arm. Completely losing the use of that arm.

The Tredinak was enraged and no longer interested in the helpless transports. It's underbelly eye lids flashed open and was quite a terrifying sight to behold. Having acquired the Mundrunche in its sights the beast turned towards the ship. Came flying slightly slower than it was before. The pain and injury caused the Tredinak to be less maneuverable than before. Its long reaching claws were in range and snapped and swung closely around the agile Mundrunche that managed by a mere half a king's thumb to avoid the massive Tredinak's claws. The vibrations of the water turbulence could be felt on the hull. Many sailors of the Mundrunche had been bracing and slipped and were thrown around some of the many cabins like rag dolls sustaining minor injuries. Even the pilot fell from his seat and impacted the hull and cut his head open above the right eye. He was gushing blood making it hard for him to use his right eye. He wouldn't let his Captain down there would be time enough to fix his wound. He snapped quickly back to his post to keep control of the helm.

Bronanes was proud of his crew taking such a tumble this close to the claws of such a fantastic monster that had missed but shook the ship with it's four massive clawed attempted strikes. Luck was with the crew of the Mundrunche just one claw could have ended their wild rampage.

Now, the Mundrunche had successfully came broad side to the Tredinak. "Fire Port Torpedo's." With that a delayed pause from the port torpedo tubes, as they had also some difficulty securing their stations. After long dreadful moments the torpedo's finally launched from the port two tubes. With one direct impact

on the Tredinak midsection and detonating by concussive force the other magics torpedo that sailed past the underbelly of the beast and under the armpit of the shoulder of the former right arm.

The Tredinak screamed in psychic pain as the direct impact ripped off two of the massive tentacles on it's left side and caused blood to come forth from the exposed bones and torn flesh. The pulsating energy of the torpedo lingered pressing closer and closer to the Tredinak tearing away tissue and bone until the energy of the blast was no more. The right arm was completely severed and filled with bone and heavy tissue that was not like wood. Flesh unless supported by fat and the air in the lungs along with the force of mussel's sinks. Sinking like the heavy tentacles that twitched and contorted with no more direction or control from the Tredinak.

Again Bronanes and his crew became staggered and half the crew-developed nose bleeds from the psychic impact to their minds. It wasn't a good feeling and Bronanes was worried about firing more torpedoes so close to this beast. Already the damage control boson was reporting some of the crew had fallen ill, unconscious or believed dead. Yet it was an acceptable number for the Mundrunche was still operational and there where two more loaded Torpedo's to aft. Bronanes could feel it was difficult to concentrate as his head was throbbing from the psychic impact and a tiny bit of blood was seen below his left nostril.

Huspecia was watching from the topside. She never knew the Mundrunche could purposely go underwater. She never seen any ship like it and was astonished yet felt her heart pounding in anxiety and fear for her Bronanes she was feeling uneasy and had to hold down her breakfast as her skin became pale and her hands clenched so tight to the side railing of the transport, watching with much concern where the Mundrunche had gone underwater. She could see in the near distance the water heave up as two massive objects had been moving under the sea. This buffeted the transport and some startled cries of the refugees, and the children came to her attention.

She had help from Ardrian and Teirdith at calming the refugees telling them to sit down and ball up into a compact fetal position and hunker close to one another and the hull. "Hold on tight and lock in!!!" She told them not sure if it was the right thing to do but seemed right enough. Huspecia wouldn't want them

falling in the water and becoming casualties of whatever was below them. Even though they are all sea elves there are dangerous predators in the deeper ocean and well most of those monsters liked sea elf flesh.

Huspecia could sense a huge predator was nearby. Then the rough sea swelling was followed by huge bubbles of water, then ruptured and sprayed their tiny transport buffeting their tiny craft. These waves caused high volumes of water to saturate the bottom of their transport, buffeting and pushing their transport nearly tipping them to port and threatened to capsize the heavy laden boat.

Just as some massive amount of black congealed and oozing blood began to float to the surface another massive exploding bubble followed immediately by another shook their transport. Filling with more spray from the ocean and oozing congealed blood that landed on Vatalorn and Rubius sending the two kids into panic, and they jumped up before the transport righted itself and fell over the side.

Rubius and Vatalorn were new at swimming and panicked they couldn't touch the bottom of the water. They were in no danger of drowning yet panicked like they would drown. It could happen if a sea elf didn't relax and just breathe underwater. This was the children still needing to understand how to swim from their parents. Ardrian hands were full with Dueith and Indirid the baby. Teirdith was packed in like a sardine trying to get to her daughter and couldn't.

It was up to Huspecia that dove in the water effortlessly and she had no difficulty gathering the two children and getting them to relax and swim with her back to the transport. She carefully pushed each back into the boat as Teirdith managed to reach the transports edge and pulled the two children back into the transport. Huspecia remained in the water and pushed herself from the boat. She needed to see what was going on below. "Teirdith take care of the refugees and the boat. I'll be back in a few." Teirdith understood and Huspecia went under the water and discarded her Yukata and belt as it felt tight and restricted her swimming along with her open toed boots and sandals that seemed awkwardly uncomfortable. It took a small amount of time for her

eyes adjusted and could see the battle unfolding beneath the surface.

The Mundrunche moved forward and was leaving the Tredinak behind and swung its aft fantail. Lining up it's aft tubes as it made a course correction to port and then starboard. Kind of sluggish in controls and response as the crew was becoming fatigued and exhausted with the battering and buffeting the ship was taking in the Tredinak's wake, along with the psychic screaming and lingering pain.

The Mundrunche had successfully pulled the monster away from Huspecia's transport and was now taking it in warm, sundown direction away from the fleet.

Bronanes could see the fantail coming around and lining up with the Tredinak's shark fin. "Fire aft tubes!!!" With a longer delay as the weapons Boson slowly responded and the reply from below decks took a bit of time. Only one torpedo launched the other misfired in the tube. The torpedo impacted the top shark fin crippling the beast and the Mundrunche was blessed to be out of the range of its psychic scream. As more blood and the concussive shock shook the Mundrunche and expanded to the surface.

There was no report on the empty tubes to the bow or port being reloaded. Bronanes only had starboard torpedo tubes, and this would mean circling back towards the Tredinak. "To starboard one and eighty hundredth's bring starboard tubes to bare."

Upon saying this, the enraged and dying Tredinak put all it's effort into targeting the Mundrunche. They were on a collision course now. There wasn't much time for the Mundrunche to alter its course or take evasive action. The crew of the Mundrunche was still reeling from the effects of the psychic scream, to sluggish and too confused to respond. About twenty more of the crew had been rendered out of service as they gave into their internal hemorrhaging. The onboard healing clerics were overwhelmed and horrified for they didn't have enough magics to help the crew.

The Tredinak closed in before Bronanes could give orders and impacted the Mundrunche hard. Even the new lacquered mithreal vibrated and a sickening crunching could be heard. Dry decks began to fill with water and if not for the submerged conditions being set and the hatches being sealed this would have

likely been the end for the Mundrunche and her crew. Yet it was a good crew, and everyone pulled their weight even the neophyte refugees conscripted into naval service onboard. Bronanes could and would only be proud of the bravery of his crew. They were a testament to the naval service of Yoranthium.

The impact caused the boiler to shift, and a crack formed in the super heated steam chamber. This shot out instantly into the boiler compartment and instantly boiled the entire boiler crew of ten. Killing them with third degree burns as the hot steam filled the chamber. Steam pressure dropped quickly and the steam engineers down in the steam controls to the burners saw this and were warned that this could lead to catastrophic damage if the fire chamber ignited the magics black rock slurry and got to the storage bins. The stokers quickly shut down the fuel as the steam engine slowed and dropped in pressure and became silent. No more water flowed into the intake. The impellers had stopped moving causing the water jets to cease to function.

The Mundrunche was dead in the water and no longer had propulsion and could not bring the starboard tubes to bear on the Tredinak as it's desperate attack ripped off those tubes and flooded the compartments more sea elves securing the tubes died and were eaten by the Tredinak, as the hull had ruptured pulling the sea elves out into the ocean before the gaping mouth of the Tredinak.

Bronanes had received the damage reports instantly and watched as the steam board dropped to zero. The Mundrunche was listing to starboard and getting worse. "Blow all ballasts, rig for emergency surfacing, Planes to surface. Up bubble angle ten. Surface the Mundrunche." Bronanes got an "aye," from his pilot and nods form his boson's that all agreed they were now out of the fight and would have to try and fight the Tredinak from the surface.

Bronanes had a different idea. Above the door was a repeating harpoon meant for hunting large sea prey. Prey like what they were fighting right now. No, he couldn't simply just shoot harpoons into the beast. It would take a lucky shot to kill it. Yet harpoons could be tied to something much more powerful and deadlier. On the fantail there where two depth charge launchers. More than enough explosive power to kill this Tredinak, he was forming a rough idea of what he intended to do. "Boson of the

deck!" This was Bronanes means to find the next highest ranking officer in the room.

The engineer was that officer. He came forward as the ballasts had been forcing the water out and the Mundrunche began ascending rapidly. The Tredinak could have attempted for another collision with the Mundrunche. That would have finished the Mundrunche if not for the rate of the surfacing was too fast for the Tredinak.

The Boson fell into Bronanes at the sudden surge of drastic change in pitch and roll of the Mundrunche went against gravity causing anyone not bracing to be thrown around their respective compartments. "Yes, sir." He said picking himself off Bronanes and looking him in the eye.

"I need you to take command of the Mundrunche. You weapons and cartographer you'll be with me once we surface." Bronanes eyed them and they were in fear of what to expect from their captain. "Don't fret any it's easy I need you two to tie rope to all the depth charges and when I say, release them into the sea. Drop them all tied together into the sea. Don't have to set the depth just time their charge for thirty sub-moments and sync them. I'll do the rest with this repeating harpoon gun."

"Sir that's very dangerous we got marines waiting to fight the Tredinak on deck five." Said the Boson sure that Bronanes had options.

"Boson the marines only have small arms and will not understand my plan and it can't fail. I will feed no more of my crew to this beast. This is something only I alone can do. It's my plan and I don't want to blame others, if I fail. You'll only have me to blame. Your job is to save the Mundrunche and the fleet and to get those surface guns to bear on the Tredinak should I fail. These will be your orders." Bronanes looked around the room and seeing the fear they all had in their eyes. His command deck simply agreed, hoping, and were certain he had a plan of action.

The Mundrunche rose quickly and shot out of the water with it's bow up and came crashing down splashing considerable water spray to all sides. Creating a quick burst of several up and down heaves and finally resting at a three bubble list to starboard and bow up of four. Damage control teams would be needed from engineering to fix the ship as the Boson took to his new command

of the Mundrunche. He barked orders to rig for surface combat and the gun only a quarter were in condition to be used were being prepared. The Boson of the deck also ordered rail guns to be mounted and lookouts to their topside and keel spotter positions.

Bronanes grabbed his weapons and cartographer boson's to his side. Opened the conning hatch to the fresh air of the blue sky above. He moved with his two companions motioning them and commanding them how to tie and string together the depth charges. He kept the rope lengths short so the barrels would be touching one another and in two clumps. Both the Weapon and Cartographer bosuns were doing a good job and understood Bronanes well as they went about their task.

Bronanes then went to the dropping station and began rigging the ramps to drop both sets within a king's length or two under the Mundrunche's fantail. He couldn't have asked for the ship to surface in the most ideal depth charge dropping position. This angle would have been difficult if the Mundrunche was unscathed. The damage caused by the Tredinak was perfect for Bronanes plan to increase its success.

He carefully prepared his repeating harpoon. Although it was repeating, he only needed one harpoon to succeed. Bronanes would likely only get one chance to fire this harpoon effectively and he needed it to hit a soft part of the underbelly and go through. Where it would not be quick to remove and move the two clusters of charges near enough to destroy the Tredinak. Looking at the sixteen barrels. He was certain that it would be more than enough firepower of black powder magics.

He just needed to get his topside bearings there was only one problem in the area he knew of. That would be the refugee transport. He looked around still trying to get his proper bearings as it was becoming mid day the sun was all the way up and it was difficult to determine which side the transport was on. He looked around and couldn't quite find it. This might be good, he thought. If they are out of range then the concussive burst wouldn't affect the transport.

He kept searching the horizon. He saw the Resolve and Spirit engaging the enemy ships in the distance with cannons firing. Couldn't tell who was winning it was just fire and smoke far away from the Mundrunche. Then he spun around and found the

transport. Just the sail of it that was down, it wasn't moving. It was several leagues off. Plenty safe distance and a relief that Huspecia was not in harms way of his drastic plan. The only real danger would be to the Mundrunche alone. If they could kill this Tredinak, then the risk was acceptable for his people's lives.

Bronanes had fastened the rope needed to the harpoon gun he was going to use. He would only get one shot at this. Needed a lot of courage for what he was going to do. Getting close to the Tredinak wouldn't be easy and he was thinking of those monstrous underbelly eyes would be the best target for his harpoon. In haste he, undid his Yukata's belt and cast off his Yukata to the side on the hatch covering the masts of the ship. He was now bare chest with a well muscular chest and defined abdomen and small waist. Baring his Yoranthium tattoo's before the sun with Huspecia's name over to the side of his heart inside a heart of the Unborn God and a lacy cross. Huspecia was written in Yoranthium that resembled a romanji gothic writing. Coiling just about two kings length of rope he put it on his left shoulder, while touching his left hand over the tattoo of his heart, with the harpoon in his right. "Are the barrels ready to drop?"

"Aye sir." Was the reply form the weapons and cartographer in unison.

"Release the charges, then." At that, the barrels one after another all sixteen barrels fell in the water and began to gradually submerge. Bronanes did not hesitate he had to go and tie off his harpoon to the two clusters and make it only one cluster of barrels as quickly as he could. The barrels would continue to descend into the depths and there was only two hundredth fathoms for Bronanes to make use of.

As he began running towards the transom and the bright blue sparkling water gleaming in the sun light and with patches of disemboweled blood of the creature rising to the surface with an awful stench of death. Bronanes kicked off his sandals that covered the bottom of his open toed boots. One of the sandals fell on the deck the other over the port side floating on the water.

His tight naval pants fastened with twine on the sides of the hip were made of a slick shiny black silk that outlined his male physique and tucked into the flopping down portion of his boots that were meant to be fully fastened above his knees and upper

thighs. Yet he preferred his boots partially laced and simply let the rest of the material dangle folded down. He ran to the transom and jumped in to the water in the cleanest possible spot he could see.

Descending in the water adjusting his eyes and getting accustomed to breathing under water with his gills behind his ears. He could see the barrels before him all neatly coming together as he had hoped. His feet and fingers filled with water and activating his stored webbed hands and toes. Making it easier for him to pull at the water and push himself through to the barrels. Once he got there he removed the coiled rope on his shoulder and let the harpoon gun dangle in the water next to him as he tied his harpoons rope to the barrels.

Having quickly done that he looked around trying to find the Tredinak. Which wasn't very difficult, as the Tredinak had seen him enter the water. Bronanes was carelessly making his way to the barrels in haste. The Tredinak saw him and the barrels. The monster surmised Bronanes must have been the sea elf that had hurt him badly for only a desperate sea elf ship captain would enter the water with such a monstrosity hunting them down.

The Tredinak had already been moving at top speed. Well that's to say as fast is it's wounded body would allow it to move at. Which would now only be about a third of the Mundrunche's speed when it was new and not disabled as one attack from the weakened Tredinak had done to the pride of the remaining Yoranthium navy. This one battle with the Tredinak gave some idea what must have happened to the Yoranthium navy if there were many Tredinak's attacking as one. The Mundrunche was lucky to have just the one Tredinak to fight.

This Tredinak sensed something familiar with this prey. It felt familiar like a deja vu a quarter of a third of a season ago when it made the initial assault on the unsuspecting Yoranthium Navy commanded by the blood of someone similar.

Yes this sea elf seemed the same, smelled the same, it was offspring of that which it had fed upon. A fitting end for that other sea elf had attacked it too. It remembered this Tredinak would get its reward before it would die from the wounds this day. It will end this line of sea elf and it shot a psychic impression to Bronanes of the fate of his father the admiral and how quickly that fleet was destroyed with the death of many a sea guard.

Bronanes knew the Tredinak was close the moment it incorrectly timed that psychic impression. Bronanes was only fazed less than a sub-moment. Duty to kill the beast took precedence before figuring out all the imagery that flooded his mind. His father taught him duty first saves lives. Bronanes only images in his mind were that of protecting Huspecia and the people of Yoranthium it's all he needed to know. Reducing the desired impact of the psychic impression from the Tredinak to nothing but a misplaced thought in his mind.

Bronanes turned around as a claw came his way and he dodged it along with the barrels, as the Tredinak exposed its underbelly. Opening the large gray sea elf eyes that had murderous intent and a huge shark like mouth just below the eyes on it's belly began to open displaying row after row of sharp and vicious looking teeth, a mouth wide enough to engulf an entire transport in one swallow.

Bronanes knew he didn't have much time. The Tredinak was already moving it's left arm and hand toward him to push him in along with the barrels towards it's mouth. This could prove to be useful to Bronanes for the Tredinak didn't see the danger of the sea elf sized depth charges. Likely the Tredinak thought the barrels was just more food. Had to be careful and quick. Can't allow the barrels to be crushed or broken into before their timer cords ran out.

Having pulled the timer cords and carefully aimed his harpoon at the Tredinak. He fired the harpoon right into the gray uncaring enormous left eye. It had gotten so close that it didn't see the real danger of the harpoon and it sailed through the water at incredible speed and plunged with great force right into the eye of the monster and continued as it tore the eye like an inflated ball and impacted the back of the soft eye socket tissue and into the creatures lower brain stem creating partial paralysis as it splattered on through the spinal column of the beast and through it's inner organs erupting through it's back before coming to a stop.

A lucky shot. Bronanes had felt that God must have guided his hand. The Tredinak pulled back in great sightless pain. It had lost it's pray. And pulled on the barbed hook of the harpoon that

tightened its rope and pulled the barrels almost hitting Bronanes in the process.

The Psychic scream from the Tredinak hit Bronanes mind hard. Giving him a pressure in his head so painful he thought it would explode as blood pooled in his eyes, and out his nostrils and from his gills. Bronanes was fighting and struggling to stay conscious as his eyes blurred. He reached to a utility pocket on the side of his pants. It contained a healing vial of some magics the healing clerics issued to the sea guard. These vials were for emergencies for some of the herbal properties to a minor percentage of sea elves these healing alchemy's had hallucinogenic effects. Fortunately only about point zero five percent of sea elves were negatively affected by healing potions and didn't know it. He quickly popped the cork and downed the contents along with the seawater. It had magically stopped the pain and allowed Bronanes to focus. He was not one of those negatively affected by the tonic.

Bronanes started to swim in the direction away from the Tredinak. The Tredinak was pulling the barrels down, down and further down in the water. Bronanes didn't notice the Tredinak's left arm was reaching towards him and almost upon him. The arm was much faster than he could swim. Closing in on him with outstretched multiple tentacles.

Then the timing cords ran out and the sixteen depth charges imploding as sea rushed in to fill the cavity of air and chemical combustion. Quickly expanded into drenched fiery explosions of great magnitude all at the same time the explosive force and concussive force was extraordinary. Bronanes was pushed through the water somersaulting head over heals and spinning in circles nearly crushed by the blast. He managed to right himself enough and open his eyes. Through blurry vision and trying to make sense of what he saw before him.

The Tredinak was the closest to the explosive charges nearly ingesting them into its maw. The force of the blast tore the poor beast apart. Sending bits of it everywhere, carapace, pincers and claws, tentacles, skin, teeth and all sorts of fleshy sickening entrails and other bone and cartilage with a massive pool of diffuse blood spreading out from the explosion. Along with the sea elf remains it had partially ingested.

Bronanes felt himself lucky and quite blessed to have lived through this amount of destruction. He managed to defeat the beast that murdered his father the admiral and got vengeance for so many sea guard and their loved ones. He was quite proud of his accomplishment, rivaled that and surpassed Rarailmuir's slaying of the dragon. He truly became the embodiment of his hero and icon. Fact is he was more heroic than Rarailmuir ever achieved and sadly not enough would ever understand.

As he began swimming up to the surface, Bronanes did not see the bit of outstretched arm from the Tredinak rising quickly below him. Just as Bronanes was about to out distance the opening hand of the severed limb the longest of the tentacles had grabbed his left ankle and foot. The Tredinak's severed limb lost all of it's momentum and was working on reflex action as the teeth of each tentacle suction cup dug into the leather of his boots and bit into the exposed toes. Pulling Bronanes back down in the depths of the ocean.

Bronanes panicked at first trying to fight for the surface but it was no use. The dead flesh and bone of the Tredinak's limb was simply too heavy. It was like having ten anchors tied to him. He was dropping fast and was quickly beyond one and fifty hundredths and descending. It wouldn't be long before he couldn't breathe as the water pressure began slowing his lungs and their ability to circulate air and water through his gills. He was in danger of drowning and remembered he had a concealed knife tucked in his boot. He reached down with considerable difficulty trying to reach the dagger. After some effort he had success and began cutting away at the tentacle fingers that latched on to him.

It was like a fight he couldn't quite describe. Each tentacle he removed another had grabbed him and then another. Removing one and two or three would attach. The ones on his exposed foot hurt the most as they tore his skin and drew blood. At last he had success. The last tentacle had been removed as Bronanes became neutrally buoyant.

He was too far down he had exceeded two and fifty hundredth's depth. His lungs filled with water he was unable to process as his lungs had too much pressure they could no longer contract. Just expand and it was now impossible to get the oxygen in his lungs he needed to work his powerful sea elf mussels.

He was simply drifting in the twilight zone of the water. Where the light from the sunny day above could not reach the transition zone between the teal blue tropical waters and into the darker sapphire blue water that was becoming darker moment by moment.

Bronanes could still see that the Mundrunche was safe and the transport with Huspecia. His dearest and sweet wife Huspecia was on was safe. He never got the chance for an heir. He never got the chance for a full life with her. This was it for him and the world was getting dark. His eyes were ever so softly closing as he filled his mind with every moment he shared with Huspecia. From the day he was beside her on his fathers ship pulling her from the sea as an infant and just today. Hearing her heart, reaching out with his soul, and dreaming of a life they could have had. Thinking as hard as he could. Hoping Huspecia could hear him so far away. 'I'll miss you my love, Huspecia.'

Then life faded away, he accepted his end. He knew he died a hero of his people, For Yoranthium. No song or story would be told of a feat greater than Rarailmuir. His eyes had closed. Surrendering to the deep ocean his soul. With much remorse the world and the sea elves of Yornathium did not see the heroic feat that Bronanes accomplished.

Yoranthium

Book One: Lost Hope

Chapter Eighteen: Spirit of Resolve

By Mark P. Bromley

Naval battles is what is common with the Kingdom of Yoranthium. This is how we divide the sea elves from shore elves and the beasts of the deep seas. Pirates, war, terrors of the sea be wary for the death's of the sea elves doesn't come cheap or free. There will be those bringing the fight to those who would terrorize the seas to preserve Freedom.

The Spirit and Resolve had received their orders from the Mundrunche. Captains Terrance of the Resolve and Zultier of the Spirit understood their orders to engage and render the two hostile ships inoperable and kill the crews. The wind was off to the cold side to their aft giving them plenty of speed. While it was obvious the hostile ships were at a great disadvantage and trying to sail against the wind. This would allow the Spirit and the Resolve more than enough power to target one hostile ship at a time with ease of maneuverability.

Having looked at the range of the ships and recognizing their design as Trooperships. It was clear these crafts must have been empty. They rode high on the water as if what they carried was no longer in their hulls. The Yoranthium Frigates gave signals to coordinate their attacks to one another. The Resolve was the first to turn port to target the starboard side Troopership. With the Spirit trailing just a little aft starboard of the fantail of the Spirit. Their speed was high enough to notice the enemy port ship was barely moving and too heavy to respond to the agile nature of the frigates. Captain Zultier could see only sparse guns on the enemy's starboard side and relayed he had only noticed six guns ports open on the hostile ship. The ship only had the two guns on the bow and seemed to have a lack of action on the deck in rearming the guns it pointlessly fired.

If the enemy ships aren't going to fight this was going to be easy thought both frigate Captain's. Suddenly the keel spotter reported to the observer boson on the fantail by sounding tube. The keel boson warned the captain on both ships. "Depth Dwellers under the water moving towards our ships. About eighty in number."

Both commanders on each ship in similar fashion relayed this message. "Prepare to repel boarders, ready the guns, and subsurface marines to the ready." This command would ready the ship to fire at the enemy ships, have all deck hands armed and on the watch for boarders. Along with getting the marines on the water deck ready to egress from the bottom of the ship to do battle with the depth dwellers. There would be one and twenty hundredths marines in the water from both ships to intercept the depth dwellers.

Captain Terrance had an idea. "Signal the Spirit. Have her hold on the marines. I'm firing port torpedo's toward the Depth Dwellers." There was a few moment pause, as the signalelves relayed and received the communications between the two frigates. Captain Terrance saw the reply was that the Spirit was holding its marines. With no risk to harming their own elves, Captain Terrance had readied starboard tubes. "Fire both starboard tubes." A slight explosion from below decks could be heard that slightly buffeted the Resolve to port.

The torpedo's sailed towards the eighty or so depth dwellers racing towards the Resolve and Spirit. Both torpedo's had luck in striking the large sized depth dwellers and exploded, the Depth Dwellers numbers were quickly diminished by thirty. Leaving about Thirty-five being harmed and injured in the expanding shockwaves and then the resulting quick imploding and expanding motion of repeated dissipating energy of the torpedo explosions. As the two repeating underwater bursts moved towards the central mass of Depth Dwellers under the surface, with fifteen depth dwellers going unscathed from the torpedo's.

As the double torpedo explosions reached the surface. The Resolve and Spirit were still far enough away to only be slightly rocked by explosive gasses leaving the surface of the water. "Dive the Marines and kill all enemies under the water." Came captain Terrance's orders. One and twenty hundredth sea elf marines had began funneling out of the dive doors on the bottom near the long keel of both the Resolve and the Spirit.

The marines were armored in a light mithreal chain mail and some sectional plating on their arms, chest and legs with curved helmets and light water treated silk skin tight leggings with their webbed hands and webbed toes exposed for ease of swimming under water. They carried long pole tridents of four prongs on their back and repeating harpoons in their arms that were tied to their waists by tethers so they could exchange weapons. Along with a dagger and short sword on their belts for in close fighting if need be.

The Depth Dwellers being larger creatures with longer foot fins, a tail and longer webbed hands were by far better and more adapt swimmers than the sea elves. Yet with the bright tropical water and the sun shining down from above seemed at a vision

disadvantage at low depths. If this had been night or the dark cloud was above them this might have turned out differently. One thing was sure the sea elves were no match for even the most injured of Depth Dwellers.

The Depth Dwellers had been armed simply with primitive sea skin leathers and shells that were formed by magics of bone. The first weapon they fired was their underwater capable crossbow's that fired somewhat haphazardly, thinks to the torpedo's thinning their numbers. The Depth Dwellers only injured a few of their own number. Enough bolts sailed through the water and killed eighteen sea elves as they got in range.

The marines did their best to return fire only killing ten depth dwellers with the repeating harpoons. Only the most injured had died. The depth dwellers had skin that was tougher than the mithreal armor of the sea elf marines. With their blubber that deflected the harpoons to be less damaging and a few harpoons barely sticking into them.

The Resolve was the first to come along side the first Troopership with cannons loaded. The first Troopership on its deck looked deserted yet on closer inspection there was a lifeless and non-energetic crew of deep-sea elves on board and some strange looking elvenoid toad Depth Dweller squatting on the fantail. Kind of a fat Depth Dweller but much more frog like and appeared to be similar to a primitive shaman. With a bone necklace, sea grass skirt and long sharp and jagged pointed crown with a large bone spear. Just languishing on the deck as if awaiting orders. No commands could be heard.

Captain Terrance ordered. "Fire, Starboard cannons!" Despite the vain useless comments of many non-military scholars whom wanted to play sea fairing pirates. The cannons were timed to fire all at once. Not in Sequential order. This would make aiming completely pointless. As the vibration and shock of one recoiling cannon would ruin any carefully aimed shots of the other twenty-one cannon. It was easier to aim and fire all the cannons at once for the shaking of the ship would not roll the ship.

The force of the cannons did not have sufficient force to push the ship firing through the air. Only vibration of the decks that created a little balancing act of the crew if they did not brace or ready themselves for the shaking caused by the rolling of the

cannons. Scholars often got this wrong and thought the wooden ships would roll over if they fired their cannons all at once. This was never the case.

For that to happen the blast of the cannons would need a surface such as the water to push against. Only a slight roll back of the cannons as the packing of the firing force pushed the cannons backwards and not the ship. Scholars were often wrong because they simply didn't have the courage to actually be in the Yoranthium Navy to learn the truth.

The twenty-two cannons fired from the Starboard side and sailed at close range raining on the deck and side hull of the Troopership. Slamming into the starboard hull, impacting a few visible cannons and shattering all sorts of matter of wood into a lot of shrapnel that flew all over the deck ripping up the ships sails, cutting the rigging and slicing up the crew that made no attempt to avoid, block or even dodge the deadly debris on deck.

Captain Zultier of the Spirit was not far behind the Resolve and noticed no guns had fired from the Trooperships and noticed the same lack of any activity by the crew on deck of the ship. "Fire Starboard Cannons!" Another salvo of twenty-two cannon shot from the Spirit rocked the first Troopership and destroyed a main amidships rigging that fell to it's port side and killed the frog like depth dweller on the fantail with the flying shrapnel and fire had broken out on it's second gun deck on it's third cannon fitting that had it's door open.

The marines had fired more repeating harpoons at the incoming depth dwellers underwater killing another four injured Depth Dweller and getting a lucky hit in the head of a full healthy Depth Dweller. Leaving twenty-one injured depth dwellers and fourteen uninjured depth dwellers. The speed of the depth dwellers would not allow any more harpoon shots to reload in time and the marines soon switched to tridents. The Tridents were only two king's length long and the depth dweller spears were four kings length long.

The first highspeed attack by the depth dwellers had the marines at a disadvantage and their mithreal armor was useless. As the thirty-five depth dweller had better reach and strength behind them resulting in the death and dismemberment of twenty-

nine sea elf marines. Reducing the sea elf contingent to seventy-two.

A long trail of blood was in the tropical and warm waters from both sides of this under water conflict. The tridents did get their turn against the Depth Dwellers. The sea elves even with all their might behind tridents only managed to kill five and incapacitate three bringing the depth dwellers numbers to twenty-seven and in such close range the depth dwellers were able to use their half a king's foot length claws to slice up another ten sea elves and even fed on them like sharks. At this rate the sea elf marines realized they were out matched by the depth dwellers. It would only be a matter of time before they would all likely die.

Then from looking behind the depth dwellers there was a startling revelation by marine lower lieutenant Geruoo. He saw several tropical razor mouths (similar to sharks but bigger with more fins) swarming in from behind the depth dwellers. Moving in quickly towards their skirmish from all the blood in the water. Geruoo ordered a retreat. Using his underwater vocal cords that the sea elves picked up and heard in their unique under water ears. Although this would end up killing another five of his elves by the depth dwellers he made for the nearest ship that happened to be the first Troopership under fire.

The razor mouths had been deadly over fifty had arrived to the blood in the water and although the depth dwellers were an even match for the massive razor mouths attacking them. Their numbers were dwindling fast. The depth dwellers lost the sight of their fleeing enemy in the melee of blood and teeth. Thanks to Geruoo's fast thinking his remaining marines made it out of the blood-infested water and away from the razor mouths and Depth Dweller bloodbath.[24]

Geruoo told his men to switch to boarding gear. Which included hand blades that fit over the top of the hands and on the feet as bands that had sharp blades for digging into wood and climbing. Fortunately the Trooperships had similar below deck openings for dropping under water swimmers. Hatches the depth

---

[24] During 2024 preparation for hardback edition I felt it was needed to illustrate to an extremist cult like congress of the USA the proper understand and use of "Bloodbath." Hopefully I don't end up as an "Insurrectionist," for my use of "Bloodbath," in a fiction novel by the extremist cults of the left insane politicians.

dwellers must of used. Many were still open and no one closed them. 'Sloppy work.' Thought Geruoo, thankful that the enemy was so ignorant for leaving access to their ship unobstructed. Geruoo could see that the Resolve and Spirit had passed the ship and were in the process of slipping back into a change of course direction towards the hostile ships.

A middle mast beam was in the water along with torn sails and wood floating above the marines, with a few bodies of dead deep sea elves above them.

Geruoo and his remaining marines would have plenty of time to capture this ship. As the fast frigates would likely take some time to return setting against the wind like the heavy Trooperships. Geruoo had commanded his group of sixty-two marines to, 'split up and one group should check out the other Troopership and take it if possible.'

Geruoo with only thirty-one marines entered the open keel hatches of the Trooperships into a larger hold. Large enough to fit ten times as many depth dwellers than what they encountered. After their eye's adjusted they noticed there was nothing else in the empty hold of the keel wet deck and that there was no watches or security set to monitor the fourth deck air locks to the upper hold. Geruoo had his unit open the airlock and went in and closed the door and balanced the pressure and gained access to the fourth deck. Repeating this procedure until his entire unit was done. Again the fourth deck was empty and no crew was noticed.

Geruoo made his way to the third deck and noticed this deck was laid out similar to function like the Mundrunche's new systems. So these Depth Dwellers it would seem had the same magics and didn't use them. No one was here except two deep-sea elves that seemed not to care or notice as their throats got slit. The two guards looked odd their eye's were lifeless and didn't seem to care. Like a set of deep dark voids had sucked their very souls from them. They seemed half starved and somewhat drained of life even before they were slain by the marines. Slaying them may have been a blessing to these mindless automatons and shadows of their former selves.

A fire was going unnoticed and unattended by another two careless and inattentive deep sea elves that were simply tied up and placed out of the way. Taken prisoner for questioning. Geruoo

ordered five of his marines to fire duty and put out the fire on the ship. As he left four to search all the decks and tie up and imprison any enemy not resisting them. They had found no more depth dwellers. Then he and the remaining twenty-two ascended to the second deck encountering no resistance. Where he placed another four on patrol.

Taking the final eighteen marines and him to the main deck. Realizing the deck was a mess and the amidships mast was in the water with debris all over and half the same careless crew was dead and or dying. There was no resistance and Geruoo ordered his men to tie up and treat any minor injuries of the enemy crew as him and five other marines took the fantail command deck. Where they found one deep sea elf tied to the wheel and had been killed along with some depth dweller looking frog.

Geruoo could see his men hadn't got to the top deck of the other ship and left his Sergeant in command of the first ship as he dived overboard and swam to the other ship to check it out. Upon swimming under the water he could see that the fight between the depth dwellers and the razor mouths had gone in his favor there was too many razor mouths and more appearing in the distance heading to the blood in the water. It would be better for all sea elves to steer clear of this area and get out of the water.

Geruoo got to the open chambers of the wet deck of the other Troopership and it was similar to the first ship and empty. His men had set a small watch of two who had been closing the egress doors. Each deck was set up the same as the first and his second force had done the same thing as the first ship for each deck. Except they had killed all enemies they encountered below decks. Lower lieutenant Geruoo met up with the second group of twenty-three about to head up to the top deck. Upon opening the hatch to the topside deck, a loud shrilled voice came from the frog looking Depth dweller on the fantail. The hand full of sluggish and slow moving deep-sea elves had vacant and pale eyes of a dark and terrible void. Turning and moaning like undead zombies toward his group appearing on the main deck and grabbed anything to use as a simple weapon and came walking, just slowly walking at him and his men.

Looking at these gray and faded purple skinned deep-sea elves lacking a zest of life and moaning. Made Geruoo feel sorry for

them. He ordered his men to take them down and knock them out and try not to kill any and just tie them up if possible. Then a dart flew by his ear. Impacting the marine just behind him and sending him to the deck in convulsions as legions began to spread over his flesh and burst into a bloody mess until he died. The poison dart came form the frog depth dweller that was slow moving and had intense dark void eye's, yet retained something of a free will of it's own and it was hostile. Geruoo called to his two of his men to go with him as another dart flew past him and hit another marine with the same effect.

As Geruoo got closer and closer the shaman depth dweller began failing to reload and aim got worse and worse as one dart impacted a deep sea elf that turned to attack his smaller group headed to the fantail. Up the steps and on the fantail the Shaman changed to just it's claws and swiped at the marine on Geruoo's left. Who blocked with his shaft of his trident, as Geruoo and the other marine thrust their tridents into the flesh of the Shaman.

The shaman gave out a scream of pain. Geruoo having difficulty removing his trident from him, then pulled out his short sword plummeting it into the Shamans belly and with some difficulty with a pull of the short sword to the right disemboweling the being and watched as life fled out of its eyes. As the shaman died so did the deep sea elves interest die with them to do anymore fighting. Just like that the deep sea elves lost their interest to live and they collapsed to the deck motionless and lifeless. The deep sea elves were noted to only have shallow slow hesitant breathing nearly and almost dead.

By now the Resolve and the Spirit had been closing in on the enemy ships about to make a run on the same side of the ship they had fired upon earlier. Geruoo had two marines trained in signaling communicate to his Captains that his Marines had successfully captured both Trooperships and razor mouths defeated the depth dwellers, at a high loss of life to his marines with only sixty remaining. Half his force remained and the unfortunate half became a feast to the sharks below them.

The captains of the Resolve and the Spirit were relieved at the ease of this battle to secure two more ships they could immediately use. The fact they were improved ships of the deep sea elves would prove invaluable in the future. Unfortunately the ships

didn't have any magics or black rock slurry onboard. Terrance looked further off and saw that the Mundrunche was listing in the water and that the sails were coming back out. From the signal colors flying off the ship indicating there was an elf overboard.

Huspecia had been watching as the Mundrunche burst from the water and slammed back down. She was shocked and awed to have seen such a thing and noticed the Mundrunche was listing. When see saw some sea guards on the deck and one jumped in the water. She wasn't aware of what was going on it took a lot of time. Suddenly she saw a huge amount of water erupt from the sea that was a good distance away form any ship in the area. The water was turbulent for a short time then returned to peace. As a pool of blood floated to the surface in various patches that meant a huge terrible sea creature must have been killed. She watched for sometime as the diver never resurfaced.

Then from in her head she heard Bronanes voice. 'I'll miss you my love, Huspecia.' What did he do? Her husband got himself in real trouble again. She immediately went under the water and started to swim in the direction her heart and her mental image of Bronanes told her to go. Desperately with all her heart and urgency, towards the direction where she saw the bursting surface of water and blood.

Down and down she kept swimming, deeper and deeper as the topaz tropical water got darker and darker. She could see her skin creating small luminous lights on her greenish blue skin. She felt her eye's getting larger and better at seeing in the dark. Her hair was changing becoming like translucent fins and helping to push her through the water.

Her clothing getting restrictive and tighter, she had to cast off her leggings along with her corset and bra. She felt new webbing from under her arms and body helping her sail through the water. She was fully naked and felt her body changing. Changing for the best as she approached the optimal depth for a sea elf.

Her hands became larger and claws had developed on her fingertips as her webbed hands treaded water and moved more purposefully. She could feel her legs becoming stronger and she could feel her feet enlarge with her toes growing in size as her small toe became the longest and her large toe the smaller on each foot.

Her legs powerfully kicking in unison as the flipper fins of her feet moved in unison pushing her effortlessly through the water. Her legs synchronized and she felt more at home than in the Grand City palace grounds. She could sense sea life hidden and far off around her. She could feel Bronanes nearer and closer to her.

She had descended below the depth of a sea elf yet she could breath and breath just fine. She was quickly looking around. She knew she had changed. Changed into what she wasn't sure. She didn't know she could shape shift. She only thought her green blue skin made her different than all the sea elves she seen along with the only one with opal eyes. She was raised a sea elf and all her life she actually thought she was a sea elf.

A unique one of a kind sea elf, her purpose to go deeper and find her Love, to find Bronanes was to the deepest depth. A depth no land based sea elf ever swam too because it would mean their death and they would drown. This is where Huspecia had to go and she felt the depth of the waters calling to her, more hauntingly than her wedding song.

It wasn't a problem for her. She wasn't even afraid. Her body just changed. Changed just like the stories of a Mermaid. Yet her legs never became one they were distinctly two legs working as one. She simply pushed herself through the water with no effort at all, at a terrific speed that passed below the Mundrunche more than two and fifty hundredths fathoms down. There he was. It was her Bronanes. He wasn't moving and tears, tears under the water began to fill her eyes. She was afraid he was dead and moved even faster to get to him flying at great speed through the water. A feeling she never knew she felt in her heart and her mind she knew what had to be done as she got closer to Bronanes. As if she was born to know.

Huspecia reached out and spun around Bronanes locking her right leg around his lower hips and pushing around with her left leg. Grabbing Bronanes behind his back and pulling him to her heart. She could feel his heart beat very faintly. He was barely alive. She took her right hand and grabbed him under his left ear and pulled his mouth to hers like the longest kiss in the world. She blew a bubble into his mouth like she was vomiting into his mouth but it was a fleshy kind of bubble that she blew and forced into his lungs as the water in his lungs came right back into her mouth and

out of her gills. Performing underwater resuscitation felt weird and sickening with mucus, stagnant water, yet was needed and she kept inflating her breath into his lungs.

Bronanes spit a bunch of mucus and fluid from his lungs. Huspecia wanted to pull away it was so awful. Tasted acidic and bad and bitter like vomit. Yet she couldn't stop doing what she had to do to preserve her husbands life. She simply let it pass through her elongated gills that transformed like her ears that became larger and of different awkward proportions to a sea elf. She had transformed between a sea elf and a mermaid. Was she half mermaid she wasn't sure. It would explain a lot. Bronanes coughed in her mouth. It tickled and was weird somewhat disgusting, she had to force herself again not to pull away. That disgusting mess too passed through her gills. Huspecia was breathing for both of them as the lining bubble strengthened Bronanes lungs.

Bronanes brown eyes began to open. He was looking at green blue skin. A face he has seen a million times. Eyes were different and large, hair was different and looked like soft back fins of a fish. Ear's were different and he reached up to her neck and felt her gills were bigger and slimy from his inner lungs being coughed up. Not caring for the remaining vomit that hadn't cleared. There was no mistake. This was Huspecia. He could feel her soul, he could feel her mind and her worry and her fear. 'My love, you look different today.' He thought to her.

'Bronanes you're alive. You are alive. I love you don't you do this again.' Huspecia thought back and was excited her kiss brought her love back to life. Her mouth on his they did not speak they simply thought to one another.

Bronanes then felt her warm naked body pressing against his bare chest and looked upon her breasts. Becoming more aroused and excited. 'So this is your real form is it? I so much love your body.' Bronanes gave her the impression of desires he's been feeling for days. Then became a little more sensible. 'How is it I'm breathing down here?'

'I put another lung in you one that is tougher and stronger. I basically threw up in your mouth.' She said with some psychic giggling.

'You threw up a bubble in me? That's gross Huspecia.' Bronanes was still kissing her and his gills and her gills were

breathing like one. 'Perhaps we should go up from here. So I can get a better look at you. My love.'

Huspecia didn't need to be told and she simply pushed up to about one and twenty hundredth's fathoms. Where she stopped kissing him and Bronanes then expelled the lining bubble from his lungs. It was gross indeed, as they had to swim away from the location a little more. Bronanes could now breathe fine and he looked at his changed Huspecia. He loved it she was indeed more like a mermaid and she was fully nude and he could see all of her and he grabbed her foot.

Huspecia was taken off guard as he yanked her right foot to look at it closely and he was massaging her foot. Going over every inch of it. As he had never seen a mermaid half fin ever in his life. Huspecia was feeling good about his touching her flipper and relaxed and as she was wetter than the ocean at this point. She had an idea. After carefully realizing no one was around them and they were finally alone and no one could see them.

No other life in the sea was near by. She didn't have to think a thought to Bronanes. Bronanes knew her and she knew him and now they could know one another more intimately than they ever had known one another.

Huspecia spun towards Bronanes left grabbing his boot and quickly and decisively removed his boots and then ascended up his left pants leg. While Bronanes had discarded his right boot to float in the water and began undoing the string on his right while Huspecia undid the string on the left and pulled his trousers off as Huspecia reached for his person and began to touch and feel what only he could offer her.

Bronanes was already pressing his body into hers and she pressed into him and their hands helped each other to touch and feel one another the way they had dreamed of the way they had wanted to feel together. They had shared desires they had always had for one another and they caressed and stroked each other to a heightened sense of awareness of arousal and lust and sharing of carnal desires. Magically Huspecia's song rang loudly psychically linked and more beautiful than the day of the wedding. As Bronanes intruded upon her and she reveled in inviting him in to her inner thoughts and desires sharing the life force of one another

and their souls mingled in strength and gentle feelings of tantalizing sensations.

Bronanes had sucked on her new ears and she played with his hair and fondled parts of his sensitivity. Until he shook and slowed and made her feel she succeeded as a female with her male as she should with her warmth of love. He felt that he had accomplished what they both had wanted and because they could feel each others thoughts they knew the explosion of their amorous ways had peaked to a zenith and that just like her song, his song was stronger and the most pulsating of any star at night and in her cosmos.

The two of them floated there in the water hugging and cuddling and digging their noses into the neck of the cheek under the ear of the other. Smelling their scent. A scent they will never forget of hormones that were driving them mad. They could only smell of one another and digging deeper in their warmth as they continued for some time as the sun lowered many times in the heavens above by many sunwanes leading to dusk.

They had felt alive, clean and a new world was born among them that bridged a gap in their hearts and made them feel fused and whole attuned to one another. In a way that only love can bind two persons and how the world could seem trivial. There was no moment in the world that meant anything. All except for what they had been feeling together at this moment in their life. Now a seed had been planted and a purpose that seemed denied was saved this very day.

For this moment was their life and a forever day that lasted from the moment they were conceived that could not ever end in their very soul and that time would pass and this moment would be fresh until there was no more time for either of them. As they were born to this moment in their life, stuck still and forever in their embrace testing the limits of the value of memory of a memory that could and would be real every day they would ever dream. This would be their rebirth and continuation of their life every time they would look at one another. Always and forever they remember this moment that they had intimately shared. Performing the ritual of life and calling upon an unseen string and spark of life that their bonding and souls summoned and welcomed in their copulation.

The merging of two loving souls ended. They relaxed spent from their vigorous exercise basking in the warmth of the ocean and the thoughts and their nakedness before one another. If Bronanes had been an artist he would have drawn Huspecia this very day. He might of drawn the moment in his mind of her pulling him from the snatches of death for she still had purpose for this sailor and she was his siren. He knew the first time he heard her song. From the very first day she was fished from the waters and he was at her side for it was the same with her. She had ensnared his heart. She was the mermaid, he would wreck his ship on the shoals for. Giving his life gladly for he had in fact done that not too long ago. He was a mere hero in comparison to Huspecia flying through the water to save him in his time of need and lifting him up to the light, his rescue swimmer.[25]

Huspecia knew she was devious and found her sailor. The soul she would find in the depths of the ocean. He rested and floated in the water beside her and would never leave her. She would always be his and she simply floated there before his eye's letting him paint her forever in his dreams and in the canvas of his thoughts. Sharing the thoughts they had this close was so clear that even if the physical exhaustion had found them. They were not done thinking to one another the sensations and feelings that went much more deeply than that of just mere physical gratification.

The sun had moved many times and eventually they both knew they had duties and responsibilities and searched the water for their clothing that had drifted in the ocean. As the depth for Huspecia was now lighter the impending demise of Bronanes was over and they became only a mere fifty fathoms down. Huspecia relaxed her form and began to shift her form and returning to her sea elf shape and size just short of Bronanes stature. Both forms was just as lovely as the one before and Bronanes thought that too her. Reminding her of the many times she taught him his old wounds now healed by the sword of Yoranthium was beautiful to her that either form or shape she would choose was one and the same. He loved her beyond just a body, he loved her in mind, spirit and soul. He loved her strength, courage, and her spirit and resolve

[25] Rescue Swimmer is art by the author available as a poster and on the cover of the softback book.

that is all that ever mattered to Bronanes. That is all that mattered to Huspecia.

Having found their clothes they returned dressed to the surface of the Mundrunche as swimmers having had no luck finding them. Had nearly called an end to finding their missing Regents. The Mundrunche was repaired and floating with its sails unfurled. Ready to depart the battles they had faced this very day. There was much to cheer about their victory and there would need to be a funeral for those who had died and would not be returning. Some had lovers. Some had wives. There were children that lost their fathers this very day and the grim reality of the choices of life to protect that, which is precious, does come at a great cost.

Huspecia and Bronanes had to return to their ships for there were many obligations they had to perform for the refugee fleet. As the bodies were collected the two new Trooperships were then repaired quickly. Over full transports were redistributed onto the new ships.

By evening the ships had a shift of wind to the warm sundown side of the ocean. Which helped the fleet find it's way to the miners that where found on the shore of the land bridge to the black mountain. They had a few more transports and had prepared to meet the refugee fleet as it pulled in at night and set anchor. Refugee after refugee arrived from the cold side miner town and tens of hundredths of more Yoranthian's families joined their numbers.

Bronanes had been on shore with the chief officers of the Mundrunche and his Sea Guards. They had set a funeral for all those Sea Marines, and fellow shipmates and the conscripted that had lost their lives in this battle along with many of the wives, children, and lovers that they left behind with their sacrifice of their life to save them.

It was a somber evening as the ships had listeners assigned to recite the words all across the bay from one ship to another for all to hear the words of their Regent King Bronanes. Tonight would be the last night for all of the refugees on the shore of their homeland and living on the transports and eight warships of the Mundrunche fleet.

Bronanes had realized his slurred speech was healed. Likely by the Sword of Yoranthium just like his burns and his scar. He

felt very strong and the love of his Huspecia made him feel even stronger than before. His actions alone saved many lives but at a great cost of his fellow sea guard and those he conscripted into service. He felt weak when it came to speaking on the matter of the love of others and the sacrifice and his voice broke when he began in the tears of the fallen. Knowing full well that he himself was nearly one of the lost that had perished this day.

Bronanes eyes had tears forming in them. "It is with grave duty of purpose as a designated Regent by Queen Kumithra. That I speak of the deeds we had witnessed for the past six days. We have faced darkness of demonic forces bent on warring with Yoranthium for an unknown purpose. We have lost fathers and mothers and children and lovers and those nearest too us. The heart of our God who is to be born beats in all of us, and our hands will be unfolded this very night. In giving back to the world of Ishormot the heart of the fallen. That we bless their souls and hope for their birth unto the heavens and that in some way they join the stars only to find their path to us so we may love them once more. So pray with me."

A pause took place. The refugees of Yoranthium had bowed their heads and placed their hands folded in prayer above their hearts. "Our God to be born. We seek your blessing, kindness, and understanding. We have faced great evil and pushed back with what we had to fight for the light of those precious to our hearts. That we beseech your guidance to bring the souls of our loved ones to the heaven's and let them twinkle like the night stars in our hearts and our minds. That the departed souls be renewed and become welcome in life anew from the heavens and cosmos. That if they their souls wish we welcome them to be reborn and to be with us in our hearts and minds, anew in our love and our hearts and mingle with our spirit and souls. Growing with us once again to make us stronger. Their sacrifice was for those they love and care for. Their souls performed a thoughtless task and they never failed in their duty even died and perished in their tasks to keep evil and wickedness from devouring the souls of their loved ones. Every one of them Yoranthian's worthy of mention and champions and heralds of angels whom we will remember. Forever and always."

At this Bronanes produced a list of all who was lost this very day and a list of names of all those who had lost someone since the

dark cloud descended upon Yoranthium. Bronanes began the very long list of names. With the name of King Sinderthion and Queen Zantkara and the Archpriest along with every person they knew or were aware of. Every person that had lost anyone they knew had filled out this list prior to the gathering. No one was missed or excluded. Many had wrapped the dead they brought with them and still had their bodies in cloth that they had with them or was provided by someone that had cloth to spare. The bodies although fewer than the lists had been placed side by side on equal pyre's and stacks of wooden kindling.

Bronanes reached the names of those on the pyres. Each was lit in order as those they loved, shed tears and cried and asked for blessings from God. Their God to be born bless them with the return of the souls to be reborn. So they will learn to love and live once again. In times when the dead could become a weapon by demons, fire on a pyre was always recommended so their souls would never return to terrify the living. The unborn God would bless their passing and expedite their time in heaven and the time they may decide to return as a new soul as new born to find and live life with those they love once again.

Bronanes finished the long list of names and the pyres were all lit a flame. "It is unto our God to be born we embrace the care of those we loved and had lived and shared our hearts with in this world. May we find them again either born to this world our in heaven and may we never forget the sacrifices of all these fine blessed Yoranthian's that had made this world a blessed and sacred purpose for us all to have shared. We will move forward with their blessing before our God in the light. We will keep their memories to find our heart, our soul, our compassion and charity for others."

Taking a moment to pause as his voice parched with welling in his eyes for the lost souls. "We will seek understanding and love and caring and bring an end to this growing evil. For it should not take the lives of those precious to us and we will return stronger. For those who sacrifice their lives for ours lives, have shown us the light and the power of love at the core of our being. Blessed is the path we follow our God and we will never forget those we leave behind us this night."

Bronanes with a determined spirit of resolve pointing out the future for Yoranthium's refugees. "Tomorrow we will set sail from Yoranthium to the land of Forumth. Leaving behind many Yoranthian's that are fighting for our very lives protecting our retreat. Bless them all our lord and God to be born and protect them from evil and spare as many of their precious lives as you can. Bless King Rarailmuir and Queen Kumithra that they find heart, love and hope to prevail against the evils of the demons that plague Yoranthium. In your name we pray our God to be born. Amen."

The voices of Yoranthium rose up in chorus and all said, "Amen." This coast was under the protection of the unborn God and no evil would befall any of the refugees this night as they refreshed themselves for a long sea voyage that began in the morning as there was now enough transports that left Yoranthium with over ten's of thousandths of Yoranthian's and many refugees from other parts of a world fleeing form the oppression and tyranny aimed at the belief of the unborn God. The hate and darkness had arrived to the shores of Yoranthium and none knew if there was any place that would be a safe haven for them now. Their exodus is evidence that Yoranthium fell.

It was not sure a smaller kingdom like Forumth would be amiable for such a large number of refugees from Yoranthium. All of this depended on the loyalty to Yoranthium of an old enemy that was now wed by the blood of Queen Zantkara and Forumth's love of a niece of Queen Kumithra that stayed behind on Yoranthium to fight. Yes they had Thernya in the group but no one knew how the ruler of Forumth would treat them. Now that he was no longer a subject of the kingdom of Yoranthium.

Yoranthium

Book One: Lost Hope

Chapter Nineteen: Days Had Passed

By Mark P. Bromley

Time changes from one event to another. Most live in a world that is apart from others and none ever see the events of days that are unknown to them. As this story grows time becomes fluid and this is just where the lapse in time begins.

Rarailmuir had thought he was dreaming. He saw Kumithra next to him. He was naked in bed. Kumithra was wearing some kind of armor he never seen before. Was it? Did she? She did have a dagger at his throat. He was sure of it. She couldn't have found out the truth. Kumithra was with Bronanes, Huspecia and Thernya an entire retinue with the purpose to keep her naive childish nature suppressed and out of the conflict. How could she even be here with a chain dagger at his throat?

Her velvet eye's full of venom and anger like amethyst vipers eyes, intense and with thoughts of murder. She smelled of blood and the secret sewer tunnels that ran for leagues to get here to the Last Bastion defenses. How could she change from a child princess to an assassin in just a few days, competent and capable of tracking him down? It made no sense to Rarailmuir. Kumithra would have had to learn these skills and as a child living her life in dreams and flights of fantasy could never have learned such things. He must give Thernya and Huspecia more credit for they had trained Kumithra well. There she was an assassin just about to slice his throat as he slept.

“Guard's to arms! To me now!” Rarailmuir quickly threw on his Yukata and boots. Grabbing his sword and ran to the door Kumithra had just ran out of. So silently that it terrified Rarailmuir to think of how Kumithra became like an assassin in the night. He thought about it and realized only one thing could have happened. Dresdie must have met Kumithra. How could she meet Kumithra? Rarailmuir's secret wife made an arrangement with him for his love. So he could become king. Kumithra wasn't to ever know or to meet Dresdie ever. That was in their deal. Or even learn of his secret marriage to Dresdie. How could she know Dresdie promised Rarailmuir for his heart and soul and would have had to break that deal, for Kumithra to have known?

How could this be? Rarailmuir was careful not to get too close that Kumithra would ever ask if he had a wife or even suspect. She would never know he married unholy by a dark ritual of blood to seal a pact for his kingdom. He distanced himself that Kumithra a foolish princess would only want him. Not be close to him. He would never had to explain himself as his duties provided the distraction for him to keep a distance.

By doing so. He would get himself closer to her father and rise in the ranks to general and then King. Now somehow she knows too much. Rarailmuir had to find her and decide what needed to be done with her. She would have to listen and not be allowed to sway the guard to her cause. She was now a danger and the Kingdom was nearing collapse with so many demons, Mechanation's and Depth Dwellers about. He could simply find her and... No, that's not Rarailmuir he couldn't bring himself to murder her. As the years passed and as Kumithra developed she became to Rarailmuir something more special and loved in his heart. She was a more suitable wife.

He didn't need Dresdie or that foolish desire for higher office to seek to be king. He didn't need that bargain at all with Dresdie. Rarailmuir knew Kumithra's heart. He knew of her soul. As he looked at the wedding binding still wrapped on his right wrist. Rarailmuir would still be who he is now without that unholy wedding to Dresdie. Without him willingly giving himself to her. Damn his lustful thoughts and carelessness. He was the very pinnacle of the Yoranthium Guard. The model of the true sword of Yoranthium in sea elf form, his magnanimous form of a forgotten hero of the three-kingdom war, that all had aspired to be in the guard. He shaped and honed the real sword of Yoranthium its Guard. Now he ruined everything by being a fool and wedding Dresdie for lies of power he could have had on his own and he could have been faithful to one person and that was Kumithra.

The Guards left their assigned post to address Rarailmuir's inquiry. Two days ago they had been at the Last Bastion and had been trying to learn where the Last Bastion guard had gone. Not a single person knew what happened to the Last Bastion guard and the records and logs didn't show anything out of the unusual. Just the day before they arrived all the logs and journals. Even the commanders own personal journal simply went blank. No one had any idea what went on. No signs of a fight. No signs that they moved. Just clean empty halls and the defenses were wide open.

Rarailmuir and his guard and those conscripted got plenty of rest that they very much needed after the fighting in the Grand City and the deadly and explosive confrontation with the Impundalu. There was ample stores here, a fully well stocked Last Bastion defenses. No Mages on duty and the newly formed thunder

staves were inaccessible, as it would take mages knowledge to open their protective enclosures. Fortunately the magics supplies were accessible and the wall defenses could be fully equipped. There was no doubt this Bastion would be a good stand for Yoranthium and Rarailmuir was positive he could hold this location for a long time under siege.

The first day here wasn't very eventful. Most of that was getting the troops properly fed and refreshed. Plenty of drinking water, bathing water, and the boilers were operational. Even the steam powered heavy defenses were in good condition, just no signs of the Bastion Guards.

The only odd occurrence is that the Map Makers disappeared without a trace from their assigned chambers. No one seen them come or go, for they are mages. No fights and no conflicts took place. The Map Makers had simply gone missing and an entire search was made and nothing was out of place. Just vanished leaving the suspect of magics known as portals. Portals, many mages and including the Map Makers must have been capable of. Why would they portal away? None of the guard knew and Rarailmuir was never informed. Mages have always been secretive and unreliable.

Rarailmuir simply had his troops take proper guard positions and conducted training on the weapons of the keep on their first day. Which went well. The Conscripted Sea Ghouls took the outer court wall and watch defenses. While they were issued camps for the outer courtyard and taught how to set up the camps shore guard fashion, which the conscripts understood as if they were guard material. It must have been the demons and the real threats of war that adjusted their attitudes to being helpful instead of insurrectionists. [26]

The Sea Ghouls had accepted their forward assigned duties just as Rarailmuir and Metiur had planned. They seem quite competent and capable under direction by Orichen extreme form

[26] Had to mention the defamatory and slander the cult of far left extremists were labeling their fellow Americans of a nation falling into decay over polarized politics. People involved in violent riot was praised and those who opposed them labeled insurrectionist's and hated although they had done nothing violent just spoke openly their concerns and criticisms that in 2020 they were being forced to put on gags over a false pretense.

of discipline, a life of a criminally enforced community. As in the Sea Ghouls if any of their elitist bosses got displeased with a lower rank, for any number of absurd and silly reasons, usually over petty matters. It was their death in the gangs or some kind of horrific and excessively cruel abusive treatment.

Punishments often designed to create fear, which hampered creativity and ingenuity and subdued imagination. Resulting often in more disrespect and more cruelty from those neglected mistreated or abused in the gangs. It was a terrible form of leadership in the Sea Ghouls. Producing forced compliance out of fear of reprisals or fear of harmful and hurtful physical discomforts. Not to mention blind obedience like that of a badly abused pet from his subordinates. Like the Sea Ghouls punishment for speaking out of turn was being bond and gagged with a face mask over the mouth as the evil bosses in the gang didn't like their lower ranks having an opinion or suggestion of how to do something better. They would force them to put on a mask as a psychological muzzle to stifle their voices and unwanted opinions. This is how the Sea Ghoul's rose in leadership muzzling their slaves.[27] An effective way to lead by fear and threats of intolerance enforced by the promise of violence, persecution by social shaming in the gangs of hate.

Fortunately the Guard under Rarailmuir was treated more fairly and respectfully elven. Infractions of duty was dealt with swiftly and based on quantity and quality of infractions. Reprimands and punishments had to be meaningful and purposeful in the Guard. Most punishments in the guard were assignments to training and development. Guards helped one another succeed. Good guards simply became more competent and better qualified for better assignments.

Terrible guards like Xern. Who ran off with the Kings Sword? Usually got treated well and offered accommodation and understanding. Yet in Xern's case the gangs messed him up. He was a product of elitism and poor leadership of organized crime ruling the back alleys and the red district. The criminal element of leadership is what Xern learned. The Guard simply was too kind

[27] Commentary on how abusively harmful 2020 modern politics in the world and how the USA abused it's people with mask mandates to force compliance and control by a globalist drug cartel agenda of oppressive socialism.

and to understanding and accommodating for those massively abused in their former criminal background lives.

Punishments usually increased in the Guard, until the crime and the punishment would become harsh and no guard wanted to be the one delivering harsh enforcement of Yoranthium law. It created a bad reputation for a command structure based on the perceived expectations of hero's in the Yoranthium Guard. Xern was a petty thug, he was going to be kicked out this quarter a third season and dishonored forever in Yoranthium for his thug mentality. Likely to return back to that criminal leadership like Orichen as his boss or worse for there were many criminals and all had their own gangs and band of thugs. Some formed by the very elites of the court itself trying to crown themselves by brutal means and hostile takeovers. The wealth they hoarded made on the backs of slaves, drugs, abuses of all kinds and theft of property even if by legal weaponized legislative means of broken government zealots. The dagger elves of Yoranthium killing their way to the top and to be crowned much like Orichen literally tried to do.

To think Xern got an innocent good supervisor dismissed wrongfully from service by his underhanded criminal deceptive practices. That supervisor of his was a good male with a nice wife and child that was no more than four revolutions old. That had worked well in his community and was of exceptional standings. The very community credits the supervisor and his family earned was proof that Xern was lying to his superiors about the supervisor's behavior. Building a good reputation takes revolutions to be trusted in a community to be offered high honors of exceptional credit based on the merit of word and deed and good performance of character. Especially when that supervisor was highly liked and got to be the representation of the heart of Yoranthium at the revolutions end festival of plenty. Selected by the most wise and good and the seat of honor and praised.

Xern was a monster of evil by nature. Hated all things better than his worthless self, for Xern had been living a lie of a life most his life. Most criminals that weaseled their way into the Guard had a knack for abusive and cruel manipulation and encouraged corruption in the ranks. Turning good guards into lying deceptive snaked tongued devils. They would incite others to complain and lie about good honest guards. Caring nothing about

the lives of good people and their families they were destroying with their defamation of character. Creating a false accusation list of events that were deceptive exaggerations of innocent behavior. Xern was the danger a silver tongued demon in disguise.

Xern was a proven manipulator and had a history of dishonesty. Living in that bar in the red district when not on duty. Gave Xern ways to meet and with sinister intent to plot the demise of his supervisor with a corrupt management in the command. Xern also had corrupted many noble's who owned recreational activities and vacation resorts. That he could bribe the supervisor's superiors with. This way by trips to the Lollygag islands bought the managers to betray the supervisor. Xern one day will have to face justice by Rarailmuir. Xern's theft from his King of the Sword of Yoranthium would qualify him for the highest and harshest of military justice. Especially in a time of war for stealing the King's sword doomed many of innocent guards to their death.

It was sad what happened to that falsely accused supervisor and his family. That supervisor never recovered. He was a good male and loved his wife and child. It was said, to try to make a living he accepted harsh work in brutal conditions. Working for more illegal unionized criminal gangs. There was no job for those wrongfully released from honorable service of the guard. The civilians believed if someone had been hated by government persecution they had to be a bad person. Often that was true but in the supervisors case he was wrongfully released from service and Yoranthium owed that supervisor and family their entire worth of life. You can't replace good lives wrongly abused and mistreated by a corrupt and twisted government. The supervisor had real knowledge and skills and ended up forced to make a living building ships in Sea Shore.

That wrongfully treated supervisor was an honorable hero in his own rights. He should have never had been treated so poorly or disrespected by that corrupted command. He had perfect performance record always on time performed his duties to exceptional merit. Excellent credit earned by decades of honest accomplishment. Kept a good uniformed appearance and was always on top of his duties. Had a unique loving family with a wife he met in a foreign land. A good child he loved and cared for. He deserved a life with his family in a good community, not the

dishonest lies his superiors leveled against him at the whims of a lowlife like Xern.

That supervisor's superior was an idiot that should have never been promoted to the higher ranks. The superior believed the lies of Xern and Xern's dishonest followers. It was understandable for the supervisor to be angry. Having to justify himself to lies and a host of defamatory statements leveled against him. When all the upper ranking superiors that weren't corrupted had to do, is witness how his family lived that should have displayed the truth the supervisor was wrongly accused. That the dishonest cult of Xern was lying; the supervisors upper ranks were corrupted and criminal just like the gangs on the streets.

The supervisor's heart was pure and his family was kind and good. Yet even in the guard mistakes of command are made. Ultimately Rarailmuir had to intervene. The entire command structure needed to be replaced in that command. Xern corrupted the entire chain of command. They had been backstabbing and harming everyone who was good in that command. Making it hard to retain and recruit guards. Hurting them because they couldn't be bought by organized crime growing in the ranks of the Guard. [28]

Xern had corrupted his entire unit and he was not of high rank. They were all influenced by the gambling habits of Xern. That entire command was dismissed and replaced with better Guard's like Metiur and Fedarious. Only Xern was left and his punishment would have been much worse. They lost a good leader in the sea guard thanks to the dishonesty of Xern and his corrupt cult of followers.

Rarailmuir sent out various recruiters for royal duties to try to fix that supervisor's wrongful treatment. Metiur and Fedarious couldn't get that supervisor back and they tried but got rejected by how angry that supervisor became after his families life was destroyed by Xern's lies while in the guard. The Kingdom was too cheap and stingy and unwilling to pay for the damages it caused that supervisor and his family. It was too awful and too painful what that corrupt command did to that supervisor's psyche. The

---

[28] This part was not hard to write. As it's based on real events in the corrupt homeland security of the USA in the state of Utah and conditions of polarized politics played in government employment to the detriment of good people and families of honorable veterans.

former supervisor no longer trusted the Yoranthium government. Viewed the government system as an enemy that was abusive and cruel for allowing such evil to exist in its ranks. He lost the respect of his life, all the good credit among his community. People who claimed were his friends turned on him wanting to believe the dishonesty that Xern caused. Or they simply turned on the supervisor simply because they feared for themselves.

Even though the supervisor didn't make much income. Him and his wife built a beautiful life on just a guards pay. The supervisor and his wife were gifted artists. They looked well off because they worked to make it look like that. It's actually really incredible what two similar minded artists forged in love could do with so little income. Simply by creating their own way of life and happiness. Love, heart, and two like minded family orientated persons are capable of greatness by the virtue of compassion. Compassion that the corrupt and evil command corrupted by Xern was unable to provide. A partisan demon like politics of hate, envy, animosity and resentment is all that good supervisor and his good family got over a five revolutions period. All because of hate crimes created by Xern.

Having a good reputation was everything to that supervisor. When he lost his posting wrongfully because of a corrupt upper command believing a dishonest Xern and his corrupt criminal cult. That reputation was torn up faster than a chicken with blood on it in a packed chicken coop. By those in the community that had envy, jealousy, hate and discrimination of mixed skinned families. The supervisor was married to a lawful resident foreigner and Xern and his cult hated miscegenation.

That supervisor met his wife in a foreign land and they were in love. Real love Rarailmuir never knew or had. Even Rarailmuir was jealous of such a couple and learned understanding and the nature of the heart. Love like that is a thing of Fantasy. It was real and that heart and love existed in his Sea Guard and got trampled on by the negative impacts of cruelty and abuse by criminals diminishing the name and reputation of the sea guard. The investigation really bridged the gulf of Rarailmuir's heart to Kumithra. He was a dark skin and she was a light skin and that Supervisor was a catalyst that grew Rarailmuirs heart for Kumithra. Everywhere that supervisor went with his family

bridged the gulf of love, heart and understanding between diverse peoples of Yoranthium.

That supervisor couldn't work for the Yoranthium government anymore. He was too afraid of the harm that could befall him. His family was no more. As his foreign wife felt Yoranthium was dangerous and an evil place. She saw what that supervisor was falsely accused of. His wife's response, "They can't be serious, it's ridiculous." Rarailmuir seen it himself and it was truly absurd and clearly falsified allegations of a cruel mismanagement by his upper command. Indicating corruption of the entire unit.

That supervisor simply dreamed of a life he no longer had with a wife and child who he deeply cared for. He became homeless and afraid of people. Realizing that outside of the guard most of the employment was criminal thugs. The same demonic politics he faced in the guard. Better for him to work for himself instead of the selfish and the cruelty of corruption on Yoranthium. He rose in the ranks because of unusually high morals and courage. That courage was taken from him when he was wrongfully dismissed. High ethics and morals can never be taken from persons of high duty and honor, courage or commitment. Just forged differently.

Yoranthium for five-hundredths revolutions had a long way to go. In understanding how to provide for good people and keep good families intact and safe in their communities. Yet the supervisor even with such hate from a nation that owed him a debt of gratitude over a service he performed revolutions ago. Continued of dreaming of winning his family back even after tens of revolutions expired. His reputation was too damaged by the demonic corruption of Xern's criminal cult in the guard that he couldn't achieve anything. The evil and corruption had been seeping deep into Yoranthium and this darkness and attack on Yoranthium is the evidence of that. War is always the evidence of a failed political system that harms good people.

Last Rarailmuir knew. That wrongfully dismissed supervisor was trying to publish a book. Having little success because of the same demonic elements in the publishing industry that wanted to rip off the author and give nothing in return. That supervisor learned hard work had no reward just impossible suffering and sad dismal loneliness. Last Rarailmuir knew of the

supervisor was that he was trying to peacefully change government to a better form of revisionist thinking to correct over five decades of bad government. Rarailmuir was hoping to see something change in Sea Shore. Apparently this darkness and war was a confirmation that the sin of Yoranthium was too great for positive change. It would be helpful if that supervisor lived, Rarailmuir could use such a person now. That supervisor's medals and actions and history made him a hero.

This incident of crime in the guard and mistreatment of Yoranthium veteran hero's had deep impacts to the guard and was a festering wound. Crime in Yoranthium began growing because of criminals like Xern and Orichen. Even localized civic and regional governance was being corrupted by a growing evil in Yoranthium. An evil that was more apparent now that a dark cloud, bad winds, appeared over Yoranthium and remained here for days on end, demons, terrible monstrosities, and unlawful combat mechanation's. War had come to Yoranthium and the level of evil had been grievous. Did Yoranthium have so much wickedness that this world deserved this awful fate?

Yoranthium's problems simply grew because of misdeeds. Misdeeds that Rarailmuir was beginning to realize for he himself. Even with his intentions of good had made mistakes and bargained with evil for something he could have done on his own and he would have not needed that dragon attack those years ago to be where he is now. Yet evil is difficult to avoid and sinning is the way of a sea elf it would seem. The God to be born was right after all. They are all sinners seeking and begging for forgiveness before they expire for passage to the next world and beyond. It would seem that Rarailmuir was not immune to corruption, as he became an accomplice to the sins of Yoranthium. One should not cheer on evil of a bully of sin on to the innocent. As those cheering evil, become enslaved to evil, and are no different than those doing the evil harmful act themselves.

Rarailmuir regretted yesterday. An enemy force did appear from Sea Shore just a small contingent of depth dwellers. Orichen saw them on the horizon approaching the main gate. There was no warning from Orichen and he opened the main gate to do combat against the Depth Dwellers that amassed in over two hundredth's in number. Orichen's men being far out matched by the Depth

Dweller numbers as they simply waited to get slaughtered. Not a single one of Orichen's elves secured the magic's on the lower or higher walls or on the inner defensive walls for the courtyard. They simply assembled right at the front of the door.

With Orichen behind them shouting intimidating threats to his own men. "This is what we have been waiting for! Take as many of these over sized lizards to their doom! You worthless pile of sea elves! You wont get what you want unless you sacrifice your lives for it!" Orichen went on and on with this kind of self-defeating speech.

For some reason his elves had agreed along with his views. Their criminal subculture must have drilled abuse and neglectful self-defeating commands in to their very souls. Randomly they would agree to all the on going insults from Orichen, like they weren't worthy of life unless they died for it. What was Orichen's plan to get his men slaughtered? They simply stood inside the courtyard waiting. Waiting to die it seemed from the inner fort Sea Guard that kept the main keep door closed and readied the magics cannons along the upper defensive walls.

As the Depth Dwellers were nearing the gun ranges on the outermost edge. Not realizing the inner keep could only fire two cannons through the open main court yard gate for the walls on the outer court were too high for line of sight, with only the inner high wall cannons to fire. Depth Dwellers began their charge towards the open courtyard.

Rarailmuir along with Metiur and Fedarious had been shouting at Orichen. "Close the gates remain in the courtyard battlements. You'll live longer forcing them to try and break the gate or the walls! We can't do much for you from here! Close the damn Gates!!!"

Orichen wasn't listening and nor was his men. It would appear that conscripted criminals were not meant for warfare. The two inner magics cannons fired explosive glowing orbs of death and destruction at the Depth Dwellers clustering to get through the door. The initial shots took out about seven at a long range. Then another eight at medium range for fifteen dead Depth Dwellers. They had large shields and because of their size and strength they could easily guard against the explosive blasts and shockwaves of the magics. Only two shots were possible from the inner upper wall

through the open gate doors as the third reloading had to be stopped. Out of fear the guns would rain down death on Orichen and his Sea Ghouls.

Fear was washing over Orichen's Sea Ghouls they knew their deaths were coming through that door any moment. Some looked relieved or they finally got their just rewards. Rarailmuir ordered for his archers to ready on the battlement. Issuing orders to use fire arrows if there was a clear direct shot only on the Depth Dwellers, not to hit any of the Sea Ghoul's. The archers had been ready and the first volley of arrows impacted the row of Depth Dwellers that still had five king's lengths before they impacted the Sea Ghouls. The Sea Ghouls looked disorganized and unmotivated. Orichen was a bad leader and taking his soldiers to their doom.

As the Depth Dwellers had switched from shields and short spear, sword bone weapons to pole mounted circular spinning bone blades. A volley of arrows rained down on the Depth Dwellers. The arrows were very much useless only killing about five and simply sticking in the skins of a few others. The main entrance was too far to throw magics from the height of the battlement. Another arrow volley killed nine more nearing the Sea Ghouls front ranks.

The Sea Ghouls front ranks quickly collapsed and the melee ensued. A few archers managed to help a few Sea Ghouls. Yet it wasn't enough only another ten depth dwellers died by arrows as the Sea Ghouls were being torn to shreds. It would take five Sea Ghouls to one Depth Dweller. Orichen finally found some courage as he realized his life was at stake. "Damn, didn't know it would be this bad! Fight you cowards, get up and fight!" He pushed his cowardly back ranks forward.

"Oh, God no! I don't want to die this way!" Orichen was seen running away from the fight as Depth Dwellers got past the final Sea Ghouls. Leaving nothing but bodily remains as some of the Depth Dwellers would only take one bite and leave the Sea Ghoul body alone. Apparently the Sea Ghouls tasted bad too. A Depth Dweller had reached out and raked Orichen's back with five claws slashing him open.

Orichen was shocked and looked puzzled as he felt the pain and turned swinging his sword at the Depth Dweller invane. Just cutting at the air wildly. "Oh, God, No!!! This isn't how it was suppose to go!" Orichen was panicking and was really afraid. With

a look like he was betrayed. Rarailmuir and his command and Shore Guard could only watch, Orichen was now to close to the inner battlements. It was his own damn fault for not supporting the outer courtyard defensive perimeter as he was instructed. If he held the doors closed and used the walls to his advantage he could have defeated that entire hoard of Depth Dwellers with ease.

The Depth Dweller stalking Orichen simply made a lunge of two kings length at Orichen and grabbed his throat and quickly snapped it like a piece of kindling. Biting into his arm tearing off his flesh and casting Orichen's dead and broken body against the inner gate of the keep. It no longer mattered now. Orichen was dead and so was the rest of his Sea Ghouls. The Depth Dwellers advanced to the main keep door and bunched up quite closely trying to push the reinforced magics sealed gate in.

"Oils and fire arrows to the ready." Was ordered by Fedarious.

"Oil's at the ready." came the response as Fedarious motioned for the oils to be dropped and Metiur then had the archers launch fire arrows onto the oil soaked Depth Dwellers. The Depth Dwellers went up in flame and fire and screamed loudly as they were burned. Oddly the same Depth Dweller that attacked Orichen fell on his body protecting his remains from burning by the oils.

The oil tactic worked well. It appeared the Depth Dwellers didn't like fire very much and went up quickly. In the distance more enemies could be seen assembling and preparing but they were far from the Last Bastion and had no intention of approaching.

Rarailmuir ordered for patrols from the upper outer battlement access gates to go out and close the courtyard doors. A contingent of twenty Shore Guard went out through the outer gate battlement hatches and around the main outer defense walls and down the stairs to the outer defense door controls. Operating a hidden steam engine that caused the outer courtyard doors to close and seal by magics. Then the squad went to the courtyard and used their spears and swords to finalize any dying of the Depth Dwellers that wasn't complete.

Rarailmuir was happy that the problem of the Sea Ghouls and Orichen was resolved just as he hoped. They had given their

lives to defend the forward defenses of the Last Bastion defenses. Metiur looked at Rarailmuir and was a little worried as he witnessed the smile of satisfaction. Sure Orichen was a terrible criminal but was this kind of terrible death really his lot in life or the other sea elves of the Sea Ghouls? Metiur was worried how this war had pressed upon Rarailmuir. Just a few days ago he was to be wed to Queen Kumithra. Metiur was losing a little faith in his new King. What actually made him a King, surely not just a mere sword or being the General of the Yoranthium guard?

"My king, are you feeling okay?" Inquired Metiur witnessing Rarailmuir's satisfaction was widening on his face a sign of his King's mental health wearing thin.

Rarailmuir realized he was near gloating over his plan with Orichen. Then he felt regret and guilt for letting Metiur witness his behavior. "Metiur you and Fedarious are in charge. I'm feeling a little under the weather. Take command and issue orders to support all the defenses possible on the outer and inner walls. Have Orichen and his men moved into the keep for an honorable funeral in the morning." Rarailmuir looked stern and serious once more regretting almost gloating at the death of the Sea Ghouls and Orichen.

Metiur and Fedarious took to their duties and sent more troops to reinforce the walls and a few guard to the storerooms for funeral dressings to honor the Sea Ghouls and especially Orichen. They had done their duty for Yoranthium and even if they were evil and wicked in their past lives. They defended their king and gave their lives in the line of duty. The Sea Ghouls earned their service to their Kingdom in the end.

"Orichen and your Sea Ghouls. May you find the blessing in the land of our God who is yet to be born, you deserved better from us and you died in the defense of Yoranthium." Metiur said as he walked over to make sure that Orichen was being given the best treatment a hero of Yoranthium deserved. Each and every Sea Ghoul was dressed in Funeral dressing in accordance with the Guards regulations.

Metiur stayed with the litter carrying Orichen while having his hands tightly folded in a long prayer to God seeking salvation for Orichen and the Sea Ghouls souls. Perhaps when life is better they return to be children to worthier parents beyond this war.

Perhaps they will not know crime. Perhaps the Kingdom of Yoranthium will be a better place for all the people of Ishormot. A lot of well wishing for Metiur knew that the truth of the world often is not what we prefer in life. Yet there was hope Metiur knew that his wounds were healed and he even came back to life by the spiritual powers invested in the lands of Yoranthium and the blessed blade of this land itself. Hopefully Rarailmuir's heart wouldn't be tainted and stayed pure.

They took all the bodies down to the lower storage where it was cold enough to preserve them from rotting and set a watch. As Rarailmuir was feeling the exhaustion he's had for days for making command choices that would determine if they lived or died. It was touch and go. Fortunately he found strength in Metiur and Fedarious and his Death Guard. Their heroism was top notch and ranked up there with the heroism of the first guard that perished in that dragon attack years ago. Just as Dresdie had said would happen. Thinking back on the dragon attack of those deaths weighed on him as well.

Rarailmuir made it down to the commander's chambers and disrobed from the day. He felt gross and sick somewhat dirty by the deeds of this day. Knowing full well Orichen and the Sea Ghouls died as hero's of Yoranthium and were placed in harms way by his very orders. It's no surprise Orichen and his sea elves made bad choices. They weren't his guard. They had no military training. He killed a bunch of civilian's. Yes they were evil awful and terrible. Orichen did kill innocent babies and terrorized to death many Yoranthium families. Eventhough. Rarailmuir should have killed him and chased his band of thugs off earlier than witness them being eaten and torn apart by the Depth Dwellers.

He had been only wearing his recently cleaned Yukata from the wedding very loosely on his nude body. No one was in the commander's chamber but him. He kept wearing the wedding Yukata even under the death armor since the wedding. Rarailmuir was attached to that day and it was a sad day of regret for him. He treated Kumithra so badly and only wanted to be King. Casting Kumithra aside like a plaything. It was shameful.

He made his way to the commander's journals and wrote the events of the day like he was keeping a watch on the Last Bastion. Annotating the deaths of Orichen and his Sea Ghouls and

wrote as many names as he could remember that died that day. Having so much fatigue he went and bathed as the hot water supply from the boilers still worked well enough. It restored some of his strength and made him feel a little better.

Afterwards he was so tired that he fell asleep wearing his Yukata the wedding band still on his right wrist that he never removed. Falling asleep completely exposed on the comfortable bed, just to be woken up by Kumithra and a knife at his throat. Perhaps being naked was to his advantage as it caused Kumithra to hesitate and reflect on how much she wanted him. He knew many times Kumithra wanted him physically. She timidly touched him many times over the past revolutions and then a day before the wedding. She acted so impulsively. She was a full female now and Rarailmuir was very much into her touch and attention out of pure attraction to her physical feminine body that had ripened and was his fruit alone.

If he had not been this sea elf and in this body, if he had been what he was before he met Dresdie. There would be no doubt she would have killed her husband to be. The dark magics made Rarailmuir strong and well defined the magics worked. Beguiling Kumithra, she looked at him and wanted and lusted for him. For that Rarailmuir was thankful. At least he can find her and tell her the truth. He has to now. She likely wouldn't understand what's happened the past few days and the deaths and fighting that had been going on.

She knows his past now. She knows some awful truths. She knows he's a liar and a thief of her heart. He only wanted the Kingdom. Rarailmuir simply wanted the kingdom easy and free without her. He was using her. He used her heart and her childish infatuation as the hero and her personal savior. He'll even have to tell her about the dragon. The truth behind the dragon attack, for so many deaths that day of the old guard was his fault. In many respects even with so many good deeds, in reality he wasn't no better than the thieving gangs or the dishonest royals and nobles of Yoranthium. All of them just like him wanted to be King at any cost and Rarailmuir's true wife was Dresdie a witch of dark magics that made his play for power possible. He was a sinner no doubt about it and Kumithra must now be told the truth. Rarailmuir wanted to be forgiven.

Where were those guards? It seemed like several awful and terrifying days just flew by so much death and a fight for life. Now Kumithra was not where she was suppose to be. She was here in this hell with Rarailmuir. A Hell he deserved and she did not. He didn't want her harmed she should be off the island with Thernya, Bronanes and Huspecia headed to Forumth. Why did they fail in their duty? Something about Dresdie his real wife meeting Kumithra went wrong. Rarailmuir was worried Dresdie would be jealous and he was right. The moment Dresdie got her hands on Kumithra she had to tell her that story of him making a deal with a demon witch.

It was obvious over the past revolutions that Dresdie and Rarailmuir's relationship was strained and stretched. Dresdie was getting increasingly angry and obsessed with Kumithra day by day over the past few seasons. As Kumithra blossomed into a real female that was attractive and forced Rarailmuir to notice her and want her. For Rarailmuir it was easy to not take interest in Kumithra when she was younger. But over the last revolution before she turned nineteen she came into her own. Giving him no reason to lust for Dresdie, as Kumithra was young, lively and tight.

Then she blossomed and Rarailmuir couldn't help looking at her or even Huspecia for that matter. Of course Dresdie was cruel and owned a parlor in town of seduction, lust, drunks, and gambling. It was that Xern's home and Orichen would go there and extort money from clients, corrupted nobles, corrupted guards and other crimes. Dresdie knew Orichen and would meet in private. It's not like Rarailmuir was the only one to have a love on the side. Now Rarailmuir was envious of Orichen and his wife. Orichen might have had the same deal or something similar that Rarailmuir made with Dresdie. He came for the crown like he was promised it too. What of Xern was he too involved?

"Guards, where are you!" Rarailmuir was getting agitated and impatient letting his mind race like it had.

With some stuttering the first guard came around the corner. "He, he, her, here sire." He was quite young and recently joined the guard. It was obvious on his face he'd been through a lot over the last few days even though he was rested and in good health. He was shaky and nervous. Along came three other guards.

All of them new and not really prepared to fight a war. Fortunate for them, they would only be tracking down their queen.

Rarailmuir had a plan. He motioned for the guards to follow him. To the right of the commander's chamber was a locker. It held many sets of forked shimmering mithreal shaped rods that glowed with magics of red. Very subtle and noticeable only in real darkness like the locker. "These rods are stealth tracers. Used to divine the location of persons who are evading or hiding in the shadows."

"My king, are we looking for assassins?" Replied one of the guards with apprehension.

"Don't talk, just listen." Rarailmuir was quite annoyed. "Your Queen Kumithra is skulking about the fortress. She's wearing some kind of strange stealth magics and hiding for reasons unknown." Rarailmuir could read the surprise on the faces of the guard. "Yes it's your Queen you are looking for. You four are to search for her."

Two more guards appeared just then. "You six are the only ones being issued three divining rods to detect a stealthy Queen Kumithra in this fortress. You will keep this a secret mission and if asked by anyone. You will tell them you are looking for weaknesses in the fortress or prior portals of mages. You are not to let anyone know your real mission is to find Queen Kumithra. She is wearing some weird magics armor and it's possessed her with some demonic purpose." Rarailmuir lied because he wanted the Queen not to be able to sway the guards.

"My lord, the Queen is possessed?" Inquired a Guard.

"Yes she is possessed and must be brought directly too me for further investigation. If you find her and she tries to resist, use your best discretion. If she becomes hostile use your best ability to render her unconscious. If she tries to use a chain dagger or a sword or weapon, again use your best judgment to immobilize and disarm her. If she is too much to handle run and get more guard but do not let her escape."

Rarailmuir was concerned if the guard understood his commands. "Do not harm your Queen, I need her for questioning. When you find her subdue her. She isn't herself and she is possessed by a demon. She will likely try to seduce or deceive you. Tie her, bind her and gag her. With these." Rarailmuir pulled out

some demon bindings from the locker and passed them out to all six guards along with the three divining rods to detect persons hiding in the fortress. "Work in pairs and comb the fortress methodically. Follow your rods as you had been trained in basic training. Got it."

The guards looked at their king and one had a question. "The Queen is possessed? When did that happen?"

"Look, I do not know the details. She woke me up with a dagger at my throat and wearing some weird armor I have never seen before. She's my Queen and my love and there is no reason except demonic possession that could teach her how to sneak past all of us the way she did. Now go find her. When you do, bind her and bring her here to the commander's chamber and tie her to the chair from the desk into the middle of the room. Understood?" Rarailmuir was irritated with the question from the guard.

The guard understood and was ready and eager to begin their search. Least they risk angering their king any further. "Yes my King, by your order it will be done."

The Guard departed in teams of two and began using their rods heading off in three directions searching the keep.

Rarailmuir wasn't sure how to handle this. If his guards were successful it would be likely in a small amount of time with the magics at work. Kumithra would be tied, and gagged to the chair in the commander's chambers. Then he would have to decide how to deal with her. It would seem she knew too much. Placing his title as King at great risk.

Metiur and Fedarious were proving very perceptive and together they could oppose him. By siding with the Queen. This would be bad for Yoranthium and there would be no way he could prove victorious in this war. Queen Kumithra was trained in matters of state not in war. She wouldn't be able to defend her people and this fortress will fall under her lack of combat experience.

She was here however. Met Dresdie, learned some secrets. Learned about his betrayal of love. He traded his oath as a husband for power. Power gained, by marrying a demon witch of the dark arts. At the time all those revolutions ago when he was younger, it appeared to be the best route. Dresdie had the power to

change the rules of the game to get ahead in a guard of experienced and professional soldiers. Ranks he could only dream of back then.

Rarailmuir was timid back then, weak and foolish. Maybe if he could do it all over again he could have avoided ever getting drunk that first night at Dresdie's. Yet she wore that red dress and had that body of hers exposed and her touch. It was the first time a female touched him the way she did. Her eyes bewitched him.

Rarailmuir didn't know anything of dark magics back then. He was enchanted by Dresdie's goals for power. Although Dresdie's goals was a little different, those goals wasn't much more different than Rarailmuir's. Kumithra didn't even exist in his world back then. He wasn't looking for love. Just a plan of action that would lead him to success to become what he wanted the King of Yoranthium. In a way corruption was in Rarailmuir too.

Dresdie held power over a dragon. She made the plan. All Rarailmuir had to do was promise to marry her and give her a night of lovemaking. By Marrying Dresdie she would inherit the title of Queen the moment Rarailmuir claimed the Sword of Yoranthium. Her promise was that Rarailmuir could then find a second wife with the help of a dragon that would burn down the old guard and old Grand City and burn the school and make him a hero that King Sinderthion would embrace as the Hero of Yoranthium. A real scandal if the truth was ever told and now Kumithra knew of the truth just part of it.

Rarailmuir would advance quickly in the ranks. He would get to forge the guard to his liking and he would be King and advert the war that just killed the old King and Queen of Yoranthium. There was only one problem with what up until now was exactly as Dresdie had predicted. Everything went exactly as Rarailmuir had expected, his advancement, his ranks. The swooning and tender moments of a growing female that followed him like a puppy all these years. She even gave him the Therica in his hair that streamed to the left of his face. Yet he betrayed Dresdie, Keeping the sword and played hero instead.

Yoranthium is now at war. It was far from over and Rarailmuir was beginning to enjoy the death of those he put in harms way. This war was to be adverted by Rarailmuir as king of Yoranthium. Perhaps it's because Xern stole the sword. If Rarailmuir could get that sword back he'd be able to end this war

and quickly. He must find out where Xern is and find out if he still had the sword? For that would end this war and he'd be Yoranthium's hero again and it's rightful King. He could denounce Kumithra as Queen and give the title to his real wife Dresdie. He'll be the light she'll be the darkness and together they will be masters of Yoranthium and solve the problems of Ishormot with that kind of power.

He's been around Kumithra too much unfortunately. He couldn't get her half undressed body out of his mind from when he arranged her wedding outfit to flee with the others. His thoughts of Dresdie paled in comparison to the lust that he had developed for Kumithra. She was younger and he did feel her breast when he caught her from fainting. She was warmer, firmer and much more of a female than Dresdie. He felt the innocence of Kumithra in his heart and felt her affection for him in her eyes. She really loved him and he had grown fond of Kumithra. She would be a better Queen than Dresdie. This was the conflict growing in Rarailmuir. Which one should be his Queen? What should he do with a foolish girl if he should stay loyal to his wife that made him the King.

This new Kingdom of Yoranthium was up to Rarailmuir and Kumithra was not the one to remove him. He was strong, he was trained and the leader of Yoranthium's defenses. By all that he has done over the years. He was still the king. Sword or no sword he was the king. Xern or Orichen was not the ones to deny or even take it from him.

Dresdie had given away their plan, for whatever reason she found Kumithra and told her. Dresdie had been a bad wife anyway. Only slept with him on one night and never bore him a son. Like she promised. Dresdie didn't even sleep with Rarailmuir even after failing to produce him a child the first time. It's been revolutions and it seemed Dresdie didn't really care for Rarailmuir's heir to the throne.

On the other hand, if Rarailmuir can undo the damage from Dresdie. Kumithra could be the one to give Rarailmuir a child. Rarailmuir junior and a continuation of him as King of Yoranthium that would be better she was much better to raise a child. Trade an old hag for a fresh new and more youthful model. He'd have to try. Repair the damage and get Kumithra's love back.

Rarailmuir began to think more and more of Kumithra and just thinking about how he touched her and dressed her and realizing how firm and fresh and new she was as a female that perfume of hers at the wedding had him wanting and excited Rarailmuir. Kumithra could bare him an heir. Yes that would be nice, Prince Rarailmuir junior heir to the throne of Yoranthium.

Yoranthium

Book One: Lost Hope

Chapter Twenty: Truth of Lies

By Mark P. Bromley

Lies nothing but lies had been told before. Truth sometimes is a twisted tale of lies and deception and a twist of fate. Hearts change like minds. One day being powerful was the goal and in the end Love and Heart is more important that living falsely.

The six guards had split up on their secret mission to locate the Queen. With only two guards to each group with one using the divining rods of detection to find hidden and concealed persons in the Last Bastion. The other two groups had been searching a long time and had not located anything of note. From time to time they would hit their divining rods on the side of a wall or vigorously shake their rod to see if it was broken. "Perhaps fixing these divining rods would be great?" They would think to themselves as they had very little luck finding anything. Their search patterns were very well planned out and covered every possible hiding spot. A thief or an assassin might hide in.

Only one group of guards was having any luck on a lengthy search. At first they were like the other two guard teams. The guards not believers in magics became skeptics that the divining rods weren't useful at all. Banging the stick around. Making jokes at how silly it was when other guards saw them. "Looking for water eh?" They often would get from the other guards and some snickers and mockery. Then a vibration began. Ever so slightly at first and the guard holding the diving rod tried to deny it was doing anything. Then that vibration sure enough got stronger and the other guard was not buying into the idea this silly stick would ever find someone hiding in the fortress.

There were many shadows and many storage and hidden locations for things to conceal themselves and go bump in the night oddly a little spooky. The previous guard kept the fortress very clean. There was no dust or cobwebs accumulating in the corners or ceiling. That would have made this night hunt creepy if there were more atmospheric arrangements of dreadful elements adorning the interiors of this dark keep. No fog on the ground. The doors were well maintained they looked into and didn't even creek. It was a fortress protected just days ago by a Shore Guard that did maintain the place. Which thankfully relieved the guards searching around the gloomy lit halls, corridors, and niches of closets and storage areas.

The divining rod began to glow brighter and vibrate stronger as they were onto someone or something. She was motionless it would seem. The guards got to a closet and opened the door silently. They saw a pile of linen in the back and heard. Snoring. It was their target. It had to be the Queen. She snuck in

here and covered herself and decided to get some sleep. This was going to be easy for these two guards.

The guard without the divining rod prepared a sap. It was a heavy weighted piece of leather with some heavy beads of mithreal inside. Saps were quite effective at subduing targets and if you hit them correctly behind the ear of the head. It would render them unconscious quite effectively. The Queen had been snoring. The guard removed the layer of cloth covering her and saw she was wearing a helmet and some strange magics imbued dark armor. He nudged the queen and realized she was a real solid sleeper. This was good for he was able to remove her helmet.

Both guards looked upon their queen's sleeping face and realized how strikingly handsome she was. No wonder why the King wanted her tied up. Anyone would want this lovely thought the guards in a room tied to a chair all to themselves. The only thing that threw them off is how bad she had smelled. She smelled like them when they got here. Days of grime built up on her and it showed and reeked. Yet pretty none for wear. The guards couldn't help but lick their lips of slight drool. Secretly coveting their Queen.

The guard with the divining rod hit the other one on the shoulder. "Hey this is our queen stop being so perverted and looking at her that way. If the King saw us he'd likely punish us for our disrespect. Let's get this over with."

The guards came to their senses and the guard with the divining rod, put the rod in his belt and then with both arms he roughly grabbed Kumithra and locked her arms together in bindings and dragged her roughly off the ground as she woke up and got spun around looking him in the eyes. She was about to move her lips. When "Wham!!!" The Sap struck her right in the back of the head just behind her right earlobe. The world spun and she was unable to protest the binding of her hands, as she was rendered unconscious. Hiding in the closet and getting sleep till the morning was a bad idea after she had attempted to assassinate her love Rarailmuir.

The guards had a lot of practice in the previous revolutions. There were many problems in the Grand City and they had been assigned to the red district. Giving them plenty of training to learn to use the saps and take down criminals. Now the queen was one of

their perpetrators. The guards bickered over how to handle Kumithra. They had some distance between here and the commanders chamber with other guards on the look out for suspicious activity.

The king wanted them to be secretive about apprehending the queen. Two guards in an all male Guard walking down the halls of this fortress. No matter how they tried to hide her. They wouldn't be able to do so, a female being taken to the commander's quarters and tied up. Explaining her was going to be tough to every guard. Some would closely inspect their prisoner and then they would have to explain their rough handling of the queen. It would be unlikely they could explain an unconscious Queen. Rarailmuir wouldn't want that much attention drawn to this matter.

After debating what to do. The Guards decided to search her body for weapons. Which required patting her down. Both guards were a little bashful about frisking the queen. She was very attractive and both of the guards were just a slight bit older than her and still had the yearnings of youthful males. Having decided that was a bad idea least they get accused of grouping and fondling their queen by the king. They simply limited their search to the Yukata sleeves, the belt, boots and scabbards they saw. Finding her chain daggers, short sword and dagger and utility items from pouches on the belt. Having grabbed her helmet they carefully put her hair back under the helmet and placed it somewhat crooked on her head.

They realized there still was a problem dragging her unconscious through the keep. There stashed in the dark corner of the closet was a royal red carpet. Used for royal visits to line the halls of the fortress. The person wrapped up and smuggled in a carpet trick. Why not, would it work? They were heading to the Kings room so who would suspect? Going to the king on the king's orders. Perfect. They unrolled the carpet and wrapped Kumithra up in it just fine. She was small and petite easy to hide in a rolled up carpet. They simply got the other guards searching for her to join them and took her directly to the commander's chambers.

Not a single guard except for one tried to find out if it was something other than a rolled up carpet. There was always one guard that questioned everything. He actually beat down on the center of the carpet with his spear. Fortunately for the guards

Kumithra was unconscious and still had her armor on. Lucked out for she felt nothing and no noise came from the carpet.

"What the hell? Do you think we are smuggling females around in a carpet? Where would we get one? We are way to far from either city, there's no farmers daughters around here." The six guards laughed at the over cautious guard. Then quickly carried out their mission. Eventually getting to the commanders chamber and knocked.

Rarailmuir greeted his retinue of guards. "Good going, you all did splendid work, quick and timely. Roll out the carpet, let's see what we got today, and tie her in that chair and gag her." Rarailmuir pointed to the chair he had picked out. It was wood and very simple with armrests, a demonology inquisition chair for interviewing common criminals in the middle of the room next to a bucket of water. It looked as if the King had his plans for questioning his queen. If she was demon possessed the instruments for demon confession wasn't present. This was the queen however. Brutal and barbaric instruments would likely not be used to find the demon possessing her. So thought the guards.

They unrolled her from the carpet and placed her in the chair. Rarailmuir was a bit angry. "Who the hell hit her on the arm like this?" He was pointing out a festering black bloody blue bruise where the guard had hit the carpet with his spear. The guards thought it was just a light tap. However it was significant. Rarailmuir checked to make sure her arm wasn't broken. "You all did enough. What were you thinking? She's your Queen and you let some guard bash her like this. Go stand watch outside and keep me notified if anything transpires around the fortress." Rarailmuir was angry with them they were not to harm her. It was their orders and the guards leaving the room felt bad for letting that happen.

"Yes my king. Sorry my king." Responded all six in unison and they left the commanders chambers and went back out the door closing the door behind them to stand watch in the main hall.

Rarailmuir was still looking at the bruise on her upper left arm. It was massive and swelling. "Animals. Just Animals. It's so hard to get good guards these days." He examined Kumithra and removed her helmet noticing the bruise form the sap behind her ear on the back of her head. She's likely going to have a serious headache from the sap knocking her out. He placed her helmet on

a nearby table. Went and got a medical kit on the adjacent wall in the commanders chambers. He checked on the bindings, which were tight but not too tight. And even found the weapons she had on her person left next to the rolled up rug the guard brought her in with. "At least they rolled out the red carpet for her arrival, the royal treatment. Fortunately I didn't get the red carpet treatment as their king." Rarailmuir humored himself.

Rarailmuir placed her weapons on the table along side the helmet that he examined and put back down. Then he looked at his wife to be with longing and regretful sadness wishing to be absolved of any wrongdoing. Noting that even with the injuries and being tied up and unconscious how strikingly beautiful she was. Even her odor of the days and the sewer without a bath didn't bother him. He still yearned for her and eyed the bed over and away from them. Perhaps he should have tied her up there. Have his way and insure his future offspring.

That was terrible thinking but Kumithra's attractiveness was tempting. Her smell was awful and she still smelled of the long sewer tunnel. "Uggh, whoo, kind of hard to ignore that smell." Rarailmuir had to clear his mind so he grabbed a glass and a bottle of Yoranthium clear rum and drank a shot of it to clear his head. It was strong rum and it did the trick. He even began to focus on the armor of Kumithra. He seen it once before. Yes it was a set of special armor Queen Zantkara ordered. How did she find that it was at the Guards public clothing sales office down by the court stable. At least she got some shopping in while Yoranthium was going to hell. How typical of a spoiled princess, yet sensible and useful had an eye for detail to find this armor.

Rarailmuir opened the medical kit and seen the magics he needed to help Kumithra recover from her wounds. He tentatively rubbed bruising ointment that had numbed and subdued the pain she would be feeling. Being generous with its application on her arm and behind her ear that got a little messy with her hair. The pain relaxing magic would take some time for it to work on her headache once she woke up. It was a pity she didn't still have on Rarailmuir's style of dress. It was likely for the best, that clothing would have been very dingy and covered in sickening filth. What she had on now wasn't too filthy, mostly clean just body odor of days without bathing and sewer sludge on her boots. He needed

another shot from the bottle. Giving him lustful thoughts of giving Kumithra a bath while she was unconscious. Well that's what the bucket of water was kind of for.

He grabbed a padded commanders chair and simply sat in front of Kumithra waiting for her to come to life. It was taking a long time and it was still early morning going on a new day. It was just Kumithra's gloved hands and sea elf booted feet that were the messiest and nastiest. He took a brush and some water to her hair and cleaned her face and ruined make-up of what remained of it after days had gone by. He took a sponge and bucket of water removed the boots and gloves and cleaned her and her clothing just a little. He was so tempted to go a little further but stopped himself and tied her back to her chair. Satisfied he remained a gentle-elf and cleaned just her face, hands and feet returning to his chair. He sat here dreaming and wishing for a different story for the two of them and fell a sleep with all this lack of activity dragging on in the early morning.

Some time near morning Kumithra was awaking. Her head was throbbing and she reached up to try to touch her head that was in agony. But she couldn't touch her head. Her arm wasn't moving like it should. She could feel she couldn't move her arms or either foot as her mouth had a saliva drenched cloth in it keeping her from speaking. She had difficulty trying to open her eyes. She felt her head throbbing and behind her ear hurting and her upper arm in agony as her muscles flexed. Yet she needed to see and her eyelids opened slowly and in agony. She was fighting to keep awake with such mind numbing pain inflaming her mind suppressing her reason and ability to rationally think.

Kumithra's purple eyes had opened and her head was sunk low looking down at her lap. Her hair was dangling before the front of her chest and forehead, concealing her face. Only she knew her eyes were open as she groaned in pain. Looking at her Yukata and chest plate armor and ropes tied around her. She was tied up. Tied to a chair. Who could do such a thing?

She lifted her head in much pain. Realizing her helmet wasn't on her head. There in front of her was the bandit master chief marauder himself. Sleeping and snoring with his head tilted back in a high padded red lined velvet chair with golden rope for

trim and in a nice white lacquered carved wooden chair. One normally owned by royals and lords of the lands.

It was Rarailmuir. She was back in his room and tied to a chair and he was sitting about a king's length from her. No doubts waiting to question her about her recent assassination attempt on his life. Likely by now he understood what she had learned from Dresdie. She had to escape. She was a threat to his kingdom and he knew it. The sword of Yoranthium did not make him king. Marriage to the Queen of Yoranthium made him King. She did not marry him. Some peasant demon witch from a brothel was his wife.

She was likely the only one that could save him like he saved her from the dragon so many revolutions ago. Kumithra owed Rarailmuir some pity, for he did save her life and in a way she was obligated to spare his. Even if the fire and all those that died from the dragon was Rarailmuir's and his wife's fault.

She could push with her feet on the floor. If she pushed hard enough the chair would tip backwards and she could hope the ropes would loosen. As she pushed the chair up to fall back the chair did exactly that. The front legs came off the floor and she tried to tilt back to tip the chair over. She failed. The chairs front legs came crashing back to the floor with and echoing bang. Resulting in waking Rarailmuir.

In his awakening state Rarailmuir was awoken from a nightmare of voices dying and screaming his name. He even witnessed one of them being Kumithra who died from some beak of a tentacle creature he couldn't make out. It seemed so real. As his betraying of Yoranthium actually was. He felt guilt strongly for his failures and mistakes. So many lives depended on him and he felt very much no longer the hero but a villain of his own story as he failed his people in his dream. The devouring of Kumithra by an unknown monster in his dream was the loss of her love.

His sun fire golden eye's opened directly on Kumithra's making her freeze and remember her desires as a young princess. His Therica that she gave him dangled in front of her like a memory of days she had hoped for. Dangling like a string to a playful kitten that she wanted to play with once more. If he didn't care of her he would have cut that off. There it remained a reminder of his love for her.

"You are awake my Queen. I was so worried about you and treated your wounds. Don't worry the blemishes will fade away and your headache will subside in a little bit." Rarailmuir sounded remorseful and apologetic. He went to her and removed the gag from her mouth to allow her to speak and returned to his chair to begin his inquiry.

"Rarailmuir." Kumithra blinked lovingly and longingly and then had to shake her own head to break the mesmerizing eye contact and forget all the foolish childish infatuation she had for.. for... this male. "You lied you have a wife! She kidnapped me using demons wanting my blood to destroy the sword of Yoranthium! She nearly tore out my heart and I did die, she did kill me!!!" Tears welled in her eyes as she began weeping like a child. Like she did when her mother and father died. Remembering the ordeal made her weak.

Rarailmuir was alarmed as Kumithra's head fell in tears. She did run into Dresdie and she did awful and terrible things to Kumithra. Things Rarailmuir didn't understand about Dresdie. Rarailmuir knew beyond the red district where Dresdie lived. Didn't know of dark rituals or anything like Kumithra was describing. Just that she practiced some dark magics that made him who he is now.

He got out of his chair and put his arms around Kumithra to comfort her like he had done a few times before their wedding day. "I'm so sorry, I didn't know."

"Get off me you deceiver. You are disgusting and sick. How could you not tell me you had married such an evil monster!!! How could you not tell me you had a child!!!" She screamed at Rarailmuir and struggled tied to the chair wanting to forcibly push him off her.

Rarailmuir let go out of shock he never knew about a child. Dresdie must of lied to her to hurt her. "Yes it's true I married Dresdie. Yet we only slept together once and she never bore me a child."

"Liar!!! I saw it… its dead and sad demise! She smashed her or it's heart on my face!" Struggling with much anger and effort to free herself from the chair. Kumithra had raised her teary eyes as Rarailmuir let her go. She wanted to see the honesty in his eyes, if he was lying. She could see even with the wet watery purple

eyes of hers that he was honest about the marriage and didn't know about the child. Of course Dresdie did kill that child before it was born. She likely never told Rarailmuir. Now Rarailmuir knew and it sent him off balance. "Yes. You had a child you bastard. She showed it to me. Her heart was of its flesh and she rubbed into my face and lips. How could you be so stupid to love a demon witch!!! Why did you toy with me? Why did you let me lust for you?" Tears flowed down her cheeks as snot began to flow from her nose she was broken over what she had learned.

Rarailmuir then saw it, the blood of his child's heart wiped on Kumithra's face. Only Rarailmuir saw his child's phantom blood for there was none there. He forgot he already washed Kumithra's face. This specter's blood had to be cleaned. He went to the table and picked up a facial cloth. He went to Kumithra and wiped her face and tears and cleaned the mucus on her face. Gently and with great sensitivity thinking of what he needs to say to explain, as he grabbed a rag and soaked it in the water bucket. Rinsing enough water out the rag and cleaning Kumithra's face. To remove the blood that she didn't deserve on her face but was on Rarailmuir's hands.

Kumithra wanted to pull away from his hand washing her face. It seemed that as he washed her face. It felt like he was trying to wipe away the defilement she felt from the child's corrupted heart pulled from Dresdie's chest. Like Rarailmuir wanted to tend to her wounds on a spiritual level seeking forgiveness for his sins. Kumithra's face was clean her spirit purified, but the rag was soaked in phantom blood and dripping into a overflowing bucket of blood. Blood covering Rarailmuir's hand and he understood the blood was on his soul and then he snapped out of the terrifying phantasm illusion. The blood was not just his child, it was Yoranthian's his actions had inadvertently killed. It was all of Yoranthium's blood he was it's mass murderer. He begged for forgiveness for he was just an innocent stupid pawn and was used. He came back to reality and the hand of Sinderthion was felt on his shoulder in spirit comforting him.

"I joined the Guard a long time ago. I had ambitions to be the smartest, strongest and fastest and best of all your fathers guard. I was stuck in the lower ranks not even a lieutenant just a nobody. I was weak, scrawny and had no real name. Oh, I had

names. Names people that let me struggle homeless as an orphan in the streets called me. None of them nice, I never knew my real name. I was neglected and an orphan without anyone since I can remember." Rarailmuir told her the sad story of his past. "I had many names and all of them were bad and terrible words. Words of how my elders mistreated me and despised me. I was not going anywhere I was nothing and no one. I simply didn't have any background to move up." Pausing to ponder his next statement.

"Stuck in low ranks that grew old never progressing in the guard. Never becoming anything but fit for guard duty and patrolling a corrupt disgusting city that was becoming twisted and distorted." Rarailmuir wanted to solicit some sympathy from Kumithra for his pathetic excuse of betrayal. "The old guard. They fought along side your father. They were hero's all, royal and noble. I was poor and just no one, nobody, and would never be anyone. This is a monarchy of royal elitist and I was of no value or merit."

"The old guard kept getting old and you had to wait for one to die before you could hope to rise in the ranks with so many just like me. All of us joined hearing of your father King Sinderthion how he fought for everything to keep this kingdom of Yoranthium. Your father was a tale we all got told Kumithra. We all got told as children. Especially us the ones dreaming of a life we could never have. Like a sick joke to remind us of our place from the streets." Rarailmuir was searching for words to describe why he went to Dresdie.

"For me there was no honor, I would likely never have courage and no place. We would only of met if you found me out on the streets like that chance encounter a third season or so ago, of yours. People like me. In the guard there was no advancement the ranks were full. Getting old and fat and living off the laurels of your father and his fathers, fathers works for five hundredth's revolutions. The story of Yoranthium was the hero's of your blood line and that damn sword of Yoranthium." Rarailmuir looked at the ceiling as if he was seeing the sky above. Trying to think how to explain his lust for power his ultimate betrayal. He had a child he never knew it, a child murdered by Dresdie and she said nothing to him.

"You were never known to me before I met Dresdie. Your name was known only by Royal proclamation. You however were a child and not my type. To young and not attractive." Looking at her and now, showing by his very look that he seen her as a real desire of feminine virtues. "Now you are very much a lady I covet. Back then you were just a name of who was on the throne. Not one bit something I understood or cared for. I had no feelings for you. I never cared or gave you a thought back then." Rarailmuir could see Kumithra was hearing him.

She broke eye contact as the weeping worsened but was muted so she could hear him. Fact is Rarailmuir was being insensitive with his story. Kumithra's heart was breaking and fracturing into tiny pieces falling away into nothingness, for she meant nothing to Rarailmuir. That's what she heard she meant nothing to him. He never cared. Faintly Kumithra was looking down and closing her burning tear drenched eyes. "You didn't love me." She hurt she wanted to die. She was a fool.

"No. You got it wrong all wrong Kumithra. Let me think." Rarailmuir was bad at telling this tale and it was going badly. His male mind couldn't let him find the feminine words to soften his explaining. "I'm going to tell you how this happened. I heard of a powerful witch from an unscrupulous pathetic lower ranking guard, an investigation about the loss of an honorable guard supervisor that was wrongfully treated and unjustly dismissed. The culprit criminal behind the shattered lives of so many honorable guards their wellbeing and destruction of their reputations. Was this sniveling coward of a sea elf named Xern. In my initial investigation I found out about Dresdie and her brothel." Rarailmuir was having considerable trouble trying to absolve himself of wrong doing but seemed to only make it worse.

All Kumithra heard was, 'Blah, blah, blah and blah, oh yeah a brothel.' Kumithra could be heard in a minor voice of disbelief. "A brothel. I should of known this story would get worse and worse."

"I'm sorry this is a hard story for me to tell. I'm not a storyteller. I don't know how to explain this for I'm a male. I'm a soldier not a scribe." Rarailmuir was trying to seek pity for his efforts at story telling, especially over this matter of the heart and a lust for power. Was he really just as bad as Xern a betrayer? "I'm

sorry Kumithra. I don't know how to tell it any other way. Yes, I went to Dresdie's, 'Den of Deepest Darkest Desires.' It was before I knew anything of you. Dresdie took a liking to me right away. She seduced and romanced me and she was a looker in that red dress she showed her skin to me and gave unto me her body. I wanted the more and became sinfully lusting after her. She demanded I marry her if I wanted power. I wanted to become the King of Yoranthium. She gave me this body you desire so much Kumithra." He flexed his muscles and displayed his magnificent body that dark rituals by Dresdie created.

"This very body of power, strength and looks. Dresdie's dark magics created and I accepted all of it. She simply wanted me to marry her for her to join me as my Queen and she even slept with me to offer me an Heir. An heir to my throne I would get from your father." Rarailmuir broke this news to Kumithra not being sensitive enough to explain it better.

Kumithra had run out of tears. Her purple eyes became red and swollen and her nose was red. She looked up with anger. She saw what that irresponsible love of Rarailmuir took him too. It took him to the inner thighs of a love sick demon of evil. Her face shot up in anger as Rarailmuir moved back from her. It was like being possessed by a demon. Kumithra's chair began bouncing and he could hear her anger welling. "You monster, you idiot, why tell me you are such a fool!!!" It was audible but muffled by the gag he placed back in her mouth, a gag that let her speak but toned down her voice as not to be heard beyond the door of the chamber. She was furious and wanted if she could, jump out of the chair and savagely attack him.

Rarailmuir was happy he replaced the gag. What came next was inaudible anger and resentment. Couldn't really be described as Kumithra went on a dark path of hateful and harmful gagged ranting. The guards outside would have heard their Queen screaming at him, if it hadn't been for the appropriate use of a muffling gag. The gag allowed Kumithra her anger but only for Rarailmuir's ears and never made it to the door to the guards outside.

Rarailmuir waited for some time until the venting ran its course. "After I cemented this marriage to Dresdie. She had a plan. It involved removing the old guard of Yoranthium to make room

for me, and my younger new guard to take their place. It was a good plan and I committed to it. It would be the only way to become a hero and rise in ranks off limits to me. Dresdie controlled a dragon. A full sized dragon. Can you imagine the power to control a dragon? That dragon nearly destroyed the Grand City and could have destroyed all of Yoranthium." Rarailmuir was now gloating at the plan. He as well as most Yoranthian's of the Grand City remembered the dragon attack it terrorized them all except Rarailmuir. "That dragon could have destroyed everything if it wasn't under Dresdie's control."

After calming down and seeming more reasonable the gag was removed again. "You were said to be the one who killed the dragon and saved me and the people of Yoranthium!" Kumithra was in disbelief as there was parts of this story that Dresdie didn't even tell her. Loud but not as loud as it could have been so the gag then returned to her very amorous angry mouth, as she was still agitated.

Rarailmuir wasn't holding any of the truth back from Kumithra's ire, he couldn't. He simply had to be open now and disclose all. Kumithra deserved the entire truth of her role in the plot to become King Rarailmuir and Queen Dresdie of Yoranthium. "You were unknowingly part of Dresdie's plan to overthrow and replace the king and queen of Yoranthium. You were the weakness of Sinderthion and Zantkara. Your heart had to be stolen and your love would conceal mine and Dresdie's plot for my rise to ruling this kingdom. When the plan began you had been to me just some kid that was the key to the throne. Not important to me just a tool. Even though you eventually changed my heart. This is why I didn't take the sword of Yoranthium to Dresdie. Why I'm here fighting for Yoranthium, Now. All because of you I have changed my heart had changed."

As if he was pleading to Kumithra, yearning for some sympathy or salvation and seeing none in her eyes. Rarailmuir continued. "I didn't see that coming. If I knew she had murdered our child. As you tell me. I would have never followed this plan and likely done something different." Regretting his decision all those years ago to assist Dresdie. Angry over the loss of his child and he wanted to kill Dresdie now.

"The dragon was a tool used by Dresdie. She killed the old guard and made the reasons for me to rise in the ranks. All of that thanks to you Kumithra, I advanced for being your hero, savior and your desire. For why not? Look at me Kumithra, just look at me." Rarailmuir waited for Kumithra to look upon his body.

Still Kumithra could not deny or hide the truth. Looking upon Rarailmuir calmed her. Dresdie imbued Rarailmuir's body with enchantments only Kumithra was unaware of. He had the body type she so much adored and there were no others on the Isle of Yoranthium as fit as Rarailmuir, a male beyond that of all the bodies on the land. Except perhaps only one she met by accident from a foreign land.

Rarailmuir was and is even now extraordinarily gifted and endowed. It's that very gift that stayed her hand from killing Rarailmuir. In so many ways his body reminded her of the dreams of her pink feathered Rarailmuir's. The real body was more tempting for it was real. She desired the dark bronze and blue skin, with golden tattoo's of the honorable guard, sun fire eyes of gold and golden mane. He said he got it from unholy dark rituals. Dresdie's witchcraft to ensnare her heart and force her to be possessed with lust and desire for no one other than Rarailmuir.

"The dragon was needed to create the proper conditions. Just so I could save you from a burning building. I will not lie. I almost faltered and turned away from rescuing a child from a burning school. The risk was great and enough support beams had made the room too dangerous to enter. By saving you. You gave me more tools to succeed in my bid for the crown. You gave me the captain of the guard Bronanes as my second from the same incident. I was able to blind Thernya via Huspecia who was also saved thanks to my heroism. To think Bronanes was a coward before he met me. Now he's married to your finest protector and sister Huspecia." Rarailmuir chuckled a little thinking how strange their fates were intertwined.

Kumithra just said nothing now. Realizing although Rarailmuir's story was sick and twisted and distorted all she knew, her appointed regents were created by Rarailmuir, Dresdie, and the Dragon's chaos all those four revolutions ago. Would Bronanes and Huspecia be who they are now if this terrible plot never took place? That could be debated. Kumithra knew Huspecia's thoughts

on Bronanes before. Her rescue by Bronanes just sealed the deal and put them closer together at the healing clerics. Without the dragon, Bronanes would have never got the courage Huspecia wanted from him. Some other suitor could have been there instead. Like Leorth, or Dabensir any number of suitable replacements that kept Bronanes at a distance and a disadvantage. Was the dragon attack really needed? It could be debated. What's done is done.

"The plan work perfectly as Dresdie had said. Got me to be your fathers favorite and last and few hero's of Yoranthium. He told me everything he wanted me to know for your hand Kumithra. Your own father decided for you the day I saved you who you would wed. You never had a choice. You have to admit I am the only suitor fit for your hand in marriage." Rarailmuir was beaming pride now in his explanation.

"If I didn't save you. I could have challenged for you hand. You would have liked that I would have bloodied the floor of the throne hall for our wedding." He was now flexing and performing a Kata a fighting stance of inner reflection and perfection of movement. Mostly to show his perfect form off to Kumithra, then he stopped.

"There had been other males that wanted your hand Kumithra. They were in that hall. All except the one foreigner I really wanted to fight for you. I saw that foreign male trying to pick you up in the gallery. He made me envious as if I would lose you!" Rarailmuir sounded jealous of some foreign male that ran away after meeting her. "Those lords and some ladies all wanted to wed you and be King too. None of them could beat me. Not even that Trovlie, or whatever that unhinged drunk called himself. He did fund a large part of that wedding with Potentates Kingdom coin. Never seen so much coin on a drunk, he likely stole it. Just like he tried to steal you about a quarter of a season ago."

Kumithra simply could not and didn't want to believe the tale. Yet it was the truth. On top of it he spied on her and followed her movements in town. He knew about that drunk noble from the Potentates kingdom that tried to teach a frightened sea elf how to pick up maidens. She almost smiled at how entertainingly funny that foreigner was. Before stopping realizing the gravity of this situation. She could see that in Rarailmuir's eyes. She calmly murmured in her gag and Rarailmuir removed it just enough for

her to speak. "What of the Dragon, everyone said you killed that dragon that destroyed the Grand City." The gag went back around her mouth again.

Rarailmuir smirked and chuckled a little. "Killed, killed the dragon. That's a lie. I never told your father I had killed, the dragon. I defeated, the dragon, I only reported I defeated the dragon. There's a difference. Defeating isn't implying I killed the dragon. I just simply let it go, with a stern warning not to return. It's still out there. Somewhere, sad and defeated." Rarailmuir shook his head in disbelief. A smirk came over his face. "So many Yoranthian's got this dragon story wrong. You think a sword and a quiver of arrows and a bow could simply kill a dragon? Even with magic tips on my arrows and demon oils. I could never have killed that dragon on my own. Dragon's are ideas the magics of concepts and thought, the very foundations of Ishormot. Dragon's are brought to life by values and meanings of life and creation. That Dragon was the protector of Yoranthium the soul of Yoranthium as told to me by Dresdie. She captured it and enslaved it. When I had finally rescued you. Dresdie stopped the dragon attack after making sure the old guard, old captain of the guard and old general were all dead. She created a power vacuum for me to fill. Fill it I did and your father approved and treated me like a father I never knew."

Rarailmuir began pacing in the room thinking how to tell the tale. "I simply caught up to where that sad pathetic weeping dragon was. On a black horse, black as coal I named Stone, from the carriage house. The Dragon was upset just like you Kumithra he was sad just like you are now. Dresdie controlled the Dragon by a demonic collar fastened to its long neck. It's front claws tried to free itself but the magics on the collar wouldn't let the dragon remove the collar. Apparently the dragon had its fill of unwanted death and destruction it never intended. The dragon was forced against its nature, like we all are. Strapped to the design of fate. The dragon could have killed me. I would have welcomed it. The tears of the dragon fell like rain and it seemed the dragon had no intention of fighting me." Rarailmuir's back was to Kumithra and he stood there like an archer and pulled an arrow from his make believe quiver. Notching it in a make believe bow and taking careful aim.

"I stood like this. I reached for a magics arrow. Pulled out my bow and readied the shot. Stood there for a long time deciding where to aim my magics explosive arrow. There was not much to shoot at until the dragon opened his mouth giving me a strait shot down its throat to where its glands produce fire. Explode the fire glands and you could kill a dragon." Rarailmuir now gave Kumithra a truth of dragon weaknesses and a means to kill one. Even contradicting his statement that dragons can't die.

"I stood there thinking it over." He was becoming quite dramatic in his motions, should he loose the arrow or take pity on the dragon. Then he moved the bow lower. "Then I saw it. There was a bolt holding the collar on, just one mithreal bolt. Protected by magics so the dragon could not remove it. It wasn't protected from my magics arrow."

"I let the arrow fly." Rarailmuir released the pretend arrow. "It sailed across the distance and struck the top of the bolt holding on the collar and exploded. The bolt fell out and the collar fell to the ground with a loud bang and dust coming off the ground. The dragon closed his mouth and moved his eyes very close to my face, to get a good look at me. Smelling my scent. Looked sad, regretful, humbled, angered and annoyed, yet grateful." Beaming with pride it was a proud defining moment of heroism.

"Then the dragon rose in the sky and headed to the Cold side of Yoranthium and disappeared into the distance. I could take you there and show you the collar. It was as if the dragon knew me but knew not him, or did I." He turned to face Kumithra as he bent down and began untying her bonds and removing her gag. "I let the dragon go and saved him from captivity. Just like you my love. I have no stomach to harm the pure of soul." Tears could be seen welling in Rarailmuir's sun fire gold eyes.

Kumithra heard him refer to her as his love. She didn't want to believe it, yet he was untying her bonds. Freeing her. While his eyes were tearing up over the dragon in captivity he freed and he never really fought. He was a kind soul and a gentle heart. Caught up in the drama of a dark and twisted plot for power he could have earned himself. He realized how little he needed Dresdie. Never believed in himself. Only now he realized he could have had that belief in himself all a long. His lie of a life was his to choose and could have been the truth of his life. So many would

have not had to pay the price with their lives. If only he believed in himself to make his own way. Instead of allowing the demonic magics deform, mutate and dictate his life. Apparently all caused by some investigation by some criminal Xern who must have gave the sword to Dresdie.

Kumithra could see her bound slavery to Yoranthium. She was a prize any male could of taken. Maybe even a maiden could have owned her as suggested by Rarailmuir. By demanding a bloody contest of combat for her hand in marriage. All it would have taken is spilling blood on the wedding floor over a challenger. Her hand would belong to the one who proved the stronger. Her kingdom was barbaric and horrifying.

Thernya told her she was a tool and nothing more for the crown of Yoranthium's King. Her playing in the gallery with males was her trying to be free. That if she was free that foreigner could have been... Kumithra wasn't free she was property and was in a trading war for power and lands. She was a bargaining asset of Yoranthium. She felt she didn't own a soul and she was like a prize cow being sired to produce better beef.

Rarailmuir sniffed as mucus filled his nostrils in sad remorse. "I failed Yoranthium the day of the dragon attack. I let Dresdie kill so many and you deserved a better knight than I for your honor of your hand. But there is no one better than I Kumithra in all of Yoranthium. I curse that day I ran into that twisted investigation of Xern."

"Xern's corruption and evil even corrupted and confused me. People died as a result of the growing evil in the guard. If I never investigated Xern I would never had been to Dresdie's Brothel. Your helmet is there on the table along with your weapons gloves and boots." With that Rarailmuir was on his knees and bared his chest and closed his eyes in a prayer exposing the unborn Gods necklace he was wearing.

Kumithra rose before Rarailmuir. Wiped the dried tears from her face and was about to reach out with an open hand and touch Rarailmuir on his head, then pulling back and clenching her fist. She understood what the dragon must of felt being used the way it had been. She was the enslaved dragon with a collar of control on her all her life. An interesting fairytale if only someone could write it, for they should. Maybe call it. 'The Dragon and I,'

or 'The Virgin and the Dragon,' even better 'The Dragon sacrificed to the Virgin.'

The deep remorse, regret and loss of life the Dragon must of felt. What it had done under the control of Dresdie. Rarailmuir was likewise under a collar of control by Dresdie and broke that yoke himself. Kumithra went through something very similar to the dragon and now she knew they had much in common. Both of them needed to be rescued and freed by Rarailmuir. Even in his twisted way, Rarailmuir freed Kumithra Queen of Yoranthium from her collar.

She walked over to the table and did her hair up noticing the bruising was subsiding ever so little but enough that it didn't hurt so much. Her headache was gone. She put on her boots. Putting her hair up and out of the way she tucked it under her mother's helmet. She fixed her belt and adjusted the pouches and the short sword and dagger. Picked up the chain daggers and hid them on her person in her armor. Finally putting her gloves back on, noticing that Rarailmuir was a gentle elf and only cleaned her feet, hands and face along with the helmet, gloves and boots and nothing more.

He didn't even touch her Yukata not even once. Rarailmuir had her to himself and didn't ravish her. He was honorable. Everything back in place, she then turned back to Rarailmuir who didn't move and was still in prayer with his arms out to his sides palm up waiting for Kumithra to decide his fate. He was sacrificing himself and welcomed his death at her hands. As treason is punishable by death.

She walked nearer to Rarailmuir and pulled her short sword. Lifted it to Rarailmuir's chest and put her left on the top of the hilt ready to push it into his heart. He didn't care he could feel the weight of the blade on his heart. It was a clear message that Rarailmuir gave his life and his heart to her, to do as she pleases with his life. She asked herself. 'Can I really win this war without my General?' The answer was, "No." She said it out loud and then.

Lifted the sword from Rarailmuir's heart and tapped him on the right and then over his head to the left. "Sir, Rarailmuir my first knight. You are demoted from King to General of Yoranthium by order of your Queen. You are to remain in title to your men as the King but you are just a General and it's your job to defend

your Queen and save Yoranthium. I no longer love you and you have failed me, and the heart of Yoranthium. We will after winning this war decide your fate and punishment for the evils you unleashed that harmed so many of your fellow Yoranthian's. You will stand trial but first you need to win this war for your Queen and the people of Yoranthium."

"Thank you my Queen. I Rarailmuir General of Yoranthium obey your commands my heart is yours to do as you please from here on forth and forever." Rarailmuir waited for his new Queen to give him orders.

"Now rise to your new post and let's save our kingdom." Kumithra seemed at first to have forgiven Rarailmuir in what she said. Yet as he rose and towered above her. He could see she was no longer in love with him and it was now professional. Like looking at her mother's eyes Queen Zantkara.

As the questioning was in progress a while ago, no one had noticed or had been standing guard over the corpses of Orichen and his Sea Ghouls. Their bodies began to twitch and their finger tip bones began to grow breaking through the tip of the skin on their fingers as sharp bone claws on their feet and hands began to grow to shy of a king's foot long. Their feet mutated and stretched as the corpses rose to stand on their toes with long clawed bone toes.

Their necrotic flesh blackened and their wounds healed over with muscle fibers and various sharp bone horns exposing up and down their bodies. The eye sockets became dark orbs and their noses had sunken inwards to two large flat nasal passages. Their teeth became long as an index finger of an ordinary sea elf and pointed and jagged as their ears fell off and blackened skin hardened like chitin. With their hair falling off and becoming jagged bone horns protruding from torn skin.

Orichen's body became larger than the other Riark's for he was the lord of the Riark's. His chest ruptured into a several jagged protruding ribs and he developed small demonic bat like wings on his back that were in the process of growing. The bones on his head formed a crown as his toothy mouth widened wider than the others and filled with more jagged long and sharp teeth.

"Yes, this is right. Power as promised by my wedding to Dresdie." Orichen was looking at his fellow and former Sea

Ghouls. Dresdie had kept her promise to Orichen and gave him power beyond death. Yet as the mutations took hold Orichen could feel his mind being deformed, his thoughts changing and becoming filled with a lust for blood, for carnage, and for the death of the tasty and delectable sea elf flesh. He wanted to own their souls, collect their skulls, devour their flesh, drink their blood and hunt them in the dark.

His words were replaced with a harsh sounding rasping that was soft and silent yet always in the mind of his blind mindless band of Riark's. They started moving around the room getting their bearings. Some skittered and crawled on the walls and the ceiling. They had become demonic and powerful.

A two elf patrol of guards heard weird rasping sounds coming from the morgue containing the Sea Ghouls. The guards entered and got shredded and torn limb form limb. They didn't even have a chance to scream. They were out numbered and quickly overwhelmed and feasted upon for their blood. Their skulls given to Orichen and he placed those skulls in his chest cavity as they were absorbed into his body. With two smaller arms growing on him and his wings getting larger.

Metiur had descended the stairs from the outer walls down to the lower level where the commander's chamber was. He ran into the guard stationed at the door who tried to oppose his approach. "What is the matter of this? Out of my way. We are under siege by all matters of demons and Mechanation's on the outer walls."

The guard apologized to Metiur. Allowing him to pass and he simply barged through the door.

Metiur was surprised he saw his Queen and King together in the same room facing one another and discussing how the war was going. Upon his barging in Kumithra was the first to notice Metiur.

"Speak up what is it?" She commanded.

"I didn't know you were here my Queen. My King we are under siege we need you now and we are under serious attack. Everything is approaching the outer walls and we had already started to fire on the enemy with magics. Fedarious is leading the defenses on his own and we need to help him." Metiur was emphatic.

Rarailmuir had spun around to look at Metiur and then his Queen. "We need to defend the keep immediately my Queen or we'll lose the Last Bastion." Rarailmuir collected his sword and began putting on his armor quickly and Kumithra recognized that the armor he had was like Metiur's and it came form those deep sea elf raiders.

"I see you recognized the armor my Queen." Rarailmuir had a smile for he knew Kumithra remembered the day they acquired these armors and weapons. "Sadly Metiur and his unit died by the torch of a Mechanation and it was the sword of Yoranthium that brought them back to life. They had no armor or weapons so I authorized this armor to be used and they are now called the Death Guard. Enough of the explanations we have to fight. A war to win."

Yoranthium

Book One: Lost Hope

Chapter Twenty-One: Fall of the Last Bastion

By Mark P. Bromley

Defense is only as good as a strong offense. Peace is a game best fought by those who prepare for war. Yoranthium was the Last Bastion of hope for a theology of the unborn God. Refugees came for the protection offered. Never knowing the problems of Yoranthium and never realizing an enemy of darkness had already defeated Yoranthium since a dragon attacked it revolutions ago. Here is the last of that hope of all Ishormot as the Last Bastion of Yoranthium fails and falls.[29]

[29] In 2024 it was recognized open borders was a failure and that this practice was ruination and poverty on an escalating level of development. In truth the real path forward is to acquire lesser nations and provide a means to bring them to the standards of American Democracy and equality by a means of colonization to statehood.

From outside the commander's chambers the guard in the hall could be heard. "Guards report! Sound off in the distance! Light your torches and magics!" As quick and hushed screams began to bellow in the lower bowels of the fortress, torches and light magics began extinguishing as the halls became dark. No sounds from the other guards and no one knew what was happening.

Rarailmuir was the first to pull and oil his Sukenobu.[30] Swiftly moving to the location of the guards protecting his chamber with Metiur following behind Kumithra. He got to the front of the guards and the torches and light magics at the start of the hall leading to the room he had came from. Witnessing that the lower floor lights had all been extinguished and hearing rasping, clattering and slithering sounds all around them except down the hall wince they came. Then some stone fell from the ceiling and pattered on the floor. His medallion was glowing just as a Riark dropped from the ceiling terrifying the guard and Kumithra let out a very terrified ear shattering and long scream.

Rarailmuir was quick he swung at the creature before him and sliced it's arm clean off at the upper joint. Which didn't matter to the creature and it came at Rarailmuir like a savage beast. Pushing its hind legs like a powerful snarling monster with tenacious gnashing teeth and claws of bone. Yet upon trying to impact Rarailmuir a bright light exploded from his necklace and burst the Riark into dust. Rarailmuir grabbed his holy relic realized what it just did for him. "Keep in Tight formation, demon oil your weapons and carry torches. The beasts are everywhere." Realizing that his necklace had lost some of its material and seemed lighter in weight.

As the group of six guards, Metiur, Rarailmuir, took positions around Kumithra. Rarailmuir took off his necklace and placed it round Kumithra's neck over her head. "What's this for?" Inquired Kumithra.

"It's a holy relic I obtained years ago once I suspected demons abounded on Yoranthium. I got it from a strange

---

[30] A sword based on Fujiwara Sukenobu in reference to a ukiyo'e artist creating a type of sword representing a style of art and aesthetics. Many historical references and used symbolically as a symbol of a strong male. In a way a perfect tool to push back against false dogma in politics of the early 21st century.

merchant and he claimed to be a healing cleric of the unborn God and apparently it works. Not so much with the lightning birds we fought but definitely works on these things at close range. You my Queen are the only one of importance here and must be defended. Even at the cost of my own life." Said Rarailmuir with a sad yet apologetic smile toward her. He touched the top of her sternum with the medallion and realized his touch was no longer welcomed by Kumithra's expression. She scowled a look of scorn back to him for tenderly touching her. "I'll do my duty my Queen and I hope you can forgive me one day." Sincerely saying as he pulled away and turned his attention, back to the problem at hand.

The torches were out all around the lower floors, the only light being that which they carried as a group. There were more than fifty guards on this floor. How did these creatures get down here? Rarailmuir didn't know. He's never seen this type of creature, black and stealthy, crawling on the ceiling and the walls. Silently until they would attack and pounce at their targets with rows of long teeth and outstretched bone claws. Pity his medallion petrified and pulverized the first to dust. Rarailmuir didn't get any time to examine the creature further.

It would be prudent for Rarailmuir's group to find more guards and more defenders. "Move to the stairs and stay close, move slow with purpose and if you see anything coming out of the dark from the floor to the ceiling that's dark and shadowy. Stab and kill it. Just be mindful of the living." They began moving with the torches and light magics at hand. Looking intensely in the dark at the ceiling to the floor from left to right as they kept their backs to the fully lit wall. The guards and Kumithra's fear was rising with dreadful horrific anxiety.

In a defended group it appeared the Riark's didn't want to attack. They could be heard in the distance as a bunch of soft hisses, and skittering around the walls, floor and ceiling as if moving to more advantageous locations for a sneak attack. Rarailmuir's group was being stalked and hunted and critically observed for weaknesses in their defense.

Perhaps that first pulverized to dust Riark by the medallion is what kept them at bay. For many opportunities to pick off a guard or two was presented to the Riarks. Yet no sudden lunge or attack took place. The air was ripe with the smell of death and fear.

Screams of terror echoed in the large chambers and down a set of stairs from outside the fortress upon its battlements.

The group rounded the corner to the upper stairs. Just as they rounded a loud hissing shriek could be heard as they ran into one of the creatures licking up the blood of a guard that was no where to be found. Just entrails and flesh, clothing, armor boots, and that guard's weapons were on the ground. The guard must have been out numbered and torn apart, as this must have been the last creature to sup on the remains. It had lunged at the first guard. The one that had hit Kumithra with the sap rending her unconscious and it had eviscerated his throat on impact and decapitated him. Which Kumithra had caught his head with her chain dagger impaling it in the eye socket and again she screamed in horror so loud that Rarailmuir and Metiur thought their ears would bleed.

She witnessed the terrified look of the guard, as he was decapitated and then the change of expression, as the separated head of the guard witnessed his impalement on Kumithra's chain dagger. That guards head made a contorted face and moved knowing what had happened. Kumithra begged for forgiveness for hastily casting his still living head to the side as his blood flew from his eye socket away from her blade. The guard's head made a loud thud on the floor and rolling into the darkness where loud hissing and some kind of conflict between the Riark's took place fighting over the guard's head.

Rarailmuir along with the other guard slashed at the Riark with a spear and sword. Stabbing and cutting the creature down, as a black congealed oozing syrup of blood flowed out of it with a stench of rotting flesh and maggots. More scuttling could be heard from behind them and up the stairs. There were more of these foul necrotic beasts around and Rarailmuir tested out his theory with fire from his torch and sure enough the Riark they slain had again burned easily. Yet it didn't stop moving it yelled in pain and agony and slashed wildly with it's claws and gnashing with its teeth it was far from dead even while on fire.

Rarailmuir slashed wildly at the remains of the creature until he batted the beast far enough away. Where it just rolled about on the ground. He like the other guard had been also swinging their torches. Two more Riark's had been lit on fire.

Knocked back on fire illuminating more Riark's. One of the guards speared another incoming Riark from the ceiling. That one simply pulled itself towards the guard while on the spear chomping away trying to bite him.

The guard, the other one who found Kumithra had pushed the creature away on the spear. By throwing it out of his hand and pushing the Riark back. Pulled out his oil covered sword that he had kept oiled from the conflict with the Impundalu. Hacking its head clean off and into the dark recesses as he climbed up the stairs. Reclaiming his dropped torch. Hearing and seeing the shadow's of other Riark's fight over and feast upon even their own.

With his back to the upper door, in a crack of lighting from above another Riark had been lurking and waiting for this mistake. The guard was ripped into from the shoulder, as the beast bit into his armor of mithreal like it was soft flesh. Ripping off his sword arm with one arm and ripping into his guts from his groin region with it's deformed beast like clawed foot. The guard was gurgling on his own blood and with his life fading he took his last action. Taking his torch and plowed it right in the midriff of the Riark on the upper stairs. Causing it to cry in pain dropping the guard to the ground and scurrying up the stairs and out onto the landing.

Kumithra was in shock remembering the looking head on her dagger as the other eye blinked. She flung the head off her dagger and into the darkness as that blinking eye set her nerves on edge. She ran to Rarailmuir and nearly into his arms. Before returning to her senses and realizing that she still viewed him as her hero and savior. Why not it was just under a quarter a third season and now she was in danger and needed her… Hero.

She had dreamed of Rarailmuir as her male protector holding her in his arms from all the evils of Ishormot for many revolutions. She stopped short and regained her senses as Rarailmuir turned to see her behind him. Where she quickly turned her back so he couldn't see her face. Her expression would have betrayed her intentions. She let loose in an undefended direction with her chain dagger and impacted another Riark that was unseen in the distance it howled in pain and Kumithra pulled hard on the chain to return her dagger as Thernya taught her revolutions ago. What came back was a slightly melted blade that

was hot and ash flying off. These demons were something else and too many of them could destroy her chain daggers. Yet the daggers worked on them just like the medallion.

Rarailmuir had suspected Kumithra was weak and needed him. He sensed it. He knew she still had feelings for him even if she was resentful of his actions. In time her heart would likely mend. Yet for that too happen he and her would have to survive this nightmare. There was still hope for him to be her King he could tell from how she continued to move backwards towards him.

He tested out a theory he had. Moved to her back and pressed up against her body and she didn't move from his back.[31] Instead she slid right into his sword arm. With her waist firmly in his grip and her hand with a chain dagger softly placed on his chest and was looking at his face as he spoke to her, her expression betraying her attitude towards him. "Kumithra move with me and stay close we are going up the stairs." Kumithra trembled in his arm and she felt very safe and protected by Rarailmuir more now than ever.

Rarailmuir could feel her trembling and hear her heart as it calmed and relaxed and she complied with his treatment of her and his sword was in a position to defend her. He was getting a little excited himself yet had to brush it off quickly as she could hear his heart miss a beat.

Kumithra felt a little ashamed she still held feelings of lust and love for Rarailmuir. Even though he betrayed her. She still cared for him and accepted her place in his arm hold. She was shorter than Rarailmuir and she looked down and sure enough the bulge of his Yukata under his belt and his trousers had grown in size. He still wanted her too and all she could do was dig her head into Rarailmuir's chest just a little more. At this moment Rarailmuir was the safest place in all of Yoranthium.

Metiur had seen his Queen and King hold each other. He had no one to hold and he was slightly envious, for he too had fear and witnessed his guards getting slaughtered by these terrifying beasts. He thought of someone but wasn't sure and he wanted to get to that person and make sure. Metiur was pleased that his king and queen still loved one another. He never got the full story of

---

[31] "Back to Back," is the hard book cover front picture. "Back to Back," is also available as a poster and other works created by the author.

how the Queen returned but it must have been one of love. The way they held each other. This was good to see, Metiur thought perhaps there is hope as long as there is love.

Another Guard next to him had been fixated on the ceiling thinking a creature would attack from there. Yet it came form the sidewall around the corner and grabbed him. Pulled him right back around the corner and he dropped his torch and spear. He screamed and Metiur was going to attempt to rescue him but then he heard many Hisses and screeching from around the dark corner it was too late as claw after claw after claw began rounding the dark corner. There was too many and that guard was likely a trap and torn to shreds. The creatures were vicious and blood thirsty and intelligent.

Metiur and the other two guards took up positions close to Rarailmuir and their Queen to protect their egress from the lower floors. One of the guards had an idea. Him and the other guard had magics on them and they tossed all their magics into the darkness down the stairs. That was a terrible mistake. Six randomized abrupt explosions ensued followed by a chain reaction of more magics that must have been littering the floor where fifty or so guards had been stationed and died in the darkness as the creature tore them apart.

Metiur yelled. "Run for your lives!!!" He yelled above the ensuing chaos above the octaves of the continuing echoing explosions. Sounding like a feminine high pitched squeal out performing Kumithra's earlier screams. The exploding chain reaction finally found the sealed chambers and stores of thunder rods they couldn't access without the Last Bastions Mages. Those Thunder rods and hidden concealed magics sealed the destruction of the central building of the Bastion as a certainty, as the explosions intensified and shook the fortress. Like a true and real natural quaking of the ground and an impending catastrophe was about to unfold.

The group headed up the stairs as loud and huge pieces of solid fused stone came crumbling down. Stone thought to be impossible to break and why the Last Bastion was believed to be indestructible. Stone that seemed like nothing more than large stone made out of soft clay. Shattering like pottery and dust and dirt following on the ends of their boots up the stairs as the lower

levels began to collapse and more explosions taking place. Not all the guards on the lower floor were dead they could be heard screaming and dying and the Riark's as well being crushed under the weight of the heavy explosions sealing their tomb of crumbling ancient stones.

Rarailmuir dropped his torch and swept the lightweight frame of Kumithra off the floor in his powerful arms. Just like a child. Swung her over his shoulder with his curved blade in front of him. Dust was covering all of them by the time they reached the battlement outside as a thick cloud of dust bellowed out following them and enveloping them. Metiur the two guards, Rarailmuir and Kumithra were coughing and choking on their knees as it took time for the dust to settle and the air to clear. Their ear's ringing from the echoing explosions that threw them off balance.

Rarailmuir was the only one to have some of his wits about him. He was experienced and known to these disasters. He realized it was a mistake issuing so many small magics to his guards. None of them had been trained adequately to understand the use of these magics. They never used them correctly and it led to many disasters and this being one of the worst by far.

The explosions continued. Floor after floor of the inner keep collapsed onto the lower level, as the supporting main beams were lost. The entire structure was unstable. Would be eventually collapsing in its entirety, as the chain reaction of explosions continued.

Metiur was able to grab a hold of Rarailmuir giving him his bearings. It was a fight for survival on the crumbling battlement. Rarailmuir searched for Kumithra and found her not far from him still coughing on the battlement floor, ear's still ringing and unable to hear for the moment. He snatched her up in one arm over his shoulder again and found his sword in the dust. Noticing cracks forming on the battlement that meant the foundations would soon fail and collapse as the fire from the explosion could be seen escaping through the gaps of broken stone.

He and Metiur looked over the battlements. Guards were locked in their own fights for their very lives. Impundalu swooping in lightning lifting tearing and killing guards and noticeably more improved in their tactics. With new Leathery bat winged, squat, three kings foot length, misshapen hairy, red eyed, elven like

demons flying all around them that were guiding the impundalu. Armed with demonic weapons and looked like demonic cupids with small bows and arrows shooting randomly. With Riark's running rampant all over the battlement. With one rather over sized winged Riark lord guiding them with hisses and high pitched screams. The guard on the battlements were doomed they had nowhere to go and some simply jumped off the wall to their deaths, the Demonic Generals where here.

Rarailmuir's command was over his hopes of a dramatic and gallant stand at the Last Bastion was over before it began. The main keep was collapsing taking his guard and demons alike to their doom. Metiur was saying something to Rarailmuir his ears still ringing as he was contemplating what to do now. Slowly his ears cleared.

".....Yard down there." Metiur was pointing. "Fedarious and the death guard they are assembled with the remaining guard. Looks like he's signaling they have a plan. I suggest we go down and join them post haste." Metiur waited for Rarailmuir's reply, relieved to see Fedarious.

Some succubi began firing arrows their way. That missed them completely. Least the one that nearly hit Kumithra in the leg that Rarailmuir caught by the shaft in his hand. Realizing it was dipped in some kind of oozing green fluid. Likely poison on it's point and was a kings finger tip from scratching his hand just below her buttocks. Fortunately Kumithra didn't know about and couldn't see it. Again Rarailmuir saved her without her knowing. Casting the poison arrow like a dart in his hand into the collapsing fortress.

Looking around Rarailmuir saw some stable stairs going down to the courtyard. "Metiur follow me and you two guards. This..." One of the guards got shot by an arrow in the neck and festered with boils across the side of his face. That grew and merged together until his head popped off. That answered the question of the poison on the arrows. Thought Rarailmuir. Amusing himself in the midst of a dire situation of death with battle fatigue setting in. "Move it or die here, follow me." Metiur and the other guard formed up tightly on Rarailmuir's heels. Kumithra saw behind them as she was being tossed like a sack of potatoes over Rarailmuir's shoulder.

Orichen had seen Rarailmuir descending the stairs. Wanted to test out his new more powerful Riark Lord body with that of his rival. His wife Dresdie was so kind to give him. Spotting his nemesis was exactly what Orichen needed, the battle of the two unholy husbands of Dresdie, Rarailmuir's turn to die and become another skull to his growing chest of skulls collection. Orichen might grow more powerful with dark magics inside Rarailmuir. He flew around the collapsing towers of the lost bastion and got in front of Rarailmuir's group descending the stairs.

Rarailmuir caught Orichen's flying out the side of his peripheral vision and coming in to full view directing his attack at him. It had to be Orichen it's the only way these monsters could have got into the Last Bastion. Rarailmuir could sense Dresdie was part of this attack. The battle of her two creations and he could sense it in the back of his mind it had to be Orichen. Wishing to now see if who was the stronger of Dresdie's dark magics.

Wings of a size that silhouetted Orichen's massive form in the lightning darkened sky like a dark angel of the most demonic a devil of the hellish sky, a deep dark Anti-Angel mocking him. Rarailmuir tossed Kumithra to Metiur like a sack of rice. Metiur nearly didn't catch her and almost lost his balance. "Take Kumithra to where the Death Guard are located Metiur. I think this winged monster has a grudge to settle with me."

Rarailmuir's eye's tightened on Orichen, readied himself, for a worthy fight against another suitor and vassal of Dresdie's lies. Orichen was of the first bloodline of the first King of Yoranthium. This would settle who the King of Yoranthium really was. So thought Rarailmuir. Feeling something more spiritual and theological and ironic that this mythical battle would be now at this time.

Kumithra found herself with her arms around Metiur. Nearly taking a tumble down the stairs. Rarailmuir did it again just flung her aside like a bushel into a silo after the harvest. Metiur felt different than Rarailmuir. Less defined, weaker, and not as competent or confident as Rarailmuir. Metiur seemed to be following Rarailmuir's command to the letter. "My queen I'll be your escort. We'll meet up with the Fedarious and the Death guard. You'll be safe with me." Metiur had said as he helped her

get her footing back as him and the other guard helped her down the rest of the flight of crumbling steps.

Just then Orichen slammed into Rarailmuir who had his sword at the ready. The impact of the speed of Orichen's descent from the sky knocked Rarailmuir back into the stonewall and on the ground. He hit his head and was almost knocked out from the impact. Orichen was unable to do much. He didn't account for the demon oil on the Sukenobu blade that Rarailmuir was wielding. Orichen never felt such a sharp folded bladed mithreal made weapon like this with demon oils. It sliced easily into the accumulated skulls Orichen had been collecting all ready the first layer turned to dust and got pulverized.

Orichen could see Rarailmuir's face and throat shaking off the initial impact of his head against the low wall. Orichen smiled wide with his row after row of jagged teeth and gleaming black orbs for eyes. His eye's glistened as he let out a shrill of victory over Rarailmuir and although the sword pained him he went in for the kill. Orichen was going to bite Rarailmuir's face clean off and claim his skull. There was nothing Rarailmuir could do he was still dazed and confused and struggling to get clear his vision.

The powerful new wings Orichen had was quite the gift, the speed at which in the open darkened sky he could get up to made his attacks devastating to his prey. He's never had so much power. Orichen loved his new form as a demonic Riark Lord an Anti-Angel of darkness and of the deep dark fiery abyss of hell.

Poor Rarailmuir he could only smell the necrotic flesh breath of the creature on top of him. Orichen’s newly transformed body was powerful even when weakened by demon oils. Orichen became supernatural in strength and power, more powerful than Dresdie's favored hero. Orichen was more powerful and now a transcended spiritual devil he could sense the eight and the one. Watching through his eyes to the demise of Rarailmuir.

Rarailmuir's eyesight was blurred and blood was flowing from a gash on the back of his head he had suffered a serious concussion from the force of the impact. He was unable to move and just moaned in agony as he fought to regain his senses. Time he did not have as Orichen's teeth neared his face.

He heard a whooshing sound through the air. Orichen pulled his teeth away from Rarailmuir's face as he felt real pain in

his back, pain from a chain dagger. Kumithra came to Rarailmuir's rescue. She flung her chain dagger at the creature that was Orichen. It sailed through the air and impacted him in the back. He was burning from the blade his demonic skin was pulverizing and turning to powder.

Kumithra took advantage of his response and agony and ran up the stairs and quickly wrapped her chain around his wing twice and then pulled it very tightly and it cut through Orichen's wing like a thin wire through a sculptor's clay. The wing fell over the balcony and became dust and the wound would eat at his back even more than the dagger. Until eventually the dagger had nothing to hold onto and it feel to the ground more melted than before with very little useful blade left on it. As the chain itself had also dissolved enough that it simply fell apart. Fortunately for Kumithra she had another chain dagger, this being why chain daggers come in a set of two.

As she reached into her chest plate to retrieve the other chain dagger, Orichen saw her clearly now and let go of Rarailmuir. Orichen did a backward kick at Kumithra and hit her armor and spraining her wrist almost breaking it. You could hear a sickening crack as her mithreal lacquered breastplate fractured and sounded like bones cracking.

Kumithra went flying and falling back down the stairs not even in contact with the stairs. She sailed three king's length down to the lowest landing in the courtyard, just as Metiur ran around trying to catch up to her. She landed into Metiur and he broke her fall that would have been fatal at the force of the impact from Orichen and the distance she fell.

This didn't matter to Orichen. Orichen was impressed with his Riark Lords body. Most of his other transformed Sea Ghouls would never have survived such attacks from demonic weapons like the chain dagger. Yet as a Riark Lord he was somewhat immune and would regenerate his wing with taking more souls this very day. Orichen was invincible and they were running out of demon killing weapons to use on him. He had to kill and claim Rarailmuir's skull. That would restore his injuries and repair his lost wing.

The beast with wings took too long gloating at what he did to Kumithra who attacked him. He would soon enough claim her

little skull and that other guard that saved her from death. Rarailmuir by this time was back on his feet with his sword in his hand. As Orichen turned to face Rarailmuir his blade sung out and cut off Orichen's right wing right hand and right leg. Fragments of former Orichen's disintegrating limbs and dust filled the air. Rarailmuir was quick and flipped the sword quickly around and committed to another effortless strike with his sword slashing his rib cage open and creating a hole in the temple of a skull near Orichen's necrotic barely beating heart and the source of the demons soul.

With that Rarailmuir's secret weapon came into play in his other hand. It was a magics that he shoved into the hole he made in the skull. Orichen lunged at Rarailmuir and he ducked as Orichen flew over the wall and with no wings Orichen fell trying with his massive claws to dig out the explosive magics near his corrupted heart.

The long claws being useless on the bone of the skull fused to his chest Orichen couldn't get the glowing magics orb before the short timed fuse went off. Half way down the side of the battlement stair well it exploded and destroyed Orichen's heart. Orichen became dark black rose petals floating in the breeze. Rarailmuir pondered on what just happened. Realizing he was more powerful than he imagined. He had defeated a devil a counter part to an angel. As a great demonic howl of defeat could be heard on the tempest of the dark clouded storm. As if a being of unbelievable existence had seen it's dark champion defeated in some kind of cruel sporting match.

The beasts got inside the keep. No. They came from inside the keep. The only thing in a backroom morgue was the dead Sea Ghouls. Having defeated who he knew as Orichen. The beasts attacking from inside the keep, was the transformed Sea Ghouls. Now it made sense why they hardly defended the courtyard. It was Orichen's plan or Dresdie's to slaughter them from inside their ranks while attacking their outer defenses. He was an unwitting fool and part of a more sinister and deeper dark plan to crush Yoranthium.

He was a pawn. Rarailmuir was hurt but would recover in a bit. He had just a throbbing headache as he touched the bleeding swelling wound on the back of his head. He was feeling the

concussion he had and it made him dizzy he lost his footing and fell to his knee. Kumithra was on his right and Metiur on his left and they lifted him off the ground. "I guess it's my turn for you to be carried on my shoulder." Kumithra had said playfully relieved Rarailmuir was alive.

Rarailmuir's head was hurting and hanging low. Low enough for Kumithra to give him a kiss on his cheek. He was relieved she might of found a means to forgive him and he was satisfied he had defeated Orichen even when he was a devil and more powerful.

Thanks to Metiur and Kumithra he prevailed and proved the stronger with love in his heart. He knew that Kumithra was becoming quite the warrior herself. As Metiur witnessed her saving Rarailmuir telling what he saw to his king in his other ear, grilled by Kumithra in the other ear as to who had to save him. To burn it into his brain that this tiny petite Queen was his savior.

Upon getting to the Death Guard's location, an impatient Fedarious looked at the group and immediately looked at Metiur and deciding this wasn't up to the king or the queen but him and Metiur. "Metiur, I got explosives and oils and fire ready to do a great defensive plan at the main gate. When I open it I'll kill the host of demons, depth dwellers and Mechanation's trying to get into the courtyard. I see we no longer have a fortress and most of our guard are now gone or dying on the battlements. They have been cut off."

Fretting he walked to Metiur, "You Metiur stand there." Fedarious pointed to a protected area of the death guard and those in the court. "When the main door goes so will that wall that isn't under attack. It's our escape route through a densely packed riverbank, where it would be hard for any of these demons, Mechanation's and things to follow or get at us. We can easily protect from all directions. We even managed to down some of those succubi fortunately I'm immune and I think you might be too Metiur. I think it's a matter of the heart that gives them power of illusion over males." Fedarious said with a smile. "I for one am glad you are okay my commander. Also charges have been set for when we leave. Once the wall is down hurry out of here and the charges will collapse those side walls protecting our retreat as this place is now a mine field so stay on the path lined out in the dirt."

“When did you and the Death Guard get the time to do all this?” Metiur wanted to know.

“I thought I told you last night about my idea as we rested on the bench. You drifted off to sleep. Only waking when the attack came. Going off apparently to warn the King and Queen. I had this idea after cleaning up the Sea Ghouls mess and seeing the Mechanation's on the horizon.” Fedarious said smiling with some sternness at Metiur.

Metiur couldn't help but smile and laugh back at Fedarious. “I think I remember something about it but feel asleep while sitting next to you on that bench.” Looking where it had been. “That's now gone.”

A distinct cloud of dust of the fallen Last Bastions central building was now filling the court yard along with the side buildings that began collapsing as the inner battlements no longer had anything holding them up began collapsing as well. With more random explosions below and fire had been erupting from the smoldering foundations. It was a terrific mess and didn't care for the guard or the demon host attacking from the sky.

Sparks of flame flew into he sky from the continuing explosions. Sporadically impacting the lighting fast moving Impundalu causing them to in turn become flaming bombs of a mess of burning soft tissue. Leaving gently falling feathers on fire that would from time to time impact other lighting fast Impundalu. That in turn would explode and continue a constant chain of fire and explosive reaction in the air all around those on precarious battlements.

These exploding Impundalu were a hazard to the succubi, the Riark's and guards alike that remained on the broken battlements that had also been crumbling and falling. Each guard still on a remaining section of battlement was in a fight for life and death and swarmed by the demonic host assailing them. It was fortunate for those in the courtyard, as the unintentional destruction by the two guards on the inner fortress steps that began this chain reaction. Created the perfect distraction to protect the exposed death guard and only remaining chain of command.

Gethia watched from a distance on the top a dead Yamazakura tree’s branches. Her Xern substance of half-life created succubi died horribly due to Dresdie's poor choice of an

Impundalu army. Gethia could see that her children would not make it past this day over the keep and would be gone before the evening came. Leaving her alone on the island. With nothing but the shades of the sick and the twisted tormented souls enlisted in the demonic dominions services once more.

Gethia was even more upset her litter was unable to enchant or entice Fedarious who was the one that organized the defenses. For some strange reason Fedarious was immune to the seductive illusions of mortal females. He had no protection that Gethia had seen. From Gethia's hiding spot in the trees she lifted up into the air and went back to her nest from where her failed progeny was born a day ago. Disappointed and sulking and upset Dresdie had created the very means of their avian armies doom and failure by choosing Impundalu's of all things.

Metiur and the rest saw the fiery, explosive and terrifying end of the inner battlement defenders. The loss of many guards was sad and regrettable. The only relief was the destruction of the demon host above on the same battlements. The luck of the purely random fires and explosion's destroying the demonic host. It wouldn't be long before the inner fortress remaining battlements would fail and collapse. Metiur was alarmed at the imminent danger and realized they had lost too much of the guard fighting for the inner courtyard. Cracks could be seen forming on the front of the outer wall as the Mechanation's went to work with their heavy flails and steam hammers. The walls of this Last Bastion were impressive, made of an old ancient means unknown to the sea elves yet still vulnerable to siege and wrecking balls mounted on the Mechanation's.

Metiur knew the keep was lost. "We'll get the King and Queen out of here. I'll get the rest of the Guard out of here. I know where that river goes and have a plan on top of your plan Fedarious."

"I've seen some troubling things that look like another demonic creature. They are called Yagrallmagrunds. Demonic tentacle monsters growing out of the ground, for now we need to go." Fedarious responded in haste as he signaled the remaining few hundredths guard to finish their assigned tasks and quickly assemble to the safe location from the escape wall. Which was a make shift barricades to protect them from the explosive debris.

Rarailmuir was becoming to weak to be giving orders. His head was in serious pain and he couldn't think. He couldn't hear clearly and the concussion he had was a fight he felt he was losing as he found it difficult to keep his eyes open.

"Please hurry with your plan Fedarious. We need to get moving. Rarailmuir is getting worse and I don't know what to do?" Kumithra was getting very worried as Rarailmuir continued to get weaker and having trouble standing. Weighing down on Kumithra more and more and she simply couldn't lift him for he was so heavy.

Metiur could feel that Rarailmuir was shifting more and more weight to his shoulder. He looked at Kumithra struggling to hold him. Her own strength would fail her soon enough and Metiur would be having to bare Rarailmuir's full weight alone. "You two!" Metiur commanded two waiting death guard to his side. As they approached Metiur gave them commands to take up his and Kumithra's support of the King. As he found a large pouch over his rear left flank hanging from his belt and pulled out the wrapped in cloth contents. Kneeling on the ground in front of Rarailmuir he unrolled the cloth and it was full of bandages and medicines and ointments.

Metiur had to work quick, He's seen this before and attended all the battlefield healing classes he could get. Rarailmuir had a very serious concussion that was progressively getting worse, perhaps internal bleeding from that impact to his unprotected head on that stone battlement half wall?

Fedarious had two other death guard run over and grab a litter he had seen by the outer defensive wall. The two ran and got it and brought it back to where Metiur had been working with the ointments and bandages and was using a syringe to administer a health potion into Rarailmuir's arm.

Metiur seen the litter being placed on the ground before their King, "Good job everyone. Now lay him down on the stretcher and you four death guard will have to carry him. Kumithra. Kumithra, my Queen." She was tearing up in her helmet and Metiur could see she cared deeply for Rarailmuir. He had to grab her shoulders and look at her tearing purple eyes. "My Queen you need to stop your crying and listen to me." He said shaking her back to her senses.

"What do you need Metiur can't you see Rarailmuir is dying." Kumithra was upset she seen his condition getting worse and all the bandages on his head an lying on a stretcher with four death guard kneeling low at the four corners of the stretcher. Getting ready for orders to move their King.

"He's not going to die. You can prevent that. I need you my Queen to keep him awake. Shake him, tap him, poke him and keep speaking to him. Just keep talking to him and say nice lovely things. Things that would keep him alive and awake, memories, stories, anything nice. The healing ointment, salve and bandages with the health potion will heal him but he needs to stay awake. Can you do that?"

Metiur asked his queen with a demanding and commanding presence for her to obey and follow as instructed. It would be critical for Rarailmuir to survive as the medicine cured his concussion and internal bleeding. He had to stay awake for all that too work. Kumithra would be that magics of heart needed to keep Rarailmuir alive.

Kumithra simply nodded and ran over to the middle of the litter and knelled down beside her King. She began talking to Rarailmuir about the time she first met him as he saved her from the dragon and what she felt and heard of his strong heart. It was very mushy thought Metiur and there were more important matters to attend too. He ordered the stretcher to be moved to the best protection from debris at the escape walls temporary barricades. Ordering all persons to the their stations. As they got ready for Fedarious plan to begin.

Having got everything in place. Metiur and Fedarious had taken the time to address and understand their current situation. The final inner fortress and battlements were about to collapse and would once the door explosives went off. The sky was full of smoke and dust but no signs of the Impundalu or the demonic cupids. The battlements became quiet. It was certain no one was alive or remaining on the cutoff battlements. There was no more movement from the creatures that the Sea Ghouls had become. Those Riark's were the essence of pure bloodthirsty evil and it was a sigh of relief that the exploding birds had killed them burned them and eliminated the demons assailing the upper battlements. At least one

thing for sure, fire was a good weapon on these demonic forces waging war on Yoranthium.

Surveying the battlefield and the courtyard everyone had a job to perform and were in their correct positions. This would prevent the remaining defenders from becoming liabilities and keep them out of harms way.

Up on the outer battlements stood two lookouts, one monitoring the door and the other monitoring the enemy forces outside the wall. The walls were beginning to oscillate and shake as the Mechanation's siege weapons had began shattering the stone. Even though the vibration of the wall had been getting worse it would still take over a day for any of these fortified walls to potentially fail.

“Conditions!!!” Cried a commanding voice of Fedarious, who began his plan in motion. The audience from behind the barricades had silenced and watched on. With Kumithra's soft voice being the only one speaking to Rarailmuir and her tale of the broken heart when it was whole and in fantasy. Which would sound like narration as Fedarious plans played out in the background.

“All enemy still just on the warm sun-up side wall trying to break in.” Came the outer wall defense report. “Mostly clustered toward the main gate.”

“ Slowly begin opening the gate to only one Kings foot high!!!” Fedarious watched as the front gate began to move and could see the Depth Dweller feet scurry closer as the door opened and could hear Mechanation's moving outside the gate.

“It's working.” Came the Guards voice watching the door.

“All enemy units moving to the opening of the gate.” Yelled the other.

“Raise the door one more kings foot!!! How is our Egress?” Fedarious needed to know.

“Clear, we are now clear!!!” The trick was working some depth dwellers were attempting to crawl under the opening door but it was still too tight as they got into one another's way.

The entire force was tricked by the door opening, that they had left the warm side of the wall all bunching around the door. The Mechanation's cared little for the Depth Dwellers some of them getting crushed by the sharp pointed feet of the

Mechanation's. Some depth dwellers got injured and didn't care as the enemy just clustering around the opening door. This demonic army although deadly wasn't very bright.

The guard watching the enemy reported. "Outer kill box is full, we can now open the door and set off the magics!!!" The guard was happy and then replied. "All clear on the Egress!!!" With that he jumped off the top of the wall and on a make shift pole that almost tipped over as he slid down it to the ground quickly taking up a position close to the kings litter.

Just as Fedarious choreographed his two guards did their duty well and exactly where they needed to be. "Open the main gate!!!" With that the guard opened the main gate. Depth Dwellers tried to rush in but got trampled on by the Mechanation's that blocked the entrance with their own girth and slowed their movement, just as Fedarious thought. Their eyes were bigger than their brains. A metaphor usually meant about eating too much and choking on it. This metaphor was fitting for what happened at the main gate. "Blow the magics!!!!"

The Guard watching the gate moved down the upper battlement flipping a set of wood levers attached to a complex set of pulleys and ropes. That set up a timed series of magics, catapults with magics, sling weapons and oils with corresponding fire braziers. Then he ran to a similar pole set for him. He jumped on it and he was too high on the pole it fell over. He would of landed in the magics explosive traps under the ground if he didn't decide to let go as he was over the safe area. He fell some distance and you could hear an audible crack as he broke his left femur upon impact with the ground.

The slings with magics fired with the catapults launching magic's behind the enemy and into their outer ranks that were now forced to pushing into the open door. Which worked well killing many and destroying a few Mechanation's and forcing the rest to push forward closer packed into a terrified massive hoard. As the next stage dropped oils over the mess pressing it's way to the door and the braziers of fire dropped onto the oils catching the depth dwellers and the Mechanation's on fire. Screeching and yelling could be heard as the hoard burned and died. Pushing harder and harder into the crowded entrance corridor. That finally it's magics

too had exploded at the same time as the egress wall came crumbling down.

The Egress wall was down and dust from the walls and the collapsed buildings along with smoke from the fires was making it hard to see anything in the chaotic courtyard. Fedarious's plan worked he was smiling and full of pride. He made his way to the injured guard that had set the magics off and pulled him up hanging off his shoulder. "Now stay between the illumination magics. Move it out of here double time and protect the Queen and Kings litter with our very lives you are all in the Death guard now and I need you all to work as one."

Metiur was proud of Fedarious. Apparently he was rubbing off on him. Metiur ordered the litter guard to lift the King all at once and he was in the center across from Kumithra who were both supporting the center of the litter. Death Guard formed all around them. The King's Litter would become the pace at which the entire remaining retinue of Death Guard would move. "Forward, move, move, move, move, Get past the egress wall as soon as possible for us to seal the enemies fate behind us and keep moving!!!"

The retinue followed Metiur's orders and they rushed through the tough to see where they were going rubble, dust, smoke. Simply staying inside the lit runway of blue lights on the left and red lights on the right with green in the center. That was only two kings width wide.

Fedarious had drilled his guard well with his plan and Metiur having been A.W.O.L. (Absent With Out Leave) for his training was doing exceptionally well at understanding what he had intended. Fedarious admired Metiur's field healing abilities. Wishing he had those skills. Metiur was a good choice for admiration from Fedarious. To think a few days ago he under scored Metiur's value to him and the rest of the Guards retinue. He thought to himself. 'Metiur, I'll never let you down again and be at your side to the end.' With a tear in his eye admiring his hero moving the king's litter effortlessly past the egress walls.

Looking behind him he could see that some of the depth dwellers and a Mechanation had made it past the main gates this was anticipated and expected. The Mechanation saw Fedarious and was centered as his target. Looking right at him and charged. The

Mechanation didn't know about the buried magics and didn't stay on the path. The guard with the broken leg watched as Fedarious kept moving back past the egress walls. The tension mounting as the Mechanation avoided by pure luck one magics and another buried magics. It seemed this Mechanation was so lucky it would bypass the minefield and catch them.

The following depth dwellers found the magics with little problem and exploded. This caused the Mechanation to stop its charge. It suddenly realized it was in a minefield. Fedarious began laughing at the Mechanation as it was now stuck and knew it. Yet it turned its flame barrel at Fedarious. Fedarious remembered what that was and out from a pouch. Fedarious quickly tossed a magics at the Mechanation and it exploded before it could fire. The Mechanation stepped back by mistake and the minefield went off and it kept stepping on magics mines until it couldn't step anymore.

Fedarious was happy and satisfied with the carnage his plan inflicted on the enemy force. His plan killed hundreds of Mechanation and Thousands of depth dwellers. More began streaming through the broken main gate and Fedarious had reached the outside of the egress wall. Where he hid another lever. Carefully reaching down with the guard on his other side. He pulled the lever up and the breached wall collapsed in a controlled explosion that collapsed and inner tower.

That tower sealed the breach and you could hear the minefield going off.

How did Fedarious get a lever outside the outer defensive wall? Carefully. He did it early in the morning. Set up the planned magics and used a small group of guards a pulley system and ropes and installed it by himself when he was lowered to the ground and then pulled back up by the guard when done. His attention to duty was magnificent. He was always well learned and detailed in his plans and careful. That's why this plan worked.

The quickly moving group of the Death Guard had been moving rapidly in the distance. Everything went as planned and nothing was following them down the side of a stream under the wooded canopy. Fedarious slowed by the guard on his side was still making good time at catching up to the main group. That litter caused them to slow enough that Fedarious would catch up to them

in no time. He thought about how good Metiur was worthy of his admiration, just as Metiur admired Fedarious for his skill at demolishing buildings and killing demon's to save their lives.

The fight retinue of shore guard lost many in this conflict. So much happened so quickly there was no time to sort out the dead and the living. The first real battle of this war unfolded. By haste and confusion and tales not told and drama unknown, it happened so fast and was quick. No matter the success the losses made this battle a Pyrrhic victory. So much loss and the Last Bastion was rent asunder and ruined in less than a day. This keep was pristine from anchient times longer than five-hundredths revolutions and now not more than ruins. Two armys clashed one of mere sea elves and another of a demonic mechanized airborne host of monsters. Mistakes made on both sides as fiction of war met the fact of real war.

One thing for certain the Last Bastion was no more.

Yoranthium

Book One: Lost Hope

Chapter Twenty-Two: Pushed to Sea Shore

By Mark P. Bromley

The war had been going badly that the onslaught of the dark forces was upon them. When you lose your veteran's you lose sight of your enemy. Training a new younger military takes time and time is costly when the forces of darkness are as old as time remembered and have been planning the demise of a kingdom. This is now to become very apparent how unprepared Rarailmuir and Kumithra was to lead this kingdom. The kingdoms demise had begun with mistakes King Sinderthion and Queen Zantkara made long ago and for not being prepared to deal with the wickedness growing in Yoranthium.

Fedarious had caught up to Metiur with the injured guard still needing help and support to keep from using his broken leg. "We need a place to rest and fix our wounded."

Metiur was concerned looking at Kumithra who had been talking to Rarailmuir and keeping him mostly awake as he faded into and out of consciousness. Kumithra was from time to time expressing a deep pain she was feeling in her chest on her right side along with the swelling of her wrist. Metiur could see a crack that had formed in her armor and it must have been where that flying creature had kicked her off the stair well. An impact capable of breaking the armor in that way, cracking it must have done some harm to Kumithra's ribs. She began coughing a little as they had been vigorously moving as fast as they could with the litter and the guard with a broken leg.

They had made some distance of a few leagues with no signs of pursuit. Yet that could change in moments if the flying demons ever returned or the long legged Depth Dwellers or Mechanation's found them. All the enemy had to do is follow this stream that was near rushing water and a main fresh water river that emptied out into a lake on the edge of Sea Shore.

Metiur as a child had been here before. He grew up near this stream and the Forested River. Matter of fact he ran away here because he wanted his parents to pay more attention to him. There was a place just down the river. It was an odd relic of a time long forgotten and mostly buried. As the riverbed covered it at one time with sediment and then shifted. Built in a time much longer than the Sea Elves had lived on Yoranthium.

There was a door that was hard to find and if you hadn't been like Metiur lost in the woods. Where he cried lost for sunwanes as a child he would have never seen the door that lead him into the place. It was dark he only had a small bit of light magics with him back then. He didn't really explore it. But it was big enough for all of them as he recalled. A place that gave him wonder for the anchient world. "Fedarious just a little further. We'll follow the river this stream empties into. I think I got a spot we can rest long enough and recover. Besides I think the Queen is also in trouble and we need to check her out as well. We can't do that here in front of the men it's too revealing."

Kumithra then coughed up a little blood in her right hand. "I agree Metiur, I'm hurt and it's my side. We need something defensible to rest at. My wrist is swelling." She looked toward Metiur and past him to Fedarious and could see the guard was closing his eye's hopping along side them in pain. "That guard there too needs to be carried." Said Kumithra.

Fedarious called for a couple of death guard to take the other guards and carry him by locking their arms together. One set of arms behind his back and the other under his bottom of his legs. Creating a kind of seat. It wasn't the best method and there was no more litters or time to hesitate to make other means available to them. His femur still was causing pain. However, the guard was not on his broken leg and was feeling a bit of more relief. The entire unit could sill move quickly down the riverbed trail. Moving and finding a safe location out of the open was a priority. The tired, exhausted and injured force of the Death Guard remembering the fight in the city when caught in the open.

The Guard commented, "Only had to break a leg to finally get the royal treatment." Taking some pain medication. The other death guard laughed and arranged to make plans with other guards to help when they got tired every ten to twenty kings length's down the path. Trading out tired guards for fresh guards. Everyone was helpful in the unit for they were all they had left.

"Down this way Fedarious and my Queen. I know of a spot I ran away too as a child. My family found me after I found it and I got scolded for running away. The place is large enough to accommodate us and it has a door that can be defended." Metiur informed them. "Just follow my directions down the river to the left. It's concealed and hard to spot unless you've been looking at the door for some time. It'll be perfect."

The group was getting more and more fatigued, as they needed to rest and hadn't took a break. They were slowing down and Metiur was seriously worried about Kumithra now as she had trouble speaking to keep Rarailmuir awake. Looking as if she was going to throw herself on the litter as she began trembling in her gait. A stream of blood could be seen at the side of her lips.

Metiur was worried as he was looking around for the door. 'Could they have passed it?' He thought with so many obligations he was paying attention too and distracted him. Such as

Rarailmuir on the stretcher, Kumithra's ribs and wrist, the broken femur and having to navigate hard terrain down the river looking for a door. While being wary of hostile enemies they expected at any moment to assail them. As they continued walking he worried that they must have passed the door it wasn't this far down the riverbank. He was getting agitated.

"Are we there yet?" Said Fedarious as his stomach began to rumble.

"Just a little further, I think. Did you think of supplies for this stage of our venture, your stomach sounds awful." Just as Metiur had said that he heard other stomachs rumbling and his too as the litter with Rarailmuir felt like they would drop it soon enough. If things couldn't get worse hunger and exhaustion was growing in the ranks.

"Yes, I do have enough hard meat and dried fruits and water on us. You did see several guards have backpacks on. Right?" Fedarious pointed out that the guards had staggered backpacks on over half of them with smaller bags over the shoulders. Others having water containers strapped to their backs while more guards with even more supplies.

Metiur was proud of Fedarious apparently his planning wasn't limited to demolishing buildings but on camping trips too. "How about blanket's and other supplies?"

"What you didn't see the rolled blankets? I got everything we should need for at least three days to the harbor of Sea Shore." Fedarious said patting Metiur on the back.

"Did you plan our escape too once we get to the harbor?" Metiur wanted to know.

"Uh, um, well, I think we'll have to still plan that one." Rubbing his hand behind his right ear with an uncertain facial expression. " I don't know much about the harbor I'm afraid, Metiur. We'll have to decide that while we are resting."

Metiur had forgotten about looking for the door. The surmounting distractions began clouding his thoughts. He was now shocked that he had been talking with Fedarious over plans. He wasn't looking for the door. Now he was certain he had walked past it.

As he turned to tell Fedarious they need to turn back. Metiur was forced to let go of the litter and he tripped on a rock.

Not a rock, it was a tree root before a carved stone. While on the ground as Fedarious was trying to pick him up. He polished it off and there was a carved arrow on it. It was a marker with some ancient unknown language on it.

Metiur looked to the left as Fedarious had pulled him back to his feet. Sure enough there was the sunken and hidden door just down the path. Since he was a kid the river shifted a little further away from the door than he last remembered. Along with some overgrowth and a blessing of a tree root that tripped him. He had rediscovered the door. That was the door and entrance to the sunken underground bunker. The door was composed of two heavy stones that slid together with a hidden activation lever to the side of the sloping column on the right.

The sloping door and framing was of a dark black looking stone. That sloped with the hill of rammed earth that covered the top like a naturally occurring short hill that would be indistinguishable from the surrounding terrain. The construction allowed dust and dirt and some blown brush to cover the door naturally as trees grew all around the structure making it hard and difficult to find.

Metiur was excited to have found it. He pushed Fedarious out of the way and ran to the door and pulled the lever only he knew about. When he first found this it took some time to find that lever. Fortunately the tree roots had been pointing at it. It was good he knew exactly where to find it this time. Thankful for the tree roots being so well placed and helping him and his unit to find sanctuary.

In the distance he heard birds and other forest animals making noise. The enemy was some distance away and on their trail, possibly more of half a day's rapid march away. They would have time to rest. But would need to explore the underground bunker and find another way out.

"Ah, here is our bunker and refuge Fedarious. I can see from the sounds of the wildlife. Our enemy isn't far behind. We have time and we can rest here but we need to explore below and hope for another escape route. It's going to be hard to cover up this door but it's fortified and sealed by more levers and doors below." Metiur had begun issuing orders to his guards and sent ten down into the sloping tunnel to check on the safety of the bunker.

An answer came back after several moments had passed and the guard below was satisfied it was safe. With that the two death guard and guard with the fractured leg went first and followed by more guards and then the litter of the King with the Queen. Followed by the rest of the guard. Once they all got into the main chamber the guard had been busy lighting magics of illumination to see all around them. Metiur got down there and showed the rows of levers in a side room to Fedarious and how to pull and activate each lever. Each one sequenced a set of additional doors on the sloped entry hall that ran for four kings lengths and sealed the entrance behind with a thick wall of ancient stones.

There wasn't much for defensive measures and after looking at the main opening and a couple of side rooms in all directions. Including a functioning toilet facility and what passed as a washing area with a basin that filled with fresh cleaned and filtered river water and disappeared back into the floor. It was clear this area was likely just a crude storehouse of some kind and had working magics. Amazing for its age and ancient architecture. No weapons just a few old wooden crates of some ancient design with old petrified food items. Rotted, useless and ruined old supply crates. Only amenity was that of fresh flowing water.

The chamber was cold. Fortunately in the middle of the main room was a simplified fire basin that had a fluted cone and chimney for allowing smoke to leave the building. Lighting anything that gave off smoke was likely a danger of giving away where they were. However Fedarious found the storage of magically imbued black rock that was treated to burn by glowing blue, wasn't of flame and gave off no smoke. That one of the guards had in his backpack he was carrying.

Fedarious filled the fire basin with enough black-rocks and lit it on fire using a flint and striker he had in a pouch. The glowing heat of the magics black-rock grew to life after burning its supply of lint and kindling and began leaping from one black stone to another.

Eventually the glow of the stones began to warm the cold room. Extending over a short period of time down the ventilated ducts across the ceiling towards all the other chambers. An ancient magically treated ducting that monitored and managed the flow of the heat from the fire pit.

Fedarious focused his efforts working on the fire pit. Metiur had placed the litter with Rarailmuir over to a side room that had a duct that fed warmth from the fire pit into the room. It would take time for the room to heat and it was still cold in the bunker. Kumithra had been keeping Rarailmuir warm by pressing her body on top of his. This sight by the other guard had been too much for the other four guards. They excused themselves out of decency and left the room.

The sight of the King having his Queen on top of him switched on their intimate feelings and yearnings. They simply couldn't remain in the same room. They felt real admiration of their queen and heard her stories of love to Rarailmuir. Wishing they could be loved by someone so special. It was only right to give them privacy.

The royal guard lived a lonely life. They had been separated from their loves. The sight of their queen and king reflected in the guard's thoughts of love and compassion. Compassion they could not see beyond this day. The guard had lost many of their own on the battlements of the Last Bastion. To many guards this could be their last days and they would not know the warmth that their King and Queen were now sharing. They wished they could be with their loves, their wives but they were stuck with guard duty. The sight of the Queen comforting her King was a painful reminder. Made them long for the fates of their own loves and children.

Fortunately for these brave guards they attended the wedding. Their loves and families departed the palace grounds with Bronanes and the Sea Guard. The Shore Guard simply had to believe the Flight guard escaped the brutal awful war with those they loved are safe. This belief alone is the thin line of a thread that kept the shore guard with a sense of duty before dishonor. They would fight and die to protect that which was precious closest to their hearts and minds, still fresh in their thoughts and memories. Those that they loved would live and love and grow. Right now left behind in that room was the physical representation of what the shore guard was fighting for. Embracing their own queens with them returning to their loving embrace of their own kings.

Fact is Kumithra didn't want to but it was the only way to keep Rarailmuir warm. Even though she hadn't told Metiur or Fedarious or anyone that they were not involved anymore. Her

responsibility to keep Rarailmuir alive and awake was simply a duty she had to perform out of compassion or he would die without her. That is what she kept telling herself at any rate. Even with the pain from her ribs on the right and her dislike of the story Rarailmuir told her. Not to mention the occasional blood she found out the side of her lip or occasional blood from her coughing. Along with the throbbing pain of her sprained wrist. Regaling the fantasy of her and Rarailmuir before this awful war. Still was the binding of her heart and charity of love for her would have been husband.

Laying on Rarailmuir was comforting to her and she was aroused from feeling his body beneath hers. She denied it but she wanted this moment, to be on top of Rarailmuir's strong and powerful chest and abdomen. With her head on his heart listening to it pump regularly and strongly. The rhythmic heartbeat was soothing to her and nearly driving her to want to sleep on his chest for his warmth and hers was so comfortable.

Metiur had come into the room. "I see you love birds are a little tired. But I need to look at your ribs my Queen. I'm worried about you. If you wouldn't mind removing your chest armor and disrobing your Yukata. I need to feel your ribs. Along with your wrist." Metiur said that and was looking at her like the royal healing cleric use to. Not one bit interested in her beauty as she could tell from her many times fooling around with Huspecia. Metiur wasn't in the slightest interested in her physically. So professional in demeanor and attitude was his manors.

As Kumithra got up she realized she had failed to keep Rarailmuir awake. His eyes had closed and he no longer whispered or said the oddest things she couldn't understand. He was motionless. Her eyes began to tear up as she frowned and a trickle of blood ran down her chin. "Oh, No Rarailmuir!!!" She began shaking his shoulders vigorously with a panicked look on her face.

Metiur kneeled in beside her and moved her gently away. "Move aside my Queen let me see."

Kumithra moved to the side and was worried that she would get some dreadful news from Metiur.

He placed two fingers on Rarailmuir's jugular and measured for a pulse. It was strong. "You did hear his heart when I came in right?"

"Yes." Said Kumithra.

"King Rarailmuir is fine my Queen. The medication made him strong again and he's doing just fine. He'll be up in no time and he owes it all to your loving care my Queen." Metiur was proud of his Queen for taking care of her King. It was so much like a fairytale.

Except usually it was the King caring for his Queen. Based off of tales told of King Sinderthion and Queen Zantkara. In that story Queen Zantkara under a different name was the one in Rarailmuir's spot and King Sinderthion was her healing cleric. Roles had reversed it would seem and now Kumithra was more like her Father.

Metiur looked over to his Queen. "I need you to remove your Armor and Yukata, Guards keep everyone out unless it's Fedarious." Metiur had a trusting suspicion of Fedarious that he would be okay to look upon the bandaging and medical treatment of the Queen. It was also a trick and test Metiur had arranged for Fedarious. Not a mean or cruel test. Just a test of mutual trust and understanding and something Metiur wanted to share to see if it was the same.

The Queen thought it was odd how Metiur thought of Fedarious yet didn't mind. Thought some rather cute thoughts of Metiur and Fedarious. 'That was absurd though, Interesting but absurd,' so she thought. Kumithra removed her helmet and let her hair fall where she was kneeling near Metiur. While it appeared Metiur liked her hair more than her and even looked jealous of her hair as it dropped upon the floor.

"You have lovely hair my Queen. You'll have to let me clean and style it for you while we have the time." Metiur couldn't help himself he wanted to get a brush and comb through the tangles and wash her hair. He always liked hair as by his own stylish hair he cut and trimmed himself.

Kumithra thought it was funny for him to pay so much attention to her hair that she had to know. She took off her armor and placed it on the ground reaching toward Metiur. Hoping he'd look at her chest as she let her Yukata sag just enough to expose her bra underneath. Metiur just kept looking at her hair.

She felt a little rejected and dramatically removed her Yukata provocatively. Metiur had to have seen it. She did it exactly how she rehearsed with Huspecia on the day they practiced to tease

the foreigner in the gallery. Yet Metiur only admired her hair. She undid her Yukata down to her waist and while pulling her arm from the sleeve screamed in pain as she removed it. There right under her right breast and ribs was a huge black, purple and red filled with blood injury.

Yes, only when she cried out in pain did Metiur look at her body. His eyes went right from her hair down to her ribs. Completely and totally not taking an interest in her bra covered breasts. It was a nice lacy bra, one of the most fanciful brassieres with lace frill on it. Still Metiur didn't even seem to care. Kumithra heard of professional healing clerics like her royal physician but usually they had been eunuchs or female.

To Kumithra's understanding when she asked Thernya. There are no eunuch's in the Guard. Metiur was way to professional for a novice healer with little skill. Then she sounded loudly in pain again as Metiur began feeling her ribs.

Fedarious came into the room with some blankets, food and water. "I got some food and water for our couple here and some blankets to keep you warm." He reached over to the vent and could feel the heat picking up through the grate covering it. "Yep just as I thought. Heating duct."

He placed the food, water and blankets by Kumithra and sat next to Metiur looking at her hair. 'Seriously why are they both looking at my hair and not my boobs?' Kumithra thought while letting out another bit of pain as Metiur was touching her ribs.

"Just as I thought that monster kick broke a couple of your ribs. You are lucky my Queen. You are lucky I caught you. That monster broke a couple of your lower ribs and sprained a few more. I'll have to bandage your ribs tightly. It's going to hurt but this magics injection health medicine should help a lot along with this magics salve. Both will reduce the pain but you'll need to sleep for it all to work. I suggest eating something now and drink a little water before sleeping." Metiur gave her the injection in the upper left arm first with a slight sting that simply dissolved, as relief was near immediate for the pain she had been feeling was subsiding quickly.

With that Metiur gave Kumithra some food and began applying salve and ointment to medicate and heal the broken ribs. Before bandaging her loosely with medical magics padding after

applying the ointment below her breast on her bruised body. That soothed the pain very quickly and she started feeling strange as the room became brightly lit. The effects of the medication began affecting her mind. She knew Metiur also tended to her sprained wrist with a tighter bandage. Not realizing she was greedily chomping away at the toughened meat that over filled her mouth and tasted like a cosmic explosion of stored juices in her mouth. She had been starving all morning.

Fedarious was looking at Metiur and spoke to him about doubling the guard with death guard they trusted outside the King's and Queen's room. He also reported that another guard with some healing cleric knowledge is treating the other guard's leg. He was doing better. All guards are being warmed and drinking water and eating and they sent a patrol to investigate the other hall in the back that had a sealed door. That they opened with a slight breeze blowing in.

Metiur and Fedarious both began caring for the queen's hair and Kumithra just let them. As it felt nice and she had no reason to object as the medication kicked in. She was feeling really good and somewhat detached and effulgent.

Fedarious didn't even look at the Queen's body not even once. He just looked at Metiur as they both fixated on her hair. It was so strange. Until another guard entered the room and was reporting something to Metiur and Fedarious the Queen wasn't able to make out. Except the guard couldn't stop looking at her bare shoulders from behind and was trying to see her breasts until he was dismissed. That was the only guard Kumithra got a natural response from and weirdly Fedarious and Metiur apologized for that guard's behavior.

Slowly he bandaged the last wound of the injection in her arm of the health potion administered to Kumithra. Metiur began to speak muffled and slow. "You're going to feel weird for a while. You got a lot of healing medications and they have been known to have side effects. Glad you had been eating and drank some water." Kumithra couldn't remember the water or the food but felt her stomach was fuller. Feeling her cheeks being inflated like a squirrel with nuts looking around for more to shove into her mouth. When did she eat or drink anything she couldn't remember but she was shoving more of the food into her mouth or was she?

The bandages were covering her waist and Fedarious was cleaning her hair as Metiur put on her Yukata just like she would of put it on herself. Covering her up not anything near how Rarailmuir dressed her, but the opposite. Not one of them really interested in her body just more interested in her hair for some weird reason. She didn't mind it felt like she went to the hairdresser and felt nice. Fedarious had a bucket of hot water and a brush. Where did he get a brush? She wanted to but decided against asking for a manicure. Fearing she might actual get one.

Metiur had spoken to her again. "There that should do it. Sorry about the weirdness my Queen. The bandages and magics should do the trick just get some rest and we'll make sure you and the king are not disturbed." Weirdness was an understatement as they both got up talking face to face to one another and Kumithra could swear they quickly touched each other hands but maybe she was imagining it.

They had left her alone in the room as she ate more food and drank some water without realizing it. She was getting groggy and very tired. She remembered kind of yawning and then eating something, kind of? The room looked weird and was glowing. She was smiling and in euphoria. Then her eyes saw the blanket and she grabbed it. Unfolding the blanket as she looked at Rarailmuir. His chest was moving up and down with each breath and she could hear his heart beating stronger half way across the room. She felt herself pulled to his body. Looked at his strong male hand with blood pulsing through the veins of his hand. The hand that touched her the way she wanted at the wedding.

She got closer with the unfolded and unrolled blanket in one hand and reached out and grabbed Rarailmuir's hand in hers. Pulling closer to him. As her face and loving eye's looked deeply at Rarailmuir who was snoring but to her it was a lovely spring breeze of air touching upon her face. Although his breath was foul and stank from days since he last brushed. It was as sweet smelling petals of Yamazakura to her. Kumithra saw the straps of his armor and quickly worked to remove his armor as her eyes danced on his body. Removed his weapons to the side and opened the chest of his Yukata as her eyes danced on his exposed skin along with her hands.

He was warm, so warm and she was feeling funny thoughts that moistened her lips and made her heart pump faster and she felt emphatically euphoric. She was trembling and thickening and could feel a change in her of lustfully wanting. She had pulled his open hand. Pressing it tight to her left breast and pushing in towards her heart. "I forgive you my love, I do love you and you are my King." She hadn't forgot the story. She couldn't conceal her true ensorcelled feelings and lust for Rarailmuir with the medication in her.

She was drugged and feeling far too good from the healing magics. Spun her head to whip her clean and newly shiny hair with a whoosh through the air. Feeling her long neck and then looking romantically down upon Rarailmuir. His eyes closed and what a pity. He would have liked the sight and vision of his queen upon him. So she thought.

Rarailmuir's body was hers for the taking like a bandit. She could do as she pleased with him and she would do just that. What was that she wanted to do? She wasn't sure for she never had any experience in the matter. Mere imagined ideas from forbidden books. Yet feeling her heart pound and fear building because she would have to disrobe and the fear of building anxiety was just too much.

Carefully she kept his hand on her breast and crawled up on top of his pelvis while still being clothed. She could feel his groin in his trousers and moved a little back and forth much ecstatic. She could do what she wanted and Rarailmuir was powerless. She then looked at his heaving chest with a smile. And began arranging herself to rest upon top of Rarailmuir she wanted to listen to the comfort of his beating heart. It made her feel alive and she kept his hand on her breast so he could feel her heart as well. She pushed into his warm chest and felt his other hand. Hoping and willing him to place his other arm and hand on the small of her back under the blanket as she lay down upon him.

With a mind of it's own, as if hearing Kumithra's inner thoughts. Rarailmuir's hand raised up and grab her waist and she loved it. As she covered them both with the blanket she brought with her. Listening to the rhythm of his heart.

It was so relaxing and exceptionally warm. She was swimming in imagination and ecstatic ecstasy. Was she doing it

right? She didn't know but it seemed she was, her eyes closed and she began dreaming vivid thoughts. Rarailmuir was all over her and she was inside him and seeking his soul. Listening to the joy of his heart and massaging his brain... In reality she had fallen a sleep and was dreaming a sequence you could only imagine in a form of extreme abstract impressionism created by an artist in oil of the most vibrant swirling and moving colors that could melt and blend and shade and separate into their base colors and create symbology of flowers and reaching in the neon as the stars of the heavens washed over her and the nature of what is and would be.

Becoming three-dimensional evolving out of two-dimensional substrata. Proliferating beyond a fourth dimension and a child growing out of the swamp filled her mind. Rarailmuir's face and body was the main theme and much of what she didn't know she didn't seem to mind.

As the dream went on Rarailmuir became distant like a memory only solidifying by a shape in form similar to that of Rarailmuir. But wasn't his skin wasn't that of a sea elf, he was from the mainland. She had seen that face before in the gallery of the Grand City a third of a third of a season ago. That face looked upon her as if the world dissolved in a bright luminous land of Yamazakura petals and trees. On a path they could only walk and only she was in that world of his. Which then transcended and reformed. From the cosmic stars a tear fell from the heavens. At incredible burning descending speeds and crashed on Ishormot in the lands of cold. Dropping onto her heart and her sole the awakening of a shared spirit from a tree planted by a mother of natural Ishormot Faefolken of the Dawn.

Glowing eyes in the distance of an alien forest she had never seen. A child abandoned, alone, surrounded by death in a swamp and lifted up in the arms of a tree. Kumithra had never seen and a child was nestled to her larger bare breast and suckled. As tree's had moved and the roots of Ishormot became living beings. Fantastical creatures of myth and legend approached her and it was a Gaiaggan. The Queen Mother Gaiaggan that was a being of the woods and nature of the first Fae. A walking tree that reached to give her a gift of life a seed not to be taken for granted. A seed of the future and the healing of a world as a marble sculpture of a female mage in a garden smiled and winked. Kumithra was happy

for the gift of life and could hear its heart just like Rarailmuir's. With the foreign elf's eyes of blue sun fire replacing that of her Rarailmuir's.

That heart became two and the smaller beat stronger and different and powerful with love. The gift was a child that was not a sea elf and then it was a sea elf. The Gaiaggan smiled at Kumithra and then disappeared into a radiant beam of sunlight as Kumithra could feel magics beyond the magics currently healing was at work. She descended from the heavens with the sword of Yoranthium that beat like her heart. Cradled in her arms with the blue sun fire eyes behind her embracing her waist and smiling together at a bundle of joy.

The sword dissolved into her hands. As a victorious saintly and Godly trumping and beating thumping of a joyous music in her head she had never heard before. An angel was seen before her. An Archangel who approved and blessed her love with love that was all too familiar.

The music tempo speed up and changed. It was primal, spiritual, angelic and gentle and yet forceful a song of power beating of a heart. As lights made shapes and images in the dark and her and Rarailmuir glowed with glowing necklaces and bracelets. Not Rarailmuir but just as massive. Neon face and body paints and they danced on one anothers skin in a crowd of strange people and places in the dark on a stage, a stage of bronze, gold, and silver walls. With an orb of reflective light dancing with reflective orbs filling the beam of light shaped rooms. Morphing and altereing as a vision of clouds and heights of what was never known danced behind them with metallic shimmering birds of oddity under the sky.

She changed and he changed, a window of massive buildings and weird flat stones and walls of glass. Her hair was metallic red with pink eyes and he was tall and wore strange clothes dressing him well. Her head twitched and he was in love with her no matter her problems. With a pounding and beating music that just became more than her mind could take and she simply in the dream closed her eyes. As her mind exploded in rapid visions of things she couldn't understand. Carriages of no horses and an ascent into the stars to a planet past a huge world of gas and rings and floating rocks beyond a red world to one that was blue. Then back to

Ishormot and the tear fell from the heavens.

Then she witnessed a moment of an angel and a face of creation and her God. There was a conversation she heard and forgot she heard and then. She couldn't remember. Was she beside herself?

Opening them to see Rarailmuir's right hand on her breast along with the wedding band that was being soiled and caked in dry blood. Her head pressed to a skin pillow of a beating heart and she heard. "Well hello my Kumithra. I thought I was just your General? Seeing you are in bed with me. Does this mean I've been promoted to King again?" He flexed his mighty right hand upon her breast.

She had become frozen in surprise.

Having no idea what just happened. Was any of it real? Then she felt something touching her in the lower pelvis. On the flaps of her delicate skin between her legs as Rarailmuir squeezed her breast ever so gently. She released his hand and raised her head at an alarming speed as she pushed and jumped away from Rarailmuir. Undoing his searching hand on her back. Leaving him without a blanket and she could see his bare naked chest and the offending appendage that had gown in his crotch area, as the blanket flew to the other side of the room next to the grate of the heated duct.

She looked at herself and was satisfied she was still wearing her Yukata, belt, long boots and pants. Oh, she still had her pants on. So did he rechecking his pup tent. She didn't want a child and she knew if her pants were gone she'd be pregnant. Thankfully that wasn't the case. She was blushing and alarmed. What did Metiur do to her, fortunately she wasn't feeling any pain from her injuries that were bandaged. Whatever Metiur did she was now healed. Apparently Rarailmuir was healed too and he seemed in very good health. From simply looking at his groin she could tell he was very healthy. She couldn't keep her eyes off…

"Uhm, Kumithra my eye's are up here." Rarailmuir had raised himself to sitting position on the litter he'd been on. Smiling. Moving his left hand fingers away from his groin to his face and stopping at his eyes. Kumithra's eyes danced on his body following his hand motion. Rarailmuir smiled. "So how did I lose my armor and get half way undressed? Apparently someone still can't help

herself. It's okay you can admit it. Apparently I like you too." He moved his hand downwards trying to get Kumithra to follow.

Which she almost hypnotically fell for it and was about to follow his hand back down to his groin. This is when he realized she wasn't falling for it so he jumped to his feet and made her look. "Yep. I knew it. You are a pervert Kumithra." He was laughing now as Kumithra blushed and turned her back at him. Annoyed at his antics.

He approached her from behind and she could feel him poking her backside while he hugged her. She was so tempted to spin in his arms and jump on him. Wanted to rip off his clothing and realized they had rested a long time and there was danger they still had to face and a band of guards to get to Sea Shore with.

"As your Queen release me!!!" She angrily commanded trying to hate Rarailmuir for his lies to her. But she couldn't. "My, my, my, King." For who else could she ever be close too? Might as well admit the truth. She couldn't avoid her feelings there was no one else here on Yoranthium. Just Rarailmuir and her in a kingdom that was doomed.

What did it matter they may not live that long anyway.

Rarailmuir came to his senses and realized she promoted him back to King. He reluctantly took a few moments to think it over and he finally released her and began backing away from her. "I'm sorry my queen. I can't take advantage of you. I did not do you justice or honor with my behavior."

She spun around with a serious expression that was very royal and commanding like her mothers. She caught his right wrist and held it up. "Keep this on you at all times. It seems to remind us what we had been to one another. I need time to think about us Rarailmuir. I was only this way because Metiur wanted me to keep you alive. I think it worked and you look.... Never mind! Your body.... You... Never mind!"

"As you like my Queen. I understand you better than you think. It'll take us time. I thank you my Queen for caring so deeply when I had not been as faithful as I should have been. I wish I knew of you before the dragon attack. Before I investigated Xern and his evil that brought me to that wicked place." Rarailmuir's hand was released and he looked at the wedding binding. Rubbed the back of his neck as he turned to collect his armor and fix his

Yukata as Kumithra admired his strong muscular back watching him get dressed and she helped him with his armor.

She gave Rarailmuir her chest armor to help her put it on right. Where he saw a massive crack on it. "Kumithra how did you survive this? An impact like this would have killed most warriors and elves I know. You are no warrior you aren't tough enough to survive this. Would have shattered your ribs and destroyed your lungs and should have stopped your heart."

"What do you mean? I have bandages and magics healing me. I feel fine right now. Metiur is better than he thinks at healing magics. He could be a healing cleric." Fact is Metiur was mediocre at best and could not of healed her wounds so well. He gave her the wrong healing potion in the injection. The reality was the Yamazakura Gaiaggan had more to do with her healing than Kumithra realized.

Gaiaggan's are nature-connected beings of mythical lore that many elves never see. They are as old as Ishormot and the first creatures to walk the land. Fae so old that time the elves knew them passed so much that the elves forgot they even existed. The Gaiaggan's of Yoranthium were of nature hidden by nature and one had been rooted to the very room that Rarailmuir and Kumithra had been in. The Gaiaggan's had been in pain in Yoranthium ever since the darkness fell and demons began destroying the land.

Kumithra was healed because Gaiaggan's can feel one another anywhere on Ishormot. She only survived and lived by a power she didn't understand. Gaiaggan's don't need eyes; their eyes are simply a glowing distraction for those with eye's to not see the roots that are the life of a Gaiaggan. The Mother Queen Gaiaggan seen Kumithra knew of her from the visions of a child. A child Kumithra was destined to meet or did meet or might meet. Saved by the power of the heavens that forged the world tree itself.

Time is a fickle thing with Gaiaggan's they are immortal and can never truly die. Kumithra was known and the healing magics of the root of this Gaiaggan healed her. With a power Kumithra did not know was hidden. The mistaken application of that healing injection drugged Kumithra. Metiur wasn't that good not one bit. Rarailmuir would have not survived the night for not of the root of the Gaiaggan in the very room and the spores it

released after knowing of their entrance into this bunker. The primordial fae had been healing all of them and protecting them from the whispered words of a higher power.

If Kumithra took the time to look up she would have seen the pinkish petals of a Yamazakura Gaiaggan hanging from a root. It was small and obscured in the dark.

"Look, I was injured too and you can see. It's a nasty bruise." At this point Kumithra wasn't too bashful around Rarailmuir. She knew he would never take advantage of her. So she undid her Yukata and removed the bandage. Rarailmuir looked at her bra and Kumithra after a moment had to motion with her finger for him to look further down with some annoyance. "Hum."

"What am I looking for?" Rarailmuir raised his palms up in the air not knowing what to look at.

The serious bruising was gone and Kumithra could feel with her hand her ribs had healed and she felt normal.

"I could touch you there if you like Kumithra. Seems you don't need the bandages." Rarailmuir was reaching towards her body again.

She slapped his hand away while tossing away the bandages. "Never mind, like I said I need time." She quickly put her Yukata on as she let Rarailmuir put on her chest armor. "I don't know anymore. Last night was weird and I had the weirdest dream. Something I never dreamt before, like a vision."

Just then a loud booming could be heard outside. Screaming and hissing could be heard this far below the mound. A commotion was taking place above the bunker. It wasn't good as sounds of different kinds of magics at work and powerful monstrosities had engaged in battle.

It was a lone Mechanation that had encountered the main form of the Gaiaggan protecting the bunker. The Gaiaggan had decided to sacrifice itself to protect a valuable asset of the Queen Mother Gaiaggan. This Yamazakura Gaiaggan had distracted the Mechanation that was going to bust through the ceiling and surprise the sea elves below. It had seen the heat of the magics black-rocks in a heat sensitive view port that the sea elves had never known about or anticipated. Part of the reasons the Mechanation knew exactly where to go and find them.

The Gaiaggan had launched a rooted boulder attack that slammed into the Mechanation. Busted a claw that fell to the ground to hinder the Mechanation's movement. The Mechanation had to move the heavy appendage like an anchor holding it back. This giving a massive advantage of the Gaiaggan to move faster than the Mechanation dodging a buzz saw blade appendage that swung in its direction. The Gaiaggan raised its two arms and lifted what passed for a head towards the sky and cried out bellowing pollen that infected every living creature for a league around the Gaiaggan.

The living creatures all infected with the spores as pinkish roots dug into them and sprouted pink five leafed budding flowers. Only self determined creatures being immune to the effects of this call of the wild. Any lesser creature became a servant and driven with a rage directed by the Gaiaggan. This included a group of twenty depth dwellers that followed the Mechanation.

The infected depth dwellers had been primitive creatures that once had been equals to the sea elves in intelligence, the thousandths of revolutions that the depth dwellers worshiped the deep dark abyss with no choice given to them. Became backward and introverted species. Their minds eroded and robbed from their kind.

Even the Depth Dweller shamans were similarly regressed and only responded to the psychic force of larger more developed deep dark creatures such as the Tredinak's and Yagrallmagrund's and many others deep dark creatures possessing dark magics of enslavement.[32]

This was perfect for the Gaiaggan to take control of the Depth Dwellers that ran up behind the Mechanation and began attacking it. The Depth Dwellers being unusually strong and could rip limbs off the Mechanation with very little effort as they were twice the size of a sea elf such as Rarailmuir. The Mechanation had to refocus and justify it's action through some kind of programmed process that took a little bit of time. Time that put the Mechanation at a great disadvantage as it lost its main siege weapon and several other cutting and pincer and claw arms. Even lost it's ability to

[32] Land of the potentate Book 3 speaks on the issue of modern inequality leading to slavery and oppressive means. The Depth Dweller topic of interest begins in the Isle of Forumth Book 4.

detect heat of other living and burning things that gave off significant heat.

Then the Mechanation adjusted it's programming and determined the depth dwellers were hostile and an enemy. It activated the most logical of it weapons. The torch. And found the central mass of the twenty attacking depth dwellers that was its support unit. Activated it's flame thrower and incinerated over fifteen of them instantly. Leaving only five that had been clinging to its outsides.

Not only that the flamethrower had impacted the woods and the massive root system of the Yamazakura Gaiaggan. Placing the Gaiaggan into a lot of pain. As it realized the saplings it had cared for since the founding of Yoranthium from the day's after it ceased to be volcanic becoming a fresh new land where trees could take root. Parts of the Gaiaggan were on fire and its forest. Becoming enraged and angered by the destruction and fire brought by the Mechanation.

The entire bunker began to shake from one set of roots to another. Cracks started to form in the bunker. Metiur had run to the room of the King and Queen. "We got to get out of here it would seem this place isn't going to last long. Whatever is going on outside it's going to crush this place."

"Where are we going Metiur?" Rarailmuir needed to know.

"There's a passage we haven't fully explored and the scouts haven't returned yet. They were to go to the end of the tunnel and report back." Metiur needed input because it was a risk to go down a tunnel that the guards sent down there hadn't come back from.

"We'll go down that tunnel. Get the guard ready to go. Before you ask. We are perfectly well and Metiur be more careful with that injecting magics." Kumithra told Metiur savagely snapping at him. He left the room going out to the guard and getting them ready to move out along with Fedarious.

The Gaiaggan knew Kumithra was below its root dangling from the ceiling. It detached its root and dropped it onto Kumithra's helmet and moved down towards her hair. Once it got there it wrapped itself in tightly tucked up and under her helmet. The Gaiaggan could feel the fire burning away at it's root system as the Mechanation turned to incinerate the Gaiaggan trying to tear off the remaining three depth dwellers still under it's control. The

Gaiaggan burned crackled and popped loudly as it's main body was burned.

This did not stop the possessed depth dwellers from tearing away at the Mechanation and finally one of the depth dwellers broke one of the fuel canisters for the flamethrower. That began spraying out fuel that came in contact with a burning root and the fire followed up the stream of flammable fluid until it reached the fuel canister and exploded followed by an explosion of the other fuel canister. Destroying the Mechanation, along with the remaining possessed depth dwellers and incinerating the entire area scorching with fire everything flammable.

This was bad for the bunker there were many roots keeping this bunkers roof from collapsing the Gaiaggan had made this it's home and laid out a vast amount of roots. It was feeding off the very magics that made the dark stone. As parts of the roots caught fire the roof was weakening and pieces of ceiling began falling. At first it was small chunks and gradually getting larger.

Kumithra could see the danger and her and Rarailmuir came out of the room. "Move out now down the tunnel!!!" Just as Kumithra gave the order, a large chunk fell on top of the wounded guard with the broken leg crushing his skull to a bloody pulp. It was no longer safe to stay in this room as more and more material was collapsing. It was shear panic enveloping all the guards and trying to fit into the tunnel all at once.

Metiur and Fedarious seen the King and Queen hadn't made it to the tunnel yet and realized the guards were in the way. They had been yelling "Make way for the king and the queen!!!" Tossing guards to the side trying to make room. It was tough going no one wanted to die like the injured guard died. They pushed Metiur and Fedarious back, as they are no stronger than any other guard.

Eventually Rarailmuir got to the congested entrance. "Make way for your King and Queen!!!" Rarailmuir's voice was the loudest voice of them all and the entire room reverberated with the echoing of his voice and the ground actually shook. It wasn't Rarailmuir's voice that shook the ground it was the support columns about to give way as the burning roots became more apparent. Down to the very bunkers foundations. With no roots down the unknown escape corridor.

The guard believed it was Rarailmuir's voice and he was big and tossing guards to the side to let Kumithra to move between them. The guard had more fear of Rarailmuir and his voice and would rather take their chances in the collapsing room than having to push or shove their own king out of the way.

Kumithra again was impressed with Rarailmuir and felt like he was saving her from the dragon all those revolutions ago and she was in the burning school. She could feel her nose shrivel and was feeling teary eyed. Fortunately no guard could see her eyes that well behind her helmet. They were none the wiser for how special she felt having Rarailmuir defending her and escorting her to the head of those trying to go down the Tunnel. She began itching at the point in her arm of the healing injection.

Rarailmuir reached Metiur and Fedarious. "Good job guys, now get the remaining guard down the tunnel behind us. You ten death guard take the lead make sure the way is clear and look for the initial scouts."

The ten guards went down the tunnel in haste with light magics leading the way. All the remaining guard made it into the tunnel as another massive quake shattered the bunkers floor and the roof along with the burning remains of the colossal Mechanation and the giant Gaiaggan came crashing down. Metiur found another lever and a door slammed shut behind them keeping the cloud of dust and dirt from filling and choking them in the tunnel.

There was a nice breeze flowing down the tunnel and it stopped once the door closed. Apparently the open door was part of a air cycling system built into the storage bunker. The real purpose of this bunker was never understood and no one spoke the ancient inscriptions on various placards on the walls and the support framing.

The group simply kept pushing further and further into the dark tunnel wondering how long their illuminated magics would last and hopefully this tunnel led to a way out.

Yoranthium

Book One: Lost Hope

Chapter Twenty-Three: All Hope is Lost

By Mark P. Bromley

So it comes to this a tragic end of a kingdom that was meant to survive until the end of time. The nightmare isn't over we need to find out the fate of the King and Queen of Yoranthium.

As all hope is lost for Yoranthium.

They had been going down the tunnel for some time. It was difficult to tell how long they had been in the tunnel. Was it sunwanes, a day, was it day or night. None of them knew they could only guess they were refreshed before they came down the tunnel. The chaos of getting all the remaining guards to safety was a little diquieting but nothing that was too discouraging. It was ordinary for panic in an emergency and Rarailmuir felt his unit of death guard's spirit was breaking. He trained the guard for emergencies not to place their own lives above others. Yet what he had to fight through to get Him and Kumithra to safety was out of character for his guard and himself.

Of course the Queen and King are the most important. Yet the guard would be demoralized by that clarification. Rarailmuir already used privilege instead of inspiration. He used raw power and the environment to his advantage to exert his dominance. He realized Metiur and Fedarious had been silent for some time. Could they be angry with their King and Queen for delegating them to care for the rear guard?

It was quite possible his command was failing. He was expecting a plausible plan of action from either Fedarious or Metiur. All he got was silence. They had been down this tunnel a long time and no one spoke. Even the ten guards ahead of them haven't been heard from. That's twenty missing guard and his guard was dwindling fast. Only seventy left with him and the queen on point. This was getting risky with not knowing what happened to the guard ahead of them.

"Hold up." Rarailmuir raised his hand in clenched fist so Metiur and Fedarious could see. Signaling a stop.

"What is it?" Fedarious was unenthusiastic and Metiur was completely disinterested.

Yes Rarailmuir made a mistake. His command was shattered. He could see Metiur being upset over how he was spoken to by the Queen over his use of injection healing magics. Rarailmuir couldn't blame him for doing his best given the situation. Kumithra could have done better handling that sensitive issue. As it made her do strange things, not that Rarailmuir objected he was wondering how it would be to have his body pressed to hers. He liked it. He liked too much and she was far warmer and firm than Dresdie ever was.

So good for Metiur he did do some repairs to their relationship. As for Fedarious he did have to get one thing strait. "Look Fedarious, we are under stress and I am still your King and this is your Queen. Our kingdom is falling and we have lost too many. I understand you are losing hope and faith but I still need you and the remaining guards do. Remember who we are as a people. Let us be brave and be Yoranthian's. I didn't award you for being anything less and I want you and Metiur to be much more. I can't do this without you, Metiur and the guard. We got to do this together." Rarailmuir could see he kind of got through to Fedarious and Metiur.

The strain of command was wearing thin on them and they found Rarailmuir's admitting to be weak and needing them comforting. It was likely the best apology Rarailmuir as a king was capable of. Fedarious signaled by pointing to Rarailmuir. His thumb pointed to Metiur and his finger pointed to Kumithra with a frown on his face.

Rarailmuir looked up and let out some air. Metiur was upset at how Kumithra spoke to him and this upset Fedarious. Metiur was owed an apology from Kumithra for her chastisement of his healing methods. Metiur wasn't a Healing cleric not even in training. He was more of an observer that had some talent for the healing arts. Kumithra owed Metiur some support and by doing so she would get them back to almost their former selves. Rarailmuir won Fedarious back by his understanding and motioned for Fedarious to have them wait, as he turned and went over to Kumithra.

"Hello my Queen." Said Rarailmuir kindly.

"What!" Kumithra snapped back. Scratching more savagely at the arm that was injected.

Rarailmuir realized she was on defense now and still unable to determine or sort out her feelings. This was bad. If he couldn't fix this mess soon he could end up with mutiny in his ranks. This could be bad for him and the queen. So much death and his unit was diminishing and still none of the forward guard arrived. They were all on edge. Having experienced too much defeat in the past quarter of days.

Rarailmuir needed to send more guard at least half to protect their front and defend their retreat. Ordering the guard

now to do this would be difficult if they couldn't get Metiur and Fedarious to buy in and help out. In this oneway tunnel they needed to know if the forward twenty had met a terrible fate.

It was quiet and no steps were heard ahead of them. "My Queen I need you to speak kindly with Metiur. You need to apologize for insulting his lack of skill. He's doing his best he's not a healing cleric you know. He doesn't fully understand those magics. So what. You got a little strange last night. I'm not complaining. You helped me live and now you and I are fully healed. We had a little moment and repaired some of our problems. Only because of Metiur and he usually does the right thing for good people." Rarailmuir spoke sweetly to Kumithra with respect and understanding. He could see she was still torn and confused with her feelings. Oddly sweating and weirdly agitated for something seeking gratification it would seem.

Fedarious seen Zantkara like this once before. He thought it was sweet that Rarailmuir and Kumithra were like this like Sinderthion and Zantkara all over again. He looked at Metiur and could see he was not impressed.

Kumithra was not listening to well to Rarailmuir. "They are your boys! You are in charge of them! Why should I apologize? I'm their Queen!" Poking Rarailmuir's chest with her index finger for each point. Never having been like this.

"Please my queen. They might be guards but they are volunteers they are your people and they were the common folk like all those we sent away with Bronanes, Thernya and Huspecia to evacuate as refugees to Forumth. We need them to help us get off of Yoranthium too. We are going into Sea Shore and the harbor that is over ran with demonic forces. I don't think we'll make it without them. If they stay behind they would likely all die. You understand?" Rarailmuir was concerned it seemed Kumithra was fighting a war of the heart in her mind.

It was the drug of that injection and now she was clearing it out of her system. She was feeling like she was missing something from that injection. She was imagining a pain in her that wasn't there. She was beginning to sweat now and shivered uncontrolled. "It's not that. Rarailmuir I need it, I need that injection again! I'm losing control! I can feel it!" She snapped at Rarailmuir harshly. Scratching at her skin where she was injected. "Get it for me! Go

get it! Make me happy!" Turning and pushing Rarailmuir back towards Metiur.

Metiur then looked at Fedarious as he heard her scream at Rarailmuir. He ran over to Fedarious. "Oh, this is bad. She was right I did mess up with that injection. She's drugged and now addicted." Metiur was warned about that type of injection. It came from a seed of a red flowering plant with a bulb.[33] If handled by the trusted healing clerics it was a medicine. Yet in the hands of the inexperienced or criminal minds it was an addictive narcotic. Even for the guard's field healers it was always a risk to use.

Rarailmuir didn't know what to do. He never saw this before. He seen people act like this at Dresdie's but never dealt with it personally. Now it was Kumithra. She's never been vulnerable and exposed to the realities of some of the shadier things in life. Now she was coming down hard off that injection that was wearing off finally. Her entire behavior was off. Rarailmuir had told Kumithra he'd help her. Went to where Fedarious and Metiur were. Hoping that they understood.

"I'm sorry, she's not going to do it." Rarailmuir approached the two whispering.

Understanding the need for discretion. "It's okay my king, I understand what I did wrong. Kumithra was right and it's really not her talking anymore. It's called a poison and sickness that people can get addicted too. About point zero five percent of people have this problem with the healing injections. Honestly I don't know all these healing potions they all look similar. It is my fault my King." Metiur was the one apologizing now realizing his mistake and what Kumithra must have been going through.

"You did as well as you could Metiur given the circumstances. It's been bad on all of us. I also apologize for my behavior earlier, you my guard are important to me. What can I do now?" Rarailmuir could see he was winning both of them over again. Even if it was at the risk of his Queen like in a game of strategy.

"I know this is nothing. Just some water and sugar in a heavy dose. I think she might relax simply by thinking she's on it

[33] Commonly the poppy seed or opium plant the first of many drugs created by drug cartels. Especially used in the USA as the reason behind brutal slavery by a certain political parties founding to harvest enslaving mass quantities.

again. It's not the best solution but she should be manageable for some time. Hopefully we buy her enough time to not need it in the future." Metiur pulled out another injection that was clear.

"Are you sure about this Metiur? I'm counting on you being right." Rarailmuir was looking Metiur in the eyes.

"Yes my King. I think this should help. You will have to keep her close to you at all times and monitor her condition. It's not going to be easy if we run into trouble. I'll do my part to get the guard to defend us along with Fedarious." Metiur was ready to inject Kumithra again.

Fedarious was concerned knowing Metiur was a little skittish over having messed up. None the less Fedarious needed to learn where they are. "Sire I wish we had the celestial mapmakers. Don't know what happened they simply disappeared at the last bastion. They would be so useful right now. We need to keep moving. I'd like to take half the guard up ahead and try and find the others if we can."

Rarailmuir forgot about the important mapmakers. Was alarmed that they got reported to as missing and disappearing. Not dead or injured just missing. A mystery for some other day and they would be useful now. Damn untrustworthy mages.

"Very well Fedarious be careful and return if you see anything out of place. If you get a bad feeling you come back. That's an order." Commanded Rarailmuir knowing he didn't want no more guards to go missing. Rarailmuir felt if he kept Metiur with him. Fedarious would want to return. It was worth a shot as he was playing a hunch about the two of them.

"Metiur you'll help the queen right now and then take command of the rear guard and help me monitor the Queen's condition." Rarailmuir looked at Metiur and got a nod of acceptance and a look of regret. Fedarious had headed off with his forward guard down the tunnel. Metiur and Rarailmuir approached the queen.

"Metiur, I'm so sorry, I love you. You got to help me." Kumithra was all over Metiur. Grabbing his hand and pulling him close so she could look him in the eyes by grabbing his shoulders, lovingly seeking his soul. "You know you could be king if you wanted to be. You got what I need the most right now. You do have

it right?" She was smiling and shivering sweating and wild-eyed looking.

Rarailmuir was perplexed never seeing this side of Kumithra. "You'll be okay, I'm right here." He tried to comfort her.

She looked at Rarailmuir with scorn. "You don't have what I need, I don't need you. You aren't the baby in my arms. You are not the child from the tree thing. Go away." Then she looked at Metiur. Bit her lip and asked again. "You have what I want don't you Metiur?" Brushing his cheek with her hand.

"Yes my queen it's right here." She wasn't his type. He didn't show it. Metiur showed her the injection magics instead.

"Quick, I need it badly." She held out her arm for the needle.

Metiur quickly injected her and then pulled it out of her arm. He was surprised as she imagined she was poisoned again. She began becoming more herself and pulled away from Metiur.

"You are dismissed, Metiur. I'll call when I need you again." Then she shot back to Rarailmuir. "Let's go, and get out of here." She bounced up and started going down the tunnel again. Humming a famed treasure raiding song of some female adventurer from a recent play at the opera house in the Grand City. A play a few quarters back where her and her parents had attended in the royal box of the theater. She loved that play because she caught that foreigner in the audience. Often gazing on him in her telescoping theater glasses. He was cute having dozed off frequently not even interested in the consorts him and his protector had with them. She envied the high-class consort next to him. Kumithra felt he missed her and perhaps drank too much from what must have been a busy day for him. She had imagined that adventurer in the play was her saving him and went skipping down the tunnel dreaming of their adventure together. Preparing her knives.

"Hurry up and follow us Metiur. You sure this is working?" Rarailmuir saw Kumithra skipping down the tunnel. "Is that all it took?" He recalled the wild and unstable seductive workers at Dresdie. They acted exactly like what he saw Kumithra just do. He never realized a simple little narcotic could twist people so quickly. He only heard stories from refugees escaping the potentate

kingdom. How the Potentate gave the people free access to narcotics and controlled substances and Kumithra reminded him of the fears the Refugees had when they got to Yoranthium. Stories of them being locked in their homes unable to come outside unless they did the drugs forced on them by the Potentate. He thought they called it a vaccine but others called it one part of a poison of genocide.[34]

"Just stay with her. She's really not that bad off. A real addict would have known the difference. She's still returning to normal. I'd say she might be tired in a short time. Other than that she should be easy to manage. I don't think she'll need another shot and I'm done with the injections anyway." Metiur had learned a valuable lesson and was better for it. Now he had some experience with this magics and his basic training had improved. Leveling up his healing abilities this day. Physical experience strengthens your character.

Rarailmuir knew this was the worst time to have a high risk like the queens condition to deal with. There was to many dangers and some Rarailmuir knew nothing of like those Yagrallmagrund's Fedarious had mentioned. Now he couldn't ask about them for Fedarious had gone on ahead of them.

Fedarious kept moving forward with his group. This was a very long tunnel he found himself in. No signs of the previous guards. Then off in the distance he had seen the twilight purplish black blue of darkness outside at the end of the tunnel. Fedarious was about to sound the return to regroup. Ordering his unit to halt. He heard one of the guards and then another scream behind them.

Upon turning to look he witnessed the two back most guards had tentacles wrapped around their bodies and they were dragged right past him and out toward the end of the tunnel. Then two more were pulled up into the air as the tentacles on the top of the tunnel with pincer claws pulled them through the air slamming them wildly against the walls and down towards the exit. Fedarious had to duck the whipping tentacles.

The process repeated and before Fedarious knew it over half his guard became ensnared and wrapped in tentacles and

---

[34] A warning that of current events that not all plandemics are for our good and can be used as weapons of a drug cartel using medicine to administer a part of a poison (Novachok) meant to manage population growth.

fighting for their lives as each tentacle ended in a claw that was snapping at them. One of the guard's arms got clipped off. While another guard lost his leg. A third got the claw right to his midsection and his guts spilled out to the ground. As the lumination of their light magics showed a grizzly sight of other elven body parts and pieces dismembered in the remainder of the long tunnel.

Another ten of his guard went chasing down the tunnel after their abducted members. That screamed in terror as they tried to free themselves with random swords, daggers and any weapon they could find. All of them simply running and being pulled and abducted towards and out the main entrance. More screams ensued and blood could be seen spraying and splattering, in the dark night salty sea air at the end of the tunnel.

Fedarious along with the remaining guard you could count on one hand. "Retreat!!!" It was clear to Fedarious they were no match for what lurked outside the tunnel and Fedarious realized what it must be. Metiur the King and Queen and the rest were headed to a well placed trap that just devoured twenty-five of his guard. No wonder why the two groups of ten never returned they were eliminated at this point close to the exit of the tunnel. Too small in number and they got devoured none had a chance to escape and report back just not enough of them to fight Yagrallmagrund's.

Yagrallmagrund's in the, "Deep sea folio of demonology," that Fedarious had only read about are massive six king tall monsters that lived their lives normally on the sea bed close to the deep dark abyss. As written about by the Archmage Deriouge, of the lolly gag, fox island. Who used magics he learned from the deep sea elves to explore the depths deeper than any other sea elf. These demons fed on creatures of all kinds at great depths. They had chitin hard scales of three progressively lengthening carapace protecting their back. Covered in a shiny mucus enzyme that was very acidic and would dissolve flesh on contact along with metals and other materials. With a kings length narrow top spike extending off the top like a long fingernail protruding horn. They stood erect with their belly exposed and made of a very strong rough textured stone and circulated and breathed through stone covered porous membranes of three above their centralized mouth very difficult to pierce with traditional metal weapons.

The Yagrallmagrund's central mass was a mouth of four beaks that could fold in and protect an inner orifice like a flower with tiny clawed and pointed tentacles for pulling prey in for it to ingest. To either side of the beak was three, two kings long bone like femur fingers of three knuckles that ended in a similar long horn on the tips of each finger that was webbed and would drip enzyme mucus in front that pooled at the creatures base. Up and down its body was covered in medium king's length larger tentacles that would aid in skewering prey and holding on to it as it fed its mouth. They were eating machines and ate anything getting to close.

The same medium tentacles would protrude from the ground at it's base were it dug into the ground to stabilize it's massive form with a pool of digestive enzymes of mucus and fluid that would allow movement. The enzymes on the ground left a sludge trail of toxic necrotic waste and anything caught in the enzymes slime trail would quickly melt and decay as mutated maggots would hatch and feed on anything in the enzyme soup. Becoming cannibalistic smaller offspring. Using very long clawed tentacles that half of eight would be used to move slowly along the ground and rooting it in place. While four more would search it's surrounding for food and sprawl out very thinly from it's original ten kings length to a great distance of over a hundredth's kings lengths as it flattened to conceal it's tentacles as feelers and traps to ensnare prey. The mage went on to claim over fifty of their apprentices had been lost to these demonic beasts of the depths.

These however were on land and wasn't natural. How did this happen the magics did frighten Fedarious. He simply knew he would have to warn the others. They would have to find another way to escape for he just lost twenty-five guards and didn't get a chance to save any of them. Let alone the two groups of ten that never returned. If there was just a few more tentacles in that tunnel he wouldn't be returning either and perhaps the camouflage should have been something that crazy wizard should of mentioned in the book Fedarious had read on this monstrosity. It wasn't as exciting as he imagined. It was a bloodthirsty insidious monstrosity of pure terror.

They didn't even dare try and see one up close. It would likely be their death if they had tried. The reason the Archmage

lost fifty apprentices to those things out of research and exploration. Just like the poor guard who tried to rescue those wrapped up in the large tentacles. Or having rushed head long to attack it's base only to find themselves stuck and trapped in the mire of dissolving enzymes that would quickly devour any organic material as maggot progeny ate at them.

Fedarious did remember one key aspect of the Yagrallmagrund it had a psychic impression of fear. Yes Fedarious and his remaining guard were wide eyed and in panic. They had felt upon their minds the psychic impression and could only run away as quickly as their feet could carry them. The fear issued from the Yagrallmagrund forced anything attacking it to run so it could thin their numbers and deal with smaller groups at its leisure.

It wasn't long until Fedarious ran right past Kumithra and Rarailmuir. "What's his problem?" Said Kumithra as the other four guards ran past them. She went back to humming a happy tune and excited about being an explorer. She was spinning her daggers around acting like she was on an action adventure in a mysterious ruin. Realizing her regular dagger was harder to spin than her chain dagger.

Rarailmuir turned and chased after Fedarious over to where Metiur was.

"Yagrallmagrund's!!!, Far too many of them. We need another way out. Oh, God we're going to die by Yagrallmagrund's!!! Metiur what should we do? We got to get out of here find another way." Fedarious was holding Metiur in a bear hug and was shaking terrified.

"What the hell is a Yagrallmagrund?" Inquired Rarailmuir.

Fedarious turned his head to his king and with wild and crazy frightened eye's in disbelief that no one knew. Which was a fact no one but Fedarious knew what one was. He quickly and wildly explained the monstrosity. To Rarailmuir and Metiur and the rest of the Guard. Except Kumithra who was humming a child's tomb finder song looking impatient at the group. Not realizing she was now the closest to looming danger.

"Who's seen this?" Inquired Rarailmuir.

Fedarious looked bewildered and shocked and snapped at Rarailmuir. "Only about forty-five other guards who tried fighting

them and died horrible blood spraying deaths. No one lives to get close to these things. You don't want to see one of these up close."

Metiur and Rarailmuir soon realized why only five guards returned. Why the other guard had gone missing and realized Fedarious was right to worry and likely correct in what he said was beyond the exit of this tunnel.

Metiur had a crazy idea. "We might be able to make our own escape from this tunnel. I just don't know what is above us?"

"What's the plan Metiur?" Rarailmuir was so inquisitive. Wanting to learn more.

Metiur had to relax Fedarious to get out of the bear like hug. Fedarious simply stayed close to him like a frightened child. "We use some of our magics to bust the ceiling and then use our daggers to dig to the surface."

"That's it. We dig our way out? I like it Metiur, do it back that way where we came. If this tunnel collapses we have at least this way out." Rarailmuir was impressed again with Metiur and Fedarious's weird ideas. Worked for him so why not entertain their plans.

Kumithra allowed her armor to conceal her as she snuck up on Rarailmuir. "Boo!!!" She dug her fingers into the sides of his ribs and made him jump with a tickle. "So what's up?"

"Kumithra we are trying to get out of here and stay right with me. Hold my hand we might have to run in a bit." Rarailmuir informed her as she was playful and took his hand swinging it. She really couldn't tell she had taken a placebo. It calmed her while she was working off the effects of the first drug.

Rarailmuir was amused and was wondering if he should tell her. Yet watching Metiur set up the magics on the ceiling was more interesting and tense. Watching how meticulous and measured and scientific Metiur was being at his current assignment.

The rest of the death guard had backed up toward Rarailmuir and took up defensive kneeling around their king and queen. A few giggled looking at the Queen swing Rarailmuir's arm back and forth like a child who was rolling on the balls of her little boot sandaled toes.

Fedarious was watching Metiur intently and didn't care to notice his queen's behavior. He was just worried for Metiur's safety as he lit the fuse and ran towards them all. "Cover your ears

tight this is going to get loud!!!" Everyone did just that and Rarailmuir had to put Kumithra's hand over her ears as he covered his own just in time.

The explosions went off one after the other as Metiur ran towards them with Lights flickering and flashing from each magics as it went off. Parts of the ceiling fell and so did lots of dirt from above the ceiling. The tunnel wind direction blew the dust and dirt away from them. Metiur had done a fantastic job. Only the ceiling and some burnt roots and dirt fell into the tunnel. There was still plenty of dirt above the open ceiling they would have to use their daggers to dig through. They couldn't use more explosives out of fear of collapsing more of the ceiling that cracked after the first magics went off.

A small group of guards were assigned to dig the tunnel up through the dirt. After some effort they had been rotated with a new set of guards. They made a ledge so they could stand on the top of the ceiling and after some time passed they finally managed to break to the surface. Those with nothing to do napped and eat and drank water and rested for it had been a long period of time down this tunnel. Many thought by now they should be close to Sea Shore. As the dirt was excavated and revealed the dark cloudy sky above them and bright enough to show it was another day. Sure enough a strong odor of salt water could be sensed among the strong tempest of wind that had been blowing dirt back down the tunnel right at them.

They could also smell the burning of the forest above them. As a flickering glow of oranges, yellows and reds created a different kind of burning light among the dark clouds above them. Burning from the direction they had fled from. The burning forest only gave them one direction to go that of Sea Shore.

Kumithra finally slept during the excavation deciding tomb work was boring. When she awoke she seemed herself again. She found Rarailmuir and apologized for her behavior and if everyone was okay. Rarailmuir was happy to see Kumithra better off as she went over to Metiur and finally thanked him for understanding her and helping her out. Metiur was attending to Fedarious as the psychic effects began wearing off.

It was a heart felt moment, as Kumithra soon realized why they were not interested in her like most of the male guards. She

smiled because she understood. Then went back to Rarailmuir as he began sending guards to the surface to scout the area.

Quickly it was confirmed to be safe enough for them to egress the tunnel. They had broken through into a garden of destroyed homes in Sea Shore. The city was on fire being destroyed while the forest they had fled was also burning out of control. It was a nightmare of cataclysmic destruction and darkness with a flaming inferno growing around them. The war here in Sea Shore was over and the dark forces won days ago. Leaving Sea Shore in ruins burning to the ground. Yoranthium had fallen into the hell fires of damnation. Half the guard Metiur and Fedarious went up first. Being the first to lose hope at the dreadful sight of a massive loss of life and destruction.

Suddenly a commotion could be heard. Fedarious had screamed louder than Kumithra ever had and much sharper in pitch which was painful to hear. He out screamed any female that Rarailmuir ever heard in shear terror upon seeing the Yagrallmagrund far down the street at the end of the tunnel to the beach that connected to the harbor pier. It was a disgusting twisted mess of dissolving enzymes sea elves, bones, maggots and tendrils at some distance away. So far away that the Yagrallmagrund didn't care about them climbing out of the tunnel. Nothing moved toward the guard. They were mostly safe.

Fedarious however wasn't he was barely recovered from his psychic impact of the thoughts of the first Yagrallmagrund. Coming to the surface reestablished his fear of the monstrous creature. Fedarious ran, he ran in fear and he just didn't look back and couldn't hear Metiur calling to him. Metiur looked down to see Rarailmuir.

Rarailmuir now understood Metiur and if it were Kumithra he would want to do the same thing. "Go my friend, go get Fedarious." With that Metiur took off after Fedarious.

Rarailmuir got most of the guard to the surface that were now standing watch, twenty-five at top and ten still at the shaft. Kumithra's turn came and the Guard became nervous for she would be likely the last female they would ever know this day. The one at the top had seen her partially nude and had fantasy's of her in his dreams. He liked his lips trying to hide it from his King. He shouldn't have impure thoughts about his queen. None of the

guards should have but they are males. They went though some traumatic and physically demanding and hard labor recently.

Their awareness of the grim and deadly situation was on their minds and they knew this was their last days and they would not likely live to see another female sea elf again queen or no queen. They all knew their queen was one of the finest beauties of Yoranthium. They knew they had to be careful and not touch her in a way that would offend Rarailmuir.

Rarailmuir saw the look on his men as Kumithra came into view. "Okay guys, be polite your queen needs your help so be on your best behavior." Rarailmuir knew his guys they had their own events and moments in the service. His guard many of them of the highest honors. They had loves and wives and children. Service in the guard called for a lot of sacrifice on their part. Their bravery was of the highest caliber, it was a great honor to lead such males in his command of the finest example of Yoranthium had to offer. He wasn't going to begrudge them any for acceptable contact with their queen.

His guard was professional as they nervously took their queens hand and lifted her by the arms and being careful not to touch her bottom or too high up on her inner legs. They had been remarkable gentlemen to their queen. Kumithra thanked each of them on her way up. Giving them a smile and a tender touch of her hand as they helped her. It was a little uncomfortable for her. She could tell the males were nervous and excited to touch their queen. In a way she liked the attention and then she seen the final guard. She knew he saw her partially naked in her bra. She could tell he couldn't get her out of his head.

Reaching her arms to him was like a dream to him as well. "It's okay, I'm not going to bite you." She shook her hands with fingers out stretched to him and he grabbed her hands and pulled her up with very little effort and she pushed herself up with her legs and got on the ground next to him. Gave him a quick little hug and a thank you. Providing him with a gentle kiss on his cheek. He was the only guard with no one in his life. This moment of surprise he had the love of his queen.

"As you wish my queen." He said with a smile and looked rewarded and bashful as she walked away from him. Then looked back down to see a waiting king and other guards impatiently

waiting for him to help them up too. "Sorry my king almost forgot."

"The Queen is unforgettable, don't need to tell me. Just get us out of here." Everyone got to the top and Rarailmuir rejoined Kumithra. "Don't stray too far from me. We are now in enemy territory. We are going to head to the ships and find a fast skiff to get out of here, from the looks of it. It's going to be rough."

The wind was blowing harsher than anywhere they had been before. Seawater spay was being pushed all across Sea Shore. Sea Shore itself was on fire burning and mostly leveled after nearly a quarter a third season had passed since the wedding ended and war began. Yoranthium's defenses had failed miserably and there was no sign of any sea elves managing any kind of defenses. Sea Shore's battle was long over. The enemy demonic forces had won.

Fortunately the lines of battle move forward as ground is conquered. They had fallen behind enemy lines. In the distance was sea wreckage of broken naval ships to be seen to the warm sunup side, with silhouettes of fantastically huge creatures surfacing in the water, Tredinak's, and fabled Megrouchin's (a strange colossus of crab like creatures). Huge platform of massive cylindrical tubes mounted on the backs of the Megrouchin's. That must have lunched the Mechanation meteors along with Trooperships of deep sea elf designs had crashed on the beach that were empty and looked like ghost ships never to sail at sea again.

The dark enemy of the deep depths must have been so massive when it took Sea Shore it simply overwhelmed their defenses. The guard here were veterans mostly the old guard as the dragon had never attacked here. No more veteran's means they never had a chance to defend Yoranthium. The entire force must have been at the Last Bastion toward the Grand City and Farmer Town and ultimately would get to Under the Rock and Worm.

Hopefully Bronanes and Huspecia had been successful with their mission. From the sight of Sea Shore Yoranthium was doomed. Looking across the bay the water break prison was destroyed and burning. From the look of it any convicts likely got killed or turned into those Riark's like the Sea Ghouls. Or even Shamblers.

The only good thing was that the skys were clear except the occasional large lighting that would shoot towards the Grand City.

No lighting would impact Sea Shore the fires here done by Mechanation's and Depth Dwellers and magics. Not only that but looking around the landscape. Several Yagrallmagrund's could be seen very slowly moving through Sea Shore leaving enzyme trails of muck behind them in their wake.

It was getting hard to see everything around them. There was so much smoke, fire, debris blown by the wind and salt water spray coming off the large waves pounding the beach and impacting the near by pier. Plenty of sailboats had been moored to the docks and Rarailmuir spied one that seemed to glow brightly in his mind as the one they must head towards. Rarailmuir had no idea if they could even get a sailboat past the incoming waves impacting the pier and the shore? At this point there wasn't many choices.

Grabbing Kumithra. Rarailmuir and the remaining guard began to run at a decent trot towards their objective. They got plenty of rest during the setting of the sun and were well enough fed and hydrated. Even with the collapsed bunker retreat they did have two days to rest. This would be perfect for the enemy had been very aggressive and likely unable to fight this far back.

Rarailmuir felt this was going to work well. Or so he thought and hoped with a spirit he had the day of the wedding before he surprised Kumithra with his hand in hers. She was now on his left as he looked to his blade in his right. Regretting he never got the chance to tie Kumithra's hand to him as he looked at the wedding band remembering the voice of a child he had never seen.

It looked as all was going well they made up a fantastic amount of distance in little time just a block from the pier. To the sailboat he had kept running. Getting over ambitious and careless. Failed to anticipate sleeping units on watch.

A Mechanation partially damaged and buried in a building spotted their heat and saw them coming. When they reached the hidden Mechanation. It came to life and blew a loud siren warning of steam. Pushing over the remains of a three-story tenement onto the guard that trailed behind Kumithra and Rarailmuir. The building killed ten of the guard instantly while only six were stuck in rubble. The Mechanation was slow with damaged legs. Moved just enough to slice and buzz saw and stab and snip killing the trapped six guard with very little effort.

Rarailmuir simply ordered the rest to not watch and keep following him and the queen. They were almost there, leaving the dying guard behind and making some distance. Then a guard slipped and grabbed the nearest guard to him. He had fallen into a pit made of digestive enzymes placed there by a Yagrallmagrund. The enzymes had attacked his web toes instantly in the open part of his boots. Quickly seeping into and soaked his leggings and dissolved his flesh working towards his bone. As kings hand sized larva latched on to anything they could attach too.

The guard he had grabbed fell face first into the enzymes and pulled up quickly in great soundless pain as his lower jaw dropped revealing a missing disintegrated tongue becoming just a skeletal partial fleshy red meaty face that was smoking and his eye's were gone along with his nose. The guard pulling him with a terrified scream looking at the faceless guard he pulled in with him. Letting him go as larva attached to him and began eating into him alive. Then tentacles came out of the soup and pierced the first fallen guard and raised him off the ground toward claw like tentacles that pulled them to the central mass of a huge Yagrallmagrund hidden in the tight alley that feasted well as seen by plenty of remains of sea elves it had devoured as it's progeny grew from the larva shells around it's base.

More tentacles lashed out and more guards another three were pulled into the direction of the Yagrallmagrund, One of the guard's was screaming yet had enough sense to pull out two of his magics and tossed them at the creature as he got pulled closer to it's leathery fingers of digestive enzymes. The magics exploded and they exploded too close to the other guards as a chain reaction of the other magics on the other guards ignited.

This block of building had its very foundations destroyed and collapsing the entire remaining ruins on the block. Yes the Yagrallmagrund was destroyed along with the larva and progeny. Yet the explosion and chain reaction was enough to take twenty of the guard. The explosions sent debris and enzyme and larva flying through the air. Fighting to stay in the air as dust and soot brought most of it back to the ground.

Rarailmuir and the remaining four guards simply kept running, as he protected Kumithra from flying debris and falling larva. "Don't look behind just let it go." Is all Rarailmuir said just

get him and Kumithra off the island. Get to the sailboat and escape.

The commotion was loud the slow Mechanation still pursued them. Depth Dwellers napping in the city had been alerted along with lurking Riark's. The Yagrallmagrund were too slow and not a threat. The remaining four guards had prepared to protect the King and Queen with their lives. Watching as the hoard moved in and tossed magics sparingly for they only had twelve magics remaining.

They had taken out large numbers of Riark's and Depth Dwellers letting the King and Queen get to safety. Noting more Impundalu in the distance rising to the sky heading their way for scraps. They thought they had secured the escape as they saw themselves finally at the pier before the sailboat. They thought they would win this day. Unfortunately they ran out of magics and the last of the guard died horribly gruesome deaths as they were overran and feasted on by starving depth dwellers and Riark's that in turn feasted on one another giving time for Kumithra and Rarailmuir to escape.

The sailboat had its mast arm down and tipped on the dock. It was a good skiff of sail enough room for ten to fit. Rarailmuir wanted to signal the others to follow quickly and get the sail craft on the water. He saw the feeding swarm at the end of the pier followed by a Mechanation that simply stepped on it's own forces not caring and killing many of it's own.

The Death Guard was gone and they had died defending him and his queen. Rarailmuir didn't know how he could get this sailboat out to sea and it seemed like any hope of that was lost. Him and Kumithra would make their last stand here for Yoranthium was lost. His head was pounding he could hear a voice he heard before. 'The time is neigh.' Repeated over and over in his head. He didn't see behind him.

Xern was on the pier. Jumping out of the sailboat. It wasn't clear how he managed to be here. Yet, there was Xern. Rarailmuir and Kumithra didn't see him at first. He had the sword of Yoranthium in his hand. As he used one of his arms to push the boom of the mast the weather and the waves did the rest using a partial sail.

The beam of the mast hit Kumithra in the head with a loud deafening boom as her head exploded in pain with a sickening crack. She fell into the sail boat unconscious but alive thanks to her mother's helmet. Lying motionless on the deck of the sailboat on her side in a fetal position.

Rarailmuir heard the commotion behind him. "Xern!!! I'll kill you!!!" He said noticing that Kumithra looked so still Xern might of killed her.

Xern had out the sword of Yoranthium. Wearing what Rarailmuir knew was his helmet. "Not if I kill you with the King's sword first." Xern tried to strike Rarailmuir.

Rarailmuir simply bent around the blade with great combat skill and backhanded Xern with his left hand that slid easily under the helmet. The sword of Yoranthium fell to the deck of the dock. While Rarailmuir's helmet fell below Kumithra's feet in the sailboat. Xern fell to the aft of the sailboat into the water.

Xern knew he was defeated and knew if Rarailmuir used the blade he would die. So he swam as hard as he could to escape to the shore not far from the sailboat. Xern was a poor swimmer and would barely make it to shore, out of breath and almost drowning on his way in four in a half kings feet of water. As a sea elf he never knew he could breathe underwater. Xern really wasn't good at anything.

Rarailmuir was amused at the sight of a drowning sea elf on the surface of the water being he could touch the bottom. Then turned his gaze at the sword and reached down. Feeling a sensation in his mind. Perhaps it's the second light. The Sword of Yoranthium was his and now victory was assured. He reclaimed his beloved sword of the King. By dropping his Sukenobu on the dock and trading it for the Kings Sword.

He was admiring the glow it was brighter than before and shined like the most precious metal he had ever seen. Shining brighter as he looked sad and longingly at Kumithra unconscious in the boat for he could protect her with this sword. He was standing with his legs wide. His right on the handle of the sword as the blood and dirt of his wedding binding was cleansed. He could feel his muscles pounding and he was getting stronger. The sword had found his heart and his love for Kumithra. It was giving him strength and not taking it. He held his left hand under the blade

admiring the blade for some time. A vortex of power ebbed and flowed through him. A power he felt was so familiar and it reminded him of his love for Kumithra and grew stronger. Knowing what he needed to do with the sword of Yoranthium for Yoranthium and for his Queen.

Then he wished to end this war and he swung the blade up in his right hand as high as his arm would go and loudly proclaimed. "I have the..."

Rarailmuir was so enlightened and ensorcelled by his newly reclaimed sword of Yoranthium that he had not been paying attention to the lumbering Mechanation behind him. A loud painful and awful simple sound is all he heard. "Snip!"

The Mechanation had used it's remaining claw to cut his right arm clean off.

Rarailmuir watched in slow motion his right arm with the wedding band and the sword of Yoranthium fall to the deck of the sailboat. As his hand fell open and the sword danced mocking him and dancing on the deck of the sail boat until it came to rest just a few kings feet above Kumithra's head and his hand appeared to be reaching for Kumithra or the sword next to her motionless form.

Rarailmuir's vision was blurring as blood flowed from the stump and the open wound of what use to be and should have connected to his right arm. He was losing blood fast. The pounding in his head increased. He saw his curved blade and went to pick it up with his right hand. He was trying to pick up his sword with is right hand. He couldn't understand why he couldn't grab the hilt of his curved Sukenobu with his right hand.

The blood loss and shock had been getting to him. Reality was no more and he just didn't understand how he could not use his right arm. He still felt he had it but couldn't use his right hand. He felt pain as blood rushed down his right side.

The Mechanation was resetting its damaged gears and resolving some minor glitches, errors in programming, and began moving its flame nozzle toward Rarailmuir and Kumithra in the sailboat. Xern had made it to shore and ran behind the break water shoal in fear of what was to come next knowing Rarailmuir lost the sword and his arm hearing it clatter in the sailboat.

The flame was glowing brighter and brighter in the chamber and Rarailmuir could not for the life of him understand

what happened to his right arm. Fire began to issue forth from the Mechanation's flamethrower. Time slowed and stopped. Then he relaxed and heard a voice. "Father, like I said and like I promised you as told to me to tell unto you. The first light will fall upon you. A gift reluctantly granted as a blessing to you father from our God."

Rarailmuir knew what was going to happen. He understood he had seen the reincarnation of his son at the wedding. A son he never knew and would have to wait some more time not knowing before he would know again. He knew his purpose and what was going to happen and he smiled knowing the future. Knowing the past. Knowing the present. Knowing he would be a saint and a name to be remembered.

Light began filling his heart and his love grew for the lives his very actions would preserve. He looked lovingly and kindly and hopefully to Kumithra and wished he had the time for one kiss but that was not to be. He knew his actions would send her where she would find the love she deserved. That was already established some time ago. Nothing ever happens without a purpose or a reason. He shed a tear one of the last he will have for a long time. He will miss his love that taught him what love should have been. Letting Kumithra go to find a love she deserved more than him. This is compassion.

A light began to grow in his heart by his love. By his deeds to protect so many in a display of God and the power that is always greater than any darkness and will defeat eight evils and the deep dark abyss. Teaching of faith in a time of the faithless. The light grew and began mending his right shoulder where no arm grew back. Just the wound closed and was like he never had his right arm as the light filled his skin. Burning off his blood to gentle petals of Sakura falling to the ground so delicate.

Time had stopped all the evil creatures surrounding Yoranthium was frozen. Rarailmuir's light had grown to a luminous level you could not make out any of his physical features and a halo formed above his head expanded from the crown of Sinderthion.

As he stood taller than ever before, light cascaded down his right side and formed a right arm of pure energy and light. He drifted up into the air his arms out to the sides and his legs

together. His right and his left crucified in the representation of God. As two luminous wings formed on his back and pulled him higher into the air. Two wings became four and then eight and then sixteen wings. He could feel the world and knew of the Gaiaggan still clinging to Kumithra's hair. Expressing a deep sense of gratitude to Rarailmuir. He could feel the life of everything and knew everything. He was on limited time for this gift had its limits and he knew that too. He was aging as he lingered in this angelic form. Mortals hadn't been meant for such gifts of the light and the heavens and the foundations of creation. Thus he aged and burned with wisdom in his mind that he never knew was already his.

With a flick of his hand, Kumithra's sailboat teleported out to a safe distance at sea. Far away from Yoranthium into calm seas and cloudless skies, Rarailmuir then turned towards Sea Shore and a bright brilliant light began building. Time was running short and he would only have a short time for his mortal coils time was short. The light expanded and grew around him and escalated forth and grew larger and larger expanding all around him as sea monsters were pulled from the sea and the light expanded. Burning all unholy things. Rarailmuir had become the angel of penance for Yoranthium, his sins where cleansed, and all the evil beings began burning as the light expanded. Buildings being leveled, all deep dark creatures could not stand up to the light and were wiped clean.

Far off in the distance in a tiny building of stone Fedarious had collapsed exhausted from running in fear.

Metiur was being pursued by a Riark, which was swinging its claws just short of him. He had followed Fedarious with his heart and not his mind. He lost sight of Fedarious a league ago. But felt this was where he went. The Riark lunged and slashed Metiur in the back making him fall to the ground.

Metiur didn't have time for this and wildly and with great luck slammed his sword right into the open mouth of the Riark burning it's head clean off with the oils. He was losing blood and strength but was at a stone building with its door wide open. He managed to crawl into the building. Closing the door. Weakly cried for Fedarious. Fedarious came to his senses and quickly pulled Metiur to him. "Metiur I'll take care of you."

"I know you will." Metiur said as the light had finally expanded to this small building on the edge of Sea Shore. Light was breaking its way through the cracks of the stone masonry and Fedarious and Metiur just smiled comfortable in each other embrace. They had known for some time and now they were happy as they were enveloped in light.

The light could be seen for some distance on the horizon. The darkness had been temporarily ended over Yoranthium. As the light orb that filled all of Sea Shore became less. A small lonely sailboat floated on the water with its sail down on calm seas. As clear blue skys and the sun shone on Kumithra. Providing warmth over her skin and dreaming of escaping the abyss of hell. She had been touched by the light of an angel and dreamed of Rarailmuir. In the dream she saw him walking with a child that smiled back behind him at Kumithra in deep regret but letting her heart go with such compassion. She was given a last, "I love you." From Rarailmuir and he walked into the light speaking to a child. The child smiled back at Kumithra. Then it was silent.

Feeling joy but deep sadness in her unconscious dreaming next to the severed right lifeless arm of Rarailmuir. The arm still had the wedding binding that was meant for them tied to the wrist as a reminder that Kumithra couldn't see. The sword of Yoranthium glowed brilliantly and pulsed a flash that could be seen for leagues across the vast ocean.

Kumithra was cast out from Yoranthium and into a bigger world she had lost everything she held dear. Her fantasy fairytale just a lie and now a tale of horror for all she knew and loved now gone. Floating adrift on tropical clear and calm waters. Alone? Her love was gone and many had died. Her kingdom was no more for the deep evils of this story have not subsided. This is just a beginning of a more complex story to tell.

For now Kumithra's world is gone and her hope is lost.

Yoranthium

Book Two:
The Book of Jintru
Book One: Epilogue
A visitor to Yoranthium
By Mark P. Bromley

Yoranthium was a safe haven for refugees and people visiting the island nation to do business and share knowledge. Many recently came looking for a safe place from lands far away that had fallen to social corruption and cruelty of the eight demons ruled by one darkness spreading across the world of Ishormot that oppressed the teaching of the one true God. This was a tale of one visitor a half of a third of a season ago before the day of Kumithra's wedding. This is the introduction to Book Two of Yoranthium. As one hero falls and one rises inspired by the courage of a heroine.

Jintru had stepped off the chartered caravel just half a quarter a third season ago. He traveled by scenic carriage to the Palace that took a couple of days. Admired the countryside, the tropical plants and the peaceful and pleasant simple life of the Yoranthian's from the windows of that carriage. This small island nation was his type of people. They were full of life and love and caring and most of all believed in the forbidden unborn God. The God to be born his own family line of the Travalion had believed in since the founding of the first elven kingdom. After the Tear from the Heaven's fell to Ishormot and created the first El that found love with the natural nature of Ishormot's Fae.

Unfortunately some twenty revolutions ago the founding first elf kingdom of Travalion Hold fell into ruins. The Potentate Verdus, a distant blood relative loosely tied to Jintru of the founding elves and Travalion Hold. Had usurped the heritage of the elven traditional culture. The new Potentate Kingdom rose on the death of Travalion Hold. Immediately forbid, banned and outlawing the following of the true God to be born.

Proclaiming the unborn God as heresy and blasphemy instilling a new pantheon of false gods called the eight and the one. The new Potentates kingdom used an incredible power of reality changing incursion magics to eradicate and burn the true history of the first elf kingdom of Travalion Hold from history. Replacing the true history with the false narrative of the Potentates kingdom and version of history. The purge of education was enacted and reeducation camps by magics inquisition became a forced reality ultimately hiding what had happened to Travalion Hold to the world.[35] Only the faithful and most loyal to Travalion Hold and those born of the Elfae of the Dawn would remember. Subsequently hunted by the Potentate when discovered. All of Ishormot forgot their true heritage caused by the incursion magics. Jintru was too young to know how this came about and didn't remember his parents and who and what the Travalion truly was. He was born surrounded by death and left for dead in the marshlands of the new Potentates world.

---

[35] Similar to the plot of Global Socialism in the early 21st century where history was being rewritten by those who bought and paid for political corruption of the same "Progress," speeches of A. Hitler about 75 years earlier.

Jintru's linage was told to him by those who found him and he was the heir apparent to the birth of the first El that mingled with the Faefolken that lived in the land of the Tear of Heaven that was a place on Ishormot and now forgotten by incursion. His line of the kingdom of Travalion Hold was born new to the world of Ishormot as the first of the Elfaefolken or Elf for short. Raised up by the Faefolken of the Dawn and taught of the goodness of the world of Ishormot. Envied by the Deep Dark evils of the Altered Faefolken making pacts with the one and the eight devils that hated the new Elfaefolken because of how they changed the world. The coming of the Elf filled the world with heart, compassion, and bringing the birth of creation to Ishormot. All things in the dark fear the coming of the light to be seen by their creator. As for the dark beings they reveled in their hate and sin and preferred to keep it all in the dark. As most who deceive love and the heart hide their evil even from themselves.

He had come here for this land believed as the Travalion. It was an oddity and curiosity and those of the Travalion Hold were running out of time and place on the main land. They had to take extreme precautions and lived a Gypsy lifestyle. Always being vagabonds[36] and traveling freely and secretively. Always, on the look out for patrols from the potentate's guard. Buying and acquiring inn's, keep's and tavern's as a roof over their heads and a way to conceal themselves during the colder seasons. They had moved to the underworlds and made their wealth as bandits that benefited the people. Only robbing and hassling the potentate's own treasury and properties giving unto those in need. All of the Potentates wealth belonged in truth to Travalion Hold and to Jintru. The Potentates lands rightfully belonged to the heritage of Travalion Hold. It was Jintru's and the people of Travalion Holds property and wealth they stole back. The Potentate Verdus stole that when he waged war with Travalion hold twenty revolutions ago. The day of Jintru's birth. Jintru didn't know who or what he was until two revolutions ago. It was infuriating and a disheartening revelation when he learned who he really was.

---

[36] Vegabond is the hero of RPG in the authors youth and late teen years where the foundations of Jintru and Rarailmuir began in many adventures of what was called Advanced Dungeon and Dragons.

Here in Yoranthium there was no cold season. There was no potentate. Jintru felt free to do as he pleased. Purchased and walked with a loose flowing Yukata of shimmering silk made on the island of Yoranthium. Silk that was the smoothest and softest cloth he had ever felt. The yukata was silver with embroidered flowers in a swirled motif and would reflect reds, gold's, and oranges very much like the sea elf scaled skins had done. Such a beautiful skin for such a beautiful people he thought. Fascinated by the wide variations of interlaced colors and double toned skins of the Yoranthium sea elves.

His Hakama was a short beach style that exposed his strong healthy legs and some sand shoes that were flat on the bottom and covered the top of his feet above his toes of the latest Yoranthium fashion. He regretted purchasing the silk under garment. It felt good but rubbed on him. It was his first item of silk underwear compared to the heavy cotton he normally wore. When the silk rubbed him, he had to stop walking and wait a few moments before continuing until the silk underwear rubbed him the right way again. It was nice underwear something he'd have to get use to and build a tolerance too. It was like drinking alcohol down there. If only it wasn't his faiths fault for trimming his extra skin down there this perhaps wouldn't be such a sensitive training program for silk undergarments.

His skin was different. He came from the main land and that his family line was elven founder. His skin was tan and lightly golden and muscular built he was Nearly a king's length tall. Short for a mainlander elf. Most original founder elves were not so tall. Thousandths of revolutions ago the founding elves had been barbaric and this cost them some of their original magics and stature. Known only as the war of the three elf founding kingdoms. That was a barbaric period of hate and warfare for the elves, one that the potentate was sure to revive. Only the belief of the unborn God saved them from degeneration and gave them purpose again.

His eyes were a deep luminosity with blue inlaid star fire around a black iris a stern and soft welcoming and commanding gaze. He had a chiseled square jaw line. That was smooth and was difficult at growing any facial hair. His Hair was a dish dirty gold and wild and wavy long and very male as it caused many females to look at him for long stares that they would try to hide once they

realized he was looking at them. The females sometimes paranoid him, for they giggled behind his back and murmured and some even stalked him and followed him. He liked it he knew the females wanted him for he was strong and rugged. They wanted to see if their souls mated with his through his gaze. The ladies would stare at him and try pretending not to look, but they loved his eyes and couldn't help themselves.

His ears were like most main land elves. Simple curved at the bottom and rounded up to a point. His was large pulled in and strong. Nothing like the Sea elves and had no protective membranes and no gills behind his ears. He was somewhat an oddity in the Grand City of Yoranthium. As many refugees and foreign people didn't see many main land elves kicking back in an outdoor bistro drinking the warm tea in simply white delicate cup the way he was. Two fingers his thumb and forefinger delicately holding the handle, with his little pinky out stretched. In his land of the potentate it was a tale of the founders. It could get him in trouble if identified and he didn't mind. He was use to trouble and escaping trouble.

Jintru had been denied access to meet King Sinderthion and Queen Zantkara. His family line of the Travalion Hold was abolished long ago and no longer showed up on the lists distributed to kingdoms like Yoranthium by the Potentate. No real kingdom just another refugee. Not worthy of an audience and he would have to go through a long process with the local magistrate to petition for an audience.[37] Time that they lacked for in a season he needed to be back in his homeland. His caravel was scheduled to leave in the next few days. Today was his last day in the Grand City of Yoranthium.

His family line was struck from the potentate's records and the official history of the elves was sealed and deemed criminal for anyone to study or know about. Even the founding language was forbidden to learn and ancient tongues taught to be dangerous and would allow demons to rule. By demons, the Potentate Verdus meant God and his Angels and the founding elves. Performing wild hunts to exterminate the Fae of the Dawn when discovered. That

[37] There is many fallen kingdoms even now struggling to be recognized in our modern world.

was the lies the potentate taught these days as the worship of eight false gods and the one dark one replaced the unborn God.[38]

It was okay that Jintru and his trusted friend Turukon had been denied an audience with King Sinderthion. He had hoped for a small parcel of land to found a monastery as they had the same belief in the God yet to be born. However there were some strange events that unfolded with the local authorities. They were all young here in the Grand City and not like the elder magistrate in Sea Shore. There was some elders but not around the central gallery or serving in the rank and file of the Yoranthium Guard. They were told the captain of the guard was the oldest and he was only twenty-seven or eight. That was their highest officer and then been told a tale of a dragon and how this Rarailmuir saved the Grand City and was engaged to the princess when she comes of age they will wed.

He thought about how quaint it was for a princess to marry at nineteen, very close to his own age. The dragon turning on elves was never heard of. Dragons from his teacher and guardian mother were creatures of the unborn God. They would never attack elves to harm them. Not God believing elves, maybe a firebreathing wyvern often mistaken as a dragon. Or a firedrake another confused creature for a dragon.

For Yoranthium to be attacked in such away alarmed Jintru. Only some kind of terrible demonic force could create such an attack here in a City that showed signs of trouble. The difficulty Jintru had here working with some of the officials and noticing that their crime problem was obvious. As some of them strutted around the streets with Sea Ghouls on the back of their black leather jackets. Clearly indicated that King Sinderthion's kingdom was experiencing some demonic problems here in their main gallery. For isn't a skull with fangs a symbol of demonic worship? Jintru and his companion Turukon almost had a skirmish with one of these Sea Ghouls as his thugs told them to make way for an Orichen apparently their boss. As the official Yoranthian Guard disappeared.

---

[38] Theological conflict began in the early politics of the 21st century. The rising of harmful, unethical and immoral beliefs originating by division of political narrative in undermining biblical churches centuries old belief systems that had founded modern civilization and feasible composition of societal function.

Jintru let them pass and pulled out a needle and stabbed it delicately and quickly into the back of the arm of the last passing Sea Ghoul. That didn't flinch or even notice he was picked by just a little prick. Jintru was pleased his skills came in handy and he pulled a jar out of a pouch hidden in his belt. The jar had a fluid in it that was clear but smelled awful as the cork was removed. Jintru dropped the needle with some blood in it. Sure enough after capping the vial and shaking it the color turned dark purple.

Jintru showed it to Turukon. "See there's problems on this island. I don't think we can settle here. We'll have to go and report back to the council of the sixteen rays of dawn. Yoranthium is under demonic attack. When that Sea Ghoul dies he's going to become a demon. They traded their souls for power and this means there's a demon witch here. Seeing just some common thug has ben mutated. That demon witch has been here for some time plotting the demise of Yoranthium." Jintru was a little sad.

Yoranthium was a beautiful kingdom. The females handsome and so lovely and he liked these two girls. One was blue-pink and the other green-blue and playful. He witnessed as those two teased other males of any age. He was also wild about the differences in their ears and range of hair colors. This Yoranthium was vibrant. The shimmer of those two girls skins really caught his eyes as they sparkled and glistened in the sun. He felt free and he could easily look at the pretty girls and accordingly the two girls didn't mind him looking. They just giggled and moved on down the street speaking to one another. Looking back at him trying to make it look like they weren't noticing him and giggling and speaking. Jintru seen it before and if he was lucky the one with the blue interlaced pink skin and white hair, he was going to find her again.

Unfortunately Yoranthium had a dangerous demon problems growing. Which brought him back to his current situation. Just like the mainland. Wasn't any safer here than where he came from. He would have to return to the Hold and prepare for a more drastic option. Relocating further to the cold. If so he should likely enjoy this tropical warmth while he could. No reason to waste this wonderful day. He had a lot of potentate wealth to spread around Yoranthium. Might as well throw a party with this coin.

Yoranthium had a small population. It wouldn't last long in a real war. Even the potentate from intelligence gathered had been making plans to expunge Yoranthium as a Kingdom. However this vial was alarming. Sea Elves selling their souls for power in the streets. Common thugs walking past posted patrols and paying them off. Twisted just like the Potentates kingdom. War would be here soon enough and they didn't know it.

Yes indeed Yoranthium outside the palace was corrupted and being demonized. Turukon looked at the vial and was disappointed. "All this traveling for nothing my lord. Well I guess we do what we normally do."

"That's right Turukon." Jintru cheered right on up slapping his protector on the back. "No more tea and pastries. Let's find us some drink and some ladies!!! Let's spend this coin and give the doomed and dying a zest for life." Jintru was smiling from ear to ear.

Turukon had smiled because it wasn't too hard for Jintru to twist his arm. "Okay, but don't forget we got to go back to Sea Shore and then in a couple of days we have to return. There are some beaches we should check out my lord. According to some sailors of their Navy there are these two sirens that sit off the rocks off the coast every now and then. Said to be quite the sight."

"You mean like a beach with Jelly-fish?" Jintru couldn't help but remind Turukon.

"At least we stayed at the beach bar and you jumped from the roof for a face first on that bounce sheet. It was a spectacular feat." Laughing, reminding Jintru of his unimpressive drunken bouncing fetes. "It was still fun with all the girls wearing nice swim suits and not being able to hide in the water."

"You going to tell everyone about that bounce pad?" Jintru needed to know.

"Nope my lord, you might get drunk and do it yourself." Turukon had said knowing it happened before. Jintru does some silly things when he's been drinking.

Jintru looked at his protector and mentor. "Turukon, stop calling me my lord. You know it has gotten me into conflict with the potentates guards more than once the past two years. Just leave the lord stuff out of everything." Then Jintru thought about it. "Unless we get invited to the palace or meet the princess or find

that legendary Sword of Yoranthium. Legend said I was supposed to see it on my visit to Yoranthium. I don't see it do you?"

"Don't put so much into some weird tale from some young Healing Cleric at that temple up the hill of the secluded glade. He claims to know the future and soothsay but really how often is he right? He's a little off most of the time. Besides you need some toughening up around the potentate guard. Sometimes I call you, My Lord, on purpose." Turukon laughed a little as they left the cafe leaving a generous amount of gold they stole from the potentate. "He told me my true love would be found in a bar. All I got was a bottle of alcohol broke over my head. If that's love he's a God. Look I got the scar to prove it."

"I remember that. It was funny. I thought you were a good fighter. You keep changing that story about your scar. I don't even know the truth about that?" Jintru remembered Turukon getting thrown out by the bar guards back in that town that he couldn't remember the name of about a revolution ago. Turukon was so drunk he couldn't stand straight. Turukon always had the scar since the two of them first met.

"That's why we need to keep our drinking simple. You pour I drink." Turukon said.

"If that's the case you might be in the same boat once again." Jintru liked drinking with Turukon he was bulky and strong. Bald with a scar on his forehead from a fight he told Jintru of as a kid and has changed many times. Turukon was supposed to be his protector as decreed by the sixteen rays of dawn. The overseers of his vast estate of Travalion Hold that no longer existed.

Turukon was over two hundredths and something revolutions. Shaved his hair off so he wouldn't look old. Had a habit of being defeated in key battles. Like the one that lost Jintru his rightful birth place. In that fight he was knocked off the outer battlement and left for dead. Apparently he was his father's protector. Now Turukon was Jintru's father, friend and protector mostly a drinking buddy. He knew so much of his father and felt regret for not being there when the potentate killed Jintru's family after he was born. It was a midwife that saved Jintru and died.

No reason for Jintru to remember the past. Only makes him moody and depressed. He had a remarkable memory and well that

healing cleric back home was a little crazy. That sword talk of a fabled sword was likely just talk. Jintru had seen many swords that were claimed to be magics they had simply been designed differently. Differently balanced. Too thick, too thin, too light, too heavy, usually it was always the one swinging the sword that made the magics of any sword work. Jintru had never seen a true or real magics sword. The scribes had written about the Sword of Yoranthium claiming it had ancient runes on it. Jintru simply wanted to see if he actually learned the old runes of the Fae and first enchanted of the Ishormot. Well perhaps another day.

They had been in the gallery for some time. Stopped at some stores and gave some wealth away to some of Yoranthian's less fortunate. From that vial these people needed some kindness if the demon blood was true Yoranthium will be fighting for it's life soon enough. Enough being so grave and worried about the future that is yet unwritten. Jintru wasn't going to settle his people here after all. There was the smaller island of Forumth. It was rocky and only a vassal kingdom of Yoranthium that would be a tough life. There still was the uncharted lands; further to the cold and it was covered in cold ice. There grew some nice brew plants. It could be fun but cold. There was another set of isles off the coast. Not to mention regions of the two other foundings too near to the Potentates Kingdom and at odds with territorial disputes.

Eventually Jintru and Turukon found a nice little sidewalk pub in the main gallery. They got friendly quickly with the bar owner who was excited to hear about mainland potentate kingdom God to be born monks of the Travalion hold. Not really it was the coin that made them fast friend. It's surprising how money can buy you friends. Being that very few mainland elves ever visited this pub and well Jintru and Turukon were the first.

They got the best seats out on the street under a canopy and were being treated well as Jintru and Turukon had been generous with their wealth. The wait staff was constantly around their table. Interested in the interaction of the foreign persons that had been visiting their neck of the world. They had never seen such skin tones that differed substantially from the soft smooth scales that shimmered like the sea elves. Mainland elves never traveled in this far and when they did they usually had business only with the lords and ladies. This was a first to have visitors not being entertained at

the palace and finding their amusement at this popular out door pub.

Sure the inside was well decorated and had been serving Yoranthium Grand City since it's creation over four and fifty hundredth's years ago. It was spared by the Dragon attack as most of the other stores burned down around it. It was full of paintings and sculptures that represented the history of Yoranthium and detailed the people who created the establishment and it's patrons.

While Jintru and Turukon were drinking the bar owner and his wife joined them and had their resident artist creating a quick painting of all of them. Which oddly enough even the artist was drinking and the painting barely looked like any of them. But they were a little drunk by the time the artist claimed to be done. That they admitted it was good. Yes. Turukon's head was pointed with rounded ears. Not to mention Jintru's eyes did look bigger on the left far bigger than the right. As his nose was a triangle on it's side.

Oh, they were having a great time the owner and his wife had to go tend to other customers as many came in to see the oddity of main land elves. Being in good spirits and very talkative. Jintru could juggle and he was amazing a crowd with his talents to entertain. Even children in the streets stopped for the show.

Jintru and Turukon quite the oddity and special guest of the bar they even picked up a few sponsors that sent them plates of food with more drinks just to hear of the lands to the cold and the world of the potentate. Jintru was quite the orator and provided a story of how the unborn God is not welcome. How he had on many adventures opposed the potentate and his evil empire. He cared for those in need. Which he proved often as less fortunate came by his table and he gave them drink, food, plates, utensils, and coin. Coin from the potentate's kingdom that still spent in Yoranthium with a better trade rate for Yoranthium coin. Jintru was the embodiment of a helping hand to all who asked and needed help.

Turukon was always watching Jintru carefully ensuring he didn't spend what they needed to report back to the Sixteen Rays of Dawn. Jintru was good for the coin. He could always acquire assets the potentate stole from his family. Travalion hold at its height and glory was the Potentates kingdom. All of the Potentates assets at one time or another was Jintru's birth right. Wealth

wasn't an object and thieving by Jintru wasn't really thieving or so the Sixteen Ray's of Dawn council perceived it. That's how the Society differed from the thievies guild in the main Kingdoms. The Society was a band of thieves that only stole back their birthright and gave it to those needing a helping hand and in true need. The Society was all that remained of the true founders and the Travalion Hold.[39]

Jintru simply became a beloved pirate tale of an anxious people of Yoranthium that had deep hearts and love of the sea and in so many ways Jintru was the inspiration of Yoranthium Navy and right versus wrong. Good versus Evil. All was right with Ishormot for the way Jintru explained his escapades. Sounded very similar to how the Yoranthian's viewed themselves on the high seas. When facing the Potentates Navy.

Then he broke into song as he found a chin and shoulder mounted four stringed instrument called a virora. He seemed to take to the instrument as he had learned to play one in his youth. Mostly he simply looked serious and played strings and sounds he understood but if you ever asked him to repeat what he played it would have been impossible. He really wasn't that good. Especially when drinking. Yet for today he was gifted with sound and endless sound that fooled everyone even the most experienced at music. The instrument made a nice 'mhm,' sound from it's strings lower than it's higher pitched chin mounted cousin and richer than it's between the leg relative.

Children danced in the street and couples danced to his playing in the bar and even Turukon found a mate in one of the bar waitresses who took a liking to him. She danced close and real close. Finding Turukon's purse. To which he grabbed her hand and whispered in her ear. "That wont work, my dear." He flashed her a sign of the Society and she knew it well, for she was one of them and they learned from the hand signal that they should be kind to another Society leader in their midst.

"I'm sorry my lord. I didn't know." She flashed a symbol of understanding and respect for how well in the organization Turukon was. She flashed the owner of the bar another hand signature and they would not roll Jintru or Turukon any further

[39] The Helping Hand a motto to live by for all of good merit.

for they were ranking members of their guild in the land of the Potentate.

The music of Jintru flew down the streets and there two courtly ladies of royalty who ran away from their duties. They heard the fun and the sounds of Jintru down the street and it sounded like some person of note was having a grand time in the Grand City. Down at a pub these ladies knew of but didn't spend much time at for it was never too busy and had a poor reputation. Apparently thieves. Rarailmuir proclaimed it off limits to them but he's just a captain of the guard and not her boss.

However today of all day's it was sounding fun to the two ladies. Huspecia was the one leading the charge and pulling Kumithra along with her. Which was typical. It was over half a third of a season before Kumithra would be nineteen and getting married. Might as well have some fun when they could Huspecia thought. She would be wedding her Bronanes soon enough to and he's been out at sea for most of this quarter. Huspecia and Kumithra being bored and wanted to flirt around town like they normally did when they couldn't be with their loves.

As they rounded the corner other musician's had joined in and it was a very groovy and bombastic band playing. Difficult to get to the street tavern as the street had filled with a party going crowd that had ended their working day. At the end of the long quarter a third season work cycle and many singles wanted something new. Something wholesome not the red district, for family, and was a good a festival a bright day and comfortable street of neighbors, kin and elven kindness.

Jintru was spent and his festive musical enchantment had worked. He couldn't make up any more tunes and ended his performance like famous musicians do by breaking the instrument to a tremendous fan fair of applause. Other musician's of real talent had taken over and Jintru gave them coin to play longer and together far into the rest of the evening. While Turukon paid for the damages to the cheap instrument from off the wall. That oddly was back on the wall as the wait staff was sweeping up the broken instrument.

Kumithra rounded the corner with Huspecia and seen the foreign Jintru and he was striking to her. Remembered seeing him at the café not to long ago. She had never seen a male from the land

of the potentate and simply had to go see this. Instead of letting Huspecia lead her, she led Huspecia for the first time. Which was unusual even for Huspecia to be pulled around like she did Kumithra most of the time.

Huspecia's right was in Kumithra's left. While Kumithra right was adjusting her fashionable loose fitting blouse to flirt and play with a young male from the potentate's kingdom. She never seen scaleless skin of a golden tanned hue. His eyes reminded her of an inverted Rarailmuir's that sparkled and danced on her memory of her love.

They entered the bar and they found themselves being compelled to get closer and closer to Jintru. As the only other table vacant was next to where Jintru was talking with some of the local youth.

One of the boys around Kumithra and Huspecia's age was interested in learning a lesson of how to be swashbuckling. He asked Jintru a question. "Can you tell me how to meet ladies?"[40]

Jintru just smiled and he looked noble and well dressed even if he was drinking a tad bit much. Trying to not be so secretive on purpose. "Sure I'll show you. I'll show all you males looking for a girl how to do it. I do it all the time." Not a single slurred word. Jintru was the life of the party and drinking was nothing to him. "First you have to decide where are and what constitute ladies." He was looking around. "They could be anywhere." As if he was going on safari hunt. "Best to find the ones you don't find with other males. Easy to avoid trouble unless looking for trouble." He was pretending not to see Kumithra or Huspecia, while doing his safari stunt. "Make sure they are not wed. Make sure they are like you, alone and free. Yes you find love with freedom in the heart and mind."

Fact is he saw them the moment they came down the street. He took an instant interest in Kumithra. As for Huspecia not so much, the table near him was open because he encouraged the staff to reserve it intentionally for Kumithra and Huspecia. He knew they were coming he saw it when he ended his song.

The wait staff hurried to follow Jintru because they knew it was their princess and her protector. Jintru had no idea what he was getting into. The owner and his wife had to be careful and they

---

[40] I admit it's a bit of a true story that happened in Japan.

alerted their own bouncer to watch Jintru and Turukon's behavior. They didn't want an incident with the royal princess and as long as Jintru was a gentle elf there would be no problem. He did claim to be a lord himself and had the coin. No reason to restrict or prevent Jintru from frolicking around with the princess. He could be a suitor. Perhaps he arrived early to size up the competition that was custom.

Turukon was aware and stopped dancing he too was watching the bar owner his wife and the bouncers. He was Jintru's protector and recognized the young Huspecia was concealing chain daggers. Chain daggers of all weapons are demon killers and weapons of the unborn God's champions and defenders of their faith. The daggers created long ago by Travalion Hold and to find such a person equipped here in Yoranthium was strange indeed for it was a weapon created by the very bloodline of Jintru.

The band was playing, people dancing, the bar was fun and filled with happiness, love and heart and most had no idea how tense a few were getting as the street became an unsanctioned festival during the day. Attracting all manners of street performances and couples and families and it was wholesome. A beautiful kind of magics at work the magics of a forgotten Travalion Hold a pact between the life of Ishormot the Fae and the EL. This was the magics inside of the line of the founding soul of the Elves at work.

Jintru didn't mind or care he was drunk on life and full of boasting and posturing. Letting the magics of the Elf and Nature of Ishormot loose on Yoranthium. Free from the sights of the potentate, free to be, and he was enamored with the love of Yoranthium this day. Perhaps it's the funny feeling from the silk underwear on his circumcision. Often he was always full of the zest of life and today more so than ever before. He was drunk.

It was the way he operated. Often never being serious even in the worst situations. He had a gift for living life. He was abandoned and surrounded by death the object of a wild hunt by the Potentate all his life. It took eighteen years for the Sixteen Ray's of Dawn to find their heir apparent. It was said he raised himself in a swamp in the wild on his own. He learned things even the most elder among them never knew. He was considered a

miracle and magics in his own right. Now he was drunk, more on life than drink.

"Now after you find a couple of ladies. Like what is this right here next to us?" He was still talking to the young male who wanted to meet girls. Jintru failed to see that the boy had recognized the princess and her protector Huspecia. He backed away in fear he wasn't of royal blood or anyone special. He knew he was being secretly watched. The young boy could get punished for jilting or upsetting either of these too. Best he left Jintru's side as not to get involved. There were rumors of real dangers if you upset those watching over the princess of Yoranthium. That King Sinderthion burned a hostile person that tried to harm his daughter the princess revolutions ago with a fireball. Or so the story went.

Jintru didn't know anything about the captain of the royal guard or that he was betrothed to Kumithra. Even if he did it wouldn't have mattered he was a great romancer. Kumithra was the lucky one today. Jintru appeared to fix his eyes on her face and Huspecia just simply wasn't his interest. Kumithra could just giggle thinking Jintru was so funny as his friend was obviously terrified. Fading into the shadows.

"Here they are two ladies of note. Dressed so lovely in their dresses and exposing their cleavage." Jintru was looking only at Kumithra. He was trying to impress the young male who was a kings length behind him by now and moving further away. "All you have to do to meet a girl is say." Jintru paused a moment so he could clearly say it looking deep into her soft lovely eyes. "Hello, I'm Jintru. My pleasure to meet you and you are?" His most remarkably effective pick line never failed and always worked.

Kumithra just sat there. Laughing. Never heard a pick up line that was so outlandishly formal. His keynote letter of introduction strait forward, precise, direct, and funny, she didn't know what to say. Jintru wasn't even looking down her blouse. He was looking at her eye's, her lips, her hair and her ears and color of her skin and scales glittering in the sun under a awning as if a stary night in the day. She could only laugh and giggle as he looked into her eyes it was humorously romantic and tickled her fancy and stirring her imaginings.

Jintru never had this happen to him before. Maybe it was the drink. Only Kumithra was in his world as the room filled to just a blinding white light around them with only him and her in the room, as the world vanished. He could sense her soul and felt he knew her. Their aura's touched and coalesced and became bright and removed the cosmos was only them. Not just now but in a life time before and before that too. It was like a vision he had when he was reading a book about Yoranthium revolutions ago. When he was twelve. It was her. It was her face. He imagined such a face and planned on traveling to Yoranthium to find her. Jintru thought it was just imagination for at twelve there was nothing but that blasted swamp. He couldn't be as big as the world. Unlikely would never travel the world.

Here he was right now. Looking at her purple eyes her lovely and beautiful painted lips and made up eyes. With a fantastic hair style and her eye's made him swoon for her soul and only she was in his world. Her laughing was music to Jintru. Her entire dress was pleasing and she was a sea elf he had dreamed of. Her skin a perfect match for his vision.

Never did he really believe this was possible to meet a legend. A fantasy of his imagination and a dream of his deepest enlightened dreaming. The face of a dream that made his heart stop beating as he finally met his match and words began to fail him. She was giggling at him. He was making a fool of himself. He couldn't find the words and he hesitated forgetting he was trying to teach a young male to impress a girl. Yes he was impressing a girl. He was impressing his goal of his heart in the worse way. The world he had to him and her and their souls had traded acknowledgment and acceptance.

Up to now he was always a free spirited kind of male. He never faltered or hesitated and just did as he willed. Living life and being free to do as he willed. Now that was changing him, he felt owned and bound to someone special. This vision of a dream from when he was twelve was real. Really in front of him and was true just like in his dream so long ago in a swamp. Trapped in a youth not to his liking never knowing who he really was. The sensory overload and he could for the first time feel another kindred soul that he was bound too.

"I'm sorry, I have to go. I had made arrangements…" He was ashamed and latched onto a true excuse to run away. He did make arrangements for a concert tonight. He had many girlfriends back in the land of the potentate. He had to set his life in order. He wasn't expecting to meet her. Not now, not ever, he was living a free life. He dated as he pleased for he believed he'd never find the dream that was she. Never would see a face he dreamed of when he was twelve studying about the land of Yoranthium. Having never believed he would find her and he become love sick and dated ladies often. He was ashamed of his reckless behavior and his femaleizing for any day he could of died and he cared not for living for he was no one. Just a rogue upstart, even the Sixteen Rays of Dawn was often disappointed in him. Archtype of selfishness a disappointment compared to his father.

How could he explain himself. In a place like this it was embarrassing he couldn't talk to her here. He was drinking and it's a bar of all places. He'd hit on her like a letch. He would touch her and try to kiss her and just make a fool of himself in a few short periods of time. He was not expecting to find her a beauty he was willing to spend his life with. Bare his soul with to have children with and be husband and wife.

Jintru had a purpose. The Sixteen Ray of Dawn said so. A destiny and duty to the deaths of his families heritage. Caught in a tactical military situation a matter of war for his kingdom. The council and care providers of what was left as the heir of his own kingdom that was stolen and lost. All he wanted in his life was her and here she was. How was this even possible? She was likely just a common girl and not able to understand the responsibility of his future his responsibility to his people and the Elfaefolken and Faefolken of the Dawn. It would be dangerous for her to be his. Even with is heart and very soul crying out to her. He had to leave and he rushed off as the music ended. Ashamed of what he was becoming and not having enough faith to truly believe. Him a would be king trying to reclaim the heritage of Travalion hold, this unknown sea elf that he dreamed of. It changed his life he needed to put it in order but could he find her again?

Huspecia looked at Kumithra grabbing her arm and pushing into her. "Look at you. I didn't think I'd ever see you put terror into any male in all this land and the most handsome of

foreign men tries to woo you and out the door they go. Good for you Kumithra you win the bet today." Huspecia was just the princesses protector. Males were allowed to approach her they only needed to fear Bronanes and his sea guard. Kumithra was their princess and her father King Sinderthion would send males who were impolite or unkind towards Kumithra to the breakwater prison.

Kumithra was entertained and felt odd. As her coming of age hasn't arrived yet she didn't know what to make of it. In her mind she could only think of that male. She seen his face before in a dream too. She seen his eye's and in that dream it was another time. A time they lived in the same world and grew up with one another. But that dream was before Rarailmuir had rescued her. Her face stiffened and Huspecia was concerned.

"Lighten up Kumithra. He's not your suitor and he's not going to challenge your one and only love Rarailmuir. I know. Let's go to the beach, I got us new swim wear you'll love it." Huspecia was prodding and poking Kumithra. Knowing they'll corner the court mage to portal them to the far away isolated beach.

Kumithra felt she had missed a moment to talk to that strange male from the Potentates kingdom. Who was he and why did she feel this way toward a strange male. All she wanted to do is trick him into looking down her blouse so she could chastise him for it. She was here to tease the foreign male and now she just wanted to pursue him down the street. That would be inappropriate for her. Huspecia would likely stop her if she tried.

Turukon simply turned and finalized the bill and paid off the bar owner. "Hopefully we'll return and have even more fun. Thanks for the wonderful afternoon. We never get to experience cultures like this." He was out of the door and running after Jintru to find out what happened. He never seen Jintru get flustered and embarrassed and take off alone like this from a bar. Usually Jintru was so good he could have three or four females under his arms and even Turukon would have one or two by this time. He was so hoping for some escorts to the Yoranthium orchestra concert this evening.

Huspecia was relieved that the older foreign male had left. She felt him looking at her hidden chain daggers. How did he even know she had them? No one ever thought of her as a threat or a

danger. That older male must have been the others protector. Even for an old drunk he was like Thernya. Who are they she wondered? Must have been someone of note and of skill. As for Jintru just a common name, not much to go on.

Too many here in this place would be silent and stiff lipped for they knew their Princess Kumithra and they would know she was her protector and there were undercover Yoranthium guards in the room. They followed wherever the princess went. As a secret service of King Sinderthion to keep his daughter safe and let Kumithra feel she was free to do as she would like. Huspecia will not get more information from any of them. Most of them are drunk anyway. She was relieved the big old male was gone. He was dangerous and Huspecia knew it for he knew about her chain blades and eyed the daggers concealed under her clothing. He seemed like a match for Thernya.

"Well Kumithra it looks like we are done here. Let's go to the beach. I got us new swim wear, you'll love it." Huspecia grabbed Kumithra's hand and pulled her away from their table and out of the pub and down the street in the opposite direction of where Jintru had gone. To the palace, find the mage and portal to the far away secret beach.

Kumithra just went along. Nothing she could do now to find that strange male. Back to their ordinary routine and the beach. Maybe a ship would show up and they could tease the sailors on it. In the new swim wear Huspecia had with her.

Jintru had been drinking a bit too much he didn't realize how quickly he went down the street. He was feeling a strange feeling in his heart. Denying something he knew was true and his heart would burst and he would soon die. That would be fine with him. That he had made a mistake. Anxiety was more like it. It made him race and speed his steps and reflect without thinking of where he was going. He had wanted to avoid people so he could weep for being so pathetic. A feeling that wasn't him.

He wanted to run back there and sweep her off her feet and kiss her. He never once in his life felt this way about any female and he knew many. Fact is he was reckless with his current dating habits. He's been caught by females dating other females just sunwanes from one anther at the same tea houses and tavern's. He

didn't care. He'd just date a new girl at the end of the frequent breaking up and finding a new love.

Jintru was indeed getting sloppy or what they called love sick. As if he was missing someone to share his life with. So he shared this void of a missing soul with females that had the same hole in their souls to fill. Thinking about it that way made it better. Yet now he met someone that could fill that whole in his heart and his soul. Not hole but whole to be made whole. Yes that was what he felt about her to fill his heart and soul and make it whole.

Then while not caring. Jintru got pushed from behind as several feet ran up and circled him. "Give us all your valuables and that Yukata foreigner." Jintru was surrounded by more thugs of the Sea Ghouls, brandishing metal knuckles, saps, and had daggers in their belts. He so much hated local criminal thugs.

"Hey look, I'm with the society." He gave the hand signal of a high ranking society member.

The Sea Ghoul's noted it but didn't care. There was no society in Yoranthium. Orichen had it destroyed and replaced it with just the Sea Ghouls in the Grand City they ran everything. The Sea Ghoul's laughed. "No Society here. Just do as we say and you wont be killed."

Daggers came out and Jintru realized he was going to have to fight them. His money was with Turukon and his coin bag was light and he'd rather keep his Yukata. Jintru wasn't going to be robbed by petty thugs. Usually he's the one doing the robbing. He spun a kick into the thug speaking to him and knocked him to the ground. Another of the four thugs attempted to grab his shoulder to place a knife in his back. Jintru twisted expecting the knife and slipped back toward the thug and grabbed his arm and let the thugs momentum propel him forward and to the ground.

The other two thugs were now a little nervous they didn't expect this to become a real investment in physical labor to get what they wanted. They simply had gotten use to soft targets allowing them to rob them and leave down these shady ally's that smelled of rot and garbage where no one normally would go.

Jintru was drunk and made a few inappropriate course changes. Was use to the shadows in the way he would accost the Potentate back in his homeland. If Jintru didn't drink so much he wouldn't of got so sloppy. He had backed up too far and right into

a sap that swung and connected with the back of his head at the base of his skull.

With the drink and the confusion over Kumithra running in his mind and now being assaulted by petty thieves. That impact to the back of his skull was a bit too much. Even for his thicker skull. He could feel his eye's closing as the ground was coming up rather quickly. He heard a booming voice shouting. Rolling over on the ground to look up he seen the thug that was about to pin him to the ground stop with a look of fear and dread. Instantly turning to run and as many steps came closer the thugs steps got further.

Eventually with Jintru still being a bit sluggish trying to focus his eyes. He felt a strong hand of bronze blue sea elf skin grab his hand and pull at him to stand up. Jintru rose and was staring at a chest just as mighty as his own yet bigger. It was bronze interlaced with blue and golden tattooed of a royal military nature. Jintru had to look up considerably at that whom had pulled him off the ground. Seeing a Therica of gold hair and then a strong face of bronze and blue sea elf scaled features with sun fire golden eyes similar to his inverted blue fired eyes. If it wasn't for the height difference and skin difference Jintru would of thought he met his brother or doppelganger if he was a sea elf.

Rarailmuir had helped Jintru to his feet. "Sorry about that. These Sea Ghouls are our local welcome wagon for wealthy foreign visitors. I'm the Captain of the Royal Guard Rarailmuir and this is my patrol."

Jintru looked around and seen about twenty or so other sea elves in royal guard outfits he recalled from the magistrates office. "I'm Jintru Lord and Heir of Travalion Hold, Thanks for the assistance I guess." He was rubbing the back of his head as Turukon had caught up to them and the Guard.

"Thank the unborn God, you are okay Jintru. Thank you Yoranthium guard for saving my lord." Turukon slapped Rarailmuir powerfully on the arm to establish his position of authority.

Rarailmuir looked at Turukon and seen his age on his face and realized that it all checked out. Visiting dignitaries often had been in this part of the Grand City gallery and would often imbibe too much spending their wealth foolishly. It wasn't the first minor lords to visit Yoranthium and get denied an audience only to get

drunk in this part of town. Fortunately Jintru was honorable and avoided the red district. Rarailmuir would have thought less of him if Metiur's patrol had to bring him in.

Normally a drunk like Jintru would if alone had to spend his time in the Royal lock up. Fortunately for Jintru he had a title and a fancy enough looking official protector to back up his claim. Not to mention he was in the wealthier part of town. Jintru likely spent enough wealth to keep him out of the stockade.

"You must be his protector then?" Inquired Rarailmuir as he sized up Turukon and imagined him to be similar to Thernya. While his twenty guard stood loosely to the sides and taking up defensive positions at the street corners breaking up any onlookers and sending them away in preparations of the shake down by the royal guard.[41]

Jintru noticed that Rarailmuir was very professional in his handling of the situation. "Thank you, Captain of the Guard Rarailmuir you do King Sinderthion proud."

"Couldn't get an audience. I've seen this before with lower ranking nobles from foreign lands getting foolish here in Yoranthium and from the looks of the two of you." Rarailmuir smelt the air. "You are both drunk. I suggest you both find a nice hotel and sleep it off until you are ready to leave. The Sea Ghoul will be looking for wealthy foreigners and you fit what they want to rob. Go get yourselves cleaned up."

Jintru could see the look change in Rarailmuir's eyes. This was out of his way and his title was more than just a rank. He had an air of the prince but Jintru couldn't recall if Yoranthium had a prince or not. Just some story in the pub that there was going to be a Royal wedding and that challengers were allowed to apply in half a third of a season for the princesses hand that Jintru couldn't remember the name of. He was also told of a huge suitor for the princess. This Rarailmuir might have been that suitor.

Rarailmuir then said. "If you value your freedom." He motioned to a nearby guard that had some pouches of coin on him. The tax collector came forward. "I suggest you give a generous donation to the Yoranthium Royal Guard."

---

[41] Still a consistent problem even in our modern times with so many cities weaponizing legislation to target and victimize it's citizens for the greed of city officials.

That guard looked like a tax collector same as in his own land he had robbed many times. Taxes they collected in the land of the potentate. Found their way into Jintru's hand as his birthright. Jintru stole those taxes and gave it back to good causes. Jintru didn't fuss and simply handed over a bag of coin. "Don't spend it all in one place."

"What?" Rarailmuir looked annoyed.

"My lord is drunk Captain of the Guard of Yoranthium. We'll give you no problem and I'll get him off the street we are staying at the finest hotel down the street my lord." Turukon was being very diplomatic even though Jintru could see he was annoyed with Rarailmuir. In his land of the Potentate this usually ended in a complete fiasco. This is Yoranthium and there was no reason to go all out and upset these sea elves. Diplomacy was nice for a change.

"Very well everything is in order. Just get this Jintru of Tavion or whatever out of here and back to his room. Save yourselves some trouble. If you can't meet the King you never will and should go back to wherever you came from." Rarailmuir was still annoyed and was deliberately baiting Jintru into a conflict as he clenched his fists ready for a bout.

"Just one more thing." Jintru had to ask.

"What?" Rarailmuir's eyes narrowed on Jintru's nose. Where he was thinking of the first shot if it came to a contest.

"I'd like to see that sword of Yoranthium. I think I can read the ancient script on it. Could you guide us to the museum it's in? A legend from my people said it was suppose to present itself to me. Yet I haven't seen it." Jintru said sincerely and hoping Rarailmuir the Captain of the Guard would know.

"If you can't get an audience with King Sinderthion. You will never. Not ever get to see the Sword of the King. He keeps that with him." Rarailmuir said matter of factually. "Its not a museum piece its real and the power of Yoranthium."

"It's real? You have seen it then?" Jintru was amazed to hear that the mythical magics weapon did in fact exist. Perhaps the only real magics weapon and Rarailmuir knew of it.

"Of Course, I meet with the King everyday and know where it is located. I'm to be wed to his daughter the Princess." Rarailmuir looked him up and down. "You know you could challenge me for her hand. I'd love thrashing you about the

courtroom and you might get a look at that sword. Hope you can read quick. Because I think you wouldn't last long Jintru of Tevil, or whatever." Rarailmuir scoffed and turned away with his guard blocking his retreat. The Yoranthium guard tax collector thanked him and wrote him a receipt for the donation they just robbed Jintru of.

Turukon saw that Jintru was not liking being made fun of or robbed. Twenty trained guard in Yoranthium would only be a bad diplomatic incident for Travalion Hold and the Sixteen Rays of Dawn would be disappointed if Jintru created a political disaster. "Come on Jintru, we got more pressing matters than this. Whatever this is." Turukon spun Jintru away and out of the back of this smelly back alley and back into the main gallery heading to sleep it off at the hotel. Then they would leave for Sea Shore in a carriage in the morning.

Jintru was feeling tired and fatigued now it was quite the day and he started this day tired. The entire Journey was disappointing and then to learn the legend was false about the Sword of Yoranthium finding him and not the other way around. He'll have to find his surrogate mother when he returns home. What a disappointing trip the only good thing was he got to meet that one sea elf female. She was the best thing he ever met in his lifetime and lost. At least he hoped to dream of her. Wished he had known her name.

This trip was wasted and nothing got advanced for Travalion Hold, maybe he wasn't good enough as the heir of the hold. The Sixteen Rays of Dawn were a good fit to manage their affairs. I guess it's fifteen rays as he was letting them down in his diplomatic skills. Turukon gave Jintru nothing but silence and they went back to their hotel. Jintru only thought of a girl he met. Knowing he had lost her and he began losing desire to want anyone else. Even though they did attend the concert with some other courtesan at his side he really didn't even speak to her. Didn't even socialize with the other females interested in the foreigner at the concert.

Jintru simply sat there in the concert in self pity and retrospect. Thinking of the girl he failed to impress. While the courtesan felt bored and rejected. Towards the end of the concert he fell asleep and began snoring. Turukon had to wake him and

saying goodbye to their dates. They went back to the boring hotel with no company. Jintru passed out and they left the next day to head home to the Land of the Potentate by Caravel a third of a season journey by sea in a cramped caravel sail ship.

Well maybe they might get to fight pirates…

This is not the end only a beginning.
Continued in.
Yoranthium Book Two: The Book of Jintru.
The next riveting novel in the Yoranthium Book Series.

Book One: Lost Hope

Acknowledgements:

Book Written By Mark P. Bromley

I would like to thank the following for making Yoranthium Possible.

<u>Thank you.</u>

My Wife. Without you this book would have been impossible. As much of my true fond memories and adventures in this world revolve mostly around you and our life together. I do suppose your cousin does deserve some credit for being right about the writer I would become. I think it's because of you my wife that my world was created with heavy influences in Japan and France as that is the world you had been a part of. Thank you for the son we share and our family was good. I know I should write about sea world and Lego land and all that good Moab stuff. With inspirations of the books and the Sodor train series I read to our son. That would be an entire book unto itself.

To my Family and friends. Without your patients and understanding this book would not of been possible and much of my research had involved the moments we had shared in a decades long quest of knowledge and understanding. If you see some of that in this book, then so be it.

Thanks a little bit to my education in Colorado at Western Colorado University the library and art education was decent. I

took many courses and perfected some of my writing abilities at the college with studies in Art history, History, Philosophy, Sociology, Science and Gothic Literature that was an honors class while being acknowledged as an excellent artist by the faculty. Being involved in Television, Radio, and Theater. Even though Western Colorado University failed to recognize my completion of credits and gave me problems with my rightfully earned degree as a BFA. There is no doubt with the Help of Advanced Higher Education in the NAVY my ACE credits far surpassed the 4 year college program. Sadly Western University is a bunch of dicks and I do not recommend enrolling there. After all if you paid more than enough money and have more real credits than they required for a degree. Should you not be given your degree? People wonder why Colorado Educators are failures. It's simply because Colorado higher education doesn't understand you got to decently pay college students so they don't have to join the US Military. Then again I liked the US Navy for it provided me a cruise ship to sail the world upon.

Thank you, US Navy. Putting me forward deployed in Japan and letting me cruise the Pacific Rim the Middle East, Australia and other coast lines around the world. I had lots of fun doing this on the flight deck of the USS Independence and USS Kitty hawk. Giving me decades of good choice material for my books. My friends in the Navy were the best and if you see something in my heroic characters that they make you think it might be you. Well to some small extent it is possible we were at one point on patrol and keeping the peace in foreign lands. I also take the time to thank the Navy for my Electronic/Electrician background and aviation and naval skills. Those did pay off and I did get a professional license working in aviation and many boat/yacht yards engineering many different systems. If you want a cruise ship I highly recommend the US Navy especially if you come from poverty and your college is a big disappointment. Forward deployed to the danger zone you get a lot of worldly experience and even get involved with foreign matters of state and Governments. Especially if you get along with the locals then you experience things you only read about in novels of high adventure. High adventures, to be presented in the Yoranthium series collection.

My Brothers and Sisters of my social fraternity of Theta Chi. Knowing you had been some of my fondest moments in my life and greatest honor. You built my leadership skills and social abilities and gave me confidence in myself from when you first found me. I also like the fact I was part of a Fraternity with greatly known persons such as the creator of ET and the Green Hornet. Giving me great confidence in my book writing.

Thanks in a small way to Homeland Security for showing me what the face of evil and terrible people looks like in the state of Utah. It would have been hard writing about evil characters if I didn't have TSA executive management to create from. Utah sucks, although I did like Moab, and Moab I highly recommend you join the state of Colorado. My dear friends in Moab you might of not understood the hate, harassment and discrimination, aimed at my family and I, that we received from the TSA's bad management out of SLC. Homeland security really hates family of color especially miscegenated families. Those TSA employees all sucked and are purely evil entities negatively impacting me on a daily basis and lets face it the job was stupid for the amount of bullshit aimed at me and my family. My only recommendation is do not take a job with TSA. Unless you want to have examples of evil characters for a book then it's great.

Now for the List of Names and Persons not in the above mentioning.

MPB Enterprises: Publications, Marine Motor Craft and Sail Craft Services, Mok Art Studios, Electrical Contracting, Consulting, Political Advising Advocacy. Without my own Entrepreneurship this book would have been impossible.

To the Christian and Mormon faith and my family up bringing. Having been and always in the study of God, Theology, Philosophy, Art and the Understandings of the metaphysical concepts of Religion and for all the Religions in this world that make this world a great place. To the Jewish community that I like and study from, thank you, for aiding me in many angelic illustrations I use in the

Yoranthium book series. To my study in Mythology and Pagan beliefs and from my friends that practice runes and have written their own metaphysical books and are published authors. Your friendships are always a highlight of my life and experience as I write with those influences of the nature of Gaia and the Earth Mother. Along with all you groovy granolas and the night of the Fire God at Hartman's rocks.

Thanks to the Religion of Buddhism from Japan. Without my wife and her connections I would have never seen it for all its diversity and teachings. I found learning the mantra's with my wife on road trips enlightinging and visiting the temples excellent memories.

To the band of my friends who were into Role Playing, LARPS, IFGS, SCA, and the entire Mile Hi Con, and Star Con and the Nerds of exceptional purpose and goals and dreams. Oh, let's not forget the Dream Buccaneers a science fiction and fantasy writers club in high school. Even though you might of gone away. I have never forgotten to be a Swashbuckling Pirate of Dreams, Nuff Said. Thank you to the table top/online gamers couldn't of explored my books concepts so effectively without the creation of so many other gamers. Yes you might run into me in RPGMMO's. If my book series works, who knows maybe we can meet up at a convention or two, as I think I made some cosplay ideas in Yoranthium. Let me know if you catch the references in Yoranthium. Be looking for the eventual release of the Yoranthium Trading Card Game.

Thank you Japan: The people of Japan for letting me live in Beauty when not on duty with the US Navy on the Aircraft carriers. Thank you for giving me your books and philosophy's and many Art experiences and my wife from Hiroshima. I met her during the time of sakura blossoms in Japan. Kind of what it was like when I met her the first time. To think it took over three years for me to see this beauty of Japan. Along with many art museums and other cultural events. Such as the Tokyo Symphony, Bon Festivals, Kabuki, first Noh play on a US aircraft carrier, and so many other events and my first experience with Avex trax and a "A Walk in the Park." I loved my time there and learned a better heart filled life. Some is only slightly depicted in this humble book.

I do have plans to write a different book but for that I need to return to Japan to write it as it's going to require permission of the people of Japan. So consider this a work for a more important book after this series runs it's course.

To all the good influences of my work, as all art come's from somewhere.

www.ingramcontent.com/pod-product-compliance
Lightning Source LLC
Chambersburg PA
CBHW060820310726
48980CB00002B/349

* 9 7 9 8 9 9 0 9 4 8 2 3 5 *